A WILD CARDS MOSAIC NOVEL

ACES FULL

The Wild Cards Universe

The Original Triad
Wild Cards
Aces High
Jokers Wild

The Puppetman Quartet
Aces Abroad
Down and Dirty
Ace in the Hole
Dead Man's Hand

The Rox Triad
One-Eyed Jacks
Jokertown Shuffle
Dealer's Choice

Solo Novels
Double Solitaire
Turn of the Cards
Death Draws Five
Deuces Down
Full House
Joker Moon

The Card Sharks Triad
Card Sharks
Marked Cards
Black Trump

The Committee Triad
Inside Straight
Busted Flush
Suicide Kings

The Mean Streets Triad
Fort Freak
Lowball
High Stakes

The America Triad
Mississippi Roll
Low Chicago
Texas Hold'em

The British Arc
Knaves Over Queens
Three Kings

A WILD CARDS MOSAIC NOVEL

ACES FULL

Edited by
George R. R. Martin

Written by

Cherie Priest
Carrie Vaughn
Caroline Spector
Bradley Denton
Walton Simons
Sage Walker
Marko Kloos
Ian Tregillis
Laura J. Mixon
Alan Brennert
Emma Newman

TOR DOT COM

TOR PUBLISHING GROUP
New York

This is a work of fiction. All of the characters, organizations, and events portrayed in these stories are either products of the authors' imaginations or are used fictitiously.

ACES FULL

Copyright © 2025 by George R. R. Martin and the Wild Cards Trust

All rights reserved.

A Tordotcom Book
Published by Tom Doherty Associates / Tor Publishing Group
120 Broadway
New York, NY 10271

www.torpublishinggroup.com

Tor® is a registered trademark of Macmillan Publishing Group, LLC.

EU Representative: Macmillan Publishers Ireland Ltd, 1st Floor,
The Liffey Trust Centre, 117–126 Sheriff Street Upper, Dublin 1, DO1 YC43

The Library of Congress Cataloging-in-Publication Data is available upon request.

ISBN 978-1-250-39689-1 (hardcover)
ISBN 978-1-250-39690-7 (ebook)

The publisher of this book does not authorize the use or reproduction of any part of this book in any manner for the purpose of training artificial intelligence technologies or systems. The publisher of this book expressly reserves this book from the Text and Data Mining exception in accordance with Article 4(3) of the European Union Digital Single Market Directive 2019/790.

Our books may be purchased in bulk for specialty retail/wholesale, literacy, corporate/premium, educational, and subscription box use. Please contact MacmillanSpecialMarkets@macmillan.com.

First Edition: 2025

Printed in the United States of America

10 9 8 7 6 5 4 3 2 1

Copyright Acknowledgments

"The Button Man and the Murder Tree" © 2013 by Cherie Priest

"The Thing About Growing Up in Jokertown" © 2016 by Carrie Vaughn

"The Flight of Morpho Girl" © 2018 Caroline Spector & Bradley Denton

"Naked, Stoned, and Stabbed" © 2019 by Bradley Denton

"The City That Never Sleeps" © 2019 by Walton Simons

"Long is the Way" © 2019 by Carrie Vaughn & Sage Walker

"Berlin Is Never Berlin" © 2020 by Marko Kloos

"Hammer and Tongs and a Rusty Nail" © 2020 by Ian Tregillis

"Ripple Effects" © 2021 by Laura J. Mixon

"Skin Deep" © 2021 by Alan Brennert

"Hearts of Stone" © 2022 by Emma Newman

"Grow" © 2022 by Carrie Vaughn

A WILD CARDS MOSAIC NOVEL

ACES FULL

The Button Man and the Murder Tree

by Cherie Priest

Chicago, 1971

SAMMY RICCA POURED HIMSELF a slug the color of old honey, spilling hardly any of it. He lifted the glass to his mouth, and the cheap whiskey rippled as he tapped it with his upper lip, pretending to drink it. He peered through the blurry amber at a tall, lean shadow in a gray suit, and he said, "I heard they were using that old tree again. Word's getting around."

"That was the idea," the button man murmured. And then, "You may as well drink that."

Sammy threw back a mouthful, as suggested. He shifted his ass so he could sit on the edge of his desk. A pen cracked under his weight, and dark blue ink pooled beneath his thigh. "This isn't about Angelo."

"I already know about Angelo."

"I could tell you—"

"Everything you know, you sang already." Beside Sammy's swiftly staining leg sat an ugly Lucite ashtray. It was emblazoned with the logo of a bar that'd burned down years ago. The button man sighed, and wished he had a cigarette.

"Raul, the money wasn't—"

"I know."

"I don't think you *do*. Before me it was Dragna, and before him, Carlo. What we had in common, it wasn't just our names on the Murder Tree, it—"

"The Deadman's Tree. Subtle difference, there." He withdrew a Colt .45, checked it, and tried not to hear how hard Sammy swallowed. "And it doesn't matter now, after the mess you made of things."

"No, I didn't make a mess. It's not Angelo. It's not the money."

"And it's not up to me."

The button man might've said more, but a warm, prickling sensation began a slow swell around his wrists. His shirt cuffs tightened. His collar was the same damn story. He wished he weren't wearing a tie. He wished it weren't so warm in the small, gray office with the creaking fan and the window that couldn't open far enough to let Lake Michigan breathe inside.

With his free hand, he tugged at the knot that pressed uncomfortably against his throat. It was his turn to swallow hard.

"Hey, Raul, is . . . is something wrong?" Sammy stalled.

He hesitated. He hadn't told anyone, which didn't mean nobody knew.

"Raul?"

"No. Nothing's wrong." His wrists felt puffy. His left hand hurt from the pressure, from the lost circulation. In another minute, it'd be numb except for the pins and needles if he didn't get those cuffs unbuttoned. He lifted the Colt and aimed it between Sammy's eyes.

Sammy drank his last drops fast and hard, like he didn't even taste them. He slammed the glass down on the desk. Then, as the Colt twitched, ready to fire, he squawked, "Wait—just wait a minute, please? One last request."

Raul's hands burned. They were swollen and marbled, white and red. "Make it fast."

"Don't dump me in the lake, would you? Leave me here, or stick me in the street."

"What do you care?"

"Elaine and the kids. It'll be easier on them, for the life insurance. Leave them something to bury. I'm asking you—in case you got family I don't know about. Promise me that, and do what you gotta."

"All right, I promise."

"And I need to tell you . . ." Sammy's voice sped up, desperate for these last seconds. "You don't even know why you're really here—"

Raul pulled the trigger twice. Sammy Ricca fell back across the desk and tumbled to the floor. A small curl of smoke escaped his forehead.

Raul checked the clock on Sammy's desk. The cleaners wouldn't come around for another twenty minutes.

He could've broken his promise if he'd wanted, but it felt like bad form, and anyway, it wasn't Elaine's fault that her husband thought he was smarter than Moe Shapiro and Angelo Licata. So the button man picked up Sammy's corpse, taking care to avoid the long streaks of ink and the sliding drips of blood.

He left it in the alley behind the newspaper, just behind the advertising division, where Sammy's shattered skull would make quite an impression on the first bum to come by for a piss. And while Sammy lay there, mucking up the pavement with his brains, the button man fought the urge to tear off his jacket and rip at his shirt cuffs, then his tie, at anything he could loosen or adjust. One thing after another, in any order that would let his skin breathe free.

But no. Not here.

Instead, he stumbled out of the alley and ducked into the onrushing glare of a car's headlamps, then out of it again. Keeping to the sidewalk only briefly, he found another dark spot between two buildings and he could've cried with relief. He knew this place—this was the back end of a restaurant Angelo liked, and the cooks kept their mouths shut unless they were taste-testing the specials. It'd do in a pinch and thank God for that, because tonight's pinch was about to strangle him.

The back door was hollow and it rang like a metal gong when he knocked. It cracked open and a round face covered in steam or grease looked at him with confusion, concern, and then the careful blankness of a man who knows when to pretend he doesn't know a goddamn thing.

"Mr. Esposito," he said. "How can we help you tonight?"

"I need a minute inside."

The door opened wide enough to let him in to a world of bright steel pots and simmering gas stoves. He dodged big-breasted waitresses with damp, round trays and kept his head down when the men at the ovens shouted back and forth in Italian or some second-generation's pidgin.

Whoever'd let him in didn't ask for details and didn't follow him back to the bathroom the staff used, a big gray box with one fizzing, swaying light bulb dangling on a wire. Raul shut the door, locked it, and leaned forward on his hands, staring down into the sink.

The taps were the old-fashioned sort: one for hot and one for cold, but shit-out-of-luck if you wanted lukewarm. He twisted both faucets on, letting the hot side steam and the cold side swirl, all of it making a friendly white noise to thwart any curious ears that might be dumb enough to come close.

Above the sink was a smudged rectangle of glass that passed for a mirror.

The button man met his own eyes as he pulled off his suit jacket and hung it on a hook that might've held meat as easily as towels. His shirt came off next, though his hands trembled as he fed the slim white buttons through the holes, one at a time, until the cotton parted with a soft, sticky sound. He knew better than to look down. He didn't want to see that he'd ruined another Van Heusen. Didn't want to look at what was growing there on his chest, not just his wrists and neck.

He stripped to the waist.

Beside the toilet squatted a knee-high trash can. He picked it up and set it on the sink's edge, then reached inside his limp jacket for the inner pocket, and pulled out a switchblade. As quickly as he dared, he sliced the bubbling lesions away.

He started at his wrists, since those growths had blossomed first, and were largest. He pruned them one by one, scraping the blade along the clustered stalks. They popped free and dropped into the steel waste bin with a spongy little *ping* that made his teeth itch. Some as small as his pinky nail. Some the size of his thumb. Brown-capped or gray, with creamy undersides and speckles.

Perfect, round mushrooms. Dozens of them. Hundreds, maybe—if he gave them another hour in the dark, and the sun wouldn't be up for another six hours if he was lucky.

They were less trouble from dawn 'til dusk, and less prolific when he kept his skin dry. That much Raul knew. He was still learning what worked and what didn't, but the truth was more horrible every day: He couldn't stop them. He couldn't manage them. He could only hide them.

He'd drawn a card, and it'd turned. Simple as a noose.

Another flick of the switchblade and another half-dozen smaller chunks of fungus fell into the bin.

It didn't hurt. Once he'd gotten over the sheer gruesomeness of it all, it was almost easy. A bit of unfamiliar pressure. A moment of disconnect, and the chilly sense that he might be bleeding—but wasn't. He couldn't carve the things free, but a simple scrape would temporarily excise them. It wasn't altogether different from trimming his nails or blowing his nose—not in principle, and that's what he told himself as he methodically filled the bin and wondered what he was going to do with the damn things. Flush them down the toilet? Cover them with paper towels, and pray nobody noticed?

He laughed, a grim grunt that didn't hold a drop of humor.

I could leave them in the kitchen.

Stick them on the pizzas, or in the carbonara. Garnish a salad, or what have you.

One more. Beside his belly button, growing almost while he watched. He picked it off with the blade and absently rubbed his thumb against the round, white patch of skin it'd left on his stomach. He tumbled this last tiny cap between his fingers and brought it up to his nose. It smelled like nighttime, like mulch and butter.

Quickly, before he could talk himself out of it, he popped the cap into his mouth and chewed.

It squished between his teeth like any other mushroom might, its texture firm but loamy, its flavor familiar but specific. He swallowed.

He knew the right mushrooms could give you visions—and the wrong ones could kill you, and he didn't know what his own personal brand might do. He felt a fast pang of fear, but it went its merry way when he told himself, *No way. It came from the outside. Won't hurt the inside.* And maybe he didn't believe that, but it kept him from sticking his finger down his throat and asking for a recount.

A knock on the bathroom door almost sent him out of his skin.

"What?" he barked, anxiously squeezing the trash can.

A timid voice on the other side said, "Mr. Esposito, sir? Are you all right in there?"

"Yeah."

"It's been . . ."

Half an hour probably. "I know. I'll be out in a minute."

He glanced around the naked little room and would've given his right arm for an incinerator chute, but the toilet would have to suffice. He took two handfuls of the mushrooms and dropped them into the bowl. The first flush took them away with a sweeping swirl, and while he waited for the tank to refill, he wondered what the hell he was going to do.

Ten minutes later he turned off the faucet. Re-dressed, if somewhat hastily, he exited through the kitchen door, and he didn't say a word to anybody.

Outside he heard sirens, so someone had found Sammy and called it in. *Good. Get that life insurance policy rolling, why don't you.* Raul's business there was finished and really, he should've been long gone—but he wasn't, and he wasn't sure where he wanted to go. Home was better than no place, but he was restless and itchy, and he wanted to walk. So he walked.

He took a rambling path through Little Italy, trusting the El to pick him up when he did eventually feel like riding. Just this once, the lake smelled clean when the wind rolled off it, sweeping through the brick jungles that would never burn again, cow or no cow; and it was probably his imagination, because the lake always smelled like cold decay and dirty sand. Maybe it just smelled better than mushrooms and blood, or sweat and the kitchen of a second-rate Italian place where people went to talk more than they went to eat.

The button man wasn't entirely sure where he was headed. It didn't dawn on him until he was right there at the clearing where the old park used to be, back when anybody gave enough of a shit about the 19th Ward to give it a park. He'd made a beeline for it without even thinking about it.

The Murder Tree. No, the Deadman's Tree.

The tree was a legacy case, and like Sammy'd said—some of his very last words—it'd been a long time since it'd been a well-used spot, but Ed Galante thought it'd be a good thing to revive. Ed liked symbols. So here was a bloody tree in a bloody ward, a leftover from when the Irish and Italians'd had it out decades ago.

For a long time, it was just an ancient poplar where kids told stories, scaring one another out of nickels and sleep. And now the gnarled branches and massive trunk were back in service, this looming giant with bark half-bare from fall's incoming wind.

That tree, it was better than the classifieds, Moe Shapiro once said. Gives people time to get their affairs together. Gives them a last chance to make things right if they can, or if they want to. Not that anyone ever does.

If he'd had a pen, Raul would've scratched out Sammy's name. He didn't. He left it there, barely legible on the thick paper that'd been nailed in place. It was too dark to see anything but the shape of the letters scrawled against the bone-white sheet, and when he looked closer, he saw something else beneath it.

A new name. He stepped closer, squinting against what must be midnight, by now.

"Harriet O'Dwyer." So it was still up to the Italians and Irish after all. "The more things change," he muttered.

But why Harriet?

He played out the possibilities as he walked away from the tree, wandering toward the nearest El stop. She was a piece of work, and she worked half the men in the syndicate. Did somebody tell her something she shouldn't have heard? Unfortunate, if so. But not unfair. She knew who she was getting into bed with, and recently that'd been a guy named Jake Corallo, if Raul recalled the rumor correctly. Jake's name hadn't gone up on the Murder Tree because he'd been shut down last month, before Ed had started up that old tradition again.

Yeah, it probably had something to do with Jake.

He didn't think about it too hard. It was easier not to. He turned on his heel and went back the way he came, but he didn't get far before he heard someone call his name. His instinct said this was a bad thing—that he didn't want to be called out on the street; but his second thoughts told him to lighten up, because it was something that happened to normal people. Something normal people didn't freak out about, because normal people don't kill for money. Normal people don't have mushrooms growing out of their skin.

He froze in his steps and then looked around. His eyes snagged on a guy named Benny Lerch, on the other sidewalk. He crossed the street in a handful of long strides for a man with legs so short. "Haven't seen you since you left for Philly last year."

"Has it been that long?"

"And then some, maybe." He grabbed Raul's hand to give it a hearty shake. "I heard you went off to New York."

"Naw, that never happened," Raul told him.

"Hey, let me buy you a drink."

"I don't need a . . . you know what? All right. I could use a drink."

Raul should've told him no, but he didn't, so he got a drink with Benny Lerch at the Waystation. His mushrooms weren't growing back too hard yet, and maybe he'd get lucky. Maybe they'd stay gone a few hours.

His clothes were a little dirty with fungal streaks, but it was dark and Benny either didn't notice or didn't say anything.

Benny was disposable, and he knew it. That was his strong suit, if he had one.

He'd weaseled into the syndicate by starting cars when he was a boy; he grew up around big men with big wallets, and he wanted to be just like 'em. Just as well for him it'd never happened. It was probably why he was still alive. That, and the way car bombs had fallen out of fashion before he reached puberty.

Benny was a fat guy, and if he were any shorter you would've said he was a fat *little* guy, but he wasn't, so you didn't. He dressed well, if cheaply, and with an excessive fondness for brown. A shaggy comb-over wasn't doing him any favors, except that it reminded almost everyone that he was harmless. It reminded Raul that none of them were kids anymore.

Benny knew better than to ask any questions about why the button man needed a drink, and he should've known better than to gossip, but he didn't. Over mediocre gin, he said quietly, "It's weird, ain't it? How the score's gone up. Not just since the Deadman's Tree went back into play—but before that, too. The last couple of months, I mean. Seems like every other night, someone's out of the game. Bunch of people I wouldn't expect to see go. People who didn't seem to be no threat. Not even players, some of them. But I don't know. Nobody tells me shit, Raul. Nobody tells me shit."

"So you've seen the Murder Tree." Raul didn't meet his eyes.

"Saw it, yeah. I saw it."

"Tonight?"

Benny hesitated, then nodded. "Yeah. They put Harriet up there, huh?"

"Apparently."

"You ever actually see anybody post the messages?" Benny asked.

"No. I don't watch the tree. Probably better for my health that I don't."

"I'll drink to that." He did, raising a glass covered in fingerprints and clinking it against Raul's. "You uh . . . you think you'll get the call? On Harriet, I mean?"

"I might." He almost certainly would, a fact he hadn't admitted to himself until just then. Must've been the gin making him honest.

"You going to be okay with that?"

He shrugged. "Nothing much happened, and what did happen, happened years ago."

"Yeah, but it *happened*. So if you do get the gig," he pressed, "can you do it?"

Raul put his glass down on a wet cardboard coaster. "More easily than I can avoid it." And that was the truest thing the gin had said yet. "Listen Benny, it's been good to see you, but I need to call it a night. In case the phone rings in the morning, you know. Our old pal Moe, he's an early riser."

"All right man, that's all right. Good to see you, Raul. Always good to see you."

♣

On the way home, sitting on the El and watching the city lights streak past, Raul thought about calling Moe tonight and getting it over with. He couldn't ask too many questions or make too many demands—no, not even him—but he and Moe were tight enough that he could risk a query or two. Of course, Moe might not know the particulars. Galante sometimes played it close to the chest—closer than the old boys, who'd known Moe better and knew how far they could trust him.

So he didn't call. Besides, like he'd told Benny: Moe was an early riser. Early risers tend to be cranky when their phones ring at 2:00 a.m.

And later that morning, Raul awoke to a ring that summoned him to Moe Shapiro's office.

Moe's office was in a nice building on a nice side of the city. Not too flashy—that wasn't his style. Tasteful and full of books, like a lawyer or a head-shrinker, except Moe'd actually read them all. Once over drinks, he'd told Raul that when he was a kid, his fellow upstart gangsters made fun of him for having a library card. He laughed it off, and kept on reading, and now he sat on top of a big pile of money—the last man left of the old guard. He'd been in the racket since the twenties, when he was one of the new guys who'd taken the game away from the big guys with narrow visions.

Behind his back, people called him "Shorty" or "Specs," and he didn't care. He was short and he wore glasses. He knew it as well as anybody. You could rib him if you liked, so long as you kept it friendly and left out anything about him being a Jew. He knew that too, obviously. But he'd be damned if he'd let anybody use it against him.

"What can I do for you, Moe?"

A brunette secretary hustled out of the way and left the two men alone together. The door closed behind her with a click. The button man took off his hat. Moe Shapiro gestured at a stuffed leather chair. "Thanks for coming, Raul. Can I get you a drink?"

"No thanks."

Moe poured out a dollop for himself, something much nicer than what Sammy'd last sipped, decanting it from a big crystal jug into a matching glass. While he worked, Raul pulled out a cigarette and lit it off a pack of matches he'd picked up at a hotel in Phoenix. "I heard the news about Ricca," Moe said as he slid a brown ashtray toward his companion's elbow. It wasn't as nice as the glass because Moe didn't smoke.

"Shame about that."

"Always is. I heard they picked him up in an alley."

"That's right," the button man said. And before Moe could ask, he added, "He had a wife and kids. Life insurance, you know how it is."

Moe nodded, but it was sometimes hard to read him. "You think Elaine knew what he was up to?"

"No. That's why Sammy didn't take a bath." He concentrated on the cigarette. He waited for Moe to decide how he felt about the small shift in plans.

Finally he said, "It's a good thing I know you're not a soft touch."

All right. Then he wasn't mad, and Raul was reassured. "So is this the part where you tell me I'm responsible for Legs O'Dwyer? I saw her name on the Deadman's Tree. A soft touch might say no to that one."

Moe shook his head, not denying anything. "A soft touch or an old flame, but if we crossed all those names off a list she'd live to see a hundred. All the same, I wish she wasn't posted. I tried to give her room after Jake bit it; I told Galante to leave her alone, let her cry it out. I gave her a talking-to, a chance to pull herself together."

"Then you played fair."

"I still don't like doing it, and I'm not sure why Ed's insisting. Something about her keeping books for Jake's operation, and how she doesn't get to walk away just because she's sad. But I didn't know she had anything to do with the books."

"Me either, but I guess it's none of my business," the button man said, and not for the first time.

Moe parked himself behind the desk with a sigh. He left his drink by the decanter, all but forgotten. For half a minute he stared into space, just past Raul's right ear. For that same half a minute, Raul let his cigarette ash creep toward his fingers without taking a drag.

Moe shook his head again. "And there's something else I've been meaning to ask you."

"Fire away."

"It's about mushrooms."

The button man nearly gagged on smoke he hadn't yet drawn. He forced his eyes to flatten, his mouth to set in a neutral line. "Good on pizza. Better with pasta. Best on meat. Otherwise, what about them?"

"Coincidence, is all. Your last two gigs. The cleaners are talking."

"About mushrooms? At my gigs?"

"You're not leaving calling cards, are you?"

"You accusing me of junior-league shit?"

"I'm asking, is all."

"Then no. I don't leave calling cards. Mushrooms, or any other kind."

"No need to snap about it."

Raul said, "Sorry," but he said it curtly. Better to sound offended than terrified. Better to act touchy than sick.

"No, no." Moe waved his concerns away with the smoke that crept in his direction. "I didn't mean to yank your chain. But you know I wouldn't be doing my job if I didn't ask."

"Hey Moe?"

"Yeah?"

"I'll take care of O'Dwyer." He changed the subject by force. He stubbed out the barely smoked cigarette and stood. "You think Frank knows where she's holed up?"

"It's no secret. She can't keep quiet long enough to hide, so you never know—she might be glad to see you. Try the boardinghouse out on Eighth—the one Anne Civella used to run. Call Frank and see if he can get you a room number." Half to himself, he asked, "What's that place's name . . . ? Can't think of it, off the top of my head."

"Three Sisters," Raul supplied. "I know the place."

"Tonight, if you can swing it. Word down low says she's got a date with some jackass from the DA's office in the morning. I'd like for that not to happen."

Raul put his hat back on and headed home to wait for night.

A stack of newspapers on his dining room table kept him company. He'd collected them over the last few weeks, and clipped articles here and there from rags he found in other cities—knowing what it'd look like if he ever had visitors.

He picked up a recent scrap and read it for the hundredth time.

NO ROOM FOR JOKERS, the headline said, and then went on to editorialize about how the whole breed ought to be rounded up and stuck on an island, like they were all a bunch of fucking lepers. MURDER ON FIFTH STREET, read another lead, and it told the story of two joker kids who'd picked the wrong ice cream shop in which to be a freak. NEW JOKER ORDINANCE, said the next sheet, and it was all about how several city blocks were being deemed "Joker-Free Zones" like they weren't even people, and never had been.

His wrist twitched. He crumpled the story and let it drop to the floor.

And then there was the exposé on Andy Sifakis, the Greek who'd set up shop on the West Side. GANGLAND HIT TAKES DOWN JOKER BOSS. That was an exaggeration. Andy hadn't been a boss, he'd only been new. And a joker. Nothing real bad, not like some of them. Andy'd had antlers, was all—that, and his hands were more like hooves. He kept everything trimmed and filed up real sharp, Raul remembered that from the one time they'd met.

Funny thing was, it wasn't the Four Families who'd taken Andy to pieces: It'd been the lower goons, guys like the button man and guys even further down the totem pole. But nobody'd stopped them. Word around town said Ed Galante might even be paying for it, and looking the other way. That's why there weren't any jokers in the syndicate—at least no jokers anyone knew about. Maybe it was only a matter of time, and maybe times were changing after all. But they hadn't changed yet.

His conversation with Benny collided uncomfortably with the scraps on the table. Some of those guys weren't even players. Andy sure as shit hadn't been.

JOKERTOWN RECEIVES CIVIC IMPROVEMENT GRANT.

And then there was New York City, where the jokers had their own quarter. Their own hospitals, restaurants, apartments. Their own gangs. Their own riots and problems, too. There was always the chance he could trade one set of problems for another, if it came to that. Take the geographic cure, so to speak.

It was something to think about.

Later.

By the time he was finished sifting through the most recent daily rags, the sun was setting low enough that he could take his chances back in the old Bloody Ward, where the Three Sisters boardinghouse waited at the edge of Little Italy.

♠

The button man took the El and then he took a cab, and then he let himself in through the back door that emptied onto the alley, because no one ever watched it. Some things you could count on. Likewise, he counted on the shifty-eyed maids and working girls who kept their heads down and their lips pursed tightly together, and he turned his face away from them, staying in the shadow of his hat's brim. He took Frank Ragen's suggestion and tried the third floor.

Room twenty-one.

The hall was empty and felt abandoned, with its ragged faux-Persian runner and dingy wallpaper that was eighty years old if it was a day. He wrinkled his nose and smelled mostly dust, mostly inefficient cleaning products and the faint, lingering tang of cheap lotion and old tobacco. The room numbers passed in tarnished metal digits, odds on the left and evens on the right. Long before he reached it, Raul knew that twenty-one would be last.

He stopped in front of it, and listened.

Outside, a telephone was ringing in a booth and two cats started up a fight. A drunk complained at a car. Closer, then. Downstairs. Downstairs, the bored teenage boy at the desk was handing out keys and making promises. A vacuum hummed across the floor. Closer still. This hallway, where nothing moved.

This room. And in it, a woman he used to know.

He heard the nearby plop of water dripping onto something that was wet already. The buzz of a radio that couldn't decide between two stations. Nothing else. No footsteps, no shifting springs in a cheap, battered bed. No furtive phone calls or last-minute sobs.

He put his hand on the doorknob and turned. The knob clicked obligingly. Didn't have to pick it or kick it down. One of his easier gigs, then, except for all the obvious reasons.

He pushed, and the door leaned inward.

He peered around the frame and saw no surprises within. A bed with an ugly blanket. A dresser no woman would choose for herself. A window overlooking the drugstore across the street. She might not be in, or Frank might've been wrong. But someone'd been here lately, he could see that much by the discarded stockings and mushed-up cotton balls. The bed wasn't made, and a smudge of beige makeup marred the right-side pillow.

He let himself inside and closed the door, leaning back against it to make sure it was shut. He slid the cheap metal bolt to lock it, knowing it wouldn't hold more than a moment if anyone insisted hard enough.

To his right was a bathroom, its door open no wider than two fingers throwing a peace sign. The dripping he'd heard . . . that's where it came from. A light burned within, casting a slim shadow in reverse. It struck into the lower-lit gloom of the bedroom, a pale yellow line like an arrow.

She was in there. He could feel it in his bones. In his skin, which already crawled with the mushrooms yet to come.

He drew his gun and steadied his breathing. This was old hat. This was the job. She'd known the rules, ignored them, and this was what it cost. He wasn't the executioner, not her friend, not her lover. Just the messenger. Same as always. No surprises for anyone.

With the back of his free hand, he nudged the bathroom door. It groaned open.

She was in there, all right. And he was surprised.

Harriet O'Dwyer reclined naked in the tub, wrists slashed and body bobbing slowly; that part didn't bother Raul. He'd seen plenty of blood and he'd already stepped in hers. He would've cursed himself but he didn't, he only took one step back and wiped his shoe on carpet the color of guacamole. The bathroom was painted with gore, and it looked like more than one woman's corpse could hold, except that he knew from experience that it wasn't.

A razor sprawled open on the floor below her dangling, lifeless hand. Obvious as can be, even before he saw the note on the mirror. She'd left it in lipstick, in handwriting barely legible, and when he saw the empty bottle of Valium, he knew why.

All it said was "Forget me."

Not "Forgive me." Not "I'm sorry." Not even "Good-bye." Raul guessed she had no one to say it to. Just a message for him, because she'd known he was coming. Or if not him personally, someone else she used to know. The odds were pretty good on that one.

He looked at her again. Her hands were scaly and rough. They reminded him of a pair of snakeskin boots he'd bought on a gig in Houston, for laughs. He'd never worn them. Her breasts were scaled too, and when he couldn't stop himself—he turned her over, her body making scarlet tides and messy splashes as she swayed and sank again—he saw the protrusion from her backside, a foot-long tail that ended in a rattle.

He jerked his hands away, letting her flop back to her original position.

And now he was soaked in bloody water up to the elbows. His knees, his stomach. No escaping it. No graceful, quiet retreat, and no more kidding himself. Legs O'Dwyer was a joker, for Christ's sake. She'd drawn a card, and it hadn't been pretty. That card had turned sometime since Raul'd last seen her.

His thoughts raced to assemble a picture that made sense, and he thought of Jake Corallo, who must've known, might've been the *only* one who knew. Jake had kept her secret, and now he was gone. No wonder she'd mourned him like that. What else could she do? Hard to play with the big boys anymore when this was what waited under the lingerie.

The button man retreated from the mirror. He turned, and he ran—all the way back down the empty hall, down the stairs, and out the way he'd come because it was always the back door, he was already unwanted and unwelcome. *I could've talked to her,* he thought wildly, the fear and disgust and discomfort stretching into crazy thoughts. *We might've made some understanding, left together if we both had to go—better than running alone, isn't it?*

And Jesus Christ, it really was time to run. No more pretending, and he'd wasted too much time to prepare so this would go by the seat of his pants and he hated that. It wasn't like him. It wasn't how he'd lived this long, and it wouldn't keep him alive much longer.

Still bloody and wet from that godawful bath, he threw himself into the nearest phone booth and jammed his fist into his pocket. He found some change. Threw it into the slot and dialed once, twice, before he got Moe's number right.

Moe answered on the first ring. "Shapiro."

"I need to ask you something, Moe. I need you to tell me the truth."

The other end of the line was silent, which was a promise of a sort—but not the one he wanted.

Raul continued. "The Murder Tree—I mean, the Deadman's Tree. The names on it, these last weeks. They had something in common. Something other than what I thought, what I was told."

"Raul . . ."

"Sammy would've blabbed if he'd lived a minute longer, and I didn't let him. I didn't have time. But he drew a card, didn't he? Nothing obvious, nothing I could see at a glance. But it must've been something. You must've known."

Pause. "I'd heard."

"You'd heard *what?*" Raul demanded. A few blocks away, a siren wailed to life.

"I'd heard he was hiding an extra face, extra mouths. Extra something, and I didn't ask for details. But that wasn't his problem, Raul. A secret like that wouldn't have put him in the morgue. I talked to Ed. Sammy'd made himself a date with a lawyer, and he was buttoning up. We've got interests to protect."

"Did Sammy even squeal?"

"He would've, if he'd had the chance."

"And Harriet, she never rang up the DA, did she?"

"Harriet too, huh?"

"Are you saying—"

"For fuck's sake, Raul. *No.* I didn't know. And you're taking this awful personal. Do I need to worry about you? Do I need to check the tree?" Then he paused and the moment hung between them. "It's the goddamn mushrooms, isn't it? You pulled a card too, son of a bitch. I'm sorry."

The button man didn't answer that particular apology. Instead he asked, "Scarfo's back from New York?"

"He got in this afternoon."

"Shit." He struggled to keep the shakes out of his voice. He steadied it, leaning his head on the glass for support and leaving a greasy smudge. He said, "You know, they can't keep us out forever. They'll have to let us in eventually. Too many of us to kill. Times'll change, Moe. They'll change and leave guys like Ed behind."

"Tell me something I haven't known for fifty years."

The siren wail drew closer. Raul turned his back to hide his face when a car came swinging around the corner, its headlights cutting through the gloom. "I've worked for you guys how long now? Twenty years almost, doing my job and nothing else."

"Nobody joins up for the pension." Moe sighed. "Do us both a favor, and get out of here. Stay gone. This isn't your fault, but I can't help you, not in Chicago. Try New York. I can make some phone calls, Raul. You can start over. You can—"

He didn't wait to hear the offer.

He slammed the phone back onto its base and cringed as another car whipped past, a cop car, this time. Its lights slapped streaks of red and blue in every direction until it made the next turn. The button man leaned his shoulder against the hard black phone. His breath was ragged; it fogged thickly against the booth's scratched-up glass. His shirt cuffs strained against the swelling fungus. Everything too small, everything outgrown.

Maybe he'd find more room in New York.

♠ ♥ ♦ ♣

The Thing About Growing Up in Jokertown

by Carrie Vaughn

THE THING ABOUT GROWING up in Jokertown is it gives you some weird ideas about what's normal.

Ma got me a job that summer at Antoine's Corner Store, just a couple of hours a day. She's been working there for I don't know how long. Like twenty years. Forever. She wants me working because she says I need to do *something,* maybe to keep me out of trouble. She and Dad are apparently worried I'm going to join a gang, like the Werewolves or the Killer Geeks, because those are the ones they read about in the papers. They read all these stories about kids running with gangs, and since I can really, you know, *run,* I think they're worried I'll get recruited by drug dealers wanting me to make deliveries across town. I'm all, "Ma, I look like a human whippet, no one's going to hire me to run drugs, I stand out way too much." One eyewitness and every cop on the Lower East Side would know exactly who they were talking about.

But when Ma looks at me she doesn't see a human whippet—five-three me with scruffy dark hair and a chest as big as a keg, with a wasp waist and the legs of an Olympic sprinter. And the fangs, don't forget the fangs. Mongoose fangs, which was what got me my nickname—Rikki. My real name is Miranda. Nobody calls me that except the teachers at school. Rikki or Miranda, Ma just sees me as her little princess, her miracle joker baby.

It could also be that Ma got me the job because she started working at Antoine's when she was sixteen, my age. Most parents who want their kids to follow in their footsteps are doctors or senators, stuff like that. But Ma wants me to work in a convenience store. Stay in the neighborhood. Support my community, because that's another thing about growing up in Jokertown—it's the only home some of us will ever have.

Jokertown gives you some weird ideas of what's normal, but if you never leave, you never need everybody else's normal. *Normal* normal.

That day, I'm restocking sodas in the cooler while Ma works behind the counter, ringing up frozen burritos and cough syrup and stuff. The bell on the door rings when someone comes in, and I can usually tell without looking if the customer is a local or not.

"Hey, June! How are things?" This is a male voice, gruff and friendly.

Ma answers, "Oh, can't complain. It's been hot, but you know that. What'll it be?"

"Gimme a pack of the Camels."

I peek over the magazine rack and see a middle-aged guy in a tank top, porkpie hat, and elephant ears the size of dinner plates, flapping just a little like he's trying to stir up a breeze to keep cool. Ma hands him his cigarettes, he gives her a wadded-up bill, and they talk some more about the weather. Then he waves, and she waves back with one of her tentacles.

Above the waist, Ma, June Michaelson, who's lived in Jokertown since her wild card turned when she was fifteen, is a forty-year-old woman with curly, shoulder-length hair dyed auburn, a round face and wide smile. She wears nice button-up shirts in bright colors and dangly earrings. She's the kind of person who asks if you've had enough to eat and if you'd like to come over for some coffee and a cinnamon roll.

Below the waist, she has a half dozen fat green tentacles instead of legs. She's like a mermaid but part octopus instead of fish. She totally walks around on those things, too. They're super strong and flexible. When she really wants to freak someone out, she'll reach over the counter with one of her tentacles to hand the customer their bag.

She always wants to freak out the tourists.

Sometimes, a nat who sees her right away will turn around and walk back out of the store because they can't handle it. Sometimes they'll already be at the counter with a can of soda and it's too late to leave, at least without being rude, and to give most people credit, they don't want to be rude. They try to be cool about it. But you can see in their eyes that Ma breaks their minds.

The guy with the elephant ears doesn't blink because, you know, Jokertown. But the next time the bell on the door rings, the guy who walks in is a nat. Or looks like a nat, maybe in his twenties, wearing a nice shirt and khakis and some kind of hip goatee. More than that, he's a tourist, like he's slumming it in Jokertown, or he thinks he's still too far north to be in Jokertown proper. He looks around nervously, sees my whippet shape, and quickly glances away. His hand taps against his leg like he wants to be anywhere but here.

He goes to grab a pack of batteries and a bag of chips and then heads to the counter, where Ma waits with her big, friendly, cinnamon-roll smile.

"Would you like a bag for that?" she asks, ringing him up on the register with her totally normal hands.

"Yeah, that'd be great."

"There you go, hon." She lifts out the bag with one of her tentacles twisted firmly around it.

"Jesus!" the guy screams, falling back three feet and knocking over half the chips display. Ma, she just smiles.

Heaving breaths like he's been attacked by a lion, the guy struggles to get his feet under him and then rushes out the door, slamming it open hard on its hinges. He remembers to grab his bag first, but holds it by the bottom, where Ma hasn't touched it.

Ma leans over the counter and calls after him, grinning, "Have a nice day!"

I stand and look at her over the magazine rack. "Ma. Really?"

"Oh, honey, it's fine! And now he has a story to take back to his friends in the Village, or Brooklyn, or wherever he's from."

"One of these days somebody's gonna pull a gun on you."

"I've been working here twenty-five years and it hasn't happened yet. Rikki, you worry an awful lot for someone your age."

I'm sixteen, and near as I can figure all my friends and I do is worry. What are we gonna be when we grow up, who's gonna ask us to prom, how the hell do you fit in when you don't look like anybody else in the whole world. We've got a lot to worry about.

I glance at the clock hanging in the back of the store. A half hour more and then I can leave. I'm supposed to hang out with my friends later. That's all I'm doing, when Ma thinks I'm joining a gang.

The bell rings again, and this time Dad comes in. A lot of days he'll stop by on his lunch break "to say hi to my girls." I smile every time.

"Hey, Dad," I say.

"How are my girls today?" He leans over the front counter for a kiss from Ma that lingers. If it weren't for the counter, it wouldn't be just her arms wrapping around him.

Dad's a manager for the sanitation department, and, like Ma, he's been working at the same place for practically his whole life. He also moved to Jokertown when his card turned. He's got lizard eyes and a forked tongue, but unless you look real close he just seems like a regular guy. He fools people. Ma says he's "passing," and that's how he got so high up in management at the sanitation department. But he says no, it's just that no one else wants to be a supervisor in Jokertown. It's the same with the cops, the utilities guys, everything.

"You working hard over there, Rikki?"

"Yeah, Dad," I say, both annoyed with the ritual and happy to have it.

"Rikki's a good worker, Nick," Ma says.

"I know it. You're a good kid."

He reaches out for a big hug, and I lean into it. I can't remember when he started having trouble getting his arms around my whippet chest. I squeeze back harder to try to make up for it, to tell him everything's okay.

Ma and Dad have been worried about me since I started high school last year. It's because I tried out for the track team and didn't make it, even though I can run faster than anyone else at the school. Than anyone in the *city*. It's because the state athletic board has rules about wild carders competing in sports against nats. Unfair advantage, they say, even though I'm just me. But my friend Beastie can't go out for football because he's like seven feet tall and super strong. He'd kick ass at football, and I guess that's the problem. The coach says there's too big a chance he'd hurt somebody. But I know Beastie. He can control himself, and he'd never hurt anybody. He just wants to go for a letter jacket like anyone else.

But in Jokertown we end up mainly competing against each other.

So my parents are worried I'm depressed. I don't think I am. I knew I couldn't be on the track team. But I'd like to show people I can run.

There's gotta be something out there for me to do, where I can run and have it be useful and not just some weird joker trick.

Dad picks out a soda; Ma gives it to him on the house. "What're you doing after work, Rikki?"

"Just hanging out," I say, like usual. He and Ma both get that worried look again, and I want to yell, "I'm *fine*."

Then it's time for him to go back to work, and we both wave him out the door, and finally it's time for my shift to end.

"I'm clocking out, Ma."

"And you're going straight back home, right?"

"No, I told you, I'm seeing Beastie and Kris and them at Seward Park, like usual."

"You'll be home by dinner." She says it like half a question, half a command.

I get exasperated. "Yes!"

She hesitates for a second, and I worry that she's going to say something, tell me no, I have to stay in and study or help with dinner or just be *around*, so she won't have to worry about me. She worries about me a lot. Dad says it's normal, but I think it's because the odds have been against me since the day I was born and she knows it.

But finally she says, "Okay. But be careful!"

I'm already out of the store.

♦

I am a miracle baby because I was a joker before I was born. The genetics of it work like this: The wild card gene is recessive, so you can have one wild card parent and one nat parent and be okay. You'll be born with the gene, but you won't be a wild carder. The only way you can get the virus is by getting infected.

But if both your parents are wild carders? If they both have the virus, and therefore the gene is written into their DNA? You're gonna have the gene, and you get the same odds as anyone who gets the virus: ninety percent chance of death. One percent chance of becoming an ace. Nine percent chance of being a human whippet, or octopus mermaid, or whatever.

I had two older siblings. They died before they were born—they got the ninety percent. "Third time's the charm," Dad used to say whenever he looked at me, until I told him to stop it. I'm the miracle baby, the one who lived, the one who beat the odds. Well, most of the odds, anyway.

I coulda been born an ace, and I wonder what would have happened then. Because the thing about Ma and Dad that no one says out loud is: They wanted a joker baby, like them. I wonder, if I'd been born an ace, with a regular human body and amazing powers, would they have loved me? I asked her that once. "Ma. What would you have done if I'd turned an ace?"

Her lips pressed into a tight line, the way they did when she had to give herself a moment to think. She finally said, "You're always an ace to me, dear."

Yeah, that didn't answer my question.

I run the few blocks to Seward Park just because I can, covering entire blocks in a few seconds, blowing past people who glare at me and shout after me to slow the hell down, but I don't care. I'm careful. I look where I'm going. I can't not run, with my lungs full of air and my legs burning with power.

Beastie's already at the park. He's hard to miss. He doesn't sit on the bench because he would break it, so he sits on the ground like a giant fuzzy boulder, hands draped on his thighs, his shirt hanging over him like a tent. He looks like a giant teddy bear until you notice the curving horns on his head and his long, pale claws. He jokes that he's gonna learn to knit with them someday.

Kris is on the bench next to him, wrapped up in her hoodie. It's a hot summer day but the hood is pulled way over her head so only her chin peeks out. Somehow, she's still able to glare. Her hands and sleeves are shoved deep in her pockets. Kris basically looks like a normal human, except for her skin. Her parents are black, but Kris's skin changes color depending on how she feels. Her mom calls her the walking mood ring, but none of us have ever seen a real mood ring so we take her word for it. Kris can't control it any more than she can control whether she's happy or sad or scared or angry. So she wears the hoodie. Right now her chin is sort of a pinkish swirl, which means she's a little bit sad, but not enough to say anything about it. She gets self-conscious when people ask her what's wrong all the time. Best thing to do with Kris is pretend you don't notice when her face goes from purple to blue to yellow because someone just said something stupid and she's furious. You can ask, but she'll just fold up and not say anything. If she wants to say something, she'll say something.

Then there's Splat. I don't notice him at first because he's under the park bench. He's part of the sidewalk, in fact. Flat. If I hadn't stopped ten feet away to look for him on purpose, I'd be stepping on his leg. Splat—his name is really Franklin Steinberg—can do something to his body that makes all his bones and organs and everything spread out until they are, mostly, flat. So when he presses himself to the wall he really presses himself to the wall. He would be an ace, except he can't actually *do* anything when he's splatted out. The way he explains it, his muscle tissue loses elasticity and he can't get the leverage to so much as slither under a closed door or lift a carpet to trip someone. He's tried. He's still trying. He practices every day but only ever has enough strength to pull himself back into his normal shape. Still, there isn't a one of us he hasn't scared by hiding behind a telephone pole and jumping out and yelling, "Boo!" He's a hoot at parties.

"I see you," I announce as I approach.

Splat picks himself up, which is weird to watch. It's like film of water spilling rolled backward, the pieces sucking toward some central point which rises from the ground to become a lanky dark-haired kid, arms wrapped around his knees, sitting under the bench and grinning up at us.

Kris screeches, jumping off the bench and launching away like a frightened cat, hood slipping off her head to reveal the skin of her face splotching between blue and red.

"Jesus fuck, Splat! Why didn't you say something?"

Beastie gets to his feet but doesn't jump like Kris. He turns to me and says in his deep voice, "We didn't think he was here yet. Hey, Rikki."

"Hey. So, Splat, learn any juicy gossip?"

He unfolds himself and crawls from under the bench. "Naw, these clowns are boring, just talking about school and stuff."

Kris hits him on the shoulder. Her skin settles back to a neutral brown, and she yanks the hood back over her short dark hair.

I slouch on the park bench. Kris slouches next to me, Splat follows, and Beastie settles back on the grass. "So what's up?" I ask.

"Nothing," Kris says.

"Nothing," Beastie repeats.

Splat shrugs. "My dad didn't come home again. Don't know when he's coming back this time."

"Aw, man, I'm sorry."

"Naw, it's cool."

Of course, if it was really cool, he wouldn't have said anything about it. But what can you say to make something like that better? He's saying it just to let it out, and we listen.

"What do you want to do?" I ask. My feet are itching to do something. They usually are.

"I dunno. Just hang out, I guess," Splat says, and the others echo it. I sigh. Hanging out it is, then. I slump back against the bench and look into the trees.

A bus pulls up to the curb on the park's east side. Its hissing brakes draw my attention. Like, a big coach tour bus, and the door opens and a crowd of people spills out and gathers on the sidewalk. They don't go any farther than that, clinging to the side of the bus like it's a life raft. A bunch of them are taking pictures.

"Tourists," Splat declares with disgust.

Sure enough, the woman in the neat skirt and suit jacket who'd gotten off first is speaking—she's too far away for us to hear exactly what she's saying, but the way she points like she's lecturing, we can pretty much guess. *Here's the street where protesters led by the JJS, Jokers for a Just Society, gathered in 1976, sparking the riots that ruined Senator Hartmann's first presidential bid. A couple of blocks that way is the brownstone where Xavier Desmond, the celebrated activist and unofficial mayor of Jokertown, lived. Our Lady of Perpetual Misery is a block in the other direction. This park has always been a gathering place for joker civil rights activists, though in recent years the neighborhood has been peaceful,* yadda yadda. I got most of the spiel from

Ma and Dad when I was growing up. They came to Jokertown after it all went down in '76, and sometimes I think they were sorry they'd missed it.

Isn't any sign of any of it now, except what the tour guides say.

Some of those cameras are clearly pointed at us, the local color, a group of joker kids hanging out in the park. Splat stands up and points both middle fingers at the tourists, scowling. Some of them look startled, eyes widening. Most just keep taking pictures. And won't that look nice in the family album? The tour guide hustles everyone back on the bus a moment later.

"We might as well be zoo animals," Splat mutters. "Stick us in a cage, put us in the zoo."

Funny he should be the one to say that, seeing as how he looks basically normal when he isn't splatting himself. It's me and Beastie, with his pelt of hair and canine face, who look like animals. It's Kris who hides under a hoodie. I think about saying something, but it'll just twist a knife. Into whom, I'm not really sure.

"It's a free country," Beastie says. Out of us all, he looks like the monster, but he's the calmest. The most sensible, even. He only scares people when they deserve it. "We're not in a cage. We can go anywhere we want."

"Yeah, right," Splat says, laughing.

We all know what he means: Sure, it's not like there are any laws that say a bunch of joker kids can't go walking up Broadway and then buy a hot dog and hang out in Times Square like anyone else. But hardly anyone actually does it. People would stare. We might not be able to find someone to actually *sell* us a hot dog. Splat would do okay; so would Kris. But Beastie? Me? A cop or two would start tailing us, and maybe even stop us and ask questions. *What're you kids doing so far from home?*—because they wouldn't have to ask where we're from. And if we were lucky, the encounter would end with them saying, "Maybe you kids ought to get on home before you get in trouble," and there'd be just a little bit of a threat in the statement.

We have Jokertown; we've had Jokertown for sixty years, so people like us don't bother the rest of Manhattan. Things like that don't ever change.

But right now it makes me angry. Maybe we're not really in a cage, but then maybe we are.

"Yeah, right," I say firmly, looking straight at Splat. "I've lived in New York my whole life and you know where I've never been? Central Park. Have you been to Central Park? Have you? And you?"

I point at each of them in turn and they all shake their heads. Suddenly, the fact makes me furious. Why haven't I been to Central Park? It's literally just up the road. Why didn't my folks ever take me to Central Park when I was a little kid? Not even to the actual real zoo that's there? Why?

Too much hassle, I suppose. Not just because of the subway ride uptown, but because of the stares, the awkwardness. The cops suggesting that maybe you ought to get on home now.

I stand, hands on hips. "I want to go to Central Park."

"*Now?*" Kris says, frowning.

"Sure. Why not?" They're all looking at me like I'm crazy, but that just makes me more determined. I can't back down now. Why not go to Central Park? We can even walk. Might take all day, but we can do it. "You guys don't have to go. I'll go by myself."

Beastie lumbers to his feet. It's like watching a mountain move. "I'll go. It's a nice day for it. It'll be fun."

I smile a quick thank you at him for backing me up.

Patting his arm, I say, "Come on." We start across the park to the sidewalk, him with his big, slow giant's stride, me with my quick, jittery one.

We haven't gotten far when Splat calls out for us to wait. He and Kris trot to catch up, though neither looks happy. Splat is surly and Kris is huddled deeper into her hoodie than ever. Her chin has gone sort of green.

"I'm bored," Splat explains. "Might as well see what happens."

"Real supportive there, jerk face," I say.

"You'll change your mind before you get to midtown," he shoots back.

Which makes me absolutely determined that I won't.

♥

We decide to take the subway.

This has a lot of pros and a lot of cons. Pro: We'll get there faster and with a lot less effort. On a warm summer day like today it'll be a lot more comfortable than walking in the sun, especially for Beastie. Cons: It'll be a lot less comfortable, especially for Beastie, being cooped up in a tiny metal car with people crowding in around him. If we get into a situation we need to get out of—well, we couldn't. The thing about walking is that no matter how long it takes or how tired we get, we can always bug out if we need to.

We leave the decision up to Beastie, and he picks the subway. The trip is a straight shot on the 6. If it gets awful we can always get out and walk back.

People clear the way for us as we go down the stairs at Canal Street. They pretty much have to—Beastie fills half the staircase by himself. People take one look at him and arc around, giving him room. Next to Beastie, they barely notice me and my whippet look. The rest of us travel in his wake.

Really, in this part of town we don't even get too many stares. Pretty much everyone around here lives in Jokertown and has scales for skin or feathers coming out of their ears or too many eyes or something. Even the nats here don't take a second look. And really, who can say that all these nats are really nats, and not some kind of ace or deuce or whatever, keeping to themselves and trying not to get noticed?

That's another thing about growing up in Jokertown: You never take anything for granted because so many things aren't what they seem.

Before too much waiting, the northbound train rolls up and we're off on our adventure.

Beastie has a method for entering a subway car. Having friends along helps, because we can get in first and kind of stake out space for him at the end, where he can lean up against the emergency door, hunch in under the ceiling and not worry about squishing anyone. As soon as the door opens, the three of us rush in and form kind of a cordon. He comes in next and has to crouch down, tuck himself under the top of the door, and pull himself through. He's done this before but there's always a moment when he looks like he might stick—he's that big. But with a twist of his shoulders, he'll wiggle his body and hunch down like some kind of gargoyle. The rest of us stand guard and glare back at anyone who might look like they want to give him a hard time. He swiped his card like everyone else, right?

The train rolls on, stopping at stops, and people get off and on. The farther north we travel, the more jokers leave, the more nats board, and the more people look over at us and scowl. Round about the Grand Central stop, a man in a business suit starts to get on our car, sees us—Beastie hunched in the back and the rest of us standing in front of him, glaring out and daring anyone to complain—and turns around to hurry to a different car. Kris's skin goes a searing red at that, and Splat presses himself as far to the wall as he can—I'm not sure he even realizes he's doing it. He looks like an ad poster.

I want to pace. I want to *run*. My feet twitch, and I tap them on the floor, first one then the other. Beastie stays calm, hunched over in a half-crouch, gazing forward with a wry smile.

"It's kind of an adventure, yeah?" he says. I roll my eyes.

"Remind me why we're going to Central Park again," Splat says, peeling himself off the wall to face the rest of us.

"To prove that we can," I answer.

"Should we have told someone where we're going?" Kris has on a permanent wince, like she's thinking this whole idea was bad. Her skin won't settle on a single color, and I'm getting kind of seasick looking at her.

"Like who?" I say.

"My mom? I should have told my mom," she murmurs.

"And if she said no, would you have just stayed home?"

She shrugs, which means the answer is yes, but she doesn't want to admit it.

"And this is why we didn't tell anyone," I declare. My own parents? They'd be horrified if they knew where I am. Jokertown is safe, and so we stay in Jokertown.

Just another couple of stops and we can get off.

As I'm thinking this, the subway car lurches, wheels screeching on tracks. Emergency brakes. Everybody in the car falls forward, grabbing at seats and poles. Beastie, sitting in the back, not holding on to anything, tips all the way forward, crashing onto the floor—and right on top of Splat.

People look around, trying to figure out why the train stopped. Beastie hurries to pick himself up, rocking back and reaching up for a pole.

"Oh, jeez, Franklin, I'm sorry. You okay?"

Splat has gone flat, compressed to the floor, limbs all splayed out. He re-forms to his regular body shape, inflating like a balloon, starting with his hands and feet, spreading up to his arms and legs, until finally he has enough leverage in his muscles to push up and climb to standing.

Beastie brushes at Splat's shirt and shoulders, wiping off dirt and grit from the subway floor.

"It's okay, it's okay," Splat says, sounding tired. "What the hell's happening with the train?"

A voice comes over the loudspeaker, but it's scratchy and filled with static, and nobody can make it out. We sit in that dark tunnel between stations for five, maybe ten minutes before the train slowly rolls forward again. So, just a temporary thing. But the whole time I'm thinking, what if we have to get out? What if someone gets mad at us for being here? I want to *run*.

The next stop, we decide, is close enough. We've all gotten claustrophobic, and this whole idea is looking less good by the minute. Besides, Beastie's legs are falling asleep.

We roll in to the Fifty-Ninth Street station—and the door sticks. All the other doors open, but our car is sealed up, and maybe this has something to do with the emergency stop. We stand by, waiting, penned in by a giant stroller and its owner, a young woman struggling to move forward, if only the door would let her out.

Meanwhile, the baby in the stroller is staring up at Beastie, real quiet, eyes round. I'm sure it's going to start screaming any minute at the big scary monster, and then the kid's mother will freak out, and station security will show up, and everything will get terrible—

Beastie starts making faces, stretching open his eyes, puffing up his cheeks, poofing breaths to make the hair on his chin fly out.

The baby smiles. Then its whole face squishes up and it lets out this gurgling little laugh.

Its mother glances over, goes pale for a second. She looks at her baby, looks at Beastie, then back to her baby. I can't tell what she's thinking. Like, she seems to want to grab the stroller and run. But the door won't open.

"Sorry," she says. "I can't get it—"

"It's not your fault," I reply. "Door's stuck."

"Here," Beastie says, and reaches over all of us. He works his claws into the crack, one at a time, then *pulls*. Wrenches back until whatever is stuck in the gears pops, and the door slides open like it's supposed to.

The woman collects herself, arranges the stroller, and smiles nervously. "Thanks," she says, rolling the stroller through the door and across the platform.

Beastie waves his claws at the baby, who is still gurgling happily.

"Let's get the hell out of here," Splat mutters, and we run.

♣

We hurry out of the station, the crowd parting in front of Beastie like magic.

Upstairs, back on the street, we all heave a sigh. Kris hunches further under her hood than ever. Beastie stretches, and I shake out my legs. We linger on the corner to get our bearings.

We're not in Jokertown anymore.

First off, we're the only jokers in sight. All kinds of people fill the sidewalks, rushing back and forth to wherever. Young, old, men, women, all ethnicities, in suits and skirts and raggedy jeans and workout clothes. None of them are jokers. It's actually weird, seeing so many people and not a scale or tentacle in sight.

We slow down traffic, with people rubbernecking to look at us. Pedestrians hesitate, look us all over, then keep going, maybe walking a little faster. Nobody says anything. They just *look*. I almost want somebody to say something so that I can yell at them.

We're on Fifty-Ninth Street. Way north from Jokertown, which doesn't even have street numbers. More than sixty blocks. Yeah, it's an adventure all right.

Across the street stands a wall of trees. Green, for the whole block. And

I can't see the other side of it, like back at Seward Park, where traffic is pretty much visible all the way around. This really is a whole wall of green.

"Well?" I ask the others. "Ready?"

"Lead on," Beastie says, smiling. If he's still smiling, things can't be that bad.

We find a place to cross the street and walk toward the park's entrance.

The whole time, Splat mutters, "Central Park. What's the big deal anyway?" He hasn't stopped complaining. Like, Central Park could be the greatest thing ever but he'll be damned if he's going to enjoy it. "A few trees and some lawn and joggers and what else? We got parks back in Jokertown—"

We enter the park. He stops and stares. We all do.

Factually, he's right. We have parks and lawns and trees in Jokertown. Little ones, squares of green bounded by traffic and buildings on all sides. But this . . . is different. I can't even explain it. It's like as soon as we leave the sidewalk, the traffic and city noises fall away. Trees rise up, lawn stretches ahead, and a calm settles. Sure, people are still around, crowds of them passing back and forth, tourists taking pictures, people with kids enjoying the day. But here they seem more spread out. Everyone, even the women in business suits and headphones and athletic shoes power walking to or from work, seems a little more laid-back.

And everything is green. Even sunlight coming through the trees turns green.

"Whoa," Splat finishes his observation.

A little ways in, on a winding blacktop trail, the trees open up to reveal a wide expanse of lawn. Here, a few people play Frisbee. Others lie stretched out on picnic blankets, reading books or talking. Farther ahead, the lawn slopes down to the edge of a wide pond where a bunch of ducks swim. Ducks, in the middle of New York City.

People look at us. They stare for a minute. And then they go back to their books and their friends. They leave us alone. After all, this is New York.

We walk for a while, following a path that loops around a hill and reveals even more park beyond. Endless park, that seems to go on forever. The path eventually brings us to a big lake. At the edge, a little kid feeds the ducks that continually squawk and ruffle their feathers. I start to think we've left the city entirely.

No one tells us to leave, and nobody stops to take pictures of us. Not that I notice, anyway. After a while, Kris picks out a spot in the sun and lies on the grass. She still wears her hoodie, but she turns her face up, squinting at the sun and sighing. The rest of us sprawl around her, and we just sit there for a long time.

"Good idea, Rikki," Beastie says, grinning so his lips curl up around his big teeth.

We've done it. An actual real quest. It feels good.

Predictably, Splat gets bored and wants to go home first. "I'm hot and tired. It's late. We walked for hours and we still have to get back home."

I'm actually thinking how good it feels to really stretch my legs. Maybe I'll take off at a run on one of those jogging trails. I can run faster than anyone here, I bet. Run the whole length of the park and see it all.

"Maybe we should go back," Kris says. "I gotta be home before dark."

So do I, but I'm glad I'm not the one who says it out loud and has to make the decision to go back.

"Ready, Rikki?" Beastie asks. He touches my shoulder with his massive hand—lightly, just a brush, because he's always so careful with everyone. He's never met anyone he can't just stomp into the ground. But he never does.

I take another look around, feeling like I'm in some kind of valley, and the tops of the skyscrapers are mountains. I breathe deep, so I can remember what this smells like. Yeah, this has been a good day.

"Sure."

Walking back, we get a little bit lost—if you told me I'd ever get lost anywhere in the city, I wouldn't have believed you. But a path curves away from where we expected it to, and it leads to a road which, it turns out, doesn't go anywhere. We double back to one of the main paths to find our way out of the park and to a subway station.

We're just about there when I hear shouting. I stop; the others stop with me and look to where I do—in the direction of uptown, where a white guy holding a backpack is running as hard as he can.

A couple of cops chase him. The shouting is them telling the guy to stop. Well, isn't this exciting? I wonder what he's done. Is this a mugging interrupted or something else?

"Why don't they just shoot him?" Splat says.

I glare at him. We ought to be happy the cops *aren't* just shooting in the middle of Central Park on a nice sunny day. The guy is fast, pulling ahead. I can see where he's headed: to the east side, cutting across the grass. If he gets over the hill, the cops aren't going to catch him.

But I have a straight shot at him.

I bunch up, clench my fists, preparing. Take a big, huge breath with my oversized lungs, and the extra oxygen lights up my system.

"Rikki, what are you doing?" Kris says warningly.

Beastie adds, "Rikki, wait—"

I launch.

Leaning forward into the speed, my legs pumping hard, I charge across the grass. Wind tangles my hair and presses against the skin of my face. Nothing but open space ahead of me, no corners to turn or obstacles to watch for. I've never been able to run like this except on a track. I grin.

I want to cut the guy off. Get in front of him so he'll have to slow down and stop, giving the cops time to catch up. Tackling him is probably not the best idea, though I'm pretty sure I could do that too if I wanted. Aim for his legs and dive. But no, I want to be smart about this. All I have to do is intercept him, making him stop or change direction, and let the police do their job. I am very proud of myself for thinking ahead and being reasonable and smart and using common sense.

The runner—with scruffy hair and a beard, wearing a leather jacket even in summer and faded jeans—catches sight of me out of the corner of his eye as I charge up the slope toward him. He does a double take, but he doesn't slow down and he doesn't change course, even as I curve around and head straight for him. We're charging each other now, and I might end up tackling him anyway in a failed game of chicken, because he doesn't look like he's going to move and I'm going too fast now to stop or turn without falling or crashing.

I put my head down, ready to take it, and then the running guy disappears. Flashes to nothing right in front of me. Flailing my arms and digging my feet into the grass, I lurch to a stop.

A teleporting ace. *Bullshit!*

And suddenly the guy's behind me, still running, not a break in his stride and not looking back. He might be able to teleport, but he only seems able to move a few yards at a time.

I should back off, then. Aces are bad news, 'cause you never know what all they can do, and if you don't want to get hurt it's best to stay away. That's what Ma and Dad always say, at least. A few aces live in Jokertown. And a few aces who look like jokers—nothing like Peregrine, you know, who has wings and can fly, but guys like Beastie who look really weird but are super strong, like ace strong. I should back off, but I'm so *angry*, I almost had him and then he pulled a trick like that. My lungs fill with air again, and my legs are on fire. I *know* I can catch this guy. I'm fast enough.

I spin on my foot and once again launch. Dig into the earth and kick my speed up a notch. He keeps running, but in just a second or two I move up behind him. I know I decided not to tackle him or get confrontational. Stay safe by keeping away from the ace, right? But how else am I going to stop him?

I lean in, reach out, grab for his sleeve—He teleports. Boom and boom, just a couple of feet away again, but enough to get out of my reach. He glances over his shoulder and he has on a wide-eyed look of panic. He's breathing hard. Maybe he can teleport, but he still has to run.

The cops are coming up behind us, shouting. I can't hear what they're saying.

The guy changes directions, keeps running. I keep chasing, not tired at all. This is *fun*. I get close, and he teleports out of my reach—and I change direction and run after him again. It's chaos, a mess, we're tearing up all the grass on the hillside and running in circles, and we aren't going anywhere. I have him corralled, but he stays out of reach.

And then, just when I go to grab him again, he teleports—and lands right in front of the pair of cops who've finally caught up with us. The taller of the two, a fit black guy, jams a hood over the guy's head while the other one wrenches his arm back and puts handcuffs on him.

The runner shouts a bunch of curses, his voice muffled by the hood.

"Shut up, Blinky, you ain't gonna die," says the cop cuffing him.

The taller one looks over at me and studies me like he's trying to figure out what to do. Both cops are nats, and I suddenly wonder how much trouble I'm in.

"And who might you be?" the tall cop asks.

"Um. Miranda Michaelson, sir."

"Well, Miranda Michaelson, hold on just a minute. We're going to need to talk to you."

The rest of the gang finally catches up, slogging up the hill like they're tired or something. "Rikki! What the hell?" Splat calls.

Beastie comes up and puts a big hand on my shoulder. "You okay?"

"Yeah, I'm fine. I caught a bad guy!"

"You could have been hurt!" he says.

"Seriously," Kris says, her face blazing red and orange with fear and a little anger.

"These your friends?" the tall cop asks.

"Yeah—we're not in trouble or anything, are we?"

"No—just . . . just come on, until we get our friend here situated."

We follow them across the lawn to the Fifth Avenue side of the park. The cops are dragging the blindfolded ace between them, and he's still yelling.

Splat hisses under his breath, "I think we should run. Before the cops get too interested in us."

"I want to see what happens," I say, and Splat huffs, scowling, but he keeps following.

"Can I ask—why the blindfold?" I ask.

The tall cop answers, "He has to be able to see to teleport. If he can't see, he can't vanish. Blinky's an old friend of ours. We have a system. He just got away from us this time."

"Like Popinjay," Splat says. Splat knows all about old-school aces and stuff like that. He reads the comic book versions.

"Not nearly as powerful. In fact, Blinky here's more like a deuce, aren't you?"

"Fuck off!"

"Hey, no swearing around the kids," says the short cop gripping his arm.

"Fuck them, too."

"It's okay," I say. "People say 'fuck' all the time around us."

The tall cop looks like he's tasted something sour.

A line of three patrol cars waits at the curb, one of them belonging to the cops who'd arrested Blinky, and the other two just seem to be there to watch. We hang out nervously while they load their mugger in the backseat. If we want to run, this is our chance.

"Are you sure they don't want to arrest us?" Kris says.

"We didn't do anything wrong," I say.

Kris glares. "No, you just went running off to interfere with some arrest—"

"They wouldn't have caught the guy at all if I hadn't helped!"

The tall cop says, "Hey. You kids aren't in trouble. We just need a statement. You're witnesses. So don't freak out. I'm Officer Dewey, and this is my partner Officer Clancy—"

By this time Clancy has stuffed Blinky in to the car and he edges over to whisper, as if we aren't right there, "You sure about them? I mean, a bunch of jokers, what are they doing all the way in Central Park—"

Dewey crosses his arms and glares. "They're not Werewolves, Clancy! Look at them, they're a bunch of kids." He looks skeptically at Beastie but doesn't correct himself.

"Hey!" Splat says. "I'm seventeen; I graduate next year!"

Dewey and Clancy look at each other, and Clancy shrugs, as if to say it's on his partner's head. Dewey sighs and goes to the car to get a notebook.

"All right. One at a time. Tell me what you saw."

♠

Being a witness is easy enough, but it isn't as much fun as actually running down a bad guy. Officer Dewey says we probably won't need to do anything else—Blinky had mugged some student; there'd been plenty of witnesses. Since he's a repeat offender, he'll likely plead guilty, so there won't be a trial or anything. But Dewey thanks us for being good citizens and offers to give us a ride home.

"Where do you kids live?" he asks.

We all stare at him. Like, is he serious?

♦

Officer Dewey has to call in a van for Beastie. I ask if maybe we can get a ride in a SWAT van, just to see what that's like, but no, they have a regular white utility van. Beastie rides in the back. The trip goes a little faster than the one uptown. That doesn't change how weird it is, riding in a cop car. We have to keep convincing ourselves we haven't done anything wrong and we aren't being secretly taken to a jail somewhere.

But no, Officer Dewey drops off Kris and Splat, and we all promise to get together in a couple of days. Just to hang out, we decide. No adventures next time. Beastie gives me a careful hug before he goes up to his apartment. He never has any trouble getting his arms around my barrel chest.

Finally, we stop at my apartment building.

"I'll walk you up," Officer Dewey says, parking the van. With the police logo on the side, he can park anywhere.

"You don't have to do that," I say. "I mean, I'm sure you're real busy—"

"Indulge me."

By now it's after dark, after supper, which means I'm going to get in trouble. I don't know what's going to happen when my folks see Officer Dewey and the police uniform. They'll think the worst; I'm not looking forward to it.

"Okay, here we are," I say, standing at the door, not opening it. "Thanks again for the ride—"

The door opens. Ma's standing right there. It's like she heard me talking. She's probably been waiting by the door for an hour, and now I feel terrible.

"Hey, Ma," I say, shrinking inside myself, blushing hard.

"Rikki, where have you been, you're late—"

And then she sees Officer Dewey. The blood drains from her face and all her tentacles go limp, flattening on the floor like a carpet. "Aw, jeez, Rikki! What did you do, hon? How many times have I told you to stay out of trouble?"

"Ma, please, it's not what you think—"

"Officer, I'm so sorry, I don't know what she's done, but I'm telling you, she's a good kid—"

I'm hoping Officer Dewey will say something soon, but he's staring. One of Ma's tentacles starts climbing up the wall as she's talking, and another reaches out to me, trembling. I recognize the signs—the tentacles all kind of quiver when she gets mad.

But I suppose this looks pretty weird to Officer Dewey.

"Ma, just listen!"

"You're gonna kill your poor father, Rikki, when he hears—"

Officer Dewey finally recovers from his shock with a shiver and manages a polite neutral expression. "Um, Mrs. Michaelson? Rikki isn't in any trouble at all."

She stops mid-rant, her tentacles frozen. "What?"

"I just gave her a ride home after she helped us nab a mugger uptown. I thought you might like to hear about what a good citizen she is. You should be proud." He smiles. I smile. He doesn't flinch at my fangs.

Ma's expression goes through a whole range of changes, from shock and upset to confusion, then to relief and finally—pride.

"I know she's a good kid," Ma says, beaming. "She's the best. Thank you for bringing her home and letting me know."

"My pleasure, Mrs. Michaelson."

Ma reaches out to me—with a hand, even—and grabs hold of my own. But she puts a tentacle around my shoulder to pull me close in a big hug. And it's totally normal.

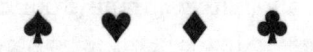

♠ ♥ ♦ ♣

The Flight of Morpho Girl

by Caroline Spector & Bradley Denton

YESTERDAY, THE DAY GHOST was kidnapped, Mom came into my bedroom after breakfast and jumped out the window.

I'd gone out that way before dawn, and I'd come back in the same way. Like, it was super practical and, bonus, Mom didn't know—which was hella best for both of us. There was no way I was telling her I'd been flying.

We're on the eighth floor, and I heard a sick thud as she slammed into the concrete below. I ran over to the window and looked down. Mom got to her feet and waved. She was fatter now.

"I love you, honey!" she called in this weird, peppy voice. I was thinking, like, please don't do that—because it was giving me the sick willies. "Have a good Monday!" Then she jogged away, and the people on the sidewalk parted for her like water.

She's been doing that a lot lately. Jumping out my window, I mean. She used to use *her* bedroom window when she wanted to put on fat, but ever since she came back from Kazakhstan she's been different. As in, *so* not normal.

Of course, "normal" for us isn't normal at all. After all, Mom's an ace. She's a totes famous ace. Between her modeling (she's been a model since she was a kid, even before her card turned) and her work with the Committee, she's either on the front page of every political website, or selling cosmetics and stuff like that to all the nats. She's always filled with the fabu—even when she's heavy. Maybe especially then.

But me, I'm a joker. I couldn't pass for a nat no matter what. My iridescent cobalt-colored wings—the same color as a morpho butterfly—make sure of that. And I still have four vestigial insect legs on my torso from when I was a little girl. Oh, yeah, did I mention that until four weeks ago I was a little girl? Overnight I went from being, like, ten to being, like, sixteen. See, the bad stuff that happened in Kazakhstan, well, my little-girl self was so frightened by what she saw in her dreams that she went into a cocoon. When I came out, I came out as something the size of a teenager. And my wings, well, they aren't just pretty anymore. They're *awesome*.

So Mom and I both emerged from that whole Kazakhstan thing... changed. And I think *my* changes have been freaking *her* out. But then, freaking her out isn't a difficult thing to do these days. Like, she went noodley over the fact that our water has started to turn a gross color kinda like orange Gatorade. Okay, so anyone would be grossed out because, ew. But she got *crazy* noodley when the super said to tell the city about it, not him. She threatened to make him drink it. Also, our HBO keeps switching to Spanish for no reason, and we've had to buy a new remote control because she got pissed about that and bubbled the old one into powder. Not pieces. *Powder*.

I guess that's why she's gone into full-blown Mom-of-the-Year mode. It probably makes her feel like she's in control of *something*. So she cooks. She cleans. She even tries to help me with my homework. Which is amazeballs, but in a bad way. For one thing, she's even worse at algebra than I am. But I have to pretend that I couldn't do it without her.

And she's pretty much gone wild with the cooking. Like, she's been channeling Martha Stewart, except Mom doesn't have a prehensile tail.

Yesterday morning, before the window thing, she made eggs, bacon, toast, pancakes, and fresh-squeezed orange juice. It used to be, when it came to breakfast, she could barely put cereal in a bowl. So most of the time we'd just grab a bagel with a schmear at the deli at Fourteenth Street and Avenue A. The deli crowd were all used to me when I was a little girl, and some of them even smiled at me once in a while. But now, if we go there at all, everyone avoids making eye contact.

Sure, I *look* like a teenager now, and my wings are a lot bigger than they used to be. So maybe I knock a few things off a table when I walk past. But I'm still *me*.

I mean, I'm *mostly* still me. I haven't told anyone this... but how I *think* is different now. It's like I got smarter and dumber at the same time. I know things I didn't know before, and I can do things I didn't do before. (I can play the bass! Really!) But I cry, like, at the drop of a hat. At stupid stuff. Like, tragic love scenes in movies. It's mega embarrassing.

"Adesina, eat up, honey," Mom said. "You're too thin." Which should have been hilarious, coming from her.

I gave a groan and pushed away my plate. "Mom, I'll be in Snoozeville, like, all day if I have any more."

As usual, she didn't seem to hear me. But she swept away the dishes and loaded them into the dishwasher. Then she polished the sink faucets for, like, the sixth time. As if that would make them any shinier.

"Mom," I said. I wanted to tell her she didn't have to do all this stuff—that it would be fine by me if she just went back to being like she used to be. But she still didn't seem to hear me. And I hated the look on her face. It was blank, and her head was cocked to one side as if she were hearing something. Something bad. But the only sounds were the usual noises coming up from the street. The taxis honking, the exhausted sigh of buses, and people yelling at each other. Nothing that would make Mom blank out like that. It was the *worst*.

I got up and went to my room. Leaving Mom alone when she got like this, I'd decided, was the only thing to do. She couldn't hear me, and getting her attention by touching her would only freak her all the hells out. I knew this because about a week before, I'd tried to get her attention that way. Just by touching her shoulder. And she had almost bubbled me.

Oh, she used to make a lot of bubbles *for* me. When I was a little kid. But they'd always be *soft* bubbles. We'd play with them in the park or knock them around the bathtub. Or she'd encase me in a bubble for a few minutes and I'd roll around in it. Stuff like that.

But there are other things she can do with her bubbles, and those just aren't funny. She can shoot iron-hard bubbles as if they were bullets. She can even make them explode. Put it all together, and she's one of the most powerful aces in the world.

Which is cool. Except when it's not.

She's my mother, but she's done . . . things. In particular, things for the Committee. Ugly things. And she tries really hard to make up for all of that. But dead is dead. You know?

So when I touched her shoulder, and she turned on me with that terrible look on her face and a bubble half-formed in her hand, it about scared the pee out of me. Not just because of the danger in her hand, but because she didn't *know* me. For a moment, I was whatever she'd been thinking of. And whatever it was, she wanted to kill it.

Then, suddenly, she was back to being Mom. Well, not exactly Mom, but that weird version of Mom that cooks and cleans. And occasionally almost blows me up.

So, yeah. We've both changed.

But I've only changed on the outside. Mostly. Mom, though, has changed on the *inside*.

And I just want her to be herself again. Like, the way that I'm still me.

Which is what I was thinking while I was getting my school stuff from my room, and she walked in. "I'm doing a job for the Committee today," she said. "They're jetting me down to Panama."

"Is it a . . . dangerous job?" I asked. I really didn't like the idea of her doing anything more for the Committee just yet—especially not if it might remind her of Kazakhstan.

Mom shrugged. "The idea is that if I make an appearance, certain people will rethink their positions. I might only need to be there a few hours, so I could be home this evening. If I'm not, Mrs. Lehman from down the hall will come over about ten o'clock, and she'll stay the night. Either way—the leftover beef Stroganoff is in the fridge. And the broccoli, too." She paused. "No. I should make you something for dinner besides leftovers."

"Leftovers are fine!" I said in a loud voice. "And I don't need Mrs. Lehman to stay with me."

For once, Mom seemed to hear me. "You might *look* like you're all grown-up, but we both know better. Text me as soon as you get home from school. And deadbolt the door."

"*I know*, Mom."

Then she jumped out the window. Which really irked me.

I mean, jeez. It's *my* room, isn't it?

Well. Two can play at that game.

♥

I had a little time before I had to go to school, so I thought about heading to the roof for more flying practice. But it was daylight now, and there are taller buildings surrounding ours. And I wasn't ready to display my aerial skills to the whole world yet. For one thing, my landings weren't always pretty. More like crash-and-tumbles. But when that happened, I just wrapped my wings around myself and rolled. My wings are hella tough, so it didn't hurt. But that didn't mean I wanted anyone to see me bouncing across the roof like a lumpy soccer ball.

So instead, I went into Mom's bedroom, reached under the bed, and pulled out the box I'd found there when she'd been at a photo shoot. Inside was a denim-covered diary.

I'd found the diary by accident. Okay, maybe not *completely* by accident. More like an accident when I had been searching her room. After the incident when she had almost bubbled me, I had decided I needed to get to know this new version of my mother a little better. Even if I had to be kinda sneaky about it.

I had read the whole thing immediately. But now I kept going back over certain entries, as if they would unlock some secret. Of course, if she'd dated anything or kept up with it all the time, it might have been easier to figure her out.

But Mom isn't really about making things easy.

She might say that I'm not, either. But I'm a teenager now. So, you know. I have an excuse.

♣

Mom's Diary

I wish Mommy wouldn't just drop me off at shoots. But today she said she had other errands to run and I'd be fine. After all, I'm ten and that's practically a teenager. At least that's what she said.

There was a new photographer today. I like Mr. B, but they said Mr. B was sick and this new man would be doing the photos. He told me to call him Tony, and then the wardrobe crew got me into the new clothes for Fall. It's Spring now, and Fall clothes are heavy and hot under the lights.

Mommy and Daddy said I had to make these ads really good because we're having money problems. But I <u>always</u> try my best when I work. And I don't want Mommy and Daddy to have to worry about money.

Mommy said we can't afford to have me out of work again. I guess things got bad when OshKosh B'gosh didn't renew my contract. They kept me after their usual cut-off because I look younger than I am. And because I was popular. But just before I turned eight I got too tall, and a lady from OshKosh said she was sorry, but no one would believe I was six anymore.

That was two years ago. Daddy was mad because he started having trouble booking me. But I knew why. I was famous as the OshKosh B'gosh girl. So who else would want me?

But Daddy found someone who did. So today I did the shoot with Tony.

I didn't like him. He kept asking me to look sexy. That's just gross. But I did my best because I'm a professional.

They dressed me up in all these grown-up clothes. Four other girls were there, too. They were like me. When they were younger, they were known for selling kids' stuff. But now no one wanted us. Not as kids, anyway.

The makeup girls seemed angry. I heard one of them say Rudolph was going too far with this new campaign. Rudolph makes these really pretty clothes and he uses all kinds of models. Most are nats like me. But he's used some aces with cool powers. Once he used jokers, but that didn't work out so well.

Peregrine posed naked for his perfume line. Her wings hid everything, but you could tell she didn't have any clothes on. Mommy said it was disgusting. Right up until Daddy said it probably paid her a fortune.

♠

Who leaves their little kid alone with strangers? I was glad I'd never met Gramma and Grampa, or whatever I would have called them. Nothing nice, I don't think.

I pulled out my phone, went on the internet, and looked up that campaign for Rudolph Haute Couture Atelier in *Vogue*.

Mom had been right. It was pukesville.

There she was all pouty-faced and made up like an adult. The clothes are gorgeous, but the way Mom and the other girls are posed—gah. I mean, it's yucky. It's a world of yuck. Did I mention the high yuck factor?

I shut the journal and put it back in the box. Then I slid the box under the bed, back into the dark, where it belonged.

♦

I wouldn't say my day at school was bad. Not exactly. The week before, and the week before that, hadn't been bad, either. Not exactly.

I mean, the high-school work isn't as hard as I thought it might be. And the teachers are okay. Also, shock of shocks, none of the other kids—I mean, teenagers—have been mean to me. For the first few days, some of them even showed me around. Being a joker probably helped my cred, since most of them are jokers, too.

But just because they haven't been jerks to me, well, that doesn't mean they're my friends. Not yet, anyway.

So yesterday, when the final bell rang, I decided to blow down to the Jerusha Carter Development Center. My actual friend, Ghost, goes to the Carter School, and I wanted to see her. Maybe I could walk home with her.

See, I *used* to be at Carter with Ghost. Then things got messed up because I got big. So now they've sent me to the Xavier Desmond High School, which is a few blocks away from the Carter School in Jokertown. But it might as well be on the Moon. I miss Carter, and I especially miss Yerodin—who we call "Ghost" because of her ace power.

She and I were both adopted after our cards turned. She was adopted by Wally Gunderson. You know, Rustbelt, who was on *American Hero* with Mom. Wally is a joker like me. Well, not like me. His skin is iron, he has bright yellow eyes, and he's about the size of one and a half professional wrestlers. And he's strong. Mom says he can hit hella hard, but that's what Mom *would* focus on. She's always into taking the damage.

Anyway, the Committee sent him and Mom to the People's Paradise of Africa—it seems like a lifetime ago, now—and that was where they found me and Yerodin. In the PPA, the both of us, along with a lot of other kids, had been injected with the wild card virus. Some of those kids became aces, like Ghost, and some, like me, turned into jokers. But the people—bad people, not that I want to be all judgy, but I really do—who were injecting us didn't want jokers. Just aces. So they either killed us jokers or left us to die. Then Mom saved me from the pit where they'd dumped me. I guess the bad people thought I'd drawn a black queen, because I was in my cocoon when they tossed me in. But really, I was just becoming my little insect-girl self.

Just like, a month ago, I would become my new insect-teenager self. The wild card virus, besides the other things it did, had been slowing down the growth of both me and Ghost, keeping us as little kids. But when Kazakhstan happened, I changed. Fast.

My first day back at Carter after my transformation, when I met Yerodin on the sidewalk, she freaked out. She went all noncorporeal, and then she ran into the building. Through the wall. And she wouldn't come near me for the next two days. She wouldn't even talk to me during gameplay on *Ocelot 9*. She did respond a few times via text, but even then, she only answered with emojis. Like, you know, steaming poops with unhappy faces.

Then I was transferred to high school.

But yesterday, I hoped that maybe enough time had passed. Maybe Ghost was feeling less weird now, and might even be glad to see me. I had to try, anyway.

To my surprise, when I got to the Carter School, Wally was there. He was lumbering out of the gate behind a gaggle of kids, but Ghost wasn't one of them. And he looked as if someone had just punched him in the gut. Assuming anyone could do that to a gut made of iron.

"Hey Wally," I said as the kids streamed past me. "Is Yerodin still inside?"

"Oh gosh, she sure isn't," he replied. His voice was thick with his Minnesota accent. Minnah-SO-dah. His shoulders were all hunched up, and he was hugging his arms to his chest as if it were winter instead of fall. And his clothes were rumpled. "We had a fight this morning about—aw, it doesn't matter. But she was mad as heck. So I thought I'd come pick her up and take her for an ice cream. But I can't find her. Mrs. Teasdale says she was here before her music class, but the music teacher says she didn't show up for it. And I know she didn't come home then, because I was there. She isn't home now, either, because our neighbor Bob has a key, and I just now called him to check." He looked up and down the street. "It was dumb to let her leave the apartment while she was mad. But I thought if she walked to school, same as every day, it might blow off some steam." He shook his huge head. "Now she won't answer her cell phone. So I don't know where she is. Or even if she's okay."

I was stunned. Wally and Ghost *never* argue. Wally is too nice, and Ghost, well, she just worships him. So what he was saying made me feel as if I were about to have a freak-out storm. Like a category 5. I couldn't even imagine what they would fight about.

"I'm sure she's all right," I said, trying to keep my voice from quavering. And I wanted to believe it. After all, Ghost can go all noncorporeal and escape pretty much anything. Also, she had been trained in the PPA as an assassin, and that made her scary as hell sometimes. What could happen to someone like her?

But Wally was beyond worried. And I didn't need him having a freak-out storm, too. Like, there's only room for one of those at a time. Besides, a guy like Wally shouldn't be scared. I mean, he's—you know, *Rustbelt,* for crying out loud.

"Neighbor Bob says he'll stick around and call me if she shows up," Wally said. "But, gosh, if she isn't there already—"

"I bet she's just taking the long way home," I said. I patted Wally's back. It made a dull thunk and kinda hurt my hand. I never would have done that before my transformation, but it seemed like a semi-grown-up thing to do. I felt stupid doing it, though.

Wally gave a shuddering sigh. "I could go home and wait, but I feel like I should be looking for her. Or calling the police. But Mrs. Teasdale says the police won't do anything about an angry child who's only been missing an hour." He grabbed the wrought-iron fence that surrounded the school, and it started turning to rust. He can do that, make iron rust. He jerked his hand back, but a three-foot section had already poofed away.

"It's going to be okay," I said. I patted his back again, and it felt a little less stupid this time. "Look, Yerodin and I have a place we like to go when we ditch class. We can check there."

Wally's mouth hinges pulled down. "You ditch class?" He sounded astonished.

All of a sudden my tongue felt thick. "Um, just a little, sometimes, during last period." Except that sometimes we snuck out during fourth period, too, because Mrs. Teasdale never did roll call after lunch. Mrs. Teasdale was a joker, sporting wiggly face and neck tentacles, and I think she was supposed to be a role model for us joker kids. But she mostly napped in the afternoon while we were supposed to be doing the day's reading on our tablets.

And that *so* didn't happen. Most of the time, Yerodin and I played the *Ocelot 9* battle version in friend mode. She beat me almost every game.

But some days, we'd sneak out of class while Mrs. Teasdale snoozed. We'd head down the street to Jinka's Juice and grab smoothies, then walk a few blocks over to our favorite game shop.

"It's called the Tumbling Dice," I said. "Ghost and I get all our *Ocelot 9* stuff there. Come on, I'll take you."

Wally's forehead crimped. The creases in his forehead had a dull sheen. If he doesn't Brillo himself now and then, he gets all cruddy and rusty. Yesterday afternoon, though, he was spotless. At least, he was at first.

"Aren't you supposed to go straight home after school?" he asked. "Your mother will wonder where you are."

"I'll text Mom," I said. "She's working late today anyhow." Wally didn't seem to know that Mom was in Panama. But I didn't see any reason to mention it. And I also didn't see any reason to mention what I would text to her.

Wally was still frowning. "I don't know," he said. "Maybe you can just tell me how to get to this Dice place."

"No!" I hadn't meant to shout, but that's how it came out. "Until four weeks ago, Yerodin and I were the same age, and we did everything together. And now—" I gestured at my teenage body. "I have to go to high school, and everyone acts weird around me. Even Ghost. But she is *always* going to be my best friend." I stared up at Wally's face and tried to beat his iron scowl with one of my own. "So I'm not going home 'til I know she's okay. Period."

Wally's frown smoothed a little. "I see. Uff-da." Then he looked up and down the street again, as if Ghost might magically appear . . . which, given her ace power, she very well could. "Let's go, then."

"Follow me." I turned to head down the sidewalk.

Then my wings began to unfurl. I tried to get them to collapse again, but it wasn't easy. I wished they would just snuggle against my back the way they did when I was little. Now it was like they had a will of their own. For example, six days after my transformation, I got all excited playing *Ocelot 9* solo, and I jumped up from the couch. At which point my head bumped the ceiling, because my wings had spread open and flapped without my even thinking about it.

So I started sneaking up to the roof to practice flying. Which got easier once I discovered I could flap up there from my bedroom window. And luckily, Mom hasn't noticed the dent in the living-room ceiling.

So, yeah. Flying. That's something. But as Wally and I headed out from the Carter School, all I knew was that we had a mission and that my big, pretty wings were trying to get in the way.

"Right behind you," Wally said, and then his jaw clanged as the upper edge of my left wing whapped him.

I looked back and started to apologize, but he hadn't even noticed. Tiny specks of rust were starting to appear on his forehead and at the corners of his mouth.

I picked up the pace and headed for the Tumbling Dice.

♥

Ever since Mom and Wally saved me and Ghost from the PPA, we've been doing our best to become normal kids.

Well, okay. Like with me and Mom, "normal" isn't an option.

But being *kids* should be. As in, not a discarded freak, and not a noncorporeal assassin. Just, you know . . . *kids*. Living the way kids are supposed to live.

For me and Ghost, in our new life in Jokertown, New York City, USA, playing games has been a huge part of that. Because that's what American kids do, right?

Besides, it's hella fun. And the most hella fun game of all is *Ocelot 9*. Which is what we were playing the day before I changed into a teenager.

"I call Baby Ocelot," Yerodin said. She had a wicked grin on her face. We were sitting on the couch at my house.

"Oh, that's so not fair!" I said with fake annoyance. She always dibsed Baby Ocelot. Usually, I just let her have it because she really liked winning.

"Watch out for my adorableness!" she cackled. You wouldn't have thought that sound could come out of the mouth of such a little girl.

"That attack is totes OP!" I said with indignation. "Even Tulip Ralph says so!" The Adorable Attack could stun or enchant an enemy, and no matter which ocelot I was playing, Baby and its AA were hard to beat.

"Hey, I've won against *you* when you've played the Baby," Ghost said. "And Ralph just likes teasing us. But I'm immune to it. Too bad you aren't immune to the Adorable Attack!"

I loved trash talking with her. "Then bring it on, doomed Baby!"

I chose Ninja Ocelot, went stealth, and started sneaking around behind her. Then, just when I came out of stealth to wallop her, she spun and hit me with the AA. It took but a few Perfume Bolts for her to finish me off.

"Boom!" She raised her hand and opened it, pretending to drop a bomb.

I reached over and tickled her. "Next time I get Baby!" She giggled, then started tickling me, too.

Our tablets fell to the floor, and we kept at it until Ghost cried "Uncle." Revenge was mine.

♣

If Wally hadn't been so worried, it might have been a nice walk. In late September, almost overnight, New York goes from smelling like melting tar and rotting garbage to crisp leaves and spiced cider. If Yerodin had been with me, we'd have been talking about what costumes we'd be wearing for Halloween.

But of course Wally didn't notice the nice day. We went down four blocks past Jinka's Juice, where Ghost and I buy our smoothies, and then I turned and headed three blocks west. And the farther we went, the worse the neighborhood got, which I hadn't realized before. But now I did, because I could tell it was making Wally tense. And the more tense he got, the more his legs clanked.

"I can't believe you and Yerodin have been skipping school," he said.

My wings twitched. "It's never hurt our grades," I said. "So we've always figured it's no big deal."

Wally's jaw made a grinding sound. "If it was no big deal," he said, "you wouldn't have kept it a secret from me and your mom."

"Wally—" I said.

But Wally wasn't finished. "And if you hadn't started doing it at all, don'tchaknow, maybe Yerodin would have come home today instead of thinking it was okay to run around down here all by herself." His shoulders slumped. "Gosh, she's still just a little kid."

And that's when I started to cry.

♠

Mom's Diary

I tried not to cry, but when the judge said I was emancipated, it was horrible.

I don't want to be emancipated. Not at fourteen. For one thing, it sounds like I was a slave or something. And I was never that. But I wish . . . I wish Mommy and Daddy hadn't done what they did.

I worked whenever they said to. And it wasn't fun most of the time. It was okay when I was a kid. But now they want me to be so skinny. I'm almost six feet tall and they've been trying to keep me at 115 pounds.

I'm hungry all the time. I know a lot of the girls will eat Kleenex because it fills them up. But I tried it once and barfed.

They spent everything I made. I must be something horrible. Because why else would they treat me like that?

I guess I'm free now. But I feel more trapped than ever.

♦

I turned my face away and managed to get control of myself. And Wally didn't speak the rest of the way to the Tumbling Dice. I was glad of that, because if he did, I might start crying again. And I was too big for that now.

Ghost and I love the Tumbling Dice. They have a ginormous inventory of RPGs and board games. The shelves are loaded up to the ceiling. They have all the current D&D modules, of course, as well as all sorts of mainstream games and some really obscure stuff. (Seriously, who's going to play an RPG where you're an amoeba?) They even have a copy of *The Game of Wild Cards* where you go along hoping you don't land on the Black Queen or Jokertown squares.

The owner is Tulip Ralph. Instead of hair, he has beautiful tulips growing out of his head, except in the winter when they go dormant. Then he has a head full of bulbs that look like gross warty growths.

But when Wally and I walked in, with the bell on the door making its *ting* sound, Ralph still had some pretty flowers left. They're always the fancy kind, all ruffly with stripes. And they change color pretty much every day. Yesterday, they matched the orange, blue, and white of his checkered shirt. Which was untucked, as usual.

He's never seemed to mind if Ghost and I hang out and watch his regulars play their games. Just so we're quiet. There's a back room set up for playing miniatures, and two tables for role-playing campaigns in the front room. At least one of those tables is always full, as it was when Wally and I came in.

"Hey, Ralph," I said, stepping past the gamers to the scuffed black counter. I hadn't been in since I'd changed, but everything still looked the same. The countertop was jammed with displays of collectable trading cards, with the super-rares in individual sleeves with hefty price tags. But *Ocelot 9* was more fun, and cheap. "Have you seen Ghost?"

Ralph looked up from his book—a biography of Abraham Lincoln—and stared over his reading glasses. His tulips bobbed, and his eyes widened. "Who's this in my store?" he asked in his usual gravelly voice. But he wasn't asking me. "If I didn't know better, I'd say you must be Rustbelt.

But what would Rustbelt be doing in my little dump?" He held out his hand. "I'm Tulip Ralph, by the way."

"Aw, gosh, Mr. Tulip," Wally said, giving Ralph's hand a quick shake. "I'm looking for my daughter, Yerodin. This is her friend, Adesina. She might've looked different the last time you saw her."

Ralph nodded. "Yeah, she was a little more compact." He nodded toward my phone, which was jutting up from the pocket of my jean jacket. "But I recognize those *Ocelot 9* stickers on her phone. That game is like crack for her and her friend." He raised an eyebrow. "In fact, Yerodin was in here yesterday, hitting me up for a free Baby Ocelot notebook. First time she's been here in weeks. I was surprised you weren't with her, 'Morpho Girl.'"

I felt a lump growing in my throat. "I wish I had been," I said. "I wish we were here together right now."

Ralph frowned. "Well, she was out on the sidewalk about an hour ago, slurpin' one of those smoothies you girls always have. Thought she was waiting for you. But after a few minutes, she sort of stretched and yawned, and then left. I assumed she got tired of waiting, and decided to take advantage of my good nature another day."

I glanced around. "That doesn't sound like her. But she can go through walls, so maybe she popped in without you noticing."

Ralph put down his book and took off his reading glasses. "I know what she can do. I've seen her zip into the back room when neither of you thought I did. You kids seem to think that just because I read books, I don't pay attention." He shook his head. "Punks."

Wally's yellow eyes widened. "Hey, fella, that's my little girl and her friend you're talking about!"

Tulip Ralph held up his hands. "Whoa, Rusty. 'Punks' is a term of affection. Like 'knuckleheads' for those guys over there." He waved his hand toward the table of four role-players—a giraffe-necked joker guy, a bug-eyed joker guy with no nose at all, a nerdy-looking little nat guy, and a lizard-skinned young woman. They all shot Ralph the finger and continued their game without looking up.

"Hey, there's a child here!" Wally said.

"Dude," said the giraffe-necked joker, "this is the rough-and-tumble world of RPGing in Jokertown. Any kid who spends time in here has seen it all."

Wally turned to me, aghast.

"He's kidding, Wally," I said, trying to give him my sweet-little-girl face. "Yerodin and I just watch the gamers play, and there's no rough-and-tumble anything. And Tulip Ralph gets us cool *Ocelot 9* stuff."

"On account of I'm a sweetheart," Ralph said.

Wally looked down at the checkerboard tiles on the floor. "Little kids. Running around town during school hours." He shook his huge head. "Once I find my Yerodin, you betcha I'm never letting her out of my sight again." He looked up. "So where else do you girls go?" He pointed a big, orange-flecked finger at me. "And if she isn't there, I'm callin' the police. And if they won't do anything, I'll call the Amazing Bubbles. Maybe a few other friends, too." He closed one hand into a huge fist and smacked it into his palm. It sounded like a sledgehammer hitting an anvil. "We can turn Jokertown upside down if we have to, by golly."

I stared at Wally. I'd never seen him like this. And I had no idea where to look for Yerodin next. Jinka's Juice and the Tumbling Dice weren't just our two main hangouts. They were our *only* hangouts.

Tulip Ralph picked up his book again. "Well, Mr. Rustbelt, before you give the neighborhood an atomic wedgie, maybe Adesina can log onto *Ocelot 9* and check for Yerodin there." He put his readers back on and looked at me over the tops. "You kids are almost never off that game, even when you're watching the knuckleheads. You're both on the *Ocelot 9* teat."

"Judas Priest!" Wally bellowed. "Watch your language!"

I snapped out of my stupor. "It's okay, Wally," I said, patting him on the shoulder. He was a lot less scary when he was yelling at someone who wasn't me.

Then I pulled out my phone and opened my *Ocelot 9* app. It automatically logged me in, and sure enough, Ghost was on. I could have smacked myself in the head with both wings.

My hands trembled. I hoped Yerodin had calmed down and was ready to come home, because I knew she could avoid me and Wally for days if she wanted to. As well as Mom and every other ace in town. Despite what Wally thought, big physical powers wouldn't be much use in finding a little Ghost.

I pulled up a chat window and nervously messaged her.

Morpho_Girl: Hey, found any new levels?
Ghost427: <cursor blinking>
Morpho_Girl: There's a hidden treasure in the jungle temple. Want me to show you?

"What's going on?" Wally leaned over my shoulder to watch, and I hunched to hide the screen. I mean, I knew he was upset, but privacy, doodle. A kid's phone is her castle.

Morpho_Girl: Pls answer if ur there. Your dad's super worried about u.
Ghost427: <cursor blinking>
Morpho_Girl: He's starting to rust from anxiety.
Ghost427: He's a big rusty dork.

I just about fell over. Ghost was answering me! Although calling Wally a "big rusty dork" didn't sound like her.

I began thumbing my screen as fast as I could.

Morpho_Girl: Not! And we've been looking 4 u everywhere.
Ghost427: ?everywhere?
Morpho_Girl: U know, like the Tumb Dice. Where R U?
Ghost427: U R a dork 2!

And then she was gone.

I looked up at Wally. His metal skin was crinkling and speckling. "She won't tell me anything," I said. "And she sounds weird. I think she's really mad at me."

Wally shook his big, blocky head. "Oh, gosh, it's not you." His voice rasped like bad brakes. "The reason we had our dustup was because she wanted me to take her out of Carter and put her in high school. So you two could be in the same class again. But I said there was no way the schools would go for it, and that made her awful mad. She was flickering in and out of being solid. And yelling."

Now Wally was crying.

The lump in my throat felt permanent. All of us who'd come back from the PPA were close to each other . . . but Ghost was my BFF.

So now I knew why she was angry. It was because I had changed. And that meant we couldn't be together anymore. Which was not something I would *ever* do on purpose.

But maybe . . . maybe she thought I had.

♥

Mom's Diary

The apartment is mine now, I guess. It's pretty much empty except for some stuff in my room. They sold everything they could before they left.

And they took MY jewelry box! And most of that was just costume stuff. I think I maybe had a little gold chain in there, and that was it.

I'm sitting on the floor in the living room now. I can't see the view because the balcony has a concrete wall and it's right in front of me. I'd be out there, but the two outdoor wicker chairs are gone, too.

They're my parents. How could they do this?

I wonder how long they're going to survive without me paying the bills. Of course, they have whatever money of mine is left. So there's that. For a while.

And I just now realized I can't stay here. In this apartment, I mean. It costs too much. And I don't have any new jobs booked. Turns out my agent really worked for Mommy and Daddy. And my court advocate is pretty much done with me now that the case is over.

So, no more high-rise city view for me. No more pretty rooms.

And next week is my birthday. I'll be 15.

Yay me.

♣

"Okay, then," Wally said, wiping his eyes and his rust-streaked cheeks. Tiny orange flakes fell away. "Where do we look next?"

I considered. "Maybe to Jinka's in case she went for another smoothie. If she was yawning like Ralph says, maybe she needed a sugar bump. Or we could wait to see if she comes back here. I mean, Ralph says she was outside, but she didn't come in. And we *always* come in."

"That's sweet, kid," Tulip Ralph said. "Of course, it'd be sweeter if you ever spent any money."

The giraffe-necked joker made a trumpeting noise, and two of the other gamers chuckled. But the lizard-skinned lady shot out her tongue and smacked Giraffe Neck on the ear.

"Shhhhh," she said. "Shhhtupid."

Wally put his hands on either side of his head. "All I want is to find my little girl and bring her home."

"Me, too," I said. Outside, the shadows were already starting to get long. And I had the sudden panicked thought that if we didn't find Ghost before dark, we might never see her again. So I made what Mom calls an executive decision. "Come on. We'll go by Jinka's and back toward Carter, and maybe we'll spot her. Tulip Ralph can text me if she comes back here. He has my number for *Ocelot 9* updates." I looked at Ralph. "Okay?"

He shrugged. "Sure. What else have I got to do?"

Then, as I stepped toward the door, my phone vibrated. I took it from my jacket pocket and saw that I had another text message from Yerodin. Excited, I slid my thumb across the screen.

The world went gray, and I couldn't catch my breath. It was worse than anything I could have imagined.

It was a photo of Ghost lying on a grimy mattress on a dirty concrete floor . . . unconscious. I recognized her orange *Ocelot 9* T-shirt, her dark purple jeans, and her pink sneakers with the electric-green laces. Her ebony skin and braids were in stark contrast to the dingy fabric of the mattress.

Someone wearing a Golden Boy mask stood over her, flipping the bird to the camera the way the knuckleheads had flipped the bird to Tulip Ralph.

A text appeared after the photo.

> We added somethin' Xtra to her smoothie at Jinka's. She don't go thru walls so good now. She's OK. But that can change.

Ghost hadn't just run off. She had been kidnapped.

My legs went weak, and I thought I was going to hurl.

But I shut down that feeling as if I were shutting down a fire hydrant. Because that's what Mom would do. At least she would have, before Kazakhstan.

"What's wrong?" Wally asked.

I held out my phone. He took it, and it was tiny in his huge hands. I thought he'd crush it when those hands started shaking. "Oh, gosh," he said. "Oh, gosh, no."

I took the phone back. It vibrated again, and another text appeared.

> U want her, 'Morpho Girl?' Come to Orchard and Stanton. Now. U alone. U get a cop, might be 1 of us anyway. But we C badges, so long Ghostie.
> Also, we h8 Bubble baths. H8 them. Know Bubbles left for Panama this AM. Coz we know. But if she comes back and U get her—bye bye Ghost.
> Just U. No cops. No suds. No Tin Man. Rusty shows up, we make Ghost a ghost.

And then a pic of me and Wally popped up. It showed us stepping into the Tumbling Dice. Whoever had taken it had been right across the street. It was hella creepy.

But I would have to shake that off. And I would have to get to Orchard and Stanton. Alone.

The "alone" part was going to be tricky. I knew if I told Wally what the deal was, he would never let me go by myself. Despite the kidnappers' threats, he would probably call the cops. He might even try to get hold of Mom.

Yeah, Mom was in Panama. But she might come running back for this. In which case, either the kidnappers would kill Ghost right off the bat, or the current post-Kazakhstan version of the Amazing Bubbles might start blowing stuff up. Maybe including Ghost. After all, Mom had almost blown up *me* a few weeks before. Which wasn't something Wally knew, and might not believe if I told him.

So I was going to have to do something I never would have done when I was little. I hoped my new teenage self would know how to do it right.

I was going to tell a huge, bald-faced lie to my best friend's dad.

I stared down at my phone. "They're sending demands," I said.

Wally held out a massive, rusty hand. "Let me see!"

I shook my head. "No, they say we have to split up right away, and that I have to relay instructions to you. I guess they think that'll make them harder to track down."

Wally pulled his own phone from a back pocket. "The heck with that! I'm gonna call the police!"

I grabbed his flaking wrist. "Wally, the kidnappers are watching us, and they claim that some of them *are* cops." That much, at least, was true. "And if we do anything that makes them nervous, they'll—" I hesitated. "You know."

Wally slumped and shuddered. Tulip Ralph and the gamers all stared. The mighty Rustbelt looked as if he were about to crumble.

I looked back down at my phone. "They want me to stay here, and they want you to go to the newsstand beside the subway stop at Union Square. When they're sure you're alone, they'll have me relay a text with further orders."

Wally's head snapped up. "Union Square! That's something like fifteen blocks away!"

Tulip Ralph made a throat-clearing noise. "Then you should get going, Mr. Rustbelt. And don't count on catching a cab in this neighborhood. There's a subway stop two blocks east, but you'll probably go faster on foot. I'll keep an eye on Miss Adesina."

Wally looked back and forth between me, Ralph, and the door. He was breathing hard. And I hated myself. But I had to do what I had to do.

"Go!" I said.

Wally gave a sudden nod and lumbered to the door. The whole shop shook. "I'll text you when I get there, Adesina," he said. "And we'll do whatever we have to do for Yerodin!"

I held back tears. "Yes. We will."

Then Wally flung open the door and barreled into the street. The door closed with a *ting* of the bell, and I watched Wally through the window until he disappeared.

"Wow," the giraffe-necked joker said. "That was intense." The lizard-skinned lady whapped him with her tongue again.

I turned toward Tulip Ralph. "I just lied to one of the nicest people on earth."

Ralph adjusted his glasses. "I know. I can tell when someone's gaming. But sometimes, that's the only way to get anywhere." He jerked his head toward the curtained doorway behind him. "So if there's anywhere *you* need to get, I suggest going through the back room into the alley."

I started around the counter. "Thanks, Ralph."

"Don't mention it. And listen, kid—text me if I can help. I'm a pretty good gamer myself, you know."

The kidnappers had said I had to do this by myself or Ghost would die. So I didn't think there was any way Tulip Ralph could help. But as I pushed through the Tumbling Dice's back door, I tried to take comfort in the fact that he *wanted* to.

It made me feel just a little less alone.

♠

Mom's Diary

I didn't mean to kill him.

I was about to give him my purse. That's how it works. They pull a weapon and you give them your money.

But he shot me. In the chest.

It hurt. It hurt worse than anything. I heard a crack and then, nothing.

Then I felt good. Really good. There was a second when it felt like my belly pooched out a little, and then the bubble shot out of my hand. It hit him in his lower left side, and bright red blood bloomed on his dirty camo-green sweatshirt.

I ran home. I guess. I mean, I know I did, but I don't remember it. Thank God Mom and Dad don't live with me anymore. They've been gone two years now, and I know what they'd do if they found out my card had turned. Probably sell tickets.

I yanked off my sweaty blouse to see if I was bleeding. But I wasn't. I had a dollop of blood on my chest, but when I wiped it away, there wasn't anything there. No bullet hole, no nothing. Just my own smooth pinkish-white skin.

Which seemed to be covering more of me than there was before.

It almost looked like I was getting fat.

♦

I stood on the southwest corner of Stanton and Orchard as the sun dropped behind the buildings. The jokers who passed by looked me over as if they thought I was selling something, and I felt a jolt of nerves every time. Was this one of the kidnappers? Were they just going to let me stand here while they did who knows what to Ghost?

See, I sort of knew what had happened to Aunt Joey that made her card turn. And I wanted to yark when I thought about something like that happening to Yerodin.

After four or five minutes, two men—one all wiry and twitchy, the other thickset with lumpy muscles—dropped from the bottom of a fire escape across Orchard. Almost every building along Orchard has a fire escape bolted to its facade, so the men had been invisible within the shadows of the zigzagging metal stairs.

As they crossed the street, I saw that both were wearing masks that looked like Mom. Seriously. They were even wearing long, braided, platinum-blond wigs. It was just . . . totes creepy.

Then I remembered that the kidnapper in the photo with an unconscious Ghost had been wearing a mask, too. Of Golden Boy.

And then I realized who had Yerodin: the Werewolves.

Mom had broken up a fight between the Werewolves and the Demon Princes several years back, and she had said how weird it was that a gang called the Werewolves always wore masks . . . but that the masks almost never depicted, you know, *werewolves*.

My stomach turned, and my palms got sticky. The Werewolves had been around for a long time, and they were bad news. They had started out as your basic street gang, like, before Mom was born. But now they were up in all kinds of nasty business. Everything from mugging to embezzlement to gambling on cockroach races. And the stories about them involved payoffs to politicians and police. No wonder they'd said that any cops we called might be theirs.

The two Werewolves in the Amazing Bubbles masks stopped a foot away from me and stared. Their eyes were watery and bloodshot behind the holes in their masks. "Sorry to make you wait," the one on the left said. "We hadda be sure you were alone."

"Well, I am," I said. "So where's . . . where's my friend?" My voice trembled, and I was ashamed I couldn't stay calmer. "Is she okay?"

The one on the left, the muscular one, spoke again. "Aw, she's fine. Fuhgeddabouddit." He had a deep voice with a thick accent. Brooklyn. So I thought of him as "Brooksie." That made him less intimidating, somehow.

"She'd better be." I let my wings unfurl. They stretched across the whole breadth of the sidewalk. And they made me feel bigger. Stronger.

The twitchy Werewolf on the right laughed. It was a high-pitched chortle that set my teeth on edge. I decided to call him "Laughing Boy."

"Why is that funny, Laughing Boy?" I asked in my snottiest tone. And I knew it might be super dumb for me to talk to him that way. But these . . . these *poop heads* had Ghost. So what I really wanted to say was, "Hey, *poop head*, give me back my friend before I stomp you into tomorrow."

"It's funny," Laughing Boy said, "because those pretty wings are the only things that'll keep your friend alive." And then he chortled again.

I wasn't sure just how hard I could hit him with the edges of my wings, but I sure wanted to find out. They jerked toward Laughing Boy's head.

"Put those things away," Brooksie said. "But don't worry, you'll need 'em soon enough."

I glared at them both, but I folded my wings. For once, they obeyed. "What do you want?" I asked, crossing my arms.

"Well," Brooksie said. "What we want are some special services from 'Morpho Girl.'"

Laughing Boy snickered. "Yeah, yeah. 'Special services.'" I could tell he was grinning behind his mask. "Like from a cute little butterfly."

I didn't like the sound of that.

♥

Mom's Diary

I don't know why I'm auditioning for American Hero. I mean, I'm no hero. But I guess I'd like to be one. It has to be better than being a model.

I know I've been lucky. The Cover Girl contract made me a lot of money. And I started getting Paris and New York runway again. I look younger than I am and they always like that. Plus I can make myself just about any size without having to diet. I just bubble the fat away and I look skinny again. And then I can jump out a window and get fat again. And it feels so good.

I don't remember when I've ever felt like I do when I use my power. I tried cocaine once, but it made me jittery as hell, so I never used it again. Same thing with pot—made me eat everything in the house—which wasn't much—and then I fell asleep for eleven hours. And all those other drugs—I don't know why anyone does them. But when I get hit and get fat, it feels wonderful.

And the bubbles, well, I'm still figuring them out. But it feels really good when I make them, too.

No. Better than good.

<u>Amazing.</u>

♣

"Follow us, sweetie pie," Laughing Boy said. Then he chortled, of course. He was totes gross and lacking with the charm. He and Brooksie turned onto Stanton, and I had to go along.

They walked half a block, then ducked down an alley. I looked around, but no one was paying any attention to us.

We went down a few more alleys, turning here and there as if Laughing Boy and Brooksie wanted to throw off anyone who was following. Finally, we ended up on Rivington between Ludlow and Essex, at the front door of the old twenty-story Hotel on Rivington.

Or what was left of it. It had once been banging. But now there were a lot of broken-out windows—not a good look for a place that's mostly glass to begin with—and stupid Devil-worship junk painted on everything that remained. *666* and whatnot. There was a pentagram carved on the door where the glass had been replaced with plywood. Plus a crude painting of some kind of bloody goat's head.

Does anybody find that stuff scary? Now, what had happened in Kazakhstan—those things that had come out of some other place and time, those things that had driven Mom insane and me all cocoony—*that* stuff had been *scary*. A pentagram and a bad drawing of a goat didn't even snuggle up close to it.

Brooksie turned toward me. "Okay, we're here. So behave yourself. Any quick moves, any wing flapping, any crap, and your friend's gonna pay. Understand?"

I nodded. "I'll behave. But before I'll do whatever it is you want, you need to prove that Yerodin's okay."

"Oh, we will," Laughing Boy said. "But *you* need to remember that we ain't on your schedule. You're on *ours*."

Then he chortled. Again. It was really starting to get old.

Mom's Diary

I can't believe it! I'm on American Hero!

I got as fat as I could before I auditioned. I also used wash-out black hair dye to hide my platinum hair. It took about five cans because my hair is so long. I hope they'll let me bring more with me.

But even if my hair goes back to blonde, I'll bet no one will know it's the famous model Michelle Pond. Even though my eyes, nose, and mouth are all the same. People think fat girls are ugly, no matter what their faces and hair look like.

My power, however, is cool and visual. They're all about the visual on TV. And maybe people can feel a little sorry for the fat girl while they're at it, because that's what people do. Or hate on her, because that's what people do, too.

But for once, I want something in my life to be about something besides my looks. If it's about how my bubbles look, though, that's another matter.

We've been divided into different "suits." I'm on the Diamonds team. There's a girl I like called Tiffani. Unfortunately, I don't think she's gay. She sure is friendly, though. And pretty, too.

Sorry, diary, I'm not taking you along. They go through everything, and I don't want them figuring out who I am.

All they need to know, for now, is that I'm the Amazing Bubbles.

And for now, that's all I need to be.

♠

The smell inside the hotel was *awesome*. Like someone had decided to use puke-scented air freshener. I gagged.

"Ain't you prissy," Brooksie said. He waved his hand, gesturing at the lobby. Trash littered the floor. There were stains on the carpet where it wasn't torn up. The wallpaper was peeling, and an impressive amount of graffiti covered everything. "But you try keepin' a place like this clean for thirty years. When you got other priorities."

"Could you both please take off those masks?" I asked. Looking at the bad latex renderings of Mom was even worse than the smell. "They're really distracting."

Laughing Boy giggled. "Sorry, honey bucket. They're to remind you not to try to involve Mommy Dearest."

Brooksie pointed at me. "Besides, you ain't in a position to make requests.

You're here to do what we say. And if you don't, little Yerodin is dead. So I'd get over being distracted, if I were you. *Capiche?*"

"For all I know, she's dead already." The hot lead in my tummy turned cold at the thought.

Brooksie snapped his fingers, and Laughing Boy grabbed my arm. He marched me to a doorway behind the old registration desk and pulled me into a stairwell. Then he dragged me up to the second-floor landing.

And there, lying on her side on the stained mattress, lit by the sickly glow of fluorescent bulbs, was Ghost. She was breathing, but otherwise still. Her eyes and her mouth were half-open, and she was drooling a little. I didn't know how they had managed to slip something into her smoothie—maybe one of them had gotten a job at Jinka's—but I did know I had to get her away from them.

Or maybe, if I could just wake her up, she could vanish. Maybe even slit a few Werewolf throats, if she could take a knife from one of them. The Werewolves knew she could go noncorporeal, but they didn't seem to be aware that she had been an assassin.

I started toward her, but Laughing Boy pulled me back. "Nope nope." He gave a little snicker. "Just looksees."

Bile rose in my throat. Okay, so I didn't really want Ghost to turn into a killer again. It looked like she was too drugged to wake up anyway.

But I had been hoping I might be able to use *my* newfound skills to save her. I had let myself imagine that if the Werewolves were holding Yerodin somewhere with a window, I could scoop her up, protect her with my wings, plunge through the glass—and fly away. In reality, though, we were in a windowless concrete stairwell. Besides which, there were two Werewolves right next to Ghost, and the ratty sneakers of at least one more a few steps up the next flight. Laughing Boy was right beside me, and Brooksie was right behind. There was no way for me to get to Ghost, even if there had been a window to plunge through.

My newfound skills were useless.

"Now you see that we're wolves of our word," Brooksie said. "So here's what you gotta do."

◆

Mom's Diary

I've been voted off <u>American Hero</u>. And, of course, once I washed the black spray-on dye out of my hair and shrank down to my modeling size again, then who I really was hit the media. Like in blogs, and on Twitter, and then the TV picked it up, too. You'd think they'd have something better to do than talk about me.

But I'm not sure I care about all that. There's something going down in Egypt. And a bunch of us aces are getting together to go there and help out.

This isn't just modeling or TV anymore. This is something bigger.

This is something real.

So I'm going to try to be a real hero.

♥

"It's simple," Brooksie said. "Once the sun sets, real soon now, you'll fly out over the harbor. Then you'll land on the deck of a container ship called the *Shanghai Princess*. It's a big boat with shit-tons of things that look like semitruck trailers."

I tried not to roll my eyes. "I know what a container ship is."

"Okay, then. There's somethin' . . . no, some*body* we want you to pick up from this one."

I interrupted. "Wait a minute. You want me to pick up a *person*? From a ship in the middle of the harbor? Are you nuts?"

Brooksie shrugged. "Maybe. But the guy you're gonna pick up has to be taken off and snuck into Manhattan. And we can't use a boat, 'cause it'd be stopped by the harbor cops. So, long story short, we told him we knew about a teenage girl who can fly." Brooksie paused. "He dug that. He likes teenage girls."

Laughing Boy started laughing like a hyena. "Especially teenage joker girls! He's gonna make us a fortune!"

It was as if an electric jolt stiffened every muscle in my body. Now I knew what this was about. The Werewolves were smuggling in a man who was going to turn joker girls into—it was beyond gross—sex slaves. He was going to hurt them the way Aunt Joey had been hurt.

And the Werewolves wanted me to fly him into the city for them. So they had drugged and kidnapped my best friend to get me to do it.

I hadn't thought I could hate them any more than I already did. But I had been wrong. Now I wished Ghost *would* wake up and slit their throats.

Brooksie looked at Laughing Boy. "Watch your mouth," he said. "We're only tellin' Sunshine here as much as she needs to know." He turned back to me. "The *Shanghai Princess* is bound for the Red Hook terminal in Brooklyn, but our guy needs to get off before it docks. Seeing as how there might be some federal types there, waitin' for him."

Laughing Boy chortled. "On account of he's banned from the country!"

Brooksie lifted a hand as if to smack Laughing Boy, then gave a grunt and dropped it. "Lucky for us, we got a Werewolf in the harbor pilots association. He took control of the *Shanghai Princess* once it reached the Narrows a couple hours ago, and in a few minutes he'll stop it dead in the water about a quarter mile south of Governors Island. He'll say he had to reverse engines to avoid plowin' into a kayak or somethin'. Then all you gotta do is pick up a guy who'll be waitin' near the bow. He's a white guy, but he might have dark stuff smeared on his face. He'll be wearing a dark hoodie, too. So let's call him 'Mr. Hoodie.'"

That set Laughing Boy off on another fit. "'Mr. Hoodie'! I like that!"

Brooksie shook his head, and his blond braid bounced. "It goes like this. You touch down on deck, and Mr. Hoodie signals you with a flashlight. When you approach, he'll ask if you want to party. If he don't ask that, he ain't our guy. You have your cell phone?"

My already-stiff muscles tensed still more. I had silenced my phone so it wouldn't buzz if Wally texted me from Union Square. But I needed to be able to contact him when I had a chance, and that couldn't happen if Brooksie took my phone. "Jeez, of course. I always do."

To my relief, Brooksie just nodded. "Good. Mr. Hoodie ain't gonna have a phone that'll work here, so we're gonna use yours to make sure he's the real deal. When he asks if you want to party, you take his picture and send it to Miss Ghost's phone, which is in my pocket. Then, if we say it's okay, hand your phone over to him. He'll type in a code, and if it's right, we'll send a smiley face, which he'll show you. And then he gets to keep your phone."

"Hey!" I protested.

Brooksie waved his hand. "Ah, fuhgeddabouddit. Your famous fat mommy'll buy you a new one. Now, after you see the smiley face, you let Mr. Hoodie grab your hands or your hair or whatever, and you fly him here to the roof of the hotel. It'll be dark, so we won't be able to have eyes on you until you get close—which is sorta the idea, since we don't want you spotted. But we're gonna give you exactly thirty minutes from the time we send the smiley face to the time when you need to have Mr. Hoodie here. If you don't show up, or you show up late, or you show up without our guy, you know what that means for Miss Yerodin. Yeah?"

I nodded. It was all I could do.

"Terrific. So, you land him on the roof, where we'll be waiting with your pal. You hand over Mr. Hoodie, we hand over little Ghost, and that's it. You and Ghostie fly home. And if you never say nothin' to nobody about this, you never hear from us again. Guaranteed."

I stared at Brooksie and Laughing Boy, utterly monkeyed. I knew what a guarantee from the Werewolves was worth. And I also knew it didn't matter, because what Brooksie had described was impossible.

"I—I can't do it," I sputtered. "I've never carried extra weight when I've flown. And I've never flown as far as you're asking, either."

Laughing Boy chortled. "First of all, we ain't asking. You want Little Missy there to be playin' with cartoon ocelots tomorrow instead of lyin' on a slab? Then this is what you gotta do. And the distance ain't so bad. I figure three and one-quarter miles, straight line from here to the ship. Hell, you can even take off from Battery Park for the first leg. That cuts off almost two miles."

Brooksie interjected. "But if you do that, you'll have to run to the park from here, 'cause time's gonna be tight. The ship can't stay dead in the water too long without the harbor cops snoopin'. So when we say move, you gotta move."

They didn't seem to understand the problem. "Look, I really don't think I'm physically able to do this! What if I crash into the water and your guy and I drown?"

Laughing Boy waggled a finger. "Then you'll be dead. And Miss Ghostie will be, too."

Brooksie gave a sigh that made a *whoof* sound inside his mask. "Look, we've been watchin' you practice. Didja think after what your mama did to us that we wouldn't be keepin' eyes on both of youse? Some days, you've done enough flights from your roof to add up to at *least* three miles."

My wings trembled. "But what you're talking about now is in the dark, over water. And on the way back, I'm supposed to carry someone who weighs—do you even know how much he weighs?"

"We've only seen pictures," Brooksie said. "But he ain't a tubbo. He's maybe a buck eighty-five."

I was dizzy now, and I almost sat down on the steps. They wanted me to carry a hundred and eighty-five pounds. Plus my own weight. For more than three miles. In the dark, over New York Harbor and Lower Manhattan. After having just flown out into the harbor, also in the dark.

There was no way. There was just no way. These yabbos were in insane clown land. It was cray-cray.

I looked at Yerodin again.

And I knew I had to try.

♣

Mom's Diary

We went to Egypt to help, and all we did was kill people. I mean, I guess we did the right thing, but it sure doesn't feel like it.

I blew up a helicopter. I killed people.

This isn't what I thought a hero would be.

But the U.N. thinks what I did was good. Good enough that they want me to keep doing the "hero" thing. They've asked, and I've joined the Committee on Extraordinary Interventions. We're supposed to be sent to places where people like me are needed. People with ace powers.

I just hope that next time I'll do better.

But I'm not so sure.

♠

I took off from Battery Park, rose to about two hundred feet, and started hitting pockets of cold air. They made me drop suddenly each time, and it felt like my stomach was trying to crawl out of my throat. But I kept flying.

I was afraid I might not be able to figure out which ship was the *Shanghai Princess,* because it was crazy dark out over the water despite the surrounding city lights and the ones on the boats and ships. But then I saw it. It was the most massive vessel in the harbor, and it was the only one stopped dead.

I began circling downward, using the air currents to reduce speed and rest my wings. I was starting to get the hang of riding the wind. And that was kewl with awesome sauce, despite the situation. But coasting only helped a little, and my shoulder muscles were already starting to get tired. Which was considerably less kewl, with zero sauce.

Even so, I managed a pretty good landing, missing the containers and touching down on deck close to the bow. I went down to one knee, but didn't take a tumble.

But I didn't have time to congratulate myself. A beefy guy wearing a hoodie stood about fifteen feet away, in front of a huge stack of containers. He had a heavy beard, and sure enough, there *was* black stuff smeared on the rest of his face. But instead of making him less visible, it had the effect of making him look pop-eyed. And the way he stared at me made me feel as if there were ants crawling over my skin.

"You want party?" he asked in a thick Russian accent. Then he gave me a gross smile and looked me up and down.

"Sure, douche," I replied. I pulled out my phone and took a picture of him. And at that moment, the ship gave a shudder and, very slowly, started moving.

I zapped the photo to Ghost's phone. Meanwhile, "Mr. Hoodie" gave me that gross smile again. "You are, ah, very beautiful." Bee-ah-yew-tee-full.

My phone buzzed: It's him. You know what to do.

I held out my phone. His fingers brushed mine as he took it. I yanked my hand back and scrubbed it hard on my jeans.

He tapped the screen, showed me the smiley-face response, and then shoved my phone into the back pocket of his jeans. It felt as if he'd stolen a piece of my soul.

"We go now," he said, stepping toward me and opening his arms. "For which we embrace, eh?"

I gave a quick flap of my wings and shot up above him. "I don't know what they told you," I said, "but I've never carried anyone. So it would be hella stupid of you to try to get handsy with me. I might dip too low, and that would end badly for both of us." It occurred to me that I sounded a little like Mom just then. Totes fearless.

Of course, unlike Mom, I was faking it.

"End badly for Ghost friend, too," he said.

Which I knew. "So I guess we'd both better behave."

He zipped his hoodie. "I will try to resist your charms," he said. "But Werewolves did not say you would be so . . . perfect."

I tried to think of something I could do right then to make him suffer for ever messing with any joker kids. But I had nothing. At least, nothing that wouldn't put Yerodin in worse danger. So I had to roll with it.

For now.

"Grab my ankles," I said. "And *nowhere* else."

A look of rage slid across Mr. Hoodie's face. Then it was covered by a Velveeta smile. But I knew what was under there.

He reached up and seized my ankles, and I tried to fly upward. But I just kept flapping and flapping, and nothing happened. Except that every muscle in my shoulders and back felt as if it were shredding. So maybe I was just too tired, and the Russian was just too heavy.

A knife-edged slice of cold slid through my tummy. I had texted Wally as I had run down to Battery Park, and had also sent a few "You'd better not be hurting her!" texts to Ghost's phone at the same time in case any Werewolves were watching me. After I'd given Wally the short version of what was really going on, we had come up with a quick plan. But the whole thing depended on me being able to pick up and carry *Wally* once I made it back to shore. And how could I pick up an extra-large-with-fries metal dude if I couldn't even get Mr. Hoodie aloft?

But I had to. I had to fly the Russian from the *Shanghai Princess* to Battery Park, and then fly Wally to the Hotel on Rivington—where, we hoped, the Werewolves would think that Wally was Mr. Hoodie just long enough for me to drop him on them.

I grunted and strained toward the sky. Sweat started rolling down my back, and the cold knife-edge in my gut turned to hot nausea.

And we still didn't move.

I looked down then and saw Mr. Hoodie grinning. He had spread his feet and crouched to brace himself, deliberately holding me back.

"Come on," he snarled. "What is holdup, smartass joker girl?"

He was showing me he still had all the power. Which made me furious. And that, in turn, made me feel . . . *stronger*.

"*You're* the holdup, you knob!" I yelled. "If you want to get off this tub, stop pulling me down! The Werewolves expect us in thirty minutes, and if we don't make it, I promise we're *both* gonna pay for it!"

The Russian gave a slimy chuckle, and he stood up straight and brought his feet together. "Okay, okay," he said. "We go now, eh?"

Then a blast of wind pushed me sideways, and I had to flap furiously to stabilize. The ship was starting to make some headway, and we needed to zoom.

Slow down, doodle, I thought. *You can do this. You can do it for Ghost.*

Be a hero, dammit.

Like Mom.

I squeezed my eyes shut and gave one hard flap of my wings, the fiercest I could muster. My shoulders would have screamed out loud if they could.

And we rose. Just a few feet, at first, and my wings trembled with the effort. But I got Mr. Hoodie into the air.

I didn't have time to celebrate, though. I had to get some altitude or we'd collide with the nearest stack of containers. We were in danger of being squished in a super smushed kind of way. So I forced more fierce flaps from my muscles, and I climbed higher. And higher.

The sky had become the color of a bruised plum, and the water in the harbor was almost black. Mr. Hoodie laughed like he was having fun, and he gripped my ankles even tighter. It really hurt. As in, I'm-going-to-kick-you-away-and-drop-you-into-the-harbor-you-hairy-snot-rag. But I couldn't do that, no matter how much I wanted to.

We cleared the containers, barely. And now I had to make it to Battery Park. The cover of night was going to help me and Wally deal with the

Russian and stay hidden from any snooping Werewolves, especially since Wally was going to knock out some of the park's sidewalk lamps. But first I had to get my cargo to shore. My shoulders were burning, and my breath was like fire in my lungs.

"Move it, joker girlie," Mr. Hoodie said. He gave my ankles another hard squeeze, and I winced. "Is too bad Werewolves have promised to let you go. I could do much with you."

A burst of rage shot through me. And it made me fly higher and faster than I ever would have thought I could.

My wings were shaking, but I didn't care. The only thing that mattered was saving Ghost . . . and making sure this gross creeper got everything he really, really deserved.

♦

It felt as if we had been flying for hours, but I knew it had been less than fifteen minutes. I sure hoped so, anyway.

My wings were almost numb now, and my shoulders hurt so much that I didn't remember what it had felt like when they *hadn't* hurt. And disgusting-douchebag Russian was like a big bag of rocks.

As we approached Battery Park, I started heading downward. Mr. Hoodie didn't notice at first because he was too busy making comments like: "You are just what clients want. Young, nice tits, enough joker to tickle pervert fancy. Wings and skin like shiny leather. Sexy slits in shirt for extra little legs. Are you joker in other places, too? That helps price, you know."

I wanted to kick him in the scrod. Just, ugh. He was hyper vile. And I knew exactly where I wanted to plant General Tiny Peen: straight into the iron railing on the bay side of the park.

A light mist had begun to fall, but it felt good on my burning shoulder muscles. And the floodlights illuminating the circular wall of Castle Clinton gave off a fuzzy glow that helped guide me. I was aiming for the sidewalk and trees just to the southeast.

I let the Russian's weight pull me down, and we began moving to shore fast. *Really* fast. Mr. Hoodie finally twigged to the fact that things weren't going as he'd thought they would. "What is happening?" he demanded. "This does not look like hotel! I think I call Werewolves!" But as long as he had to hold my ankles, I didn't think he'd be using my phone to call the Werewolves or anyone else.

Then his ankles slammed into the railing. He didn't let go of me right away, so the collision twisted me around and sent me skidding across the sidewalk on my wings.

But like I've said, my wings are tough. Captain Craptastic, on the other hand, smacked the wet sidewalk hard, and his hoodie wasn't much protection. That was when he finally let go. "Filthy joker bitch!" the Russian howled. Then he tried to stand up, but fell again and shrieked. His ankles might have been broken. I sure hoped so, anyway.

I picked myself up and kicked Butt Monkey in the knee as hard as I could. That made him shriek, which was nice. There was just enough light for me to see the shocked look on his ugly face. And that his mouth was bleeding.

Then Wally came running from a clump of trees, grabbed Fuck Face (Aunt Joey has *really* rubbed off on me) by the hoodie, and started dragging him off the sidewalk. Wally was now wearing a dark hoodie himself, ready for the next part of our plan.

But before Wally could reach the trees again, a gravelly voice called from farther down the sidewalk.

"Mr. Rustbelt," it said. "You can drop that piece of garbage. We'll take care of the side quest, and you and Miss Adesina can finish the main mission."

I turned toward the voice and saw five darkened figures, backlit by a single unbroken lamp, approaching through the mist. They were the only other people in this darkened part of the park.

"I'm glad you made it," I said. "But I didn't know you were bringing company."

Wally picked up the Russian by the hood and held him off the ground, dangling and flailing. He stepped closer to me and peered toward the approaching figures. "Do I need to do something about them, Adesina?"

I shook my head and plucked my cell phone from Mr. Hoodie's back pocket. "No, Wally. You aren't the only person I texted before I flew to the ship."

The lead figure of the five stopped a few yards away, shook drops of water from the flowers on his head, and then took off his glasses and wiped them with the tail of his checkered shirt.

"Tulip Ralph!" Wally exclaimed.

Ralph nodded. "Hope you don't mind that I let these knuckleheads come along. But when I told 'em the game you two were running, they wanted in."

The giraffe-necked guy came up on Ralph's right, and the lizard-skinned lady came up on his left. The bug-eyed guy and the nerdy nat joined them.

"Is that the dirtball who sells joker kids?" the giraffe-necked guy asked.

The dangling Russian spat a bloody gob at him. "Don't worry, big-nose," he said. "You and lizard bitch would not bring enough money to be worth trouble."

The lizard-lady hissed. "Oh, yessss," she said. "That'sss him."

Ralph put on his glasses. "Seriously, Mr. Rustbelt," he said. "You and Miss Adesina can go. As a Jokertown businessman, I know which cops are honest. So I'll make a call, and the knuckleheads and I can, uh . . . look after this person until they get here."

"Gosh, thank you!" Wally said. "I was gonna tie him up, but I lost my rope when I was busting out lights." He chucked Mr. Hoodie to the sidewalk at Ralph's feet, and the Russian lay there like a discarded, filthy rag.

Ralph cleared his throat, and his four knuckleheads grabbed Mr. Hoodie and dragged him toward the trees. The Russian started to scream, but then the nerdy nat produced a roll of duct tape. So Corporal Dingus was quiet by the time they got him out of sight.

"I owe you one, Ralph," I said.

Tulip Ralph shrugged. "You and Miss Yerodin come into the Dice as soon as you can, and we'll call it even." He started for the trees, then looked back at us. "You punks kick some ass, okay?" He vanished into the foliage.

I checked the time on my phone against the time stamp on the smiley face. We had thirteen minutes.

"We gotta go, Wally," I said, sliding my phone into my jacket pocket. "You ready?"

He gave a rust-raspy nod. "I am if you are."

Then I had to swallow hard. "I am. But Wally, I'm—I'm sorry I had to trick you."

Wally's eyes grew wide. "Aw, geez, there'll be time for that stuff later. We have to get my daughter!"

So I fluttered into the air so he could grab my ankles the way the Russian had. I'd struggled flying with that Butt Monkey, and he weighed a lot less than Wally. Even so, I was pretty sure I could get Wally aloft—but could I get him high enough and keep him there long enough? And fly fast enough?

I mean, I was *tired*.

Wally grasped my ankles. His hands were bigger than Mr. Hoodie's, and they made a slight *clang* as his fingers clasped. I could tell he was trying to be gentle. But still, hey, metal hands. Owie.

I flapped my wings, and nothing happened. Again. It was the same as when I'd tried to get the Butt Monkey up into the air, only worse. This time, I knew my passenger wasn't messing with me.

But one way or another, we had to go. So I gave a grunt and flapped my wings as hard as I could. I swear I felt something pop, but we went up about five feet. Then every flap took us a little higher until, at last, we rose above the trees.

And ever so slowly at first, but gaining altitude and velocity with each flap, I began flying us over the park, and then over the streets, toward the Hotel on Rivington.

"You got this, Morpho Girl!" Wally cried. "You betcha!"

I gritted my teeth and strained.

Hang on, Ghost, I thought. *We're coming.*

♥

Mom's Diary

I guess I might become a hero after all.

When Drake couldn't control his power, I absorbed the massive explosion and went into a coma. I saved New Orleans from being destroyed.

I'm out of the coma now, but when I was unconscious, I dreamed about a lot of weird stuff. I dreamed about a little girl.

Her name is Adesina.

♣

Time slows down when everything hurts. With each flap of my wings, my muscles screamed a little more. My legs turned numb from Wally's weight. Breathing was torture.

When I went into my cocoon as a little girl, it was because I was afraid and in pain. But now, I couldn't hide in a cocoon. I had to keep moving. And I had no way of knowing if I was moving fast enough.

Then, through the pounding in my head, I heard Wally shout.

"There it is!" he cried. "Half a block! Six Werewolves on the west side of the roof. And oh, gosh, a Werewolf with Yerodin on the other side!"

I blinked to clear my eyes of mist and tears. We were about thirty feet higher than the roof of the Hotel on Rivington, which was illuminated by floodlights. Near the eastern edge, several yards from a clump of Werewolves, Ghost was lying unconscious on the tarred gravel. She was guarded by a Werewolf in a Golden Boy mask.

With what felt like the last of my energy, I put on all the speed I could muster. But I didn't let myself descend. Not yet. I didn't want the Werewolves to see that Wally wasn't the Russian until it was too late.

"Wally," I rasped. "I'm going to drop you on the one beside Ghost! You throw him at the others and hold them off so I can pick her up. Then I'll hover so you can grab hold again, and I'll fly us all out of here."

"Oh gee, no!" he replied. "If you try that, one of them might grab you first." Then he gave a grim chuckle. It didn't sound like anything I'd ever heard from him. "Besides, I need to stay long enough to give these boys something to remember me by. You just fly Yerodin away from here and meet me at our apartment, okey dokey?"

And now we were less than a quarter block away, so there was no more time to discuss it. "Here we go, then!" I yelled. "Like, gravity isn't just a good idea—it's the law!"

I went into a dive, and we came in hella fast. We were only ten feet over the cluster of six Werewolves when we shot across them and streaked toward the one in the Golden Boy mask.

"Shit!" Golden Boy yelled. He had seen that Wally was *not* the Russian. But it was too late. Wally let go of me, dropped like the mother of all rusty bombs, and crashed down on him. They hit the gravel two feet from where Ghost lay, and it sounded like every pot and pan in Williams Sonoma falling to the floor all at once.

With Wally suddenly gone, I bounced up another ten feet, and that wiped out my forward momentum. I spun in the air, managed to stabilize, and found myself hovering.

Wally leaped to his feet, grabbed the flattened Golden Boy Werewolf, and flung him at the six who had now started toward them. Golden Boy hit two, and they went down. The others all stopped where they were.

Wally's hoodie and shirt had ripped apart, and anyone else's skin would have been shredded. But not his. If anything, he looked shinier and stronger. Some of the day's rust had been scraped away.

He charged the cluster. But then five more Werewolves surged out of the roof exit behind them. And the three who had gone down were getting up.

Wally stopped four yards short of the twelve Werewolves. He balled his right hand into a fist, then punched it into his open left hand. There was that sledgehammer-hitting-an-anvil sound again.

The reinforced Werewolves wore masks ranging from puppy dogs to demons to Golden Boy. To, of course, the Amazing Bubbles. They were armed with chains, knives, pipes, and baseball bats. And a few guns.

A wiry Werewolf in a Bubbles mask pointed a pistol at Wally and chortled. Laughing Boy. "You weren't invited, lead-for-brains!" Laughing Boy crowed. "So we'll have to show you the way out!" He pulled the trigger, and there was a loud *pow*.

And then a *ping* and a puff of rust as the slug bounced from Wally's forehead. "Well, gosh darn it," Wally said. "I'm only here because you fellas went and hurt my daughter, don'tchaknow. So pardon me for bein' rude!"

Then he charged again, like a locomotive with legs.

The Werewolves were about as distracted as they were going to get. So I dropped into a sudden dive, plunged behind Wally, and landed on the roof with a skid that almost tore off my shoes. I slid right into Yerodin, and she almost rolled into the low steel lip at the edge of the roof. But she stayed limp, and there was a horrible moment when I thought she might be dead. Then we came to a stop, and she groaned. I reached down, scooped her up, and held her tight.

Then, over the clanging and screams from the other side of the roof, I heard a crunch of gravel behind me. One of the Werewolves had managed to avoid Wally. "Fuhgeddabouddit, you double-crossin' bitch." I didn't have to turn around to know it was Brooksie. "You ain't goin' nowhere."

But, yeah, I was pretty sure I was.

I leaped straight up, spreading my wings with a *whoomp*. Compared to Wally, Ghost felt like nothing. But my arms, shoulders, and wings still trembled with fatigue. And before I could get totally clear, Brooksie was able to grab my left foot.

I kicked at him with my right and tried to keep heading up and out. But he was dragging me down and keeping me from crossing the edge of the roof into open air, holding me back just like Captain Craptastic the Butt Monkey had. And a Golden Boy Werewolf, broken free of Wally's attack, was now running toward us—and if he latched onto Brooksie, they would pull me down to the roof again. For sure.

I grunted and flapped my wings with every ounce of strength my shrieking muscles could muster, pushing through the pain. Then my left shoe slipped off. Brooksie fell back with a shout, and both he and Golden Boy went down to the gravel while Ghost and I popped up high above them.

Thank God for clogs.

We spiraled upward, and I hugged Ghost to my chest as I felt her arms slip around me. Down below, Wally had been surrounded by the rest of the Werewolves. They began to swarm and pile on, and he vanished beneath them.

I paused in my ascent. I was, like, two seconds away from diving back down to try to help.

Then I heard a metallic roar, like a road grader revved up to drag-racing speed, and the piled-on Werewolves exploded outward. It was as if a grenade had gone off in a mound of marionettes.

One of the Bubbles-masked Werewolves went over the edge of the roof, screaming and crying as he fell. I recognized the voice even though it wasn't chortling now.

"So long, Laughing Boy," I muttered. And maybe this makes me a bad person . . . but hey, I didn't feel sorry for him at all.

Wally looked up at me and Yerodin as he windmilled his arm and brought his huge fist down on the head of a puppy-dog Werewolf who was trying to kneecap him with a crowbar.

"Cripes!" Wally shouted. "You two get out of here! This is just gonna take a while, that's all."

He clunked a couple of demon-Werewolf heads together, then stacked the demons atop the puppy dog. Then a few more Werewolves attacked, and they were added to the pile.

"Later, Wally!" I called, and made a shallow dive to gain enough airspeed to turn away.

Wobbling and slow, I flew away from the Hotel on Rivington toward the Lower East Side. A couple of shots rang out behind me, but I only felt one slug hit my wings. It bounced off almost as neatly as the one that had bounced off Wally's forehead, albeit with less *ping*. I had known my wings were tough—but this was the first time I'd realized they could deflect bullets.

Yup, the New Teenage Me was lots tougher than the Old Little-Girl Me had been. And that was pretty cool.

But maybe a little confusing, too.

I wasn't a full-strength grown-up yet. But I wasn't a vulnerable kid anymore, either. And it had been a really rapid transition. Even after all that I had just managed to do, I still wasn't sure what to make of it.

And if I wasn't . . . well, I knew Mom wouldn't be, either.

♠

Mom's Diary

I'm a mother now. I never thought I'd be one. But Adesina's real parents are dead, and who else is going to take care of her?

Besides, we're connected in some way. I'd still be in the coma without her help.

And we saved those children. That counts for something. It has to. I'm not saying it was a perfect victory, but some good came out of it. Maybe even a lot.

And now there's Adesina . . . and me.

Plus, I sure did like beating the hell out of Tom Weathers's Monster. That was the best. Filled to the top with chocolatey goodness.

Turns out that being a hero has an upside, after all.

Who knew?

◆

I touched down on the roof of the Gundersons' apartment building with an "Oof," kicking off my remaining shoe to keep my balance. And then I saw that Yerodin's eyes were wide open and staring up at my face. So I set her down and released her. She wavered a bit, but stood on her own.

"How're you doing?" I asked. My voice sounded hella nervous. I was still scared that she might be mad at me.

She gave me a big, goofy smile. "You came and got me!" Then she swayed, and I put my hand on her shoulder. Her eyes blinked slowly.

"Of course I did," I said. "Well, me and your dad. He kinda helped."

Her eyes widened, and her forehead crinkled. "Did he tell you about our fight?"

"Yeah," I replied. I nudged my lone shoe with my bare toe. "And I told him about us skipping school. I mean, I kinda had to."

Ghost nodded. "I get that." Then she smiled. "I almost feel sorry for the Werewolves. Dad's *really* strong."

"Oh, hells yes!" I said. "Once he got hold of them, I wasn't the only flying joker in the neighborhood."

She laughed, but then gave me a worried look. "Are we okay, Adesina? I miss you so much, and I've been afraid we won't be friends anymore now that you're . . ." She waved her hands in circles in front of me. "All this."

I put on a deliberate smirk. "Maybe I've changed a little, but I can still kick your butt at *Ocelot 9*."

She stabbed an index finger toward the sky. "I call Baby Ocelot!"

"No way," I said. "No dibsing after you've been kidnapped. Totes unfair!"

"Too late!" She pirouetted like a drunken ballerina. "C'mon. The Werewolves still have my phone, but my tablet is downstairs."

I was suddenly happier than I'd been since before I'd changed. "All right, but I'm going to pwn you. You're way too third dwarf right now. You know—Dopey!"

We went down to her and Wally's apartment, where their neighbor Bob was still waiting to see if Yerodin would show up. So now he texted Wally, said goodnight to us, and went home. Ghost retrieved her tablet, and we sat on the couch to play.

She slaughtered me. And I loved it.

Then my phone buzzed. It was a text, but there were no words. Just an emoji of a tulip, followed by a thumbs-up.

I grinned. Tomorrow, my best friend and I would have to pay a visit to the Tumbling Dice.

♥

"Daddy!" Ghost exclaimed when Wally came in. She jumped up and gave him a jumbo hug. His clothes were torn and dirty, and his face looked a little dinged-up. There was a new dimple in his forehead, and even a couple of small rips in the iron skin of his arms. But they didn't seem to bother him.

"Oh, gosh, I didn't 'spect to see you awake." He held her close. "I've sure been worried, don'tchaknow. And we're gonna get you checked out by a doctor right away, you betcha."

Ghost was steady on her feet now. "Okay, Daddy," she said softly. "But in the morning, please? I promise I'm all right. I'm just so sorry I scared you. And it's not your fault I'm not big enough for high school."

They both looked at me, and I wanted to sink into the floor. "I'm sorry, too. If I hadn't changed—"

Wally shook his huge head. "All that matters is you girls are both okay." He wiped a tear from his cheek. It left a rusty trail. "You did good today, Adesina."

That embarrassed me. But I had an easy out. "I should be going. It's after nine, and Mrs. Lehman is supposed to come stay with me if Mom isn't back by ten."

"Golly," Wally said. "Speaking of your mom. Uh, maybe we don't need to tell her about today's business. She has enough on her mind, don'tcha think?"

I was super glad to hear him say that. "Yeah, I do. So telling her about any of this would be *such* a bad idea."

"Okey doke, then," Wally said. He breathed a sigh. "We're on the same sheet of the funny pages."

Ghost gave him a suspicious look. "Daddy," she said. "You're giving the feeling that maybe, just once in a while . . . you used to skip school."

♣

Mom's Diary

I'm not sure who I am anymore. What I did in Kazakhstan was unspeakable. How could I have done those things? How?

Madness. There was nothing but madness.

But wasn't it pulled from somewhere inside me?

Am I a monster?

Can anyone ever forgive me?

♠

When I got home from the Gundersons', I decided I wasn't hungry. Not even for yummy leftover beef Stroganoff.

Instead, since I still had a few minutes before Mrs. Lehman would come over, I pulled out Mom's diary again. I kept coming back to the last entry. See, that Kazakhstan madness had tried to catch me, too. But I protected myself in my cocoon.

Mom, though, was there in the flesh. It ripped her mind apart, and that's why she's so . . . broken now.

As I stepped out of her bedroom, I heard the front door open. I assumed it was Mrs. Lehman, using the key Mom had given her. But when I came into the living room, there was Mom with a bag of groceries in one arm and flowers in the other.

"Hi, Mom!" I took the groceries from her. "I guess stuff in Panama went okay? And you called Mrs. Lehman?"

She shrugged. "I sent Mrs. Lehman a text. As for Panama, there was nothing to it. Turned out the people the Committee thought were going to be a problem were just being paid to be obstreperous for a day. They 'fessed up when I put one of them into a bubble and offered to roll it into the canal. But none of them seemed to know where the money had come from, or why they were told to stall."

I had a pretty good idea, myself. But of course I couldn't say. "Maybe someone just wanted a celebrity encounter with the Amazing Bubbles. Oh, and what's up with the flowers?" I hoped that would change the subject.

"I thought they might brighten up the place." She looked sad for a moment, and then there was that blankness again. I'd been sure she'd look at me and know I had been up to something. But no. Nothing.

"Mom." I put the groceries on the kitchen counter, then waved my hand in front of her face. "You okay?"

She blinked and was back. She gave me a wan smile. "Yes, dear. Panama was nothing. I'm fine."

But she wasn't fine, and there was nothing I could say to change it. I didn't have the right words.

And then I realized that even though there was nothing I could say . . . there might be one thing I could *do*.

"Hey," I said as we put away the groceries. "I know it's kinda late, and a school night, but . . . just for a little while, maybe we could get out of the house and do something totes fun."

She gave me a falsely bright smile. "What's that, honey?"

"We could go to the Statue of Liberty."

A confused expression crossed her face. "I don't think the ferry runs this late."

I took her hand and gave a tug, but I couldn't move her. She was pretty pudgy at the moment.

"C'mon, Mom," I said.

She shook her head as if she were just waking up. "Okay, fine, if you're going to insist." She half laughed and almost sounded like the old Mom. Then she let me pull her into my bedroom.

I let go of her hand, cranked my window open, and climbed onto the sill. The mist had stopped, and the sky was almost clear.

I stepped out onto the narrow ledge and turned to face Mom.

Her eyes were wide. "You can't," she said. "You never told—"

But before she could finish her sentence, I jumped backward, letting my wings spread wide. Mom gave a little squeak, then ran over and stuck her head out.

"Why didn't you tell me?" she asked. There was both wonder and annoyance in her voice. Definitely more like the old Mom. "How long have you known?"

"Not long," I replied, hovering. I looked down and saw people on the sidewalk stopping to squint up past the streetlamps. Oh well. It was going to come out sometime. "Let's go, Mom. It'll be fun!"

Now she looked dubious. "How do you know you can even carry me?"

"Well, we can try," I replied. No need for explanations about that.

And yeah, I was exhausted from the day's torturous adventure. But the thought of taking Mom flying made me feel like I could do anything.

"You could bubble off some fat," I said. "And even if you fall, well, I mean . . . so what?"

That made her snort-laugh—nothing ladylike about it at all. I loved that laugh.

Then she started bubbling through the open window. Some of the bubbles floated around me, and some drifted down to amaze the pedestrians. They were all like the ones she used to make for me. Soft and pretty. Shiny, too.

"Okay," she said, climbing out onto the ledge when she was a bit thinner. "How do you want to do this?"

"Just wrap your arms around me." She reached out to pull me close, and I let her embrace me.

Then I gave a few strong flaps, and we rose into the air. It smelled of autumn. The wind changed direction as we ascended, and I knew I'd have to compensate for it. But hey, no prob. Not for Morpho Girl.

I liked Mom's arms around me. It made me feel like a little kid again. But now I was the one carrying *her,* and that felt like . . . something new.

So maybe we could never be normal again. Never like the way we used to be, I mean.

But maybe we could be . . . okay.

I flew upward until we were high above the city. Below us, the jumbled buildings of Lower Manhattan were bathed in electric radiance. It was freaking gorgeous.

Then Mom and I looped around, rose higher still, and flew through the darkness toward the bright glow of Lady Liberty.

♠ ♥ ♦ ♣

Naked, Stoned, and Stabbed

by Bradley Denton

OUR THIRD NIGHT AT the Bowery Ballroom, Liam punched me in the gut. But I was happy to let him do it, for the sake of the gig. Besides, I hoped it might take my mind off a few things.

Such as the fact that we were in the city where my half sister lived. Who didn't know I existed. And whom I'd sworn I would never try to meet.

Trouble was, after three days in New York, I was finding that a tough resolution to keep. It turned out Big Sis lived just seven blocks from the Ballroom, a fact I discovered because I couldn't stay off Google. And I reckoned if I walked in that direction, I'd do better to turn around, step into Sara D. Roosevelt Park, and alter my motivation with the cheap K2 its denizens were hawking.

Of course, I'd already heard that some of that K2, the stuff the locals called KX or Xeno, would drive you starkers. Among other things, it was blamed for various incidents of violence, especially nat-on-joker or vice versa. But that was the sort of thing prigs said to scare you. My own experience, though limited to one party in London, told me that K2—or Spice, or KX, or whatever—was just mild synthetic pot.

On the other hand, my gaffer in chief, Liam, warned that whatever was being sold in an NYC Jokertown park wasn't going to be what I'd had back home. And since Liam had tried and quit more drugs in more places than I'd ever heard of, I guessed he would know.

Besides, if I got baked, I might be even more likely to wind up at Big Sis's apartment. And then I'd tell her who I was, which would also mean telling her that eighteen years ago, her dad had cheated on her mum with *my* mum. Not an auspicious icebreaker.

Especially since Big Sis just happened to be world-famous as a fashion model, reality-TV contestant, and, hang on, what was that other thing? Oh, yes: insanely powerful, civilization-saving ace.

Given some of the barmy fans I'd encountered in almost two years as a

Maximum R&B roadie, I reckoned someone like Big Sis would have delusional wankers claiming personal relationships almost daily. So knocking on her door and saying, "Hi, I'm yer secret baby brother," might be problematic.

Still, I couldn't help thinking it might be nice to have a sister. Half or otherwise. After all, it was a safe wager I'd never see my mum again. Since, if I did, one or both of us could wind up dead. I hadn't run off to join the circus on a whim.

In short, I was a bit torn. The one thing I was sure of was that as long as the Who were in Manhattan, I would be arguing with myself about it. So I was ready for Liam to punch me.

But I wasn't ready for the Bowery Ballroom to catch fire, and I wasn't ready to electrocute myself.

Or to die and meet an angel.

Or to be attacked by a psychotic mob.

Or to be smacked to oblivion by an insanely powerful, civilization-saving ace.

So I suppose what I'm saying is:

Getting punched would be the easiest part of my weekend.

♦

Mr. Daltrey had screamed like a fiend on Thursday and Friday nights—in December, in New York City, in a drafty venue—so by Saturday, his throat was as raw as if he'd swallowed a hedgehog. But for the 2018–19 tour, the Who are playing multi-night stands in small to medium halls, and profit margins are slim. We ain't about to cancel a show due to minor illness. Which means the band and crew must find ways to carry on.

For one thing, the lads might play fewer rusty-fork-and-chalkboard numbers. But even so, they always close with "Won't Get Fooled Again," which requires the nuclear apocalypse of all screams. And they absolutely must do it, Mr. Townshend says, because otherwise "the arse'oles won't leave." By which he means the audience.

My own favorite tune from *Who's Next* happens to be "Bargain," and I always wish they'd end with that one. Or "Pinball Wizard" from *Tommy*. But "Pinball Wizard" always shows up in the middle of the set, and some nights they don't play "Bargain" at all. So Liam has told me not to bother suggesting it as a closer. "It's always gonna be 'Won't Get Fooled,'" he says. "And 'Won't Get Fooled' has always gotta have the 'Eee-yaaayyyy' so the Wholigans can end the night screamin'."

So on Saturday night at the Bowery Ballroom, during the recorded synthesizer break near the end of the song, while the lights and lasers were flashing, Liam and I slipped behind Mr. Entwistle's Hiwatt bass cabinets at stage right. It was the thirteenth time we'd done it in the year and a half since I'd shown Liam what I could do.

Liam got down on one knee. In the strobes, he looked like a bushy-bearded Buddha. Assuming Buddha had ever worn a black T-shirt emblazoned with a bull's-eye roundel. Or if Buddha had ever flattened a bartender for calling me a "freakish little wog."

Now, Liam himself had once said that my spiky white-blond hair, wheatish complexion, and silver-gray eyes were an "odd mishmash." But that didn't mean he'd let an outsider insult one of his crew. Even if that crewmate happened to look as I do, or sometimes happened to sound more like a Yank than a Londoner. But Liam knew I couldn't help that. I learned how to speak from my mum, who had spent much of her youth in the States. And that was no doubt where she would have stayed, modeling and having tons of fun, if I hadn't come along.

Which explains her resentment of me. Not that my childhood was consistently dreadful. For one thing, in addition to my odd speech patterns, Mum also gave me an appreciation for classic rock—since my naptimes were always accompanied by the Kinks, the Rolling Stones, or the Who. And after my card turned, that appreciation would help me make my getaway.

But I would always be an odd duck, and I couldn't get away from that. In fact, it was right after Liam's "mishmash" comment that I'd taken to wearing round, blue-tinted spectacles. I couldn't change my skin, my hair, or the way I spoke. But I could cover my eyes.

Mr. Moon started the drum buildup to the "Won't Get Fooled" climax, and Liam tapped his earplugs. "Ready, Mr. Fullerton?" he asked.

Which I knew by reading his lips. I don't wear earplugs myself—don't need 'em—but I still can't hear shite over those Moonie drums.

I made sure my old gray jacket was open, so I'd get the full impact, then gave Liam a nod as he drew back his fist. I looked toward the front of house, adjusted my specs, and tilted my head up. I stared over the speaker cabinets and took careful aim at a dark point out at the center of the Ballroom's high ceiling, midway between the balconies on either side. The place was packed with five hundred strobe-lit Wholigans on the floor, jumping and jostling, plus another hundred at tables on the balconies . . . and I didn't want to bash any heads together. The audience was a diverse mix of nats and jokers, all of whom seemed to be having a fine time. But that might not hold steady if I knocked them into each other.

When Mr. Townshend's big guitar chord slammed down and Liam's fist connected with my belly, just below my own T-shirt's bull's-eye, it was perfect. Mr. Daltrey mimed my scream with precision, and the noise bounced off the ceiling, shook the Hiwatt cabinets, rattled the lights, rang through the cymbals, and roared from the walls. The whole joint was shakin' all over. But nothing collapsed or burst, and Liam remained on one knee in front of me instead of being swatted away like a tennis ball. Best of all, it sounded like Mr. Daltrey on a good night, if a bit louder. The Wholigans cheered.

Liam was grinning as he stood up. And my headache, though immediate, wasn't terrible. I could walk it off. This had been one of our best "Won't Get Fooled Again" saves. And no one in the audience would guess that the scream that had ripped their knickers had come from an unamplified roadie.

But as the lads hit the "Meet the new boss, same as the old boss" bit, a blazing yellow flash washed out the stage lights, and a tremendous *ka-wham* overwhelmed the music. It was even louder than my scream.

Then the amps and PA went dead, Mr. Moon dropped his sticks, and the only sound was a sudden cacophony from the audience.

Liam's grin vanished. He peered out between the Hiwatts.

So did I. That was when I saw the flames at the foot of the stage, between the band and the audience.

The cacophony turned to shrieks.

Then came a second yellow flash and another *ka-wham*. This time I was blinded. I heard the shrieks become panicked as the audience stomped the floor and slammed into each other.

It was the beginning of a stampede.

"Bloody Jeezus!" Liam bellowed. "I told that Russian bloke 'No pyros, and no smoke!' I don't think the sod was even allowed to be in here. I see him again, I'm gonna tear off 'is arms!" He slapped my shoulder, but not so hard that it triggered a shout. "Right, Freddie! We'll bugger off out back. Arnie and I will get the lads, and you and Bruce grab amp heads. Two apiece if you can, but move fast!"

"And take 'em where?" I asked. We'd planned to load out to a hired lorry in the morning, and it wasn't there yet.

"Carry 'em up to the hotel!" The band and crew were all staying at the Public Hotel a few blocks up Chrystie Street. "But stay out o' the park, or them dossers'll take 'em. Leave the drums and cabinets, and we'll get 'em tomorrow. If they don't burn!"

My vision was starting to clear. I caught a glimpse of Mr. Entwistle calmly unplugging his bass. Beyond him, below the lip of the stage, the flames were licking higher. I didn't know what had exploded down there, or what was fueling the flames, but the fire was spreading. The stage monitors in front of Mr. Daltrey and Mr. Townshend were alight, and the heavy curtains at stage left were starting to catch. And there was smoke. The mingled chemical stinks of burning cloth, plastic, electrical wiring, and God knew what else filled the air.

Out on the floor, illuminated by flames and by bobbing cell phones, hundreds of flickering Wholigans were shoving, shrieking, and falling. They were all trying to get to the lobby doors at the far end of the house. But those doors were closed, and dozens of shadow-people had already clustered there, shoving outward. No one was escaping. And the fire was spreading.

I grabbed Liam's arm. "We can get some of the audience out with us!" I had spotted a gap below our side of the stage where there were no flames, and where people might be able to climb up.

Liam's scowl was tinged with something frantic. "No way to tell 'em!" He had to shout so I could hear him over the screams. "The PA's knackered!"

He was right. I could see Mr. Townshend, his face glowing with weird orange light, trying to yell to the audience through his mic as he waved his red Strat over his head. But there was no sound except the noise from the crowd.

"We can't do nothin' but look after our own!" Liam yelled. "That smoke reeks, and Mister D is gonna asphyxiate! So snag a couple o' bass heads, and come on!"

He pulled away and ran around the Hiwatts to the front of the stage. I watched him grab both Mr. Entwistle and Mr. Townshend, who held on to their instruments as Liam dragged them back to the stage door that led to the green room and rear exit. Our crewmates, Ginger Arnie and Bald Bruce, came onstage from that door just then, and I saw Liam bellowing orders. Arnie collected Mr. Daltrey and Mr. Moon, who was wandering around behind the drum kit, and he got them out while Bruce yanked the speaker cables and power cords from Mr. Townshend's two amp heads and carried them out as well.

That left me onstage alone, behind the bass cabinets, unplugging speaker cables from Mr. Entwistle's three big Hiwatt heads. The vacuum tubes inside the top head glowed the same yellow-orange as the flames below the stage. The grille that had once covered the back of the chassis was long gone, so those tubes shone as bright and hot as tiny furnaces.

The amp was still getting juice. And it was one of Mr. Entwistle's vintage units from the 1970s, so the power cord was hardwired. I couldn't just yank out the cord, grab the head, and take off. I had to disconnect it at the mains.

The cord snaked down to a block of outlets bolted to the floor at stage right, and I scurried over to unplug it. But as I bent down, I heard crashing noises and still more screams. I looked out through the flames and smoke and saw people, nats and jokers alike, jumping from the balconies. Their chairs and tables were going over, too. So everyone below, already panicking, was now being hit from above. Some Wholigans were falling to the floor, and others were collapsing on top of them.

It looked as if one of the doors to the lobby had been torn from its hinges. But it was still nothing but colliding shadows back there. So the main doors to Delancey Street were still closed, and no one was making it out of the building.

For a few seconds, I froze with my hand on the plug of the power cord.

All I could think was that everyone who had come to see the Who that night was going to die. All those people. All those Wholigans.

And I remember what I did next. But I don't remember deciding to do it.

So I guess I didn't consider how much it was going to hurt.

♥

I left the power cord plugged in and jumped back behind the Hiwatts. Then I made sure I had a line of sight to the western wall of the main floor, beyond the far edge of stage right. There was still a gap there with no flames. The wall was about thirty feet from me, and I hoped that was close enough. Luckily, no one was in my way because the entire audience was clustered at the other end of the house.

I reached into the amp head. Just to the left of the little glowing furnaces, I found the metal cover over the filter capacitors. It came free with a tug. Ginger Arnie, our lead amplifier tech, has to work on the guts of Mr. Entwistle's amps almost every other gig, so he always leaves the screws loose.

After flinging the cover away, I reached back inside with both hands and grabbed the exposed capacitors. There were five of them, and I tried to squeeze them all into my fists. Then I yanked.

Filter capacitors look like small sticks of dynamite. I wasn't looking at them just then, though, because I had to face that western wall. But I knew I had them. Arnie had pointed them out many times.

"Now, these little thugs," he'd said. "You lay a finger on these 'fore you bleed off the charge, and they'll kick yer bollocks up through yer skull."

Which was his way of saying filter caps carry tremendous voltages. Sometimes they'll even hold those charges for hours after the amp has been switched off.

When it's switched on, though, there's no debate. Grab 'em, and you're dead.

Or most of you are.

I levitated. It was as if I were suspended in air on a skewer of lightning. Every cell in my body burst into a fireball.

Even so, I stayed on target, although the shrieks of my various internal organs kept me from hearing the actual noise of my shout.

But I saw the result.

A rough oval section of wall, eight feet wide by ten feet high, blew out as if punched by a gigantic fist.

And at that, I collapsed to the stage with my muscles convulsing and my head being crushed by a pneumatic press.

It was bad. Almost as bad as the day my card had turned, the day my mum had lost her mind and slapped the shite out of me. The day I had tried to suppress my first big shout—thus saving Mum's life, but sending myself to hospital.

I had been all right with that. And I was all right with this, too.

The shock wave had knocked over the Hiwatt cabinets, so I still had a clear view to the hole I had made. It was a pretty thing, having been blasted through the shared wall into the building next door. That building appeared to house a showroom for commercial kitchen equipment. The lights were on in there, and as the brick and concrete dust settled, I saw gleaming pots and pans scattered on the floor where they'd been blasted from their shelves. The brightness stung my eyes, because my tinted specs had been knocked askew.

Then I saw some of the Wholigans come back toward the stage and begin to make their way out through the hole. There were just a few at first, but then ten, fifteen, thirty. One bloke who looked like he might be almost seventeen—my age—a dark-haired kid wearing Buddy Holly glasses and a kilt, took it upon himself to pull two limp fans through the hole. Then he pushed his way back to help two more. He moved so smoothly and so fast that he looked as if he must have been skating on air.

You can always count on a floating Scotsman, I thought.

Then I saw that his legs ended in wheels, joined by some sort of cartilaginous axle.

So I guessed my mind was not cogent. In fact, I reckoned I was in rotten shape overall. But I managed to turn my head enough to look out at the main floor. I wanted to see the entire audience find their way out through my new door.

But only those closest to the stage had seen what I'd done. Everyone else must have assumed the noise was another explosion. Now most of them were even more panicked than before, and they kept surging toward an escape that wasn't there.

I had saved perhaps fifty out of six hundred. The rest were still going to be killed.

Unless I did more.

The amp head that had given me my jolt was on the floor beside one of the fallen cabinets. I tried to crawl toward it, but then I saw it was useless. Its tiny furnaces had gone out. Mr. Entwistle's other two amp heads were nearby, but they were dark and defunct as well. So the people who didn't find the new way out were doomed.

As was I. I had crawled just a few feet before collapsing into porridge. There was no way I would make it to either the stage door or the hole in the wall. The fire would get me first. And by the time my crewmates realized I hadn't joined them outside, they wouldn't be able to return. I could feel my smartphone buzzing in the hip pocket of my jeans, and I assumed it was Liam asking what was taking me so sodding long.

The smoky air was becoming hot, thick, and ever more bitter. So at least I would fall unconscious before I burned.

In the meantime, with my chest and cheek pressed against the boards of the stage, I could look out over the surging throng and take a shred of comfort in watching a few of them escape.

I supposed I should have tried to meet my sister after all. While I'd had a choice.

And then I knew I was dying, because over the rims of my skewed spectacles I saw an angel. She rose from the tumultuous shadows and flew toward me on cobalt-blue butterfly wings.

She was like a perfect holy creature carved from obsidian and come to life. As she soared over the flames, the smoke swirling away from her beating wings, she was the most beautiful sight I had ever beheld.

Now that, I thought, *is even better than a floating Scotsman.*

Then the angel fuzzed into darkness, and I was done.

♣

I awoke as she lifted me from the stage. Startled, I twisted away and crumpled into a flat sack of bones again.

Now I was lying on my back, and my specs had popped back into place.

I found myself looking up at the "angel" hovering over me, and it occurred to me that she might really exist. She still had huge blue butterfly wings, and she still looked as if she were carved from obsidian. But now I saw that she was also wearing a long-sleeved Union Jack–patterned THE KIDS ARE ALRIGHT T-shirt and bright red stovepipe pants. Two slender appendages like insect legs stuck out through extra holes below her shirtsleeves, and they wiggled. As did a pair of foot-long antennae sprouting from her forehead.

But more striking than any of that were her long, coppery dreadlocks glowing in the light of the fire. Her eyes were that same coppery color—and I could have sworn they glowed, too.

Other than that, she had the face of a deeply annoyed teenage girl. Perhaps a year younger than me.

"Cheese and crackers!" she yelped. She landed on the stage, her purple high-top Chuck Taylors on either side of my waist. "Dude, I'm trying to save you!" She was yelling. "A little cooperation, maybe?"

So she wasn't an angel. She was a joker. But she was a joker who had flown to me on brilliant blue wings, so she still looked bloody angelic to me. Also, she had those red pants and purple Chuck Taylors. I myself stuck to black jeans and Doc Martens, but I could appreciate red stovepipes and Chucks. I wondered where she'd snagged the purple ones.

Then she coughed, and I realized the smoke had become still heavier and more pungent. The heat from the flames was getting aggressive, too. My right cheek was trying to decide whether to blister.

I looked toward the hole I had blasted. The bloke in the kilt was helping more people through, but it wasn't going to be enough. In a few moments, he would have to give up and save himself, because the fire was about to cut off his access to anyone else. Which meant there wasn't any point in trying to widen the hole or make another beside it, because no one else was going to reach that spot.

So I forced myself up to my elbows and looked toward the opposite wall. But there was already too much fire and smoke over there.

Nor was there any use in blasting through the back of the building, behind the stage. There was already a door there that no one out on the floor could reach.

I was too far from the main doors, and there were too many people in the way, for me to try to punch a hole there. Over that distance, the shock wave would spread too wide and weaken too much, and I'd only clobber the Wholigans instead of helping them. The same was true for the wall space under the balconies.

Besides, I couldn't give myself another electrical jolt anyway.

All of that left just one option. And there was just one reason it was an option at all: The angel was real.

I stared up at her. My head was about to split open because someone was hammering an invisible iron wedge between my eyes. But the good news, I supposed, was that I was already hurting about as much as I could hurt.

Which was a dumb thing to suppose.

"A lot of people are about to die!" I said.

The butterfly girl reached toward me. "Some of us are going to make it, thanks to you! My boyfriend and I saw you blast the wall. It was loud! So he's helping people get out, and I came to help *you*. I'll fly you to the hole. Trust me, I can totally carry you!"

But I was already counting on that.

I pointed upward. "You can help more people if you fly me to the ceiling. Then drop me."

I thought about the venue stats Liam had quoted as we'd prepared for sound check on Thursday: "Room echo won't be bad once the Wholigans pack in. We've got just five thousand square feet, and twenty-four feet to the ceiling."

A twenty-four-foot ceiling was fine for a music hall. But it might not give me what I needed. It wasn't a sure thing, like the filter capacitors.

The angel interrupted my thought with a non-angelic snort. "You want me to *drop* you? You already look two-thirds dead!"

I tried to nod, which only drove the iron wedge deeper. "Yeah, but don't just drop me. *Kick* me straight down, hard as you can. Find a spot with some empty floor, and make sure I land on my back. But get out of the way before I hit!"

She stared at me for a second, then looked out at the main floor. The bulk of the audience was still surging against the doors and trying to jam into the lobby, and the rest had made it to the hole in the wall. So a small space in the center of the room was empty, and the fire hadn't reached it yet.

The angel looked dubious.

"Are you—" she began.

Then she stopped. She knew I was sure. And we didn't have more time to waste.

I dug down for some strength, then grasped her arms and hooked my heels behind her calves. Those glorious blue wings spread wide and pumped hard. We shot upward, and I gasped at the acceleration. But I held tight as we arced out over the main floor, all the way up, as high as we could go.

The butterfly girl paused then, her wings brushing the black iron braces that crisscrossed the ceiling.

We were at the point where I had aimed my "Won't Get Fooled Again" scream. I was looking up at the angel's face, and she was looking down at mine. I saw from her expression that she was afraid for me. I thought that was nice of her.

"I'm Adesina," she said.

I made myself give her a smile. "Freddie."

Then her wings pumped again, and she pressed her spine against one of the iron braces. She brought up her knees and jammed the soles of her Chuck Taylors against my chest as my heels slipped from her calves. I released her arms, and she kicked downward. Hard.

I watched her shrink and dive away as I tried to suck in as much smoky air as I could.

Then the sun exploded, and the earth crumbled. The darkness above me blew apart, and all the sky was stars.

♠

I awoke, coughing, with my back against the concrete base of a streetlight pole in the middle of Delancey Street. Or rather, in the middle of the wide median that split Delancey Street. I was halfway between Bowery and Chrystie in a section of the median with planted greenery, although there was nothing green about it right now. Low shrubs stood stark and leafless on either side of me, and my rump was in the frigid dirt. My breath came out as fog in the cold night.

The heels of my Doc Martens were hanging over the street, and I was looking across four lanes of asphalt at the green iron railing surrounding the Bowery station subway entrance on the sidewalk. Beyond that was the limestone facade and the tall, arched, wired-glass window of the Bowery Ballroom. The window reflected steady white streetlights punctuated with flashing red and blue. The steel double doors on either side of the window were still closed, and I thought I heard shouts and screams from inside. But I wasn't sure because an FDNY fire engine, its siren winding down to a growl, rumbled past me and stopped beside a hydrant just west of the subway entrance.

Then I saw her.

At the east end of the subway entrance, turning toward the Ballroom as she emerged from beneath the street, was my sister.

For a few seconds, I thought I must still be unconscious. After years of wondering what it might be like to be in her presence, what were the odds that she would appear right in front of me, right now?

It was far more likely that I was still blacked out. Or perhaps dying. And my scrambled brain was performing one last act of kindness before closing up shop.

But then I shivered with considerable force, and icy needles shot through what felt like every shattered bone in my body. Also, I was pretty sure the iron wedge had succeeded in splitting my skull wide open.

So I was alive, and conscious. Painfully so.

And my half sister, Michelle Pond, the Amazing Bubbles, was standing right across the street.

Her back was to me now, and she was wearing a bulky, oversized gray sweater and black leggings with knee-high suede boots. So how could I know it was her?

How could I not?

She was tall and broad-shouldered, and her long silver-blond hair was flying in the chill breeze. Her arms stretched upward, spreading in a wide V, and an enormous bubble formed between her palms. It gleamed with flashes of color from the FDNY lights.

As fast as an eyeblink, the bubble was larger than Bubbles herself, and it rose from her hands with the speed of an express lift.

"Adesina!" she cried. "Soft landing for your next passengers!" Her voice was clear and commanding. She sounded exactly as I'd imagined.

I looked up, my eyes following the huge bubble as it reached the top of the Ballroom's facade. At that moment, the butterfly-winged angel appeared above it, flying through a thin veil of smoke with two hefty middle-aged nats, Wholigans for three or four decades, dangling from her hands. She didn't struggle with the weight. Carrying me must have been a doddle.

She let them go, and the two men fell into the bubble, which sucked them inside with a loud kissing sound. Then they floated down to the sidewalk as gently as a tuft of goose down.

"Awesome, Mom!" Adesina shouted. "This'll go faster now!"

Wait a minute, I thought. *What—*

The bubble disintegrated as it touched the concrete, and the rescued men stood there dazed. Then a firefighter leaped from the truck and shouted to them to hurry across Chrystie to Roosevelt Park. "EMS is setting up a triage station! They'll look after you!"

By this time another huge bubble had reached the roof, and Adesina dropped a lizard-scaled woman and a three-legged boy into it as the two nats stumbled eastward.

"We have to be even faster!" the Amazing Bubbles shouted as the woman and child floated down. "If they can walk, just bring them to the roof and tell them to run to the front of the building. They can jump into a bubble on their own while you're flying back down for someone else!"

Adesina, hovering, gave a quick nod. "Okay, Mom!" She shot backward, out of sight.

Wait a minute, I thought again. *What'd she call her?*

"But hold your breath down there!" Bubbles yelled. "And stop if the smoke is too thick for you to see!"

I tried to call out that I didn't think Adesina had heard her. But now the firefighters were shouting too, and there were more sirens. Plus the roaring in my head, and my coughing. I couldn't even hear myself.

"You over there, on the wheels!" a firefighter cried, waving her arms. She had a fleshy flap in the middle of her face instead of a nose, and it bounced with every word.

She was looking west. The fire engine partially blocked my view in that direction, and another engine pulled up and blocked it further. But then I glimpsed a kilted lad leading a string of stumbling, coughing people southward across the intersection of Delancey and Bowery. He had gotten them out through the restaurant supply showroom. And, sure enough, he was rolling along on two wheels joined by a cartilaginous axle at his ankles.

"Good man," I tried to say. I was relieved that I hadn't hallucinated the wheels. And I was even more relieved to see he had managed to lead thirty or forty people to safety.

"We've set up triage for injuries and smoke inhalation at the plaza that cuts through the park at Rivington!" the firefighter yelled at the wheeled lad. "You know the spot?"

The wheeled lad nodded and waved.

"Okay! Bring everyone along the south side of Delancey, cross north at Chrystie, and head for the flashing lights!"

The wheeled lad gestured to his flock, but not everyone chose to come along. A few abandoned the group and staggered off on their own. I hoped they didn't wind up regretting it.

I looked back up at the Bowery Ballroom facade, despite the fact that a hot spike shot through my brain every time I moved my head. Enormous bubble after enormous bubble was floating up to the edge of the roof, and Wholigan after Wholigan, young and old, male and female, nats and jokers, were jumping off into the rubbery spheres and floating down to the sidewalk.

The firefighter who had shouted to the wheeled lad now ran up to the Amazing Bubbles.

"There are a *lot* of people inside, Ms. Pond," she said in a rush, the flap on her face bouncing wildly. "You won't be able to get them all out like this. And Morpho Girl isn't wearing a respirator, so she needs to get *herself* out."

Wait a minute, I thought yet again. *What kind of girl?*

"We can't just leave people in there!" Bubbles snapped.

"We won't!" the firefighter said. "That's my job! But someone chained those doors on the inside, and we need them open—faster than we can pry them, because if anyone tries to come through that glass, it'll be ugly. So if you could blast 'em, that'd be great!"

The Amazing Bubbles released another giant bubble as two more popped on the sidewalk and their occupants fled eastward. She lowered her arms and faced the firefighter. I could see her in profile now. Her nose was the shape of a small, inverted strawberry, and her jaw was like the corner of a shoebox. Both looked just like mine.

She was much slimmer than when she'd come up from the subway, and her sweater was hanging like an empty sack. She had "bubbled off" most of her fat while making the rescue spheres. That meant she'd have to jump off a roof herself, or have some big bloke punch her a few times, before she would bulk up again. Which was what made her one of the world's toughest aces: If you tried to hurt her, you just made her stronger.

Bloody hell, how my screaming head, ribs, and spine made me envy that.

"I would have already blasted the doors," Bubbles said, "but there are people on the other side. I could kill someone!"

The firefighter shook her head. "We're on a phone call with one of the trapped individuals. He's conveyed our order to move back, and we believe they have. We have to breach *now*!"

At that, Bubbles didn't hesitate. She faced the Ballroom and thrust out her arms in another V, this time horizontal. A silvery bubble the size of a cricket ball shot from each of her palms, moving so fast that I heard the air sizzle. The bubbles hit the double doors on either side of the arched window, and the doors blew inward with a tremendous clang. But they stayed on their hinges, and one of them swung back. I saw a heavy chain dangling from its inside handle.

The firefighter had been right. Someone had chained the doors.

Someone had meant for all of us to be locked inside while the Bowery Ballroom burned.

♦

I expected smoke to start pouring from the open doors. Instead, there was a sudden low whistle as air began rushing *into* the Ballroom. I looked up and saw a wide column of smoke rising from the roof, venting through the hole I'd blasted.

Four firefighters entered through the east doors and began hustling people out, while eight more firefighters in respirators went in through the west doors with a pair of hoses. They shouted for the civilians to head for the east exit, and a steady stream of coughing, crying Wholigans complied. Firefighters from the second truck began giving oxygen to some of them as a third truck stopped in the street between me and the Ballroom. Some of the third truck's personnel began helping the escapees toward the triage station in the park.

I heard more sirens coming. NYPD cruisers and motorcycles had already closed Delancey to civilian traffic from both directions, and they were also stopping vehicles from turning north onto Forsyth at the far side of the park, more than a hundred yards from where I sat. There was no traffic entering or emerging from Chrystie on the near side of the park, either. That meant Chrystie was closed not only at Delancey but at some point to the north, probably Houston Street. So fire and rescue vehicles had a clear path, and so did the people fleeing the Ballroom.

With the third FDNY truck sitting in front of me, I could no longer see the Ballroom doors or the Amazing Bubbles. But I saw a ladder go up the center of the building facade, and firefighters ascending to the roof. Four more giant bubbles of rescued people floated down past them.

The noise of trucks and sirens, and of shouting and screaming, was making my skull reverberate like a church bell. But the rest of my body was beginning to hurt a little less. So I pushed against the base of the streetlight, and managed to get my feet under me.

I wobbled as I stood, but steadied myself on the streetlight pole and took inventory. My boots were still tied. My jeans were soiled, but only with dirt. I hadn't embarrassed myself. My T-shirt had come untucked. My trusty gray canvas jacket stank of smoke, but it had kept my shirt and skin intact when Adesina had kicked me to the floor. My head still swiveled, my mouth tasted only slightly of copper, and my blue specs were, somehow, still seated on my nose. All my senses seemed operational.

So despite my initial agony and blackout, I had come through this evening's big shouts better than I'd come through the first one, on my fifteenth birthday. That had been worse because I'd tried to clamp my mouth shut. So some of the force had been directed down at my own guts, resulting in a hiatal hernia and what a laconic sawbones had called "just a touch" of internal bleeding.

"Nevertheless," the doc had continued, "whatever caused this, I advise against repeating the activity."

But even if I had understood what that first shout had been, I still would have tried to push it down. No matter how things had degenerated between us, I couldn't very well kill my own mum. As it was, the small portion of the shout that had escaped my lips had thrown her across the flat and given her a radial fracture.

So as soon as a nurse had told me I was about to be released from hospital, and that my mum would be notified, I'd slipped away. Fortunately, I'd already stashed a few hundred quid from repairing guitars and amps, using one of my clients as a bank. It had been just enough to purchase a birth certificate and passport from an East End artisan, with both documents indicating I was three years older than I was. So if anyone were to ask, I was eighteen.

Then my "banker" had informed me that an old mate of his, Liam, was hiring crew for a certain iconic rock band's upcoming Continental and North American tours. Minimum age requirement: Eighteen.

That tip had gotten me out of the UK for a good long while, which was just what I needed. Because if I had stayed in Britain, I might have been tempted to go home. And if Mum were ever to hit me in the face again, with all those rings she wears . . . Well, it wouldn't be a good job. Not for anyone.

Which was what I was thinking as I leaned against the streetlight pole and watched Adesina fly out over the edge of the Ballroom roof again. This time, she wasn't carrying anyone.

"Everyone's getting out the regular way now, Mom!" she called.

And that was why I'd been thinking about my mum. Because Adesina, the angel who had saved me, kept addressing my secret big sis as "Mom."

As the Yanks say, it was messing with my head.

"Come down, then," Bubbles said, "and we'll leave the rest to the professionals." Her voice was strong enough that I could hear it through all the noise, despite the fact that a truck was sitting between us. "We'll have the medics look you over, and maybe then we can go home. After which you're not allowed to date again until you're thirty. And I mean your real age, so we're talking another two decades."

Adesina began to descend, high-fiving a firefighter on the ladder on her way down. "I'm fine!" she said. "I hardly breathed any smoke. And we have to find Peter. He was helping people get out through the hole in the wall, but I don't know what happened to him after that. He hasn't answered my texts."

So the kilt-wearing lad on wheels was her boyfriend, and his name was Peter. My head was clear enough now to understand that much. But I was still having trouble with the Amazing Bubbles being "Mom." And with Adesina being—what, ten years old?

"Oh!" Adesina exclaimed. "We also need to make sure Freddie is okay!"

That made me feel a bit better. She hadn't forgotten me.

"Who's Freddie?" Big Sis asked.

"Come on, Mom! He's who I told you about in my second and third texts. The dude who blasted the holes."

"Well, it's no wonder I didn't catch who *that* guy was," Bubbles said. "See, after your first text that said 'Fire,' I was sort of focused on getting out of the tub."

"That guy is Freddie!" Adesina said. "He got knocked out when I helped him make the hole in the roof. But then there were a lot of people I had to try to rescue, so I just flew him out here and—"

Adesina dropped out of sight behind the fire truck, and her voice blended with all the other noises flooding Delancey.

It occurred to me then that where I was standing right now, where Adesina had left me, was the first place she and Big Sis would look for me.

I wasn't ready for that. So I pushed away from the streetlight and headed east, struggling through a dead shrub and then wobbling along the wide concrete median. I wanted to get away as fast as possible, but didn't think I was steady enough to run. And if I fell, I might give a yelp and blow a crater into the pavement. Also, a lot of other people were running, and if I ran and then collided with one of them, that might do something worse than blowing a crater. I had just now been electrocuted and kicked to the floor to save dozens of Wholigans, and I didn't want to spoil it by turning any of them into pulp.

My phone buzzed in my back pocket again. Astonished it was still working, I brought it out as I turned left past a cluster of NYPD cruisers and headed north on Chrystie. I was in the lanes meant for southbound traffic, but at the moment, the street was wholly occupied by a few hundred coughing Ballroom escapees, all stumbling northward.

Most of them were making for the triage station, but not I. My plan was to head up another block to the Who's hotel at Chrystie and Stanton. From what the Amazing Bubbles had said, she would be bringing Morpho Girl—"Morpho," like the butterfly, I realized—to the park plaza to be examined. And I didn't want them to find me there any more than I'd wanted them to find me in the median. Nor did I want them to spot me on the street. But I blended in well with the throng, since I was just one of many who were staring down at phones as we staggered along. The glowing rectangles joined with the streetlights to illuminate the small fogs of our breath.

My phone screen had a thin crack running across it, but it still came to life when I gave it a tap. Liam had sent me two texts—one, as I'd guessed, from just after I'd electrocuted myself. The second was from just now:

FUK IF UR ALIVE IM @ MEDIC IN PARK LOOKN 4 U. GOT LADS 2 HOTEL N CAME BAK BUT THINGS GETTN BARMY. WAS SOMETHN IN SMOKE. WHOLIGANS STARTN 2 GO ROUND THE TWIST.

I tried to text a reply and tell him we could just meet at the hotel. But for that, my touchscreen wouldn't work.

Bugger it. I would have to stop at the triage station after all.

And then, when I was twenty seconds from the plaza, another text popped up:

SPOTTD SCUM WHAT SET PYROS W POISON SMOKE GNNA CRAK SKULL.

I heard a shriek ahead, and it multiplied and rippled toward me from scores of throats. In the middle of the shriek came a metallic crash.

So now, wobbly or not, I began to run.

♥

The forty-foot-wide brick plaza had become a scene from Bedlam.

Dozens of jokers of all shapes, sizes, and sorts, some of whom I recognized from the Ballroom—jokers with extra arms or legs, jokers with tentacles, jokers with scales, jokers with flowers sprouting from their heads, jokers with necks like giraffes or heads like hippopotami—all were pressed with their backs against the ironwork fences on the northern and southern boundaries of the plaza, all the way across the park to Forsyth. They had terror in their eyes. They were being shielded by two thin blue lines of cops and medics, jokers and nats standing together. The medics had linked arms with some of the cops, and the rest of the cops had batons at the ready.

Between those blue lines, in the middle of the plaza, more than two hundred nats were rioting. They had overturned an emergency medical services van that had pulled onto the bricks, and now they were swarming over it, ripping off the doors and emptying it of every piece of equipment, all of which went flying into the air like jagged confetti. As it came down, most of the rioters dodged it. But a few didn't, and they fell to the bricks, bleeding. They lay among dozens of dropped smartphones, some of which were glowing and buzzing, and some of which had already been trampled to pieces.

The only reason the fallen nats weren't trampled themselves was because more and more of the rioters were joining screaming nats at either side of the plaza. They were lunging at the trapped jokers, and they were only just being held at bay by the thin blue lines.

A few of the jokers closest to Chrystie tried to escape into the street, but were driven back by a swarm of nats on the asphalt. I found myself in the middle of that swarm, which just moments before had been Wholigans running up the street with me. But now they swirled, stomped, and screamed.

Whatever had turned them into a psychotic mob hadn't affected me. And at first, none of them seemed to notice. They all surged toward the plaza, and I stumbled backward to get away from them. But I collided with a patrol car blocking the entrance to Rivington Street, and six or seven stragglers turned toward me. They hunched over, cocked their heads, and sniffed the air. Then their lips curled back from their teeth. And over the shrieks of the mob, I heard them snarl.

One was wearing a black hoodie that said PINBALL WIZARD in jagged silver letters, and another was wearing a QUADROPHENIA T-shirt. I caught glimpses of Union Jacks, blue latticework, a can of baked beans, and flying doves as they all moved toward me.

Then I heard Liam's rough roar to my right. "Freddie!" he bellowed. "Fer God's sake, get over here!"

I dove toward his voice, and the gang of half a dozen Freddie-hating maniacs lunged for me. A few of them slammed into the police cruiser and fell to the street. One tried to grab my arm, but he got my jacket, and I shucked out of it. Goodbye, faithful jacket. Then a maniac closed a fist on my T-shirt to the left of the bull's-eye. Another grabbed it on the right. I pulled backward, spun away so the shirt ripped, and left them with scraps. The air hit my bare chest like ice water.

Then a big, meaty hand grabbed me by the collar and dragged me up from the street. I found myself standing on the sidewalk in front of an oak-and-glass restaurant entrance that said LE TURTLE. For an instant, a horrified waiter stared at me from the other side. Then he flipped over a CLOSED sign and cut the inside lights, and I saw my reflection. I looked like a half-naked, wheatish ghost with round blue eyeglasses and colorless hair. My T-shirt consisted of the sleeves, the collar, and the top of the bull's-eye, plus a ragged curtain down my back. The tattoo of a Fender Deluxe Reverb amp on the right side of my chest was raked with red lines where a maniac had clawed me. But I hadn't felt it, so it hadn't provoked a shout.

I looked to my left and saw Liam's bushy-bearded face looming over me. He was standing with his back against a brick wall, and he had my collar bunched in his left fist. Meanwhile, his right arm, as thick as a small goat and almost as hairy, had an orange-haired, hatchet-faced man pinned to the wall by the throat. The hatchet-faced man was wearing a green tracksuit that made his skin look yellow. He was gurgling and thrashing, holding a glowing smartphone in one hand.

"This bag o' shite drugged us!" Liam bellowed. "I knew it soon as I got into clean air. We were lucky to hustle out before gettin' a full dose. So forgive the Wholigans, Freddie, for they know not what they do." He sniffed the air. "Jeezus, lad, you stink like Satan's bum." He let go of my collar.

The hatchet-faced man stopped thrashing. And despite the fact that Liam's arm was across his windpipe, he sneered.

"You got *some* dose, bear-man," he said. He spoke with a Russian accent. "Xeno smoke lets natural person smell what others are. Joker smells like vermin, so must kill. Ace smells like hyena. Foul, but dangerous to touch. Boy is ace, yes? But not strong ace. Stench can confuse at first, if ace not strong." He managed to nod toward the street. "Look now."

I turned toward Chrystie. The nats who had tried to attack me had followed as far as the curb. But now they were backing away and shaking their heads like dogs trying to get rid of skunk spray. I took a step toward them, and they shrieked, spun, and ran to the plaza to join their fellow maniacs in threatening the terrified jokers.

In that instant, I was overwhelmed by a cold fury. I whirled back toward Liam and the Russian.

"Gaffer," I said. My voice was hoarse. "Hit me. I'll take off his head."

Liam snorted. "Not on your Nelly! You'll take off my arm as well. We'll let the coppers have him."

"He's beaten the coppers!" I waved at the scene behind me. "He set fire to the Ballroom and nearly killed us all, and he's poisoned the nats so they'll finish the job. And he's proud!"

The Russian was pinned to the wall, so he couldn't shrug. But his face took on an "oh well" expression. "Sorry about fire. Was supposed to just be smoke, with jokers locked inside so natural persons could kill. Will fix next time. But situation now is working also, yes?" He sneered again. "Xeno may fade in hour or two, but will be enough. Purge of jokers will have begun. So sure, give me to police. Comrades will see what Xeno can do, and continue liberation."

Liam's big left fist swung around and caught the Russian square in the face. The Russian's eyes rolled up to the whites, and his arms went limp. His phone clattered to the sidewalk. Liam took his right arm away from the Russian's throat, and the berk crumpled into a green and yellow pile.

"Shut yer gob, you tosser," Liam said. He leaned over, picked up the Russian's phone, and put it into his back pocket. "Rotter was makin' a video of all this and smirkin' like he was shootin' a snuff film."

The shouts and shrieks behind me intensified. I turned toward the plaza again and saw that fifty or sixty of the drugged nats had boiled back into the street. Half of them charged north, and the other half charged south.

I looked north and spotted the kilted lad, Peter, barreling toward us at high speed. He had somehow acquired a robin's-egg-blue NYPD motorcycle helmet. The maniacs tried to converge on him, but he dodged and wove between them like an Olympic skier on a slalom course. At his first dodge, his axle compressed, and his two wheels merged into one. He leaned to the left and whipped around his first set of attackers, then leaned to the right and whipped around another. Then he did it again, and again. They couldn't lay a finger on him.

"Adesina!" he shouted.

That's when I looked south. Seventy yards away, my blue-winged angel was trying to rise from the street. But Xeno-drugged maniacs clawed at her legs to drag her down. And it looked like they were going to do it.

♣

One of the enraged nats grabbed Adesina around her knees, and he rose a few feet with her as she struggled to ascend. Then a second nat grabbed the first one, and a third grabbed the second. Two or three more joined in, and they started pulling Adesina back toward the asphalt.

I took a step toward her as Peter came abreast of me—but then a silvery bubble the size of a grapefruit shot up from the center of the nat cluster, and it caught the first maniac in the spine. He shrieked and lost his grip on Adesina, and the whole string collapsed. Adesina zipped upward.

"Stay there, Peter!" she cried. "I'll get you!" The street was full of shrieks, and more and more sirens were coming closer. I heard a helicopter closing in. But Morpho Girl's voice rang out over all the noise.

Peter twisted sideways and skittered to a halt a few yards ahead of me. His axle expanded as he came to a stop, his wheel splitting in two again.

Adesina flew toward us, and she spotted me.

"Freddie!" she called. "You're okay!"

Peter looked back at me. "Freddie?" Then he recognized me and rolled closer. "You're the dude who blew the holes in the wall and ceiling! Nice work!"

I was nonplussed, and I became excessively polite. "Er, well, thank you very much indeed. And you did a fine job helping others exit. Well done. Peter, is it?"

Liam stomped past us into the middle of the street. "Write each other a couple a epic poems, why don'tcher," he said, and knocked down two charging maniacs.

"Thank you!" Peter said to Liam. Then he turned back to me. "It's Peter, but some of my friends call me Segway." He pointed at my chest. "Cool tattoo. What happened to your shirt?"

I gestured toward another crazed nat Liam was fighting off, and then at the screaming mob in the plaza. They were coming closer and closer to overwhelming the thin blue lines protecting the jokers, and some of the cops had started swinging their batons. I saw one make contact, and the nat went down to the bricks. Which enraged those around him even further.

"A riot happened to my shirt," I said.

Peter grimaced. "Yeah, we need to get out of here. I was just at Houston Street, and the cops up there said SWAT teams are on the way. They don't know what's made the nats go berserk, so they're just gonna zip-tie everyone and take 'em to the Tombs. But I don't see how they can do it without a bloodbath." He tapped his helmet. "One of the cops tossed this to me when I started back. They don't expect the night to end well."

Morpho Girl landed between us, her wings brushing me as she threw her arms around Peter's neck. "Thanks for finally answering my texts!" She sounded irritated, but the neck-hug said something else.

"Hey, I was kinda busy!" Peter said. "None of the people I took out of the Ballroom went crazy, so I had to help them get clear. Where's your mom?"

Adesina pointed back down the street. "Moving slow. Those psychos are trying to stop her, but whenever she gets close, they shake their heads and back away. Then they swarm in again. But none of them will hit her, which is totes frustrating 'cause she burned off almost all her fat making rescue bubbles. So, obvs, I was gonna fly her up and drop her—but the nats got between us and started grabbing me. I had to take off, and I think Mom used her last bit of fat to knock them away."

"Can't she just throw herself down on the pavement or something?" Peter asked.

"That might give her enough to bubble two or three psychos," Adesina said. "But look how many there are! Somebody needs to, like, attack her."

Liam was still keeping the maniacs away from us. "I knew that had to be Ms. Bubbles over there!" he yelled. "Once she gets here, it'd be my honor to give her as much of a thumping as she likes. Then she can machine-gun-bubble all these nutters!"

I tried to imagine how that would work out. The mob in the plaza extended all the way across the park. Even if the Amazing Bubbles could reach us and fatten up, there was no way she would be able to deal with all those maniacs before the SWAT teams arrived and the violence escalated. Not without seriously injuring or killing people herself.

The sirens were getting louder, and I could see more flashing red and blue lights to the north. The SWAT units would be on us in two minutes. At most.

"No," I said. In that moment, it was the only word I could muster. "No."

As maniacal as all those nats had become, Liam was right: They knew not what they did. The only thing they had done of their own free will was attend a concert—a pretty damn good one, too—and they'd been happily enjoying the show along with everyone else. Nats and jokers alike.

In fact, for a few hours, there in the Bowery Ballroom, there hadn't been any nats or jokers. Or aces, either.

We had all been Wholigans.

And now a lot of us had been hurt. But "hurt" was as far as I was going to let it go.

No. It was as far as *we* were going to let it go.

I looked straight up. Le Turtle was on the ground floor of a six-story apartment building. It was maybe seventy feet to the roof. That would be enough.

"Morpho Girl!" I said. "Do you and your mom have your phones?"

Adesina looked at me, startled. "Well, sure."

That's what I'd thought. "Okay, good. And after what we did in the Ballroom, you trust me, yeah?"

She frowned. "I—guess so."

It wasn't quite a vote of confidence, but it would have to do. I looked at Peter. "Segway! We have to clear a path to the Amazing Bubbles. Roll toward her, fast, and get close enough so some of those nats around her come after you. Then zip up the street to draw them away. Go just far enough so that when you wheel around and come *back* this way, you're rolling as fast as you can when you're here at Le Turtle. Top speed!" I looked at Liam, who had a moment between maniac attacks. "And when Segway rolls past, both ways, don't let the nutters slow him down."

Liam looked gobsmacked that I was giving him orders. But he gave me a sharp nod and said, "Right, mate."

Peter was staring at me. "And, uh, where am I supposed to stop when I come back here at top speed?"

I used the sternest tone I could muster. "Stop at Adesina's mom. Put your head down and ram her with that helmet. Hard."

Peter's eyes grew wide as saucers.

"Oh, *hell* no," he said.

More of the nats from the plaza, and stragglers on the street, were coming at us now. The cluster around the Amazing Bubbles was getting bigger, too. More batons were swinging in the plaza. And the SWAT teams were drawing near.

"Segway, please—" I began.

But I didn't have to finish, because Morpho Girl shouted over me. "*Peter, go!*" she yelled.

His eyes still wide, Segway took off toward the cluster.

I looked at Adesina and pointed up. "Get me to the roof." Then, as she launched into the air and hovered over my head, I gave Liam a glance. "You got this?"

He gave me a feral grin and, without looking, clotheslined a shrieking nat the size of a mountain gorilla. "Whaddaya take me fer?"

I reached up and grasped Adesina's ankles. I remembered how fast she could accelerate, so I held on tight.

As we shot upward, I saw that her purple Chuck Taylors had silver shoelaces. Why hadn't I noticed that before?

♠

In seconds, I was standing on the metal flashing at the lip of the roof. A sharp breeze hit my skin and made me shiver.

I released my grip on Morpho Girl as I looked down at the melee below. I could see the entire park plaza and the swarming maniacs therein, plus those in the street, all illuminated by streetlights. To the south, I could see two police vans and three cruisers with flashing lights approaching on Delancey, and to the north, three more vans and five cruisers on Houston. One of the vans had already turned from Houston onto Chrystie.

Segway had reached the cluster of maniacs surrounding the Amazing Bubbles, who was an island in the eye of a hurricane. Segway zipped back and forth along the northern edge of the storm, his two wheels compressing to one again, and then he spun and rushed northward with at least fifteen of the nats giving chase. The northern edge of the hurricane had been broken.

Adesina landed beside me. She pointed straight down.

"Who's the guy in the green tracksuit, lying on the sidewalk? He's, like, right behind where you were standing."

I was watching Segway, Liam, and the mob. "That's who did this," I said. "He drugged the nats with the smoke in the Ballroom. Some Russian arse."

Adesina gave a gasp. "Another one?"

I didn't ask what she meant, because I had to keep track of the action below. Segway had made it past Liam, zigging and zagging around numerous maniacs, and Liam had helped him out by booting a few of them toward the park. But now the first police van coming down Chrystie had almost reached Stanton, just a block north. And more vans and cruisers were turning onto Chrystie from both Houston and Delancey.

The mob in the park was still screaming and lunging against the thin blue lines. And the lines were breaking. Jokers were being attacked, falling to the bricks.

The synthesizer break from "Won't Get Fooled Again" started playing in my head. We were already in the middle of the drum buildup.

"Adesina, phone your mom."

"I can text—"

"She'll need to hear you."

I kept focus on the street and the plaza. So I didn't see Adesina take her phone from her pocket. But I heard her say, "Mom?"

And I saw the Amazing Bubbles press her hand to the side of her silver-blond mane. She was looking up at me and Adesina.

I glanced to the north. Segway had turned back before reaching Stanton, and the first police van had been forced to slam on its brakes to avoid hitting him. Good. That bought us a few more seconds.

Now Segway was streaking southward.

"Morpho Girl!" I barked. She was standing to my right, and much too close. "Take off! Get away! And tell your mom that the moment she gets fat, the very instant, she has to blast me. One shot, everything she has."

Adesina gasped again. She lowered her phone and gripped my arm.

"Freddie, you don't know how much that can be," she said. "I mean, you *really* don't know!"

I shook off her hand. "You said you'd trust me. Tell her!"

"But she won't!" Adesina said. "I know her, and she won't!"

I was staring straight at the Amazing Bubbles now.

In my peripheral vision, I caught the blue-helmeted blur of Segway directly below.

The Moonie drums in my head were approaching a climax.

"Yes, she will," I said.

I put my hand on Adesina's neck and threw her off the roof.

She gave a short, startled scream. Her mother heard it.

Adesina dropped below the edge of the roof. If she had been a regular kid, she would have fallen to the sidewalk and died.

But she was Morpho Girl. I kept my eyes on Bubbles, but I felt the rush of air from Adesina's wings as she began to swoop up and away.

By then, I had raised my right middle finger to my big sis.

And Segway hit her. Head down, full steam. Right in the solar plexus.

I heard a *whump* and saw concentric rings of vapor radiate out as if blown away by a sudden explosion of heat. Peter bounced back as if he'd hit a wall of rubber, and he tumbled arse over teakettle, bowling over two or three maniacal nats in the process.

Meanwhile, in the tiniest fraction of a second, of a nanosecond, the Amazing Bubbles *expanded*. Her oversized sweater stretched to its limits, and her white-blond mane became a spiked corona around the enraged visage of a goddess.

Her tree trunk of a right arm shot out, and I saw a shining, silvery globe burst from her palm and blaze toward me.

I wasn't sure of its size, because it was coming straight at my head. Maybe a football. You know, a proper football. Or maybe it was three times larger. Five. Ten. Fifty.

The synthesizer and drums reached their peak.

So I looked toward the plaza, and across the raging sea of maniacs to Forsyth. If I aimed at the buildings there, the Wholigans wouldn't take a direct hit. They would catch the spreading lower edge of the shock wave, and then the reflection from the buildings as the leading edge bounced back. And maybe there would be no deaths.

Well, maybe one.

In an instant, the black sky turned crimson, then golden, and then an unbearably brilliant white as every star in the Milky Way went nova. A hundred thousand spikes of lightning stabbed into my skull, my eyes, my throat, my lungs, my heart. My arms spasmed outward. The tattoo on my chest caught fire, and the fire rushed to the rest of my flesh like burning magnesium.

The lights came up, and the guitar, bass, and cymbals came crashing down.

And I *screamed*.

Limbs blew off the trees in the park and flew through the night to splinter on distant walls. Windows shattered, and glass sleeted down for blocks. Streetlights burst, and steel poles swayed like bamboo.

The edge of the shock wave hit the plaza, and almost everyone, nat and joker, cop and criminal, sinner and saint, new boss and old boss, fell to the earth as if blown down by a puff of breath from the lips of Shiva.

Then the reflected wave returned, and those few who had been left standing joined the rest down on the asphalt, down on the concrete, down on the bricks. Even Liam, and even the Amazing Bubbles. They toppled like mountains chopped down by the edge of an invisible hand.

And then the reflection hit me, too. It almost blew me backward, back onto the roof of the Le Turtle building. But my last shreds of reflex fought it, and they fought too hard.

So I fell forward. As I went over, I saw the police vans and cruisers approaching the plaza. If they hurried, maybe all would be well. Maybe they could zip-tie the fallen nats before any could rise. Maybe no one would be hurt too badly. I had tried to stun everyone, to knock them down and take their breath away. But I knew there would be injuries. Maybe some bad ones.

But no deaths. Please, no deaths.

And maybe all the Wholigans drugged by the Xeno smoke would come back to themselves. So we could all see each other at another show sometime.

I tumbled, glimpsing a brick wall and spinning lights and broken windows and then the concrete squares of the sidewalk. I would hit it right beside the crumpled Russian.

Then I tumbled over once more, so I was looking up at the sky. It was dark again, just as a night sky should be.

High above, I caught a glimmer of cobalt-blue wings.

◆

For the longest time, I was Nothing.

It wasn't that I was suspended in Nothing. I *was* Nothing.

Darkness. Emptiness. No light, no music. Nothing.

And then:

I dreamed of my mum.

Except she wasn't Mum. She looked like her, with her smooth, dark hair and chestnut eyes. And she sounded like her, her voice tinged with faint hints of Welsh and Punjabi, with a broader streak of American popster.

But this Mum's eyes were bright, her brow unfurrowed. And when she reached toward my face, I didn't flinch. She gave me a light caress with her fingertips.

Perhaps she was the Mum I had known when I was small. Until I was about eight.

That was when her London modeling jobs, already few and far between, had evaporated. That was when she'd started taking the waitressing and cashiering jobs. Which, soon enough, had become few and far between as well.

And she'd become angry. All the time. Mostly at me. After all, I was the thing that had changed her life, and not for the better.

But that wasn't who we were in the dream.

In the dream, I'd been accepted to university, and was preparing to leave.

Mum, her fingertips still on my cheek, said she was proud. But that I must phone her twice a week, and text more than that.

I held up my phone and showed her the crack in the glass.

Then Mum took her hand away, and she turned to smoke.

I jerked awake, threw off the covers, and shouted, "Wait!"

My voice was a croak.

I was in bed, propped against the headboard with pillows. Across the room, in a big cream-colored chair in the corner, Adesina looked up from her phone. Her expression, much like the first time I'd seen her, was one of annoyance. The light from the floor lamp beside her chair made me squint.

The blue edges of her wings were visible behind her shoulders. But she wasn't wearing a Union Jack T-shirt or red stovepipe jeans. Now she wore a dark green pullover—which still had small slits for her insect legs—with khaki slacks and fuzzy orange socks. No shoes.

She set her phone on the chair's armrest, then raised an eyebrow. Her antennae gave a twitch. "Do you need me to, like, show you where the bathroom is?" she asked. She tucked a coppery dreadlock behind her ear. "I mean, again?"

I looked around the room. A chest of drawers, a dresser. Art on the walls, including a watercolor of the Statue of Liberty and a framed photo of Adesina at nine or ten. A window looking out on a Manhattan street, maybe SoHo or Jokertown, with a sky turning to dusk. We were on the seventh or eighth floor of . . . somewhere.

The bed was queen-size, with half a dozen soft pillows, a couple of cushy blankets, and a comforter. To my right was a walnut nightstand with a reading lamp, along with my blue spectacles and a glass of water.

I would have expected to wake up in hospital, which I would have hated. Assuming I woke up at all. But this was someone's bedroom.

Every joint and muscle in my body reacted as if stuffed with broken glass. But I managed to push out from the pillows and swing my legs to sit on the edge of the mattress. Then, with my head starting to throb, I had a quick look at myself.

I was wearing white socks, gray sweatpants, and a too-large navy blue T-shirt. The shirt had a gold logo that I pulled away from my chest to read. It said JOKERTOWN MOB!

"That's my school jazz band," Adesina said. "I'm the bass player. Peter plays trumpet. By the way, I'm missing practice right now. Not that you should feel guilty about that."

I smoothed out the shirt. "You guys any good?"

She gave me a sardonic smile. "We're *hella* good. And if you start acting like someone who isn't a poopyhead, I'll show you our YouTube channel."

No doubt about it. Adesina was a musician.

"That explains why you were at a Who concert," I said. "Our demographic skews a bit older, but bass players of all ages seem keen to watch Mr. Entwistle at work."

Adesina rolled her eyes. "Well, yeah! But Peter wanted to go, too. I mean, OMG, great music is great music, right?" Her eyes narrowed. "Besides, I bet you're not much older than we are. And you're one of their roadies."

I picked up my specs from the nightstand, grimacing as the jagged bits of glass in my arm shuffled about. "Yes, well," I said. "I'm mature for my age." I put on the specs with my hands shaking. But the throbbing in my head eased a tad as the tinted lenses dimmed the light.

Adesina pointed at her photograph on the wall. "That was me a year ago. You got nothing on me in the 'mature for your age' department."

I looked down at the logo on my shirt again. The MOB! part was ringing in my head. "I have nothing on you in any regard," I said. "If not for you, everyone at the concert . . ." I tried to swallow. My voice was thin and ragged, and I was thirsty. But I didn't think I could lift the glass of water from the nightstand.

Adesina stood. "Freddie, don't you jump down that bunny chute again. We totes do *not* want you to go lights-out so we have to start all over."

I was confused. "Bunny chute?"

"Rabbit hole, or whatever! Jeez!"

Okay. Stay above ground, then. Ask the question.

But it was as if my throat were trying to close around a wire brush.

Then Adesina was standing in front of me, holding the glass of water to my lips. "Just a sip," she said. "Don't gulp it, or you'll get all spewy again, like when I fed you that oatmeal this morning."

A sip helped. "What happened to . . ." I took a painful breath. "Everyone in the park?"

She set down the glass. "I think you just like hearing it. You pretty much saved everyone, okay? I mean, some people got concussions, and there were a few broken arms and wrists. Some ruptured eardrums, duh. And a couple of skull fractures, but you didn't do those. Anyway, it's been three days, and something like thirty people are still in the hospital. Twitter says a few of the nats are having psychotic episodes, but everyone else seems to be over it. Oh, and there were maybe ten or twelve nats who ran off before the cops could stop them. So no one knows if they're all right, or if they're still smoke-crazy."

The smoke. That evil shite.

"What about the Russian?" I rasped.

"That creep disappeared. I mean, he was still on the sidewalk when you fell. I saw him. But by the time the cops showed up, like a minute later, he was gone."

Hell and damn. "So he got away with it."

"Nope, he's ska-rewed," Adesina said. "Your boss had his phone. So now the cops have his contacts." She made a low noise in her throat. "Also, it looks like he knows this other crook-type Russian I ran into a few months ago. *That* jerkface was trying to enslave joker kids—so guess what, he wound up on Rikers. And now with this Xeno thing, the cops think there must be a whole gang of them." She gave a shudder. "The good news is that the police think they can get the smoke guy. The bad news is that I didn't tell my mom about my run-in with the first guy, and now she knows. Lucky you, you were still unconscious when we had *that* discussion."

It was as if the broken glass were trying to shred my brain. "I'm sorry," I said, lowering my eyes. "Especially about everyone who got hurt."

Adesina put her hand under my chin and tilted my head up. It wasn't painful at all, which is a lie.

"Jeez Louise," she said. "That's not on you! Besides, nobody got killed. Things were starting to get super violent—but you gave that ginormous yell, and then everyone just sorta lay there like stunned tuna while the cops cuffed them." She released my chin and took a step back. "Course, a bunch of people are pissed about their broken windows. Funny thing, though. Nobody knows who broke 'em."

My joints, muscles, throat, chest, and head still ached. And I had more questions. But they could wait. A tension that had been twisting my gut had decided to relax.

"Right," I said. "Now you can show me the bathroom."

♥

It was one door down the hall, which was good. When I finally emerged, another door across the hall opened, and Adesina peeked out.

"You alive?" she asked.

I nodded, which hurt. "I'm okay. But I'm concerned."

Adesina stepped into the hall. "About?"

I rubbed my neck. "When I woke up, you were angry with me. And I don't know why."

She rolled her eyes again. "Dude! You pushed me off a roof!"

Somehow, I hadn't realized that would be a problem. "Well, I did know you could fly."

She crossed her arms. "It was mean. And when you hit the sidewalk, you yelled straight at me. I was tossed up, like, another two hundred feet. I almost hit a helicopter."

I suspected she was exaggerating. But we had met in the midst of trauma, and then I had fallen unconscious for three days. During which she'd apparently been required to feed me.

"I apologize," I said. "But you're wrong about one thing."

She raised her eyebrow again. "Oh, really?"

I nodded once more. Extreme pain. I had to stop doing that. "You said I saved everyone. But it was you, and Peter, and your mother. And Liam, the big hairy git." I shrugged, and winced. "You played the music. I was just the instrument."

Adesina rolled her eyes a third time, but now she was smiling.

"No way," she said. "You were, like, the *amplifier*." Then her expression changed. "Speaking of which, my bass amp has been making a stupid stinky buzzing noise. You know anything about stuff like that?"

As it happened, I did. Her amp and bass were in the living room, so we went out to have a look. The buzz was a ground-loop issue, easy to rectify. But I noted that the amp was a low-watt practice unit, and I thought she should have something with more punch. Especially since her bass was a lovely purple-sparkle StingRay. So we talked about small yet muscular amps she could get away with in an NYC apartment.

At some point, I remembered to ask if she knew whether I still had a job. She said the band and crew had moved on to Philadelphia—but that Liam had promised to rent a car and make a side trip to collect me the next Saturday, if I had recovered. Then we'd drive to Boston in time for the show that evening.

Adesina had taken out her phone and was showing me a game called *Ocelot 9* when the apartment door opened and the Amazing Bubbles entered with two bags of groceries.

"Mom!" Adesina chirped. "Look who's up!"

Bubbles was the same size as when I'd first seen her. She was dressed much the same, too, except that today's big sweater was lavender. And her platinum hair was tied back in a ponytail. She hip-checked the door shut behind her, then crossed the living room to the open kitchen. She was giving me and Adesina a look I couldn't read.

"This worries me," she said at last, setting the bags on the kitchen counter.

My throat started to close around the wire brush again, and I had the urge to run for the exit. But I knew if I did, I'd flop over like . . . well, like a stunned tuna.

"No, it's okay!" Adesina said. "He went to the bathroom by himself and everything."

Bubbles began unpacking groceries. A whole chicken. Rice. Celery. Pasta. Black grapes. I focused on all of that so I wouldn't look at her face. If I did, she might turn me to stone.

"I mean," Bubbles said, "I'm worried because your bass is beside the couch, and you're ignoring it. So I'm wondering if this rock-band roadie has talked you into wanting a new one."

Adesina gave a short laugh. "God, no! He knows the StingRay's awesome." She tilted her head. "But he does think I need a new amp."

There was a brief moment of silence. Then Bubbles said, "Of course he does."

I risked looking at her, and tried to get enough air to speak. "It's, you see, it's not that her amp is *bad*, it's—"

Bubbles didn't seem to hear me. "At least we can all sit at the table for dinner. And then I can have my bedroom back."

Adesina jumped up. "Mom! You can't kick him out! He's our guest! Besides, you're the one who wouldn't let them keep him in the hospital. You, like, insisted—and what were they gonna do, say no to *you*?"

The Amazing Bubbles regarded Adesina with a look of motherly reproach. "That isn't quite true. Liam said Freddie hated hospitals and would recover faster elsewhere. But the doctors wouldn't listen, since Liam was just a friend. So he asked if I could do something. Which I did, as soon as I—" She began folding the first grocery bag. "—realized I could. But I didn't threaten anyone. I don't do that." She frowned. "At least, I don't make a habit of it."

It looked as if I was getting the boot. I wasn't sure where I would go now . . . but I was grateful to Bubbles and Adesina for taking me in. And I didn't want to cause further strife.

"Ms. Pond," I said, "thank you so much for having me. But I've imposed quite enough, so I'll take my leave."

Or rather, that's what I tried to say. But nothing came out except "Ms. Pond," followed by a wheeze.

The Amazing Bubbles rolled her eyes, and now I understood how Adesina had gotten so good at it. "Four things," Bubbles said. She held up a finger. "One: Adesina, I'm not kicking him out. I'm saying, now that he's better, I can have my bed back, and he can have the couch."

"But Mom!" Adesina protested. "He's a guest—"

Bubbles added a second finger. "Two: He's not a guest. And he'll have his own space here, whenever he wants it, as soon as we clean out that room we've been calling an office, but which has really been the junk room. We'll need another bed, too. For tonight, though, he gets the couch."

Adesina stood silent and still. She blinked. Her antennae twitched.

Bubbles began emptying the second bag.

Then Adesina said, "What? Huh?"

Bubbles set a loaf of French bread on the counter.

"Freddie," she said, looking down at the bread, "is your mother named Farishta Fullerton?"

It took me a few moments to answer. I'd almost never heard anyone use Mum's given name.

"I—she—" I gulped air. It hurt. "Yes."

Bubbles nodded. "When Liam told me your last name, I knew why you looked familiar. Doubly so." She paused, and when she spoke again, her voice was quieter. "Your mother and I did some shoots together when I was fifteen. She was eighteen or nineteen. My so-called father came to those shoots, so I assumed he was keeping an eye on me. I thought he'd realized I was about to file papers to become an emancipated minor. But that wasn't why he was there."

Adesina and I were both staring at the Amazing Bubbles, and the Amazing Bubbles was still staring at the bread.

Finally, she looked at Adesina. "I'm sorry to spring this on you, honey. But it wouldn't have been fair to him if I'd told you before he was awake."

"Huh?" Adesina said again. "What?"

Bubbles gave a slight smile. "Adesina," she said. "This is your uncle Freddie." She looked at me. "Freddie, this is your niece, Adesina."

Now Adesina was staring at me instead.

"It's traditional to shake hands when introduced," Bubbles said.

I stood up, wobbling like a buoy in the wake of a speedboat. Adesina and I managed to shake hands, and she looked at me as if I had materialized from the ether.

"Uh, Mom?" Adesina said, sounding dazed. "You said 'Four things.'"

"Oh, yes." Bubbles held up three fingers. "Three: Adesina, please come help with dinner. I'd ask your uncle as well, but he still looks shaky. And we have things to chop."

Adesina released my hand. She walked to the kitchen with her wings quivering.

I swallowed. Ow. "Um, the fourth thing?" I asked.

Bubbles didn't hold up four fingers. Instead, she pulled a cutting board from a cabinet and dropped it onto the counter. Then she reached into a drawer and produced a large, gleaming knife.

"Four," she said, cutting the wrapper from the chicken. "I'm not 'Ms. Pond' to you, Freddie, any more than you're 'Mr. Fullerton' to me. My name is Michelle. Got it?"

I nodded. Ow again.

"Yes, ma'am," I said.

She pointed the knife at me.

"I mean—yes, Michelle."

Michelle slapped the chicken onto the cutting board and attacked it. "Damn skippy," she said.

♣

My new phone buzzed as Michelle, Adesina, and I came into the apartment late Saturday morning. We were stuffed with blintzes from Katz's and loaded down with bags from other stops, including one straining with eight LPs from Bleecker Bob's. One Jethro Tull, one Kinks, two Stones, and four from my employers: *The Who Sell Out*, *Tommy*, *Live at Leeds*, and *Who's Next*.

After we'd discovered a turntable stashed in the "junk room," I'd told Adesina there was only one way to fully appreciate classic rock: on vinyl. So we'd set up the turntable in her room, and now she had some records. They were all in decent shape, too. Of course, Michelle had grumbled about there being more than enough noise in the apartment already, what with the bass playing and the bandmates coming 'round. But she'd paid for the albums.

As we'd left Bleecker Bob's, Adesina had asked me which song on which album was my favorite. "That's a sticky wicket," I'd said. "I don't think I can answer."

She'd rolled her eyes. "What if I threatened to push you off a roof?"

"Side one, track two," I'd said. "*Who's Next*."

It had been a long morning's hike, and I was sore. But we were all puffing a bit. The day was sunny for December, but the air still had a chilly bite. Michelle's cheeks were pink, and once she'd hip-checked the door, she shuffled to the couch, dropped her bags, and flopped onto her back.

"This is mine," she said, groaning. "You two can have the floor."

Adesina hefted the bag from Bleecker Bob's. "No, I'll be in my room with the volume turned to—" She grinned at me. "What was it?"

"Eleven," I said, setting down my own bag.

Michelle groaned again. Adesina and I fist-bumped.

Then I took the new phone from the pocket of my jacket, which was also new. The jacket was almost like the one I'd lost in the riot, and Michelle had wanted to buy it for me. But I'd done it myself, since she'd already paid for my phone.

I had a text from Liam. CAN U MEET ME RATHR THAN PIKN U UP? FOUND SHOP LAST WEEK HANDMADE GUITAR STRAPS N LADS ORDRD SOM. NICE LADY FINSHNG THM UP BUT TIME SHORT MUST GO SOON AS SHE FINSHS F WE R 2 GET 2 BOSTN SOUNDCHK. 195 CHRYSTIE NEAR WHERE WE HAD ROW W YANKS N RUSSIAN. BE HERE IN 30? TELL MS BUBBLES N MORPHO GRL SRRY 2 MISS EM.

Bollocks. I'd thought I'd have another hour. Enough time for a proper goodbye.

But then, a proper goodbye might be too much like a goodbye.

I tapped my answer. BE THERE IN 30 MATE.

"What is it?" Adesina asked. But she knew.

I gave her a smile, hoping it didn't look forced. "It's Liam. I'm to meet him on Chrystie, not far from where I tried to throw you into a helicopter. Am I right that I can walk there in fifteen or twenty minutes?"

Adesina looked into her Bleecker Bob's bag and didn't answer. But Michelle sat up. "Twenty, if you don't window-shop," she said. "We can walk you. Do you have to leave right away?"

I nodded. "'Fraid so. Liam sends apologies." I looked from Michelle to Adesina. "I want you both to know, these past few days have been . . ." I took a moment to find the right words. ". . . the best of my life, other than my seventh birthday, which was the day I rode a pony."

Adesina actually laughed. That was a relief.

"Let me put these records in my room and go to the bathroom," Adesina said, with just a touch of a quaver. "Then we'll walk you to Chrystie, and Mom and I can give you a genuine New York goodbye."

"What's that?" I asked.

Michelle stood. "It involves the same one-fingered salute you gave me a week ago."

Now I laughed. Or chuckled, at least.

"Much as I hate to miss that," I said, "I'd rather say farewell here. If you were to come along, I . . . might be tempted to miss my ride." I was suddenly aware that my throat was still a bit ragged. "And I do want to keep my job."

Adesina set down her Bleecker Bob's bag and wrapped her arms around me. Then her wings wrapped around me as well. It was like being inside a warm blue cocoon.

"But you'll come visit," Adesina said into my neck. "Lots."

"Of course." I pushed away as gently as I could. Her arms released me before her wings did.

"If you don't," she said, "I'll send Mom after you."

I glanced at Michelle. "Good Lord. Nobody wants that."

Adesina picked up the Bleecker Bob's bag. "You better believe it." Then she turned, went to the hallway, and vanished.

♠

Michelle reached behind the couch and picked up my olive-drab duffel. "I'll walk you down."

We took the stairs, and neither of us said another word until we were in the lobby. No one else was there.

At the door, she handed over my duffel. "I know Adesina told you how I came to adopt her. So you know that, for us, the mother-daughter thing has been forged in fire. Which means you also need to know: If you're going to be my brother, you can't just be Adesina's friend or bass-equipment guru or anything else teenagers might be to each other. There's a duty. You know?"

I knew.

"You've only been aware of my existence for a week," I said. "But my mum told me about you almost from the day I was born. So, for me—" I dropped the duffel, took a chance, and hugged her. "You've always been my sister. And now Adesina is my niece."

Michelle hugged me back. "So if anything should ever happen to me . . ."

"Nothing could. But I'm her uncle. Always."

"Good." She broke the hug. "You're gonna text us both, right? Maybe even phone or FaceTime once in a while?"

"I think I'm obligated, since you bought the phone. Besides, Adesina's hooked me up with *Ocelot 9,* so I'll be playing online with her and her friends."

Michelle gave a mock grimace. "You're braver than I."

Then she held out a fist and opened it. A bright silver bubble lay in her palm. "This is a reminder," she said, "that you have a place here. Whenever you have a break. I'll buy the ticket."

I plucked it from her palm. It had weight, like steel.

"Cor blimey," I said. "It's a pinball! I reckon that makes me a wizard."

Michelle frowned. "Say what?"

I dropped the bubble into my jeans pocket. Sometimes music skips a generation. "Ask Adesina."

She rolled her eyes. "Oh, fine. Make me feel like an out-of-touch mom." Then she gave me a steady gaze. "Speaking of which. It might not be my business, but . . . maybe phone your own mom, too. You wouldn't have to tell her where you are or what you're doing. But let her know you're alive, okay?"

I scuffed one of my Doc Martens. "I sent her an email once. She knows I'm alive."

"Like I said, might not be my business. But you kept her name. So I'm thinking, maybe you want to keep her, too."

I nodded and picked up my duffel.

Michelle made a throat-clearing noise. "One more thing. Last week, when you were up on that roof . . ."

She looked at the floor. "I bubbled you pretty bad. Right afterward, I knew it was what you wanted. But that wasn't why I did it." She shook her head. "Adesina had already told me what you did in the Ballroom. And I knew my own daughter could fly. But when you pushed her, I lost control. And I hit you."

She sounded torn up about it. Which surprised me.

"Well, I knew you would," I said.

She looked at me again, her face tight. "Is my reputation that . . . monstrous?"

I realized she had been through some shite that would always make her doubt herself. And maybe, sometimes, that was a good thing. But in this case, it was a load of crap.

"Michelle, your reputation had sod all to do with it. I knew you'd do it because I knew *I* would." I shrugged. "And you're my big sis. So I kind of *am* you."

Michelle let out a breath. "Poor bastard."

I put my hand on the door. "That's accurate."

She crossed the lobby to the lift. "By the way, Little Bro," she said as she pushed the button. "That bubble in your pocket will be stable for about six months." The doors opened, and she stepped inside. "After that, it could explode at any moment. So you might want to come back before that." The doors closed.

I pushed out into the crisp air and started south on Lafayette. But I'd only gone twenty feet when I saw the kilted figure of Segway coming toward me in one-wheel mode, zigzagging around pedestrians and saying "'Scuse me!" to anyone who seemed startled. He was wearing his NYPD helmet, which he'd been allowed to keep, and was carrying a trumpet case. He waved to me with his free hand, so I paused as he expanded to two wheels and slid to a stop in front of me. I saw that the NYPD shield on his helmet had been replaced by a JOKERTOWN MOB! sticker.

"Hey, Amplifier!" he said. "You leaving?"

I nodded. "And you're on your way to see Adesina?"

He hefted the case. "Yup. We're gonna play a little. Band practice at school is all well and good, but you gotta put in the hours if you wanna be a badass."

That was true. "I'm glad Adesina has a boyfriend as serious about music as she is."

Peter's jaw went slack, and his face flushed. The lenses of his Buddy Holly specs fogged a bit.

"I, uh, I—" He gave a cough. "I wouldn't say I'm her boyfriend, exactly."

"Ah," I said. "But *she* would. So have a care." I lowered my own specs and looked at him over the rims. "Don't make me raise my voice."

He swallowed. "I hear you."

"Good man," I said. I gave him a clap on the shoulder and started on my way again. "But it's 'Mister Amplifier' to you."

This time, I had walked just another ten feet when the sky above me rang with the majestic noise of side one, track two of *Who's Next*. Turned to eleven.

I looked up and saw Morpho Girl hovering above me. She was eight stories high, just outside her open bedroom window.

"Uncle Freddie!" she called down through the music. "It's a love song! But it's, like, about more than that, right?"

I gave her a wave. Exactly right.

Now I had to hurry. So the nearer I drew to Chrystie, the more I became aware that my joints still ached. That my legs still had pangs. That my head still throbbed, and my throat and chest still rasped. That it was still going to be a while before I was strong again. Before I was free of pain.

Well, no wonder. I had been punched, shocked, kicked, dropped, pummeled, bubbled, and knocked about like a small silver ball being flipped and battered between bumpers and buzzers. And then I'd tilted into a darkness where I hadn't even known whether I still existed.

But after all that—

I'd awakened into a new life. In a new world.

And like the song says: I'd call that a bargain.

The best I ever had.

♠ ♥ ♦ ♣

The City That Never Sleeps

by Walton Simons

New York, New York
December, 1986

SPECTOR KNEW HE WAS being followed. The tail was a young man who clearly wasn't up to the job. His dumbass shadow was well groomed, had a nice blue suit, and was keeping in back of him by about thirty feet. Spector paused at the corner of Second Avenue and Tenth, the cold wind whipping his lank hair. New York City at Christmastime wasn't as bad as it was in January, but it was still no picnic. A trio of Salvation Army folks sang "God Rest Ye Merry, Gentlemen," but not very well. There was an A&P a couple of blocks away. If the person following him came inside looking for Spector that would be his mistake; if not, Spector would do some grocery shopping.

He'd been back in the city for less than two weeks. After Wild Card Day he'd decided Manhattan was just too dangerous for him. Lots of people wound up dead that day, including big-name aces like the Howler and the Astronomer and some lesser-known ones like the dino kid. Spector had done the Astronomer himself, feeding his former boss his death memory hard and fast, and leaving the old bastard's corpse fused inside a brick wall. That helped him sleep a little easier, but there were still plenty of people who wanted him dead again, not to mention the politicians and cops who were howling for the blood of the aces who'd brought terror to their fair city.

So Demise had gone back to Teaneck and lain low for a couple of months. Still, he needed a roof over his head and food on the table, so he'd done a few random jobs for the local mob. He'd told them he was a chemist with a drug that could simulate a heart attack. His employers weren't particularly curious about his methods and paid on time. The rubouts weren't enough for Spector to live well, but he kept them on a scale small enough that he didn't draw much attention, either.

He ducked into the A&P and moved quickly to his left and down an aisle. The place wasn't crowded, which suited Spector to a T. He heard the door squeak open and knew the man had been dumb enough to follow him inside. Spector headed for a corner of the produce section where the lighting was poor. He heard slow, uncertain footfalls the next aisle over. Spector couldn't figure why anyone who knew who he was would follow him, much less confront him. Unless the guy was an ace; that could be big trouble.

The man turned the corner.

"Can I get a light?" Spector asked.

"Uh." The young man seemed surprised to see Spector pop up in front of him.

"Following me is a bad idea." Spector pushed his horrific pain inside the man's mind. The agony of Spector's own death from the black queen took hold. The man's eyes rolled up in his head and there was a fresh corpse on the floor seconds later.

Spector glanced around and saw no one. He heard the squeak of a grocery cart closing in and bolted around the corner. No one noticed as he exited the store. Still, someone knew he was back in town. Maybe they wanted to hire him; maybe they wanted to kill him. He'd know for sure soon enough.

♦

Spector bought a mask at the first vendor he saw. In Jokertown, masks were easy to come by. He was tempted by a really ugly Santa mask, but instead picked out an angry-looking bird head. Spector didn't particularly like birds, but the eye holes were large and gave him a decent field of vision. He'd downed a pint of Jack Daniel's Black Label the night before to help with the pain. It took the edge off, but that was it. Pills would be better if he could find some.

He felt reasonably safe looking for drugs in Jokertown, where they were as common as misery and deformity. Spector ducked into an alleyway and shoved a couple of wadded-up tissues under his mask, giving the appearance of a misshapen face underneath. He heard a wet, unhappy noise behind him and moved back out onto the sidewalk before it could close in.

The sky was clear and blue, and there was only a hint of a chilling breeze. He decided to stretch his legs and take a long walk through Jokertown. Most people, other than jokers, would be scared to take a stroll here; too much ugliness and potential danger. Spector wasn't nervous though. He might well be the scariest person in Jokertown at the moment. He didn't like it here, but Jokertown was comfortable in a smelly-old-shirt kind of way.

He hit Jube the Walrus's newsstand first, not for any particular reason. The Walrus was one of Jokertown's oldest citizens. There was a large joker under a pair of stitched-together coats picking up a newspaper with a pink, furry hand. It tossed a coin at Jube and wobbled away as Spector approached.

"Want a *Cry*, friend?" the Walrus asked.

Spector picked it up and scanned the headlines. "What? No 'Hideous Joker Baby Eats Own Head' story? Must be a slow day."

The Walrus shrugged, his skin rumpling around his neck. "That's yesterday's news. Got to keep current. Everything you want to know is inside."

Spector set a quarter down and picked up a paper. "If you say so." He tucked the *Cry* under his arm and turned away.

"Do I know you? Something about you seems kind of familiar."

"Probably not," Spector replied. "Better if you keep it that way."

He headed for the Crystal Palace, in spite of the fact that it was a long walk. The Victorian décor wasn't to his taste, but a man could get a drink or two there and generally be left alone. He'd keep his distance from Sascha the bartender, though. Sascha was an eyeless freak who could get into your head and pick up some thoughts.

A joker crossed the street in front of him. It looked like someone had thrown a greenish-purple tarp over a group of giant scrubbing bubbles. The thing had more legs on either side than Spector could count in the short time he saw it, like a centipede. Other than the noise of legs on the sidewalk it didn't make a sound. Yep, he definitely needed a drink or three.

The Palace was done up for Christmas. There were matching human-sized nutcrackers flanking each side of the door into the main room, with holly strung across the arch. Sascha was behind the bar when he entered, wearing an off-kilter Santa hat. Spector avoided him and headed to the saloon area. The air inside was warm and he inhaled deeply. After breathing the December chill for so long his lungs needed it. He found an unoccupied booth and slid onto the comfortably padded bench. There was a birdcage filled with ornaments in the center of the table.

A waitress walked to his booth, but before she could open her mouth, he said, "Get me a double shot of Jack Black and don't be a stranger." He handed her a ten and paged through the *Cry*.

"Yes, sir. And a happy Yule to you."

The headlines were the fun part of reading the Walrus's rag. JOKER TRAPPED IN FREEZER EATS THREE OF HER OWN LEGS TO SURVIVE, MIKE TYSON, ACE OR JOKER?, and Spector's personal front-page favorite, BAT BOY AND FAMILY FOUND LIVING UNDER JOKERTOWN PRECINCT BUILDING.

The waitress arrived with his order, setting the glass carefully in front of him. She attempted to hand him his change, but Spector waved her off.

"Keep it. Like I said, don't be a stranger." He liked the way she smelled. At least, he thought it was her.

He heard heavy footfalls approaching his booth. A broad shadow fell across the tabletop. Spector sighed. Would they just once leave him the fuck alone?

"She wants to see you."

Spector looked up from his newspaper. It was Elmo the dwarf, the bouncer at the Crystal Palace. Elmo was crazy strong and very good at his job. He was wearing mirrored sunglasses.

"Let me finish my drink," Spector said.

"Bring it with you. She won't mind." Elmo turned toward the bar. "Sascha, you too."

"Not him." Spector didn't want that mind-reading asshole around. He could lose the ability to take the initiative if things were going to get ugly. "Or I'm out of here."

Elmo shrugged. "You're fine where you are, Sascha."

Spector, drink in hand, followed the dwarf into a large back room. The interior looked the way Spector would imagine Buckingham Palace looked if he'd ever bothered to imagine Buckingham Palace. Chrysalis sat behind a large desk, hands folded. Her transparent skin revealed muscle, sinew, and an occasional glimpse of bone. She had on mirrorshades, too. He wondered how she slept with transparent eyelids. Some people said she looked creepy or ugly. Spector had seen plenty of both and to him Chrysalis was neither. She was a powerful person in Jokertown, though, and could make his life harder if she wanted to.

"Mr. Spector, or should I call you Demise?" Her accent was phony British. It sounded funny coming out of her mouth. She motioned him to sit in the chair opposite her desk.

He took a seat. "Call me what you want. I'm more interested in why you want to see me in the first place." Spector got the sense she was into formal niceties, which was not how he operated. He killed his drink with a final swallow of Jack Black.

"Since seeing you can be the last thing some people do—" She paused. "—you can assume I want something else."

Spector nodded. "Who do you want killed?"

"No, you don't understand. I was informed by an anonymous person that you were back in Manhattan. This person would like to meet with you to discuss a business matter. They asked that if I encountered you to put you in contact."

So someone Chrysalis knew wanted someone killed. There was no other reason to contact him. It was all he did. "Fine, you can give me their phone number and I'll call them or I won't." He set his empty glass on her desk. "What's the payoff for you?"

She smiled, or appeared to. It was hard to tell without being able to see her skin. "I deal in information and favors. One often leads to the other. By arranging a meeting with you, I now have a degree of credit with this person. If the meeting is beneficial to you, perhaps you'll be inclined to help me at some point in the future."

"There's never a shortage of people other people want dead." Spector felt on familiar footing now that he saw the entire game.

"That's not exactly what I was implying. As I said, I deal in information. A person who travels in the circles you frequent might come across some interesting tidbits now and then." She handed him a card with a local phone number written on it. "Elmo will show you out."

Spector took the card and stood. "Maybe so. You could give me a bottle of Jack Black to keep me sweet if I do happen across something."

"Sascha will take care of you when you leave."

♥

Spector had made his way halfway through the bottle and still couldn't make up his mind. After surviving Wild Card Day, he'd decided to work for himself. That wasn't a practical idea, though. He had exactly one marketable skill—killing people—and he couldn't exactly set up a storefront to do that kind of business. No matter what way he turned it around in his mind, he'd be taking risks for other people. Doing their dirty work. Maybe if he strung together a bunch of high-profile jobs he'd have enough money to retire. He'd been an accountant, although not a very good one, before the Wild Card took him, and knew a little about investing money and making it grow. With a nice nest egg he could kick back, relax, and stick to killing the people who pissed him off. There was no shortage of those.

Spector knew the law wouldn't be a problem. He didn't leave any evidence behind when he took someone out, so there was nothing the cops or the DA could make stick in courtroom. He also knew this was a world of aces, with people like Fortunato and the Astronomer, people who also didn't care about the legal system and could kill him easily enough. Low risk–low reward versus high risk–maybe dead. What the hell, he was an ace. He could handle pretty much anything.

He grabbed the phone and set it on his lap, then punched in the number on the card. It rang for a while before someone picked up.

"Hello. How may I help you?"

Spector recognized the voice. It was the smooth-voiced, nameless asshole who'd sent him after some notebooks and mob bosses on Wild Card Day. He thought about hanging up, didn't. "I think I'm the one who's going to be doing the helping, if my information is correct."

"Ah, I'm so glad you decided to contact me. We have unfinished business."

While he was in Jersey, Spector had asked around with his mob employers and they had given him a possible name, St. John Latham. Latham was a big-time attorney with suspected underworld connections. "No shit, Sherlock. You owe me."

The man cleared his throat. "I can hardly be blamed for not making payment in light of your disappearance."

"So you tracked me down to pay me?" Spector didn't think for a minute this was the case, but he didn't see a need to be an open book when dealing with someone this slippery.

"No. Not entirely. I have a something of significant mutual benefit to propose."

"Maybe I should come to your office. I'm guessing you have one, right?"

"That won't work. Let me think." There was a long pause. "It's problematic for me to be seen with a person of your reputation. Perhaps I could send an intermediary."

"Bad idea," Spector said. "Remember what happened to the last punk you put on my trail. He was a total amateur." The last part was a guess, but obviously an accurate one.

"He was a temp, whose only job was to determine if you were, in fact, you. In that regard he was a success."

"Whatever." Spector didn't mind dealing with cold-blooded assholes. He wouldn't mind putting them down if it came to it. "No more go-betweens. I'm dealing with you, or I'm not dealing at all."

"Well, that would require a location with sufficient privacy."

"Jokertown. You can wear a mask. I've already got one."

Another pause. "That's not exactly ideal for me."

"How about the Crystal Palace? They know you there."

"No. The bartender is a problem. Our discussions wouldn't remain private for long."

So he knew about Sascha. That made sense. "Okay, the Dime Museum then." Spector expected a pause. Got one. "It's only two bucks, and you can wear a mask." Jokers were welcome at the Dime Museum. Some rich-guy joker supposedly owned it.

"I suppose that could be workable."

"Okay, a couple of things. First, meet me at four in the afternoon. I'll be wearing a bird-head mask, hanging out by the Turtle's shell. Second, bring my fucking money."

"Four o'clock."

Spector hung up the phone and took another swig of bourbon. That had gone about as well as he could have hoped.

♣

The doorway to the Famous Bowery Wild Card Dime Museum had fake holly draped above the doorway, strung from plastic ace and joker heads. He paid the two-dollar admission fee and entered. There were only a few people wandering around when Spector arrived. He'd made a point of being ten minutes late, just to emphasize that he could take this job or leave it. A couple of kids, a boy and a girl, were slowly making their way around the Turtle's Volkswagen shell, pointing and smiling.

"He's dead, you know," Spector said.

"Nuh-uh," said the taller of the two kids, a scrawny, sandy-haired boy. "People have seen him."

"You're a liar, Mr. Bird-Face," the girl chimed in.

"Swamp gas, kid. That's what people saw." He leaned in close, his mask almost touching the boy's face.

The girl took the boy's hand and hauled him in the direction of the Four Aces display. She gave Spector a hard look he figured she usually saved for teachers or her parents.

"If looks could kill, sir," came a cultured voice from behind him, "you'd be on your way to the grave."

Spector recognized Latham's voice and turned around. The man was wearing a perfectly tailored dark gray suit and a gold human-faced mask. He inclined his head slightly to one side, giving Spector a slow once-over.

"Maybe the Turtle really is dead," Spector said. "People get that way all the time."

"Indeed." He passed Spector a heavy envelope. "For your previous efforts on our behalf. I assume you prefer cash."

"That works best."

"Before you decide whether or not to continue your relationship with us, I'd like to explain some of the potential benefits we can offer."

"I'm all about the benefits," Spector said. He wondered if those included a regular supply of drugs.

"Yes. Since you're officially dead, you're required to work on a cash basis. We could provide you with a new identity; including ID, bank accounts, a passport if you chose to leave the country, investment opportunities, and so on. You would be free to move around and your funds would be much more secure than stuffed under your mattress."

Spector hadn't really thought about all this long-term. He was mostly focused on staying alive and taking care of the pain. Still, there was something to be said for it. "Lots of people do fake IDs. And I know something about accounting myself."

"There's a difference between accounting and finance. Stay with us and you'll see just how much of a difference that can be." The man's tone oozed confidence and conviction.

"Let's say for the sake of argument I'm interested. Are you planning on sending me to Paris for the job?"

The man shook his head. "Hardly. Our current concerns remain here in the city. As before, your efforts would be directed against the fading criminal power structure."

Spector nodded. They wanted him to keep going after the mob. Potentially dangerous work, even for him. "I might be interested."

"Excellent. I'll send one of our people to your apartment to get the ball rolling." He turned away, then paused. "Please try not to kill this one."

"No promises."

♠

He was annoyed. The line at the bank wasn't particularly long, but it was moving slowly. His pain was acting up more than usual and Spector was having a hard time concentrating. All he wanted was to be back at his place with a bottle of JD.

The flunky had come by just like the smooth-talking slimeball had said. Carl was young and well-dressed, like the corpse Spector had made a few days back, but had the good sense to wear mirrorshades. Spector had grimaced at that and knocked the sunglasses clattering to the floor with a quick sweep of his right arm.

"You'd better staple those to the side of your head if you want them to do you any good," Spector had said. "I may have a stapler around here if you need the help."

Carl had scrambled to get the glasses back in hand and looked like he was going to piss himself. "No, no. I'm just here to help."

He'd given Spector a fake Social Security card under the name Thomas B. Stone. Whoever came up with that must have thought they were being clever. Carl had also set up a couple of different-colored background screens and had taken some photos of Spector for a New York driver's license and a passport. He had taken off as soon as the work was done, but had come back a couple of days later with the driver's license and some instructions about the upcoming job Spector was supposed to do. As always, someone was in need of getting dead.

"May I help you, sir?" The teller's tone was friendly in a tired, rote kind of way.

"I need to open an account." He handed over his fake driver's license and a creased envelope heavy with bills.

"I'm sure we can help you with that."

Spector looked the teller over while she was walking him through the paperwork. She was youngish, but clearly old enough to have been around the block a few times. Her eyes were bright and intelligent; she was too smart for her job and there was no way she'd last.

He stopped at the Strand on his way back to the apartment and found his way to the travel section. Spector had never really imagined himself leaving the NYC area, but it was an interesting notion. Why couldn't he travel some, see the world? He picked out some dog-eared travel guides for Australia, England, a few other European countries, and Tahiti. He tried to imagine anyone needing to be killed in Tahiti and couldn't, so he put that travel guide back on the shelf. Spector headed to the counter to check out.

Later, on the sofa at his apartment, he paged slowly through the guides while emptying a pint of bourbon. There really was a great big world out there, and if it took a few random bodies to see it that was a price he was willing to pay.

◆

Spector's mark, a Mr. DiCiccio, was a Gambione lieutenant. Back on Wild Card Day, Spector had had a run-in with some Gambiones, and he didn't much care for them. His target was in a high-rise apartment, holed up with several other people. Mostly bodyguards, from the info he had. They sent one guy out every day or so to buy groceries. He always wore the same dark blue suit. Spector's associates had made an identical garment for him to wear, which would make getting inside easier. Working with an organization of professionals had its upside. He stalked the man from the grocery store and caught up with him outside the high-rise.

"Down the alley, friend." Spector put a gun in the man's back, although he had no intention of using it. Guns left evidence; his power didn't.

"You're making a mistake, mister." The man walked with a grudging slowness into the mouth of the alley. "A big mistake."

"That's my lookout, paisan." Spector herded him behind a pile of garbage twenty yards in. "Set the bags down, put your hands up, and turn around."

The man did as he was told, then looked Spector directly in the eye and said, "Whatever you've got in mind, you're a dead man, you know."

He flooded the gangster's mind with the memory of his death, pushing it in so fast the man's body hit the ground before his face had the chance to register pain, surprise, or anything else. "Yep. Been that way for a while, tough guy."

Spector picked up the two sacks of groceries and moved to the building entrance. He entered the code he'd been given and elbowed his way inside. There were fresh fruits and vegetables in one of the sacks. For a moment, he remembered being a kid at the supermarket. It was just a corner grocery, but it had seemed so big to his young eyes. He pushed the memory away. It was time to focus. There was a room of people several stories up, where he was headed now. Those eyes were the last thing they'd ever see. Tough break for them, maybe. He imagined what it was like in Paris about right now.

The elevator was slow and creaky and his arms were getting tired by the time the doors opened. He moved quickly down the hallway and pressed the doorbell on room 817. Spector held the groceries up higher and turned away from the door so they couldn't see much of his face.

"Come in, Antonio." The voice belonged to an older woman. She turned her back to him and headed into the kitchen. "Just put the groceries on the counter. We'll eat in an hour or so if you'll all just leave me alone."

Spector deposited the bags on the Formica countertop and padded into the living area, where there was a TV playing a basketball game. There were two men on the couch, one old and heavy, the other young and heavier. The older man was watching TV and turned, expecting to see Antonio.

"What the . . ." he managed to say before Spector put him down.

The young man peered up from behind a magazine. His reflexes were fast and he almost made it to his gun before Spector locked eyes. Almost. Spector smiled in a thin, crooked way. This was going better than he could have hoped. The fact that they'd been on a couch meant no sound of bodies hitting the floor to warn anyone else. He would prefer not to kill the old woman, although he'd do it in an instant if he had to. One thing he couldn't do was leave a witness. The way he offed his victims didn't create any actual leads for the cops to use against him, but a witness could be trouble.

He glanced over at a mostly empty bookshelf on the far side of the room. A porcelain clock noisily ticked away the seconds. His target was almost certainly in the bedroom beyond, and had no idea how few seconds he had left to breathe.

Spector advanced to the doorway of the bedroom and stuck his head inside. An old man in silk pajamas sat propped up on the bed. He turned to the doorway.

"Antonio?"

Spector tried to lock eyes, but for some reason it wasn't working. He felt fear; his power was the only thing he could count on. The old man put on his glasses and craned his head forward. Spector connected immediately. The old man's final breath took a long time to leave his body, a leisurely rattling cough.

The bathroom door opened. A wiry man with graying hair stared momentarily at the bed, then went for his gun. He got the weapon out fast and fired the first shot without looking. The bullet missed Spector and thudded into the wall behind him, spraying bits of Sheetrock. The man squeezed off another round before Spector was able to catch his eye. Then it was over.

"Fuck," Spector muttered. Now he'd have to kill the old lady in the kitchen. Her bad luck, but there was nothing he could do about it now. He walked quickly back into the living room and was almost to the kitchen when she shouted something in Italian.

For an instant he saw her. She was holding something and her arms moved, then it hit him. Water, scalding hot. He screamed and clutched his face. As much as he hated his death pain, he was used to it after all this time. This was worse for being so unexpected. She'd nailed him right in his eyes and he couldn't see anything. He reflexively kicked out his right leg and caught nothing but air, setting himself off-balance. She grabbed him under his armpits and pushed him backward. He heard glass break, and then there was nothing under his feet. In spite of the pain, Spector knew he was falling. If he landed on his head from eight stories up, that was it. He twisted his body, trying to get his legs underneath him.

Spector felt a blow to his midsection and all the air went out of his lungs.

"Just in time. Good thing I was climbing up the building or we'd both be out of luck." The voice was strange, not quite human.

He didn't spend much time trying to figure out why he wasn't a smashed heap on the pavement. In addition to everything else, one of Spector's left ribs was broken.

"Get me out of here," he said through his blistering lips.

"I can take you back where you came from." The voice definitely wasn't human, probably a joker.

"Someone just tried to kill me up there. Get me someplace safe. I'll pay."

"You're already paying, or I wouldn't be here."

Spector couldn't tell how long it took for his rescuer to get him where he was going. His face was a mass of scalded nerve endings. The important thing was that he'd survived. He'd heal up soon enough. In the meantime he'd just have to endure. That was his life in a nutshell, getting from moment to moment and day to day. He could do that.

He heard a door open and the whatever-it-was set him down on a couch. Spector felt a broken spring underneath his ribs and rolled over on his other side. The radio was on, playing the Byrds' "Turn! Turn! Turn!" His eyes were still a mess. He couldn't see squat out of them. "Do you have any liquor?"

"Sure."

He heard some rummaging around and felt a bottle pressed into his right palm. Spector unscrewed the cap and pressed the rim to his lips, taking as many quick swallows as he could manage. It was vodka, not bourbon, but he didn't care. Enough of it would do the job.

"You need anything else? I've got places to be. Busy, busy, busy." The voice wasn't just inhuman, it was quick and staccato, like the words were racing to get out of its mouth.

"I'll survive." If Spector had a motto, that was it.

"Later."

Spector heard a door close and continued knocking back enough vodka to take the edge off the pain. He'd been badly burned once before and had figured out that dead skin can't heal, it just sits there. He'd had to peel it off to jump-start the regeneration process.

There were bits of pasta stuck to his face. Pulling them free was uncomfortable, but not excruciating. Then he put his hands to his eyelids. They were rippled, bloated, and stuck to his eyeballs. "Fuck me," he said, draining as much of the bottle as he could. Spector pulled off his coat and put it over his head. That, at least, would cut down on the light. He worked a fingernail into the corner of one of his eyelids and began pulling it away from his eye. At first it came off in little bits, then the entire piece of ruined flesh peeled away. He screamed and forced the bottle back between his lips. It was empty by the time he finished the job.

♥

Spector staggered through the doorway of his joker-rescuer's hideout and made it about ten feet before vomiting the first time. There were still some dead patches of skin on his face he'd have to pick away, but his eyelids were working again and that was what mattered most. He threw up twice more before making it to the corner. The cold wind drained the warmth from his body, adding to his misery level. Spector took note of where he was; it might be useful in the future, having a place he could duck into if the heat was on. Of course that was contingent on how hospitable the joker was at that point.

He managed to flag down a cab and huddled silently in the back for the entire trip to his apartment. The cabbie wasn't talkative or annoying, so Spector not only let him live, he gave the man a healthy tip.

The springs on his beat-up sofa groaned as he flopped down onto it. He looked around his living room and realized that he finally had enough money to make some improvements. The place was a wreck, much like its occupant, and it would be hard to know where to even start. Spector closed his eyes; he'd think about it later. Right now sleep was the first order of business, and for once he didn't expect any trouble drifting off.

♣

The door buzzer went off three times, spaced at intervals of several seconds. The signal meant Carl, the kid he wasn't supposed to kill, was downstairs. Spector hobbled to the door, glancing at the kitchen clock; he'd been out for four hours.

"Damn," he muttered to himself, then opened the door after hearing footsteps up the stairs.

Carl poked his head in tentatively, not bothering with mirrorshades this time, and tried to smile. "May I come in, sir?"

"You woke me up."

Carl's face lost a shade of color. "I'm very sorry. I won't take more than a moment of your time." He handed Spector an envelope. "There's a check inside for the agreed amount payable to you from one of our holding companies."

Spector took the envelope and opened it. He pulled out the check to make sure it was payment in full. It was. "Are you afraid of me, Carl?"

Carl paused for a moment. Spector could feel the kid's mind searching for the answer least likely to get him killed.

"Tell your boss I almost got killed again. My enthusiasm for this partnership is waning. Now get the fuck out of here."

Carl hit the doorway like a thoroughbred racehorse.

♠

Spector didn't know what he was doing, or why he was doing it. He'd gone to the bank to deposit the check, but instead he'd taken half out in cash. He planned on giving it to the joker who'd helped him out. He wasn't the kind of person who was big on gratitude, but maybe that was because nobody ever did anything for him. People did shitty things to him pretty regularly. Not that they got a chance to do much else after that. Nobody actually helped him out, though. He'd felt strange, having some kind of obligation to another person, even if it was accidental. He didn't much like the feeling and was happy to buy his way out of it.

He was wearing his bird mask when he knocked on the door to the joker's place. If there was no answer that was fine, he'd have tried to do something and that was good enough. "Anybody home?"

"Just a minute, minute, minute."

The joker opened the door; Spector saw his rescuer for the first time. It was big, half again the size of a normal person, and its skin was dark and moist. The face was a cross between a human's and a newt's, with slitted yellow eyes. Its arms and legs were long and muscular, with knobby tips at the end of the fingers.

"You got my pizza?" it asked, then looked with disappointment at his empty hands. "Who are you?"

"It's me, from yesterday. You saved my life when I fell out of the building."

The joker blinked its eyes rapidly, then cocked its head. "Oh right. The paper said you were dead, Mr. DiCiccio, so I was confused. I hadn't made clear how big I am, so I was going to do my bodyguarding from outside the building." He stared off into space for a moment. "Kind of muddled right now anyway."

The dime dropped for Spector. DiCiccio, his mark, must have gotten word there was a contract on him. So he hired Mr. Big-and-Ugly, who showed up just in time to save Spector's hash. What fucking luck. Spector would have felt warm and fuzzy if he were able to. "Yeah, I'm supposed to be dead, safer that way. That's why I'm wearing the mask. Can I come in?"

"Sure, sure."

He was uncomfortable and wanted to get this over with as quickly as possible. Didn't want to know the joker's name or anything else about him. He fished in his pocket for a wad of hundreds. "What you did yesterday was kind of above the call, so I figured a bonus was in order." He peeled off several bills and placed them in the palm of the joker's hand. Spector didn't really want to know his benefactor's name, on the remote chance he had to kill him at some point.

"Hey, great. Much appreciated." The joker tucked the money into the pocket of a coat hanging on a rack in the corner. "After I have some pizza we should go out for a few drinks."

"That's okay, thanks."

"No, no, no, really. It'll be fun. I don't have anything on for tonight. I know a place where you can wear your mask, no problem. They serve drinks with straws if you want. I've seen people do it plenty of times." The words streamed out of its mouth like a sibilant auctioneer's.

Spector sighed and pressed his thin lips together. He could always use a drink or three. "What the hell," he said. The pizza came soon enough, and Spector waited, fighting off second thoughts, as the joker quickly consumed a sizable portion before wiping his face with a napkin and both went outside.

"I can't exactly use a car, and people on the subway just freak out, so climb aboard," the joker said, pointing to his neck and shoulders.

Spector clambered up the joker's broad back. The skin was actually pleasant to the touch, soft and not slimy. He'd expected it to feel weird. He grabbed its shoulders on either side of the neck. "Ready whenever you are."

The joker took off with a jolt. His bounding stride took Spector a while to adjust to, but soon he was bobbing his body up and down in sync with his amphibian carrier. Spector had never done any horseback riding, so he didn't have anything else to compare it to, but imagined it to be similar. He felt strange, though, and couldn't place the sensation. Then he realized he was having fun. It had been a long time since he'd felt this good without killing someone. He might even be smiling. More likely it was just the icy December night numbing his lips under his mask.

The blocks sped by as they moved deeper into Jokertown. His ride was nimble, but didn't put too much effort into avoiding obstacles. Trash cans were trodden or kicked and left emptied of their contents. He'd even jumped on an old '68 Dodge Dart and crushed the hood.

They were halfway down a particularly narrow alley when a police growler stopped in front of them and flipped on its rotating red-and-blues.

Spector was surprised for an instant. Normally cops from the Jokertown precinct didn't make waves. *Must be a couple of go-getters.*

A moment later the joker was effortlessly scaling the wall. Spector hung on for dear life until they reached the top and sped away over the tops of the buildings.

"Don't like cops?" he asked.

"They can be a pain slow us down who needs that?" The words butted together like cars on a gridlocked freeway.

After Mr. Newt's wild ride finally came to an end, Spector smelled Chinese food. "Are we eating?" he asked.

The joker shook his head as Spector dismounted. "Need a drink. Squisher's." He headed down the stairs, opened the door, and squeezed himself through the doorway.

Spector guessed pizza was off the agenda, at least for now. Spector had heard about Squisher's Basement, but had never been particularly interested in going there. Still, he walked down the stairs, making sure his mask was securely on his face. Being recognized as a non-joker would probably lead to trouble.

The interior of Squisher's smelled like week-old fish sticks soaked in urine, but the atmosphere was still homey in a battered kind of way. Behind the bar was a massive fish tank inhabited by a manatee/octopus joker. Squisher himself, no doubt. The place was decently crowded, a few jokers at the bar and a couple opposite each other in a booth. There was a crowded table where a group of albino-looking jokers crowded around another joker with a giant head. Looking closer, he saw their faces were smeared with greasepaint. The pasty-faced bunch was uniformly muscular and dressed in similar clothing; a gang, maybe.

Spector hated gangs. On first glance he thought they were octuplets, but on looking a bit closer he saw that they weren't actually identical, just similar.

"We should get one of the big-boy booths in the back," said Spector's amphibian companion.

The big-boy booths were clearly for jokers in the extra-large range. Spector stood over six feet, but had to hoist himself up onto the bench seat. His legs swung like a kid's beneath him. The joker eased in comfortably opposite him.

"A pitcher of beer and a shot of whiskey," he said. "My friend will have . . ." He turned to Spector.

"A double shot of bourbon, with a straw. And keep it coming."

The waitperson was a short joker with multiple arms and a semitransparent, ghostlike appearance. It placed the drinks down in a practiced manner. Spector handed it a twenty. The joker nodded and bobbled away.

Spector slid the straw through the mouth-hole of his mask and took a long, satisfying draw of bourbon. It wasn't Jack Black, but it would get the job done.

"So, what do you do for fun down here?"

The joker shrugged. "Same as anyplace else, just a little dirtier here. And cheaper," he said, raising his glass.

"I'll drink to that." Spector clinked his shot glass against the joker's beer mug and took another swallow.

Spector's friend pulled out an amber bottle and poured a half-dozen pills into his oversized palm. He then downed them with a massive gulp of beer.

"What exactly are those for?"

"Energy, plus keeps the sandman away."

Speed, Spector thought. "Do you know where I could get something for pain? Still pretty beat up and I can't go to the doctor. Someone might spot me."

The joker cocked his head and belched. "No, just these. I did know somebody who had pain pills: who that was can't remember."

Spector sighed and took another slug of bourbon. If he could find a pain-med supplier it would make his life easier. Hell, he'd even let them live if they weren't too much of an asshole. Drug dealers usually were, though.

"Let me know if it comes back to you."

An eyeball floated past Spector's left shoulder and pivoted so that the business end was facing him. He wondered if he could kill the orb's owner. Probably.

Newt-man snatched the eyeball out of the air, tossed it into his mostly full beer glass, and gave the glass a shake.

There was a scream from the table with the gang and several members stood angrily, each assuming a fighting posture.

Spector's friend fished the eyeball out of his beer and blew the foam off it, then let it go. The eye floated quickly back toward the joker with the massive head. Each of the muscle-punks was standing and pointing in a way that might be threatening to the average Joe.

"Keep your eyes to yourself, Sue," he said matter-of-factly.

Squisher poked his head out of the top of his tank with what Spector figured was a really unhappy look on his manatee-like face.

"Hey, how about those Knicks?" Spector said, turning his back to the oversized aquatic joker. A stream of water caught him in the back of the head.

"Let's get out of here." Newt-thing pushed himself up from the table and finished his mug of beer in a couple of swallows.

Spector followed him outside, turning up his collar to the biting cold. "So, who is this Sue?"

"Sue Maroo. Joker with lots of detachable eyes. She snoops for certain parties, yes parties. Other things, too. Nasty things. Her boys help her. Mostly rejects from other gangs. Little shits. Sue and I have had a couple of run-ins. She wound up with the short end of the stick. Yes, yes." He blinked his eyes rapidly. "Hey, speaking of the Knicks, I've got some tickets to tomorrow night's game with the Celtics." He inserted a pair of knobby fingers into a pouch on his waist and produced a ticket. "You should come. We'll have a great time."

Spector took the ticket out of what might have been politeness. The joker's enthusiasm was a tough headwind to buck. "The Celts are great again this year."

"Yeah, but the Knicks have Patrick Ewing."

Spector shrugged. "I'll think about it."

"Sure. We still need to eat, right. Let's get a pizza."

His companion was crazed as far as Spector was concerned, but he was still hungry. "Why the hell not."

◆

The movie wasn't what he'd hoped it would be. One of the art-house theaters was showing *An American in Paris* and Spector had figured watching it might be a good way to put himself in an international state of mind. It wasn't working. Gene Kelly could sing and dance. Hell, seemed like everyone could sing and dance. Nothing was real, though. It was set in Paris, but it was pure Hollywood.

Spector fished the few remaining bits out of his popcorn and chewed them silently, then left his seat and walked across the sticky floor to the exit.

Outside, the frigid wind whipped his clothes and chilled his exposed skin. At least the sun was out for now. Spector looked around slowly. New York felt the way a big city should: cold, filthy, oppressive, and uncaring.

He had plenty of cash, so Spector flagged a cab for a ride back to his apartment. The cabbie didn't have anything to say, which was good because Spector was in the mood to kill someone and he didn't feel like grabbing another ride just to get home.

Spector had the cab drop him a block away from his apartment. He was feeling uneasy and didn't know why, so he let his paranoia get the better of him. He spotted a black Olds parked outside his apartment building, engine running. As he walked by he saw a young woman in the back seat looking at a notepad. Probably a grad student from NYU or Columbia doing her thesis on how the other half lives. He moved carefully up the stairs, which were coated in half ice, half slush, and entered the building with a backward glance at the car. The young girl was watching him, but looked away when he returned her gaze.

His apartment was cold, so he turned up the heat and poured a tumbler with a few inches of Jack Black. A couple of swallows helped warm and numb him. He dropped himself onto the couch and turned on the TV. He didn't bother to change the channel from the soap opera that was playing.

Someone rapped on his door.

Spector hauled himself up off the couch and cracked the door open. It looked like the woman from the car, but he wasn't sure. She had shoulder-length brown hair, thick-lensed glasses, and more attitude than a person her age was entitled to.

"Who are you?"

"I'm Ms. Davis. I'm Carl's replacement. He's afraid of you. For the record, I know who you are and I'm not afraid of you." She lifted her chin and narrowed her eyes.

Spector shook his head. "Then you're too stupid to be a lawyer. Or much of anything else, Miss Davis."

"Ms."

He partly wanted to punch her and partly wanted to kill her. Spector didn't want a corpse in his apartment, though. And he didn't much like killing women. Not that women didn't deserve it just as much as men, but tombstoning one made him think of his time with the Astronomer. Those were bad times he wanted to put in the rearview mirror.

"We have a very lucrative opportunity for you. The benefits would include not only cash reimbursement, but also many of the items I understand have been previously discussed with you." She looked directly into his eyes. "Are you interested?"

"Depends," Spector replied, moving over to the table to pick up his bottle of Jack Black. He took a swallow. This kid was trying too hard. People with too much to prove were almost always more trouble than they were worth.

"All the information you need is in this folder." She presented it to Spector, who ignored it. "The subject is a high-priority item as he's an ace. Just freelance, but we want to remove any enhanced individuals from the opposition side of the board. He may already be working for them."

Spector snarled at her, "Fuck no. No aces." He pushed her toward the door and opened it, then shoved her hard through the doorway. "Aces can get me killed."

"I hope you'll reconsider. His name is Cro—" Spector slammed the door shut before she could finish another syllable. They didn't care if he got killed again. What the hell did he need financial experts for anyway?

He refilled his tumbler with bourbon. Maybe he'd go to the Knicks game and take his mind off things for a while.

♥

The crowd outside the Garden was cold and surly, holidays be damned. Spector didn't like crowds. If a situation got out of hand it was hard to decide who to kill first. Plus, he just didn't like people much. Inside the arena smelled of dirty slush, and, once the people removed their coats, the dank sweat of partisan hatred peculiar to sports fans. The talk from the people around Spector wasn't optimistic. The hated Celtics were the best team in the Eastern Division, with a frontline of Bird, McHale, and Parish. Plus Ainge and D.J. at the guards. The Knicks had Pat Ewing, who was great but still somewhat new to the league. The Knicks had other good players, but it was still likely to be a slaughter. Spector had never been a big Knicks fan. He'd seen Dr. J play for the Nets back in the old ABA. The ABA was long gone, and Julius had decided to hang it up at the end of last season.

Spector got in line for something to drink. Beer didn't do much for him, but he had some Jack Black to sweeten it up once he took his seat.

He spiked his beer with bourbon and finished it before warmups were done. There was no way a giant crazed joker was going to make it into the Garden, so he'd have room to spread out if he wanted.

A young, bearded guy with thick glasses was sitting a few seats down. His orange and blue cap marked him as part of the home crowd, and he chanted "Let's go Knicks! Let's go Knicks! Let's go Knicks!" for upward of a solid minute. Spector was getting irritated—not homicidal irritated but please-shut-the-fuck-up irritated. The Knicks fan finally quit yelling.

He was comfortably numb by the time tip-off arrived. The crowd noise, which had been little more than a buzz, grew to a roar as the game got underway.

On their first possession the Celtics worked the ball around until it wound up in Bird's hands in the left corner. He lowered his shoulder into the defender to make space and shot. The ball swished through the net to a groan from the hometown fans.

The rest of the first quarter saw the lead change hands several times. Neither team led by more than five points, but the Celts were up three at the end of the first twelve minutes.

Spector heard a commotion from the upper deck. There were a few screams mingled in with the general hubbub. He craned his neck to see what was going on. A large, dark form clambered over the upper deck railing and jumped, landing with a massive thud in the aisle between his section and the adjacent one.

It was the joker, of course. Spector had really thought there was no way for him to get inside, but he'd underestimated the creature's determination.

Newt-thing had purchased three seats and Spector was in the center one, which was clearly a mistake.

"Mind moving over, buddy buddy," he said, gesturing with his oversized hands.

"Not at all," Spector replied, "just keeping it warm for you." He took the next seat over.

The joker gingerly tore the armrest from between his two seats and dropped it on the floor. He leaned over. "Would you mind buying us a couple of beers, and maybe some pizza? If I try to move, people will make trouble."

"It's on me, big guy," Spector said. He figured this situation was going to be trouble no matter what. Being in the concourses right now was probably his best play.

The line at the concessions wasn't bad. Spector had a pizza and a couple of beers in less than five minutes. He hadn't heard any crowd noises that were out of the ordinary. Nothing that resembled the death screams of people being torn to pieces by a giant newt.

As he headed back down his aisle, Spector spotted a couple of security guys talking to each other, but they didn't look like they were inclined to do anything. Yet.

Spector made it back to their seats and realized there was no way he was getting by the joker. He handed him the beers and said, "I'll get by behind and come over."

"Okay. Pizza, goooood. So hungry."

As he was sliding by two men to reach a place where he could step over a vacant seat, one of them said, "You know, your friend is making it really hard to see the game."

"Feel free to tell him about it," Spector replied, dropping into his seat.

He didn't give them another thought. The joker daintily handed him a beer between a massive thumb and first finger.

The Celtics started to pull away in the second quarter, mostly by feeding the ball to McHale and Parish down low. At one point Ewing sent a Parish shot into the second row. That drew a thunderous cheer from the Knicks fans. Spector chugged his beer.

"Might want to take it easy with that." The joker pointed to Spector's cup. "I put a little pick-me-up in there. Great for staying alert."

Spector felt a tingle under his tongue. "Speed?"

The joker nodded. "Helps keep me awake. I'm going to crash before too much longer if I don't keep a bunch in my system."

Spector stared into the cup. What remained of the foam was dissipating into small clumps of bubbles. He'd never taken speed before. His whole deal was deadening his senses, not pushing them to the max. He felt the pain surging inside him. It hurt more than usual, but felt different. Normally the sensation of sharing his death was like pushing goo into another person's mind. Now he felt like lightning in a bottle. The sensation of power almost made up for additional pain.

"You can't stay here, big guy." Spector looked over and saw a couple of security personnel talking to his newt companion.

The joker let out a rumbling laugh. "Feel free to drag me out if you can. It's not even halftime yet and I'm here to see the game."

The uniformed men looked at each other, hopelessness and anger on their faces.

"We'll help you get this ugly fuck out of here." One of the men sitting behind Big Newt stood and thumped his sizable chest. The man next to him got up, too. "We haven't been able to see shit since he sat down."

The joker stood quickly, a slice of pizza disappearing into his mouth. "You just need a different seat, friend." He took the man under the armpits with his blotched hands and tossed him screaming into the upper deck of the Garden. He grabbed the man's buddy by his jacket. "What about you?"

"Don't throw me up there!"

Newt-man looked around several times, then smiled. "Fair enough." He turned and launched the man into the Celtics bench, knocking players and staff onto the court like bowling pins.

Spector laughed out loud. This was better than any game. The entire Celtics bench charged the stands. The Celts on the floor looked at each other for a second then followed their teammates in the melee. Danny Ainge was screaming.

Spector felt something wet and cold hit the back of his head. Beer. He turned and saw a man pointing at him and smiling.

"Fuck you, buddy." He killed the asshole in an instant. It felt good. The dead man dropped onto the seat in front of him like a sack of potatoes.

People in the stands around Spector were going apeshit. A knot of Celtics fans had poured down the aisle and were whaling away on the joker, but it wasn't going well for them. The joker picked up one man in each oversized mitt and smacked them together, then head-butted another. Uniformed security officers were trying to intervene at courtside, but several of the Celtics players were fighting their way up the aisle. Danny Ainge's green uniform was spattered in blood. It looked very festive. Spector was thinking it might be a good time to kill his way out of this mess when he caught a sucker punch to the right side of his head and a couple more to his ribs. He fell breathless to the concrete and looked for his assailant.

An instant later a middle-aged man with a beer gut and a Celtics shirt bounded gracelessly down from the row behind Spector and glared down at him.

Spector blew the life out of him and put a leg up, making sure the man didn't fall onto him, then pushed his body over backward. The corpse made a heavy noise as it hit, punctuated by a nasty thwack when its skull impacted the concrete.

In addition to the security forces near the floor, a large group of uniformed men were shoulder-cutting down the aisle toward the brawl in the stands. They were making headway at a slow but steady pace. Before long they'd be in Spector and his friend's lap. *Might be time to think of an exit strategy. It could mean a lot of corpses.*

Spector turned back toward the court to see if that was a reasonable way of retreat. Nope. The angry Celtic contingent was smashing through the Knick partisans, fists flailing. Spector saw Larry Bird; if only the Celtic star would look his way, he could deal the Boston Greenies a fatal blow. Bird looked his way, just for an instant. Spector locked in and pushed, but lost contact as he was gathered up by a massive newt hand.

"Time to go, go, go. Yes indeed."

The joker leaped to the upper deck. Spector hadn't really seen the extent of his jumping power. It was impressive, and almost made him heave the contents of his stomach onto the fans underneath them. The joker vaulted upward again into the girders and catwalks that formed the upper skeleton of the Garden. Spector eyed a large hole in the roof, figuring that was where the joker had made a forced entrance. It was now their way out from the melee far below. Spector hissed as they exited the building into the biting Manhattan air. It was quite a view.

♣

The sound of sirens had receded into the distance behind them. The joker carried Spector like before as they sped across the rooftops and across walls.

Spector's massive companion was beginning to move in stops and starts. The speed must be wearing off. Not the case for Spector, who was brimming with pain and sharp as a tack. It was beyond uncomfortable, but in a powerful way. Not something he'd want to do again, most likely.

He wasn't familiar with the rooftop views, but Spector could tell they'd been in Jokertown for a while by the smell.

"Almost there," the joker said, shaking his head. "Time to head to the, uh, street. Don't want to fall."

"Good idea," Spector said. It would be ironic if the joker saved him from a bone-shattering fall a couple of days ago only to drop him several stories now. Spector wasn't into irony, unless there was a nice payday attached. He dropped off the joker's back when they hit street level. His arms and shoulders were sore and aching from hanging on much of the way.

"Gotta get home," the joker said.

Spector looked around. Jokertown in the dark wasn't easy for him to navigate, but he had a fair sense of where he was. "I think it's a few blocks that way, then hook a left and you're there."

"Right," the joker said slowly. He turned and started walking down the cracked, litter-strewn sidewalk.

Spector shrugged. He figured the joker would make it back one way or another. For now, he was cold and hungry and needed a few more shots of liquor. Not much chance of catching a cab here, so he turned in the direction of the nearest subway stop. He hadn't gone more than fifty feet when a van screamed out of a nearby alley. Before he could jump out of the way, Spector felt the side of the vehicle slam into him. The impact knocked him several yards back into the wall of a nearby tenement. He howled, all too familiar with how broken bones felt. This was just a couple of ribs, and they'd mend in a hurry, but he was going to make these fuckers pay if he could catch them.

He got up and staggered after the van. His hip hurt, too. Spector had all the pain in the world to share with the asshole driver. When it came to killing people, joker or nat, it didn't make any difference to him. The van came to an abrupt halt, tires squealing. The doors slammed open and several people piled out. Spector's suspicion that they were armed was confirmed seconds later when he heard rounds popping off. A bullet to his head could . . . well, he wasn't sure exactly what it could do, but he didn't want to find out.

He heard a scream and a body flew over his head and bounced hard off the sidewalk. Spector moved toward the person to get a closer look. A young man got shakily to his feet and pointed a gun in Spector's direction. The man holding it was one of the pasty boys from Squisher's. Nearby Spector saw broken glass and smoking cement.

Spector grabbed the man's gun arm and pointed it away from him, then pulled him close. There was just enough illumination from a dirty streetlight for Spector to see his face clearly. He locked eyes and killed him in an instant. When the man's head hit the sidewalk something popped off. Spector picked it up—headphones connected to a battery pack in the dead guy's pocket. He put one headphone to his ear, letting the battery dangle. He heard a woman speaking.

"Get his eyes. Who had the acid? Get it in his eyes."

"I think it was Jesse. He's gone," a voice replied.

Spector dropped the headphones. He'd heard enough. These bozos and Sue Maroo were looking for payback. He limped forward as fast as he could, gritting his teeth. They hadn't counted on him when they decided to kill his joker friend, or whatever he was. That was their mistake.

There was no one behind the wheel of the van, so Spector walked around front. The punks must have run out of ammo, as they were attacking the joker with knives and clubs. Newt-joker was holding his own for the moment, but the numbers were against him. The massive joker staggered into a badly lit area. Spector shook his head. It would be nearly impossible to lock eyes unless the battle moved back into the light.

Something small glided noiselessly by his shoulder. One of the joker's attackers wheeled and charged Spector, knife in hand. Spector dodged, but the knife caught him on the elbow. More pain. He was about to give it back in spades. He caught the punk's eyes and put him down in a heap.

Another eye floated by, just out of his reach. Sue was pretty smart. Spector jumped as high as his meth-pumped body would go, extending his arms. His fingers closed on empty air a few inches short of the orb. It was like the damned thing was taunting him. More likely it was keeping him busy so the other creeps could take down the joker, who was now down on one knee.

Spector dodged around the back of the van, scrambled up on top of it, spotted the eye, and pushed off as hard as he could in its direction.

He felt something soft struggling in his palm as he hit the pavement. Spector opened his fingers up a bit, and was surprised and annoyed at what he found. The eye had a lid, and it was closed tightly. He stuck a dirty thumbnail under the lid and slid it upward, prying it slowly open.

Another one of the thugs turned from the joker and headed his way. The eye was fully open and Spector gazed into it, hoping this would work. He forced his death into the eye and it went still in his hand. There was a soft wheeze from somewhere nearby. The punk who'd been headed his way paused and turned his head with uncertainty. He tapped his ear.

"You are so fucked, buddy," Spector said, catching the man's eye. A moment later, one more corpse was now getting cold in the winter air. The other punks scattered.

The joker got back to his feet. His wounds looked superficial from what Spector could tell. "Saw what you did. Thanks."

"The Knicks didn't win tonight, but we did." Spector motioned to the open van. "Climb in. I'll drive you home."

Unfortunately, his giant newt body didn't fit inside, so the joker climbed on top, crumpling the roof over the back part of the van.

Spector jumped in behind the wheel and started the engine. The trip was only a few blocks, he'd been right about that, but the van groaned under the weight of the joker every foot of the way. One of the rear tires blew out and they had to make the final hundred yards riding the rim.

"Home again, home again," Spector said, as the joker tumbled from the top of the damaged van.

"Get me inside."

Spector guided and talked the joker into his place. Big Newt collapsed heavily on the floor, his eyes already closed.

"Turn on the radio."

Spector located the radio and flipped it on. A light behind the dial flickered to life. The music wasn't anything Spector recognized. He set the door lock and headed out into the freezing New York night.

♠

Spector was sitting in a booth at the Crystal Palace with a cup of coffee and a bottle of whiskey. The light from outside was soft. It was early still. The meth had kept him up all night. He had hoofed it to the nearest subway stop, making it there without further incident. Later, he'd picked up a large pepperoni pizza. That and half a bottle of Jack Black had gotten him through the night. When he left his place to come to the Crystal Palace Spector had had a good reason for doing it. Now he couldn't remember what that was. He had the sports section of the *Times* open in front of him.

BIRD CONSIDERS RETIREMENT AFTER NEAR-DEATH EXPERIENCE, the headline read in bold type. Too bad he hadn't killed the fucker, but at least Bird would think long and hard before putting on Celtic Green again.

Elmo, wearing mirrorshades again, walked up to his booth and coughed. "She wants to see you again."

Spector couldn't imagine why. He didn't think he knew anything that Chrysalis didn't. Still, the last time he visited with her he'd gotten some free whiskey, so why the hell not?

Chrysalis was seated in her chair when Spector entered her private room. As expected, she also wore mirrored glasses. "Mr. Spector," she said, "how decent of you to join me."

"Sure."

"Quite a lot of excitement last night." The muscles in her chest moved slightly as she took a deep breath.

Spector held up his sports section. "Yeah, I was just reading about it."

"I wasn't referring to the incident at the sports arena, Mr. Spector. Have you ever heard of Sue Maroo?"

He decided to play dumb. "Nope."

"I see."

Chrysalis was impossible to read. Spector had denied being involved and he was going to stick with that. "You mind if I get back to my newspaper and pick-me-up?"

She gestured toward the door with a bony finger.

"One thing," Spector said, turning back. "My gut feeling is there's a war coming. A big one. Blood in the streets kind of a deal. You might keep an ear to the ground."

Chrysalis cocked her head slightly. "My ear is always to the ground, and a war sounds like a situation you might be able to—exploit."

"A man's gotta eat," he said, heading back to his booth. "Happy holidays," he added in parting.

"Enjoy the Yuletide, Mr. Spector."

Spector lingered in the Crystal Palace for an hour or so, nursing his coffee and drink, mulling over his brief adventure. He'd had fun, and it wasn't just killing fun.

His mind drifted to wondering what it would have been like to be an international assassin. Probably a pain, having to learn languages and deal with customs. Jet lag, too. He was better off right here. There were millions of people in New York City, and plenty of them needed killing.

He got up from his booth and left the Crystal Palace. The bitter New York cold embraced him like a long-lost child who'd finally found his way home.

♠ ♥ ♦ ♣

Long is the Way

by Carrie Vaughn & Sage Walker

Long is the way and hard, that out of Hell leads up to light.
—John Milton, *Paradise Lost*

JONATHAN TIPTON-CLARKE—ALSO known as Jonathan Hive, also known as Bugsy, and probably also known as a lot of other things that no one actually said to his face—drove up the impossibly picturesque country road with decreasing confidence that he was going the right way. The direction app on his phone had been silent for too long, which probably meant he'd lost the signal. The road grew narrower and narrower, curving through one tiny Provençal village after another, until the villages ran out, replaced by hillsides covered with olive groves and vineyards, and the soft, golden light that had given Impressionist painters ecstatic fits. He ought to be enjoying this. The assignment—track down and interview a "person of interest" who might or might not have been involved with a terrorist attack on Jerusalem almost twenty years ago—had been an excuse to spend time in the South of France on an expense account. He didn't expect to actually find Zoe Harris.

While he might have had romantic spy thriller notions about chasing down leads across the Middle East, the task had been bureaucratic and dull. Old-fashioned detective work, poring over records, asking the right questions, offering a bribe here and there to get a look at files he maybe shouldn't have seen. He hadn't even had to use his ace, much. Fortunately, Harris had spent a lot of time in countries without strict HIPAA requirements. He started with her last known location—Jerusalem, 1994—and her last known associates. The problem was, most of them had died in the disaster. The sheer scale of it—five thousand dead from a biological attack, a weaponized version of the Black Trump virus that killed any wild carder who came in contact with it—meant records were spotty. A lot of people disappeared. But Harris popped back into the record once or twice over the years. A couple of arrests, a couple of hospitalizations—she'd apparently had a rough go of it.

Then he found a mug shot from a hospital in Cairo. Didn't have a name attached to it, but the ash-blond hair and angry expression matched an earlier passport photo. Harris was an ace who could animate small objects. According to the hospital records, her power was out of control. She was a danger to herself and others and had been kept sedated for years. Then she disappeared, again. Released, homeless, most likely. She was probably dead at the bottom of the Nile.

Except . . . a decade ago, a woman named Zoe Harris popped up as the president of a small chemical company in Toulouse, France. Couldn't be the same person, could it? This Harris was reclusive. He couldn't find any pictures of her. So he asked for a meeting, and now he was on his way to meet her. Assuming he could find the address.

He rolled down the window, set his arm on the edge, and let loose a couple of bugs. Bottle-green wasps popped from his hand and were whisked away by the wind of the car's passage. That was Jonathan's own weird and occasionally surprisingly useful ace: He could turn into an equivalent mass of wasps and his consciousness could follow along wherever they went. He sent them straight up, high enough to give him a map-eye view of the road ahead, to make sure he was really going the right way and wasn't about to end up in some cowshed.

The place wasn't even that far ahead, turned out, and he'd been going the right way the whole time. Trust the app. Hidden behind a hill and an uninviting stone wall, Harris's enclave was disguised as a remote country farm. No one who didn't have a reason to be here would find it. And here he was, driving through a gap in the wall and up to a set of buildings arranged around a gravelly courtyard. Some of the structures were old, maybe even medieval—weathered gray stone, cracked Spanish tiles on the roof. One was very modern, glass and steel, with wide windows and skylights. That must hold the labs.

A small, unassuming sign placed in front of the modern building read *Zephyr* in a very expensive-looking font. He hesitated a moment, hands on the steering wheel, engine idling. Did he really want to go in? Probably this Harris woman wasn't even who he thought she was. She probably hadn't had anything to do with anything. He'd ask her a few questions, maybe get a rundown on her perfume business, and write a puff piece for an airline magazine. Expense account justified.

He sent his already-released bugs ahead, along with a few more of them besides. Just to look the place over. Got the layout pretty quick. Apart from the main building, there were a number of cottages and more typical country buildings, with whitewashed walls and tile roofs, the little kitchen gardens and trash bins of any residential neighborhood. He gathered that a lot of the people who worked here also lived here. Middle of the day, no one much was out and about.

Zephyr was involved with processing ingredients used in perfumes, which seemed an arcane business but somebody had to do it, he supposed. The sleek modern building was the centerpiece of the estate, and a couple of the bugs skimmed over the roof. They found a vent and slipped inside. The sharp tang of volatile chemicals—alcohols, esters, solvents—almost knocked them out right then, and back in the car he shivered in response, until they got their wings back in order. If this lab really did belong to Zoe Harris, maybe-former-terrorist, was she hiding anything in plain sight here? Maybe cranking out something else besides overpowering smells? The bugs flew on through the ductwork. He was hoping he could pop them out into a room—some actual lab or even a secret storage closet—but it turned out the interior vents all had really good filters on them. He couldn't find so much as a loose seam to crawl through. He'd have to find another way in. He diverted a couple of bugs to wait by the front door, right at the top where no one ever looked.

Back in the driveway, he stepped out of the rental car, shaking out his jacket and running his hands through his dark hair to make sure he didn't look too respectable. Made him more approachable, he thought. Or maybe he was more nervous than he wanted to admit.

A man left the modern building and approached Jonathan. Middle-aged, with Mediterranean features and a brisk, practical walk. An eye patch over his right eye. He looked a little like a pirate. So the place had surveillance. They'd known the minute Jonathan arrived.

The man said, *"Puis-je vous aider?"*

"Ah . . . *Je ne parle pas français.*" That was most of the French he knew right there.

"Oh yes, of course. You're American."

Jonathan tried not to feel insulted. "My name is Jonathan Tipton-Clarke. I have an appointment with Ms. Harris. I assume I'm at the right place?"

"You are; she's expecting you. Right this way." The man smiled thinly and gestured for Jonathan to follow him. With one last look around the yard, he did so.

A pair of bugs went inside when they did, and quietly buzzed off looking for whatever they could find.

Windows along one side of the corridor looked into a laboratory, stainless steel tables filled with glassware—flasks and bottles, the intricate tubing of distilling apparatus. Several people shrouded in white lab coats, caps, and masks seemed intent on their work, bent over metal trays, carefully lifting bits with delicate forceps.

The clean rooms were really clean. The wasps couldn't find a way inside. Not that Jonathan would have known what he was looking at if they had. Be helpful if he could find a box labeled DANGER, EXPLOSIVES, a package with a return address from the Twisted Fists, but he didn't.

"Not what people imagine when they think of a perfume factory, eh?" his guide said, with obvious pride. "Not very romantic. This isn't really a perfume factory—we don't make perfume here. We make what makes perfume, yes? We can draw the essence from nearly anything."

There was a metaphor there that Jonathan chose not to chase down.

One bug caught a glimpse: a woman approaching . . . and she saw him. Them. She was a joker, with a face that looked melted on one side, average white middle-aged matron on the other, with brown hair tied in a ponytail. She held a tightly coiled newspaper in one hand. The pair of bugs crawled along the ceiling—well out of reach of the universal weapon of "death to insects."

And then her arm stretched. She whipped it back and flung it out, once, twice, and both wasps smashed into spots of goo. Well, then. Jonathan felt the buggy deaths as an itch. He decided not to send out any more bugs, at least not right now.

The corridor turned away from the lab, then ended up at an open door, which they passed through. His guide announced, "Zoe? Mr. Tipton-Clarke is here."

"Ah. Thank you, Tarek." The man gave a little bow that somehow didn't seem anachronistic, and slipped back out, leaving Jonathan to confront his interview subject.

The office was like something out of *Architectural Digest*. Nothing but clean lines, glass and steel, a soft carpet in a comforting shade of gray. The desk and credenza were black lacquer, and several available chairs seemed somehow soft and repellent at the same time. Zoe Harris, a woman of late middle age, with short-cropped hair and a tired, severe expression, wore black slacks and a gray silk blouse. She'd been studying her large computer screen—only the screen sat on the desk, and a small cordless mouse was tucked under her hand. She clearly ruled this domain.

It *was* her. That ashy hair, the shape of her face—this was the Zoe Harris from Jerusalem. The terrorist.

He waited while she finished whatever task on the monitor held her attention. After a moment, she stood. "Please, come and sit." Her accent was American. New York. She didn't offer her hand for shaking, and Jonathan didn't press the issue.

"Thanks for agreeing to speak with me, Ms. Harris."

"Zoe, please."

"Do you mind if I record our interview?" He held up his digital recorder.

"I'd rather you didn't, if that's all right."

It made things harder, but he understood. He'd even offer to let her speak anonymously. He was imagining an artistic photo to accompany the article, her face shrouded in shadow. He traded the recorder for a pad and pen. "I'm looking forward to hearing more about your work here, and how you got started—"

"That's not why you're here," she said bluntly. "I read up on you, you know. I had people on the lookout for your, ah, associates."

Jonathan smiled wryly. He was years past being embarrassed at his spying. People generally knew what they were getting when they invited him in.

"Can't blame a guy for trying," he said.

"No, of course not. But we can't be having outside contagions cluttering up our clean rooms. You understand."

He spread his hands to say yes, he did. In a way, he was relieved. No pretending he was something he wasn't, and no dancing around the subject. "So. I'm here about Jerusalem."

"And?"

"And you're one of the loose ends. You had contact with the major players. Then you disappeared. A lot of people assumed you were dead. Then you pop up here?" He took in the quiet, professional surroundings.

"Are you working for the police? The CIA?"

Jonathan laughed. "No, no—I'm exactly what I said I was. I'm a reporter on assignment for *The Atlantic*." It was the highest-profile gig he'd ever had. They were doing a whole issue of think pieces on wild cards–related terrorism and its aftermath. A lot of retrospectives, interviews with people who'd been there. Trouble was, given the nature of the topic, there weren't a whole lot of survivors to interview. Jonathan was shocked they'd called him—his usual gig, *Aces!* magazine, was generally considered a tabloid rag, all celebrity gossip and scandal. But he'd been one of the aces to ditch *American Hero* to battle the Righteous Djinn in Egypt, back in the day. Five, six years ago now? Seemed longer. He had front-line experience, so to speak, and if an editor thought that made him qualified to tackle the subject, well, he'd give it a shot. This was going to be a coup. *If* he could get the interview.

"All right, then. What is it you hope to learn, Mr. Tipton-Clarke?"

Why did you do it? was never the right question. It was too big, too prone to pat answers. He had to come at it backward. Find out who Harris was then by figuring out who she was now.

"I want to learn about all this. Zephyr. How did this start? What is it you do here?" He was thinking of a nice lead-in, contrasting the pastoral beauty of the place with the violence of the woman's past.

Her gaze narrowed, as if she had made a decision. This was usually the point where Jonathan got kicked out of places. "What is it you think we do here?"

"Uh . . . it's a perfume business?"

"No. This is redemption."

He hesitated, taken aback. Now *this* sounded like a story. "What do you mean? What are you redeeming?"

She might have been a little surprised by his attention. Like she expected him to be uncomfortable with that kind of declaration. She pursed her lips, gave a little nod. And then she told her story.

◆

There have been no criminal charges against me, yet. The penalty I deserve is death. If I thought an eternity of torment, of fire or torture, awaited me after death, that would be comforting. I'm stuck with a rationalist's disbelief in immortality. My hell is that I have memories of what I've done and didn't do to stay alive.

When I left Jerusalem, my plan was to somehow find ten people who were cursed with generosity and the power to forgive. I'm a secular Jew at best, but the mythology is that ten good men are required to keep the world from destruction. I wanted to get ten people out of living hell and into a place where they could live and thrive. Everyone I employ here at Zephyr is a joker. I was born in Jokertown, you know. The people there, the people in jokertowns all over the world, need a leg up more than most. If I can do this little bit . . .

But I think I might be getting ahead of myself. I'll start again.

You're here about what happened in Jerusalem in 1994. The Black Trump. The Card Sharks. There are some words, some memories that cause physical reactions, even after years have passed. See this? I'm trembling, even now. I remember too much.

I was working with the Black Dog—you know the name? At the time he led the Twisted Fists, and I know you know *that* name. I imagine you sent your little spies out to look for signs of them, to see if maybe I'm still working with the most notorious terrorist ever to crawl out of Jokertown. You know about their "five for one" policy? They'd kill the killer and four others for every murdered joker. It was justice that no one else was seeking at the time. But no, I have no ties with the Fists, not anymore. The incident you're here about was the Black Trump, the moment Jerusalem was held hostage. The Card Sharks wanted to release the Black Trump, kill every wild carder in the area. So the Fists had a bomb, a nuke. Retaliation I helped haul to the Mideast in an old Blue Bird bus. And then I tried to stop them from using it. So, no, I'm not working with the Twisted Fists.

I'm a murderer. I've slaughtered people in anger and killed in self-defense. I saw a moonlit desert, an ambush, a forever-anonymous man with a rifle, his outstretched arm clouded by needle-sharp grains of a private and deadly sandstorm. My vision of that arm would replay for me that night or on some other night soon, a nightmare view of forearm and wrist and finger bones, scoured blue-white and fresh, falling to the sand.

His screams.

I did that.

I didn't save Jerusalem, or children who depended on me, or my mother. I went to Pan Rudo's camp, I even had sex with that genocidal monster, but I didn't manage to destroy the Black Trump virus. Other people did. A virus that could have killed every ace, deuce, and joker on Earth had been destroyed. The quantity of evil in the world remained much the same. Its forms remained banal.

You're here about what happened to me after Jerusalem. How does one get from that to this?

The first thing I did—I went mad.

I had a list. Jack Braun. Thomas Tudbury. Nephi Callendar. Tachyon. Tachyon was off-planet. I managed to learn that much. Others. People who could have done, should have done, and didn't. But I couldn't manage to get close enough to anyone on the list to even sneeze at them. Those were pre-Google years, remember? No, you wouldn't. You're young.

I have powers, Mr. Tipton-Clarke. You must know that about me. But I still couldn't save anyone. And then I realized I was one of those people I hated. I should have done more, and I didn't, I couldn't. Self-hatred grew in tandem with my desire to lash out at the perpetrators of so much violence, so much slaughter. I had nightmares, and my nightmares . . . fear fuels my power. I'd wake to a bedside lamp rocketing through the air, smashing into the wall above my head. Lumps of dust would grow huge, sharp teeth and chatter in Arabic under my bed.

The flat in Jerusalem was crowded with beds, and all of them were empty but mine. I forgot to eat. I stopped bathing, stopped cooking, lived on canned food I didn't bother to heat. I left Jerusalem, thinking if I could just get away from where the horror happened, the nightmares would end. They didn't. I ended up in Cairo. But it was the same. This went on for years. I was arrested—I destroyed the flat I was living in. And then I was institutionalized. You know they really do have padded rooms? I should have been safe, in a room with nothing in it. But during my nightmares, my power pulled the stuffing out of the walls and turned it into shrapnel.

I spent a lot of time drugged. That was probably for the best.

And that's the state I was in when Croyd found me.

♥

"Wait," Jonathan interrupted. He'd written down just a few key words. *Black Trump. Card Sharks. Black Dog. Twisted Fists. Jerusalem.* But this . . . "Croyd Crenson? The Sleeper?"

"Yes. You know him?"

"Can't say that I do," he answered. "But . . . everyone knows Croyd Crenson."

"Yes," she said, wearing a smile that was incongruously gentle. They'd slept together, Jonathan realized suddenly.

"And he was in Cairo," Jonathan prompted. "He found you?"

"Yes."

♣

"Jesus, Zoe. What the hell happened to you?"

I didn't recognize the man who said this to me. The fact that I didn't recognize him told me who he was. The voice was familiar. That hurt.

"Croyd?" My own voice was small and unused.

"Come on, let's get out of here."

Croyd changes every time he sleeps. Sometimes he wakes normal. Sometimes he wakes with powers, an ace. Sometimes . . . well, sometimes he tries to go back to sleep as quickly as he can. In this manifestation, he was the height I remembered from years before, medium tall. He had dark hair and eyes when I knew him, and a wedge of nose that was slightly left of center. I liked that nose. This Croyd was bald as an egg and his jaw boasted three days' worth of black and gray stubble. His eyes were pale in the harsh hospital light, but I knew him.

One of his arms seemed to be missing, though. No, not missing. Translucent. A ghost. I thought my drug-drenched brain was playing tricks.

"We can't get out, they'll stop us—"

"No they won't," he said. "I need your help, Zoe. I need you."

He was wrong; no one had needed me for a very long time.

"You knew where I was this whole time and didn't come visit?" It felt like so long since I'd talked at all.

"I didn't know. It was Needles, and he didn't tell me until—I don't have time to explain!"

"Needles?"

Croyd's translucent hand passed through the door, into the locking mechanism, which clicked back, and the door swung open. He unlocked the last two doors the same way. We passed a couple of orderlies, a couple of doctors. But Croyd was wearing a white lab coat. He had his solid arm around me, as if he was guiding a distraught patient back to her room. Smiled and waved at hospital officials. No one questioned him. People trust men in white lab coats. They shouldn't, but they do.

We walked out of the hospital. It felt like being reborn.

It was autumn—dark, raining. Croyd hustled me into a jeep and drove straight out of the city, then onto a path that zigged and zagged and tracked across wet dunes and through a marsh.

There was a boat, sleek and fast, with four seats and a lot of inboard motor, hidden in a stand of reeds. It was black and had too much gold striping on it, like a prized drag racer from some paint shop in Jersey. Its engine was loud in the quiet. Some ducks woke up and yelled at us.

I noticed Croyd didn't have a key. He used his translucent hand to reach into the ignition, to start the motor. He'd done the same with the jeep.

"Did you steal this?" I asked him. I'd missed a couple of doses of medication by now. I was starting to really wake up. "And the jeep?"

"Yeah." He shrugged.

There was enough light for me to get scared of what I might see if I could only see better. It came from some sort of reflection from the lake, a strange shade of brownish gray. Even now I can smell the living water, see swirls of mist and the white wake behind us, feel the splinters of rain jabbing my face. We went through dark stretches of open water and twisting paths through low stands of what I thought might be papyrus. I didn't know if papyrus was a thing of history or if I was looking at plain old bulrushes. Whatever they were, they were growing in shallow water. I tried not to think about what would happen if we hit a sandbar.

I grabbed for a handhold when Croyd hauled into a steep turn that lifted my side of the boat out of the water. He hit reverse and the boat crashed back to level and braked itself fast. We plowed through a stand of reeds and onto wet sand.

There was a hut. It seemed to be built of weathered gray boards. It had a tile roof that slanted back from a sort of porch. Water was pouring off a low spot in the roof and falling into a plastic barrel. A man came from beneath its shadow and ran toward us.

It was Needles. Needles, one of the kids I took care of in Jerusalem, but all grown up. He's a joker, with sharp claws for hands and teeth like baleen. He looks . . . different now. Well fed, fit.

"How is she?" Croyd demanded.

"Not good," Needles said. "Zoe. Hi."

"Hi," I replied wonderingly. One of them made it. At least one of them is alive.

Croyd hauled me out of the boat with his solid arm and I felt a faint tremor in his hand. Uh-oh. He'd been awake for too long. What a pair we were.

"Croyd. Why are we here?"

"Zoe. Zoe, I couldn't think of anyone else. She has to get help and she's so afraid." He grabbed me by one elbow and tugged me toward the hut.

She, I heard. We'd been lovers once, Croyd and I. We'd been through a lot. *She.* Damn him.

The slanted roof of the hut made the interior seem like the inside of a tent. It smelled clean. There was an oil lamp in one corner with a small, steady flame, scented with cassia and camwood, warm scents for a cold wet night. There was a sort of pallet bed on the wooden floor, its red-striped cotton covering squared off and carefully tucked in. A woman sat beside it, her feet tucked under her. Her arms were braced on the floor beside her, palms flat, to support the weight of a huge, painfully pregnant belly. Her eyes were closed tight and her fingers were puffy.

"Rima," Croyd whispered. "She's here. Zoe's here, the woman I told you about. She'll help."

She opened her eyes, the huge sloe eyes of a beauty from *One Thousand and One Nights*. She was in her twenties, perhaps. Her hair was hidden by a scarf of green threaded with gold. Her perfect amber skin was beaded with sweat.

"No one can help me," she said, in English. She clenched her jaw and held her breath, listening to something inside her that hurt. "But the baby? She can take the baby?"

"You, she'll help *you*."

At the time, I didn't know what that meant. Or I ignored what that meant.

Oh, dear God. We were in the middle of nowhere. Really nowhere. I'd seen no lights during the journey from shore to this place. The woman was in labor. I'd had an EMT course years ago, in another life. I'd seen videos of a delivery but I had never seen a live birth.

Needles stood like a statue at the doorway. Croyd stayed frozen where he was, crouched on the floor an arm's length away from the woman. She breathed again. When she did, he moved no closer and said nothing at all. I think it was terror.

Hospital was my first thought. *We have to get her to a hospital.* My vision was of sterile tiles and clever machines and brisk, efficient people in scrubs who delivered babies every day. The reality was that we were in muddy wilderness, a long way from any sign of the crowded, sprawling chaos that had been my experience of towns in the Mideast. We had a speedboat, and two men who looked ready to run like rabbits at any sudden noise. It was not a good time for me to lose it.

"What am I supposed to do?" I asked stupidly. I was coming out of the sedative haze. My head hurt. My stomach turned over. "I can't . . . I don't . . . I can't . . ."

Croyd said, "I thought . . . your power. You know. Maybe you can help things along. Like, move the baby out?"

I stared. "Croyd, that's stupid. My power only works on inanimate objects."

The woman, Rima, groaned.

"Please, Zoe."

I knelt by the woman. "When did the pains start?"

"Yesterday," Rima said.

I thought I knew that first babies take longer to get born, that labor for a first-time mother takes hours, even a whole day. I sincerely hoped I wasn't making that up. "How far apart are they?"

Rima gazed directly at me for the first time. She looked a little startled. "I don't know," she said.

"Let's time them, then."

"I have a watch," Needles said from the doorway. He held a finger above the face of his watch, ready to punch a button on it.

"One's starting now," Rima said. She pinched her lips tight together. Her nostrils flared.

"Breathe," I said. "Slow, deep breaths." It was tempting to hold my own breath until whatever this child, this woman, was feeling went away. But I knelt beside her and rubbed her shoulders.

We breathed.

"Tell me when it eases," I said.

Rima nodded.

Another breath. Another.

"Better," she said.

"Two minutes," Needles said.

Croyd finally approached and stroked Rima's forearm from elbow to wrist, a gentle touch, but he stayed where he was, at arm's length.

I looked at his translucent hand. "Maybe you could . . . with that hand . . . like you did with the lock."

He huffed a nervous laugh. "It only works on inanimate objects."

"Needles, keep your eye on that watch," I said. "We'll tell you when the next one starts."

He nodded and didn't look up at us.

"I'm thirsty," Rima said.

Croyd patted the back of her hand and got to his feet. "I'll get you some water," he said.

There were shelves along one wall, and a Coleman two-burner camp stove on a counter.

"How long would it take us to get to the nearest hospital?" I asked.

"Two hours at least, Zoe," Needles said. "There's a canal that leads to a little harbor. No hospital. Maybe there's a clinic there or something, but there's been fighting in the village. Some shelling. I don't know about tonight."

Croyd opened the cap on some bottled water and brought it back to us. Rima drank deeply and handed the bottle back.

"No. Tell her," she said to him.

"We can't go to a hospital. If her father . . . If any of her brothers or her father find her, they'll kill her," Croyd said.

Ritual murder, a tainted woman, a disgrace to the family. I knew that story. *Croyd, what have you done, and why?*

"We'll lie about her name," I said.

"It's starting again," Rima said.

"Four minutes since the last one," Needles said.

"I have to go outside." Rima grabbed a little sack from beside the bed. She clambered to her feet and beneath the hem of the white cotton layers of her dress, I saw them for the first time, her bare little swollen feet and chubby toes. Babies' little fat feet are pretty and healthy. Swollen feet on a pregnant woman can be an okay thing, but her ankles and her calves were swollen, too.

"I have to—"

The next word was in Arabic. I went with her to the porch.

She limped to the side of the house and squatted. I didn't know if a baby would fall out. I wanted to panic about that, but baby horses slid out on the ground, didn't they? And they lived through it. I supposed there was nothing to do if that happened other than pick it up. I was extremely scared, but I couldn't think of anything to animate that would help any of us. This would be a good time for an ace to show up and perform miracles. Didn't look like that was going to happen, and I seemed to be all this poor girl had to cling to, so I shoved the panic aside and tried to keep on thinking.

In the dark and the rain, she pushed, she pooped, and her water broke. The little package was some sort of sterile wipes, and Rima used them and managed to get to her feet. There was no baby on the ground, but her dress was soaked. She began to sob.

"Somebody bring me a towel!" I yelled.

Needles brought me one. I lifted Rima's skirts and dabbed her legs and we helped her walk inside.

I remember how warm the little hut felt after the cold wet air of the outside, how the scented lamp cast its faint golden light.

She was preeclamptic, but I didn't know that then. I didn't know what it meant. I got her out of her wet clothes and wrapped her in blankets. We shoved the bedding in the corner and I got Croyd to sit with his shoulders braced against it so Rima could lean back against him. I asked Needles to heat water, because it's traditional and because it kept his back to us, and I wanted some warm soapy water around for Rima and the baby. He brought water in from the barrel outside. Rima probably didn't want any men around, but as things got busier I don't think she cared.

That's how I saw it then. Now I think her indifference was an early stage of delirium.

I tried to distract her. "Tell me how you and Croyd met." *How you got into this predicament.* Between the two of them, I got the story. They traded off, corrected each other on little details. The way couples do.

Rima Naji was a student at Columbia. She wanted a master's degree when she finished her B.S. in sustainable development. Her family wanted her to come home to Port Said and marry the man they had chosen for her. She thought the prospective husband would turn down the match if she wasn't a virgin. She went into Jokertown to find someone who could make her inconvenient hymen go away. She found Croyd in a coffee shop, freshly wakened and eating a dozen donuts.

It was sweet, he said. She was fascinating, and exotic, and very bright, and she had a lovely laugh.

I have a clip of her that I've saved for Jorah, a Q&A after a C-SPAN lecture where she gave an opinion disguised as a question. She was articulate and persuasive. And she was beautiful. Her dark curly hair wasn't covered, not when she was a student in New York. I understood why Croyd fell for her. One thing led to another, and then to bed.

"She insisted," Croyd told me. "It wasn't until after, until a couple of weeks after that first night, that she told me why."

He had been her lover in a working city in a busy time, in a country at peace. I envied her that. When I remember the first time Croyd and I made love, I remember the fear that we did our best to escape in each other's arms, the hope that we'd make it to shore, the smell of seawater crashing over the decks, the growling thump of the engine. We were on a creaking ship in a Mediterranean storm. The blankets smelled of diesel.

"And then she was just gone. Poof. Gone." As Croyd tends to be once he can't fight off sleep anymore. "She told the guy at the coffee shop she was going to Toronto."

Rima murmured, "There was nothing you could do."

Holding her hand, he stared into the past. "When I woke up the next time . . . No, two times later; those two were bad wakeups. I tried to find her in Toronto, her name, where she lived, anything."

"I refused to go back to Egypt," she said. "So my father came himself and hauled me onto a plane."

Croyd said, "I got a message from a cop in Jokertown. He found me awake. She'd sent it weeks before. It said she needed help in Egypt."

He didn't say he was sorry he'd been asleep, or crazed, when she needed him. He knew I knew how life worked for him. There's no way out for him, no escape from the cycles.

"You found me," Rima said. Her smile was beautiful.

"I got a one-way ticket to Alexandria and gave this guy with a truck the name of the place she'd written down, and the next thing I knew he stopped at the side of the road by a lake." The corner of Croyd's mouth twisted in a sardonic smile. "Rima found *me*. When I saw her . . ."

Croyd had never looked at me the way he looked at Rima.

I think Rima didn't know she was pregnant when she left New York. When that news slipped, one way or the other, and she knew her father and her brothers knew and would kill her, as required for the honor of the family, someone gave her enough money to get away from Port Said.

It may have been her mom. She couldn't buy an airline ticket in her own name, so she went west to a place she knew from her childhood. The hut was abandoned, part of a research station at a bird sanctuary. A comfortable place for rich Alexandrians to wait until it was time to get in the duck blinds for a morning's sport. At least she and Croyd had found each other again.

Rima groaned. "I need to push."

I held her feet so she could brace against my hands. Croyd locked his arm in front of her chest like a bar for her to hold and whispered to her, little terms of endearment that I knew from long ago.

It went too fast. It was the first time I'd seen how huge a baby's head looks on its way out. Jorah's head was a sliver of gray bulge sliding forward with contractions and then retreating again, and each push made it larger. *This isn't going to work* was what I thought. This can't ever work; human babies are too big.

Needles brought a basin of warm soapy water and a pile of towels he'd found by rummaging in a cabinet. He sat down beside Rima and kept one supporting hand on Croyd's bicep. Needles rattled off some Arabic. Rima replied.

"She says she's trying to be brave," Needles said.

Croyd whispered something in her ear. The girl smiled and then clamped her jaw and pushed again. He tried not to tremble but he was truly wired, and I saw the effort he was making.

It's like kittens, I told myself. I've seen kittens born. Things get born and it's usually okay. There was black silky hair beneath the membrane that covered Jorah's head. That was a relief. It was a head coming out, not a gray monster. I guided Rima's hand down to feel it and she smiled. I picked up a towel and held it tight against her stretched vaginal skin. *Support the perineum,* that long-ago video had said. Something was going to tear, and Rima was bellowing, and Jorah's head slipped out, facing down, the back of his head on top, a little chin where I couldn't see it well, and membrane over it all. I wanted to get his nose free so he could breathe and his mother was no kitten; she couldn't reach down and tear the sac away with her teeth.

"Scissors?" I called out. "A knife? Something?"

Croyd rummaged in his pocket and brought out a folded pocketknife with a black-and-ivory handle. It looked like the 1950s to me. I got it open and let it fall into the soapy water. That would have to do for sterilization. Carefully made a hole in the membrane with the knife tip and pushed the cowl away from Jorah's face. I turned his head to the side a little and wiped his nose and mouth. He blinked and stared, as calm as a Buddha. I found myself smiling.

I could feel Rima's relief in the way her muscles relaxed, in the different rhythm of her breathing.

"The head's out," I said.

Rima tried to lean forward to see. The motion pushed the rest of Jorah out into my arms, wet and slick and purple, and I thought, *My God, he's dead.*

There's this thing about holding a baby by the heels and slapping him to make him breathe. *He's too slippery,* I thought. *I can't do that.*

Jorah opened his mouth, all gum and tongue, and sighed, and began to turn pink.

I lifted him onto Rima's remarkably deflated belly. She reached down and stroked his head, and everything was wonderful and my next obstacle was the umbilical cord. The video had stressed that you don't have to cut it first thing, that if you just left it where it was for a while, nothing bad would happen. But the damned cord was in my way and it looked as big as a garden hose.

Croyd stared at the baby wide-eyed. He looked completely dazed.

"It's a boy," Croyd said. Jorah was most definitely a boy, and since I'd never seen a baby boy's genitals at birth before, I was a little worried. They looked huge. Maternal hormones, I learned later, are the reason baby boys' genitals are so big, relatively speaking, at birth. And they were a nice healthy red, as was the rest of him.

I tied the cord, in two places, as tight as I could, with dental floss, and cut between the knots with the blade facing up. The texture of the cord was tough, much like a chicken's windpipe. Croyd kept a nice edge on his knife.

The baby was making sucking motions with his little mouth. I lifted him and Rima took him in her swollen hands. He found her nipple like an old pro, bless his heart, and I grabbed a towel to wipe him down a little, and then covered him with another one.

"Oof," Rima said when the baby began to suck. As it's supposed to do, the breast stimulation gave her one more contraction and the placenta slid out, a purple and red mushroom the size of a big seder plate with a long stem of cord. It smelled meaty, like a slightly warmed steak. I bundled it into a plastic sack, because the video I'd watched so long ago said to do that.

"Okay, guys," I said. "Go out and smoke cigars or something while we clean up."

They tromped out. The rain was heavier than it had been before I had stopped listening to anything except Rima's breathing between contractions and, later, the screams that she tried not to make.

"He's beautiful," Rima said.

He looked small to me, but I didn't know how big or little a newborn was supposed to be. Like a nat whose skin was covered with a splotchy layer of white cheese, but a standard human, not a variant. I finished giving Rima a bed bath and pulled the coverlet up to her shoulders.

"Take care of him," she whispered.

There was something wrong with her eyes. Glassy, staring, wrong. *Really* wrong. I leaned closer to look and got the baby out of her arms when the first convulsion began.

♠

Jonathan stared at her across the desk, his notepad sitting forgotten in front of him. "Croyd Crenson has a kid," he said bluntly. This was news. This was *huge*. The Sleeper, a kid. This was the cover of *Aces!*. The story of a former terrorist made good was okay, but one of New York's ace legends with a secret child—people loved stories about babies.

But this one wasn't finished yet. Zoe Harris looked at him with a kind of forced serenity. This was a woman who had killed people. Who had planned to kill more. If she wanted to kill Jonathan, she could, and he had a sudden thought—that was the only reason she was telling him her story, because she planned on killing him. Likely, she wouldn't be able to. Whatever she threw at him, Jonathan Hive could disintegrate into a cloud of bugs and flee. Sting her good on the way out, too.

"There's more," Harris said.

"Of course there is. This doesn't end well, does it?"

"It could have ended worse," she said calmly.

♦

Rima might have died even in a hospital. Eclampsia still kills women, despite the sterile and steel hospitals of the so-called first world. The hypertension may have caused an intracerebral bleed, and that's what killed her. I didn't know that then. I didn't know what had happened to her, the name of the disease that had killed her, or even, really, who she was.

"Rima?" Then, "Rima, Rima, no no no—"

The basin that the soapy water had been in flew, hit the ramshackle wall. Water sprayed behind it. A tin cup followed it. The baby cried, and I bent my head over him and tried to get myself under control. This was me, my stress and fear. My power, out of control. Croyd never should have smuggled me out of the hospital.

The door slammed open, Croyd and Needles storming back in. "Rima!" Croyd choked out and rushed to her bedside, but there was nothing he could do, nothing anyone could do.

"Zoe, it's okay. Calm down, Zoe. Please." Needles talked me down. Things stopped smashing into the wall. The weight of the baby in my arms anchored me.

The rain stopped. The hut was quiet. And Croyd murmured, "She's gone."

More quiet. For a long time. Croyd stayed frozen where he was, crouched over Rima, ready to brace her when the next seizure began. But there wasn't another one. At last, he sat back. He fumbled inside his jacket and I knew he was searching for pills before he brought out a bottle and chewed three of them. He always wants to stay awake as long as he can. Sleep for him means he'll wake as a different person—deuce, ace, or joker. Or he'll draw the black queen and be dead. He knows more about amphetamine psychosis than anyone should have to know.

I'd have thought he'd want to sleep, just then. I did.

"We should go," Needles said hoarsely. "Her family might still find her here. But if we leave now they won't follow us."

"We can't just leave her—"

"Yes, we can," Needles said.

"If nothing else, he'll need a bottle," I said. "Formula, diapers, surely there's something if there's no breast milk bank—a wet nurse, if we can find one."

"Croyd?" Needles pressed.

"Yeah, okay."

Too quickly, we were back in the speedboat, leaving the hut—and Rima—behind. Needles opened the throttle and the motor roared. We were in open water. Brushy little hummocks or islands broke its surface here and there. Rain tapped down on the canopy of the boat, on the surface of the lake. I thought there was a horizon ahead, a smudge of lighter sky at the edge of the dark watery world. The rich littoral smell of the water had changed. I smelled the sea.

"What do you think?" Needles asked after a time. "The village, or back to the jeep?"

Croyd jerked at the sound of Needles's voice and began turning his head to scan the water, first on one side of the boat and then the other.

The jeep meant a long drive back to Cairo. At the village . . . surely there'd be something there for the baby. Blankets. Milk.

"Village," I said.

"Okay," Needles said. "Village. Croyd, help me look out for the lights. Croyd?"

The man was huddled up in his seat, hugging himself, his stare vacant.

"I'll help," I said softly. "Croyd? Croyd. I need you to hold the baby. Your son, Croyd." It was the only thing I could think of to get Croyd to focus.

"What?"

"Here." I went to him and pressed the baby against his chest. His one substantial arm went around him automatically, balanced him on his lap. Croyd looked startled, but he took his son and held him close. Even with one arm. He fiddled with the wrappings and pried a tiny fist out into the air. So help me, he counted fingers, which seems to be one of the things people do. The baby grabbed Croyd's finger and held on tight. Croyd fished for feet, two, and assessed the number of toes. Five on each foot. I was counting, too.

The baby began to cry. Croyd wrapped his son's feet up again and patted his little back. He tried to rock him, in a jerky sort of way.

"Zoe? What do I do?"

"Put him inside your jacket, for starters. We don't want him cold."

"He's *wet*!"

He didn't mean rain. Oh. Diaper-change time. We didn't have any diapers and we were running low on dry cloth when we left the hut. "It'll have to wait."

"Jorah. She wanted to call him Jorah."

Needles steered around a hummock of reeds. The patch of lighter sky I had seen before was brighter now, beams of white light strobing in smoky dust. It wasn't dawn. It was the village, and something had gone terribly wrong there.

"This complicates things," Needles said. "Croyd. Whose boat is this?"

"I don't know," Croyd said. "I stole it. Berth seventeen."

Needles sighed. "Zoe, there should be some papers near where you're sitting. See if you can find the registration or something."

There was a clear plastic folder with papers in it in the glove compartment, or whatever it's called in a boat. The papers were in Arabic. Needles stopped the boat and took them from me, leaning over to read in the faint yellow glow from the battery compartment light. None of us had a torch, a flashlight.

Needles whistled through his baleen teeth. It's quite a sound.

"Okay," Needles said. "When we get to shore I'll do the talking. Pretend you don't understand a word I'm saying."

I remembered a little Arabic from my time in Jerusalem. Croyd? He might or might not speak it. *Look like you don't belong here and we might live through this,* Needles meant. Right. Got it.

The baby began to fuss. Croyd passed him back to me. "I can't," he said.

"What?"

"I'm sorry. I can't do this. Rima knew I couldn't do this, but you . . . I'm sorry." He looked at Needles and me, took one last look at the baby, then rolled over the side of the boat, into the water.

"Croyd!" I yelled. Needles kept driving the boat. As if he had expected this.

I wasn't worried that Croyd would get hurt, or that he wouldn't be okay. Croyd was always okay. But if there is one thing Croyd Crenson can't ever be, it's a father. He can't stay in one place. He can't hold a job. Some of the jokers he's been are monsters who could not in any way cook a meal, hold a child, even throw a ball to a kid or catch one with whatever flippers or tentacles that version of him happens to have. And Croyd has to be on the run from time to time. He's good at hiding when he has to, and sometimes no one knows where to find him.

"We can do this," Needles said. "It'll be fine." Last time I saw him he'd been a teenager. Now here he was, taking charge. Taking care of us.

I let the baby suck on my knuckle. He had a strong suck and that surprised me. He seemed really hungry. I thought babies needed to get calories every couple of hours or they'd starve. He'd die, too, like his mother. I'd never felt more helpless.

Jorah fell asleep again.

Newborns really don't need to eat for the first twenty-four hours. I didn't know that then.

Needles steered the boat up to the weathered boards of a slip. Strobing torches blinded us, and uniformed men with guns stood on the jetty. They looked as big as giants, looming above us. The charred remains of a town lined the shore. A breeze came off the salt harbor and kept most of the stink of destruction to the land side of us.

I was suddenly glad we'd left Rima's body at the hut.

It's been eleven years since Needles climbed out on that sagging pier to a face-off with the local authorities. I huddled in the boat with Jorah inside my jacket. Needles didn't outrank Magdi Shenouda, the Alexandrian official on the dock, but he could match him in rapid and adversarial chatter mingled with effusive praise and many honorifics. There was much shouting. Needles pointed to the boat. More discussion. They walked a few steps away and then Needles came back and reached down to help me out of the boat.

"He wants to see the baby," Needles said.

As ordered, I climbed out and got the baby out of my jacket.

"It's a boy," Needles said. "Unwrap him, Zoe."

It had stopped raining. Shenouda stepped closer while I demonstrated Jorah's undoubted boy-ness to the cold wet air. Jorah squirmed and gave an outraged yell or two. Shenouda smiled and chucked Jorah under the chin. I wrapped Jorah up again.

I saw a wad of cash pass from Needle's spiny hand to Shenouda's. Then it disappeared.

"Congratulations on the birth of your son, madame," Magdi Shenouda said. "I fear there will be no papers regarding the kind return of my friend's stolen speedboat or your accouchement. The chaos of war. I'm sure you understand."

I don't know how things would have gone if the baby had been a girl. Or a joker. No matter. Jorah Harris is a de facto French citizen because Magdi Shenouda was a decent man. They do exist. Another factor in our survival may have been that if there was one thing he didn't need that morning, it was more bodies to deal with.

There were body bags lined up on the beach. I'm sure Rima's body became one of them, eventually, but I've never heard about it.

After that, Needles somehow found us an ancient farm truck, and drove us out of the war zone.

"Needles, where did you get that money?"

The truck rattled, its decrepit engine thunking along. "Croyd gave it to me. It's like he knew. He knew, Zoe." Crying, Needles wiped his nose on the shoulder of his shirt. "There's enough to get you to . . . well. To wherever. Both of you." He nodded to the baby in my arms. Jorah.

They never even asked. They just knew I would take care of him.

Not every memory is ugly. The fields of Egypt are tended and lovely and flat, and the sunrise that morning was beautiful, pinks and purples and touches of gold burning away the mist. A falcon, the sign of Ra-Horus returning with light and life, flew by on his way to the waking lake.

"France," I said. "We'll go to France."

The mythology is that ten good men are required to keep the world from destruction. I had a second chance. I had survived madness. I wanted to do more. I wanted to get ten people out of living hell and into a place where they could live and thrive.

I wanted to raise Jorah to be a good man.

It took years. I got a little start-up business going with Croyd's money. I hired locals in the first years and made them part of the business. They got a share of the profits. Greed is a great motivator. When Zephyr became known as a good place to work, I went looking for my special ten, nats and jokers with talent and the ability to work and histories that read like horror porn. A half-Asian woman and her husband, who had built and owned a rice-paper factory in Free Vietnam before Tom Weathers went totally psychotic and left for Africa. A former lay sister and her bastard son, driven out of Tanzania. Her brothers later became child soldiers and then, very soon, dead child soldiers. An attorney from Nairobi, who was born in some unpronounceable hamlet on the Congo before it became a river of death. My dear Tarek—you met him when you arrived. You know he has a degree in chemical engineering? Gadi, his wife. Amanda Ann, always both names, from N'allins, US of A. She has a lovely drawl. Mateus and Victor, a couple from Brazil.

And I have a son.

Croyd does what he can. He sends money when he has some. He comes from time to time, to Zephyr, to see his son. Jorah knows who his father is, and that he can't be here very often. I think he knows more about Croyd than he's willing to tell me yet, because Google. They seem to have a bond, Croyd and Jorah, when they get together, and the different versions don't seem to bother my son at all.

I don't know if Croyd looked like Jorah at any point in his life, but the boy Croyd may have looked something like this before the virus changed him for the first time. There's something about Jorah's voice . . . Their voices are similar in some ways, and there's something silky and dark in Croyd's voice that seems to hold through the transformations he goes through.

I'm a murderer and a fool. I regret many things. I fell in love once, and I don't regret that. While my son lives, I will keep on living. That's all I can promise myself, ever.

♥

Jonathan Tipton-Clarke sat for a moment, trying to take it in, playing it as a movie in his mind—it would make a pretty good movie. He might even suggest to Zoe Harris that she write a memoir of the whole thing. If, you know, her life story weren't tied to the Twisted Fists and littered with bodies. If she didn't have a kid to take care of.

And Croyd Crenson's son. As Harris had said, the Sleeper was great at hiding. There were a lot of people who wanted him dead, who might settle for hurting his kid.

"I—I can't publish this story," he said. "That's why you told it to me. You knew I wouldn't jump on it."

Smiling serenely, she glanced down at the surface of her desk, her hands flattened on it. Contemplating the blood on them, maybe. Or maybe admiring how clean they looked these days.

"Was it enough?" he asked. He might not be able to publish the story, but he was still going to push. In fact, not publishing the story gave him even more reason to push. "Has all of this been enough to clear the slate? To get yourself some of that redemption?"

"That's not for me to decide," she said softly.

"And . . . where is Jorah now?" he asked.

"He's at school. I'm sorry you won't get to meet him."

He didn't think she was sorry at all. In fact, he was pretty sure she'd planned this to keep the reprobate journalist away from her kid.

She moved the mouse, tapped a couple of commands, and then turned the monitor around to show him a snapshot. She had it set as her computer's desktop image: Zoe Harris, mid-laugh, hugging a child of eleven or twelve, a boy in a school uniform, sweater vest and charcoal trousers. He was also laughing, hugging her back with gangly pre-adolescent limbs. Jonathan guessed that Jorah more resembled his mother: He had thick dark hair in an untamed flop over his forehead, light brown skin and fine features. No one knew what Croyd Crenson really looked like. Probably not even Croyd himself. But hey, there was a project—Croyd had grown up in New York City. There had to be a school picture somewhere. Maybe he could find it. Send it along to Zoe and Jorah.

"Nice kid," Jonathan said, and meant it.

"Thank you." The woman in the picture seemed completely different from the poised, precise executive sitting in front of him. He suspected Jorah was really the only person who ever got to see the other Zoe Harris. "Well, Mr. Tipton-Clarke, I shouldn't take up any more of your time."

And there it was, the pointed exit. The part of the script where he walked out the door and tried to figure out what to do with this secret he'd been given.

Nothing. He'd do nothing with it.

"Thank you for your time, Ms. Harris."

She still didn't offer a hand for shaking. "I'm sorry you came all this way and won't have anything to show for it."

"No, you're not. But hey, I got to spend a week in the south of France."

"I'll have Tarek show you out." She reached for a phone, presumably to call the man. One of Harris's ten good men.

He was about to insist that he could find his way out, but was clever enough to realize that it wasn't about him finding his way out but about making sure he *left*. "How about this? How about I interview Tarek about what it's like to have a degree in chemical engineering and work at a perfume lab." He'd get his puff piece, dammit. "A guy who benefited from the generosity of a good person."

Ms. Harris smiled. "I would read that story, Mr. Tipton-Clarke."

♠ ♥ ♦ ♣

Berlin Is Never Berlin

by Marko Kloos

THE PLANE WAS ONLY three hours into its flight when Khan was entertaining the thought of a massacre for the first time.

The surroundings were posh, and it was easily the most comfortable air travel he had ever enjoyed. Sal Scuderi's private jet had the full executive luxury package, and the club seating in the Lear was so roomy that even Khan, all six foot three and three hundred pounds, could stretch his legs a little. There was a bar stocked with premium liquor, and he didn't even have to pour his own drinks because they had a flight attendant on staff. The surroundings were more than fine. It was the company that triggered homicidal thoughts in Khan before they had even made it out over the Atlantic Ocean.

Natalie Scuderi, Sal's daughter and Khan's protectee for the week, traveled with an entourage. There were only three friends, but Khan suspected that she had picked her friends after a long and thorough vetting process to find the vapidest rich kids in the country. They had started with the champagne right before takeoff. Five minutes after wheels-up, they had commandeered the impressively loud luxury entertainment system in the cabin and started listening to Top 40 shit at high volume. It was a seven-hour flight to Iceland and then another three-hour hop to Berlin from there, and Natalie's entourage seemed determined to party all the way through the trip.

A simple job, Khan thought as he watched the scene from the front of the plane, where he had a spot to himself next to the bar. Babysitting a bunch of spoiled kids. *Easy money.*

The center of the cabin had a four-seat club arrangement and a leather couch, and Natalie's friends were all piled on the couch, glasses in their hands, talking loudly over the music and giving Khan a headache. Natalie herself was sitting in the back of the plane, in the single seat next to the bathroom. She was wearing headphones the size of canned hams on her head, and she was typing away on the computer she had propped on the little tray table in front of her.

Sal Scuderi was a high-risk insurance salesman and one of the main money-laundering outlets for the Chicago mob. His daughter dabbled in acting and singing, but as far as Khan could tell, she was mostly famous for being famous. They were on the way to Berlin, where Natalie was booked for introducing a new fashion line and opening a nightclub. Having a joker-ace as a bodyguard conveyed a certain image, and plenty of entertainment industry celebrities were willing to shell out money just to rent that image for a night or a long weekend out on the club circuit. Khan didn't mind those jobs—they were all easy money, just hanging out in clubs and looking mean for the cameras. But even milk run jobs had their hazards, and one of them was a migraine headache. He spent some time extending and retracting the claws of his tiger hand a few times while looking pointedly at the big-screen TV on the bulkhead above the couch, and someone turned down the volume a little. Just to make sure it stuck, he got out of his seat and walked to the bathroom at the back of the cabin. When he was between the couch and the giant TV, he took the remote and clicked the volume down a few more notches for good measure.

When he emerged from the bathroom, Natalie Scuderi had taken off her headphones and closed the lid on her laptop.

"How do you like the ride?"

Khan closed the door behind him and shrugged. "Beats the hell out of flying coach," he replied.

"I've never flown coach." The way she said it wasn't boastful, just a statement of fact.

"Count yourself blessed."

Khan noticed that Natalie's gaze flicked from one side of his face to the other, and he knew that she was looking at the tiger half without being too obvious about it. Khan's left body half was that of a Bengal tiger, and the demarcation line between man and cat went right down the centerline of his body. For a mob bodyguard, the tiger half paid many dividends. It gave him the strength, reflexes, senses, teeth, and claws of a tiger, and it made him look dangerous and imposing. Not even the roughest or most drunken blockheads wanted to test their mettle against a guy who was half apex predator. Claws and teeth had a way of triggering people's primal fears.

Travis, Eli, and Melissa—Natalie's friends—had been in such awe of Khan that none of them had even tried to make small talk with him. Now that he was standing next to Natalie and talking to her, someone had decided that he wasn't going to tear off any heads on the spot. Melissa got up from the couch and sauntered over, champagne glass in hand.

"Hey, can I ask you something?"

"Sure," Khan said.

She gestured at the line that bisected his face, fur on one side and skin on the other. He had grown out a beard to match the fur fringe on the tiger half of his jaw, to keep his looks symmetrical.

"Does that go, like, *all* the way down your body? Right down the middle?"

She tried to make it sound light and casual, but he knew what she was trying to ask because he had gotten the same question hundreds of times. Under normal circumstances, he would have given her a clever or flirty reply, like *You'll have to buy me drinks first to find out*. But she wasn't a paying client, and her gaggle of friends had been annoying Khan too much for him to tolerate a personal question like that.

"That's none of your business," he said. "Buzz off."

The girl beat a hasty retreat to the lounge area. Next to Khan, Natalie chuckled and opened her laptop again.

"Now she won't talk to you again for the rest of the trip."

"That is fine with me," Khan replied. "She doesn't have to talk to me. She just needs to listen when I tell her to do stuff."

Back on the couch, Natalie's chastened friend shot Khan a glare. Then she picked up the TV remote and turned the volume up again.

This is going to be a long fucking week, Khan thought.

♣

There was always some security bullshit involved when a joker-ace like Khan traveled by air, but it was increased by a few orders of magnitude when international borders were involved. Scuderi's private plane meant that Khan hadn't had to suffer the enhanced screening before their departure in Chicago, but the Germans weren't going to let him skip a damned thing. He'd had to file his plans in advance, and when the Lear stopped at the private terminal at Berlin's shiny new Brandenburg Airport, there was a welcoming committee waiting for him at customs and immigration.

"What is the purpose of your visit?" the customs officer asked when he checked Khan's passport.

"Business," Khan said. "I'm a bodyguard. My client is going through your no-hassle line over there right now."

"Are you bringing any weapons into the country at this time?"

"No weapons," Khan replied. He knew they'd go through his luggage anyway and check thoroughly. He carried a gun back home when he was working—no point disadvantaging yourself in a fight—but when he traveled out of the country, he didn't pack so much as a nail file. Foreign cops got twitchy enough when they saw the teeth and claws, and if they hadn't been firmly attached to him, he was sure they'd have made him leave those at home as well.

"Very well," the officer said. "In accordance with laws and regulations regarding the admission of foreign persons with enhanced abilities, I have to ask you to follow my colleague back to the room for your entry screening. You can choose to decline, but in that case you will be denied entry into the Federal Republic."

"Lead the way," Khan grumbled. The world had had seventy years to get used to jokers and aces, and they still got civil rights parceled out to them like the nats were giving them treats for good behavior. Khan wasn't the type for political activism, but something in him bristled at having to ask permission to come and go from some pencil-necked bureaucrats when everyone in the room would already be cut into bloody ribbons if he had violence on his mind. The security kabuki existed to make the nats feel safer, and they knew that as well as he did.

The inspection was Teutonically thorough. They made him strip down to his underwear, snapped pictures of him with a sophisticated spatial camera array mounted on the wall of the screening room, and took prints and iris scans.

"You sure you don't want to put a tracking bracelet on me?" he asked when they rolled his tiger hand over the electronic print scanner—once with claws retracted, once with them extended.

"We only use those for certain criminal offenders," the police officer taking his print said, mild pique in his voice. "You are not an offender."

Could have fooled me, Khan thought, but he decided to keep it to himself. Customs and border police everywhere had a low tolerance threshold for humor and sarcasm.

The circus started almost right after Natalie's entourage left the private aviation terminal. They had transportation waiting outside, two big Mercedes limousines. There was a small crowd of fans and photographers by the exit, snapping pictures with cameras and phones and yelling Natalie's artist name excitedly when they spotted her. Natalie went by the mononym "Rikki," which sounded like the annoying call of an exotic bird when it was shouted by dozens of people at high volume.

Khan stepped ahead of Natalie and walked between her and the bulk of the crowd. When they all caught sight of him, there were some audible gasps. He put on his most humorless face and rasped a low growl when the front rank of excited fans came a little too close for comfort. None of them dared to come within an arm's length, and he ushered Natalie to one of the waiting limousines. As she climbed into the backseat, he stood guard and looked around. The situation was innocuous enough, a bunch of teenage kids squealing and taking pictures, but something made the hairs on the back of Khan's neck stand up a little.

Over in the group of paparazzi standing twenty feet away, there were two guys who Khan thought didn't quite act right. They weren't shouting at him or Natalie's entourage to pose for shots like the rest of them. They weren't even particularly engaged in taking photos, and when they did, they seemed to focus on him rather than the celebrity he was guarding. When they noticed his attention, they shifted their lenses and snapped shots of Natalie through the car window like the rest of them. Khan tried to get their scents, but this place was full of new and unfamiliar smells, there were ten or fifteen people between him and the two not-quite-right photographers, and his group had almost finished entering the cars. Khan held out an arm to keep one of Natalie's friends from getting into the front passenger seat.

"That's my spot," he told him. "You ride in the back or in the other car."

The kid moved off to the second waiting car. Khan closed the rear passenger door and lowered himself into the front seat next to the driver. He made sure to keep eye contact with the two fishy photographers, just so they'd be aware they had been noticed.

I don't know who you are, but I see you, he thought. As they rolled off past the squealing crowd of fans, one of the photographers lowered his camera, pointed a finger, and cocked his thumb like the hammer of a gun.

Pow.

♠

Khan's tiger half didn't sweat. This was something that he hadn't known about canines and felines before his card had turned. Cats and dogs shed excess heat through panting, and through the pads on their paws. If he dressed to keep his tiger side cool, his human side was too cold, and if he dressed to keep his human half warm, his tiger half was too well insulated. Finding a happy medium was difficult even on temperate days. In the middle of a nightclub, the heat from hundreds of bodies contesting with the building's inadequate air-conditioning, it was downright impossible. Half an hour after the start of Natalie's first engagement in Berlin, Khan's button-down was soaked in sweat. He was standing close to his charge, shielding access to the booth where she was holding court with her entourage, while the crowd was mingling and hopping around on the floor to relentless Europop tunes.

The new nightclub was ostentatiously exclusive. All the patrons wore designer clothes and expensive watches, and Khan was sure that the cocaine being done in the bathrooms was high-grade stuff. He wasn't much into pop culture these days, but even he recognized some of the celebrities lounging in the booths that surrounded the dance floor. One of the nearby booths held a group that was even more conspicuous than Natalie and her entourage. In the center of it was a playboy princeling from the one of the oil-rich Gulf states that had been swallowed up by the Caliphate, someone whose face was featured in the tabloids on a regular basis. He was tan and toned, with a thousand-dollar pair of sunglasses on his face and a Swiss watch on his wrist that was worth more than Khan's car. Khan watched him trying to get Natalie's attention for a little while. Finally, the princeling got out of his booth and walked over to Natalie's corner, two bodyguards in dark suits immediately trailing three feet behind and on either side of him.

"Hold up there, sport," Khan said and held out an arm to bar the way into the booth. The princeling looked at him with an irritated expression. He turned toward his bodyguards and said something that made them laugh, and Khan let out a slow breath and flexed his muscles to get ready for a tussle.

"It's okay," Natalie shouted from behind. "You can let him in. Only him, though."

"You heard the lady," Khan said to the princeling, who still regarded him like he was something rotting the dogs had dragged in. The princeling waved his hand curtly over his shoulder without turning around, and his bodyguards took a step back.

The princeling squeezed past Khan and sat down in the booth with Natalie's group. For a while, they talked and drank together; Khan tried to ignore the insipid conversation while the princeling's bodyguards tried to ignore him. Like their boss, they wore their sunglasses inside, which made them look like jackasses.

Khan smelled the trouble flaring up at the moment it started behind him, that unmistakable whiff of adrenaline and high emotions right before a fight breaks out. He started to turn around just as some liquid splashed the back of his neck and the tiger side of his face. One of the girls had voiced her anger at the princeling and emptied a drink in his direction, and some of the splash had hit Khan instead. From the way the prince's hand recoiled from Natalie's friend Melissa, Khan could guess the reason for the sharp and sudden outrage. And then, almost reflexively, the princeling slapped Melissa. The strike was hard enough to make her head rock back. Blood came gushing from her nose, and the metallic smell of it permeated the air.

Next to Khan, one of the princeling's bodyguards caught on to the action and tried to wedge himself past Khan and between Melissa and the princeling. Khan yanked him by the collar of his suit and tossed him away from the booth and onto the dance floor, where he fell on his ass with a yelp and skidded backward a foot or two.

Behind Khan, the second bodyguard let out a curse in his own language and reached underneath his suit coat. Khan seized the hand holding the pistol with his tiger hand and wrapped his fingers firmly around the wrist of the other man. The second bodyguard dropped the gun with a strangled yelp. Khan caught it with his human hand before it could hit the floor.

"No guns," he growled.

The pistol was one of the new lightweight European cop guns, with a frame made of reinforced polymer. He let go of the bodyguard's wrist, transferred the gun to his tiger hand, and crushed it right in front of the man's face. The frame buckled in his fist and then started spilling little metal tabs and springs from its insides. Khan hit the other man in the face with the barrel assembly. He shook the plastic bits of the frame to the floor and flung the broken gun parts aside as the second bodyguard dropped to the floor.

With Khan blocking the exit of the booth, the princeling scrambled over the back of the seating corner to get away. Khan took two long steps and hauled him up by the back of his shirt. The princeling yelped as Khan spun him around and tossed him onto the seat. Then he wrapped his tiger hand around the princeling's neck and extended his claws just a little, enough to let the man know that hasty movements were now unwise. Khan smelled fear coming from him in big olfactory waves, and his heart was racing. It felt like holding a panicked rabbit by the ears. Next to them, Natalie's entourage was in a headless, noisy panic, trying to stay out of Khan's way and tend to Melissa at the same time.

"Touch them again, and I'll rip your head off, you little chickenshit," Khan said to the wild-eyed princeling. He finished the statement with a low, rasping growl and was rewarded with the smell of fresh piss wafting up from below the man's waistline. Natalie's friends were annoying as hell, but they were *his* charges, and men who hit women ranked lower on Khan's vermin scale than plague-carrying sewer rats.

He lifted the princeling off his feet and threw him toward the first bodyguard, who was still sitting on the floor and dusting off his dignity. The two men collided hard and went down in a tangle of limbs.

Khan closed a hand around Natalie's arm and pulled her to her feet.

"We have to go," he said. "Right now."

He was glad to see that Natalie seemed too shaken to argue, because he didn't want to have to carry her out of the place like a sack of playground sand. Her retinue rushed to follow when they saw that Khan wasn't stopping to wait, and they hurried across the dance floor toward the exit.

They were halfway across the floor when the doors of the nightclub opened and half a dozen angry-looking guys in suits pushed their way into the crowd. All of them were wearing earpieces and grim expressions. The crowd around the periphery of the dance floor was densely packed, and the newcomers were pushing people aside with force as they came through. Khan turned and looked around for the fire exits. Things were about to get complicated, and Khan didn't want to wait around to see whose side the cops would take.

There was a bouncer stationed at the fire exit. He stepped in front of Khan and his group as they approached the door and held up his hand in the universal "hold it" gesture. Khan wasted no time trying to figure out language commonalities. He grabbed the bouncer by the wrist of his outstretched hand and yanked him aside. The bouncer stumbled and went to one knee with an indignant yelp. Then he got back to his feet and lunged at Khan, who stopped him cold by raising his tiger hand and extending his claws in front of the man's face.

"Don't," Khan snarled.

The bouncer blanched and backed off. Khan pushed the exit open, and the fire alarm started blaring instantly. The noise felt like a physical thing assaulting his ears despite the earbuds that kept the volume to tolerable levels for Khan, and once they were out in the cooler evening air of the street and the decibel level subsided a little, he almost sighed with relief. Behind them, the bouncer appeared in the door and yelled something in angry German, but made no move to follow them.

God, I fucking hate nightclubs, Khan thought.

◆

Outside, Khan led the group away from the nightclub's back entrance, which proved to be a more difficult task than putting the princeling's bodyguards on their asses. Natalie was surprisingly helpful and collected. She was propping up Melissa and holding a wad of tissues underneath the other girl's nose. Melissa and the two boys, however, acted like they had just survived a flaming plane crash. After the tenth high-pitched "Oh my *God!*" in fifty meters, Khan lost his patience.

"Would you shut *up*," he told them. "She got slapped in the face, not shot in the head. Now move your asses before someone sends those cops after us."

"He broke my fucking *nose!*" Melissa wailed, her exclamation only slightly muffled by the tissues Natalie was pressing against her face to catch the blood.

"We'll have the front desk at the hotel call an ambulance," Natalie offered. Melissa glared at Khan, but kept pace with the group.

Khan never used valet services. He had parked their rented luxury SUV in a garage half a block away from the nightclub. He rushed his charges to the garage as fast as he felt they could go without having to carry Melissa, who was still acting like someone had cut off half her face. The club was in a hip part of the city, and the sidewalks were still busy with foot traffic, but most people gave Khan and his group a wide berth.

He led everyone up the staircase onto the rooftop parking deck and had them get into their SUV. When it was Melissa's turn to board, he held her back and turned her to face him.

"Let me see that nose," he said. She grimaced and lowered the tissue wad she had been pressing against her nose for the last five minutes. The tissue had some red splotches on it, but the trickle of blood coming from her nostrils had already stopped. Khan had seen a lot of busted noses over the years, and hers was as straight as it had been on the plane yesterday.

"That's not broken," he told her. "He just gave you a little nosebleed, that's all. Now let's get out of here."

The parking garage had three levels, with a ramp setup that required Khan to make a full circumnavigation of every deck before descending to the one below it. It was all ninety-degree turns, and the traffic lanes were narrower than the ones in American parking garages, so Khan had to take extra care every time he took a turn with the big seven-seat SUV they had rented. Back home, the size of it would have been nothing out of the ordinary, but over here, it felt like he was driving a monster truck.

He was making yet another right-hand turn at the end of a downward ramp when he saw headlights coming at them from the right. The strike was perfectly timed. Even with his reflexes, he had no chance to react and get the SUV out of the way of the other car, which had been shielded from his view by the concrete wall to the right of the ramp. Before he could even yell a warning, the other car plowed into their SUV. It struck the front of the car and caved in the passenger door. Khan felt the SUV lurching to the left with the force of the impact. To their left, the wall of the garage's lower level wasn't far away, and the driver's side of the SUV slammed into it with the dull crunch of metal on concrete. Behind Khan, Natalie and her entourage shrieked in unison.

The look of tense concentration on the face of the other driver told Khan that this was an ambush, not an accident. The SUV was pinned in a sideways vise between the wall and the front of the other car. To his left, the concrete wall kept Khan from opening his door, and to his right, the other car's bumper had dented in the passenger-side door.

"Get down," he shouted at Melissa and her crew. Then he made a fist with his tiger hand and punched out the spiderwebbed windshield of the SUV. Khan sliced his seatbelt in half with one claw and climbed out onto the hood.

A second car pulled up behind the one that had rammed them into the wall and came to a stop with squealing tires. All the doors seemed to open at once, and several people came rushing around the first car and toward the SUV. Khan leapt over the hood of the car that had rammed them and placed himself in front of the right rear passenger door of the SUV. Someone in the SUV tried to open the door from the inside, and he pushed it shut again.

"Stay there," he shouted through the glass. "Call the cops. Number's one-one-zero."

He figured they'd send their biggest bruiser against him first, and the attackers did not disappoint. The guy who lunged at him was clearly a wild card. He was easily as tall as Khan and looked half again as heavy, with arms that were as wide around as Khan's thighs. His face was dark gray, the skin ashen and rough like the bark on an ancient tree. Khan dodged a massive gnarled fist and raked his claws across the man's side. It felt like taking a swipe at the trunk of a Pacific redwood. Then Tree Guy swung his arm around and caught Khan in a backhand that sent him flying over the hood of the attackers' car. He tumbled across the dirty concrete of the garage deck and crashed into a parked car, taking out a taillight in the process. Khan scrambled back to his feet. His right arm felt like it had been smacked with a railroad tie.

In front of him, Tree Guy hooked one of his huge hands underneath the wheel well of the car Khan had sailed over. Then he lifted the car off its front wheels and pushed it out of his way in a motion that almost looked casual. His companions seemed content with letting Tree Guy do the heavy lifting of the fight. They were all over the rental car now. One of them yanked on the handle of the one door that was undamaged and reachable. When the door didn't open, he flicked open a collapsible steel baton and swung it at the window, which cracked into a spiderweb on the first blow. Tree Guy wedged himself through the gap he had created between the cars and walked toward Khan with heavy, unhurried steps.

Khan extended his tiger arm to one side and let his claws pop out with a flick of his wrist. The flick wasn't a necessity, but it always made him feel like he was getting ready for serious business, like pushing the button on a switchblade. Usually, even the big mob bruisers flinched at the sight of Khan's curved three-inch claws, but Tree Guy's expression didn't change a bit. Khan bellowed a roar, and one of the nearby parked cars started bleating its alarm as if in fearful protest.

So you're strong but slow, Khan thought. *I can work around that.*

His right arm was out of commission, but his legs still worked fine. Khan tensed his muscles and leapt sideways just as Tree Guy was about to reach him. He landed on the hood of the wailing car fifteen feet away, then pushed himself off for another leap toward the rental. The unknown goons had succeeded in smashing the rear passenger door's window. Khan landed on three of his four extremities right behind the two men who were now fumbling to get the door open. He grabbed one of them by the collar of his shirt and yanked him away from the car as hard as he could. The man flew backward with a yelp, arms flailing.

The other man was still holding the baton he had used to smash the window. He barked an obvious obscenity in some Slavic language—Russian, or maybe Ukrainian—and lashed out with the baton. Khan had expected a swing, and the straight jab aimed at his chest took him by surprise. Even with his reflexes, he barely managed to deflect the jab, his claws clicking against the hard steel of the baton. The other man didn't drop the weapon. Instead, he pulled it back and brought it down on Khan's hand. The pain shot all the way from his hand up to his elbow, and Khan roared again. He made a fist and drove it into the other man's face as hard as he could. Baton Guy's head rocked back and smacked into the doorframe of the rental car, and he went down hard and dropped to the ground with a muffled thudding sound. His baton dropped from his hand and clattered away on the concrete.

Khan sensed the blow aimed at him from behind and ducked out of the way just in time. Tree Guy's arm barely missed the top of his head, whistling by so close that it ruffled his hair. Then the swing landed against the upper frame of the car door and crunched into it hard enough to rock the vehicle on its suspension and dent the roof in by half a foot.

Tackling Tree Guy was only marginally less futile than swiping at him. Khan went low and put all his body weight into the move, three hundred pounds of enhanced feline strength, but he only managed to rock him back on his heels. Tree Guy's right arm came down, and Khan aborted his tackling attempt and rolled out of the way to avoid getting his spine pulverized. The last goon still standing decided to join the fray. He came around the back of the attackers' car and closed in on Khan.

"He is stronger than you. You will not beat him," the goon said in heavily accented English. Khan saw that he was holding a knife.

"Don't have to beat him," Khan snarled. "Just you."

Tree Guy was almost upon him again, so Khan advanced against the last goon, who widened his stance a little and planted his feet. The utter lack of fear or concern from these men was a little unnerving. At home, nine out of ten bush league crooks would turn tail and run at the sight of his claws and teeth, and these guys stood their ground against him in a hand-to-hand melee, armed with nothing but blades and impact weapons so far. They had to be supremely stupid or very sure of themselves.

With the blade in the game, Khan felt free to bring his own cutlery into play. The goon feigned a jab with his left, and Khan obliged the ruse by raising his tiger arm to protect his face. When the man's other hand flashed forward to plant the blade between his ribs, Khan brought his arm back down in a short and swift arc that was perfectly timed. The knife bounced to the ground, along with two or three of the goon's fingers, and the blow forced him to one knee.

Nearby, the sound of distant police sirens reached Khan's ears. He allowed himself a small grin. Another minute, and the German cops would be all over this parking garage.

Two rock-hard, unyielding hands grabbed him by the fabric of his jacket collar and the waistband of his slacks. He flung the elbow of his good arm backward in an arc and smashed it into Tree Guy's head, but to no effect. His feet left the ground as Tree Guy lifted him up. Khan felt like a kitten someone was shaking by the scruff. Tree Guy lifted him over his head seemingly without effort. Then Khan was airborne. He tumbled in midair, trying to roll around to land on his feet, but the boost he had just gotten was so violently forceful and sudden that even his cat reflexes failed him this time. He sailed over a long row of cars and smashed into the side of a minivan, and the impact knocked all the breath out of him.

When he came to a rest on the glass-strewn garage deck, all his body's warning lights seemed to be going off in his brain at once. He rasped a cough and tasted blood. The car alarms and the police sirens were still blaring, but everything sounded distant now, weak and faded, as if he had stuffed his ears with cotton balls. He tried to draw in a deep breath and muster the will to get up again, but the excruciating pain shooting through his chest made him abandon that impulse. People were shouting somewhere nearby, but he couldn't make out the words. Somewhere in the noise, Khan thought he heard Natalie's voice. Then there was the sound of slamming car doors and squealing tires. He tried to will himself to get to his feet, but his body refused to obey. When darkness finally washed over his consciousness, it felt almost comforting.

♥

Khan woke up to the scent of alcohol and the sharp pain of something piercing the skin of his left arm. He tried to jerk the arm away from the source of the pain, but found that he couldn't move it. When he opened his eyes, he saw that he was strapped down on a gurney, and a medic in an orange uniform was trying to insert a needle into his arm. The medic pulled the needle back when he saw Khan move and said something in German.

"Don't speak the language," Khan mumbled. His arm still hurt like hell, but it no longer felt like it had been worked over with a sledgehammer. He hadn't lost consciousness since he had been sick with the effects of the virus when his card turned.

"Don't move," the medic replied in English. "You have broken bones and a head injury. Your spine may be injured too."

Khan flexed his leg muscles against the pressure of the restraining straps. The buckles creaked under the force.

"Nothing wrong with my spine. Arm's gonna be fine in a few hours too. Save your meds."

"But you are badly injured. You may die without treatment."

"I'm not dead," Khan said. "That means I'll be good as new tomorrow morning. Now take that needle away and unbuckle these straps before I tear them to shit and you have to buy new ones."

The medic looked from Khan to someone else nearby and rattled off a few words in rapid-fire German. A moment later, a police officer walked up to them and looked down at Khan.

"You wish to decline treatment? We can not be held responsible if you do."

"I'll be fine. I'm a fast healer."

The policeman exchanged a few words with the medic, who proceeded to unbuckle the gurney straps. Khan sat up and swung his legs over the edge to test them. Everything hurt, but nothing seemed broken below the waist. He put some weight on his feet and stood up with a grunt. The policeman and the medic took an involuntary step back as Khan unfolded himself to his full six foot three. He looked around to see that the parking deck was lousy with cops. There were at least a dozen of them, and several blue-and-silver police cars were clogging up the passageways of the deck and the nearby ramp, blue emergency lights flashing and radios squawking. The rental SUV stood alone and abandoned, its side dented in from the collision. The car that had rammed them was nowhere to be seen. Khan walked over to the SUV with slow and careful steps. It felt like someone had rubbed down his legs with broken glass, but he had gotten hurt in enough fights to know that he was already on the mend. The medic began to gather his supplies, but the police officer followed him, staying three steps behind.

"There were four people in this car. Two women and two men. Where are they?"

"There were two men and a woman in the car when we arrived. They have been taken to the hospital already."

Khan didn't have to ask which member of Natalie's entourage was missing.

"You're looking for a dark blue luxury sedan with front damage," he said. "I didn't see the brand because the front end was already in my passenger door by the time I saw the car. They kidnapped my client. Natalie Scuderi."

"You will have to come with us to explain what happened and answer some questions."

"Am I under arrest?" Khan asked.

"Not yet," the officer said. He looked over to his colleagues, and Khan saw that he was nervously fingering his duty belt in the vicinity of his holstered pistol. "But we must insist."

The last thing Khan wanted to do right now was to play twenty questions. Natalie's trail was getting colder by the minute, and he had no time to waste. But there were lots of German cops in shouting range now, and they all carried guns and wore dour expressions. There was no way to decline the directive without starting to hurt people, and getting arrested for assault on police officers wouldn't do a damn thing to get Natalie back either. He let out an annoyed sigh.

"Lead the way, then," he said.

♣

It wasn't an arrest, but the whole affair wasn't just a cordial exchange of information either. As soon as the German cops brought Khan into their police headquarters, a pair of officers in body armor appeared by his side and escorted him to an interview room, submachine guns held loosely by their sides but obviously ready for use. As they walked through the halls of the police station, passing officers glanced at Khan and gave him a wide berth. When they reached the room, Khan's escort had him sit down on one of the chairs in front of the table inside. Then they took positions on either side of the door. Two people in plainclothes walked in and sat down on the other side of the table. Neither offered to shake his hand when they introduced themselves, and they started asking him a barrage of questions.

Half an hour later, Khan started to reconsider his earlier decision to comply without violence. The two cops across the table—he had forgotten their names almost right away—seemed to have a fetish for hearing the same information reiterated in twenty different ways. He was sure they were taking a page out of the police interview playbook, to see if they could catch him in contradictions and poke holes in his story, but Khan grew increasingly irritated.

"And you did not know these people at all?" one of the cops asked. "You had never seen them before since you got to Germany?"

"No."

"What about the person you said was a"—he consulted the notepad in front of him—"joker-ace? The man who looked like his skin was made up of tree bark?"

"No," Khan said. "Trust me, I would know if I had. Bastard picked me up and threw me fifty feet. Haven't met a lot of joker-aces who can do that. Look, I love chatting with you fellas, but you really ought to be out there looking for the people who kidnapped Miss Scuderi. I think you won't much enjoy the media shitstorm that's about to come down on you."

"The criminal police are already investigating," the other cop said. "We have set up a dragnet to look for the car you have described, and for anyone matching the description of Frau Scuderi. But in the meantime, we have to be certain that you are telling the truth."

"Of course I'm telling the fucking truth. What, you think I helped kidnap my own client?"

The cop shrugged and smiled in an apologetic way that seemed entirely insincere.

"I don't know how such things work where you come from, but over here, that would not be unusual. We have many organized crime groups.

Germans, Russians, Italians. Chechens, Serbians, Turks. There is a lot of competition. People cross over sometimes. For money or power."

Khan felt the blood rise in his face.

"I've been in this business for ten years. The people I deal with, they go by reputation. Loyalty is everything to them. You betray their trust, you end up on your knees in a junkyard somewhere while they take your fingers off with a fucking pipe cutter. *That's* how such things work where I come from."

He extended his claws a little and drummed them on the table in front of him. They made a tapping sound that seemed very loud in the small room.

"Arrest me and inform the American embassy so they can send someone over. Or get off my ass and let me get back to my job. I have a missing client, and I don't see you people doing jack shit to find her."

The two cops exchanged a few sentences in German. Khan wondered what he'd do if they took him up on his challenge and locked him up. Finally, one of the cops rapidly clicked his pen a few times and dropped it on the notepad in front of him.

"You are not under arrest, Herr Khan. But you will need to keep yourself available for further interviews. We have asked for assistance from our colleagues at the federal office for special abilities. They are sending someone from Kassel to talk to you."

"Great. Tell them they can find me at the Hotel Adlon. If I'm not out and about."

The two plainclothes officers got up from their chairs, and Khan rose with them.

"You will find that we here in Germany do not like it when people try to bring justice about on their own. Leave the police work to the police."

"No worries," Khan said and flexed his tiger hand slowly. "I'm just going to do some tourist stuff. Sightseeing. Maybe get some souvenirs."

♣

They'd handed him his stuff back when they released him, and his phone never stopped buzzing with incoming messages on the entire half-hour taxi ride back to the hotel. In her Rikki persona, Natalie was a big enough deal in the pop culture scene that her violent kidnapping would make front-page news on both sides of the Atlantic. Back home in Chicago, they were seven hours behind Berlin time, which meant the news clips reporting on the incident would make the evening broadcasts.

When they were almost back at the hotel, his phone chirped again.

This time, it wasn't the chime of a message, but an incoming call. Very few people had his mobile number, and those who did were people who wouldn't react well to being ignored. The caller ID was "unknown," but that wasn't unusual. A lot of his clients were allergic to easy identification. He swiped to accept the call.

"Hello," he said.

"The fuck have you been," Sal Scuderi said, in a voice that was just one or two decibels short of a shout. "I've been trying to get ahold of you for hours. What the hell happened?"

"The German cops had my phone," Khan replied. "Event last night went sideways, and we got jumped in the parking garage when we left the venue."

"They said you were the best in the business. That's why I fucking hired you. To keep shit like this from happening."

"It was three nats and a joker-ace," Khan replied. "They knew what they'd be up against. And they brought just the right guy for the job."

"I don't give a flying fuck if they hired *Mighty Joe Young* for the job. You were supposed to keep her safe. You find my girl and bring her home. If you want to ever get another job in this town, you bring her home and fix what you fucked up."

Khan gritted his teeth. Scuderi was an insurance salesman, not a mob boss, but plenty of people in the Chicago scene relied on his services. Losing the man's daughter on the job would be a fatal black mark on his professional resume. Khan had never lost a client, and he wasn't about to start a habit.

"I'm going to find her," he said. "That was a kidnapping, not a hit. They'll come to someone with a ransom demand. Makes no sense any other way."

"They already did," Scuderi said. "I got a message this morning. They want thirty million. I have forty-eight hours to come up with the cash."

"Did you take it to the feds?"

"Fuck the feds. The message said they'll cut her up into small pieces if I involve the cops. Whatever you do, don't fucking tell the Germans anything."

"I may have to," Khan said. "Not sure I can do this by myself. This isn't Chicago. I don't know the local players."

"Then find someone who does," Scuderi said. "You've worked for enough high rollers around here. Gotta be some favors you can call in. Just don't run your mouth. If they kill my little girl, you're going to be in a world of shit."

"I'll get her back. They won't . . . oh, fuck *me*." The car had slowed down and taken a turn into the driveway of the hotel, and Khan looked up to see a throng of people under the awning of the entrance, most wielding cameras or microphones.

"What is it?"

"I just got to the hotel. Fucking reporters everywhere. I'll call you back as soon as I can."

Khan ended the call, glad for an excuse to exit the conversation. If he wanted to find Natalie and determine who snatched her, he would need a clear head and no distractions.

The throng of reporters streamed around him as soon as he stepped out of the taxi. A dozen different people stuck microphones in his direction and asked him questions in both German and English. He tried to ignore them and quickly make his way to the entrance, but he found his way blocked by people and camera lenses. His frustration manifested itself in an unhappy growl deep in his throat, and the path ahead magically cleared enough for him to pick up his stride. The crowd of newspeople moved with him, but nobody tried to block his way again, and they all kept at least an arm's length away.

Natalie's talent agency had rented a huge three-bedroom suite on the top floor of the hotel. Khan half-expected to find the place tossed and ransacked, either by the cops or the people who had taken Natalie, but when he walked in, it looked just the way it had when they left it. He went into his own bedroom and changed out of his suit, which was now in tatters and smelled of medical disinfectant. When he peeled his old clothes off his body, he looked at himself in the mirror. The fight with Tree Guy had left its mark in the shape of a dozen bruises of various sizes and colors, from light red to angry purple. Khan's wild card had given him the gift of rapid regeneration and recovery from injuries, but for some reason the quick-healing factor didn't extend to bruises, which took just as long to disappear as before. He stepped into the bathroom and turned on the shower, cranking the temperature adjustment as hot as it would go, then ran the water until the room was filled with steam. The scalding-hot water hurt his bruises as if someone was punching him all over again, but the sensation wasn't unwelcome. It kept his anger simmering, which was where he wanted it so he could bring it to a boil quickly.

It felt good to be in a clean suit and smell like himself again. Khan went through his luggage and took stock of the gear he had brought. There were no weapons in his bag, but even if he had brought any, he doubted that anything in his gun safe back home would make a dent in Tree Guy, who had shrugged off slashes from Khan's claws that could have gutted a steer.

He remembered the blows the other joker-ace had dished out, and the feeling of getting tossed over several rows of parked cars like a half-eaten bag of chips. This was not a fight he'd be able to win with his claws or teeth, but his brain wasn't serving up any solutions to the problem, and the bag in front of him held no answers either.

Out in the suite, Khan heard the soft click of the main door lock and the voices of Natalie's friends. They stopped their chatter when they saw him emerge from the bedroom. It took him a few seconds to recall the names of the two boys: Travis and Eli. Travis was wearing a large adhesive bandage above his eyebrow.

"You guys all right?" he asked.

"We're okay, man," Eli answered. "They didn't do anything to us. Travis just got cut by some glass from the window. But they took Natalie."

"No shit," Khan said. "Tell me what you saw after they smashed in your window."

Between the three of them, Khan was able to assemble a sketchy picture of what had gone on while he was busy getting the tar whomped out of him by Tree Guy. The attackers had bashed in the rear passenger window, dragged Natalie and her three friends out of the car, and made off only with Natalie, who had struggled against her abductors while they had stuffed her into the back of a second car that had pulled up while Khan was tied up fighting.

"Did they say anything?"

"Not to us," Melissa said. "They were just talking to each other. Just a few words."

"Any idea what language?" Khan asked.

Melissa and the boys shook their heads. He sighed and sat down on the couch next to them. Everything about this shouted *mob hit* to Khan. But why would the foreign mob here in Berlin have any interest in a socialite rich girl from Chicago? Kidnappings were usually high-risk, low-reward schemes thought up by desperate bush-league amateurs, not pulled off by professional enforcers.

"I need to find out where they took Natalie," Khan said. "If any of you have any ideas or remember anything else, tell me now. I want to know all the details. Even if you think it's not important."

"Have you tried her phone?" Melissa said.

Khan shook his head.

"That's the first thing they would have taken from her. Unless they're dumber than dirt. Everyone knows you can track a cell phone's location."

"Well, let's see anyway." Melissa pulled out her phone and tapped away at the screen. "We use that friend tracker thing. So we can find each other when we're out together."

Khan watched her mess around with her phone for a few moments. There was virtually no chance the kidnappers would have forgotten to strip Natalie of her phone, but he was fresh out of ideas at the moment, so he decided to humor Melissa. As expected, she let out a disappointed little huff and showed Khan the screen of her phone. It showed a map, and the last location of Natalie's phone was marked with a gray dot. Khan took the phone and zoomed in on the map to see that the spot where her phone had last connected to the data network was the parking garage where they had gotten jumped.

"They turned it off. Or probably smashed it right there," Khan said.

"Hey, I wonder if they got her watch too," Eli said.

"What watch?"

"She bought one of those watches that connect to your phone. So she can track her workouts. You know what I'm talking about."

"I really don't," Khan said. "But go on."

"It's like a computer on your wrist. You can even make calls with it."

"Does it need the phone nearby to work?"

Eli shook his head. "Not the kind she's got."

"Can you track that thing?" Khan asked Melissa. She looked at her phone's screen again and shook her head.

"It's not on here."

"You gotta be the owner," Eli contributed. "Natalie could do it. From her laptop. It's set that way so you can track down your stuff if you lose it."

"Well, she's indisposed," Khan said.

"But her laptop's here," Melissa said. She got up and walked over to the bedroom the girls shared. A moment later, she came back with the laptop Khan had seen Natalie use on the plane. She handed it to Khan, who opened it and put it on the coffee table in front of him. The excitement that had been welling up inside of him died down again when he saw the login screen.

"Fuck. It's locked."

"I know her password," Eli offered. "I set up all her tech stuff for her. Unless she changed it recently."

"Give it a shot," Khan said. He turned the laptop around and slid it in front of Eli, who hunched over the keyboard and started typing away.

"Got it," he said.

"Holy shit." Khan grinned at him. "So you *do* have some useful skills. Now I'm glad I didn't chuck you out of the plane on the way here."

◆

The tracking map on the laptop looked like a bigger version of the one on Melissa's phone. Eli logged in, toggled a few settings, and turned the laptop so Khan could see the screen.

"There's her phone," he said. "Same place. And there's her watch. It's gray too. If it was turned on right now, it'd be blue."

The dot that marked the position of Natalie's watch was right in front of a large square building labeled as FLAKTURM.

"What the fuck is a Flakturm," Khan asked. Eli took the question as a directive and did a search, then scrolled through the results.

"Whoa. It's a thing left over from the war. Big concrete tower, for air defense."

"You mean like a bunker?"

"Look." Eli brought up an image. The structure looked square and brutal. The concrete was stained and dirty from decades of weather exposure. There were no windows or other external reference points, but judging by the height of the trees lining the pathways around the building, he guessed the concrete monstrosity was at least six floors high.

"Does it say what's in that thing?"

Eli closed the picture and scrolled through a few more pages.

"It says there's a museum inside now. Some artist commune. And a nightclub. Looks pretty cool, actually."

Something tickled Khan's tiger instincts, and he felt the hair on his neck bristle. Over by one of the windows, there was a soft scraping noise. Khan looked up and saw a hint of movement in the corner of the window, like a fluttering drape. Then it was gone. He heard another sound, the faintest ticking of something hard on metal, this one from above. Their suite was on the top floor, and there was nothing above them but the roof.

Khan got up and walked over to the window. The windows in their suite stretched from floor to ceiling and opened onto a narrow balcony that ran the width of the suite. He made a shushing gesture at Melissa and the boys. Then he opened one of the windows and stepped out onto the balcony. The night air was pleasantly cool and carried thousands of city smells with it. In front of the hotel, on the other side of Pariser Platz, the columns of the Brandenburg Gate glowed in the darkness, illuminated by dozens of spotlight fixtures.

Khan turned to look up at the edge of the roof and sniffed the air again. There was a presence up there, something bigger than an enterprising raccoon. Something was up there in the darkness, quietly breathing.

The part of the roof above the top floor was a sloping face of green-tinged copper sheeting, topped by a rail. The rail was just at the limit of Khan's vertical leaping range. He flexed his leg muscles a few times and extended his claws. The copper roof slope was almost too smooth for him to get traction, but he managed to get a hand on the rail at the top. He hauled himself up and dropped onto the roof.

The rooftop was flat and lined with rubberized material. Every few dozen feet, Khan saw the dome-shaped bubbles of transparent skylights. There were two small sheds in the middle of the roof that looked like maintenance shacks, and a large tripod antenna was anchored between them. In the darkness above the sheds, Khan saw a shape crouched on an antenna crossbar, twenty feet high.

"Don't make me jump up there and pluck you off that thing," he growled.

"Good evening, Herr Khan," the shape said, in a dry and reedy voice that put the hairs on the back of Khan's neck on edge again.

"So you know who I am. Not too hard to figure out, I guess."

"We know who you are. We have been keeping an eye on you ever since you entered the country."

"Who's *we*?"

He walked closer to the base of the antenna to decrease the range between himself and the stranger, to improve his chances at making good on his threat and snatching him out of the air if needed. The rooftop visitor shrugged. A pair of leathery wings unfolded and blotted out the stars of the night sky behind him. He stepped off his perch and landed in front of Khan silently, with just a single flap of those enormous wings.

Close up, he made Khan's hairs stand up even more. He was clearly a joker-ace. His body was squat and short, and covered with coarse black hair except for his wings, which looked like leather sails. Even his eyes were uniformly black, and when he opened his mouth to speak again, Khan saw that his teeth were pointed and very white, the only part of his body that wasn't the color of spilled ink at midnight.

"I have several colleagues in the area, and they would not like it if you tried to hurt me," the stranger said.

"I won't pick a fight if you don't," Khan replied. "Again—who the fuck is *we*?"

"*We* are with BDBF," the visitor said. "Bundesamt für Besondere

Fähigkeiten. The federal office for special abilities. What you at home call SCARE."

♥

"I just flew in from Kassel, and boy, are my arms tired," Khan said with a chuckle. The man in front of him either didn't get the joke or wasn't in a jovial mood, because he merely cocked his head quizzically.

"My name is Fledermaus," he said. "And five thousand meters above us, my colleague Überschall is keeping an eye on things from above. Rest assured that he can be here very quickly."

"Fledermaus," Khan repeated. "And Überschall. Sounds like the title for a sitcom."

"I am not familiar with that word."

"Never mind. They said you'd come. Are you here to ask me questions about my client's kidnapping, too?"

"You claim there was an enhanced individual involved. So far, the only such person confirmed to be involved was you. That is why the Berlin police asked us to assist."

"There *was* someone else," Khan said. "Three nats—regular people. And one wild card. Big, strong guy, looked like a tree. Bark for skin and everything. He held me off while the nats grabbed my client."

"Looked like a tree," Fledermaus repeated.

"Yes, a tree. Rock-hard skin. And strong as shit. He threw me over a whole row of parked cars. Couldn't make a scratch in him, not even with these."

He held out his tiger hand and extended his claws, three inches of curved black keratin knives glistening in the moonlight, then retracted them again so Fledermaus wouldn't feel threatened.

"If that is true, it would be very interesting," Fledermaus said.

"So you know the guy?"

"I have heard of him, yes. That is our main task at BDBF. To keep our eyes on people such as him. And you. But the man you speak of, he is not known to be in Germany."

"Well, unless I got beaten up by his twin brother, I'd say you're wrong. Who is he?"

"We do not know where he comes from. Some sources say he is from Ukraine. We know he works as hired muscle for many groups. Sometimes for the Chechens or the Serbians, but mostly for the Georgian mafia. They call him Mukha. The Georgian word for 'oak.'"

"Georgian mob. *Super*," Khan said. Back home in Chicago, the Georgians were not to be fucked with. They were not as numerous as the Russians or the long-established Polish mafia, but they had a reputation for stomach-churning violence.

"You think the Georgians took your client?"

"I'm not sure. They were Eastern European, though. I've been around that kind long enough."

"I do not think I have to warn you about these people, then," Fledermaus said. "They have no respect for the local authorities, and they are very violent. If you go after them, the police may not be able to protect you."

"The police sure weren't any help in that parking garage," Khan said. He hesitated, then decided to throw caution to the wind. Time was running short, and he couldn't shop around for allies. "Do you know anything about a local place called the Flakturm? Big, ugly concrete tower in the Tiergarten park?"

Fledermaus cocked his head a little. His ears were large and pointy, with tufts of coarse black hair sprouting from the tips.

"I know of it, yes. A relic of the war. They had three of them in the city. I think this one is the only one left. Apparently it was too large to blow up. The walls are very thick."

"They say there's a museum in this one now. And a nightclub. Know anything about that?"

Fledermaus shook his head.

"I'm afraid not. I am not from Berlin, and I do not frequent nightclubs. The noise, you see." He flashed an awkward-looking smile. "But I do know that the criminal element often uses legal places such as this to cleanse the money from their other activities. The Italians use restaurants. The Arab clans have their tobacco lounges. And the Russians and Georgians—"

"Bars and clubs and gambling," Khan finished. "Same as back home."

"BDBF can only intervene in law enforcement matters if we are asked to do so by the local authorities," Fledermaus said. "I cannot help you with whatever it is you are planning to do. You are in our area of responsibility. If you commit any offenses, we will not need a request from the police to deal with you."

"That guy who looks like a tree. Mukha. You must have a file on him. Any idea if he has any weaknesses? Unofficially speaking, I mean. Since you know for sure he's not even in the country right now."

Fledermaus considered Khan's question for a moment. "Officially, I cannot help you, as I said." He smiled again in his awkward way. His teeth were very bright in the darkness. "*Unofficially,* I can point out that he is very much like a tree. You cannot take down a tree with claws and fists. But there are other ways."

Fledermaus shuffled to the edge of the roof and put a hand on the railing. In the light coming from the square and the Brandenburg Gate beyond, Khan saw that he was wearing some sort of high-tech ballistic armor, cut out low on the sides to make space for his enormous wings. He swung himself over the rail and looked back at Khan. "Just ask yourself, Herr Khan. If *you* were a tree, what would be your worst fear in life?"

Fledermaus nodded a curt goodbye and jumped off the roof. Khan walked over to the railing to watch the German joker-ace glide over the Pariser Platz and soar through the space between the central columns of the Brandenburg Gate before disappearing in the darkness of the park beyond.

"Squirrel shit," Khan said into the silence.

♣

The Flakturm was a foreign presence in the calm tranquility of the Tiergarten. Somehow, even the peaceful trees and meadows that surrounded it didn't mellow its massiveness or the complete lack of aesthetic concern evident in its architecture. As Khan walked toward it, he felt something like existential dread at the sight of the thing. Near the top of the tower, four round gun platforms jutted out at the corners like the leaves of a giant concrete clover. It was a structure built for war, and it looked out of place here in this park in the middle of a modern, cosmopolitan city. Khan walked around it twice at a distance to get an idea of the layout, and it struck him that nobody had ever tried to pretty up that ugly block of concrete, as if they knew all these years that no coat of paint or architectural surgery could make it look inviting.

Whenever he wanted to get into a place without an invitation, Khan would scale the fire escapes and get in from the roof, or pop open a window on the way. But this place had no windows, no fire escapes, and the roof was more than a hundred feet above ground, atop sheer concrete sides without handholds or other features. There were thin concrete beams jutting out of the walls near the gun platforms, but even those were much too high for him to reach. The Flakturm truly was a fortress by design, with only one obvious way in and out. Khan watched from a distance as late-night revelers arrived and walked into the entrance vestibule, and others left and noisily made their way to the distant parking lot at the edge of the Tiergarten. Every time the front door opened, he heard a smattering of thumping electronic music. He spent half an hour looking for alternative entry points before deciding to throw plan B out the window. On the eastern horizon, the colors of the sky had started to shift from black to dark blue and purple. The best time to bust into a place was this exact time of the night, when everyone was tired and winding down, and reflexes and reaction times were at their worst.

I hope you're really in there, kid, Khan thought as he cut across the lawn and briskly walked toward the entrance vestibule.

The entrance was a set of double doors, one each on the inner and outer edges of the exterior wall. He pushed open the outer door and walked inside, past a group of clubgoers on the way out. The wall of the Flakturm was at least ten feet thick, and when he walked through the second set of doors and into the foyer, the temperature dropped by a dozen degrees. He pulled out his phone to confirm a hunch and saw that his reception had dropped to nothing. No radio signal would make it through that much concrete, which was why Natalie's watch had dropped off the map as soon as they had brought her inside.

As Eli had learned online, it was a multiuse building now. The interior looked far more welcoming than the outside. The foyer was two floors high and looked like a boutique computer store, all white wood and tasteful accent lighting. There was a broad staircase leading up to what looked like an art installation, and down to a pair of glass doors that had a pair of broad-shouldered guys standing in front of it. Beyond the glass doors, Khan saw the reflections of flashing strobes and neon lights. On the right side of the foyer, there was a bar that had throngs of people standing in it, chatting and swilling drinks. A few of the patrons looked over at him, and some nudged their friends to draw their attention to him, but the stares were curious, not concerned. Berliners seemed used to seeing weird and unusual things.

He walked down the steps to the club. The two bouncers looked like they were unsure how to deal with him. One of them fidgeted with his lapels while the other put a hand under the jacket of his dark suit and tried to look casual about it.

"You can try to draw whatever the fuck that is," Khan said when he had reached the door. "Or you can let me in there without losing a hand."

The second bouncer removed his hand from his waistline and held it up in a placating gesture. Khan saw that he had been reaching for a pepper spray dispenser on his belt. The first bouncer opened the door for him.

"Just looking for someone," Khan said. "I won't be long."

Even at this hour, the club was packed. Dozens of people were gyrating to thumping electronic music, and dozens more were watching from the edge of the floor or hanging out in the seating groups tucked into alcoves along the periphery of the room. The air smelled like weed, spilled booze, and sweat, and the room was radiating warmth, the collective body heat of all the late-night revelers dancing and drinking and groping each other in the corners. It was everything he hated about nightclubs, turned up to maximum intensity. As Khan skirted the edge of the dance floor and walked deeper into the bowels of the club, a smoke machine hissed and spewed a stream of thick fog onto the dance floor. The cloud temporarily displaced all the awful smells of the place, and it cut visibility in the vicinity of the dance floor to three feet or less. He went to the left until he found the row of seating alcoves on that side of the room, and started to map out the periphery of the place. There had to be other exits.

It took him five minutes to find all the doors in the room. Most of them were fire exits that led to dirty concrete stairwells where people were making out or smoking joints. One was behind the bar, and Khan could see people going in and out every few seconds, carrying armfuls of glasses and empty bottles. There was only one door that was locked, secured with a keypad. He concluded that if they were hiding anything in this place, it was behind that door.

Khan looked around to see if anyone was paying attention, but saw nothing except for club patrons lost in their own worlds. If the bouncers had called for backup, it hadn't found him yet. He waited until the fog machine blasted another thick cloud of water vapor onto the dance floor. Then he turned toward the door and wrapped his tiger hand around the knob.

The door was reinforced with steel liners, but Khan could max out the weight plates on the gym machines with just his feline arm, and he strained only for a moment before he wrenched the lock out of the frame with a dull crack. The handle came off in his hand, and he dropped it onto the ground and kicked it aside. Beyond the door, there was a long, dimly lit hallway that had more doors leading off to the left and right. He counted them: four left, four right. Then he stepped into the hallway on light feet and closed the access door behind him.

The first door to the right was a janitorial closet, shelves of cleaning materials and a bunch of mops and buckets. The first door to the left was an office, a desk with a computer screen and a filthy-looking keyboard, an ashtray overflowing with cigarette butts, and shelves with stuffed binders and untidy stacks of papers. Khan moved on to the second set of doors. Natalie wore a particular perfume, something that smelled like waving a freshly cut lilac over a warm blueberry pie, and he hoped that the whiffs of it he caught in the stale air of the hallway were not just his wishful imagination. He reached for the handle of the second door to the right and yanked it open.

Inside, three men sat around a table littered with ashtrays and bottles. There was a TV set in a corner of the room that was showing a news report. The air was thick with the smell of old cigarette smoke and body odor. One of the men turned around to see who was standing in the door, and his eyes widened. Then he muttered a curse, which got the attention of the other two.

"Shit," Khan said.

For just a moment, the space between them practically hummed with the anticipation of the impending violence. It was that split second before a fight Khan knew all too well, the moment that felt like everyone was holding their breath before committing to action. There was no way to talk these men down, and if he hesitated, he'd give them an edge. He flicked out his claws just as the first guy grabbed a bottle off the table and threw it at him. Khan jerked his head to the side, and the bottle sailed past him and smashed against the wall of the hallway behind him.

There was no grace to the fight. The room was only ten feet square and had a table and a bunch of chairs in it, and there was no way for anyone to execute any fancy maneuvers. It was like an attempted assassination in a phone booth. Two of the men pulled knives and the third swung his fist at Khan, and only his reflexes kept him from getting shanked on the spot. He recoiled from one knife and slashed at the hand holding it, then drove his fist into the face of the second knife's wielder. The bare-handed one of the group was the only one to connect with Khan. His fist cracked into Khan's eyebrow on the human side of his face, and Khan saw a burst of stars exploding in his field of view. He roared, and in the confines of the room, the sound was so loud that it made the ashtrays on the table bounce and clatter.

One of the knives was on the floor now, but the other was still in play, its owner slashing with quick and practiced moves. Khan jerked away from the edge of the blade and bodychecked the bare-handed fighter into the TV shelf in the process, and the man went down along with the screen as the shelving collapsed. The knife made another arc and stabbed into Khan's shoulder blade, then skidded off the bone to carve open a few inches of his tiger fur. Khan lashed out and raked all five claws across the remaining knife wielder's face and neck. He leapt back, bounced off the doorframe behind him, and collapsed in the hallway with a wet, gurgling sound. The smell of blood was suddenly thick in the air.

The guy who had held the other knife was doubled over and shouting incoherently. Khan saw that his swipe at the knife hand had taken the hand off at the wrist. He picked the man up and hurled him against the concrete wall, then did it again. After the second impact against the rough concrete, his opponent crumpled to the floor and stopped his pained shouting. Maybe ten seconds had passed since Khan had turned the door handle, but he was panting for breath, and his heart was pounding like he had just run a hundred-yard dash. Blood was running down from a gash in his right eyebrow and clouding his vision, and he used the sleeve of his sport coat to wipe it out of his eye.

The man in the hallway was a mess. Khan had opened him up along the whole length of his collarbone. The puddle of blood spreading out from him was already pooling from one side of the hallway to the other. Khan wondered about the depth of the shit he was likely to find himself in over killing someone on foreign soil, even in self-defense. But he'd have to be around for them to charge him, and that was a shaky proposition at the moment. All it took was another room of mobsters, but ones who were packing guns instead of blades. He had come here to find Natalie, though, so Khan steeled himself and went back to opening doors.

Two of the remaining rooms were stockrooms, haphazardly loaded from floor to ceiling with boxes and crates of supplies, and thankfully devoid of armed men. Khan went to the end of the hallway, where the last two locked rooms waited. He hadn't smelled the scent of Natalie's perfume again, and for a moment, a sort of deep, dark fear gripped his mind as he convinced himself that he'd find nothing, and he would be stamping license plates in a German prison for absolutely nothing in the end.

Then his heart skipped two beats when he saw that the last door on the right had a security keypad next to the handle, just like the entry door had.

He grabbed the door handle, wrenched it down, and threw himself against the door with all the force he could muster. It popped out of the frame, spraying bits of the lock, and swung inward with the grinding sound of steel against concrete as the bottom edge of the door, now crooked in its hinges, dragged across the floor and left a chalky white scrape mark.

Natalie was lying on her side on a field cot on the far side of the room. There was a little table and a folding chair, and a chemical toilet in one corner. She didn't wear a gag like a kidnapping victim in a movie. They had tied her wrists and ankles to the frame of the cot with several loops of commercial plastic ties. She had her back to him, but turned her head at the sound of the door busting open. He could tell that she couldn't turn far enough to make out who had just entered the room.

"Motherfuckers," Khan growled. He peeked into the hallway to make sure he wasn't about to get jumped by reinforcements. Then he rushed over to Natalie's cot.

"Are you okay, kid?"

He saw recognition in her eyes, and she murmured something, but it was slurred gibberish. Her eyes were glazed over and she looked like she was having a hard time focusing. He cursed again. They hadn't bothered with a gag because they had sedated the shit out of her to keep her quiet.

"Let's get you out of this place."

He used one of his claws to snip through the plastic ties, carefully stripping them off her wrists and tossing them to the ground one by one. When he was finished, he put his tiger arm behind her shoulders and helped her to a sitting position.

"Soft," she mumbled. "'S like you're a cat."

"Half right," he said. "Can you walk?"

She swung her legs over the edge of the cot and tried to get to her feet, then stumbled sideways almost immediately. Khan caught her before she could fall, then raised her and draped his arm across her shoulder again. "This is going to be a mess," he said. "We have to go, kiddo. Can't call the cops from in here. Gotta get outside. Come on."

He practically carried her up the hallway back to the entrance to the main part of the nightclub. She was holding on to him, but clearly out of it, and the toes of her white linen shoes touched the ground maybe three times in the entire awkward twenty-meter shuffle to the door.

Almost there, Khan told himself. *Across the dance floor, out the main doors, call the cops once we're outside.*

In the nightclub, the thumping music was still churning up the crowd. The flashing lights of the dance floor illumination painted the fog from the machine in bright streaks of red, green, and blue. He went for the most direct route to the exit, straight across the dance floor, bumping people out of the way left and right.

In the space between the dance floor and the exit door, a familiar shape was making its way through the fog toward him: thick arms and legs, short hair on a square-looking head, beady eyes in a face that looked like it was hewn out of a petrified tree trunk. Mukha moved without hurry, but Khan knew that he would not be able to get past the bastard and through those doors, not with Natalie to safeguard.

He lowered Natalie until she was standing on her own very unsteady feet. Then he drew a deep breath and roared at Tree Guy, the loudest roar he had ever squeezed from his lungs and vocal cords. In the confines of the Flakturm, it sounded like a slowly imploding building.

That got the attention of the crowd. They retreated from his vicinity like the tide pulling away from a shoreline at the onset of ebb. Mukha didn't seem impressed, however. He kept up his infuriatingly unhurried gait, advancing without any hint of hesitation: *stomp, stomp, stomp.*

When Mukha was ten feet away, Khan reached into his sport coat and brought out the bottle he had prepared in the hotel room's bathroom before he had set out for the Flakturm. It held a mixture of gasoline, procured by Eli at a nearby service station, and high-proof alcohol, all mixed in with hand soap and a few scoops of laundry detergent. In his youth, back when Khan was still scrawny Samir Khanna, he had experimented with many flammable and explosive substances with his friends, and he hoped that he had remembered the ratios for this particular cocktail correctly. He granted himself the luxury of an extra second to aim. Then he hurled the bottle straight at Mukha.

The cocktail hit the joker-ace right in the middle of his chest. The bottle shattered, and the flammable liquid inside sprayed, and left globs and droplets on the floor in a wide arc in front of Mukha. Most of it, Khan was happy to see, remained on Mukha's body, soaking the clothes he had draped over his bulky frame. Khan reached into his pocket and pulled out one of the road flares he had brought along. He ignited it with a quick swipe on the leg of his pants. Mukha hesitated, then stopped and looked down at the sticky goop that was covering the front of his torso.

"*Step aside,*" Khan shouted in Polish, the only Slavic language he knew. He had no idea whether Georgian had any similarities to his mother's native tongue, but he guessed that Mukha spoke Russian, and maybe he knew some other language that was similar enough to Polish to get the gist. Mukha raised his head again and looked at Khan with an unreadable expression.

"Step aside," Khan repeated, and waved the road flare for emphasis. "Or I swear I will burn you down along with this shithole. I bet you'll stay on fire for days."

Mukha's face showed no indication that he comprehended the threat, but Khan guessed the smell of gasoline and the lit flare in his hand conveyed the message clearly enough even if this guy didn't understand a fucking word of Polish after all, because a few heartbeats later, he raised his hands slowly to chest height and walked back half a dozen steps. Khan loaded up Natalie again and headed toward the exit, road flare extended toward Mukha.

We may make it out of here alive after all, he thought. But the brief glimmer of triumph he felt was extinguished a moment later, when the front door opened and four broad-shouldered guys with pissed-off expressions hurried through. They spotted Khan and Natalie, and one of them shouted something at his companions. Then he pulled out a handgun and held it low as he was advancing.

"Shit," Khan said.

He tossed the road flare in Mukha's general direction, not aiming to hit the guy but not particularly concerned whether he did. Then he scooped up Natalie and carried her over to the nearest emergency exit he had spotted earlier. He kicked the door open at a run and catapulted two of the stoners behind it into the staircase. A few people were hanging out on the stairs, and Khan barged through them, ignoring their yelled protests as he knocked them aside. He took four and five steps at once, up onto the next landing, and then up the next staircase. Below him, the door banged open again. He peered over the railing to see the four broad-shouldered goons huffing up the first set of stairs. Behind them, Mukha filled out the doorframe and followed the goons with heavy steps that kicked up cigarette butts and concrete dust. One of the armed goons looked up and spotted Khan. He raised his gun and cranked off a shot. Khan flinched back and heard the bullet smack into the concrete somewhere above his head. For the first time since he had walked through the front doors of the Flakturm, the thought came to him that he could die in here. Too many bad guys, a joker-ace who couldn't be beaten in a stand-up fight, no weapons, no allies, and now nowhere to go.

Make it up to the roof, he told himself. *Take it from there. At least the phone will work again up top.*

He raced up the stairs and the landings. Natalie's weight wouldn't have slowed him down much even under normal circumstances, and with adrenaline flooding his system, it was like she was barely there. By the time he got to the top landing on the sixth floor, their pursuers were only halfway up the stairwell.

A steel door with large rust stains marked the end of the escape path. Khan put down Natalie and threw himself against it. It took several attempts to dislodge the rusty piece of shit from the frame, but on the fourth body blow, it popped open with a sharp metallic squeal.

Outside, the night air was warm and humid. The stairwell door opened onto one of the circular gun platforms Khan had seen jutting from the top corners of the tower. The guns were gone, of course, and nothing but rust-stained concrete remained where the gun pits used to be. Khan could tell that there used to be concrete catwalks connecting the gun platforms, but someone had demolished large chunks of them, and there was nothing left to get them safely across to the next platform. He had run into a dead end, and the only way out was a hundred-foot drop they wouldn't survive. The gun platform had a waist-high concrete balustrade, and he lowered Natalie in front of it so she wouldn't fall off the roof, and away from the door so gunfire wouldn't hit her by accident.

Behind him, the pursuers were almost at the top of the staircase. If he wanted to hold them off, he'd have to fight them while they were trying to make it through the door, not when they had space to spread out and hit him from several directions.

"Call the cops," Khan told Natalie. He hoped that she was awake enough to understand what he was saying. "One-one-zero."

He handed her his phone and turned toward the door. Then he took off his sport coat to free up his range of movement, unsheathed the claws on his tiger hand, and roared a challenge at the unseen pursuers who were just now making their way onto the top staircase landing.

They didn't do him the favor of coming through the door single file and letting him pick them off one by one. Instead, the goon with the pistol stuck his head around the corner of the staircase and aimed his gun at the doorway. Khan leapt sideways as the shot rang out, losing sight of the top landing.

"Come out and let's settle this shit," he yelled through the doorway. The reply came in Georgian, and it didn't sound like they agreed with his proposal. He glanced back at Natalie, who was still looking like she had just woken up from a deep sleep.

For the next minute or two, they were at an impasse. It was a true Mexican standoff. Every time Khan stuck his head around the corner, the mobster with the gun would fire a round in his direction. He couldn't rush them without catching a bullet or two, and they couldn't come out to finish him off without getting cut to ribbons. But time was working against Khan, because he knew that with every passing moment, Mukha made his way farther up the stairs. And there was nothing he could do about it, because he had gotten them stuck in a dead-end kill trap like a fucking amateur.

Khan could smell and hear Mukha as he lumbered up onto the top landing and toward the door. He reeked of gasoline-and-soap mix, and his footsteps echoed in the staircase. Khan bared his teeth and growled. Then he backed up to the low balustrade where Natalie was still hunched and took a running start toward the door just as Mukha filled out the doorframe with his bulk. Khan put all his weight and force into a flying leap, three hundred pounds of pissed-off ballistic feline, thousands of foot-pounds of energy, and slammed his feet right into the middle of Mukha's chest.

It felt like trying to dropkick the front of a speeding truck. The shock of the impact traveled from Khan's feet to the top of his skull. He bounced off Mukha's chest and careened into the doorframe, then back out onto the gun platform, where he landed flat on his back. He turned his head to see that Mukha was on his back as well, lying in a cloud of dust a few feet inside the staircase landing.

Mukha sat up, slowly shook his head once, and started to get to his feet.

"Come *on*," Khan groaned. "What does it fucking *take*."

He fished for another road flare, but his hands couldn't find a pocket, and he remembered that he had just discarded his coat. It was on the ground by the edge of the platform, fifteen feet away. Khan stood on aching legs and staggered over to the coat, but it was too late. Mukha was already at the door again, and behind him, three mobsters brought up the rear. They followed Mukha onto the platform and fanned out behind him. One of them aimed his gun at Khan in an infuriatingly casual manner.

He flexed his leg muscles for another jump, even though he knew that he'd never take down all three men in time, not even if they didn't have the fucking Mukha as a shield.

Sorry, kiddo, he thought. *I fucked this one up for both of us.*

In the cloudless early morning sky above the Flakturm, a thunderclap boomed. It seemed to come from everywhere at once, and it was so loud that it made Khan's teeth rattle. He felt the impact of something heavy landing on the gun platform behind him. Khan turned his head to see a man in a military-type flight suit straighten himself out as if he had just landed a mildly challenging acrobatic routine. The newcomer was wearing a helmet with a gold-tinted visor that made him look a bit like a robot. The helmet was white, and it bore a call sign written onto the side with stick-on vinyl lettering: ÜBERSCHALL.

For a heartbeat, time seemed to be frozen.

Then the mobster with the gun raised his arm and moved the muzzle of his weapon from Khan over to the newcomer.

The guy in the flight suit clapped his hands and pushed them outward in a shoving motion. There was another thunderclap, this one so unbearably loud it made Khan roar in pain. When he looked up again, all three mobsters were on the ground, and Mukha was on his back again, twenty feet inside the staircase hallway beyond the door. This time, he didn't try to get up again.

Khan heard the soft rustling of very large wings behind him. He turned around to see Fledermaus come to a soft and gentle landing on the gun platform right near Natalie, who recoiled at the sight of the white-fanged German joker-ace.

"He's all right," Khan assured her. "He's with the good guys."

The man in the flight suit took off his helmet and ran a gloved hand through his hair, which was ash blond and cut short in the military fashion. He looked like a runway model, blue eyes over chiseled cheekbones. When he spoke, his diction was perfect, even if his accent was so German that it made him sound like a war movie villain.

"Is everyone all right?"

"Yeah, we're okay," Khan replied. "They pumped Miss Scuderi full of sedatives. She'll need to get to a hospital, and soon."

"This is my colleague," Fledermaus said. "Major Florian Lambert, also called Überschall. Also with BDBF."

"I figured. Very nice of you to drop by," Khan said. "Could have shown up a bit sooner."

"Like I said, we were keeping an eye on things from above. Pardon my late entrance, but my colleague here is a bit faster in the air than I am."

"So you knew where we were all along?"

"We were tracking you since you left the hotel. But we are not allowed to intervene unless we have positive verification of a special abilities target."

"This oaf over there," Khan said, and nodded at the hallway where Mukha was lying. "I told you he was around."

"Unfortunately, our rules of engagement make no allowance for hearsay," Überschall said. He walked over to the goons he had knocked senseless and began to tie up their wrists with plastic restraints he fished out from a pocket on his flight suit. The pistol was on the ground next to one of the mobsters. Überschall picked it up, ejected the magazine, racked the slide to clear the chamber, and fieldstripped the weapon with quick and practiced motions. Then he tossed the parts of the gun into the concrete dust. Khan watched him walk into the staircase vestibule to the spot where Mukha was laid out, still motionless.

"Not that I'm holding a grudge," Khan shouted after him. "But if that fucker moves, stick a match up his ass and let him burn until Christmas."

When the adrenaline subsided, Khan felt utterly drained. He stood next to Natalie while Überschall played field medic and checked her overall condition. Now that the fight was over, the top of the Flakturm was an oddly peaceful place. The sun had started to rise above the eastern horizon, painting the sky in shades of deep purple and orange. Down below, life continued as if nothing had happened. Khan heard the laughter and chatter from nightclub patrons as they left and made their way through the park, and all around them, the city was starting to stir from its brief slumber.

"What's going to happen to Mister Woody over there?" Khan asked Fledermaus and nodded in the direction of the unconscious Mukha.

"He did not register with the authorities when he entered the country," Fledermaus said. "That is a violation of our law. I imagine we will have strong words with the authorities in his home country. As for him, we have a facility in Butzbach for people with special abilities. I think he will spend a bit of time there as our guest."

"That's a lot of risk they took. Six guys, two cars. And a joker-ace smuggled in. A lot of effort, and no guarantee of a payout. Why would they do that?"

"They told me," Natalie mumbled behind them. Khan and Fledermaus turned around in surprise. She was sitting up with her arms wrapped around her knees, and she merely sounded drunk instead of incoherent.

"They told you what?" Khan asked and sat down next to her.

"They said my father owed them money. Lots of money. Said they weren't letting me go until he paid up." She shuddered a little and hugged her knees tighter. "Told me they'd start cutting off fingers if he didn't. Send 'em back to him in a box, one by one."

Khan looked over at the still-unconscious mobsters and suppressed his sudden desire to grab them by the neck and throw them off the gun platform. He didn't much care for her music or her social circle, but Natalie was just a kid, barely out of her teens, and no threat to anyone. He had killed mobsters and other dirtbags in cold blood before, but he'd never lay a hand on an innocent, especially not one so close in age and appearance to his little sister Naya. All of a sudden, he didn't have any more scruples about the mook he had slashed to shreds down in the nightclub's back hallway.

In the distance, sirens cut through the tranquility of the park. Khan looked over the balustrade and saw blue lights flashing. At least a dozen police cars were rushing up the access road from the nearby parking lot. The German police sirens had a two-tone pattern that was somehow even more annoying than the shrill ululating wail of the cop sirens back home:

BEE-DO, BEE-DO. The blue lights cut through the semidarkness of the early morning and drew erratic light patterns on the concrete walls of the Flakturm.

"Some things are the same everywhere," Khan said.

"What is that?" Fledermaus asked.

"The cavalry always shows up five minutes too late."

Forty-eight hours and an interminable amount of police interviews later, Khan and Natalie's entourage were in the air again. He had fully expected to join Mukha, the Tree Guy, in whatever high-security facility BDBF had set up for wayward wild cards in Butzbach. But the BDBF guys seemed to have a great deal of pull with Germany's federal police. He'd had to sign a legal paper obliging him to return for a court appearance if the prosecutor decided to file charges, and then they released him on his word and returned his passport, much to Khan's astonishment.

There was no Top 40 music blaring in the cabin of the Learjet on the way to Keflavik. Natalie and her friends were huddled on the lounge seating and talking while sipping drinks. Khan knew the shell-shocked look in their eyes all too well. He spent most of the flight to Iceland thinking about the kidnapping and of all the ways he screwed up. In reality, he knew that he couldn't have done much better, but he also knew that the open wound on his professional ego would take a much longer time to heal than the bruises on his body.

Half an hour before their descent into Keflavik, he called Sal Scuderi from the onboard phone. "We're on our way back," he said when Sal answered. "Two-hour layover, then four more hours. She'll be home by dinner."

"How's my girl?"

"She's doing all right," Khan said. "Still shaken. It'll take a while."

"I can't even tell you what kinda state I've been in the last few days. You dropped the fucking ball, my friend. I mean, I'm happy you got her back. But you let them take her to begin with."

Khan sighed heavily. "How much do you owe them?"

"The fuck are you talking about?"

"The Georgians. They told Natalie that you owe them a shitload of money. Said they'd send her back in little pieces if you didn't pay up."

"You know that's bullshit tough guy talk. You don't damage the valuable goods."

"Sal," Khan said. "Cut the crap. How much?"

There was silence on the line for a few moments. Then Sal Scuderi let out a shaky breath. It sounded like the remaining air escaping from a flaccid old balloon. "Twenty mil."

"You borrowed *twenty mil* from the Georgian mob? Are you out of your fucking mind?"

"They were about to get it back," Sal said. "It would have been okay. If only..."

"If only what?"

It took a few seconds for Khan to understand, and when he did, he felt his anger welling up again. "You took a policy out on her. A high-risk one."

"Geez, Khan. The kid has had a policy on her since the day she was born. It's what I *do*. I got a policy on the wife too. And the fucking dog. What kind of asshole do you take me for?"

Khan looked over at Natalie, who was curled up in her seat, looking like someone who needed about two weeks of uninterrupted sleep.

"The kind of asshole who'd try and pay off his debt with his kid's life insurance policy," he said. "I knew you were shit, Sal. I just didn't know you had no fucking soul left."

"You're one to talk. How many people have you killed for guys like me?"

"Too many," Khan conceded.

There was another long pause. Then Sal cleared his throat.

"You have a rep. You get paid well because you do what you're told. You want to see any of your fee, you keep your mouth shut about this. In front of Natalie, or the media, or the cops. You fuck me over, and I'll make sure you never get another job in this town again."

"Don't ever fucking threaten me," Khan said. He could have growled into the phone for emphasis, but right now he was too tired for theatrics. Instead, he just ended the call and turned off his phone.

Across the cabin, Natalie was watching him with concern on her face. He smiled in what he hoped was a reassuring manner, and she returned it.

He got up from his seat in the back of the plane and moved past the entourage to the Learjet's bar. He uncorked the Scotch decanter and poured two fingers' worth of whisky into a glass, then repeated the process. Then he walked over to Natalie and held out one of the glasses.

"Got a minute to talk?"

She looked at him in surprise. Then she nodded and got to her feet.

"Sure. Let's go in the back."

He let her walk ahead. Before he followed, he picked up the remote from the lounge table and turned on the TV.

"Turn it up as loud as you want," he told Melissa and the boys.

On the way to the back, he glanced out of the window. Outside, a steel-blue sky flecked with clouds was meeting a restless ocean, sunshine glittering on waves.

Fuck the fee, he thought, and went to talk to Natalie.

♠ ♥ ♦ ♣

Hammer and Tongs
and a Rusty Nail

by Ian Tregillis

"CALL DARCY."

The voice was faint but crystal clear, in exactly the way Mordecai Albert Jones sometimes imagined would presage the creeping onset of dementia. He paused in dismantling an Imperial LeBaron land yacht, straining to listen past the fading shriek of torn metal. But the scrapyard was quiet; he heard only the thrum of a chill spring wind and clinking of chains somewhere nearby. With a shrug, he tore the junker's hood down the middle like a piece of tissue paper, extracting the mercury switch from the trunk light.

It was getting difficult to find spare mercury just lying around these days. Many of the heavy metals, really. Either they were valuable, and people stole them—like the platinum in old catalytic converters—or toxic, and over time manufacturers had stopped using them. He couldn't begrudge a change from the old days that was so much better for the environment, but it meant a growing portion of his diet had to be ordered from sketchy suppliers in eastern Europe. For some reason, a lot of strontium had flooded the market after the horrific events in Kazakhstan. But he wouldn't touch that stuff with a ten-foot pole. Never would.

"Gosh dang it. Call DAR-SEE."

Mordecai paused again, his prize pinched between thumb and forefinger. That was definitely a voice. Louder this time. Actually, two voices. It sounded like somebody was having a conversation with a mentally challenged robot.

"Okay. Dialing the pharmacy."

"No. *DAR-SEE.*"

"I'm sorry, I don't understand."

The first voice started to giggle. "Doll Carcy."

"Shall I search for car seats?"

Mordecai glanced at the glass bulb in his hand, its thimbleful of mercury gleaming in the sunlight. Consuming heavy metals was how his ace kept him strong, his bones unbreakable, his flesh impervious. The unusual diet had certainly never seemed to be deleterious to his health. Strontium was better, but increasingly difficult to get without a high tax in moral compromise. Mercury would do in a pinch. But now, listening to the faint surreal conversation unfolding around him, he remembered *Alice in Wonderland*. Lewis Carroll's Mad Hatter was supposedly inspired by the mercury poisoning that commonly afflicted hatters of his era, something to do with making felt. *Hmmm.*

"Tall horsey—aww, nuts," said the giggly voice. Something plopped to the dirt a few yards from Mordecai, kicking up a cloud of dust with a muted *crack.*

Okay, that wasn't a hallucination. Or if it was, Mordecai was already too far gone to worry about it. He walked a few strides and picked up a phone. Fractures spiderwebbed the glass screen.

"Hey there, fella."

Mordecai held the phone to his ear. "Yes?"

More giggling, but it didn't seem to be coming from the phone. "Any chance you could call someone for me? It'd be real swell of you."

That voice . . . there was something vaguely familiar about it. Which, Mordecai supposed, did nothing to rule out a delusion.

The wind kicked up, and with it, the creak and rattle of chains. "Oh, cripes."

Aha. Yes. He'd definitely heard that voice before. It'd been a few years, but Mordecai remembered now. He looked up.

Wally Gunderson hung thirty feet overhead, splayed across the face of an electromagnet. The breeze had it swaying like a carnival ride. "Call my friend and tell her—" The metal man broke off in a giggling fit. "—tell her it hap, it, it happappenened again, would ya?"

He sounded drunk, which seemed a little out of character for the ace known as Rustbelt. Not that Mordecai knew him particularly well. They'd been on TV together, kind of, more than a decade ago.

Mordecai frowned. "Are you okay up there? Is that healthy for you?"

It was difficult to read the expression on the iron face. But something about the set of the steam-shovel jaw suggested mild relief. "Whew, you're real. It sure gets confusing up here."

Yeah . . . he didn't sound right. Poor kid needed help.

"Hold on," said Mordecai. He set the damaged phone on a stack of tire rims, and the mercury switch atop it. He leapt atop the crane arm holding the magnet, and shimmied to where Rustbelt hung helpless as a pinned butterfly. Mordecai flipped around so that his knees were hooked over the chains, wedged his hands under Wally's shoulders, then braced his feet against the magnet.

"Oh, they gotta cut the power or I'll be up here all day, ya know." Another gust set them twirling like a lazy pinwheel. "Wheee!" said Wally. "I'm kinda strong but—"

"Ready? One-two-three!"

Mordecai yanked on Wally's shoulders. The joker-ace clanged free. Mordecai launched himself into a backward summersault and landed on his feet.

Wally face-planted in the junkyard's oily dirt. "Oof." He lay there for a moment, silent and still, which Mordecai found unnerving. But then the metal man rolled over, saying, "Holy smokes. You're *really* strong." He winced, rubbing his shoulders. It sounded like two cast-iron frying pans scraping together. Wally now sported a pair of perfect handprints pressed into the metal.

Mordecai winced. "Should I take you to the hospital?"

Wally saw his frown. "Oh, don't worry, fella. These bruises'll go away in time. Tick tock." Another giggling fit took him. "Hickory dickory dock."

The stack of steel rims toppled over. The nearest bounced across the dirt to clunk against Wally's legs. He laughed, pantomiming the exaggerated movements of steering a car. "Vrooom, vroom!"

More rims followed. And an ominous creaking came from various piles of junk and scrap metal, as the taller ones began to sway toward the temporarily magnetized metal man like flowers seeking the sun.

"Let's get you out of here." Mordecai grabbed the broken phone and the mercury switch. "You said there's somebody I can call for you?"

♠

Wally lay sprawled on the concrete apron of a repair bay as if making a cement angel, belting out the Minnesota Rouser. Loose tools—wrenches, screwdrivers, and a cordless drill—dangled from his arms, chest, and face.

A pickup truck pulled up on the street adjacent to Mordecai's motorcycle shop. The woman who emerged from the driver's side stood practically half of Wally's size; she cast a disapproving eye over the expired meters of the other cars on the street. Her passenger was clearly too young to drive. Mordecai didn't have daughters, so it was hard to judge, but he'd put her at about twelve or thirteen.

"RAH, RAH, RAH, FOR SKY-U-MAH! RAH! RAH oh hi, Darcy." Wally's head lolled sideways as if his neck were pneumatically actuated and had sprung a leak. The look on his face (Mordecai decided most of the heavy lifting was done by Wally's eyes) went from a carefree looseness to something a little more focused, almost tender, when he looked at the tween. "Hiya, kiddo."

"Hi, Wallywally."

He reached up to touch her face. Mordecai winced, but the girl didn't recoil from the iron fingers. Wally was surprisingly gentle despite his current state.

She asked, "Did you get stuck again?"

"Yeah."

"Ugh, *Dad*." She rolled her eyes.

Dad. Adoption? Wally definitely hadn't been a father when he was on the show. If he had, then that other contestant, the winner (What was his name? Jamal . . . Norwood. He died in Kazakhstan. Mordecai had read about it in the paper. Very sad.) never would have gotten away with his claim against Wally. Not that a guileless kid like Wally ever really had a chance on that stupid show. (Unless the adoption was a response to the accusations on *American Hero*. Now *that* was an ugly thought. Also difficult to square with the young man who up and turned his back on TV to go defend helpless strangers halfway around the world. But . . .)

The tween said, "You have to warn people before you go wandering into scrapyards. Darcy told you."

"Yeah, I did," said the driver. "I feel like I was pretty clear on this."

"Sorry, Darcy. I forgot." Wally started giggling again, but then his demeanor turned on a dime and he looked ready to cry. "I broke the phone you gave me," he sniffled.

The new arrivals shared a look. Darcy said, "Ohhh, super. It's weepy Wally."

"Guess he was up there awhile," said the tween. "Watch out for your credit cards." She shrugged, pulled out her phone, turned slightly translucent, and floated out of earshot, her toes dangling a few inches from the pavement.

Darcy placed her hands on her hips and frowned at Wally moaning woozily on the ground. "You always know how to show a girl a good time on her day off, don't you."

Mordecai felt bad about not letting him inside, but it had been a job getting him to the shop, and it seemed a bad idea to bring Wally anywhere near the computers. He opened the screen door and stepped outside.

"You must be Darcy." He smiled, extending a hand. "I'm Mordecai. I'm the one who called you?"

"Thanks for the call." As she shook his hand, her gaze darted to the sign over the door. He could see the gears turning. And yet, she didn't flinch from his handshake. Sometimes people did, even if they didn't mean anything by it. Just a natural self-preservation instinct, he supposed, when you're meeting somebody who is, quite possibly, the strongest ace in the world.

"Hey, are you—"

Mordecai shrugged. "Yeah. I'm him."

"Wow." Darcy nudged the metal man with the hard toe of her shoe, making a *gong* sound. It wasn't a kick, really, and was perhaps even mildly affectionate. Or, at least, within arm's length of affection. "Hey, dingbat. Do you even realize who rescued you?"

"My pal from the junkyard? He's, really really strong." Wally sniffled. "Do you think we'll ever see him again?"

"Oh, for crying out loud—"

Mordecai said, "It's fine. Will he be okay? I gather the magnet kind of . . ." He tapped his temple.

"Yeah, it always wears off." She glared at the prone ace. "*Eventually.*"

Mordecai lifted Wally to his feet. Then the tween came back, slipped her phone in a pocket, and took one of Wally's arms from Mordecai. It was touch and go for a moment, but she and Darcy managed to keep the metal man upright without getting crushed. The unlikely trio wobbled toward the pickup; Mordecai opened the tailgate for them. Loading unconscious Wally into the pickup bed was another job, owing to the magnetism. Mordecai wondered how Darcy and the tween would have managed on their own.

Wally's eyes opened. His gaze cast about, and then he focused on Mordecai. "Harlem Hammer."

Mordecai dipped his head in acknowledgment. He didn't exactly love that title, but he'd let it slide. Poor kid had a scrambled brain.

"Thank you," said the metal man.

♦

Jube, the walrus-joker who had owned and run the corner newspaper stand in Wally's part of Jokertown since long before Wally's card turned, gave him a friendly nod. "Wally Gunderson. Haven't seen you in a while."

"I've been feeling kinda crummy the last few days."

The day after his magnet misadventure, he still wasn't feeling like himself, so he'd asked a favor of his friend Michelle. Ghost (Wally had given up using her real name, Yerodin, otherwise she bristled, and when she bristled she played with knives) was getting the better end of the deal, a sleepover with her friend Adesina, who could fly. It made him feel like a lousy parent, but then, in his addled state, if he'd tried to be a parent to Ghost just then, he would've done a real bad job, and felt even lousier.

"Sorry to hear it. How's the little one?"

"Oh, gosh. She's good. So good. Yeah . . ." Wally paused, looking for a natural way to turn the conversation. "Real good. Um, hey, speaking of all this stuff, do you happen to know a real strong fella who's got a motorbike-fixin' store up in Harlem?"

Jube raised his bushy eyebrows to the point it looked like they would disappear under his hat. Wally had asked him about it once, and remembered it was called a porkpie hat, though he still didn't know why.

"Mordecai Jones? Of course I do." Jube's wire-brush mustache twitched into a frown. "Oh, Wally, tell me you're not tussling with him. I know you can take care of yourself, but Mordecai, you're not in his class. He'd ball you up like so much tinfoil."

"Tussling?" It was Wally's turn to frown. "Oh, you mean *fighting*. Heck no! Gosh. No, he did something real swell and I want to say thanks," said Wally, hoping Jube wouldn't pry for details. If pressed, he'd end up telling the whole story. Truth, he often felt, was like steam. It always leaked out eventually. Especially from himself, who in that regard was little better than a rusted-out teapot.

Jube looked relieved. "Everybody knows Mordecai or, at least, knows of him. But he generally keeps a low profile. I recall he was a little more active back in the old days, though I think even back then he was never entirely keen on the adventuring ace thing."

Jube paused to make change for a joker woman with kaleidoscopically shifting paisley patterns on her skin; she bought gum, cigarettes, and a copy of the *Financial Times*. Wally thought the pink newspaper was kinda neat.

"He's never been a regular customer," Jube continued, "not being a Jokertown resident. But I do see him once in a while. Loves the *Times* crossword puzzle, that one."

Wally perked up. "Oh, that's super. Thanks, Jube! I know the perfect thank-you gift. Heck, one time I even went in disguise as the president of a crossword puzzle club."

Jube stared at him, unblinking. "I . . . How's that?"

And just like steam, the story started leaking out. Wally was proud of this one; he considered it one of the more clever ideas he'd ever had. "It was back when all them folks were getting snatched. Remember that? Well—"

"Mr. Gunderson!"

A man in a tan suit waved at Wally across the street.

"Aw, nuts."

Jube rubbed a sleeve of his Hawaiian shirt across one tusk. "Friend of yours?"

"Not really. But he sure acts like it sometimes."

The man, who appeared to be a nat (though Wally tried not to judge people on their looks), dodged traffic to join them. He was quick on his feet; despite crossing against the light, he didn't get a single horn honk or finger. Wally hadn't known that was possible.

"Mr. Gunderson. I wonder if you've given any more thought to my suggestion?"

"Uff-da." Wally sighed, running a hand across his face (*grind, clang*). "Look, fella, it's nice of you to think of me, honest, but I'm just not the kind of guy for politics."

Wally got more than his share of politics with his work for the Committee. So much so that sometimes he wanted to quit and spend that time at home with Ghost—the large amount of time he spent out of the country had been a knock against him during the adoption process. But he never did quit the Committee because it was kinda his fault it existed in the first place. And sometimes it did good things.

Though it wasn't entirely steady work. As he'd once told his friend Jerusha before she died, the only thing he was really good for was wrecking stuff. Which is why he had been so glad to get the offer to do demolition work for Mr. Matthews's company, Aces in Hand. That wasn't steady, either—it wasn't every day somebody needed a building torn down—though it had picked up recently.

Jube's eyebrows did that thing again. "Politics?"

Tan-suit man gave him a wide smile, nodding like his neck was one of those paint-can shakers at the hardware store. "Morlock-and-Eloi is stepping down from the city council. There's going to be a special election to fill the empty Jokertown spot."

Jube, who knew the neighborhood better than anybody, shook his head. "This is news to me. Why's she quitting?"

Tan suit shrugged. "Illness, I gather." He looked down, shaking his head the tiniest bit, the way people do when they hear that the friend of a friend's cousin's pet died and don't want to seem callous.

"You seem to know a lot about J-town politics."

"Randall McNath, Joker Anti-Defamation League." Tan suit gave Jube a vigorous handshake. "A pleasure. Your reputation precedes you, Mr. Jube." Jube chuckled. "You're clearly already acquainted with Mr. Gunderson.

So you don't need me to tell you that he'd be a fine representative for the people of Jokertown."

He always said things like that. It was nice and all, him being so concerned about the neighborhood, and a member of the Joker Antidefathingy, and not even a joker himself. But just because it was flattering didn't mean it was true or, frankly, very well thought out.

"Well, it's real swell of you to say such nice things, but I tell ya, buddy, I wouldn't be a good fit." Wally looked at Jube for support. The walrus-man was staring at Wally hard, his eyebrows low over his eyes. "Right, Jube?"

Jube fiddled with a pile of magazines, absently squaring and re-squaring it. "The more I think about it . . . It doesn't sound so crazy to me, Wally. Nothing against Morlock-and-Eloi, of course, salt of the earth that woman, but if I had to be honest, she was never quite the same after the fight club took her. And you'd probably be the most honest guy to ever stand for any public office."

"Aw, nuts. Not you, too?"

Jube shrugged. "I'm just saying."

Mr. McNath launched into his paint-shaker nod again. "Exactly! So am I." He turned again to Wally. "As a member of the Committee, you've traveled around the globe, trying to make things right for people. But on the city council, you could do the same for your friends, your neighbors, even your family. Like your work for the Jerusha Carter School—which I applaud, by the way. Little acts of betterment every day, without people shooting at you. It's getting merchants to shovel their sidewalks promptly, not stopping genocides. It's improving signage for school crossing zones, not dodging Exocet missiles in a border dispute."

Wally frowned. "The genocide stuff is important, too."

For the first time since he crossed the street, Mr. McNath stopped fidgeting for a moment. He just stared. But a moment later he was nodding again. "Yes, yes, of course it is. So, think of the city council as in-addition-to, not instead-of." He sure talked fast.

But he was sorta convincing, too.

♥

As an apology for ruining her day off with the mess at the scrapyard, Wally took Darcy out to breakfast. Hollandays was her favorite place for sit-down morning food, and he often felt the need to apologize for something, so they were regulars. The food wasn't too bad, though the corned beef hash didn't come with a slice of Spam on the side the way his dad did it back home. But that was okay.

Their table was quiet but for the clinking of silverware in his hands and the occasional crinkle of folded newsprint. Darcy always read the paper while she finished her coffee.

She sipped, then clinked the cup back into her saucer without looking away from the paper. Once again, their server seemed to appear out of thin air, swooping by to replenish Darcy's nearly-full cup. The service was particularly attentive today: because Darcy would have to go straight to the precinct from the restaurant, she wore her uniform. Wally wondered if maybe she'd timed it that way on purpose. People got real nice when they saw the badge.

He spread boysenberry jam on another piece of toast, then used it to mop up the last of his eggs Benedict. He could never remember what it was called, but he liked the fancy yellow sauce they poured on top of the eggs. He had the impression it might have been invented there.

Darcy sat up, sloshing coffee. "What the hell is this?"

Wally started. The stainless steel butter knife in his hand dissolved into a fine orange powder. "Oops," he said, scattering rust across his plate, the formerly white tablecloth, and her coffee.

Looking for their server, he said, "What is what?"

Darcy held the paper up between them, smacking it lightly with the back of her fingers.

He leaned forward, squinting. "Oh, yeah! I forgot all about that. Neat, huh?"

She glanced at the paper again. "You forgot that you're running for city council?"

Wally caught their server's eye, pointed at the rust on the table, and the remaining silverware, and shrugged, mouthing, "Sorry." To Darcy he said, "I mean, I forgot to tell you about it. Only Ghost knows. Oh, and Jube. And that real nice fella who suggested it in the first place. And now you. And I suppose all the people who see it in the paper. But it's only"—he checked his watch—"seven thirty in the morning. So you're one of the first." He grinned.

Darcy placed the folded newspaper over her plate. "Okay. Walk me through this. You hate politics."

So he explained the whole thing. He liked the way it made him feel, helping people. Everything the Committee did got so complicated, no matter how obvious and necessary it was. And his other job was just work. It wasn't a cause and didn't have a goal, except to make money for Mr. Matthews.

After he finished, Darcy asked, "Did this 'real nice fella' give you his card?"

"Nope."

"Did you ask for one?"

"Nope."

"And you weren't the least bit curious about who he was or why he sought you out?"

"Nope." She watched him as if waiting for more. So he added, "I figured he'd heard about me. Maybe from the other parents at school."

"But if you wanted to talk to him again . . ."

"Oh, I see him all the time lately. We just keep running into each other, like, one coincidence after another. Crazy!"

"Uh-huh. But if somebody wanted to go talk to him, how would she do that?"

"I'm sure he's in the phone book. Oh! I remember now. He works for the Joker thingamajiggy."

It took a while to unravel that, but she eventually figured out what he meant. He didn't understand why she was getting grumpy about the whole thing. After all, her job was all about helping people. He said as much.

At that, her expression softened. She put her hand on his arm. "Hey, I'm not trying to rain on your parade. You're a really good guy and I know you'd take working on the city council as seriously as you take raising your daughter. And thanks to you she *probably* won't grow up to be an axe murderer. You'd pour your big stupid heart into it. And probably drive people crazy and maybe, just maybe, do some good along the way. But have you really thought this through? The city council in New York City is a world apart from the city council in Mountain Iron, Minnesota."

"Back home that was Mr. Lacosky, the principal, and Mrs. Pikkanen, who owns the gas station and bait shop."

"See, that's exactly what I mean." She squeezed his arm before withdrawing. "Are you sure about this?"

He thought it over. "Yep."

"Then I wish you the very best of luck, and I hope the people of Jokertown will soon be fortunate enough to have you in their corner." She picked up the paper again. "And anyway, your opponent is completely off her nut. So that's another point in your favor."

"Opponent?" That made it sound like a boxing match. He didn't like that. He'd had the impression there wouldn't be anybody else. Truth be told, that had been no small part of the appeal of running in the first place. The eggs Benedict turned a little bit sour in his stomach.

Wally leaned across the table, giving the small item in the paper a more careful read-through: Local Activists Throw Hats into J-Town Council Race. He wondered which of his hats he'd have to give up. The fella in the suit hadn't mentioned that part. He also hadn't mentioned Jan Chang, who was listed as another candidate for the empty Jokertown seat.

"You know her?"

"Oh yeah. She once accused me of using parking tickets as a cover for attaching extrajudicial GPS tracking units to prominent citizens' cars without a warrant. Said I was working to usher in a one-world-government junta by making it possible for the Illuminati drones to know exactly where to find and kill those same prominent citizens in a 'decapitation strike.'" Wally didn't understand any of that. Darcy raised her cup as if to take a sip, then saw the rust floating on it, and put it down again. "If there's some crazy claim going around, Jan is probably behind it. Everybody knows better than to believe her, of course."

That was sad. It made him feel sorry for this lady.

Darcy balled up her napkin and tossed it on the table. "The more I think about it, I'm almost looking forward to the round-table forum. Between you and her, it'll be one for the record books. I wonder if my DVR can record public-access cable."

He missed most of that. "What kind of table?"

"I mean the candidates' forum." Darcy ran her finger to the very bottom of the little two-inch piece about the special city council election. "There's a list of events."

So there was. He sighed. "Aw, cripes."

♣

Mordecai was popping the fuel tank from a 1960 Moto Guzzi Cardellino when a battered, rust-splotched Impala came to a noisy stop (squeaky brakes) on the street nearby. Mordecai knew from the parking job that it wasn't Darcy behind the wheel. Plus, she didn't seem to be the kind of woman who tolerated unfixed fender benders and naked Bondo.

Wally blinked in the sun, looking a bit confused, as if he didn't remember being here a few days ago. He definitely had been, as the cracks in the concrete floor of the repair bay could attest. He took a few steps toward the shop entrance, then froze, looking up. He turned in place, head craned back, presumably searching for magnets. Wiping his oily hands with a rag, Mordecai went to the office.

Rochelle, who managed and kept an eye on the front of the shop when Mordecai was working (though it had been a very long time since anybody had tried to rob the Harlem Hammer), turned as he entered. She indicated Wally behind the counter, the shifting of whose jaw suggested a smile.

"This gentleman is here to see you."

Wally waved. "Howdy! You probably don't remember me, but I was here a few days ago. I'm Wally, by the way."

"I remember. You seem to be doing better."

"Gosh. I was in a jam and you sure helped me out."

Mordecai shrugged. "You clearly needed help. I'm glad it worked out and that you're okay."

Wally offered his hand. Mordecai moved to shake it, but then he realized the metal man's iron fingers were curled around something. A frayed tuft of green ribbon dangled from his palm. "I brought you this to say thank you for pulling me down and being so swell about it. Here."

He turned his closed hand over Mordecai's cupped palms. The ribbon had been used to bundle together a collection of mechanical pencils, click erasers, and ballpoint pens. A mismatched collection, but new and nice.

"Uh. Thank you. But it really isn't necessary."

"I heard that you're a crossword puzzler fella, so I thought, what does a guy who does crosswords need? Pencils! And then erasers, too." Wally pointed at the click erasers. "But then I also thought, he seems like a sharp one, and I heard sometimes real smart people even do the puzzles in pen. So I got them pens, too." He pointed again, elaborating, "In case you do the puzzles in ink, see."

Rochelle, turning red with the effort not to burst out laughing, excused herself. As she headed for the break room, Mordecai said, "Thank you, Wally. This is very nice—"

"Oh! I forgot the extra leads. For the pencils, you know." Wally fished around in the breast pocket of his denim overalls and retrieved a little plastic cylinder.

Mordecai took this, too. Wally seemed to be waiting for something, so he said, "You know what? I'll use them every day. I haven't missed the daily puzzle in years. Thank you."

"You betcha." Wally looked around. "Sure is a nice fix-'em-up shop you got here."

"Uh, thank you."

"You know, I was in that scrapyard the other day because I sorta accidentally rusted up the handlebars on this other fella's bike. He got kinda sore about it so I was looking for a replacement . . ."

Mordecai laughed. "Hey, that's what we do. If you have the model information, leave it with Rochelle, and have the owner call us."

"Oh, that's swell! I'll pay, 'cause it was my fault." Wally beamed. Or seemed to. (Damned if it wasn't tricky, reading that metal face.) But he didn't appear in a hurry to go anywhere.

"Would you like a tour?"

"Gosh, that'd be neat."

So they went through the side door into the repair bay containing the partially disassembled Moto Guzzi and the ghostly scent of gasoline. "Neato," said Wally, not really looking at anything. Speaking over the radio, which Mordecai hadn't bothered to turn off and which was now playing something from the Dave Brubeck Quartet, the joker-ace said, "Um. So, hey, fella, this'll sound nuts, but did you know we've met before? I mean, before the other day. Years ago."

Aha. So *that's* what this was about. Mordecai wanted to hash this out even less than he wanted to chow down on a barrel of accursed Kazakh strontium. But even though he could see the slow-motion train wreck coming from a mile away, he felt powerless to avoid it. Even the strongest man in the world couldn't change the path of a loaded freight train once it was barreling down the tracks. Not without hurting a lot of people. He sighed.

"On the TV show."

"Oh. You do remember *American Hero*." The metal man's tone of voice suggested he hoped nobody remembered.

"I sort of regret doing it. I thought I'd have more opportunities to mentor younger folks." Mordecai figured he had a good thirty years on Wally.

"I wish I'd never been on the show at all. But I'm still glad I applied to be a contestant. I mean, it was exciting at first and all, and I suppose that without it I wouldn't have the life I have today, with a daughter and all." Wally trailed off. "If not for the show, I'd be working in an iron mine right now."

"I bet you'd be good at that. You certainly have the, uh, look for it." Did they still use steam shovels? Mordecai didn't know the first thing about mining. He supposed that nowadays everything was diesel or electric.

Wally took a deep breath. Rivets creaked when his chest swelled. "The thing is, that fella who won? He said I said some stuff I didn't say. So I just wanted to say that I didn't say the stuff he said I said."

And there it was. Way back on the first season of *American Hero*, Rustbelt had been eliminated from the contest ("discarded," ugh) after being accused by the eventual winner, Stuntman, of hurling a racial slur at him.

Mordecai closed his eyes, pinching the bridge of his nose. Wally seemed decent. Guileless, at the very least. Mordecai remembered the incident, and the flap at the time, and his doubts about the accusation. But the show's producers had latched onto the narrative twist—it was manna from heaven for people whose livelihoods involved spinning plotted drama from pointless contrived interactions—and that was that. So Wally had gone off to Egypt to defend the helpless, taking a bunch of contestants with him.

But people were complicated. You could never truly know what lurked in somebody's heart. And Mordecai was so damn tired, furiously tired, of the "I'm not racist, *but*" types.

When he opened his eyes, Wally added, "Honest." His skin made a grinding sound and even threw a couple of sparks when he drew his fingertip in a little "x" across his chest.

Mordecai's gut told him Wally was sincere. He wanted to believe it, at any rate. So he made a decision. Surprising himself a little bit, he said, "Let's watch the clip, then."

The shop had several laptops for pulling diagnostic codes from bikes a lot more modern and sophisticated than the Moto Guzzi. And Rochelle had dragged their credit card processing into the twenty-first century with a wireless network. So, after wiping the worst of the grease from the nearest keyboard (an inevitability in a repair shop), Mordecai started searching for "american hero season 1 clips rustbelt stuntman."

It took a bit of digging to find the desired needle in a haystack of manufactured drama. But after a few minutes he landed on a listicle titled, "The 15 Most Shocking Moments on *American Hero,* Seasons I-IX." Merely reading that made him cringe. He could feel his crossword skill leaking away.

He clicked play. The screen filled with slickly edited footage of Jamal Norwood, aka Stuntman, scrambling to get somewhere ahead of Wally. Mordecai recalled nothing of the hokey weekly challenges, only that they were uniformly inane. And, like this one, often loud. The as-televised segment showed the two aces coming close, Rustbelt's jaw moving, and then Stuntman whirling toward the cameras, releasing his hold on the Jetboy statue that had been the object of the hunt. Faintly, over the hurricane whoosh of the helicopter, he could be heard screaming, "Did you hear what he called me. What kind of racist shit is that?"

Mordecai turned up the volume as high as it would go and hit replay. It took more than one rewatch, but Mordecai eventually convinced himself he might have heard a barely audible "n—" coming from Wally.

He turned. "Well?"

"I called him a knucklehead." Wally's gaze went to the cracked floor. "It wasn't nice of me. He, just, gosh, that fella was being so mean. I guess he got under my skin. Maybe he did it on purpose."

Sadly, there would only be one side to this story, as Jamal had given his life in the line of duty, working for SCARE. But Mordecai felt confident that if the man standing next to him was one thing, it was sincere. On balance, he decided, his gut reaction from way back then was affirmed.

"Yeah. I figured as much."

Wally deflated like a rusted-out lead balloon. "Whew. I'm so glad."

Mordecai closed the laptop, eager to get back to work. "Worry no more. Go forth and keep doing what you're doing."

"That's actually what I wanted to ask you about."

Good heavens, there was *more*?

He nodded at the laptop. "I thought that was it."

"I thought maybe there'd be no point without clearing up the TV stuff first."

Jerking a thumb at the disembodied fuel tank, Mordecai said, "I do need to finish this today, so . . ."

"I'm running for city council so I need a campaign manager," Wally blurted.

That took a moment to sink in. "I'm sorry?"

The younger ace explained, in a not particularly eloquent but thoroughly transparent way, about a special election in Jokertown.

"Well, I'm flattered. But, for one thing, I abhor party politics, and for another, obviously I don't live in Jokertown." Mordecai spread his arms, indicating the shop and, by extension, the neighborhood around it. The spot where they stood was miles north of J-town.

"Nope."

"Then why ask me?"

"Because you do crossword puzzles and I . . . don't. It's, you know, there are some people who do puzzles and some who don't. I'm not the kind of person who knows stuff like"—Rusty gestured at the bundle of pens—"I dunno, the French word for 'beret.' But I bet you do." He sighed. "I want to do a good job. But I also know I'm not the sharpest fella. People don't think I understand that. But I do."

Despite his better judgment, Mordecai found that admission genuinely touching. And he had no doubt Wally would do the utmost for his constituents. Maybe he wouldn't have such a healthy skepticism of political games if the players were more like Wally.

"I'll need to think about it. But first, tell me what role your daughter will play in this campaign."

"Ghost? Nothing! I mean, she knows I'm doing it, but that's it. It's got nothing to do with her."

"It will until the election. And after, if you win."

"No it won't. Not ever." Wally shook his head. "She was one of them . . . have you ever heard about them child soldiers? When she was pretty young, some real bad people exposed her to the virus and then they gave her a knife and taught her . . ." He shuddered. "It's not what she is, but it's what they tried to make her. They made her do some bad stuff. Real bad. So I figure, gosh, she's seen so many bad things in her life. She's still just a kid, I guess I'm saying, and if I do one thing in life it's make sure she never again gets wrapped up in grown-ups' baloney."

Mordecai never would have guessed the eye-rolling phone-obsessed tween he'd glimpsed a few days ago had been the progeny of a war zone. That spoke volumes about her resilience, but also spoke extremely well of her father.

What the hell. Wally wasn't exactly a born front-runner. He needed a mentor. And how difficult could it be?

"Good answer," he said, offering his hand. They shook.

"Cripes," said Wally, wincing. "You're strong."

♠

Ghost was haunting the kitchen when Wally emerged from his bedroom. Normally this alarmed him: when she sleepwalked, it meant she'd been having nightmares about her early childhood again. Sometimes Wally had to go through the apartment, count all the knives, and, occasionally, apologize to the neighbors. (She didn't have many friends for sleepovers. Bubbles and Adesina were *real* understanding.) He tensed: she was holding something long and thin. But after rubbing the sleep from his eyes he saw it was a paintbrush, not her favorite stiletto. He relaxed.

"Whatcha doing, kiddo?"

When Ghost was deep in thought, the very tip of her tongue stuck from the corner of her mouth. Like it did now. The kitchen smelled like paint.

She leaned over the table, arms outstretched as if she were going to hug her craft project. "Don't look! Not yet!"

"Okey dokey." He turned his attention to the coffeepot which, once again, he'd forgotten to set the night before. He resolved to be more organized. If he got on the city council he couldn't be the kind of guy who forgot to make coffee. He'd have to be the kind of guy who remembered coffee and made sure everybody got some, if they wanted it, but also made sure the people who didn't like coffee got something else. Like tea, or milkshakes.

He figured the city council was like that.

Once he managed to get a cup filled, he rummaged under the sink for the S.O.S pads and lumbered into the bathroom. He kept the door open so that he could keep an eye on Ghost, balanced the coffee on the vanity, and set about inspecting himself in the mirror for signs of rust. Every blemish got a quick scrub with lemon-scented steel wool.

When finished, he called out, "Can I look yet?"

"Wait!" He heard the scraping of a chair, and Ghost blowing on something. "Okay. You can come back now."

She floated in the middle of the kitchen table, holding a large piece of poster board in her outstretched arms. It was blank and almost too big for her. But then she spun in midair to show him the other side. She'd written

GUNDERSON CAMPAIGN HEADQUARTERS

in puffy glitter paint.

"Oh my gosh. You made this for me?"

She bobbed up and down.

"Well now it's official, isn't it? This is super."

It took a bit of rummaging to find a hole puncher and a good length of yarn, but Wally had it hanging squarely over the kitchen table by the time Mordecai arrived. The dripping had mostly stopped by then, although the "S" in HEADQUARTERS looked a little smeary.

In response to a firm but unaggressive knock, Ghost drifted across the apartment, settled on the floor as she rematerialized, and opened the door. Mordecai stood outside, holding a valise.

"Good morning, young lady. I believe we've met. I'm Mordecai." He offered his hand. Instead of taking it, she curtseyed (where in the heck did she learn that?) and stepped back, motioning him to enter. The boards creaked under him. Wally was glad their apartment was on the ground; he was hard on floors, too.

"You helped Dad. I'm Ghost."

"Nice to meet you."

"Hi, guy!" Wally waved from the kitchen.

Mordecai joined him, gaze flicking back and forth between Wally and the sign hanging over his head. For a moment, the look on his face got real hard to read. But then he said, "You, uh, have some . . ." and gestured at his head.

"Nuts." Wally tore a paper towel from the dispenser. It came away from his forehead smeared blue and stippled with red and green glitter.

He pushed out a chair for Mordecai. But the other man took one look at it and said, "I'd better stand. That'll break if I sit in it."

Wally stood. "Here. Take mine. I got the same problem sometimes." His chair was reinforced. "I insist."

Once at the table, Mordecai got down to business. From the valise he produced a sheaf of papers, a laptop, and one of the pens that Wally had given him.

"First things first. I went to City Hall yesterday to file your intent-to-campaign form. Here's the receipt for your check. I can send you a digital scan if you're doing your campaign accounting electronically. Or should I just give these things to your accountant?" In response to Wally's blank look, he added, "Or maybe you have a dedicated file for expenses?"

"Oh, sure." Wally thought about it for a moment. Then he reached over and pulled the empty cookie jar off the counter. "Stick it in here. This'll work."

When the crinkling stopped, Mordecai cleared his throat. "Given this is a low-level affair, I think it's unlikely that anybody is going to come back later and demand to audit your campaign books. Not for something that'll run its course from start to finish in a few weeks. That kind of thing is usually reserved for big campaigns with official fundraising organizations. And even if there were enough time for the entire process, I'm guessing you don't want to go through the hassle of filing for a 501(c)(3)."

Wally didn't get the joke, so he just nodded. "Anything more than one hundred sounds pretty expensive."

"Uh-huh." Here Mordecai gave the cookie jar a meaningful glance. "Nevertheless, and just in case, it wouldn't be a bad idea to use an accounting system that's a little more official. If you see what I mean?"

"Oh, sure. Good thinkin', pal!"

Wally slid the jar closer and, using Ghost's paintbrush, covered the word "cookie." Then in red glitter paint he wrote "money" on the lid. He beamed at his campaign manager over the newly created and very official Money Jar. "I knew you'd be the right fella for this job."

"Time will tell." The next set of papers Mordecai produced was fringed with about a dozen yellow adhesive tags. "Okay, speaking of the financials, next is your conflict of interest statement and disclosure forms. By signing these you're asserting that you don't own or are invested in any ventures that would directly benefit, financially, from your being on the city council. In other words you're not doing this to secretly make yourself rich."

Wally could understand the need for this. He'd seen firsthand dictatorships where the folks in charge got rich while their people had it real real bad. He stole a glance at Ghost, bobbing in a corner as she played on her phone.

"That's easy. Where do I sign?"

They were still going through the disclosure forms when Darcy arrived, phone to her ear. She gave Ghost a wink as she entered, saying, "Yes, I'll hold."

"This is quite a sight," she added, and then to Mordecai, "Nice to see you again. Welcome to Wonderland."

Mordecai gave her a friendly nod. "Ma'am."

She sniffed. "It's 'Miss,' thank you very much."

She helped herself to a coffee cup and, filling it, said, "Yes hi good morning, I recently met one of your staff members and he gave me his card"—this she punctuated with a meaningful glare at Wally—"but I'm afraid I lost it. If he's there could you put me through to a Randall?"

Mordecai tucked the signed disclosure forms away, and replaced them on the table with minutes from every city council meeting of the past eighteen months.

"We don't have to go through these right now, but it would be a very good idea to study them. They'll give you a good sense of how the council operates, what the major issues have been, and where the various councilors come down on those issues. You'll see who work with, and against, each other. Knowing the lay of the land will give you a leg up."

"Holy smokes," said Wally. The stack was over an inch thick. There sure was a lot of reading to do.

"Oh, by the way, I think this will help when you're reading those." Next from the valise Mordecai produced a little booklet titled *Robert's Rules of Order*. "City council meetings are run according to a particular method," he said, tapping the booklet. "It'll seem strange at first but you'll get the hang of it."

Wally leafed through the booklet. (Rules for holding a meeting? Gosh.) "Huh. Meetings of the Committee are done differently. People just yell at each other."

Meanwhile, Darcy listened to a voice that was only faintly audible to Wally in bits and pieces. But whatever she heard, it made her face twist up in confusion. "Are you sure? Huh, that's so weird. I could have sworn he said his name was Randall. Can you hold on a sec while I check to see if I jotted it down correctly?"

Then she cupped her hand over the bottom of her phone. "Psst, hey, Mr. Politician, what was this guy's name? The one from the JADL?"

Wally concentrated. "I'm pretty sure it was Randy. Or Randall? Yeah, that sounds right."

Darcy frowned and, still looking at him, uncupped the phone. "Well, 'Randall' is what I scribbled here. Would you mind checking one more time? Please?"

Wally's wristwatch started to beep. "Aw, heck." Across the apartment, he called, "Hey, kid, we gotta go," and across the table he said, "I'm real sorry, fella, real sorry, but I gotta take her over to the school. Her scout troop is selling cookies. Fundraiser for a camping trip. Ghost volunteered to help unload the truck."

"No I didn't," she objected. "You volunteered me."

Wally winced. She'd been "volunteered" for the experiment that killed all of her friends and turned her into a killer ace, too. "But you're excited to go camping, right?"

"I already know how to live outdoors."

Yeah . . . she did. Wally was pretty sure that nobody else in her troop could survive in the jungle on her own for weeks. Maybe he'd chosen the wrong activity for her.

"I'll only be gone half an hour. Promise."

Darcy, still on the phone, nodded, mouthing, "Of course." Mordecai said, "This sounds important. You guys go. I'll keep working on your calendar while you're gone."

◆

After the door closed behind Wally and Ghost, Darcy looked up from her book. "I have to say, you deserve an award for how well you're taking all of this in stride." She nodded at the Campaign Headquarters sign and the Money Jar.

"It's definitely an interesting challenge."

"Well, Wally's lucky to have you on his team."

"What about you?"

"You mean why didn't I step up and offer to do what you're doing? Two reasons. First, I'm a cop and there's this thing called conflict of interest. Second, I didn't want to." She pointed at the Money Jar. "That's pretty much exactly how I figured this would go down."

"That's not very supportive."

"Don't get me wrong. Wally is probably the best human being I've ever known. But he can be a lot."

Mordecai sighed hard enough to make his chair groan. She wasn't wrong. "I'm getting that."

"But he'd fight tooth and nail and rivet for his constituents. It really is too bad he's going to lose. And that is where my job will come in."

"Lose?" Mordecai scoffed. "Miss, I have not *begun* to flex these yet." He curled his arms, making his legendary muscles bulge until the stitching in his shirt sleeves complained. Even the floor creaked.

They shared a laugh.

♥

The campaign strategy discussion continued over a pile of take-out containers. Darcy had sprung for the meal and, after Mordecai explained to Wally how it was a good idea to categorize things, the receipt had gone into the Money Jar with "campaign contribution: Darcy" scrawled on the back.

Even when he didn't understand everything, Wally never wavered in his attentive listening. Mordecai could tell he was taking it all very seriously. He found that encouraging.

Working down the checklist on his laptop, Mordecai said, "Okay. Next item. While I was at City Hall, I called up all the other intent-to-campaign forms that had been filed." Mordecai pulled up a digital scan he'd taken with his phone camera. "The first and, as of yesterday afternoon, so far only other person to join the race is a Jan Chang."

He turned the screen around so Wally could see. There was no photo but the forms, of course, had her address.

"I oughta go introduce myself."

Darcy shook her head. "That's noble, but I know from direct personal experience with her that it won't go over the way you're expecting."

"I sure would like to shake her hand. Just so she knows me and knows I won't be mean or anything."

("Yeah, but what about her," Darcy muttered.)

"I think it's a great idea," said Mordecai, surprising them both. "Perfect way to set the tone for the next few weeks. And because you're the one taking the initiative, it makes you look good. Even better that you do it informally, without a press release, so people can't accuse you of a publicity stunt. It's just two people shaking hands and promising a clean fight. Like boxers before a match."

"Yikes!" Wally shook his head. "I'm not gonna punch her or nothing like that!"

"Well that's even better," said Mordecai, standing. "And if we walk over there, you can meet and interact with your future constituents along the way."

"Oh, most of 'em already know me." Wally clanged a knuckle against his forearm. "I'm the metal guy." He paused for a moment, the look in his eyes momentarily going distant. Then he returned from wherever he'd gone. "Ooh! That should be our slogan! *'Vote for the Metal Guy.'*"

"Hmm. Let's not settle on it just yet, in case we have other ideas we like. But I'm glad you're thinking about slogans. Now you're thinking like a politician," said Mordecai. "We should settle on one in the next day or so, so we have time to get it printed on your signs." He nodded at the Money Jar. "That'll be another campaign expense, by the way, and one of your larger ones."

"I hope the jar is big enough."

"But anyway, the people of Jokertown might know and think of you as Rustbelt, founding member of the United Nations Committee on Extraordinary Interventions—"

"Gosh, I'd forgotten the whole name."

"—and Rustbelt, champion of the Jerusha Carter School, and Rustbelt, local dad."

("And Rustbelt, menace to parking meters," said Darcy.)

"But they don't yet think of you as Rustbelt, city councilor. That's what we want. When people think of you, we want them to associate you with the guy who's going to listen to their concerns. The guy in their corner."

"Okay, but like I said, I ain't gonna punch nobody."

"That's for the best, I think." Mordecai zipped his laptop into the valise. "Let's hit the pavement, team."

They were almost out the door when Ghost, who had ridden the subway back with her troop leader, said, "Wallywally, your special hat."

"Cripes, I almost forgot! I got the perfect thing for being a politics guy." He disappeared into his bedroom and emerged a moment later with a gray silk top hat perched on the iron dome of his head. An elastic chin strap hooked under Wally's jaw kept it from sliding off. "Snazzy, huh?"

Mordecai looked him up and down. The combination of denim overalls and opera hat was undeniably eccentric, but it wouldn't merit a second glance in Jokertown.

"You know what?" Darcy said, her mouth curling into a rare smile. "I kinda love it."

♣

The seven-block stroll to Jan Chang's brownstone took forever because Wally—to his credit—embraced his public debut as a candidate and paused to shake practically every hand, foot, fin, frond, trunk, tentacle, cilium, stalk, pseudopod, antenna, mandible, gill, and claw they passed on the street. (It did go a little more smoothly once they convinced him to stop bellowing "*WALLY GUNDERSON FOR CITY COUNCIL!*" every thirty feet.) And he chatted with anyone and everyone. But it was a pleasant spring day, and the cherry trees on Bleecker sweetened the breeze with a blizzard of white petals.

While Wally discussed PTA drama with a fellow parent from the Jerusha Carter School, Mordecai turned to Darcy.

"So. Police officer, huh?"

"Mmm-hmm. The thin blue line, that's me."

"What's your beat?"

"If that's your roundabout way of asking if I work the Jokertown precinct, the answer is yes. And it's okay to call it Fort Freak. Everybody does. But it's not okay to call me a meter maid, even though everybody does that, too. I'm a parking enforcement officer."

Quietly, watching Wally converse with a person who had the head and neck of a giant earthworm and what appeared to be a humanoid body covered in mackerel heads, Mordecai said, sotto voce, "An endorsement from your fraternity would be a boon for his campaign."

"I saw this request coming from a mile away."

"Well, what are the chances? He seems to know lots of people. Does that include your colleagues?"

"Oh, everybody at the precinct knows Wally. Maybe not in the way you'd prefer, though."

Mordecai started. "You're not telling me he has a criminal record? I can't believe that."

"No, but you should know that for a period of time his list of parking citations was the stuff of legend. Relax, they're all paid now. I made sure of that. But you know how after he got magnetized you were reticent to bring him inside your shop? Well, let's just say our budget for paper clips and hard drives went through the roof the last time he visited the precinct."

"Oh."

"People still talk about it."

"In a funny reminiscence kind of way?"

"No. More of a 'I had to let my perp walk when we lost all the witness statements' kind of way."

"So—"

"They're endorsing Chang. At least until somebody less batso comes along."

He'd been running the campaign for less than two days, but that stung. "And you?"

"I can't campaign for Wally inside the precinct any more than I can anywhere else. But we have a few weeks. I'll work on them. I can change some minds between now and then."

"Okay. You're our woman on the inside."

She shushed him. "Don't say stuff like that. It's like catnip to IA."

Wally's interactions with passersby dwindled a little as they neared Jan's place. Halfway down the block, he waved at a familiar figure descending the stairs to the basement of a brownstone. "Howdy, Jube!"

The walrus-joker paused in the act of unlocking the door. He spun, hiding something behind his back. "Oh, well, hey, look at that, it's Wally Gunderson." His gaze flitted between Wally and the doorstep of the neighboring building. Under his breath, he added, "On this street."

"What are you doing here, buddy?"

"I, uh, live here," said Jube, eyes scanning the windows of the neighboring building. The drapes twitched. He reached for his door. "Well, good to see you, I'd better—"

Darcy stepped forward. "Jube, one moment, please," she said in what was clearly her cop voice.

The walrus turned again, tipping his hat to her. "Afternoon, Officer Ackerman. Didn't see you there. Well I'm sure you've got places to be—"

She spoke over him. "I believe that on Monday of this past week, you and Mr. Gunderson together encountered a person who expressed enthusiasm for city council politics. Is that correct?"

"Yes—"

"I don't suppose you recall his name."

Mordecai had to admire her technique. Everybody knew Jube never forgot a face or a name or the tiniest crumb of gossip. By indirectly challenging this, she hooked him by the pride. He stopped inching toward the door. "Of course I do: Randall McNath. From the Joker Anti-Defamation League."

She frowned. "Are you absolutely certain?"

Jube looked pained. "Come on."

"Thank you for your help, citizen."

He glanced at the neighboring house again. "Well, if that's everything—"

"Enjoy your day."

Jube spun for his door, unlocking and opening it at the same moment his neighbor's door swung open. A woman wearing extremely thick dark glasses stormed onto the stoop of the adjoining brownstone. Jube's shoulders sagged.

"A-*ha*," she declared, pointing at him over the railing. "I knew it. I *knew* it. I caught you red-handed."

Wally looked at the number on the mail slot, then compared it to the number written on his arm in puffy glitter paint. "Oh my gosh. Are you Miss Chang?" There was a brief grinding of metal when he scratched his temple, as if trying to remember something. "Oh, hey, I know you! You were in Texas with all them band kids. Me, too!"

The newcomer ignored him, anger focused on the walrus. "I knew you were spying on me for the enemy camp."

Mordecai raised his hands in what he thought would be a supplicating gesture. "Whoa, hey, we're not—"

"I won't be threatened." Little arcs of electricity leapt the gap between her teeth when she raised her voice, exhorting random passersby to take out their phones and record her assassination. "They can't get all of us!"

"—enemies," he finished quietly, backing away.

(Darcy said, sotto voce, "I warned you guys.")

Jan saw Darcy and, finally, Wally. "Oh, I get it. I get it. I see what's happening here. The NYPD cites me for some made-up offense, the paper injects me with their subcutaneous tracking technology, and then *he* watches me through the holes in the walls, reporting every move until the time is right to take me out. Then they install their robotic minion—"

("Hey," said Wally.)

"—and before you can say 'Annunaki overlords' the rest of the city council has been mesmerized. Then, boom! Rents spike up to a thousand dollars per square foot while economy-destroying tycoons chew up our neighborhoods and turn us into hyper-abstracted financial instruments in a gigantic spreadsheet somewhere."

Jube asked, "Why would I have to watch you if they're already tracking you?"

Good question, thought Mordecai. But, having read the room, so to speak, he kept this to himself.

"Well, the joke's on you, Jube. I'm installing steel plating over the drywall. Every inch." She tapped her temple. "Try drilling through *that*! Ha."

Wally stepped forward. "Gosh. I think we got off on the wrong foot. I just wanted to introduce myself and say—"

Though he was twenty feet away, she shrank from his outstretched hand. "I won't fall for that. You think *I* don't know that *they* know that a walking Faraday cage would be the perfect assassin for *me*? Ha." She leaned forward, sniffed the air, then retreated against the wrought-iron bannister, where the snap and crackle of corona discharge filled the street with the metallic stink of ozone. "What's in that microsyringe, Mr. 'Wally Gunderson'?" She raised her gloved hands and waggled her index fingers in the air when she said Wally's name. "Polonium? Weaponized anthrax? Xenovirus Takis-H? Yeah, that's right, I know all about strain 'H.' Or maybe it's something special cooked up by your reptoid shadowmasters in Majestic-12."

"I don't know what any of those words mean, ma'am."

"Stooges never do." Jan stepped inside. "I'm sweeping for bugs after you leave, so don't bother dispersing your aerosolized drones." Then she slammed the door. A fading glow of St. Elmo's fire limned the door.

Silence, like the fading echoes of a thunderclap, enveloped the street.

"Cripes," Wally sighed, effectively summarizing the encounter.

Darcy nodded. "Yeah. Definitely recording the forum."

Wally noticed the package behind Jube's back. "Hey, whatcha got there, fella?"

"What, this? Nothing."

"It looks like a sign. Hey, you know, I'm gonna have some signs printed up real soon. Maybe you could . . ."

Wally trailed off when Darcy laid a hand on his arm. She pointed at the windows of Jube's brownstone. All but one held a sign reading

JAN CHANG FOR CITY COUNCIL

Wally's shoulders slumped.

"Don't take it personally. And she's really okay most of the time. It's just, since the city council thing . . ." Jube shrugged. "I can't keep replacing my appliances."

♠

Wally lay in bed, reading the city council minutes that Mordecai had acquired.

It was slow going. He didn't read real fast, for one. And for another, everything the councilors said involved quorums and motions and seconds and points of order and yeas and nays, so he had to keep *Robert's Rules of Order* in one hand and the minutes in the other, practically reading both at the same time. It was like a different language. But he kept at it. He had to know this stuff.

He soon noticed that Jan Chang appeared frequently in the public comment sections. She used a lot of terms like "amortization," "Bohemian Grove," "credit default swap," and "Illuminati." He'd found he needed a dictionary on the nightstand, too, to piece through the meeting minutes, but even this didn't help with a lot of what Jan said.

He paid particular attention to the places where the councilors for Jokertown spoke up a lot. In addition to Morlock-and-Eloi on the council, there was Mark Benson, whose dentist's office was just down the street. When it came to Jokertown issues, he and M&E usually agreed, though they'd been on opposite sides of a debate over something called the Annex Nine Phase Two Redevelopment. Whatever it was, M&E had been dead set against it. Vocally so.

Overall, she seemed to have taken seriously her responsibility for Jokertown and its residents. Too bad she'd gotten sick.

◆

"It's as if he doesn't exist."

Mordecai bent steel pipes around a frame, listening to Darcy. One advantage his repair shop had over many others was that he could bend all the metal by hand, thus faster and cheaper than shops that had to use torches and hammers. It was also the only motorcycle shop in the city—and the only establishment in Harlem, period—with a **WALLY GUNDERSON FOR JOKERTOWN** sign in the window (*"THE METAL MAN WITH THE METTLE TO SOLVE YOUR PROBLEMS!"*).

"Maybe the JADL fired him," he said. "That would explain why he's not in their phone book."

"No." Darcy shook her head. "I went down there. They'd never heard of him. And you don't think that's weird?"

"If he really did claim to work there . . ." Mordecai conceded the point. "Yeah, it's weird."

"At first I thought Wally had misremembered—"

"I can understand how you might have thought that."

"—but then Jube confirmed what Wally had told us." She was pacing now.

"It's not as if this Randall person, or whatever his name is, actually committed a crime. Just to play devil's advocate, all he did was convince Wally to run."

"First of all, are we really sure that's not a crime? And second, he did so under a false name, claiming false credentials. Honest people don't do that."

"Well, sure. I'm not saying it isn't hinky. But I don't see the play here.

Wally is honest to a fault. It's not like they're installing somebody who can be bribed."

"I don't have an answer for that yet," said Darcy, "but here's the really worrisome thing. Not only did he give Wally and Jube a false name, he up and disappeared after Wally joined the race. Wally said he kept running into this person. But in the past week? Vanished."

"Maybe he doesn't live in J-town, either. Like me."

"Then why does he give a toss about who represents it? And why claim to work for the JADL? Because it opens doors in Jokertown. Even people with compound eyes can read the papers and watch the news. Many places in the world, jokers don't have it very good." She stopped pacing. "I am telling you, as a cop, something doesn't smell right about this."

"We'll get to the bottom of it. Or you will, anyway." Mordecai paused in bending another pipe so he didn't have to speak over the groan of distressed steel. "Wally's lucky to have you looking out for him."

"It's why we make the big bucks, you and me. Speaking of which, dare I ask how fares the debate preparation?"

Mordecai winced.

♥

The candidates' round-table forum was held in a community room of the local library and sponsored by the *Jokertown Cry*. The paper had wanted to use the auditorium of the Jerusha Carter School, which was larger and had better facilities, but Jan had refused on the grounds that Wally's relationship with the school offered his agents ample opportunity to install psychotropic agents in the HVAC.

Tables had been angled at the front of the room so that Wally and Jan could face both each other and the audience at the same time. At Jan's insistence, she and Wally were seated as far apart as the width of the New York Public Library Jokertown Branch's Xavier Desmond Community Room would allow. Something about Wally's body acting like a "subharmonic refractor for ionospheric HAARP beams."

Ghost and the others sat just behind the moderators' table. Wally waved at them. A stand mike had been situated in each aisle, for the public Q&A portion of the forum. The moderators' table didn't have a microphone, owing to its proximity to Jan and the pretty lights under her skin.

Near the back of the room, a technician fiddled with a digital video camera on a tripod. Wally tugged at his hat's chin strap. Looking at the camera made it tighten, like it was trying to choke him.

He recognized a few parents from the Carter School. Mrs. Trelawny gave him an encouraging smile. Leaning against the rear wall, maybe so that his bulk wouldn't block the camera, was an out-of-uniform Officer Bester, one of Darcy's coworkers. A cryptic look passed between the two police officers; Bester shrugged at her. If she had convinced others to attend, Wally didn't recognize them.

Mr. McNath hadn't come. That was a bummer. He'd been such a fan of the campaign, even before it started.

Jan's supporters had turned out, too. Wally didn't see Jube anywhere, but three of her fans sat in the same row as Ghost, wearing JAN CHANG FOR CITY COUNCIL T-shirts. He knew the slightly rubbery guy on the end; Mr. Ruttiger had been one of his fellow chaperones during the band trip to Texas. Wally tried not to look disappointed. It woulda been nice to have more people on his side of the aisle. He'd called Bubbles but she was down in Brazil, doing a fashion shoot in Rio de Janeiro and fighting forest fires in the Amazon. It felt crummy wishing she was here instead.

Maybe he should've worn something other than his John Deere overalls. Wally tugged on his top hat again, glancing at the camera. Gee whiz, he didn't like being on TV.

"Relax," Mordecai said. Ghost gave him a thumbs-up.

The room was approximately a third full at ten minutes after the official starting time of the event, so the fella from the *Cry* stood up and addressed the crowd. He introduced the candidates and explained the format of the discussion. He had what looked like spider legs for arms. Wally couldn't remember if he'd seen him around the neighborhood, but then, he didn't subscribe to the *Cry*. Or any other paper.

Maybe he shouldn't mention that.

The moderator took his seat and opened a binder. "We'll begin by asking the candidates to describe briefly their motivation for seeking a seat on the council, and why they feel they are better suited to serving the people of Jokertown. Mr. Gunderson?"

Mordecai had anticipated the forum would begin this way, so he'd spent hours over the past few days helping Wally practice what he wanted to say and how he wanted to say it. His campaign manager had insisted that Wally's motivations were "above reproach" (a good thing, Wally learned, after consulting the dictionary on his nightstand), so all he had to do was practice the delivery.

Don't be intimidated by the audience, Mordecai had said. *Just pretend everybody in the audience is naked.*

Wally remembered that now, and blushed. The chin strap pulled tighter still. And had they turned up the lights, too? It sure seemed warm.

A camera shutter clicked. The moderator cleared her throat. "Mr. Gunderson?"

"Yep. I mean, 'Yes.'" He took a deep breath. "I, uh, figure lots of you know me, but maybe some don't. I wasn't born here, but this is where I've made my home. I have a family and I pay taxes and all my parking tickets, all of 'em, even though, gosh, it sure was a lot of money—"

A frantic motion in the front row caught his eye: Darcy drawing the edge of her hand across her neck while Mordecai rolled his index fingers around each other in the little gesture they decided would mean "move on."

"Anyway, when I'm not here in Jokertown I've traveled all over the world with the United Nations trying to help folks who need it. Like the jokers in Egypt some years back, and some folks in East Timor, and those poor kids in the place that used to be the People's Paradise of Africa" (Ghost betrayed no reaction) "and a buncha other places, too. But sometimes the help people need isn't facing down tanks and bullets and bad guys. Sometimes it's fixing potholes or making parking meters that don't break so dang easily." (Darcy rolled her eyes at this digression.) "That makes people's lives better, too. On the Committee, we come and go and sometimes I don't get to see how what we've done made things better for the folks living there. But this is where I live. And I'm not going anywhere." (Mordecai wrote that part.) "I like making a difference in people's lives. I've done it around the world, and I will do it here, too. If I can survive getting machine-gunned in a war zone, I can survive city council meetings." (Hold for laughter. Mordecai wrote that part, too.)

After polite applause, it was Jan's turn.

"Okay. We don't have all evening, so I'll give you the executive summary. Guys, my visual aid, please?" The trio with JAN CHANG T-shirts slid a long cardboard tube out from under their seats. Mr. Ruttiger stretched like a rubber band, bobbing over the moderator's table to hand it to Jan.

She said, "I've been tracing the secret currents of power in this country, and in this city, for years. At tremendous personal peril and cost, I might add. So, why am I running for city council?" Jan asked, sliding something from the tube. "I think my research speaks for itself."

With a flourish she unfurled a large sheet of butcher paper. It was full of little pictures, handwritten phrases, and newspaper clippings, all connected with different-colored pieces of yarn, like a tie-dyed spiderweb. The diagram-collage thingy had a few large labels written in capital letters and circled in black Magic Marker: FEDERAL RESERVE, MK-ULTRA, BILDERBERG GROUP, REPTOIDS, PAUL MCCARTNEY/WALRUS. A tangle of yarn connected these to each other and to dozens of smaller labels on the poster: *mortgage-backed financial instruments, water fluoridation, Jokertown city council, chemtrails, 2008 recession.* Wally didn't get most of it, but the tangle was real pretty, like the cat's cradles that Ghost sometimes did on her fingers.

"Wow," said Wally into the sudden silence. "Was I supposed to make a poster, too?"

Jan held the butcher paper aloft until only her fingertips were visible, awkwardly angling it toward the camera. From behind the poster, her slightly muffled voice added, "By the way, everybody in this room is now a target. That's the curse of knowledge. But they can't get us all!"

Then she lowered it again. "When I'm on the city council, I'll . . ." She cast about, looking for something. "Guys, my prop." They passed a pair of scissors to her. Little arcs of electricity danced between the open blades as she raised her voice. "When I'm on the city council, I'll cut this Gordian knot spun from generations of middle-class financial subjugation!" And with that, she set about sawing through the thickest tangle of yarn. Maybe the scissors weren't sharp; she gave up after a moment and tossed them on the table, saying, "Well, you get the point."

Wally couldn't tell if the applause Jan received was as confused as he was, but it sounded like about the same amount as he got. He figured that was a pretty good sign.

"Also," she added, "rents are too damn high."

The audience really liked that. Somebody even whistled.

As Jan re-rolled her spiderweb poster, Wally noticed that one of the little text bubbles hanging off *Jokertown city council*—a scribble of red ink wedged between yarn-tags labeled *polio vaccine* and *Count of St. Germaine*—read *Ann. 9 Phase II Redev.* Something about that seemed familiar, but he couldn't say why.

The moderated portion of the forum mostly focused on issues before the city council, and a few hypotheticals. (Moderator: "Numerous cities across the country have passed ordinances banning single-use plastic grocery bags. Some support this move on environmental grounds, but retailers argue this raises their costs, which are then passed to consumers. Candidates, where would you stand on this issue?" Wally: "Well, them plastic bags don't look so nice in the spring when the winds blow and they get stuck in trees." Jan: "Retailers' plastic bags usually derive from various ethylene polymerizations including high-density or HDPE, low-density or LDPE, and linear low-density or LLDPE. All are highly stable with extremely long lifetimes to degradation, meaning they stay in the environment for decades. Beyond the immediate environmental risk, however, the military-chemical-industrial complex infuses these items with synthetic hormones that are easily absorbed through the skin. These hormones are capable of permeating the blood-brain barrier to attack the pituitary gland, where they prime the victim's brain to receive the transmissions hidden in digital television broadcasts." Wally: "Gosh.")

Then the moderator opened the floor to questions from the audience. The first was addressed at Jan:

"You make a lot of unverifiable claims, so it's hard to know if what you're saying is true. You're very vocal about being targeted and having your life threatened. Why should I vote for somebody who sounds so paranoid?"

"You want evidence of the conspiracy, right?"

Her questioner nodded, then returned to his seat.

"Okay. The evidence is sitting right in front of you." Jan removed her gloves, waggling her fingers until little arcs of electricity danced between them like the science stuff in the old black-and-white Frankenstein movies. "Some of you call me 'Sparkplug.' Don't you think it's odd that my only opponent in this race is a metal man? A metal man whose body functions as a natural Faraday cage?" The more she spoke, the louder her voice, and the brighter the arcs between her fingers. They appeared between her teeth, too, as she built to a crescendo. "A metal man who is, therefore, completely immune to my abilities? Who better than a metal man—who, by his own admission, has ample experience with combat and regime change—to assassinate me?"

Wally, trying to remember all that complicated wordy Robert's Rules stuff, jabbed a finger in the air. "Objection, Your Honor!"

Jan cocked her head, peering at him through her thick sunglasses. "Do you understand we're not in court?"

"Oh." He lowered his finger.

The next question was for Wally. The lady at the microphone read her question from an index card.

"You've repeatedly emphasized your association with the United Nations Committee. Yet you were absent from recent events in Kazakhstan, arguably the greatest humanitarian crisis since the Card Sharks released the Black Trump. How do you respond to those who accuse you of abandoning your colleagues, and who say that Aero, Doktor Omweer, and many others might be alive today if you had joined the fight?"

Silence, heavy as a wet wool blanket, fell across the audience. It was as though the air had been sucked from the room. ("Whoa," Ghost whispered. "That escalated quickly.")

Jan's supporters in the front row looked at each other and shrugged. Both Mordecai and Darcy turned in their seats, craning their necks to get a look at the questioner.

(Jan scoffed. "Kazakhstan was a false flag.")

Wally tugged on his chin strap. It felt like the elastic was cutting through his jaw. The strap snapped. He removed his top hat, placed it on the table, lowered his head, and ran his hands across his face. He knew people didn't like the grinding sounds his body made sometimes, but he needed to process the question.

Not because he hadn't wondered the same thing himself. He had. But because he couldn't answer the question without bringing Ghost into it. He chewed on this, looking for a way to keep his personal promise to himself and his vow to Mordecai without dodging the question.

The *snick* of a camera shutter punctuated the silence. Somebody coughed. People started to whisper to each other.

Wally raised his head. Everyone was watching him.

"Nobody knew what was going on over there. Not at first. It took a few days before people understood how bad it was. And by the time I heard about it . . . I, uh, I got scared. See, I'm responsible for somebody, you know? Maybe you are, too. Well, my person, she doesn't have anyone else. And I worried, gosh, what if I go and I don't come back? What happens to her? Now, those fellas you mentioned, I didn't know them much but I think they were good folks. Thinking about 'em and all the others makes me sad. But if they didn't make it back, I wouldn't have, either. Sometimes making the world better means keeping it from getting worse for just one person." He looked at Ghost, who sniffed and rubbed her eyes. "I know I made the right choice."

Darcy broke the ensuing silence. "Holy crap," she said, and clapped. Mordecai joined her. Wally didn't really hear the applause, though, because he was busy watching Ghost.

The forum concluded soon after that. Mordecai scooted over to shake Wally's hand, followed closely by Darcy.

"You did a fantastic job. You should feel proud."

"Thanks, fella," Wally said. "You sure helped me out. All that reading, oof, it was tough, but . . ."

Reading. The meeting minutes.

As he watched Jan pack up her visual aids and props, Wally suddenly remembered where he'd seen something similar to the weird abbreviation on her poster.

He raised his voice over the hubbub of people chatting, putting on their coats, and bumping into chairs. To the moderator, who was finishing up his notes, Wally said, "Hey there. Are we allowed to ask you questions, too?"

The newspaper guy blinked. "What?"

"I was just wondering something. You asked us about all sorts of city council stuff, but how come you never asked us about Annex Nine?"

Darcy frowned. "What the hell is—"

Jan's poster tube clattered on the floor. The sparkly lights under her skin went dark, like somebody had flipped a switch. "How do *you* know about that?"

♣

Mordecai and Wally were hunched over the kitchen table, aka Gunderson Campaign Headquarters, when Darcy burst into the apartment, weaving a sheaf of papers like a pennant.

"I've got it. I've got it."

She plunked the papers on the table. "Check this out."

Mordecai did. The top half of the stack comprised financial disclosure forms, like the one he'd helped Wally fill out. The bottom half pertained to a company called Twenty-First-Century Retail Group. Flipping through these pages, he glimpsed the SEC logo.

He showed Wally. "'SEC' stands for Securities and Exchange Commission," he said.

Wally nodded. "Sure."

"They're like the police, but for banks," said Darcy.

Wally nodded. "Sure."

"I know how to pull disclosure forms," said Mordecai, "but how did you get all this other stuff?"

"Um, I'm a *cop*?" She pulled up a chair. "At first I thought there was nothing to her ranting after the forum. But I kept thinking about what Jan said about some kind of real estate swindle, so I went over to the detectives' desks and asked around. Franny Black has been keeping tabs on these guys. If he's right, they are into some shady stuff."

She nudged Mordecai aside and used his laptop to pull up an image of the board of directors of Twenty-First. Five men stood in a conference room. The four with crew cuts were so bulky they must have been sewn into the suits. They flanked a more stereotypical business type at the center of the picture: tan suit, perfect hair, dead-eyed smile full of blinding white teeth. Probably normal-sized, but he seemed a child beside his juiced-up business partners.

"Recognize anybody?"

Wally's lips moved while he studied the photo. Then he pointed at the guy in the middle. "Oh, hey! That's the fella from the Joker thingamajiggy. Randall whatshisname."

Darcy relinquished control of Mordecai's laptop. "His name isn't Randall McNath. Or, at least, that's not what he called himself fifteen years ago. Meet Patrick Wilhelm Howard. He's rumored to be the best three-card monte dealer the five boroughs have ever seen." She shook her head, looking at the boardroom photo again. "Same game, larger shells. I swear, the pair of balls on this guy."

She split the stack into two piles, and tapped one.

"Annex Nine is a wholly owned subsidiary of Twenty-First-Century Retail Group. It was spun off six months ago as the overseeing contractor for a major construction project. Luxury high-rise condos with built-in retail space, the usual gentrification crap. Of course, there's no room for that anywhere in Jokertown . . ."

". . . Unless you knock down a few buildings to make room for it," Mordecai concluded.

Wally asked, quietly, "Did I do something wrong?"

Darcy put her hand on his shoulder. It was the most affection Mordecai had yet witnessed from her. "No, Wally. Not even close."

"We might not like it," Mordecai sighed, "but the tear down/build up cycle you're describing is pretty common."

"Annex Nine, Phase Two is Our Lady of Perpetual Misery. And much of the rest of that block."

"Oh." Mordecai whistled. "That's . . . bold."

"Bold enough to require some back-room dealings."

♠

Wally crouched in the cosmetics aisle of a drugstore, the only place from which he had a clear view of the street and the roadster that Darcy said belonged to their guy. Mordecai and Darcy got to enjoy a bright spring day sitting at a sidewalk café because Randall McNath or Patrick Howard—Wally was a little confused on that point—didn't know them on sight.

A shopper sucked in his breath to slither past.

"Howdy!" Wally whispered, offering a hand. "Wally Gunderson for city council."

So it went for a couple of hours. Then:

"Holy smokes! That's him. That's him!"

He wished they had brought walkie-talkies.

But it didn't matter, because Darcy and Mordecai were already on the move, sauntering up the street as the man from the photograph unlocked the car. Wally felt bad about lurking in the store all afternoon, so he got in the checkout line and bought a neck massager, compression socks, and a jar of vitamin C pills. By the time Wally got outside, the guy was too busy yelling at Darcy to notice him.

"I've broken no laws. I'm leaving now."

He reached for the door handle, but Wally's campaign manager was faster. Mordecai leaned forward, wrapped his arms around the hood, picked up the car, and walked it across the street to lay it gently across two of the drugstore's three angle-in parking spots.

That done, he flagged down Darcy. "Officer? Excuse me, Officer? I think this car might be parked illegally."

She made a show of checking the license plate and looking for a parking placard. "My goodness. Thank you for bringing this to my attention, citizen."

"You can't do this," said McNath. "It's entrapment."

"Actually, it's not," she said, brandishing a wheel lock. Wally had known her to boot cars even when she was off duty. It had even happened to him, before they were friends. "Nobody enticed you to park illegally."

McNath moved to intervene, but Mordecai gently laid one fingertip on his chest. "Speaking of enticement, I think you know my friend here."

Mordecai jerked a thumb over his shoulder. Wally waved. "Hey there, fella."

Mr. McNath looked unhappy, but he recovered quickly, launching into that paint-can-shaker nod of his. "Mr. Gunderson! Well this is a bright spot to the day. And may I say congratulations on your city council campaign? I've been following the coverage in the *Cry* and I am just tickled knowing the people of Jokertown will soon have you as their most passionate advocate. And perhaps when you're on the council you'll be in a position to do something about these rogue elements of the law enforcement community."

"Okey dokey. But how come you lied about working for the Joker antithingy? You work with them real estate guys."

McNath cleared his throat. "Well, you see, public advocacy doesn't pay the bills—"

"Now you tell me," Wally said. This wasn't going the way he thought. But, as usual, Mordecai had his back.

"How will your fellow directors of Twenty-First-Century Retail Group react when they find out you confessed to poisoning Morlock-and-Eloi as retaliation for her stance against Annex Nine Phase Two?"

The poison was a guess, but a good one, apparently.

Now McNath looked scared. "You wouldn't do that. You can't! They're all tied up with the Brighton Beach crew. Alexandrovitch, my god, he'd pull my head off."

Wally frowned. "But did you? Did you hurt M&E?"

McNath looked around as if seeking an escape path. But finding himself sandwiched between Mordecai and Wally on the sidewalk, and with his car immobilized, there was none. McNath's shoulders slumped. "Please, don't tell them you heard it from me. Please."

"Judas priest," said Wally. "That's rotten."

"Phase Two seems like it would be controversial," Darcy added. "How fortunate for you that my other city council representative was on board with the project."

McNath shrugged. "Mark Benson is a major investor in Annex Nine."

A look passed between Darcy and Mordecai. Wally didn't understand. "What?"

Mordecai said, "Think back to all the forms you had to fill out."

Wally concentrated. Politics was hard. "So . . . this other fella who represents Jokertown . . . and who argued with M&E about Annex Nine . . . It's like he had an extra money jar. A secret one that nobody knew about."

Mordecai smiled. "Exactly."

"Huh." But now that Wally was thinking in politician style, he couldn't stop. "But I still don't get it. How come you were so keen for me to run in the first place?"

McNath hemmed and hawed. Mordecai loomed closer to him. Wally knew Mordecai wouldn't hurt a fly, but McNath didn't.

"Two reasons. We knew that hiring Aces in Hand for the demolition phase of the work meant you'd be involved. That would give us leverage against you. But we didn't expect to need it, because we thought you'd be easy to trick. We'd slip Phase Two right past you and finally get the vote we needed to proceed. You're not somebody known for looking deeply at things."

"Yeah, I guess so." It hurt, but not much. Wally already knew this. That's why he'd gone to Mordecai in the first place. "But you didn't know I have these guys! Holy moly. I sure am lucky."

Wally pulled a flyer from the pocket of his overalls and tucked it on McNath's windshield. Then he knelt on the asphalt and touched the wheel lock. As it dissolved into rust, he said, "Don't forget to vote on Tuesday."

♦

Though he wore his politics top hat, Wally was uncharacteristically quiet on the walk back to Campaign Headquarters. Mordecai felt bad for him. When McNath told Wally to his face that he was a dimwitted patsy, he might as well have been kicking a puppy.

Wally broke his silence as they neared the apartment. "I guess Jan was right."

"About the Nazi UFOs piloted by Satanic reptilian Freemasons from the hollow earth? Probably not." Mordecai shrugged. "But about the real estate stuff, yeah."

"Gosh. People should be nicer to her." Wally's shoulders slumped. "Does all this mean I have to drop out?"

Darcy laughed, hooking her arm through his. "No, you dingbat."

"It means that after we head over to the *Jokertown Cry* and explain how you and Jan both uncovered evidence of Benson's illegal enrichment scheme," said Mordecai, "there will soon be *two* open spots on the city council."

Wally thought this over. "I guess I'd better work on gaining her trust, then."

"You'll be quite a team," said Mordecai, feeling immensely satisfied.

♠ ♥ ♦ ♣

Ripple Effects

by Laura J. Mixon

JOHN MONTAÑO HADN'T BEEN sleeping well as it was, but his last night on the *Queen Margaret* was a doozy.

It was early evening before the night shift, their last night aboard, and John was dreaming. He'd gotten lost in a big hospital and was wandering through the halls. Screams issued from the rooms he passed. People were trapped behind thick walls of glass. Their faces contorted as they pounded on the glass, trying to warn him. Someone had sealed them in there, and was now hunting *him*.

He looked to his left. His enemy stood there, face and body in shadow. John yelled—his enemy had hurled a whirling mass of glass shards at him. Then his alarm went off and he awakened to see—and feel—yellow fire streaming from his palms. His pillows were airborne; he'd attacked them in his sleep. "*Fuck!*"

He leapt off the bed, buck naked, as his flame struck the pillows in midair. One smacked into the wall by the bathroom and the other two bounced back onto the bedcovers. Feathers scattered, trailing smoke. Flame residue dripped from his fingers onto his feet. He hopped back. "Ow!"

A fine fucking mess, Juanma.

Then his training kicked in. He marked the beat of his heart and made a wrenching *twist* around some corner of his mind. Spacetime spun away, carrying his body with it. Now he faced out into a different place entirely. The place where his ace powers grew.

John could still feel his body back there somewhere. His heartbeat—that meat metronome in his chest—had grown louder, and the atrial beat, the *lub* half, had ended as he'd twisted loose. But the ventricular beat, the *DUB*, came on languidly, and deepened to a pitch more felt than heard as it slowed almost to a halt. He was fully *here* now: outside of his body, outside of time. Now he could pause to think. To plan.

OK, he'd *somehow* triggered his ace without meaning to and set the frigging room on fire. The headline sprang into his head, unbidden: CHUBB'S ACE ART DETECTIVE FUELS PANIC AS FLAMES SPREAD THROUGH OCEAN LINER. Or, worse: NOCTURNAL EMISSIONS! CANDLE'S NIGHTMARE FLAMES BURN DOWN THE *QUEEN MARGARET*.

He visualized the cabin in his mind. Pillows down *there* and over *there*—smoke detector up *there*—window *there*—door across the cabin. Burning feathers airborne. This called for red flame, he decided. And blue. Lots of blue.

John moved into the vast energy forest. Cables and spires of flame—reeds and bundles—columns and jets of fire sprouted up and vanished. They seemed to sense him, somehow, and moved as if responding to his attention. Or perhaps he was the one who moved. It was impossible to tell because nothing here behaved the way it should. Perhaps the flames floated in some arcane energy flow he couldn't detect, the way kelp in an ocean current might (if those kelp were blazing-bright and multicolored, say; if they grew to the size of sequoia trunks and city 'scrapers, and were supercharged with trillions of volts of raging energies . . .). Perhaps the cause of the movement was those unseen giants, passing through.

His first trip here had been involuntary. The virus, as it triggered, had thrown him into this inferno-world. That had been almost half his life ago, when he was a boy of seventeen in Boston. His body had lain in a hospital bed long enough to get bedsores (the traces of which still scarred his ass) and for the doctors to declare his state permanent, vegetative, before he'd figured out how to get back.

Nowadays, while here, he counted his heartbeats, as fervently as his mother had counted her rosary beads back then. He never stayed longer than he had to. For one, he couldn't afford to. At five heartbeats, his body collapsed like a puppet with cut strings. At a hundred, his lungs stopped working on their own. Besides, this world . . . dimension . . . whatever it was . . . wasn't what you'd call human-friendly. More lived here than just the fire tendrils. Beings so immense, so monstrous it was impossible to know what to call them. To even *see* them all in one go. He'd long since learned to shut them out.

Nope—nobody down here but us fire motes!

The tendrils, though: *those* he could bear to look at (some more so than others). He still wondered what had possessed him to reach out for a thread of fire that first time, when he was caught in the grip of the primary wild card infection. It had certainly saved his life. He'd still be stuck here—or, more likely, dead; long since unplugged from life support—if he hadn't touched that first cord of flame.

It was the yellow he'd reached out to first, and its force had blasted him all the way back into his body—nearly killing him in the process. But the green had happened to be nearby and had moved into his body with him, healing the damage the yellow had done.

That first encounter with the flames had been so traumatic that it had taken John a long time to work up the nerve to try harvesting other flames. Red, green, and purple weren't *so* bad—not by comparison to the other three. But without his green, he'd have been simply another wild card statistic. What followed was months and years of figuring out which colors he could touch safely and training himself to wield them. First green. Then red. Then yellow. Blue. Purple. Black. (There were flames of other colors, as well. He still hadn't tried any of the others. Truth to tell, he was afraid to.)

Six is plenty. More than enough.

The individual fire strands peeled away from the red fire trunk he'd found and rejoined it, pulsating languidly: carnelians, burgundies, crimsons, roses. This crop looked good. He teased out a clump of cherry red, and the energy tendrils gravitated toward him: syrupy flames licking at his hands, rolling over themselves in gobs.

Red fire, despite its appearance, wasn't hot. In fact, it was cool to the touch and easy to snare: a mild sensation, compared to some of the other flames. It was also incredibly useful; he could use it to create structures. Including, for instance, a smoke barrier to minimize damage and seal off the room while he harvested the more challenging blue to quell the fire.

John coaxed streams of pulsing cherry loose from the thicket and lured them into a swirling sheath around him as he let his life force pull him back toward his body. You had to be patient with red, though, and it took a while for the threads to find the entry point and latch on. Eventually the tendrils found the entry at the crown of his head. They tried to suck him back into his body as they flowed in, but he resisted, and hovered at the threshold. Doing so bought him more time, and while suspended partway *there*, he could tolerate the pain of the flames better.

They pressed through the blood vessels in his scalp and collected in pools behind his eyes, sinuses, and ears like the world's worst migraine. They slid, molasses-slow, through his facial veins and internal and external jugulars, and from there down into his chest, lungs, and heart.

He'd seen videos. To the outside world, when he summoned the fire he looked like a man lit up from the inside. The first time, the red flames' pressure in his face, limbs, and chest had been agonizing. He'd thought his heart would explode. "Mild"? By comparison to most of the others, perhaps. But he had adapted. Now it was little more than a throbbing ache that spread through his head, chest, belly, and limbs as the fire followed the trails of his blood vessels.

Time and space continued to tug at him while he collected more of the red. His first heartbeat had just finished, quarter-speed, and a second beat was about to start. *Clock's ticking. This'll have to do.*

He shut off the flow, *twisted* back into himself—and shoved the red stream out through his blood vessels with the full force of the second heartbeat. As fire surged into the arteries lacing his lungs he opened his eyes—it coursed up the brachial arteries and then down, through his arms and into wrists and hands. Already, he saw, yellow flames were licking at the covers, and smoke coiled upward from bedding and floor.

He shot a stream of crimson flame from his right hand, sealing instructions into it as it left his fingers. Blazing, cherry-red tendrils spun up and encased the smoke detector in a translucent, flickering dome of light. More of the glowing red spilled out from the dome and spread across the ceiling. With his left hand, he sent a second batch of streamers to coat the upper walls: burning red snakes struck the ceiling along its edges and traveled out and down. He shot one last stream of red at the desk, coating his laptop. Then he was out of flame, and his third heartbeat had finished. *Get a move on.*

He *twisted* away again, back to the other place.

Finding a good patch of blue, as usual, turned out to be more of a challenge. The energy fields shifted unpredictably here, and distance behaved even more strangely than time did. He couldn't simply look at a tendril and will himself over to it. Objects that seemed nearby one moment were far away the next, or would vanish entirely, while another set of energies appeared suddenly somewhere else.

He got lucky. A blue flame trunk soon moved into view: a whipping cable of eye-piercing indigo—dark brilliance, bigger around than a city block. It swung near, shedding waves of deadly blue fire. Even the other fire cables steered clear. He didn't reach for it (he never touched the main trunks). Instead, he gestured-called-teased the crackling flame coronas that arced out from its boundary layer. Soon a large tendril budded off. He called to it and it spun out from its parent, blazing sapphire, and slithered toward him.

Blue flame here wasn't heat. Nor cold, either, not exactly—though it certainly froze what it touched. Rather, it was a *nothingness*. An anti-energy. A stillness so complete it seared worse than the hottest flame.

He tugged at the tendril, backing up, nudging other cords and clumps out of his way, and the hostile blue energy surged-lurched-coiled after him. As John approached the entry to his body, the blue fanned out and enveloped him in cold fire, and the force poured in and lanced his skull. It *hurt*.

Blue preferred to trace its path along the bone structures, the ligaments, and the tendons: it etched frigid agonies across his nasal bridge and cheekbones and jaw—pierced the tiny bones in his ears—sank icy daggers into the rotator cuffs at his shoulders, spread across his collarbone. His lungs sucked in a sharp breath. He tasted smoke in his throat, and coughed.

His fourth heartbeat had begun by now, a deep thrum in his chest, and the smell of smoke was stronger than before. *Better hurry.* He closed the entry point—dispelled the indigo-bright cord attached to his crown, back *there*—and with a dizzying yank turned all the way into his body.

John opened his eyes. Flame had taken hold at the end of the bed, and smoke was billowing up, spreading along his red barrier on the ceiling. Angry blue snakes ran the maze of his bones, demanding an exit. John obliged. He shaped the power as it spattered outward from his curled fingertips—he was forcibly pinching off the flow to control its rate; he didn't want to blow a hole in the wall. He snared the flames in a spiral long enough to shape a sphere of blinding-dark sapphire, then released it with a snap of his hands.

The first blast struck the burning bedding and caused a flurry of carbon dioxide snowflakes to burst out in a puff. In the blast's wake came a clear liquid stream that splashed violently onto the bedding, knocking it askew and coating it in a thin layer of ice. The stream was liquefied air, cooled to minus 320 degrees Fahrenheit. It raced across the frozen covers in beads and sputtering rivulets—pooled in crannies—and then a wave spilled over and splashed onto the pillow on the floor, instantly snuffing out its flames. The last of the liquid air skittered around like manic beads on the carpet till it re-vaporized.

John had broken out all over in gooseflesh. The cabin's temperature must've dropped by a good twenty degrees. He delivered a smaller spray of blue flame out to chase down the last of the burning feathers, which were still settling onto the dresser, desk, and carpet. Another snow flurry fell throughout the cabin.

He used his last bout of blue flame to make a small ice devil. It spun around inside the room, gathering remaining wisps of smoke and condensing them into a ball of soot, which it dumped onto the fancy burgundy carpet. John frowned at it. *Oops! That'll leave a stain.*

He dusted ash and ice crystals from his hair and went in search of his phone. It had gotten buried under the tourist brochures for Miami, Myrtle Beach, and Baltimore, all the stops the *Queen Margaret* had made while on her way up from Havana to Manhattan. A Gideon Bible had fallen from the drawer of the bedside table, which had gotten knocked onto its side. He didn't remember doing that.

He snatched up his phone and sent a text to his second-in-command on this detail, Rashida Thorne.

Can you come by? I need a hand.

While he was texting, the red shield began dribbling off his desk, as well as the walls and ceiling. It oozed down in red filaments, flame confetti streamers. They pooled on the carpet here and there but did no harm, merely flickered like dying embers as they melted away. Rashida responded.

Be right there. Uhhhh . . . everything okay?

He spent a few seconds with his thumbs over the keys before giving up the attempt at words, and just sent her a poop emoji and a shrug.

♥

John had time to pee, tug on shorts and a T-shirt, roll the singed bedding up in the mattress pad, and drag it onto the floor before Rashida's tap landed on the inner door. He let her in, put out the DO NOT DISTURB sign, and latched and bolted the door.

"Brrr! Turn your AC off, John—it's not *that* hot out." John caught a faint whiff of her hair oil as she passed. He nipped at his lower lip with his teeth. *Down, boy. You* boss, *her* employee; *remember?*

They were both bi (well, technically *he* was bi; *she* was pan), nonmonogamous, and . . . well, there was chemistry. She was full-figured, Black and Native American, with a background in modern dance and criminal justice. He loved her dark-skinned face and wide, freckled nose, and he loved her full-throated laugh, which never failed to disarm him. She had insight into people, and a relentless pursuit of truth that often made him feel secretly that she should really be leading the team—not him.

They'd flirted mercilessly, back before he'd been promoted, and had had a brief fling after the death of one of their team members. Once the gig was over they'd gone out for drinks to talk it through, and fallen into each other's arms for a weekend in the sack—cried, comforted each other, and had amazing sex—and then agreed not to do it again. (Chubb was strict about coworker coitus, even *before* he'd gotten promoted and the power differential had entered the mix.)

She surveyed the room now. "Bad sleep, I take it?"

He grimaced and rubbed the back of his neck. "Something like that."

She eyed the scorch marks on the bed and the sodden mess of burned fabric and feather and foam on the floor. The beads of water dripping down the walls. The knocked-over furniture. The spray of soot on the carpet.

"Jesus, John." She struggled for words; gave it up. "At least you didn't set off the smoke detector." She looked at him. "Did you?"

"No. You would have heard." Probably everybody on the ship would have heard. "My bad. All my bad. Look, can we just . . . fast-forward through the color commentary?"

She laughed. "Sorry. Whatever you say. I'll call the Beef in."

"Not just yet. I need Arry out there with the horn till I can get this taken care of. Just because we haven't seen trouble yet doesn't mean we won't."

The gig this time was providing security for a traveling art exhibit. John led a five-member team—two aces, two nats, and a joker. Arry ("The Beef"), Ariadne Cerigo, was John's other direct report—though you could really count her as a team of four all on her own.

Her card had turned almost ten years ago, in her mid-forties. Strictly a joker; no special powers, but a two-ton minotaur with wicked six-foot-long horns, an impenetrable hide, and a battle mace the size of a battering ram could rack up a lot of hit points pretty damn quick. Not to mention that as the mother of five, she had inculcated a deft blend of other talents: de-escalation skills and bullshit-put-up-with-which-NOT attitude, in the face of which even the most testosterone-fueled disagreement tended to resolve itself quite readily. Extra bonus points: she played a mean hand of poker and never got drunk or did stupid shit or created drama. So, yeah: her specific dietary and structural support notwithstanding, he wouldn't trade her for a dozen aces. The fabulous needlepoint she doled out after every mission was just the lovely Maraschino cherry on top.

"Sooo . . . feeling better tonight?" he asked. Rashida had gotten hit with a bad case of stomach crud from something she ate in Baltimore, and had been hugging the porcelain throne for the past two days. Now their watches were all out of whack.

"Much. Why?"

"If you feel up for it, I'd like you to run a quick read on the room."

"*This* room?" He nodded. Her brow furrowed. "Why?"

"Just a precaution."

"John." Ras stood five foot ten, but John was a good head taller at six foot three, which gave him the edge in a stare-down. But she wasn't his second for nothing, and he felt his fib fraying before her *don't-fuck-with-me* gaze. "What gives?"

He glowered.

"As your second, I have a right to know if something could be putting the operation at risk. And this"—she encompassed the room in a gesture—"qualifies. Especially if you suspect an intrusion."

"It's just a *precaution!*"

She folded her arms. Tapped her foot. John sighed. "All right, fine! Sometimes I have . . . vivid dreams. I'm partially awake when they happen. It's a sleep disorder. It's called hypnopompia."

He caught her suppressing a smile. "Hypno-*what?*"

Ordinarily he'd share the joke, but right now, not so much. "It's perfectly normal. I mean—it's normal *for me*. But it's never been this bad. In fact, I've never manifested my ace during an episode before." He paused. "Er, except the once."

"Oh?"

"When it first manifested."

"'It.' You mean your flames? When your card first turned?" He nodded. "Hmmm. I don't think you've ever told me your origin story."

Damn straight. "I don't like to talk about it. Bad memories."

She punched him in the arm. "Why didn't you say so, dummy? But that still doesn't explain why you want me to do a read on the room."

He shook his head with a frown. "I don't know, Ras . . . I've been jumpy as a cat since we left Cuba. Or . . . look, I was sure someone was in the cabin with me." He thought about that tornado made of glass shards. "I just need to be sure that it was *only* a dream."

"It couldn't possibly be that we're transporting a priceless historical artifact on an ocean liner with obsolete, appallingly bad security and trotting it out nightly for hundreds of tourists' entertainment?"

"Oh yeah . . ." He snapped his fingers. "Whose idea was this, anyway?"

They looked at each other, morose. "Triple hazard-duty pay!" they said in unison. Ras removed and pocketed her hoops, bracelet, and rings, and looked around. "Any spots you're particularly interested in?"

"Over there. On the left side of the bed." That was where his attacker had come from, in his dream. "I know I'm being paranoid," he said again.

She waved him off. "Relax. I've got this." Rashida crouched. Her clothing collapsed onto the carpet as corporeal became particulate, and a cloud of shiny motes slid out of the gaps with a sandy *swo-o-osh!* They amassed before him, dense and glittering, and shaped Ras's face long enough to whisper, "Be right back . . ."

The cloud drifted over to the far side of the bed and divided in three. One portion settled onto the carpet, mattress, and duvet; another gathered where the wall and ceiling shared an intersection; and the third clump settled onto the wall, headboard, lamp, papers, and bedside table.

Ras's ace handle was Patina. She could transform at will to inorganic matter. Usually particles: sand, dust motes, glitter, pebbles, glass or porcelain beads, metal shards; things like that—though with effort she could form larger objects for short periods of time. If it didn't have carbon in it, she was your ace—though John *had* observed over the two years they'd known each other that she had a pronounced preference for shiny over dull and round over spiky.

A trick she'd discovered recently was that while in a metallic form, she could pick up impressions from certain surfaces—visual flashes or auditory impressions, and sometimes both—of prior events that had occurred within arm's reach.

Her awareness didn't extend far, only a few hours back and a few feet away from the spots where she settled. And it only worked if she was in contact with metallic or crystalline surfaces. She'd theorized to John that perhaps the molecules she came in contact with while in her inorganic state formed some kind of bond that held onto traces of the interactions she was detecting: she said it felt like shifts in lattice energies—tiny dislocations. Perhaps sound vibrations that had reordered the solid matrix and briefly lingered there, too faint for human instruments to measure, or some such thing. Molecular memories.

Whatever. It all sounded like New Age bullshit to him, but she'd nailed at least one criminal mastermind with it to date. Besides, who was he to judge? *He* spent *his* time harvesting power from a massive transdimensional cropland, in a land of hyperplex, Brobdingnagian horrors so immense and hideous he couldn't bear to even perceive them.

While he waited, John called up the app for their on-call scene documentation and cleanup, Vigilant Response, and filled out the form.

He opened the picklist for Response Type and chose "Site cleanup," then, with a wince, "Damage documentation." More expensive, and he *hoped* the insurance company wouldn't deny the claim as a result but . . . well . . . it was best to be sure.

Task Summary:
   Satchmo art transport detail: clean up fire damage on *Queen M.*
Location:
   Cabin 4.045, RMS *Queen Margaret*
   at sea, Atlantic Ocean, N 39°35'40.30', W 73°32'34.44'

Account No.:
  544-0772322-01
Priority:
  03—Medium (respond in 12-24 hours)
Damage Assessment:
  Size: ~200 sq. ft.
  Severity: 05—Low (est. <$5k damage)
Contact:
  John Montaño / 212-555-0062
Description:
  Burned bedding. Scorch marks on bed & carpet & dresser. Soot stains on carpet & mirror.

He sniffed, grimaced, and added, *Residual smell.*

John shot pictures with his phone of the bedding, bed, and carpet, and took a couple of the curtains and chairs, as well. He uploaded them and noted under special instructions: *Replace mattress and bedding; clean carpet and furniture. Inspect walls and ceiling to confirm no further action needed. Meet ship at Pier 88 Manhattan at 6:00 a.m. Match cabin decor as closely as possible.*

By the time he had finished uploading the photos and submitted the cleanup request, tendrils of Ras-glamour were rising up from where they had settled. They all coalesced into a single metallic cloud, which swooped over and slipped back into her clothing through the various openings. She re-formed, stood, and shook out her tight black curls, which lengthened and braided themselves into a neat, beaded knot at her nape.

She grimaced. "Yuck. I'm going to have to shower again." She tucked her silk cami into her capris, straightened her linen jacket, and slipped her patent leather pumps back on.

"Well?"

"Nothing much," she replied. "I picked up a visit by ship maintenance to check the HVAC system. You called them?"

He nodded. "This morning. It went on the fritz."

"And an argument out in the hall a while ago, but it had nothing to do with us." She paused. "It was—well, blurry—around the headboard and on the mirror. I had a hard time getting a read."

"What do you make of that?" Smooth surfaces were where she usually got her best information. She shrugged. "I've encountered it before, once or twice. Sometimes I can't get anything." She hesitated, then stopped herself from saying more.

"What?"

"Well... the other times I've encountered this effect were around you, actually. I think it may have something to do with your ace. It feels like..." She paused. "Like something goes out of focus in your vicinity. Echoes of some kind." She laced her fingers together. "It's like there's an interference pattern of some kind. I don't know." She dropped her hands. "I wouldn't worry too much about it."

"Hmmm." John kept his expression still, but wished now he hadn't asked her to check. He couldn't help but wonder if his journey to the other place, or the energy he brought back with him, created those echoes. He hadn't told anyone about where he went to harvest his flame powers. He didn't want people getting too curious; he often had the feeling he shouldn't be there. Someone might try to make him stop, if they knew.

"Well, thanks. I owe you."

"I'll find a way to cash my chips in later, Candle-man. When you least expect it." She paused at the door. "Leave a giant tip."

He gave her a thumbs-up. She flashed him a big, gorgeous grin and left.

♣

Six weeks earlier, ace art thief Titus "Ripple Effect" Maguire ("Call me Rip") and his newly minted accomplice, Megan "Tiffani" McKnee (actress/model, ace, and former *American Hero* contestant), boarded the *Queen Margaret* at Havana.

For Tiffani, this cruise had mostly been just a big old romp, thus far. She'd seen little of Rip since they'd boarded. He spent his days doing "reconnaissance," as he called it, using his weird ace power, while she went on tours and visited local food fairs and craft shows. She had a spa treatment every day. With her complexion there was no point in trying to tan—all she did was turn the color of boiled lobster and get more freckles. She did enjoy sitting out on deck in her beribboned hat and bikini, though, glammed up with her own ace version of sunscreen: a diamond layer no thicker than a hair, but with enough crystalline microfractures in it to bounce the UV rays right back out. Added bonus: it made her skin sparkle like diamond dust. She would sit sipping sweetened ice tea while watching yachts and fishing skiffs float past, while gulls and herons skimmed the surface waters of the ports.

She fancied she still looked good in a bikini, even at twenty-eight. She still had it. She could tell by the way men's heads still turned. Not as many as when she was younger, maybe, but she figured she could enjoy herself for a bit longer before landing a good catch and settling down to start a family.

She loved to lean out over the railing, showing as much of her cleavage as possible, and wave with her sun hat, shouting a friendly *Yoohoo! Hi, y'all!* at the smaller boats as they passed, water piling up on their bows. They'd even blow their horns at her sometimes. *Boop-boop!*

So all in all, good times on the old *Queen Margaret*. All she had to do to earn her keep was act like Rip's girlfriend and when he returned from his daily "reconnaissance," answer his questions about the Candle. He assumed she must know a lot about the Candle from their time on set way back when, competing in the first season of *American Hero*. That was ages ago, and she couldn't see why it mattered now, but it did to Rip. Meanwhile, he would pull out maps and diagrams and mark them up, and scribble notes in his journal, scowling like a guy who couldn't figure out what 64 Down on the crossword was.

Granted, the questions got to be a bore. He'd kept at it, night after night. Tiffani knew herself to be a patient woman, but today, day five of this, she lost her cool. He hadn't shown up for dinner so she went by herself, and when she returned to the cabin he still wasn't back. So she set the carry-out she'd gotten for him on the desk, curled up on the bed with a pile of pillows, and picked up her tablet to get caught up on all the juicy celebrity gossip.

A while later she looked up. He was doing that thing he did: standing there inside the mirror—or a reverse image of him, anyway—staring at her and looking weird, because people's faces always look kind of weird when they're reversed. She let out a shriek and put a hand on her chest. "Rip, honey, don't do that! You scared me half to death."

His mirror image was rippling. Then for a second it was like she could see a hundred reflective panes all at once, each with a flat version of him in it. The tumbling panes spilled out from the mirror and shiny reflections spun around like an aluminum disco ball, only cylindrical—vaguely human shaped—scattering the room's light. In a flash he was back. He strode over and unlocked his briefcase, then flipped through the papers in there. He seemed agitated.

"What's wrong?" she asked. No answer. He wouldn't look at her, despite her efforts to catch his gaze. "I brought you some food." She waved a hand. "It's over there on the desk. You should have a bite."

"Quiet!"

"Fine. Whatever."

She picked up her tablet and pretended to read while watching him out of the corner of her eye. He was a piece of work, this one. At the start, he'd been so sweet that sugar wouldn't melt on his tongue. He'd been a real charmer. But something had changed after that first night, when he came back from one of his "outings." Ever since, he'd been surly as a dog with hemorrhoids.

He spread his materials out on the bed, nudging her foot out of the way. She oh-so-slowly put her foot back where it had been, and rubbed his thumb with her big toe. Finally he looked at her. She wiggled her eyebrows and patted the mattress next to her. But he only frowned. *Here we go again,* she thought, and suppressed a sigh.

He said, "This time I want real answers. *Details.* Tell me what you observed about how he used the different flame colors. *Why* does he use more red, blue, and yellow? What about the other three? What exactly do they do?"

She sighed. "I *told* you. He uses the yellow for heat, the red to build things, and the blue to freeze things."

"I know that. Everybody knows that. I need to know *why. How* they work. And what do the other colors do? Why is there no public record of him ever using the others? Did you ever see him use them on people or things? What do they do? What are their limits?"

"For Christ's sake!" she burst out. "Rip, you've asked me *a hundred times.* It was *ten years ago!* He wasn't even on my team on the show! I was a Diamond; he was a Spade. I've told you everything I know."

He stared at her, leaning on his hands.

Maybe I pushed him too far, she thought. Rip was a lot bigger than she was, with his muscular chest and big arms. She said, in an even tone, "I can't tell you what I don't know." A flare of defiance slipped out, despite herself. "And anyway, the episodes are all on YouTube. You can see for your own self." She'd been going to say *your own* damn *self,* but thought better of it. Then she looked down at her tablet, trying to get her breathing back under control.

"If I can get everything I need from YouTube, remind me again why I need you? You seem to be trying awfully hard to talk yourself out of your fee."

OK, definitely went too far.

"Let's not fight." She crawled off the bed and went over to give him a hug from behind, but he turned and gripped her arms, and dug his fingers deep into her biceps.

"I'm running out of patience, Megan."

"Ow!" she yelped. "Hey!" She tried to jerk loose, but he merely tightened his grip. So she summoned her ace, and with a crack, turned crystalline, two inches deep. A flawless, faceted, diamond-like shell coated her from head to toe.

His grip slipped, throwing her off-balance, and her diamond-coated heels hit the floor with a thud. She found her footing, and straightened with her crystalline fists on her hips. *Squeeze me now, asshole.* "Hands off the merch, please."

Rip laughed and slow-clapped. "So she has a backbone." The sound carried through the crystalline coat over her ears, albeit muffled. Sort of like a bad case of swimmer's ear. "I wondered how far I'd have to push you." He looked her up and down. "Quite striking, I must say—much more impressive than it looked on TV."

Way to neg a lady, jerk. She reverted to flesh and rubbed at her arms where he'd grabbed her. He returned to his plans on the foot of the bed. She quelled the urge to recrystallize her arms and choke the fucker till he begged for mercy. Not a good idea. Especially not with how much she stood to make on this gig, if she kept her cool.

With a noisy sigh, she snatched her tablet up and sat down in the chair at the desk—facing him, of course; you don't turn your back on a man with a temper. She tucked a leg under herself and scrolled in a slow progression, trying to calm herself down.

If she was honest, this gig was turning out to be a much bigger headache than she'd expected. She'd figured, you know, a nice cruise, earn some cash, give Rip a few inside tidbits on the Candle—nothing too damaging, of course; she had nothing against John—and get the hell out, a couple stacks richer. The man was easy on the eyes and had been quite charming when they first met. Normally she didn't jump in the sack with a man right away, but that first night Rip had gotten a bit weird and scary, and she'd decided she'd be better if she seduced him, to get a better handle on the situation, so to speak. Unfortunately, that hadn't worked out all that well. Most men, you could count on them giving more attention to their little head than they ever did to their big one. Not this guy.

Oh, they'd had sex. She'd pulled out all the stops: fancy lingerie, butt plugs, the works. And he'd seemed to enjoy it well enough, but he sure wasn't all gah-gah over her all the time. The minute he got out of bed, his mind would turn to other things. This whole trip, he'd seemed distracted or wound up. And on a short fuse, to boot.

He also had bad burn marks on his chest and abdomen, and along the underside of his left arm. She'd asked, once, but he hadn't answered. Maybe he was traumatized. *Or maybe you're losing your touch,* that nasty little voice in her head said. *Maybe he's just not that into you.*

Tiffani hadn't gotten to know John Montaño on the show except to say hi to on set once in a while, and to pass him in the halls in the Discard Pile. They hadn't run into each other much on-camera, either—no big encounters—which had made it easier to sell Rip on her lack of knowledge. But truth to tell, this ignorance of his powers was, well, a bit of a fabrication. She'd watched the rushes every day to keep up on who was who and what was what, and had paid careful attention to everyone's abilities—including the gossip. So she had a pretty damn good idea what the Candle could do.

Once she'd seen him enter the bathroom limping, his face and arms cut up pretty good. She saw a green glow under the door, and a few minutes later when he came back out the injuries were gone and he was walking normally.

And then there was that evening Pop Tart had come out of his room so stoned she couldn't find the door to the lounge, exhaling lavender lightning bugs out her mouth and nose. So Tiffani had her suspicions about *that* flame's nature, too. As for the black fire, well. She didn't know what it did, but after seeing how the Candle totally lost his shit at Spasm and Stuntman when they'd teased him so mercilessly that one time about being afraid to show them what it could do—and the look on his face when he turned away—what*ever* it did, the mere *thought* of using it scared the fuck out of him.

The Candle . . . now *there* was a guy who knew how to put his little head to good use.

I do mean, she thought with a sigh. Not that she herself had partaken of his charms, but most everybody else on the set had, seemed like. If they exhibited signs of life, and were into *him*, he'd been into *them*. Male, female, nonbinary, genderfluid; joker, ace, nat. It made no never mind. And a lot of guys like that are players, but not John. She didn't know how he pulled off sleeping with so many people in such close quarters without anybody wanting to throttle him, but he just had the knack. He'd been sweet, like a puppy. A large, terrifyingly powerful puppy.

Frankly, she thought, Rip could usefully have some of that attitude rub off on him.

Well, push was obviously coming to shove with Titus-the-Rippler, here. She'd driven the dumb-bunny buggy about as far as it'd go. *You don't owe the Candle anything,* she reminded herself, *and this guy is tilting toward being a hazard to your health.*

Still . . . Rip wouldn't be spending all this time and money on a fancy-ass ocean cruise, days and days of his mirror-reconnaissance, and all this note-taking and map-marking, if it wasn't going to be a big haul. Starlight Jewels in Miami had just dropped Tiffani's modeling contract and no one else had picked her up yet; she needed the money. Maybe she should just play ball. But she wanted to know what she was getting into before she jumped.

She crawled onto the bed again, giving him a little "insight" into her décolletage. "Rip, honey?"

He looked up, irritated, so she dialed the sweet-thing routine down several notches. "Look. I know you have been frustrated with me not giving what you need to beat the Candle's flame powers. It's just . . . I feel sure I could help you better, if I knew just a *little bit* more about *exactly* what you're looking for—what kind of a job you're planning."

"So you can remember, but only if I tell you my plans. That it?"

"Now, don't be that way. How well do *you* remember events from ten years ago?" She could tell that one landed. "It'd give me more to work with. Help me visualize his fighting style, you know, if I had some situations I could picture him in to help me along."

"I thought you'd never seen him fight."

"Not in person, no. But I watched the show and I heard the other contestants talking. I'm sure all that would come back to me, with your help. And as you saw, I have my own ace powers. Sure, they're not offensive, but I *excel* at defense. I'm hard to harm. You must have seen me on *American Hero,* back in oh-seven."

He burst out laughing. "What you excelled at, darling, was betrayal."

Tiffani bit her lower lip. She *had* betrayed Bubbles, her teammate, who'd had the sweetest crush on her. The memory still burned. "You *have* to vote people off in those shows. And I couldn't afford to lose. My family was counting on me. I did what it took."

He chuckled. "I'll give you that. The fat chick never saw you coming."

"Don't disrespect her!"

His eyes widened at her flare of anger. Then he rubbed his face with a sigh.

"All right, fine. I presume this is an attempt to renegotiate our deal. What do you want? A cut of the profits, or what?"

"Oh, I'm just glad to help out," she said, letting her Appalachian drawl creep back in. "Of course, if I did more to help out than just give you information, and you were satisfied with my performance, cutting me in would be nice. I mean, I'd be purely flattered . . ." She examined her nails. She quite liked the crystalline pink she'd glammed over them. "I have many talents."

"Uh-huh..."

His dismissive tone irritated her. "Well, you think it over and let me know, hon." She returned to the chair and snatched up her tablet, making a big show of swiping between articles.

He watched her. After a pause, he walked over and pulled the outer door open. Warm, muggy summer air flowed in. "Walk with me."

"In this?" The diaphanous micro-mini nightie she wore had quite the décolletage. Not to mention the matching thong, faintly visible underneath it.

"Relax. You look fine. No one's going to care. Those that do . . ." He gave her a little smile. "Will enjoy the view."

She eyed him, skeptical and still a bit miffed, but the compliment seemed genuine. Tiffani felt her cheeks warm, despite herself. She'd brought her best wardrobe with her, but this was the first time he seemed to notice. "Oh, all right." She slipped on her sandals and pulled on a sarong over her lingerie, and followed him up the outer stairs to the promenade deck.

The night was humid and overcast. Tiffani brushed a damp curl off her forehead. Their cabin was near the stern, and she caught sight of the great liner's wake roiling the water behind them. Beyond the circle of the *Queen Margaret*'s deck lighting, the ocean was black as pitch. She couldn't see much of anything out there, other than sparse flecks of light on the far shore.

"Let's check out the view from the bow," Rip said. He led the way. She followed, hurrying to match his much longer stride, wondering what he was up to.

At the front of the ship was an open area where you could look out ahead. It was close to midnight. Not many people were out. One couple sat on a bench, engaged in some serious PDA; one or two others strolled by. On the top deck by the bridge, a couple crew members were chatting. A jazz tune drifted out into the night from the showroom.

Rip leaned on the rail. "I'm trying to decide how far I can trust you, Megan. We both know you're not nearly as dumb as you act. You have your charms and your ace talent, which could be useful for what I have in mind. And I know you can be ruthless, when need be. All good. The question is . . . how loyal are you? Nobody gets onto my team who I can't count on, one hundred percent."

She laid a hand on his arm and brought all the sincerity she had in her to show. "Rip, honey, if we can come to an agreement, you can *totally* count on me."

"That's what I was hoping you'd say." Rip checked his watch, and turned around to look at something. She turned, too. The necking couple had just gotten up and were walking away, fingers interlaced, eyes only for each other, leaving Rip and Tiffani alone on the bow deck.

"I've never told you what my ace does, have I?" he asked. She shook her head. "Well then, I'm going to let you in on my secret."

She leaned backward on the rail, propped by her elbows. "I feel flattered! Please, do tell."

His lips quirked up in a smile. "Let's just say the virus gave me an unlimited lifetime subscription to streaming videos from the future."

"How handy! So is it like cable? A zillion channels on and nothing good to watch?"

He chuckled. "I begin to like you, Megan. I can see into the future. Fu*tures,* to be exact. There are a *lot* of them. And I can visit them, any one I choose, and see what might happen at any point along the way."

"Sounds useful." Tiffani kept her tone and posture casual, though a sense of foreboding nudged at her. With that kind of ability, he would not be easy to fool. Not that she would do that, of course. Not unless she *absolutely* needed to . . .

"It's not as great as it sounds. For one thing, I can only see future events in the vicinity of where I'm at when I enter the mirror." Ah . . . so *that* was why they were here. She'd snooped around among his notes the other day, and found a reference to an upcoming cruise on this very ship: a cruise that the Candle would take later in the summer. Rip must need to be on the *Queen Margaret now,* so he could spy on the Candle's actions here *in the future.* She looked at Rip with new appreciation. This here was some world-class sneakiness. "I can't directly affect anything while I'm up there poking around," Rip was saying, "and none of it is set in stone. They're all probable outcomes. *Possible* futures. Many different timelines, each with their own turning points and individual outcomes. There are an impossibly large number of them, and I can only guess which ones are more likely than the rest. It's rather maddening, actually."

"I can imagine." This was the first time he'd ever opened up like this. She got a feeling he was a lonely man, under all that obsessive grumpiness.

"And I can only see scenes that I'm not part of. If I try to look at any future event with me actually there? Ka-*BOOM.*" He expanded his hands rapidly, mimicking an explosion. "It blows up the whole causal chain. Or if I make a decision here in the present that changes that future moment?" He clapped his hands together. "Implosion. Timeline collapse. Schrödinger's cat croaks and I go time-blind till the ripple effects finish their belly roll through the multiverse. I call them causality shadows.

"Honestly," he sighed. "It's a huge pain. You have no idea."

"Poor dear..."

"What this boils down to is, I can see all these possibilities the future might hold, but I can't be sure how *likely* each future is, I can't see anything with *me* in it, and I can only see up to the point where I make a decision beforehand that affects that moment in the future. So I'm *very* careful about the decisions I make."

"Why not just buy lottery tickets?" she asked. "Why all this art-thievery rigmarole?" She waved her hand. She had no idea what he was planning to steal, but he'd mentioned it had to do with a painting or something that the Candle would be in charge of guarding, sometime soon. "Just check out the lotto, hon. Get the winning numbers and make a mint that way."

He rolled his eyes. "Wow, thanks. I never thought of *that*. That was the very first thing I did, and I've socked away quite a lovely nest egg over the years. But there are organizations out there that keep an eye on newsworthy events. Like lottery winnings and repeat offenders at casinos and the like. Too many lucky coincidences and you might get black-bagged and locked away under the desert by SCARE." A pause. "And... you know? The life of the idle rich gets boring, especially if you've got an ace talent like mine. You want to do something with your life. You want a challenge. Me, I like to mix things up. Get creative. And, well, I've always been an art lover, so..."

Tiffani was feeling that urge to throttle him again. What she'd give to live a life of ease, spend all her days on the beach or shopping on Madison Avenue. *Men and their adrenaline highs. Such a waste.* But Mama always said there's no point fighting with the lightning about where it wants to strike.

"Anyway, my gift has all these devilish constraints," Rip was saying, "and I've had to learn how to work it in ways that help me find the best path to my goals.

"So, there you go. I'm laying my cards down, right here. Right now. In some futures, you become my ally, and you could be a real help. In others, you betray me. I need to know which future we're headed to." She started to reply, and he gripped her arm again, hard. "Shh! Listen, for once. I can offer you a future you can't even *begin* to imagine. Inconceivable wealth. Fame and fortune. The world at your feet. You'll be worshipped by the masses."

He checked his watch again. "Come on. Let's head back," he said, and continued as they walked. "You'd be able to help your family members. Help your mama get the best possible care for her diabetes. Maybe even a liver and pancreas transplant. Your Mamaw and Pampaw could get into a quality assisted-living facility. And there's Uncle Bertie and Auntie Tamara, right? Annabelle? Charlie and Jess and the triplets." She looked at him, suppressing a spike of fear. "Everyone you care about can join you in a life of luxury. But, as I said . . . first I have to know how far I can trust you."

They'd reached their cabin.

"Can I trust you, Tiffani?" Rip asked. "Can I trust you to keep your mouth shut and do what I say?"

He opened the door. She'd left her phone on the dresser, and it was ringing.

"That'll be Annabelle. Here." Rip handed her a crisp new five-hundred-dollar bill. "Her boyfriend got picked up for drunk-and-disorderly and she needs help with bail money. You'd better pick up."

She gave him a look of alarm, and hurried over and accepted the call.

"Hey babe, it's me," Annabelle said, voice tense and breathy. "Listen, can you spare five hundred bucks? Tommy got in some trouble . . ."

Tiffani went numb. She felt Rip's gaze on her. "Sure, Belle. I'll wire it to your account right away. No, it's no trouble. No, I won't tell Mama, I promise. Okay, call you tomorrow. Gotta-go-love-you-bye."

She hung up and looked over at Rip. He smiled at her. *Yeah,* she thought. *Message received.*

She drew a long, deep breath, stuffed all her thundering rage down and locked it away. She leaned against the dresser and smiled back at him, with full sincerity and not a jot of goodwill. "Of *course* you can count on me, Rip honey. I'll do everything you ask."

♠

Two hours after setting his bed on fire, the Candle had finished dealing with the fire's aftermath, gotten moved to a different cabin, showered, and changed. (Chubb security detail dress: black suit, tailored and, like all his clothing, made of specialty fabrics impervious to his flames; white or light shirt. He accessorized with a few of his own touches: a fire-opal bolo and his favorite cowboy boots, black with blackened silver studs and a subtle rainbow glaze that matched the colors of his flames.) Last, he strapped on his radio, tucked the speaker into his ear, and headed up to the main deck.

It was 9:40 p.m. and the showroom was packed. Beauteous Maximus was on stage in the bar, warming up the crowd with some decent blues on harmonica, piano, and drums. A big sign next to the stage announced, LAST ONBOARD PERFORMANCE: TUNGSTEN PARADOX, STARRING PULITZER-WINNING

JAZZ MASTER WINSTON MARCUS ON SATCHMO'S GOLDEN TRUMPET! ALL PROCEEDS GO TO CHARITY!

John spotted Horace and Gil, his nat detail, covering the rear entrance. The *Queen Margaret* had provided their own security as well; two crew members each guarded the side entrances between restaurant and bar. In the long room's center, below the big chandelier, stood Louis Armstrong's instrument, encased in glass on a black base replete with hidden, deadly tech.

The trumpet seemed suspended in air within the lit sphere, flooded in a pool of light, as though it truly had the mystic powers of Gabriel's horn. No one was looking at it at the moment, however; the passengers had all had plenty of chances to view it by now and no day visitors were around, not while they were at sea. Arry and Ras stood guard in the shadows behind the exhibit.

"Security lead on site," he said. "Give me a comms check, everyone." The security team all turned to look at him—Arry quite slowly (the first night on board, she'd accidentally taken out the chandelier above the display). Their voices came through his earpiece, confirming. As they spoke, John made his way amid the crowd to the display, to Rashida and Ariadne.

Rashida wore her black suit jacket with a midi skirt, a cream silk top, a single strand of pearls, and several pearl-and-diamond studs in her ears. Her hair was tied back in a braided knot. Classy and formal, but with her badge, gun, and radio as well.

And as for Ariadne, well . . . what can you do about dress codes for a two-ton minotaur? Arry was the size of an Asian elephant, and all ruminant from the waist down, with reversed knee joints, tail, cloven hooves, and luxuriant auburn fur in loose curls. The showroom's ceilings were high enough that Arry could stand upright—just barely—without hunching over, as long as she avoided the ceiling fixtures. When she moved, the air currents shifted. When she laughed, the dishes rattled. You couldn't ignore the Beef.

Chubb had of course cut her slack on clothing requirements: her black suit jacket was more like a jacket-tunic covering most of her torso. Beneath it she wore a black midi spandex skort, with alterations to allow her tail out. Her face, as supersized as the rest of her, was lightly furred, with a broadened brow and nose and bovine nostrils, but her eyes and mouth were fully human. With her oversized reading glasses and her inquisitive expressions, she looked as if she'd be as comfortable in a library, surrounded by books, as on the battlefield. Her horns, though, were all warrior. They curved outward, sweeping an area six feet in diameter, and ended in metal-shielded tips. Her dark chestnut locks, a luxuriant mane, streaked with silver, tumbled down between her ears and horns, framing her face, and across her shoulders. The musculature in her shoulders, back, and chest and her massive, elongated arms were the envy of linebackers everywhere. She wore wrist and hand guards that enabled her to walk on all fours if necessary—i.e., in most nat-adapted spaces—but her hands were human. And she had a musky, pleasant herbivore scent.

Per company regulation, as were the rest of them, Arry was armed. Her battle mace jutted up at her left shoulder, harnessed against her back. When on duty Gil and Horace were also armed with handguns and Tasers. John didn't carry a weapon; his flames sufficed. The ship security team had no sidearms but had flashlight batons and radios.

John reached his two seconds. "How went the watch?" he asked Arry.

"Long! But uneventful," she whispered, in a near-subsonic rumble. She had had to cover for John after the flaming pillows incident, which meant she'd been on duty for almost fifteen hours straight now. Her stiff posture and the shadows under her eyes told him how weary she was. Probably hungry, too; she needed to eat often to sustain her metabolism, and that could be challenging for a ruminant on duty.

"Patina told me about your exciting wake-up, dear," she went on, in a rumble intended to be inaudible. "How did our hosts take it?"

He grimaced. "You can probably imagine," he replied. "But we got the initial details settled. They've moved me to a different cabin and a cleanup crew comes in when we dock. I'm sure they'll be glad to see our backsides tomorrow."

"Speak of the devil." Ras elbowed him and gestured with her chin. The musicians had just entered, with Captain Leemans escorting them.

Winston Marcus's renown as a musician rivaled that of Louis Armstrong himself. There could be no better choice to play Satchmo's trumpet on this tour. And his three younger siblings, the Tungsten Paradox Jazz and Blues Band, had several gold and platinum hits of their own. Jake and Lou were dressed, like Winston, in fine navy suits, and Ellie Marcus-Black wore a formal gown of midnight blue with a subtle spray of sequins across it, like the Milky Way on a clear dark night. The crowd swamped them, and they stopped to shake hands and sign autographs.

"Here come our star performers. You're relieved!" John told Arry. "Go get some shut-eye."

His mention of sleep triggered the yawn Arry had been trying to stifle, which emerged as a muffled roar. Silence swept through the room and all eyes went to her. Arry's dimples appeared. She covered her mouth. "Well, pardon me, folks!"

She dropped to all fours with a thump that made the room sway. People scooted chairs back and crowded out of her way as she lumbered through the room. "Pardon me," she repeated. "Excuse me." A mother shrieked and snatched her child up as Arry's enormous head passed near. "Your child is safe, ma'am," Arry told her. "I'm vegan."

John hid a smile behind a cough as the Beef eased her way through the double doors at the back of the bar. The ship rocked and water sloshed against the hull outside as she made her way down to her sleeping space in the hold.

Meanwhile, Ellie, Jake, and Lou approached the stage. Marcus came over to join them at the display. People were crowding around.

"Security detail, on alert," John said quietly. "Eyes on the audience." They confirmed.

Captain Leemans lifted her handheld mic. "Folks, please step away from the case and clear the aisles! Thank you. You'll have plenty of opportunities to see Mr. Marcus with the trumpet."

The room grew quiet; everybody on board knew the routine by now.

"Rashida, you present," John murmured. "I'll guard."

"Copy that."

He scanned his badge at the panel in the back of the display case, and keyed in his code. Rashida followed suit. Then she stepped around front, and he stepped back.

The sphere had two glass layers, which opened in reverse directions to allow access in a widening wedge. Rashida used a rouge polishing cloth to remove the trumpet from its glass mounting. She carried the horn over and handed it to Winston. He wiped the horn down with practiced ease, swept it to his mouth, and blew a few notes as mellow as whipped cream on mousse. The crowd burst into wild applause. He lifted his arms wide with a smile.

Winston headed to the stage, and stepped up onto it, horn in hand. "Thank you! Shall we get this party started?" Cheers, screams, stomping. It was the fifth night of this, and John still couldn't get over it, the love the audience felt for this man and his music. Winston gestured to the other band, now standing off to the side. "Let's hear it for Beauteous Maximus, and their bee-you-teous blues!"

The crowd clapped and whistled, and they departed. Winston went on, "Performing with me are my family. Ellie, on the flute and voice!" She played a few notes like a swirl of sprites. "Jake on bass sax!" A low, smooth progression. "Lou on keyboards and mouth harps!" Syncopated chords and percussion.

"Now, this is our last night aboard the *Queen Margaret*. A callout to the captain and crew!" Whistles and shouts. "And you've been a great audience. We dock tomorrow for one day and two nights in New York City. Tomorrow evening, we wrap up our Golden Jazz tour with a big, blowout charity event on New Liberty Island, beneath the Golden Lady herself. You are all invited! I hope you've already bought your tickets, because it's sold out. All proceeds will go to help refugees escaping the horrors in Kazakhstan. So drink up! Eat up! Open up your wallets for a good cause! And enjoy the show." With that, he lifted the horn and played the opening notes of their first song.

"Off to a good start," Rashida said in John's ear. He had started his evening rounds checking the room's passive security systems. They'd tricked out the liner with the latest anti-ace-power detection and security tech. The company had a contract with Royal Flush, LLC, Clara van Renssaeler's security software company, which had reverse-engineered Takisian science to detect different kinds of abilities. Readouts showed nominal conditions here: no unusual gravitational fluctuations, no unexpected or abnormal electromagnetic or psionic or sonic patterns detected; no megafauna or -flora or animated nonliving matter showing up on radar in the vicinity. Nothing behaving outside standard parameters.

So why the hell were all the hairs standing up on the back of his neck?

♦

Many of the audience members were older, or parents with young kids, and the crowd thinned around midnight. John and Rashida stood guard at the stage while the band members took a fifteen-minute break. By the time Tungsten Paradox returned for their second set, a younger crowd had wandered in from the casino and dance hall. John checked the readings again, and then had a few words with the guards covering the exits.

Rashida found a seat near the exit while John found an empty stool at the bar. He pulled out his phone and checked the monitor reads one last time, and then allowed himself to relax. He ordered a tonic and lime and leaned back to enjoy the show.

After a bit, the guy sitting next to him leaned close. "Hey, you're that guy, aren't you? The Candle, right? The ace from that reality show."

John glanced over. The man was big—as tall as he was, and broader in the shoulders. Not Hollywood looks, exactly, but he had a rough magnetism. He looked to be about the same age as John, maybe a year or so younger, and in excellent physical shape. He also had a shock of dark blond hair, eyes as green as a cat's, and a hawklike nose. And he was eyeing John with an intent focus that gave John a delightful shiver. John had always been a sucker for green eyes.

Settle down, there; he may not even be into men.

John muted the mic on his comms—he'd be able to hear the security team, but the team wouldn't hear him. Rashida looked over and gestured: *What gives?* He gave her a hand signal: *All clear; it's personal; cover me for a few minutes.*

"That's right." He set his drink down. "*American Hero,* season one. That was a long time ago, though; you've got a good memory." He held out his hand. "John Montaño." The other man gripped it. The touch lingered. As did the eye contact.

"Call me Rip." He gestured at John's glass. "Can I buy you another drink?"

"Thanks, but . . ." John rattled the ice cubes in his glass. "Tonic and lime, buzz not included. I'm on duty. Where are you from?"

"New York. A village in the Hamptons."

"Long Island, eh?" John hadn't made this guy out as having a lot of money. He supposed not *everyone* from the Hamptons was filthy rich.

Let's see where this goes. John moved his forearm close enough to Rip's on the bar for the other man's arm hairs to tickle. Their shoulders were side by side. Both were playing it cool, just two guys sitting next to each other, watching the show, enjoying a casual conversation.

"And you?" Rip asked. "Where are you from?"

"Colorado, originally. Durango." He had lost every trace of his Boston accent years ago. That had taken a lot of work. "I live in New York now. And you? What brings you to the *Queen*? Jazz fan? On vacation with the wife and kids? Or husband, or . . . ?"

"No, I'm single." A sidelong glance.

"Me, too."

The other man smiled. "I was in Havana on business. I'm an art collector."

"Collector? Or dealer?" Art *dealer* was a job. Art *collector* was a hobby—and typically meant lots of discretionary income.

"A bit of both," Rip replied with a shrug. So he *did* have money.

"Really? Cool! I was a professional artist myself for a while, before I took up the day job full-time."

"Oh? And what business are you in now?"

"Still in the art business—but as a detective. I'm an investigator and security operations lead for an insurance company." John gestured at the stage, where Winston Marcus was playing a sexy jazz solo on the golden trumpet. "Authenticity certifications, fraud and theft investigations, transport security, that sort of thing."

"Ah, yes. The famed trumpet I read about. Is it truly solid gold?"

"Almost entirely—fourteen carats. Though some of the working parts are ten-carat or brass, of necessity."

"Even so, twenty million seems a bit on the high side," Rip replied, referring to its estimated market value.

"It's more what Armstrong did with it than what it's made of." At the other man's blank look, he stared. "You mean you've never heard the story?"

"Wait, you mean—Louis Armstrong was that guy? The Black ace in the sixties who brought a bridge full of jackboots down with his trumpet?"

John smiled. "It was quite a bit more interesting than that. They say Satchmo had the ability to manipulate and amplify sound waves. He was world famous as a jazz and blues musician, as I'm sure you know, and that had nothing to do with his powers. But when his card turned in '46, he used his ace to primarily enhance his performances. He could make it sound like there were ten of him playing at once. Amazing, if you've heard the recordings.

"He wasn't political early in his career, but in the late fifties he began speaking up to oppose segregation, and in early 1965 civil rights leaders asked him to join them at the protest marches in Alabama. The state and local cops confronted the protestors on a bridge between Selma and Montgomery and tried to force the marchers to disperse, Old Satchmo whips out his golden trumpet—that very horn, they say"—John jerked his thumb as Winston played a rising note to audience applause—"and drives the cops back off the bridge with a blast of music. If you believe the stories, the music actually lifted the cops up in the air and dumped them in the river. But there's video so we know that part's apocryphal.

"The police regroup and so do the protestors, on opposite halves of the bridge. Then the cops start to advance again. Satchmo has a private word or two with Dr. King and a couple of the other civil rights leaders. They pass the word along for everyone to lock arms and march in place, in rhythm, and Satchmo picks up and amplifies the marchers' footsteps with his music. It's as if there are thousands and thousands of feet pounding on that bridge. The Edmund Pettus starts bucking and weaving like it's in an earthquake, and again the cops are driven back, stumbling and falling over each other. Every time they come after the protestors, Satchmo blows his horn and the marchers march to make the bridge shake. Eventually the cops finally have to give up and let the protestors through, with Armstrong at the front with King, playing Havana jazz in three-four time to keep the beat.

"They still had to bring the National Guard in to get the state and local governments to back down, but that was a big day for the movement. Pretty soon people were saying that Gabriel himself came down from Heaven that day with the trumpet for Satchmo to play, in answer to the people's prayers.

"There was a huge stink over what Satchmo did, of course. He'd been really popular with white audiences before, but whites staged boycotts of Armstrong's performances after that, and white supremacists firebombed his house in Queens and smashed his LPs. They nearly drove him out of the music business for several years. But if anything, he ended up selling *more* records, because Black people spend money too, and a lot of folks were grateful to him. It was a big deal at the time."

"And now you're guarding the horn. Quite a responsibility."

John shrugged. "It pays the bills. And I get paid to spend my time around lots of really cool art pieces and ancient artifacts."

"You said you were a professional artist. Why'd you quit?"

"I got tired of having to promote myself." He tossed back the last of his tonic. "Besides, being broke all the time is a pain in the ass."

Rip took a swallow of his drink. "What was your medium?"

"I was a sculptor," John said. "Of sorts."

"'Of sorts'?"

John shook his head. "My medium is . . . was . . . ephemeral. I finally resorted to holography, to create something that could be put in an exhibit or go out on tour. But it was a huge amount of work to try to capture them, and it was never the same as actually seeing them. So I gave it up." On impulse, he said, "Here, I'll show you."

John *twisted* into inferno-world and harvested small bursts of the brightest hues he could find. Returning, he fed them in careful, compartmented order through his body, and from there in tiny bursts and flares into the space between his hands.

Fiery shapes blossomed there: an obsidian cliff, dark-bright fire; next, ocean waves of sapphire and seafoam and lavender, which billowed out and surrounded the black, churning at its base. At the center atop the cliff sprouted a burning carnelian lattice: a lighthouse. Yellow flames jetted up inside the lighthouse's red frame, brightening it from within. Then the outer layers of the outcropping morphed into a mighty black crow, which spread its wings and rose aloft, trailing smoke, and spiraled up around the lighthouse. It landed atop the structure, and from its beak burst lemon-bright flame.

The metaphor was a *little* on the nose, John thought. Still, he was pleased with it. He held it between his hands a little longer, trickling gouts of different hues to maintain it. Rip was staring at it, rapt, his face lit by its colors.

The other man reached out to touch it, but John slapped his hand away. "Careful!" The fire sculpture dissolved with a *shh-whoop!* and fizzled out. "It's not entirely safe."

Others at the bar near them were looking over. Murmurs rose at the nearby tables, above the blues song Ellie was singing.

OK, maybe that wasn't such a good idea. The security teams at both doors were looking at him, and Rashida spread her hands with a *what the fuck, John?!* look.

"Impressive," Rip said. "Quite evocative." Their gazes locked, and John got a sudden erection. It lodged at a painful angle. He stood, trying not to grimace or squirm.

"Listen . . . I need to get back to work. Uh . . . I'm on deck five, cabin four. Why don't you come by later? The performance should be wrapping up in a half hour or so. I have a fifth of Glenlivet single malt that needs some attention. And we can talk about"—he smiled—"art."

"Sounds like a plan." Rip glanced at his watch. "Say one thirty, then?"

"It's a date."

After Rip left, Rashida asked in John's ear, "Care to elaborate?"

He turned his mic back on. "On what? You mean him? Just some guy. Wanted to know the story of the horn." He got another tonic and lime and between songs, joined her at her table. She was side-eyeing him. "All right," he said. "I shouldn't have let myself get distracted."

"Mmm-hmm. Just some guy." He felt his face warm up. She muted her own mic. "You know . . . I don't think I've ever seen you do that."

He muted his mic too. "What? Flirt with a cute guy while on duty?"

"Not *that*. You do that plenty. I'm talking about your flames."

He felt his hackles going up. "What about them?"

"Well—" She bit her lip. "Don't take this personally, but—"

"Go on. I won't get angry."

"You already are." She gestured with her chin, and he followed her gaze down to his hands. Which were leaking dribbles of yellow flame from the knuckles down. *Shit!* He shook off the flames and shoved the yellow energy away, back in inferno-world. Then he installed a placid smile on his face and lifted his palms toward her. "I'm all good. See?"

She propped her chin on her interlaced fingers. "If you *pinkie swear* you won't yell at me, or write me a bad performance review." She crooked her pinkie at him, eyebrows raised.

He hooked her pinkie with his. "Of course not! No reprisals." Then he sat back. "So hit me, Doc. What's your analysis?"

She rolled her eyes at him. "When was the last time you actually had *fun* with your flames?"

He flung a hand back toward the bar counter. "Um, just now?"

"Before tonight."

"What was *American Hero*? Liver pâté?"

"A, that was for money. And B, that was *a decade ago*."

"I'm always using my powers! 'Hey John, could you light the barbecue for me?' 'My battery's dead; could you give it a quick jump?'" He snapped his fingers. "'Hey John, let's get high! Gimme some of that purple stuff.' 'Hey Candle, my knee injury's been giving me trouble. Could you throw some of that green fire at my MCL?'"

She shook her head. "But that's exactly my point! You only use your ace when other people ask you for a favor. Or for the job. Oops. 'Scuse me." She transformed to a cloud of beads that swooped under the table, and when she returned she had her napkin back in hand.

"But—but—what about my flame sculptures? The MoMA still has one of my holograms on display . . ."

"That's cool. I've seen some of your sculptures. They were great. But you know—" The musicians finished a song as she spoke, and people burst into applause, drowning her out.

"Well, that's it for tonight, folks!" Winston said into the standing mic. "You've been a great audience! We hope to see you tomorrow night at the Golden Lady!" He held up the golden trumpet. "It'll be a big show—we have some surprise guests who will join us there. And who knows?" He blew a tune. "Maybe Satchmo's ghost will return and bring the house down!"

John approached the stage as the musicians took a bow amid raucous applause. Winston sat down to clean the horn while his siblings cleaned and put away their own instruments. "Give us five to clean up," he said.

"Whenever you're ready."

John returned to the table. Ras was sucking the last of her soda through her straw, watching him over the rim of her glass. John sat back down. "It looks like you have more to say."

"I do. Do you know what the art dealers I've met say about you? Practically every professional of standing has told me that you have enough talent for ten other artists, but that just when you were starting to build up a name for yourself, you bailed. Your output dropped into the toilet. You missed deadlines. Blew people off. So don't try to tell me nothing's going on with your ace."

The waitstaff were clearing the tables, cleaning them, and stacking the chairs. The showroom had mostly emptied of tourists. "There's a much simpler explanation. The well dried up. I ran out of ideas."

"Sure. Whatever you say." Her tone was light, but he caught a hint of exasperation in it. "You are probably one of the most easygoing people I've met, John. You're downright sweet. And smart and funny and gorgeous. If I was into monogamy, I'd snap you right up off the meat market—company rules be damned." She tapped her fingernails on the glass and looked at him with her beautiful big dark eyes, and he shifted to ease the pressure of another erection. *Dammit.*

She leaned forward and tapped his temple. "Now, I don't know what you have locked in there, but it wants out. And someday, if you don't uncage it, it's going to eat you up inside, and do real harm. To you or to the people you care about." She sat back. "And now I'm done."

"Thank God." John waved her incipient objection away. "I know, I know. I asked for it."

Up on stage, the musicians had finished with their instruments, and the physical security guys were gathering nearby. He stood. "Come on. Time for us to put trumpet-baby back in its cradle. It's your turn to babysit tonight."

"No slack for a woman just getting over a tummy bug?"

"Nope. I've taken the last three graveyard shifts in a row because of that bug, and you've clearly recovered."

"Hey! I thought you said no reprisals."

"I have a date with a hot blond. Besides . . ." He turned on his mic and motioned the security team up. "Rank hath its privileges."

"That it does," she said with a smile. "That it does."

♥

At precisely 1:30 a.m. came the knock. John opened the deck-side door.

Rip said, "I thought I'd take you up on that drink."

"By all means." John gestured for him to come in.

Rip hadn't changed: he still wore a green button-down shirt with rolled-up sleeves, khaki shorts, and sandals. But he'd shaved and used some product in his hair. He smelled good, too; hair gel and something else—aftershave or deodorant. *Nice.*

He caught Rip checking him out as well.

John had changed to a black T-shirt, a little on the snug side. (His musculature was more long and lean than bulked up, but he worked out regularly, so he had decent pecs and abs. And he thought the shirt showed his biceps off nicely.) He was barefoot, freshly shaved and showered, and had on his favorite pair of button-up jeans. No briefs. He had laid out a few condoms in an array of sizes and types on the bedside table, as well as massage oil. Rip noticed them.

"Make yourself comfortable." John went to the dresser to pour them each a couple fingers of scotch. If Rip sat in the chair near the door, he hadn't made up his mind yet; if on the bed, anchors aweigh and full steam ahead. "How do you take it? Rocks or neat?"

"However I can get it," Rip replied, so close behind him that his breath tickled John's neck. He slipped an arm around John's waist.

OK, option three: this guy wants to get right down to business.

John turned and handed Rip a glass. Rip downed its contents in one go, set the glass on the dresser, and entangled his fingers in John's hair and pulled him close. They looked at each other for a second. *Those green eyes. Wow.* This guy was really doing it for him. John slid his hands around Rip's nape, too, and pressed his lips to Rip's. He flicked his tongue across Rip's teeth. Rip moaned.

After a moment, John pulled back and ran a finger along Rip's jawline. "You don't waste time."

"Making good use of time is my specialty."

Rip pressed his hand against John's crotch, over his jeans, and then shoved him up against the wall, causing John to spill his drink. "Packing a nice load, I see."

John winced—Rip's fondling was a bit much; the buttons of his jeans were pressing into a very sensitive area. "Easy, friend." He laid his hand over Rip's and peeled his fingers back. "Not that I don't appreciate the attention, but the equipment only *feels* like it's made of titanium."

Rip wasn't listening. He shoved John against the wall again, hard enough to knock John's drink from his hand, forced John's mouth open with his hand, and pushed his tongue deep inside.

Enough of this.

John shoved Rip away, and when Rip came for him he moved off to the side, grabbed Rip's wrist from behind, and gripped his collar. With a twist from the hips, he flung the other man across the room. Rip stumbled, banging his shin on the bed frame with a curse, and went to his knees on the floor. John landed on top of him before he could rise, grabbed Rip in a half nelson, and bore down with all his strength. Rip fought, but went down onto his belly.

John sat up. He gripped the base of Rip's neck with one hand and pinned the man's arms with his knees.

This had sure taken a weird turn. Did he think this was rough play, or was it a fight? He was struggling silently, lurching hard enough to nearly buck John off.

"Would you calm down?" John said. "Take a breather."

At that, the other man stopped fighting. It sounded like he laughed. "All right." His head was to the side and John could see he was grinning. "Better?"

John planted a hand next to Rip's head to brace himself. "You know, I like a bit of rough-and-tumble as much as the next guy, but we need to talk about our safe words."

As John spoke, Rip slammed his head back and pain exploded in John's face. He felt the bones of his nose go *crunch*. "Ow! *Fuck!*"

He shoved himself backward over the bed, rolled, and came up on his knees on one side of the bed. He put his hands to his nose and then looked at them: blood filled his palms. He'd left a trail of blood spatters across the bedcover as well. Rip came up onto the other side of the bed. John rose to his feet, staggered back, and smacked against the door. Rip stood, too, breathing heavily.

John shook his head. "You *do* know you're picking a fight with an ace, right?"

Rip grinned. "Just friendly foreplay."

The pain radiating across John's face was causing yellow flames to gather near him at the other place. He displayed his bloodied palms to Rip. "This? Not my definition of friendly." He *twisted* away to harvest a gout of yellow flame and a clot of blue. Returning, he ignited both hands—one yellow, one blue—then shoved them to a spot above Rip's head. The resulting flash-hiss-*BOOM!* came complete with a miniature thunderclap, lightning flash, and raindrop microburst.

Rip wiped water from his face. He chuckled. "What's the matter, can't take a little roughhousing?" He walked around the edge of the bed. "You're what I call a *cloacal* ace. You're nothing but chicken shit."

John rolled his eyes. "Haha. How old are you, ten?"

"Your flames *look* impressive, all right. Bright and shiny. So sexy. So gay. But they're all for show." Rip jabbed a finger. "You were a *loser* on *American Hero*. You were a *loser* as an artist. What is this, your third job in seven years?"

"Odd that you would know that . . ."

"And what kind of an ace name is 'the Candle,' anyway? It sounds like someone should light some incense or toke a doobie or something."

"Maybe someone should explain to you how this works." John called up more flame and juggled the different colors. "They call *me* the Candle, but *you're* the one who ends up as a human torch. Or a corpsicle. Or a lightning rod. Fortunately for *you*, I'd never do that. Not without extreme provocation." He flexed his hands. "But you know . . . I'm starting to feel just a little *provoked*."

"Yeah? Go ahead, then. Hit me with all you've got." Rip edged closer and slapped his chest with both hands. "Pussy. Faggot. Mangina."

"'Mangina'?" John couldn't help it; he laughed. He clapped, and his flames snuffed out. "*You* were the one who stuck his tongue down *my* throat, darling."

Rip went white with rage and lunged. John *twisted* away again, and the pain of his broken nose faded with the sound of his heartbeat. He wound through roaring towers of conflagration. *Purple or black?* Either would do. *OK, then . . . whichever I see first.*

He found and harvested a jagged bouquet of black flame. It crackled in along his spinal cord and through his somatic nerves, making his muscles twitch and jump. He turned back there again, and summoned a batch of green flames.

As he reached the threshold to his body this time, he saw something he'd never seen before. He saw movement in the gap that separated inferno-world and his own.

In his own world, his first heartbeat was ending, and Rip had moved perceptibly nearer. But he could afford another half beat. He returned his focus to the threshold's edge. And saw light—but not flame. Something else. Something that shifted and spun, like a coin spinning. It was another world.

It unfolded under his scrutiny beyond this edge, yet another world—like nothing he'd ever seen back home, nor like inferno-world, either. Beyond the crack were many two-dimensional versions of scenes from his life—as if Flatland itself had broken into a million fragments. Or a castle of vast mirrors in a strobe light, all in black and white. Beyond the threshold, planar worlds splayed out in constant motion, in fans and branches. There were far too many to count and more every instant; new ones appeared as the older ones receded, as if each moment were shedding its past and generating new possible futures. These snapshots stacked up on one another at impossible angles, overlapping, spinning around, and spreading out and away in an endless procession.

He caught glimpses of the images nearest the gap. Strangely, the images were of him—but not the moment he'd left just now; rather, they were of a moment earlier in the evening, with him and Rashida, right before Rip had entered the showroom.

Which reminds me . . .

He did a half-*twist* again and the threshold to his own body came into view. The green had already begun to course through his lymphatic vessels to settle in his adenoids, tonsils, thymus, and spleen. He slid back into his body, pointed his right forefinger and middle finger at Rip, and drew the black from his spinal column. Dark agonies rippled along his nerves and John screamed as the power shot out with a crack, smelling of ozone. The black fireball (it wasn't truly black, but there wasn't a better word for what it looked like) caught Rip in the chest, mid-lunge. Now it was his turn to scream. He smashed into John's midriff, stiff as a plank, and slammed him against the wall.

John caught him and lowered him to the floor—not as carefully as he might have. Pain makes a person cranky. He stared down at Rip—breathing hard, dripping blood onto the other man's shirt. *What the fucking fuck?* Rip stared up, panting as well. His heart still beat, of course; black fire attacked only the somatic nerves, which controlled voluntary muscles. So he was locked in.

John allowed himself an instant of vindictive glee. *You'll be sore as hell later, and it serves you right.* He pulled out his phone and snapped a photo. Then he swiped over to video, made it selfie mode with the time-date-location stamp visible, and hit Record.

"This is Johd Bodtadyo, recordi'g evidedce of ad assault od be, just seco'ds ago by"—he flipped the camera around—"this persod, who goes by the dabe Rip. I idvited hib to by roob for *codsedsual* sex. But he decided to attack be idstead. I've disabled hib, id self-defedse."

He transmitted the photo and video to his work server, then tucked his phone away. He was still dripping blood on the carpet and the pain in his face was making his eyes water. *You're a mess, Juanma.* He pressed fingers against the pressure points in his jaw and temples to stanch the flow of blood and stepped into the bathroom.

His face was straight out of a horror movie.

John pulled the green up into the flesh behind his face, tilting his head back. Emerald healing passed in waves across his face, first burning, then feeling the way mint tastes, and casting an interference pattern on the ceiling as it did its work. In its tingling wake came a massaging, bone-cracking pressure. "Ow! Ow! Fuck!"

He gripped the counter and bent over, stamping a foot to distract himself from the agony while the blood vessels and tissue in his face mended, torn flesh melded, and bones knitted themselves together.

Green healed fast, but it didn't come with Novocain.

Finally he straightened, as the green glow under his skin ebbed and flickered out. He turned his head to both sides and checked his reflection, pressing his fingers against his nose, orbital sockets, and cheeks. Though he still looked a fright from all the blood, the nose had returned to its own shape and he had no swelling or tissue damage. Not even tenderness.

John sighed with a nod. *We loves our green fire; yes, we does.* He washed up, came out, and changed his T-shirt. Then he squatted next to the Pinocchio-stiff man on the floor. "You did quite a number on me," John said. "The question now is, what am *I* going to do with *you*?"

Rip's gaze tracked him. From the subtle movements in his facial muscles, John guessed he'd begun to regain voluntary control. Small sparks and embers of black fire still surfaced on and submerged in his exposed flesh, but with less intensity than before. Most people would stay immobile for another ten or fifteen minutes, but it varied, and Rip seemed like the type to play possum. Best not to take chances.

John worked his arms under Rip's armpits and with a grunt, dragged him over and levered him up into the easy chair. He shoved Rip in the midsection, and the other man bent into an L shape. Then John *twisted* away to inferno-world to harvest more green and black. He socked the flames away on the other side and pulled the desk chair over.

"Way to ruin a perfectly good roll in the sack, dude. I gave you every chance to bow out gracefully." John reversed the chair and sat, leaning his arms on the chair's back. "The big question now is, are you just some rando homophobe? Or is this a *professional* visit?"

"As you've discovered, my black causes your muscles to seize up. Its effects can take a while to wear off. Think of it as a fifteen-minute plank. But we haven't got all night—we'll be docking in New York City in a couple of hours and I've got other fish to fry. So I'm going to wake your body up now, to have a little chat before I turn you over to Captain Leemans." As he spoke, John drew out the green. It coursed into his right hand, slithered over his knuckles, and blanketed his arm in a gauntlet of gouts and rivulets of lime-dark fire. He played with it, rolling it back and forth over his hand and arm, holding Rip's gaze.

"The green fire will return muscular control, and help ease some of the soreness you're going to have. But in case you're feeling the need to get frisky again"—he drew out the black and swirled it around his left hand—

"I've got more black waiting. And I have a few other tricks up my sleeve as well, because as you have probably guessed by now, *this* isn't my first circus and *you're* not my first monkey. But I'm hoping we can dispense with further primate threat displays and have an adult conversation instead. What do you say?"

John tucked the black flame away again and spread the green between his two hands, weaving a mesh of fire, and cast it over Rip like a fisherman's net. As it settled over the big man, his eyes went wide. Luminous green traced patterns beneath his skin, dispersing the black. Rip's shoulders dropped. He closed his eyes and drew a long, shuddering breath.

The last of the flames exited the top of his head in a flash of lime and a puff of smoke. He sat up and tested movement in his legs, arms, and hands. Then he wiped the spittle from his chin. The look he gave John could have fried him from low Earth orbit.

"So," John said. "You want to tell me what you're really doing here?"

At that, Rip burst into laughter. "You still don't recognize me, do you, Juanma?"

John managed to keep his jaw from falling open. Barely. His answering laugh sounded hollow even to his own ears. "The name's *John*, friend. Not—whatever it was you called me. I think you must have me confused with some other brown guy."

Rip smiled. "So you're disavowing your mother's Irish blood now, Juanma? For shame." He tsked. "What would she say, if she knew?"

The words fell like one-ton bricks. *OK, so he's not guessing.*

Rip stood, and so did he. "She's still alive, you know," Rip said. "Your mom. Still in Southie. She remarried, and you have a half sister now, who just turned ten. But you probably knew that." John stared. His fists clenched. Fury waged with terror in him.

"I visited them a while back. I thought you might have been secretly in touch. But nope, she still thinks you're dead. She's even built a cute little shrine for you in the living room, next to your dad's. So touching. If she only knew what a nasty piece of work Juan Maria Montoya Cavanagh turned out to be. She probably suspected it, though, the first time you got arrested at fourteen." Rip's lips skinned back over his teeth. "What would she say, knowing her prodigal son is alive and well, hiding in plain sight? The big ace celebrity! While his family is barely scraping by. Would she forgive you? Or would she know you for the selfish prick you are?"

While Rip spoke, John's thoughts were racing. *Play dumb? Or blast the shit out of this fucker and dump him into the sea?* John shook his head and unclenched his hands. Nah. He had plenty of options for dealing with this asshole. *Just be patient, Juanma. Find out as much as you can.* He forced himself to relax, and leaned against the wall. "You've built up quite a delusion to go along with your homophobia," John said. "But do go on. I love a good story."

"I admit," Rip said, "your appearance is different enough now that it took me a long time to recognize you. Nice handiwork." He scrutinized John's face. "No scarring at all, not even up close. I'd assumed it was multiple plastic surgeries. But it must have been your green fire that healed you and changed you. Wasn't it?"

Both, actually. "Sorry. Not a clue what you're talking about." Meanwhile he was racking his brains for a connection. Everyone from his boyhood in Boston thought he was dead. No body, but the supposed death-by-wildcard made that not an issue. And there was a death certificate and a gravestone and everything.

"They told me you'd died in the blast," Rip said. He made air quotes. "'Obliterated by otherworldly energy.' That's what they said. Imagine my surprise when I learned that wasn't the case. That you'd run off and left me there, and started a life somewhere else."

Finally the sneering mask peeled away. The edges of his mouth tugged down. "We were going to get out together, Juanma. We were going to escape *together*. And I come to find you ran off alone. You left me *crippled*, you asshole! You let me think you were dead."

And as he spoke, John knew. Bigger and beefier, now; he'd been a boy then, for all his height. And he, too, wore a different face than he had when they were boys. But he had the same intense green eyes, the same blond hair. The same Boston accent. And he was the only one who'd known of John's desire to get out of Southie at all costs. Because he'd shared it. He gasped. "*Titus?*"

Rip gave him a thin smile. "Took you long enough. Though admittedly, I had some work done, too. Want to see more of your handiwork?"

He unbuttoned his shirt and stripped it off. A patchwork of grafts and scarring—the remnants of melted flesh—mottled the musculature of his chest, neck, and abdomen. He lifted his arms; the burns extended around into both armpits and up the underside of his left arm past the elbow. "*This* is what you did to me that night."

John rubbed his mouth, covering his shock. Rip pulled the shirt back on. They just stood there looking at each other across those seventeen years. "I was in the room with you when your ace turned the rest of the way. Or whatever it was that happened, that second time they manifested.

"I came by every day to check on you after you fell into your wild card coma. Were you aware? I was waiting for you, Juanma. For months. I wanted to be there when you woke up. And I was *right next to you* when you exploded into flame. I saw you open your eyes and look at me, and yellow flames were shooting everywhere. I tried to put you out but the blankets caught fire too, and so did I. I passed out, and when I woke up I was in the burn unit, with burns over nearly twenty percent of my body, and you were gone.

"I spent *months* in the hospital, Juanma, just for trying to save you. I lost count of the operations. The hospital bills put me so far under with Fagan it was a life sentence.

"You know how skin grafts work? They strip flesh from other parts of your body, like the inside of your thigh. They patch them onto the burned areas, bit by bit. They let those patches heal and then take more. Before you know it, you're one big walking scar. And of course there were the infections. And the multiple plastic surgeries to return my boyish looks, because this part of my face was burned too." He laid a hand on his lower left cheek, chin, and neck. "And there were those years of physical therapy to give me full use of my left arm back. That was a barrel of giggles. When you could have healed me with your green flames *at any time*."

The silence stretched. "Titus . . . I had no idea . . ."

"No. You didn't. Because you never bothered to check."

John pressed his lips together and said nothing.

"Well." Rip clapped his hands together. "This has been real. And we have a lot more to talk about. But I must be going. Lady Liberty is coming up soon. From there it's just a short way to Pier 88." Rip checked his watch. "It's going to be a busy day. We should both see if we can get a little shut-eye. Meet me at Battery Park, at precisely eleven fifty-two a.m. Not a minute before, not a minute after. By the Staten Island Ferry, but don't worry, we won't be going to Staten Island. Come alone. I have something important to discuss."

"Why should I? Why should I do *anything* you say?"

Rip shrugged. "Up to you. But if you don't show precisely at that time, I'll release the evidence I've compiled regarding your secret past."

"What evidence? There *is* none." He'd made sure of it, long ago.

"None? Really?" Rip tapped his chin with a finger. "I bet if someone knew your true identity—knew who your mother was, say, and where your father was buried—it would be a fairly simple exercise to collect a bit of familial DNA to compare yours to.

"And if it comes down to that, we'll let the public weigh the evidence for themselves. The great and powerful Candle is linked to a notorious

Boston crime syndicate? He has a pretty impressive criminal record from his youth and he's been lying about who he is all these years? Wow. Ace celebrity art cop turns out to have been a street punk all along. Should I give the story to *TMZ*, *Deadspin*, or *Aces! Online*? They'll eat it up. 'Should this guy be entrusted with safeguarding priceless artifacts for the world's top art insurer?' I'm betting the answer is no.

"And at that point . . ." He walked to the door and laid his hand on the latch. "I imagine certain people from our shared past might get very curious about what you recall about them. And they know where your family lives, too."

A muscle jumped in John's jaw. "*Fagan.*"

"Bingo! So unless you're up for public exposure and taking on Riley Fagan on your own, seriously consider my offer. I'm good either way."

"Wow, Titus. That's low."

"When it comes to you, Juanma, I've had a lot of years to explore just how low I can go." He pulled the door open. "Ta!"

He stepped out and shut the door behind him.

♣

At five in the morning, the *Queen Margaret* docked on the Hudson at Pier 88. Tiffani stood at the curb in front of the pier, waiting for Rip. She wore her favorite summer cardigan wrap, a lightweight, silver-gray raw-silk weave that went all the way to her knees. Even at this hour, the air was a bit too hot for the sweater, but more importantly, it hid what she had on underneath: a pair of grease-monkey coveralls with AEROLUX AIRSHIP TOURS stitched on the breast pocket.

A nondescript gray sedan with smoked-over windows pulled up. The passenger door opened. Rip was in the driver's seat. "C'mon, hustle! We're on a tight timetable."

She scooted in and, as he pulled away from the curb, wiggled out of the cardigan and stuffed it into her bag. *Tug, tuck, glam, and roll,* she thought, ignoring the gibbering animal fear in the back of her mind. She pressed a shaking finger under her nose so she wouldn't cry. *Tug, tuck, glam, and roll. I can do this.*

He drove to an empty warehouse on the outskirts of Jokertown. The flatbed driver met them there, an older man—rotund and taciturn with a bald head and big ears—who let them inside. Rip called him Brody. While Brody climbed into a forklift and loaded the catapult onto the flatbed, Tiffani tied her auburn hair back in a ponytail and pulled on a baseball cap, and tugged the end of the ponytail through the gap. She did some big arm circles and deep knee bends, more to get rid of nerves than anything else. "Rip, hon, are you sure I won't need a crash helmet? Have you seen it?"

"You'll be fine." Rip popped the trunk and pulled out a package. "Here." He removed a box from the bag and handed it to her.

Tiffani nearly dropped it, it was so heavy. Her eyes went wide. "Jesus, what's in this? Gold bullion?" The box was about the size and shape of a medium pizza box. THRUST BEARING, the label said, and below it, in big red letters: *URGENT SAFETY RECALL—REPLACEMENT PART.*

Tiffani stuffed it into her messenger bag. Then she looked over at Rip. *Not gonna ask,* she thought. *No point in knowing what it does. It wouldn't change anything.*

"OK, let's do a final equipment check," he said. "Gloves?"

She pulled out a disposable nitrile pair from her right pocket and wiggled them at him.

"Spare turbine part." She showed him the box in her messenger bag.

"Change of outfit?"

She felt around in her messenger bag for the items she'd brought with her, per instructions: makeup kit, heels, clean blouse, and slacks. "Check," she said.

"All right, then. Looks like you're good to go."

She grabbed his sleeve as he started toward the car. "Rip—"

"Ah-ah. No second thoughts," he said. "I've kept your family safe and I've spent a lot of money caring for them."

She released her grip with a sigh. "I know."

"Trust me. I've run through a hundred different scenarios, and this is the only way that works. I need that part to be on board the dirigible before shift change at six." He took hold of her arms. "I've worked out the physics and the timing, Megan. You've practiced this a hundred times. Just remember."

"I know, I know. Tug, tuck, glam, and roll."

"OK. One last walk-through?"

She hugged herself. "Sure, OK."

"How do you get in?"

"There's an outside stair. I go in through the window—*after* I put on my plastic gloves," she added, holding up her hands, "so I don't leave fingerprints."

"And once you're inside?"

"I find the key card in the supervisor's office and use that to get into the airship. Leave the card on the stairs. Find the machine room." She paused. "Where . . . ?"

"Where there'll be a big spherical tank next to a panel of blinking lights."

"That's the helium."

"Right. And there's another machine in back of it, that looks sort of like a jet engine lying on its side."

He was nodding. "The thrust turbine. Next?"

"Next I swap out the pizza box by the machine with this one." She touched her messenger bag.

"And then hide where I showed you—"

"I know, I know—in the storage locker in the corner, just outside the machine room."

"And you have to be out of that room and in the storage locker by what time?"

"Six oh four."

"Six oh *three*."

"That's what I meant!"

"Don't mess it up, Megan."

"I won't. I mean, you've seen this, right? I make it through?"

"You make it through. As long as you play it *exactly* the way I told you."

"I will. Just like you said."

"Good girl." He laid an arm across her shoulders and they stepped out of the way to allow Brody room to finish strapping the catapult down. "Now, after they're done with their maintenance procedures," he told her, "they'll fly the airship from Jersey to the Empire State Building to pick up the passengers. That'll be at ten till noon. Then, when the airship reaches its cruising altitude, the flight attendants start serving drinks. What do you do next?"

"I'll hear two bells—"

"That's right, when the airship reaches a mile up. And what time is it then?"

"Twelve oh one and fifty seconds, plus or minus five seconds."

"Correct. And at that point, your passage will be clear, for exactly one minute and twenty-two seconds."

She nodded, and ticked the steps off on her fingers. "I get out of the locker when I hear the 'ding-ding.' I take off my shoes and coveralls and leave them there and put on my change of clothes. I open the hatch, close it behind me, and quietly descend to the gondola."

"Right. And?"

"Make sure the flight attendants aren't looking, then walk normally through the kitchen like I belong there."

"Yep! Then you can just join the other tourists. Take an empty seat anywhere—there'll be several open. And relax! Have a lovely tour of the city, with free champagne and catering. Hobnob all you like. You'll return to watch the concert from the air at sundown.

"And it's going to be quite a show, you know." He touched her jaw and gave her a searching gaze. "They have giant windows and you'll be able to see the whole thing from above. Plus they'll be broadcasting it onto big screens and speakers inside the gondola. Best seats in the house. And afterward, there'll be fireworks."

"That doesn't sound so bad." She gave him a phony smile and hated herself for showing him her fear. But existential terror'll do that to a person. Over the past six weeks, since they'd stepped off the *Queen Margaret* from their own cruise, she'd learned way more about Rip and his proclivities than she'd ever wanted to know.

It was too late to back out now.

For my family, she thought. *I can do this for them.*

"That's my Tiffani." He squeezed her shoulder. "Now, it'll be a long wait in that locker. Did you bring something to read?"

She nodded. The latest issues of *Cosmo*, *Aces of Hollywood*, and *Rock and Gem* were rolled up in the bottom of the bag. And she'd bought one of those super-chargers for her cell phone, so she wouldn't run out of juice.

"I have to get going. You follow my instructions *to the letter,* just like we practiced. We'll meet back at the hotel after the concert, and make a clean getaway."

"Maybe I can find a way off while folks are boarding the airship. That way I can help you with the heist."

"Uh-uh. We can't risk being seen together. Just get the turbine part to the spot where it needs to be, get down into the gondola, and enjoy the ride." He kissed her on the forehead and then on the lips. It was a good-bye kiss—a real one—the first kiss he had ever given her that felt one hundred percent like it came from the heart. She'd touched her fingers to her lips as she watched him drive away, and nodded to herself.

You're over me already, she thought. *But not over the Candle yet, after all these years.*

And now it was a quarter past five a.m., and she sat in the flatbed cab with Brody, making their way down Hook Road in Bayonne. The truck's headlights flashed on a sign: AEROLUX MAINTENANCE HANGAR ENTRANCE: 1 MI. Brody turned onto a gravel road that ran alongside the security fence. He shut off the engine and turned off his headlights. "Now we wait here till the security service finishes their rounds."

The dirigible hangar was there in the distance. A car drove slowly out from behind it, shining a floodlight across the surrounding field. It looked like a cop car, but Rip had said it would be a private security company doing the rounds. The car disappeared behind the building and several minutes later, a car with the same markings passed by on the highway behind them.

"All righty, ma'am," Brody said. "You're up. You'll wait for my signal, yes?" He showed her a fist, held up where she'd be able to see it through the cab window. She nodded, and climbed out and scrambled up onto the flatbed.

The catapult was a platform with handrails on both sides. The right handrail held the launch pull cord: a red triangle that dangled at its front end. She pulled her cap down tight, swung her messenger bag in front of her, and took hold of the launch pull. Then she gripped both rails. Over Brody's shoulder, the dashboard clock said 5:32. No time for a do-over—it was now or never. She waved so Brody could see her in the mirror. He nodded. The truck started moving.

Tiffani held on tight as the truck lurched onto the gravel road. Brody sped up. She tried to stay upright, and suppressed shrieks every time Brody hit a bump. He followed the road along the fence. The road would curve away and then back as they neared the far end of the property, and they needed to be going at least sixty, Rip had said, so that by the time they swung back toward the fence, she could clear the top. Brody was in charge of making sure she jumped at the right point, at the right speed.

The bag banged against her midsection, heavy-laden with the spare part. Bits of hair escaped her scrunchie and whipped in her face. The security fence whizzed by alongside them, about a hundred feet away. Twenty feet high, with razor wire on top of that. *Aw, shit.*

"Timing will be everything," Rip had said. A burst of anger broke through her resolve. *I'll give you "timing," the next time I am anywhere near your sorry ass.* Mama wouldn't believe this. Little Meg wouldn't even climb a tree.

Here came the jump point. She could see it in the headlights through the bug-spattered windshield of the cab. She closed her eyes. *Jesus Christ on a Harley knockoff—what have I gotten myself into?*

Brody turned hard into the curve, and the truck's wheels skidded, flinging gravel. Her feet slipped across the catapult platform. As he straightened out of the curve he held up his hand. Three fingers—she released the left handhold and clutched the bag to her belly; two—she crouched; one—she tensed—and *go!*

She yanked the triangle and—BANG!—the platform shoved her up into the sky.

Tiffani soared high above the truck as it braked and skidded around the next curve in the road. She drew her legs up and hugged them tight, with the bag between legs and belly. Her diamond coat snapped on with a *crack*. Four inches deep in hard-polished glam, tip-to-tuchus, she tumbled in an arc. Razor wire whispered a kiss on her crystalline-coated ass, and the world and sky spun cattywampus, till the ground came up and slapped her silly.

She bounced and rolled across the field like the world's biggest, shiniest croquet ball, kicking up dirt clods and tufts of grass. Finally she rolled to a stop, and dropped her glam. She leaned back, knees up, gasping for air, dizzy and knocked about.

Oh my God—I'm still alive!

She felt her limbs. Nothing seemed broken. "Well, Rip honey," she said to the early morning air, "you were right about that part, at least."

She stood, brushed off the dirt, and slung her bag onto her back. *Tug, tuck, glam, and roll. Check.* The moon, a quarter past full, hung low in the west. In the east, a dull maroon glow had appeared above the line of trees. Directly before her, not a hundred yards away, stood the hangar, lit up by ugly orange sodium lights. Shit and shebangles; it was HUGE. *What the hell am I doing here?*

Keeping your family alive. Get a move on.

She pulled on her disposable gloves (check), hiked across the field—as light-footed as she could so as not to leave big tracks—waving away the clouds of mosquitos—and climbed up the metal stair along the side of the big hangar (check). It was at least a ten-story climb along the long back side of the hangar. And she could see right through the pressed metal stairs, all the way to the ground. Thank goodness she'd worn her good sneakers. She had to stop more than once to catch her breath.

Up near the top of the stairs, as promised, she found the window, open just wide enough for a small person like her to wiggle through (check). She shoved her bag in, scrambled across the window's threshold, and dropped to the floor with a loud *thunk*.

"If you're back there in the past watching, honey," she said, "you *really* owe me."

She used her phone's flashlight to locate the key card hanging over the supervisor's desk, and slipped the lanyard around her neck. Then she exited the office onto the catwalk. The dirigible sat below.

A sigh escaped her. "Oh, Rip. You didn't tell me . . ."

It was massive. It was glorious. In the rosy, predawn light entering through the hangar's row of high-up windows, the airship gleamed like the world's biggest Mylar balloon. Standing here, just above its tail, she could barely see over it. It was wider than it was tall, too, and all but filled the hangar, over a football field's length down the way. It was a flattened cigar shape with fins on its tail, kind of like a submarine. In big powder-blue letters, below *AeroLux Sky Cruises,* was its name: GOSSAMER SPIRIT.

Somehow, for all its mass, if she went down there to the bottom and gave it a push, she felt sure it'd float right up off the ground.

The stairway to her left went only one direction: down. It had two intermediate stops on its way to the bottom. About fifteen feet below her was a landing with a gate, and a catwalk that ran alongside the cruiser. A second landing came about two-thirds of the way down its back end, maybe forty feet above the floor. That was her destination.

She descended to that second landing, and on impulse, farther down, nearly to floor level. Below the dirigible's belly, between four squat legs, hung a long, sleek gondola. The gondola was enclosed, with big picture windows all around: a space big enough for at least a couple hundred people to sit and walk about comfortably. Through the windows, she could see a second, much smaller gondola, way at the front end of the dirigible, which must be the pilots' gondola.

And then, through the windows in the hangar door, she spotted a pickup, headed this way. Her heart jumped. She raced up the steps.

Everything that came next felt like it was happening to someone else. Back to the cargo bay landing and open the door with the key card (check). Duck inside and close door (check). Find the machine room. Her phone flashlight showed her a door labeled MACHINE ROOM at the end of a short corridor. Before it was the T-shaped intersection Rip had told her about, with the storage unit she was supposed to hide in, a big footlocker-type thing. She spotted a row of orange coveralls like the pair she had on, hanging on hooks above the locker. Across the way in the other nook stood the ladder with the hatch at its feet, which led down through the lower hold and into the passenger gondola.

Now that she had the lay of the land, she headed down to the end of the corridor and tried the machine room door. It was unlocked (check). She slipped inside and left it ajar.

The jet engine–looking machine squatted beside the big spherical tank. It had a big green diamond on it with numbers. Tiffani hurried over. The tank was up on a low platform, with big pipes coming out of it. She spotted the box Rip had told her to look for—it was on the corner of the platform, close to the jet engine machine.

Swap out the part, she thought. But—*damn it!*—the key card lanyard brushed against her arm as she set down her bag. She'd forgotten to throw it onto the stairs.

Too late for that now. She fumbled around in the bag for the part she'd brought. Her hands were shaking. *Calm down, Megan. You big baby.* She drew a breath, pulled out the part she'd brought, and shone her light on the original. The two versions looked identical. She picked up the original—and heard faint rhythmic clanging on the stairs, and muffled voices.

Shit, shit, shit! She shut off her light. They were right outside the hold. She'd taken too long with her little detour earlier.

In the dark, her hands held both boxes. And in that moment, she knew. *Nope. Can't. Ain't gonna happen.* She set the original box down where she'd found it and stuffed Rip's phony one back into her bag.

Then she turned on the faint light from her phone display and made it to the machine room door, scrambled past the ladder as the outer door clanked, and rolled onto the storage locker in the nook. The lights came up as she stood, oh-so-quietly, among the hanging coveralls. She eased one in front of her face. The other coveralls were much bigger than hers. They were also dirty. *Ugh.* They reeked of oil and dirt and body odor. The hold was air-conditioned and she tried not to shiver, pinching her nose with her hand. Two men were talking. Their footsteps grew louder.

They entered the machine room and the machine room door latched shut. She peeked out. No sign of them in the corridor. She slid down off the locker, opened it, and climbed inside.

Shoot the bolt, Rip had said, *before closing it.* That way the lid would fit over the rim of the locker rim, but wouldn't latch, so she could breathe and get out later. She dug out her cardigan and put it on to stave off the chill, and then hunched over her knees in the dark.

It had been too dark in the machine room for Rip to see that she'd defied him. Could he know what she'd done? How could he know? There was no way.

Either way, though, she was dead. She'd known that for the past two weeks, since he'd told her what plan B was.

She'd pretended this whole time—even to herself—that she believed him. That as long as she followed his instructions today, she'd be okay, and so would everybody else. It wasn't true. He wanted to bring the airship down tonight. He wasn't just out to steal the golden trumpet—though he surely wanted that, too. He wanted to draw the eyes of the world to New Liberty

Island, with the Candle in the center. He wanted to utterly destroy him. To lay him so low before so many that he'd never be able to get back up.

And if Rip wanted her to stay aboard so bad, his intent there was clear, too. Tiffani had served her purpose. He was wrapping up loose ends.

Well, she'd foiled *that* part of his plan, at least. She'd saved the airship. But now she had no escape—she had to stay here till it was time to leave, per Rip's instructions; if not, he'd have seen it and would have laid a different trap for her. Whether she liked it or not, she'd have to spend the day a mile aboveground until the show tonight.

She couldn't even warn her family about him, even if she'd had cell phone coverage—which she did not, out here in the boonies inside this little metal box. If she contacted them now, past-Rip, again, would've long since seen it, and set up one of his little traps for them. She couldn't let him see *now* that she was defying him, or that she knew what he was up to. Otherwise, by the time she *could* call her family they'd already be dead.

But one possibility sprang to mind. She'd had a chance to look at his plans that night he'd left them out. She had one single thread of hope—if not of saving herself, at least of saving *them*. At 11:52 a.m. today, he planned to meet the Candle near the Staten Island Ferry terminal in Manhattan. He'd had the time and date marked in one of his temporal maps. For some reason he had to be there precisely at that time. And he'd had two probability paths mapped out from there. One he'd use if he decided it was necessary to tell his old lover what his ace power was, to force his cooperation; the other, if it turned out to be unnecessary.

According to his notes, the discussion would take less than ten minutes. In that time window, he'd have to make a decision. And he'd told her himself that he couldn't see past a decision point till after his temporal blind spot resolved.

So from 11:57 at the earliest and 12:02 at the latest to about an hour after that, a time shadow would be cast over his future-vision. And within that shadow, she had a chance to warn her family without him ever knowing. But to pull it off, she'd have to time it perfectly.

Guess he's right, as always. Timing is everything.

♠

John spotted Rip standing at a corner in Battery Park, just east of the Staten Island Ferry terminal. A sign on a building across the street had a time-and-temperature display, and the time changed to 11:52 a.m. as he walked up.

"Right on time. Good." Rip looked John over. His hands went to his waist. "Wow, you must not have slept a wink. Something eating at you? Your conscience, perhaps?"

"In your dreams, Titus."

John *had* slept, but not nearly enough. He'd had to get up early to deal with the cleanup of the cabin he'd damaged the night before, and then he'd run through his company's various investigative databases to dig up whatever he could about Titus Maguire.

"The name is *Rip*," the other man said.

"And *my* name is John. John Julius Montaño."

"Have it your way, '*John*.'" Rip made air quotes. "Down to business." The walk light at the intersection turned green and he stepped into the street. John followed. "I asked you out here so we could talk in private. What with your security team crawling all over the *Queen* and your surveillance equipment on board . . ." They'd reached the other side; he stepped up onto the curb. "Easier to arrange for a tête-à-tête outside the ring of security." He broke off and looked to the south, across the bay. John looked, too, and saw the dirigible rising into the air across the river in Jersey, beyond the Golden Lady and the wharfs of Jersey City.

"Impressive, isn't it?" Rip said. "They're pulling out all the stops. Tonight should be quite a show."

John made an impatient circling motion with his hand. "Get to the point, Titus. I haven't got all day."

"As you wish. I'm going to steal Armstrong's fancy gold trumpet tonight, and you are going to help me do it."

"I figured as much. And if I refuse, you'll reveal your 'evidence' of my criminal youth. Mustache-twirl, evil laugh, yada yada."

"Pretty much."

"Well, tough break. I'm not about to lift a pinkie to help you. See, I've been doing some checking on *you*. You've amassed quite a fortune over the years. There is no way in hell you did that legally."

Rip smiled widely. "All too true. But proving it . . . there's the rub."

"I don't need to prove it. All I need to do is plant seeds of doubt in the right places. I know a lot of people in law enforcement. If word gets out of *my* youthful indiscretions, what's to stop me from revealing *yours*? Maybe the IRS or the SEC would like to have me as a cooperating witness about where you got your start. Maybe they'll take a closer look at your activities. You're on the board of directors for three Fortune 100 companies, I noticed. I imagine they wouldn't be thrilled if you ended up under investigation."

"I'd sue your ass for defamation. And my pockets are a hell of a lot deeper than yours, Juanma. I guarantee it."

The light changed and a truck honked. Diesel fumes cloaked them both as the truck splashed through a water-filled pothole nearby. The dirty water spattered John but not Rip, who had stepped back just outside its reach.

"Sue me all you want," John said. "Hard to get blood from a stone. Either way, I'm sure the attention would be unwelcome."

"Maybe. But *I* haven't assumed a false identity. I *bought* my way out of Fagan's grasp, fair and square. He has no beef with me anymore. Everything's been on the up-and-up for my adult life, best anyone can tell."

John scoffed. "No way you could've bought Fagan off. He wouldn't let you out of his grip. We knew too much."

"Oh, you'd be surprised." Rip checked his watch and glanced at the bank sign across the way. *He's waiting for something,* John thought. "I've been debating just how much I should tell you. But the timing seems to be working out, and you know? I really want you to know. So I'm going to let you in on my biggest secret." He leaned close. "Turns out, I'm an ace, too."

John folded his arms. "What a remarkable coincidence."

"Funny you should say that. Because it's *all* about coincidence. I call it future-vision. I can manipulate events to get whatever I want. Hence my ace handle. Ripple Effect." He spread his arms. "Cool handle, huh?"

John gave him a bored look. "Is that supposed to worry me? When I can fry you in a heartbeat?"

Rip glanced at his watch. "You know, I never had you pegged as someone with no imagination. Observe. I stand here." He pointed at his feet. "Someone lives. I stand there?" He pointed at the edge of the curb. "Someone dies. That's all it takes."

"Uh . . . I hate to break it to you, Ripples, but we were standing right there just a second ago, and"—John cupped his hand and stage-whispered—*"no one died."*

"True. But timing"—Rip stepped into the gutter at the intersection—"is everything"—just as a cyclist shot out from behind the building. The cyclist shouted and swerved—"Hey!"—and barely missed Rip, veering into the intersection as Rip stepped back onto the curb.

"That's Ripple *Effect,*" he said. "As in, 'cause and.'"

John pushed past him with a gasp—a white pickup had entered the intersection as the cyclist swerved, and caught him on its front bumper. The cyclist flipped up. Rip didn't bother to look behind him. "You g—"

But John had already *twisted* away. Red to block traffic. Green to heal. Purple to dull pain. For the second time, as John returned to the threshold of his own body, trailing fire, he caught that flickering of mirrors around its edge again. He didn't spare a glance this time, only dove back into his body, pulling strands of fire in with him, as fast and hard as he could, batch by batch.

"—et it?" Rip finished.

The cyclist's head hit the hood before John could blast a shield, and he went under the wheels. Tires squealed and blue smoke went up. John ran into the street.

The truck was screeching to a halt. Other vehicle brakes squealed too. More car crashes. Horns blared, burnt rubber and blue smoke filled the air. The cyclist rolled out from underneath the truck in mid-intersection, broken and bloody.

John whirled in the middle of the intersection, throwing up a blazing crimson barrier. Nothing fancy—no time. The red flames stacked up in mounds and pillars, like the world's most garish stalagmites, in a sloppy L-shape, blocking all oncoming lanes. An instant later, a car slammed into the barrier less than a foot from the cyclist's head, destroying it. John shot more red flame into the gap to repair it. Then he skidded to a halt by the young man and went to his knees, pulling the green from his lymphatic system.

The cyclist was white, with a long, neat braid extending from under his helmet. His condition? Not good. Eyes half open, pupils blown. Right side of chest caved in. Blood was spreading across his orange jersey and mingling with the oily water on the asphalt.

John had never used fire on an injury this bad. But if even a single heartbeat remained—a single breath or brain wave—the green should work. It *must*.

Healing tendrils sailed out from John's hands and settled onto the cyclist, while John pulled more green in through the entryway at his crown—and yet more. No response. He kept it up, weaving and casting, till fire jetted from beneath the cyclist's skin and clothes, turning the young man's body into a shamrock-bright torch. In a second or two the cyclist began to twitch. A low moan came. His voice rose in pitch, and he arched his back, keening. John could hear the bones crackling.

"Sorry, kid. Believe me, I get it." He exhaled a swirling cloud of purple fire into his hands and spread it across the cyclist's face. The haze soaked into his eye sockets, his ears, nostrils, and mouth, and the man slumped with a billowy, lavender-tinged sigh.

"Oh, my God. What *is* that?" a woman asked. John looked up to see a middle-aged Black woman, dressed in slacks and heels, by the tailgate.

The truck's left cab door stood open; she must be the driver, and she was staring in alarm at the green inferno lighting up the cyclist's torso.

John sat back on his heels and wiped grit and sweat from his forehead. "It won't hurt him. The green fire heals."

"Does that green flame heal broken vertebrae? Look there." She pointed at the cyclist's helmet, which was cracked and holding his head at an angle that couldn't be good for his neck. "I'm a nurse," she said at John's startled glance. "Got any more of that red stuff we can use to brace him?"

"Good idea! When I give the signal, lift him up." John *twisted* away to harvest more red, then returned. She knelt behind the cyclist's head. "I'm ready."

"All right... *now*!" She lifted the cyclist's head and shoulders as he spun out the red in a saddle shape—but flinched as flame filled the gap beneath her arms. "Don't move! Red doesn't burn."

Once the cyclist was braced, she levered her arms carefully out and stood. She bit her lip, looking down at the cyclist. "He came out of nowhere."

"It wasn't your fault. I saw what happened. He veered right into you."

The cyclist started making warbling noises and waved his hands languidly.

"I'm the Candle," he told the woman. "My friends call me John."

"Yes, I recognized you." She laid a hand on her chest. "Samiyah Morretty."

He smiled at her. "Glad to meet you."

The young man opened his eyes and blinked at them, bleary-eyed. Samiyah knelt.

"Lie still, son." Lavender fireflies sparkled in his eyes and swirled in and out with his breath. John knelt on his other side and gave him a second dose. "Lie still. You've been in an accident."

The cyclist broke into a drunken smile. "Cool..."

The woman gave John a worried look. "Concussion?"

"No, thank you," the cyclist said.

John replied, "I *think* it's just the happy juice I gave him. It should wear off in a bit."

Samiyah got a medkit from her truck, took the cyclist's vitals, and jotted some info on his chest with a black Sharpie. Meanwhile, parts of the red-flame traffic barrier were beginning to collapse and cars were creeping cautiously past through burning red puddles. On the sidewalks and along the pier, a crowd had gathered. People were taking snapshots and selfies and videos. Rip, of course, was nowhere to be seen. John added smaller red-flame lumps as flares. Samiyah pulled the smashed bike out from under her truck's wheels, then pulled her truck into a nearby lot.

By this time a cop had arrived. He left his shop lights flashing. "What happened here? What are all these?" He poked with a toe at a nearby red-flame pillar, which had shrunk considerably and grown gooey.

"A barrier I put up to protect the crash victim from oncoming traffic." John gestured at the driver who had smacked into the barrier, and was now using his phone to record a video through his windshield. The man waved. *At least he doesn't seem pissed off.*

"You're an ace."

"Yes, Officer. I saw the crash and stopped to render aid. This young man was riding his bike into the intersection, there." John pointed. "A pedestrian stepped into the bike lane right at that instant, and the cyclist had to swerve to miss him. He ended up in front of this woman's truck." He gestured at Samiyah, who was walking over to rejoin them. "She had no time to avoid him. Neither of them was at fault. It was the fault of the pedestrian who stepped into the street. He was crossing against the light."

Samiyah was nodding as John had described the impact.

"Officer," she said, "he got thrown right under my wheels before I even had time to react. He'd surely be dead if not for *him*." She touched John's shoulder. "That green fire of yours is a blessing, Candle! He used it to heal the man," she told the cop. "It's a miracle the Candle was here."

John just shook his head, lips drawn taut. *It wouldn't have happened at all if I hadn't been here.*

The cop looked around. "Where is the pedestrian now?"

"I didn't get a good look at him," Samiyah said.

John replied, "He left immediately after the accident."

"Well, first things first." The cop knelt next to the cyclist. "I see blood here. Young man, can you hear me?"

The cyclist looked up at the cop. He patted the cop's faceplate and said in a puff of purple sparks, "Nice panda."

John told the cop, "Those purple sparks have a hallucinogenic and sedative effect. I healed him as best I could with my green fire, but the repair may not have been complete—I've never used it on injuries this severe. He should be checked out right away. Ms. Morretty and I rigged a neck brace for him, but it will melt in the next few minutes."

"EMTs are on their way," the cop replied. "We'll take care of him." John heard the sirens even as he spoke.

John stood. He thought of the trumpet, and his team, who would be transferring it from the *Queen Margaret* to the amphitheater on New Liberty

Island soon. Rip had vanished, Armstrong's gold horn was at risk, and his team had no clue what was going down. He came to his feet and pulled out his wallet.

"Officer, I'm a private investigator with Chubb Insurance." He showed him his PI license. "We're here on a protective detail for an exhibition aboard the *Queen Margaret*. I was heading to the ship on an urgent security matter when this happened and I need to get back there right away. With your permission?" He handed the officer his business card. "You can reach me at this number if you have further questions."

The cop jotted down John's license number and tucked the card into his clipboard. "All right. We'll contact you shortly. We'll want to get a description of the pedestrian."

"Of course. Thank you, Officer." John accepted a thank-you hug from Samiyah, which he appreciated, but which did little to calm him down. "Take care of yourself," he told her. Then he stalked to the cab stand across the street. People moved out of his way—probably because small jets of multicolored flame were shooting out from his head, hands, and arms.

He caught a taxi to Pier 88 and the *Queen Margaret*. As he climbed out and paid the fare, a glint in the sky caught his eye. The tourist airship had risen high into the sky over the harbor and was floating slowly up the river toward the pier.

As John moved toward the water taxi, a gust came up, and a fast food napkin tumbled over to land under the ball of his foot. It had writing on it in black Magic Marker. He stooped and snatched it up.

It had to be Titus. The message was their old shorthand from back in the bad old days, when they'd ditched school to tag buildings and subway walls, pick fights, and do other stupid and/or illegal shit. *Eyeball-specs-down-arrow-sunset* meant *watch for instructions this evening*. Presumably at the concert venue, on New Liberty Island. *Dime-ghost-target* was a threat: *Snitches and deserters get dead*.

John looked around. Longshoremen were removing sound equipment from the *Queen Margaret* with a portable gantry near the ship, about to load it onto a water taxi en route to New Liberty Island. But they were too far away to have caused it, and the only other people nearby were, like, eighty or something, and only had eyes for each other as they strolled toward the river walk a short ways away.

Titus could have paid someone to release the napkin. But at the precise spot it would have had to be when they released it? For the breeze to catch it at just the right angle and just the right instant for it to land under his foot, as he stepped onto the curb? When it could have could have as easily tumbled off into the water or blown off down the way?

No. The delivery method was as important as the content. Titus was nailing his point to John's forehead with a staple gun. *I can get to you anytime I choose. You won't see it coming. There's not a damn thing you can do about it, much less prove it was me.*

◆

The magazines were a total waste; Tiffani couldn't find the concentration to read during her morning-long sojourn, crammed in the locker. She alternated between playing *Candy Crush* and staring at her phone's clock. At precisely 12:03 p.m. and six seconds, the double tone sounded and she sprang up, pushing the lid open. She *really* needed to pee. She climbed out of the locker and scrambled down.

The *Gossamer Spirit* was airborne—she could tell by the gentle rocking under her feet—and the corridor was empty. As promised. She had a strong signal now. It was past the ten-minute window. Rip should be in his blind spot. *Please. Please be future-blind.*

She called her sister, Annabelle. "Belle? It's me, Megan. It's an emergency. Can you talk?"

"Oh, hi, honey! We got the card you sent with that last check. And all those lovely gifts! Thank you so much!"

"You're welcome. Now keep quiet and listen. The family is in extreme danger—"

"Say *what?*"

"I said, the family is in danger! I need you to call *everyone*. Right away. Tell them they have to be out of their houses and on the road, quick as they can. Get to Charleston and pick up Mamaw and Pampaw, too."

"Well—OK, I'm hearing you, but—why? Are you in trouble, honey?"

"*Yes*, I'm in trouble! The man who gave me the money for those gifts—he's not a good man, Belle. And I've defied him, and he's going to do something terrible to the family if you don't all *get out*."

She could hear Belle's breathing on the other end of the phone.

"What did you do, Meg?" Her tone was harsh.

Tiffani dug her manicured nails into her palms. Then she hung her head with a sigh. "I made a deal with the devil, Belle. I purely did."

"And the bill came due."

"Yes." Tiffani broke down. Her body shook with messy sobs. But she gulped them back in. No time for that, either.

"Now, Meg," her sister was saying. "That's a big old shame. But nobody is holding us hostage. He can't hurt us. He's just made you fearful, or your own conscience has. We've all been there. It's never as bad as it seems. You just need to leave this man. Come on home. The good Lord will forgive you, and your heart will heal in time."

Gahhh! "No! This isn't about my soul! It's about your safety!" Tiffani lowered her voice with a nervous look around. "Things are *not* going to be OK," she whispered into the phone. "He's going to *come after you*. After *everybody*!" She swallowed another sob. "He's done it to others and not gotten caught. I've seen it. *You have to get away.* Load everybody in the car and go. Please. NOW."

A long pause. "Well . . . but . . . all right, hang on." Tiffani heard her talking to someone else. "It's Meg. She's having a meltdown. Said her new beau has turned out to be a real douche-noodle, and he's threatening the family."

Thomas came on the phone. "Now, what's all this about?"

Tiffani sighed. "Never mind, I'll explain later," she said, and hung up.

She needed to get out of here, one way or another, and her chance to go below had passed—her hand that gripped the ladder down through the hatch felt a vibration. Someone was ascending.

I get found now, she thought, *and it'll turn out he's known since the beginning. There'll be another trap waiting. It'll all be over by the time the airship lands.*

Her gaze fell on the cargo door at the back of the hold. Her hand went to the lanyard with the key card she'd forgotten to leave behind. The handle on the hatch turned at her feet. *Well, you were ready to die anyway. Now or never!*

"Fuck it," she said. She dropped her bag and bolted for the door.

WARNING—DO NOT OPEN DOOR IN FLIGHT, the sign on it said.

A shout came from behind her. She didn't bother to turn and look. Instead, she swiped the card and shoved at the bar latch. The door flew open and carried her out. An alarm blared and a light flashed. Her back bumped into the bulkhead. She hung on.

Cat's out of the bag now. She looked down. A mile below her dangling feet, she could see the Golden Lady, the shining new Statue of Liberty they had thrown up after the old green one of her childhood had been destroyed in the Rox War. The amphitheater that would host the charity concert was at the lady's feet. All around were the waters of New York Bay.

Tiffani let go.

At least try *to survive. Slow yourself down.* Tiffani grabbed the edges of her cardigan and flattened onto her belly, the way she'd seen flying squirrels do, and her cardigan billowed up, like a parachute, slowing her a bit. But after a few seconds it tore loose from her hands and the wind ripped it off her. The water was getting close.

She'd read once that if you fell from a plane, even to water, it would be like hitting concrete. But diamond could cut through concrete.

Get vertical! Make a knife. Feet first—point toes, arms up!

Crack! She called her ace—and *ka-BOOM!*—she hit the water.

Tiffani came to in a coughing fit with stabbing pain in her ears and water streaming into her nose. She coughed, and spat, and swam for all she was worth toward what she thought must be up: the glittering light she saw amid murk and bubbles still boiling from the impact. Finally, she emerged into air and treaded water, coughing till she could breathe. Fish surfaced around her, belly up. *Oops. Sorry, dears.*

She turned in the water, looking around. New Liberty Island was maybe a quarter mile away. *I can swim that far,* she told herself, though her head pounded so hard she could barely think and her limbs trembled from shock and cold and pain. *Sure. Why stop lying now?*

But she could tell she'd broken bones, despite her diamond armor, and was going into shock. She could barely move her arms. After a minute or two it just seemed like too much trouble. The bay closed over her head.

♥

New Liberty Island was three times as large as the original island had been, the one that had been home to the first Statue of Liberty, before it had been washed away during the Rox War. Its five-thousand-seat amphitheater, an open-air quarter-cutout of a bowl, nestled at the feet of the Golden Lady, with the towers of Manhattan behind her. A twenty-foot retaining wall lay between the stage and the harbor bank. The water taxi had dropped John near the backstage area. From here, he could see straight through the stage and up into the stands—though people were installing panels behind the stage that blocked the view.

He headed up the slope to the amphitheater's rear entrances. Stairs led up to the top of the stands on either side of the skybox entry. Rashida and Arry stood conferring outside the east entry passage beneath the stands. The underground secure complex housed amphitheater operations as well as equipment and machine rooms, and air-conditioned locker rooms and green rooms for performers. John's team had co-opted the equipment room and installed further security. That was where they'd house the horn and case till after the performance.

Rashida saw John and waved. Both had their comms on.

"The horn?" he asked.

"Secure inside," Rashida replied. "Gil and Horace are on duty with it."

"Any surprises?" he asked, and his seconds looked at each other. Arry rumbled, "Not at all, dear," and Rashida asked, "Why? What's wrong?"

He released a breath he hadn't realized he'd been holding. "Just wanted to be sure."

Arry cocked her giant head as if listening to something, and Rashida touched her ear. "On my way," Arry replied. She dropped onto her hands and lumbered down the passage to the freight door. A production company guard there opened the door for her and she moved through, tilting her head to make sure her horns didn't gouge the doorframe. From inside the door, she turned and bent down so they could see her face. "You two could both use some rest. We gotcha covered. See you at six."

"Thanks, Arry," John said. "Call if you need us." He and Rashida started along the sidewalk toward the boat.

"You get into a fight or something?" She gestured at the filth on his clothes and hands.

"Long story," he said. "I'll explain later. Right now I want extra security assigned to the concert. Let's see if we can get a couple of the *Queen Margaret* crew out here."

"Why? What's going on?"

John started to reply but someone screamed near the western shore of the island. A family stood on the bay shore, staring up at the airship floating overhead. Sunlight flashed off a falling object as John shielded his eyes to look—something faceted and bright. A crystal statue? He barely had time to register its shape before it struck the bay in an explosion of water.

They scrambled down across the rocks to the shore. Out on the bay, someone's head rose above the water. "Someone *survived* that?" he gasped.

"I'll get to them. Get ready to shoot me some red!" Rashida particulated and rose in a swarm of tigereye beads, which raced out over the water toward the swimmer.

John reached behind into inferno-world and brought back the strongest reds he could find. He shoved the wine-red energy out through his body, as fast as he could, weaving the strands into a stout cable. Then he readied it, swirling it above and in front of himself. It coiled in the air like a nest of burning snakes. But when Patina reached the spot where they'd seen the person's head, no one was there.

She shaped herself into a giant brass articulated hand-and-arm, and dropped into the water. A moment later, something bobbed up to the surface in a splash: a shiny, black-rubber version of that hand and arm, with a woman's still form curled in Patina's palm, the giant thumb, pinkie, and ring fingers holding on to her with her head pillowed at the base of the forefinger. The forefinger crooked itself at John—*Throw me the rope!*

John cast the red flames out as hard as he could, drawing flame and casting again and again, fighting to keep it aloft, till the blazing cable reached Patina. As the flames coiled around the massive hand, its fingers grew smaller hands, which caught hold of the cable.

"Hold tight!" he yelled, and tossed a section back for the nearby family to grab. "I need your help!" he told them. "It's safe to touch. *Pull!*"

They grabbed hold. Others ran up and joined in, and soon Patina Raft-Hand and her passenger were skimming toward shore. John waded out to meet them. He pulled the raft in and Patina re-particulated to a tigereye bead cloud. John caught the woman as she sank into the water. He carried her to shore and lowered her to the ground.

Dead? No, she still breathed. He rolled her on her side—*twisted* to find green flames—and cast healing tendrils over her. In a moment, she coughed up a lungful of water. Her eyes opened. She looked surprised. "Well, well, the Candle. Aren't you a sight for sore eyes?"

John hardly recognized her through the schmutz and sodden, torn-up clothes. "*Tiffani?*"

"The very same." She propped herself up on her elbows and wiped her forehead with a trembling, dirty arm. Rivulets of muddy water ran down her face. "Holy fucking hell. What a day. I must look a fright."

He helped her sit up. For some odd reason she was wearing orange work coveralls. She had only one sneaker and her hair was a mess. She felt along her legs. "Huh. I was *sure* I'd broken bones."

"I took care of that," he said. "What are *you* doing here? And more to the point, why did you just fall out of the airship?"

She looked at him and then lowered her gaze. "Long story."

He folded his arms. "I've got time."

She looked up again. "In fact, you don't."

By now a small crowd had gathered. Some were taking photos and selfies. Tiffani scooted to the side, maneuvering so he was a barrier between her and the people trying to film her. He stood and turned around. "All right, folks. The incident's over. The lady is fine, and would appreciate some privacy." The lookie-loos began to disperse.

Rashida had rejoined them. Tiffani took her hands and gripped them tightly. "Oh my gosh, you saved my very life. And you too, Candle. Thank you. I'm Tiffani," she said to Rashida. "John and I go back a ways."

Rashida gave her hands a squeeze and released them. "Rashida Thorne. Also known as Patina. So glad you're OK! You sure gave us all a fright. What happened? Do we need to radio the airship?"

"Please, no! The fewer people who know, the better." She turned to John and lowered her voice. "Might I impose on you for the time?"

John glanced at his phone. "Twelve twenty on the nose."

"Good. We're still in the shadow."

"Shadow?" Rashida asked. "What shadow?"

Tiffani gave her an unconvincing smile. She brushed herself off. "Listen, I'd love to stay and chat but I've got prior commitments . . . places to go. You know!" She stood and started to wobble off. The look on her face made the hairs on John's neck bristle.

"No we *don't* know. Tiffani—wait! I have more questions."

"Well, I'm afraid I don't have time right now to give you answers. I really must be off." She was power walking—or trying to—but given that his legs were about half again as long as hers and she was missing a shoe and had just plummeted from more than a mile in the air and nearly drowned, he had no problem catching up.

"Maybe we can help you."

"No, I'm afraid not."

"Tiffani, slow down." John grabbed her arm. "For fuck's sake, what's *wrong*? *Talk* to me."

At his touch, she spun with a snarl. "*Don't touch me!*" He released her. She stared at him, then covered her mouth with both hands and crumpled to the ground, sobbing great big gulping, body-racking sobs.

Rashida had caught up. She and John looked at each other. "This day just keeps getting weirder and weirder."

John knelt next to Tiffani. "I have a feeling we have a common enemy." She gave him a hollow look, holding her sleeve to her nose. "If you'll just take a minute to let us in on what's happened to you, we might be able to help each other."

She wiped her eyes and nose on the sleeve of her coveralls, and gave him a bitter smile. "All right. I can spare a few minutes. But then I really *must* go." She leaned closer. "And we should find someplace more private."

"Follow me."

He led the way inside the museum at the base of the Golden Lady. Not many people were around. At the gift shop John bought her a souvenir T-shirt and sweatshorts to replace her torn coveralls. While she ducked into the bathroom to change, Rashida edged closer. "You want to clue me in?"

"The short version? There's a new ace in town. A powerful one. A total psycho. Something tells me *she*"—John gestured with his chin toward the bathroom, where they could hear the water running—"is connected to him in some way. I don't know how yet."

Ras looked alarmed. "Wait. *What?* A dangerous ace?"

He shushed her. "You know that guy who approached me in the bar?" he asked.

"The blond?" He nodded. Her eyes widened. "You sure know how to pick 'em."

"You don't know the *half* of it."

"What are his powers?"

"He *says* he sees possible futures. He uses it to spy on people and manipulate events in his favor. Calls himself 'Ripple Master' or 'the Rippler' or something."

"Ripple Effect," said Tiffani, emerging from the bathroom. She leaned against the wall nearby. "I've seen what he can do, Candle. He's deadly."

"Agreed," John said. "Today he asked me to meet him in Battery Park and caused a truck to crash into a cyclist before my eyes. He nearly killed the guy. And . . . this will sound delusional, but . . . I was headed back to the ship not ten minutes ago and a napkin landed under my foot." He pulled it out of his pocket and showed it to them. "I mean, he was *nowhere* around. The breeze just blew it there. He couldn't have done it. And yet he did."

Rashida took it. "What are these symbols?"

"Just a sec." John looked at Tiffani. "He recruited you, didn't he? Why? For the goods on me?"

"Yes." Tiffani's color rose. "He wanted me to tell him all the skinny I could on you, from our time on the show." At his frown, she shrugged. "Sorry Candle, but I needed the money.

"Looking back, I think it's because he can't get as good a read on you as he'd like. There's a blurring effect or something. He says your 'fates are entwined.'" She gnawed at her lip. "He's been threatening my family to make me help him. This morning he tried to force me to sabotage the airship. But I didn't do it. And when he finds out, my family will be in danger. Which is why I have to go save them, *now*, before he can kill them all."

"Whoa, whoa—slow down," John said. "The people on the airship are in danger?"

"Not anymore. I didn't switch out the part like Rip told me to."

"'The part'?" Rashida repeated. She and John exchanged a look.

"For the 'thrust turbine.'" Tiffani made air quotes. "Don't ask me, but it has to do with the helium they use to make the airship float. He wanted me to swap out the real part for one that I guess he had messed with or something. But I—I couldn't go through with it. And now he's going to punish me. My family, I mean. He'll kill them first and then he'll hunt me down and kill me. That's what he does." Her lips quivered again, but her expression remained impassive.

"But I mean—what's his aim?" Rashida asked. "Why is he doing this?"

"He wants Satchmo's horn," John replied.

Rashida frowned. "I don't get it. Why go to all this trouble? Why drag John into it? If he can manipulate events as he says he can, why not just arrange it so there's a crash or flat tire while the horn is in transit, and just walk away with the goods while one guard is changing the tire and the other one's tying his shoe, or something? That's how *I'd* do it."

Rashida was looking at Tiffani as she spoke. Tiffani looked at John. "I don't think I'm the best one to answer that," she replied.

He sighed. "Because this guy has it in for me. Because he knows me from our childhood. Because"—deep breath—"John Montaño is not the name I was born with. It's an alias. Like in witness protection. Only I did it on my own. He told you, didn't he?" he asked Tiffani. She nodded. John turned back to Rashida. Her eyes had widened. "There's no time for all the details now," he said. "But there was a good reason."

"Oh, *hell* no. You're not getting off that easy. You're going to tell me *exactly* what's going on, John. Or whoever you are."

He flinched. "Ras . . . you *know* me. This was a long time ago. Can't it wait?" But the stern lines in her face didn't soften. "All right. Fine. This guy, Titus—"

"He calls himself Rip now," Tiffani said.

"Right. Rip. He was someone I knew back when I was a kid. He was my best friend. My first love." He felt his face heat up as he said it. "The virus hit when I was seventeen, and I entered a coma for three months before my card finished turning. And Titus, Rip—whatever—he was in the room when I came to." He hesitated. "Unfortunately, I came out on fire and burned the ever-loving shit out of him. I gave him burns over twenty percent of his body."

Rashida gasped. "That . . . that's messed up."

"Honestly, Ras, I didn't even know about his injuries until last night. I woke up with the room on fire, and I fled.

"But I *did* ditch him. He's right about that. And my mom, too—though she'd given up on me long before my card turned." He paused. "I was a real asshole when I was a teen. A thief and a forger. A dropout. I spent as much of my teens in juvie as I did out of it. And it wasn't because we were poor or lived in a bad neighborhood. It wasn't bad influences. I just was pissed off after my dad drew a black queen, and I decided, *Fuck it.* I made a bunch of shitty choices. And this guy Fagan, he's a crime lord, he made us all kinds of promises that we were suckers enough to believe." John shook his head at his younger self. "He had his claws in us good and deep by the time my card turned. That was why I ran.

"So. Since everyone thought I'd self-immolated, I stole a bunch of money from one of Fagan's dealers and got out of town. I bought a shiny new identity in Colorado. Next thing I know I'm trying out for *American Hero*, I'm on the show, and my future is set. No more crimes since, Ras. I promise."

The horrified look Rashida wore shamed him. But she said only, "Is he going to try to kill you and make it look like an accident?"

"No, he wants to humiliate him," Tiffani said. "He wants to reveal John's past and make him out to be a criminal. He wants him alive, so he can make him suffer."

"Well, I *am* a criminal," John said, but Tiffani shook her head. "You don't get it. He will steal the trumpet and frame you for it. And he'll probably kill off all the people you care about while you're in prison. Or force you to do terrible things for him . . ." She lowered her gaze. It sure sounded like she was speaking from personal experience.

Rashida put her hands on her hips and looked from Tiffani to John. "Well then, we'd better stop him."

The clock above the cashier read twelve thirty-five. Tiffani pointed. "We don't have much time. His power has limits. We're in what he calls a causality shadow right now. He can't see his *own* future—it sets up a feedback loop. And he can't see what happens after he makes a decision that changes his future. Not for a while, at least. In both cases he gets thrown out on his ass and has to wait for a reset before he can go back in and future-snoop. But things'll reset soon. We need to leave."

"He gets thrown *out?*" Rashida repeated. "You mean he actually leaves the room with his power?"

"Yep! He walks right into mirrors. Anything shiny. They're doorways for him. You can *kind of* see what he sees, for a second, when he comes and goes. It's like a glass pinwheel, only bigger and stranger."

John started, remembering his dream last night, and the effect he'd been seeing at his own dimensional threshold.

Rashida was focused on something else. "So he needs a shiny surface big enough to get through to use his power?"

Tiffani nodded. "He can see out through mirrored surfaces, while he's up there poking around in people's business. But where there's nothing shiny, he can't see you. And he has to come *out* the same mirror he goes *in*. He has some other limits too. It's his 'temporal physics.'" She made sarcastic air quotes.

"Oh, really?" John said. *Hmmmm . . .*

"Mmm-hmm. We're in a causality shadow right now. That's why I keep looking at the time. Up till he met up with you, Candle, he wasn't sure he was going to tell you about his ace. He hoped not to. Almost no one knows, and I think he'll kill anyone who finds out, if he can't control them. That's why *you'll* be in danger, yourself," she told Rashida, "once he finds out you know. And he *will* find out." She turned back to John. "Candle, when he revealed his ability to you, I figure lots of people were affected. Yes?"

John nodded. "Absolutely. Not only the cyclist who got hit, and the driver, but everyone whose commute was delayed. And there was the motorcycle cop, and the EMTs and all the people they would have come in contact with. Plus the people in the hospital where the cyclist was taken . . ."

"Good! All those are the 'ripple effects' that went out from his choice." Tiffani made spiraling motions with her hands. "The more of those the better. He's created a humdinger of a blind spot."

"How long do we have," Rashida asked, "before he comes out from behind this 'causality shadow' of his?"

"They usually last an hour or so." They all glanced at the clock this time. Twelve forty-five. John's skin crawled. A few minutes before 12:03 p.m., Rip had shown John his ace. They had a maximum of fifteen minutes. It could be less; Tiffani didn't sound all that sure about the timing. And the gift shop was filled with shiny surfaces.

Tiffani said, "I'm thinking . . . we may have a way to get away from his spying eyes, even after the blind spot ends. He said once he can only see futures for places he's physically near—within walking distance. He has this fancy smartwatch that helps him find future versions of people by tracing their cell signals, but he has to be close to them for it to work.

"He's already surveilled the shit out of New Liberty Island, because he knew the concert would be here tonight. So this is the first place he'll look for us. But now that he's hit the reset on the timeline . . . I've never tested this, but I don't see how, if we're far enough away before the shadow lifts and he doesn't know *where* we're going to be, he could surveil us."

John massaged his temples. "This is making my head hurt."

"How do we even know that's true?" Ras asked Tiffani. "He could have been lying to you."

"We don't. But here's the other thing. There's no escaping Rip forever,

Patina. Even if we could get away—and maybe we can; I'm not saying we can't hide for a good while. Believe me, I'd much rather run than fight. But I don't think we'll ever get a better chance at defeating him than now. Each of us could run to different corners of the Earth and huddle alone like rats in a sewer drain, but it'd only be temporary. He's a billionaire. Who can *see into the future*."

"Uh, he's a *billionaire?*" Rashida repeated, and John felt the blood drain from his own face. Tiffani nodded, grim.

"A multibillionaire. He could buy a country and barely make a dent in his net worth. Hell, he's only not a *trillionaire* because he doesn't need to bother. And you know what? Even if we lived a lifetime hidden away from him, he'd still be right up here." She tapped her own forehead. "No, thank you! I have had more than enough of Titus 'Ripple Effect' Maguire. I want him out of my head, and out of my life. And yours, too, Candle." She took John's hands, and looked right into his eyes. "You listen to me. He's obsessed with you. He'll never stop hunting you. And I've seen him at work. He *can't* be stopped. No prison can hold him. We have to *end him*. There is no other way."

John jerked his hands free, staring in alarm. Rashida cleared her throat. "John, a word with you?" She glanced at Tiffani. "Privately?"

Tiffani shrugged. "Whatever. But I'm getting off this island in the next five minutes. With or without you." She went back into the bathroom and shut the door.

Rashida pulled him close. "I don't think we should be trying to do this ourselves, John. If this guy is all that dangerous, shouldn't we call Chubb? Or . . . the police or, or SCARE, or the Committee? *Someone?*"

"And what? Try to convince someone in middle management in one or more major bureaucracies that we're being targeted by a billionaire time-traveler who can murder people using the beat of a butterfly's wings? With no proof except some scribbles on a napkin?"

"Stranger things have happened."

"Ras, the only two people who have actually *seen* what he can do are me and Tiffani. A 'gay-ish' guy living under a fake identity with a criminal youth, and a B-list actress-slash-model famous for being self-serving and untrustworthy."

"*Hey!*" Tiffani's head popped out of the restroom door. "Bubbles again? It's always poor Bub-Bub-Bubbles. What about poor *me?*" The door slammed.

John told Rashida, "By the time SCARE even opens a file, Tiffani and I will be dead of 'natural causes.' Maybe they'll *eventually* catch him, but I don't want to end up as an entry in somebody's murder book. No. Tiffani is right. Time is his advantage. Surprise is ours. We have this one shot to stop him. But"—he forced the words out—"I think you should bow out of this, Ras. It isn't your fight, and you probably aren't a target yet."

"What? Oh, *hell* no! How could you even *think* that? It's my job to protect that damn horn. And you're not just my boss, John. You're my friend. Even if you're a fucking jerk for lying to me, you asshole."

John winced. "You're right. I'm trash. I'm sorry."

"We'll hash that out later. But I'm not going to stand by while you get framed. Plus, you know? *Fuck* this 'Ripple Effect' guy. He's a hazard to public safety. He needs to be stopped."

He gave her a grateful look. "Thanks, Ras."

Tiffani came back out. "All righty, then. Now we need to find a place he won't think to look for us."

Rashida said, "You could have, you know, at least *pretended* not to listen."

"Sorry. Guess I'm too riled up about *getting the hell out of here.*" Tiffani tilted her head toward the clock above the cashier. It said 12:53. "We need to go *now.*"

Rashida fiddled with her phone and swiped through some screens. "All right. Follow me." She led the way out of the gift shop to the wharf, where a tour boat was disembarking visitors. "That boat is headed to Manhattan. If we run, we can catch it."

♣

With sunset came the crowds, and after sunset, a show—if not quite the one the audience was expecting. John watched from the amphitheater's west side, just offstage, where he could see the performers and the crowd, as well as all the approaches from the amphitheater's west. Arry covered the approaches and stage from the east.

It was a clear night. Spotlights pirouetted across the dark sky. Twilight had not cooled the air nor made it less muggy, though the promoters had installed giant electric fans that bracketed the stands and piped the air up atop them with big ducts that blew the hot air around. The secured building below the stands had an exit in a pit that separated the stage from the audience. There they'd installed a cooling unit with a duct that came up alongside the stage and blew chilled air onto the performers from the catwalk. John, standing at the top of the stairs from the pit, was glad to be an unintended beneficiary: wearing the requisite suit jacket was sheer misery in this weather, and he was dripping sweat.

Thousands had crowded into the stands over the past forty-five minutes and now sat shoulder to shoulder, fanning themselves. Their conversations added up to a din you could hear even over the fans. City and state officials sat in air-conditioned comfort in the skybox at the back, behind glass. The airship had returned from the Empire State Building around sunset, and had sunk like a giant soap bubble from high overhead to a few hundred feet above the skybox. John looked up. New York City's skyline was reflected on the dirigible's near side.

Halfway up the stands, two lighting towers held spotlights that swept the crowds. The stage was cast in shadow. John wore his own earpiece, mic, and radio, as well as a walkie-talkie the stage manager had provided him so she could cue him when it was time to bring out the horn.

They hadn't dared brief Arry about Rip's plans, nor Gil or Horace, nor the *Queen Margaret* security staff, nor the park rangers, nor the police—that causality shadow had long since passed, and they couldn't risk it. John paced in the darkness offstage till the stage manager's voice came through on his radio handset, amid a wash of static.

His walkie-talked crackled. "Angel now at standby position." ("Angel" was the code name they'd agreed on for the trumpet.) John acknowledged, and said into his security mic, "Bring Angel on up, Patina. Stand by, Beef. Leads acknowledge."

"Roger that," Arry said. "Approaches all clear from the east."

"Roger," Rashida said. "Angel and saints now leaving secured area."

The seconds ticked by. John's neck hairs were bristling again: Rip *had* to be watching, both at this moment *and* through some window from the past.

A clanking came from below. Rashida said, "Angel in the pit."

The amphitheater's lights shut off and a hush fell across the crowd. Onstage, a pool of light appeared, and within its triple circle stood Peregrine. Her gown of red sequins and stiletto heels of crystal tossed sparkles across the faces of the crowd as she turned to acknowledge their applause. She was well into her sixties now, and maturity had inflected her lifelong charisma with a commanding calm. Her hair, chestnut brown with a white streak at the temple, brushed her shoulders.

Peregrine unfurled her feathered wings with a snap and soared into the air. People gasped as she swooped over their heads, and a flurry of camera flashes chased her into the darkening sky. There she joined the searchlights' pirouettes, and then returned and alighted, silk-soft, in the pool of light onstage. "Hello, New York City!" she said into her hand mic. The crowd sprang to their feet with applause, shouts, and whistles.

By the time Peregrine had finished her grand entrance, the security team had reached the top of the stairs and were approaching. John couldn't read Rashida's face, but her posture was as tense as violin wire. "Angel arriving at offstage left," he reported into his handset. Rashida gave him a querying look. *Any sign of trouble?* He shook his head. *Nothing yet.*

"All right," he said. "Patina, you're the running back. Horace, Gil, you're the linemen. I want you all to stay alert. You make damn sure to cover her."

"Roger that."

"Roger."

"And I want you to draw your weapons," John told the two men. "Got it?"

Ras grimaced at him. *Really?* He scowled back. *Yes, really.*

Gil looked surprised. "That violates protocol, boss."

"Not when I've got probable cause to worry about a breach," Candle replied. Horace and Gil exchanged worried looks. Then Horace elbowed his junior partner. "Best not argue. The Candle has a hunch." He drew his gun and removed the safety. "At least out here there's less of a chance you'll incinerate the bedding, boss."

"Haha, very funny. As a matter of fact, I *do* have a hunch. And it's a bad one. I'd just as soon not lose anybody tonight. That goes for you, too, Beef."

The Beef was leaning on her mace at the far side of the pit, at offstage right, in partial shadow. She rumbled, "Oh, you know I'm always up for a bit of a melee, dear. But I'll be mindful."

John acknowledged Arry's wave and then headed around the corner with the other three. They'd decided to move the horn into place by going around the outside, away from the stage crew, and taking it in through the rear entrance. This was in essence an invitation to Rip; John wanted to make it easy for him to make his move before the performance, under conditions that put the fewest people at risk. They'd have a crunch getting the trumpet back inside and into Winston's hands on the stage director's timetable, but taking the interior route inside the enclosure would have put dozens of people at all manner of risk: the place was crisscrossed and hung with lighting and weights and equipment; collapsing stage sets and panels; trapdoors; wiring, ductwork, and cables. The area surrounding the back end of the amphitheater was restricted access, and the grounds were clear of anything Rip could use to cause "accidental" harm.

They'd also have much more room to maneuver in a fight. Down the hill to the south, behind the stage, were a concrete pad, a strip of grass, and a seawall with a gravel shoreline. There was no way Rip could pen them in here. Other than his future-vision, Rip was a nat. With no need to worry about hostages, they should be able to defend against most physical attacks.

As Peregrine alighted, the stage manager's voice came over John's handset. "Security, ready for Angel backstage in sixty; acknowledge."

"Roger that," John said into his handset. He gave the trumpet bearers the hand signal and they set out along the walkway outside the amphitheater stage: Gil and Horace in the lead with guns drawn, pointed at the ground, fingers off their triggers, and Rashida carrying the horn. John faced southwest, away from the stage, toward the shadowed stretch of land and the waters beyond. The trumpet escort trio rounded the curve toward the backstage door.

"Tonight," Peregrine said, "we celebrate the era of jazz, and the life of a legend . . ."

A roar of applause rose and as it swelled to a deafening roar, John heard several pops in succession. He started running even before it registered that the sounds were gunshots, and reached the backstage door in time to see a scene playing out in silhouette against the faint light reflecting off the Golden Lady. Rip stood behind the backstage wall, on the concrete pad above the retaining wall. He was taking aim at Rashida as Gil crumpled. Horace was already down.

"No!" John yelled. Rip fired.

But Patina was already changing—a cloud of metal shards burst outward as the bullets reached her. Bullets ricocheted off the stage wall at her back and clattered onto the pavement. Some of Patina's shards struck Rip and he threw an arm up belatedly to protect his face. The golden trumpet in its polishing cloth landed in the pile of her shoes and clothes.

"Ah—so we're on *that* track," Rip said, and then screamed as the shards that had struck his face, arms, and torso tore free and followed the rest of the Patina-shards into the dark sky above the theater.

Peregrine continued, "One of our greatest musical stars of the past century was the dean of jazz, wild card ace Louis Armstrong, also known as Satchmo, or Pops. Born near the turn of the twentieth century, his career spanned over five decades . . ."

John heard Arry's voice in his ear. "What's going on, boss? Everyone OK?"

"Beef, *keep station!*" John yelled, his voice hoarse. If she responded to the scene now, she was dead. Rip would have planned for it. John *twisted* to inferno-world to gather green and purple for his team, and a crackling blast of black for Rip, which he would stuff down that fucker's throat. The spinning reflections at the threshold caught his attention again, and he paused for the barest second to focus on the other world beyond the gap.

This time he saw a shadow moving in front of the mirrored scenes: a two-dimensional figure of shades of black, white, and gray, in the size and shape of a man. A cardboard cutout, in effect, of Rip. The scene beyond that figure in the mirrors was from up on the stands at amphitheater's top, looking down at the stage where Peregrine had stood seconds ago. To the right in that future-image was Arry, who stood guard with her mace, facing northwest. At the left side of the stage, he saw himself keeping watch, facing southeast. And Rashida was there with the security detail, nearing the backstage entrance.

So that's *how it works.*

He *twisted* back into his own body—where the flames tore free from his control and ripped through him, searing nerve endings, blood vessels, skin, and flesh, outside the channels he'd trained to contain them. John buckled in agony. The flames, intermingled, shot out from him every which way.

He forced himself to his hands and knees, and saw Rip's entry, lit by his own green-and-black-bright incandescence. It was just as Tiffani had described: a man-shaped *thing*—all sheets and edges of mirrored glass, rippling around a center of gravity, turning from a hall of horrors into a man. Ripple Effect stood on something shiny. From the way his feet rumpled it, Mylar. Blood streamed from Rip's face and arms. He dodged a wild bolt of John's black flame, and another—and dove into a rampant green blast that issued from John's mouth. The green engulfed him and the gashes on his face, chest, and arms began to heal as he tumbled.

At the instant Rip became flesh again, John regained control of his flames. Rip dashed toward his Mylar sheet—John *twisted* back to pull more green in for himself and the guards. But once more, the tourmaline-green fire spewed out as if he were a sieve, from every pore and orifice. And again, he saw, Rip had turned into a spinning set of mirrored future-vision blades.

Our fates are entwined, eh? he thought. *When he transforms near me, my flames go berserk. And when I go to inferno-world, his future-vision goes haywire.*

Rip had re-embodied yet again. He wiped blood from his mouth with a grin at him. John launched himself at Rip—summoned black en route—and stumbled through air as the other man vanished into the Mylar at his feet. John rolled onto the pavement; his back arched, racked with seizures as the black energy slipped from his control and attacked his nervous system.

John somehow fought his way back into inferno-world and dragged more green to himself, enough sheer volume to block the black energy waves' destructive force. Then he returned to the world and—keeping the entryway open at his crown—blazing green, with no control whatsoever—he crawled back to his fallen men. Blazing green, he ran his hands over them, trying with the misfiring flames to give them enough to heal. *Not enough!* So he used his whole body. He lay across Horace, who was nearer. Next Gil. The flames slowly poured into each. But they both had bullet holes in their heads and were unresponsive.

Rip walked over and picked up the trumpet from Rashida's clothes pile, pulled out his own polishing cloth, and wiped the blood off the horn. He slid it into a messenger bag he wore. Then he walked over and looked down at John, still lying between Horace's and Gil's bodies, spewing green flames.

"Give it up, Juanma," he said. "They were dead before you got here."

In the background, Peregrine was saying, ". . . has come to stand for freedom. Equality. Justice. Courage and resilience."

John's handset had fallen off his belt and lay on the sidewalk nearby. The stage manager's voice was saying, "Repeat, cue Angel onstage. Security lead, acknowledge! Where *are* you guys?"

John released the last of his green flames, spent, and rocked onto his heels as Rip knelt near him. John felt a pressure in his palm and looked down. Rip had pressed the gun into it. He also saw the sticky fluid all over his white shirt and his hands—his men's blood, black in the ebbing green pools of flame. He shook his head to clear it.

I'm supposed to do something. I'm waiting for a cue. But half his team was dead on the ground, and he couldn't think.

"Oh, don't torment yourself. I made sure you couldn't save them." Rip pointed a finger at John's forehead and mimicked pulling a trigger. "One shot to the head for each. And I researched their body armor, of course, and chose the weapon and ammo needed to penetrate it. Plugged them each a couple times in the chest, too. Hollow-point bullets. Not much left of the crucial organs but jelly. You really should have had them in stronger armor, Juanma. Of course . . ." He shrugged. "In that case I would have used a full-auto rifle and larger-gauge bullets. I admit that would have been more of a hassle, though."

Rage carried John to his feet. He was still clutching the handgun; he examined it. A semi-automatic; a Glock of some kind. He glanced from it to Rip, who chuckled. "By all means." Rip spread his arms. "Let's see you try."

Rashida's voice came to his ear. "John, I've briefed Arry and I'm in position. We're a go for Phase Two on your signal."

John ignored her. He checked the safety; it was still off. He took aim at Rip through the sight. He'd never shot anyone before, but he'd trained on guns and was a decent shot. It was a requirement for his investigator's license, with annual recertification. He'd never needed to carry one, though, much less fire it.

More to the point, John had never killed. Fagan had been grooming them for it. But John had gotten out before he'd crossed that line. He still had the nightmares.

He also remembered Tiffani's words from earlier: *You'll have to end him.* The thought made him sick. He ejected the gun's magazine and the chambered bullet, then locked the slide back and tossed it all to the ground.

He caught the flicker of disappointment in Rip's gaze. Interesting. Suicide-by-ex-lover? Maybe the guy was getting tired of being an evil fuckhat.

"Let's see you step away from that Mylar."

Rip smiled. "I'm not an idiot."

"That's debatable." John gestured at the bodies on the pavement behind him. "Why, Titus? What's the point of killing my men? They were no threat to you."

"I had my reasons."

"I repeat," came Rashida's voice in his ear, "we're a go for Phase Two, over here. What the hell are you waiting for, John?"

"Who's dead?" Arry demanded. "What's going on? Is that our cue?"

"Hold fast, Beef," Rashida said.

"Oh?" John said to Rip. "Enlighten me."

"By all means. First of all"—Rip pointed at him—"*you* don't decide who lives and who dies, Juanma." He jerked a thumb at his own chest. "*I* do."

"And tonight we have a *very* special treat for you," Peregrine was saying. "To play Satchmo's own golden trumpet, we have another music legend with us. In fact, we have four!"

He's every bit as dangerous as Tiffani said. "And it gives you a big, juicy boner, doesn't it," he asked, "to play God with people's lives? I bet you even take pictures and jerk off to them later. You always had a bit of trouble getting it up, as I recall. Is this what it takes for you, now?"

"Awww, you used to *like* my boner. Oh!" Rip snapped his fingers. "That reminds me. The cyclist you saved earlier? Dead. Fluke accident at the hospital. Someone gave him a transfusion of the wrong drug. Medication labeling error. A few other patients died too, alas. And after all the trouble you went to."

John's hands spasmed into fists and yellow fire, unbidden, engulfed them. Rip said, "Careful there," gesturing with his chin at John's hands. "You wouldn't want someone to get hurt."

John shoved the yellow back and the flames guttered out.

"Still waiting for our cue, Candle," Rashida said in his ear. He shook his head hard.

Rip glanced at his watch. "And the cop? Died, too. A few minutes ago. A buddy called in sick and he took a second shift for him. Got called in on an armed robbery and . . . *bang*! Rotten luck."

Up on stage, Peregrine was saying, ". . . personal heroes. He made his first professional recording at age eleven. He had his first platinum hit at seventeen. He has won a record-breaking *ten Grammys*, and is the first Black musician—and the *only* jazz musician, *ever*—to win the Pulitzer Prize for music. Ladies and gentleman, please welcome Winston Marcus, performing with his Grammy-winning siblings, Ellie, Jake, and Lou Marcus, of Tungsten Paradox!"

A rising wave of applause.

"As for the driver—" Rip held up a hand at John's start. "Relax. *Her* I've kept alive. For the moment. See? I could tell you liked her."

John flexed his hands and forced himself to look away, out at the skyline to the east. *Calm down. Stick to the plan.* "You know, that's the one thing I didn't expect," he told Rip. "I didn't expect you to become a *death merchant*."

"Death merchant" was the phrase they'd agreed on to trigger Phase Two.

"Confirming, Patina go for Phase Two," Rashida said in his ear in a clipped tone. "One minute out. Hang tight."

"Confirming, the Beef standing by," Arry said. "Ready on your order, Candle."

"I was a terrible influence on you, wasn't I?" John told Rip. "I was the one who got you tangled up with Fagan. I figured once I was out of your life, you'd get out, too. The *last* thing I expected was that'd you'd become a bigger dickwad than he ever was."

Rip started laughing. "Oh, dear. Oh no. That's rich."

"What's so funny?"

Rip straightened and wiped away tears. "Someday I'll have to tell you."

"Whatever." John stepped toward Rip at an angle. Rip pivoted, watching him warily. "What I don't get is all this." John swept a hand back toward his dead team members. "It all seems so crude. Unworthy of your talent."

John took another step and caught a glimpse of movement beneath the Golden Lady. He summoned yellow fire and held it back in infernoworld, at a safe distance. Rip, frowning, converted to spinning mirrors anyway.

"Whoa—paranoid, much? Settle down there, cowboy." John turned his hands over for Rip to examine and gave him a peek inside his suit cuffs. "See? Nothing up my sleeves. We're just having a conversation."

Rip returned to human form and opened his mouth to reply—and John snapped a yellow fireball right at his mouth. *Eat heat, fucker!*

But it passed through Rip with a hiss as he transformed back to mirror-fans—in the nick of time—and John shoved the rest of the stream back into the other world, barely in time to avoid getting cooked himself. He wiped at the sweat on his lip and forehead with his sleeve.

But he'd seen fear in Rip's eyes. *You haven't forgotten the yellow, have you?*

"You're only hurting yourself," Rip replied, "trying to fight me. I'm keeping count. Each act of defiance will result in someone else you care about dying. Starting with that woman, I think: the driver of the pickup. And maybe your mother after that. Or your little sister; how does that sound?

"Or how about your lieutenant instead, Patina? Or that ridiculous minotaur with the granny glasses. The Beef, is it? Ariadne. Yes, Ariadne Cerigo."

John gritted his teeth. *Hurry up, guys.* A dark shape wafted down toward them from the direction of the Golden Lady. *Only another few seconds . . .*

John said, "Nah, that's not your game. You kill whoever you feel like killing, whenever you feel like it, and use their deaths to manipulate the living. Until you get bored of toying with them, of course, at which point you kill them too." John shrugged. "So whatever. Do what you're going to do. That's on you.

"But back to my earlier point. *Guns?* Really? This from a guy who can supposedly kill with a gust of wind and a gum wrapper? Not too impressive an ace, if you can't finish the job without resorting to a hail of bullets."

"It's true," Rip replied; "I take pride in my ripple effects. I think of myself more as a death *artist* than a death *merchant*. But you know, Juanma, it's an *awful* lot of effort. Money, time, research . . . sometimes it's easier to just"—he made a gun of his thumb and forefinger, pointed at John, and jerked his hand up—"cap them. Besides, in this case, it's all part of my plan. Which brings me to the second reason I took out your guards."

"Which is . . . ?"

"To frame you," he said, pulling something out of his pocket.

While he spoke, Tiffani landed on the concrete pad behind them and released the handle of the black-camo hang glider she'd ridden down on.

"Hello, Rip, darlin'," she said.

He spun. "*Tiffani?* What the—how did—"

"I have hidden depths." She leaned forward and repeated herself, jabbing him in the chest with each word. "Hidden. Depths."

He started to reply but jerked his head to stare at John as a mellow, clear tone rose from the stage. It was a trumpet, playing the opening notes of Louis Armstrong's hit single, "Hello, Dolly," with Ellie's contralto voice accompanying it.

Rip opened his pack. The golden trumpet inside dematerialized and rose in a cloud of shards, which whipped around him in a miniature tornado. He screamed and beat at them.

John ran and rammed him in the gut. Rip stumbled off the Mylar sheet and John snatched it up, and shoved it into his pocket. "Beef," John said, "outside south quadrant, backstage door. *NOW!*"

The hang glider frame and nylon had risen up in a cloud of particles when the shrapnel tornado had struck Rip. Now they and the shrapnel reunited and coalesced into Rashida's shape as the ground began to tremble. Arry galloped up in a thunder of hooves. *Boom! Boom! Boom!* Two tons of angry Beef bore down.

Arry skidded to a halt behind Rashida, pelting them all with rocks. She took in the sight of her team members' bodies, the spilled blood, the backspatter against the stage wall. Her face contorted with anger; her arm muscles bunched and she gripped her mace handle so hard John feared it might crack. She looked at John, who tilted his head toward Rip. Arry's bellow shook the air. Her horns began swaying. She bellowed again, and stomped her right hoof rhythmically, cracking the cement.

"YOU KILLED OUR BOYS!" she thundered.

"Stand down!" John ordered. *Sorry, love. This one is mine.*

"You pulled a switch," Rip said to Rashida. "How? There wasn't time."

"Sure there was." Between *sure* and *was* she had sloughed off enough Patina essence to shape a trumpet in her hands. "The real one I dropped"—she let it fall—"and caught"—she obscured it in a swirl of dust near her feet—"and carried away with me while"—she spawned a second trumpet, which she held up—"leaving the fake for you to find. In the dark, it was easy."

In the light of John's fireballs, which he was lobbing every so often to keep the area lit, he saw Tiffani standing back a bit. She had been looking from Rashida and John to Rip to the bodies on the sidewalk. Now it was as if something in her snapped. She stalked over and whacked Rip in the face with a diamond-crusted hand, hard enough that John could hear the *crack!*

♠

Rip put a hand to his cheek. "Ow! What the hell—?"

She laughed. "I have been wanting to give you a smack like that since day one."

He balled his fists. "You lying little *shit*. How *dare* you?"

"How dare *I*? Oh, honey. I haven't even started." Her anger was incandescent. Glorious, like a fury-filled Pomeranian facing down a nervous pit bull. "You know what my mama would say about you, Mr. Titus 'call-me-Rip' Maguire? That you wasn't worth pickin' up in the road for *stew*, if you was hit by a *truck*. You sorry *son of a bitch!*"

She slapped him across the other cheek. Rip put a finger in his mouth and drew it out bloody.

"You should've just followed my directions, Megan. Now there'll be hell to pay." He reached out to grab her by the arm, but Tiffani slapped his hand away, hard enough to break bone. "Don't fucking *touch* me, you animal." She jabbed a thumb over her shoulder toward the dirigible. From where they stood, the stage structure obscured all but the upper edge of the giant balloon. "You put my family at risk, to try to make me kill all those airship passengers. And you intended for me to go down right along with them."

He sighed and shook his head. "Not true. If you'd just done what I'd asked, woman, you would have been fine."

"Don't 'woman' me—I ain't your damn woman. Besides, no way I would have been fine! You would have had me stay on that airship with a bad part on it."

He had something in his hand that he was fiddling with—that object he'd pulled out of his pocket a moment before. John started in alarm and lunged, but Rip stepped backward, down the slope, and tossed the device into the air. John caught it. It was a remote the size of a pack of gum. He tucked it in his pocket.

Rip was saying to Tiffani, "I'd already switched the parts out during the recall, actually. The replacement part I gave you was just a little test. I might have found a way to save you, if you'd shown any loyalty. How *did* you get off the airship, anyway?"

"You 'might have' saved me? Fuck you. You and your damn shitty loyalty tests." Then her eyes grew wide. "Wait. You mean—"

"Correct! It didn't make any difference to the outcome. I just wanted to see if you'd actually do it for me. I couldn't tell in the dark whether you swapped them out. And apparently you did not . . . ?"

She only glared at him. He sighed. "I never could get a good read. Still, it was all very entertaining, watching you go to the trouble you did on that caper. Jumping over electric fences and climbing through windows, getting all grubby for little ol' me? Your mama wouldn't have believed it." He laughed. "I wish I'd been able to film it."

She balled her fists. "Titus Maguire, you're a terrible, *hateful* person, and someday—if *I* have anything to say about it—you'll have your comeuppance." She turned away. John saw the haunted look beneath her anger.

"It's like I said at the very beginning," Rip said. "In some scenarios, you become a trusted ally, not in others. It wasn't to be. A shame." Without warning, he bolted and leapt off the retaining wall. John ran to the edge. Rip was staggering to his feet.

John blasted a red fireman's slide from the edge of the retaining wall down to the gravel shore, leaped onto it, and summoned blue as he slid. Patina swooped down off the retaining wall in a cloud. John fired a raging sapphire blast at Rip's receding back as his momentum propelled him off the slide and onto his feet.

Rip must have heard the crack of the blast's release—he dove aside and the frigid bolt skimmed past, carrying ice chunks and boiling liquid air. The blast struck the waters of the harbor about a third of the way to the far shore, and plowed an ice wedge several yards long through the water. The force of the blast caused the wedge-shaped iceberg to rear like an unruly horse and land with a splash. Fog billowed out and carbon dioxide snow fell along the blast's length, then vanished in the hot night air.

John's last light globe had fizzled out, but the lights from the amphitheater provided enough illumination for him to see Rip scramble back to his feet. The Beef landed behind John with a ground-shaking boom and a grunt. Her mace flew past John at Rip. The spiked ball grazed Rip between shoulder and head, close enough to take off an ear, and landed in the mud near the water's edge. Rip stumbled again, but he had covered most of the distance to the waterline.

John pursued, drawing more blue from inferno-world as Arry thundered past him at a four-limbed dead run, her hooves throwing mud and gravel high. She took care to stay out of his line of sight—*Good play, Arry!*—and he loosed another blast of blue at the spot between Rip's shoulder blades. But he hadn't been paying attention to Rashida, behind him. As soon as Arry had struck she'd made her own move, from the left, and a field of steel marbles now bounced across the sloping hillside into Rip's path.

Rip's heels struck the marbles and he staggered. John's next blue blaze caught Rip's right arm as it cartwheeled up—but the bulk of the ice blast sailed on over his head. Rip threw his hands in front to catch his fall and his right arm snapped off at the elbow. John recoiled as Rip tipped over and bashed his head on the ground.

But he barely seemed to notice the amputation. He clambered over the handle of Arry's massive mace and rolled down to the water's edge, into the water—

—and at its touch, turned to spinning-mirror fans—

—and the dark water lit up in a rapidly expanding wave, revealing two-dimensional planes that spun off from that point where he'd entered—further self-spawning planes fanning from the present instant into endless futures in black and white and shades of gray—as far as the eye could see. Then all went dark again. The ripples in the water settled. Rip was gone.

John's fists went to his hip bones. He shook his head. "Well, *shit*."

"Sorry, Candle," Rashida said as she reformulated. "You would have had him." She was slowly growing as her Patina marbles bounced back to her and soaked in where they struck.

"No." John rubbed his head with both hands. "I should have had a closer eye on what you were doing. Too pissed off to think clearly." He called up red flames to build them a staircase up the retaining wall and then green to heal their injuries. Rashida floated up and reassembled next to Tiffani, who was sitting on the ground crying, while John and Arry hustled up the makeshift, burning, gooey stairs.

The stairway wasn't a great batch of red; the flames lasted only long enough for Arry to scramble up beside him onto the platform, then collapsed in smoldering puddles on the shore. "Did you know he could do that?" John asked Tiffani, gesturing out at the harbor. "Use water as a mirror like that?"

Tiffani shook her head. She used her wrist to rub mascara off her cheeks. "It appears there was much I did not know about that man."

"And now he has thousands of miles of continuous mirrored surface to exit from," John said. "Fucking great." He went over and knelt next to Horace's and Gil's bodies.

"Candle, hon," Tiffani said. He looked over at her. "From what he said . . . I think the airship is sabotaged, after all."

"*What? Is that* what you two were talking about?"

"Yes! He was saying he'd already sabotaged the airship himself. That whole swapping-out parts business he had me do was just him messing with me."

John headed toward the front of the stage. People wouldn't have noticed what had happened to the water—the amphitheater and the Golden Lady would have blocked their view—but the fireworks might have been visible from the edges of the upper amphitheater seating.

Winston Marcus said something, his sister Ellie replied, and laughter rippled through the stands.

As John came around toward the stage entry point, a sound like multiple bells chiming came from the dirigible above, and then a growl that grew louder, like a giant garbage disposal chewing metal. John looked up. First came a loud clanging and then the sound of ricochets. Black spots appeared along the dirigible's side. Correction: *in* its side. The airship's frame shuddered and it listed sideways.

"It's coming down!" He spun. "There'll be a panic—too few exits! Beef, you're on audience evacs—stop a stampede if you can. Patina, rescues! Tiffani, backstage evacs! Now go! *Go!*"

His two seconds ran forward and Tiffani yanked open the backstage door. John followed, dodging through the clutter and commotion and out onto the stage. Peregrine and the musicians were still there, but he ignored them. Ignored the crowd's screams, the shouting. Nothing mattered now but the airship.

The airship was maybe five hundred feet up. Tears were opening in the dirigible's near side as well, as its front end swung around. The airship was dropping fast, coming forward. It would plow headfirst into the stage in seconds—eight, maybe ten.

John marked his heartbeat and *twisted* back into the forest of fire. And he caught that glimpse of spinning mirrors at the threshold of the inferno.

Oh, so you're still around, are you? I'll deal with you later, then. If I survive this.

Wandering among the vast, coiling energy towers, he tried to work up his nerve. Gobs and rivulets like he was used to weren't going to cut it. He'd have to try something new. *Oh, hell.* His body, back there on Earth, was standing at ground zero, anyway. *No point in drawing this out.*

A wine-red cable swung near, blazing bright and strong, cool and pliable as he could hope for, as big around as a sequoia. One of the smaller ones, in fact, for a primary firestalk. That was some consolation. He put a hand out. Paused. *Here goes.*

The cable bent toward his outstretched hand. He could feel its ferocious, brilliant presence. Something there *knew*. Responded. Maybe sentience, maybe not, but there was a *beingness*. A purpose. *Maybe* it would understand. Couldn't hurt to ask. "Try not to kill me, would you?" he said, and drew it in.

♦

People were already clearing out of the backstage area by the time Tiffani got there. She ran past them and looked through the wings. "What the—!"

The musicians were still out front! She saw Peregrine loft herself up, and ran out onto the stage. Winston Marcus was shouting into his mic, trying to get everyone to calm down, but it was hard even for her to hear him over the screams and shouts of the crowd beyond the pit.

Beyond the stage, pandemonium raged. This was a losing battle—people had lost their minds. They pushed and punched and trampled each other. The airship's downward drift was arcing more sharply into a fall. Tiffani could see the faces of the people in the gondola. Her heart rate leapt. That could have been her, up there.

Like her falcon namesake, Peregrine dove, grabbed two little kids from their parents' outstretched arms, and carried them out beyond the walls toward the Golden Lady. Patina swooped over, cushioning someone's fall when they got shoved over the edge of the wall as people pushed their way down the stairs.

Then the Candle, standing mid-stage, erupted in flame.

Tiffani had never seen anything quite like *this*.

Oh, sure—sometimes you might get a look at traces of his fire before they emerged—a glow under his skin, or flames flickering along his flesh. You might catch a fuzzy glimpse of bone or organ lit up within. Then the flames would stream from his hands—or his head or butt or wherever, if he was goofing off. Maybe he'd use the full length of his arms sometimes, if he wanted a bigger blast.

But now he *was* the fire. A blazing figure from which a dozen jets of burgundy flame thick as tree trunks snaked out, so bright and fast you had to shield your eyes, with a crackling roar so loud you covered your ears. The fire figure swayed and spun, flinging energies out across the stands and back. The fire cables over the stands coiled together, weaving themselves into a massive mesh. They soared up to ensnare the lighting towers—piled up along the skybox's roof—entangled themselves in flaming knots along the front rail of the catwalk—looped and wormed along the eaves at the front of the stage.

The airship, meanwhile, grew bigger, and yet bigger.

"*Holy fuck,*" Tiffani said.

The airship was truly falling by now—massive, twice the size of the amphitheater. It headed toward the net nose-first. People below were screaming, pushing each other. As the last gouts of red flame dripped from John's arms, she saw him look up at the ship. He was wobbling at the stage's front edge. Right before a two-story drop into the pit.

Shit—he's going down. She ran all out, leaped over a knocked-down chair and music stand, and skidded to her knees—just in time to grab his belt and yank as he buckled. Instead of pitching forward, he toppled back into her lap, unconscious.

Meanwhile, the dirigible had bounced up out of the net, bowed in the middle, and with a buck came back down. Its nose struck the stage roof with a crunch that drove cracks through the ceiling and down the walls. She shielded John's head and upper torso, and went full-on glam till chunks of roofing stopped falling on and around them. Crashes came from backstage as the backdrops collapsed and equipment got knocked over by falling debris. Up in the stands, the metal lighting towers groaned and bent as the airship settled. The flaming red safety web sagged under its weight. Screams went up again from the people beneath the airship. But the web held.

Well, the pilots are goners unless they got out beforehand, Tiffani thought. Their gondola had struck the stage roof smack in the middle on that second bounce. But the passenger gondola had by some miracle escaped being crushed. It hung sideways at an angle now, its front pointed down, and was gradually settling toward the empty chairs of the auditorium, as the wine-colored flame mesh stretched and began to melt under its weight.

Behind her, a loud fanfare pierced the commotion. Winston Marcus held up the trumpet and spoke loudly. "Folks, I'm no ace, like old Pops, and this here horn isn't magic, either. But music itself has power. So let's use the power of Satchmo's music on this historic trumpet to gather up our own courage and save each other's lives. How about we get everybody out safely?"

Some quieted and turned. Ellie said, "That's right, we'll stay right here with you till everyone is safe. Y'all help your elders, now, and all those folks that need more time, who might be using wheelchairs or canes or walkers. Help those folks with younger kids and babies."

Winston lifted the trumpet to his lips and started playing the blues number "Everybody Needs Somebody to Love" to a lively beat. Ellie sang while Jake came from the wings playing his sax, with Lou on his mouth harp. People in the stands and aisles had calmed down. They started to sing, too, as they stood, helping up those who had fallen. The lines began to move.

Before she started the second verse, while her brothers kept playing,

Ellie said, "Now folks, I spy Ms. Ariadne up there in Row P, and looks like she could sure use your help to evacuate some folks who are stranded in the gondola. Could we get half a dozen of our stronger and younger folks to help her?"

Tiffani saw that the Beef had braced herself on top of the seats and was reaching up as far as she could, extending the handle of her giant mace upward with both hands. This gave her a good eighteen feet of reach. The gondola door hung open, mostly downward, a few feet above that. The first gondola passenger was sliding down the handle to grab onto the joker's horns. Patina and several nats came over to assist her down, and Peregrine came over, too. Another group of people were forming hand-swings to carry out the wounded as they were lowered to the stands.

Tiffani scooted out from underneath John and laid his head on the floor. Every inch that wasn't covered in clothes was covered in webs of busted blood vessels, swelling, and bruises and torn skin. He looked like he'd been beat up from the inside out.

"Candle?" she said. No response. She touched his arm and he groaned. His eyes opened. His sclera were filled with burst capillaries, and blood leaked from his eyes' corners. She feared he might have blinded himself. More blood trickled from his ears and mouth. His suit jacket and shirt were in tatters, and so was the flesh of his torso, where high-pressure flames had torn through him.

"Candle, can you hear me? John?" She tried to help him sit up, but no go—he emitted an anguished scream and collapsed. Tiffani bit her lip. If only he could get some of that green flame for himself.

She heard sirens. "Help's coming. Hang on."

She stood to see if she could find a medic, but the Candle started flailing his arm behind him, as if reaching for something, groaning. Then he was encased in brilliant green flames, and thrashing and yelling fit to scare the livestock. Winston and the others broke off and looked over, alarmed. Tiffani waved at them to keep on playing. "It's OK! Green heals! He'll be all right."

Soon the Candle grew quiet, and the flames ebbed. He moaned and opened his eyes. With Tiffani's help he sat up, and looked out at the vast, fiery mesh.

"Wow," he said.

"Wow," she agreed. She looked him over. His body was completely healed. "I hope you brought a change of clothes, darlin', because we're all getting a damn fine view. Not that I mind . . ."

The Candle looked down at himself, at his tattered, bloody clothes.

"Damn. That was my best suit." He stood and tried to drape the tatters strategically. He looked around. "Where are my shoes?"

"Your guess is as good as mine!"

"Oh well. Just—do what you can to help, would you?" he said. "I'll be back." He started past her toward backstage.

"Wait!" Tiffani grabbed his arm. "Where are you going?"

"I have to stop Rip before he gets away."

She sighed. *If only.* "But how? He's long gone."

"Not yet he's not. And I know where he is." He dropped his earpiece and radio into her palm and pressed her fingers around it. "Tell Patina and the Beef, would you? I'll be back as quick as I can."

♥

John stepped onto the concrete pad outside the enclosure. Lower Manhattan's city lights shone across the water. A Coast Guard boat approached from the north. Help was coming for the wounded. Good.

His red flames were fading now, but they seemed to have done their work; the airship gondola looked empty. So did the amphitheater, from what he could see. People had dispersed across the grounds below the Golden Lady's pedestal on benches or hill slopes or in clusters along the walkway that encircled the monument. Vendors were passing out ice and free snacks. It was all starting to take on a carnival aspect. Maybe the casualties would be lower than he'd feared.

A police helicopter shone a searchlight down onto the dirigible's deflated remains. The fabric draped across the amphitheater's front and its own damaged structure like a satin shroud over shattered bones. Arry had gotten up onto the stage rooftop somehow—*Holy shit, Ma, there's a minotaur on the roof!*—and was using her mace handle and a cinder block as a lever to raise the dirigible up. A cloud of Patina particles slipped into the gap beneath.

John hesitated, then got going. He circled the amphitheater and entered the restricted area at a run, past where Gil's and Horace's bodies lay, to the southern seawall, and leapt down onto the rocky shore where the drop was shallowest. He crossed the sloping gravel as swiftly as he could. No one was in sight. All the helicopter and speedboat action was on the other side of the amphitheater.

How many have died because of you, Titus? How many more will?

He reached the southernmost point of the island, where the waters of the bay lapped at the shore, and lobbed a yellow fireball skyward. There it was! The iceberg, right where it had been in the image he'd seen just a moment ago, in Titus's whirling mirror-blades future-vision. The berg bobbed along about a hundred feet out or so, headed toward the Verrazzano-Narrows. A small dark shape showed up against the white ice.

If I never touch red flame again it'll be too soon, he thought, and shuddered, but still he *twisted* back and harvested enough to make a net with. Then he cast it out to snare the iceberg and pulled it in—and harvested-wove-cast-and-pulled again, and again, and again—till the ice scraped up against the shore nearby, dripping red flame. He waded over.

It was Rip, all right. The other man lay atop the ice, dead or unconscious. A web of dark runnels fanned out atop the ice—that must be blood from his injury. The rivulets had spread the length and width of the fifteen-foot-long ice wedge. But it was best to be sure.

John bound Rip up in red flame till he glowed like a Christmas ornament, dragged him off the ice, and pulled him the rest of the way onto the shore. He checked for a pulse. Rip was still alive.

"What the—?" Rip opened his eyes and saw John. "Well, shit."

John said, "Guess there wasn't as much blood as it looked like. Pity."

With a grunt, Rip struggled to sit up. He wiped his mouth with his left hand and laughed. "Hell of a thing." He leaned over, cradling the stump of his right arm. He'd gotten his belt around it, John saw, but blood was still dribbling out. His skin was so white it was almost transparent in the dimness, and his lips were blue. He wiped his mouth with his left hand, looked over at John. "Well . . . I *almost* made it."

"You wanted me to find you."

Rip rolled his eyes. "Uh, no . . . I really didn't."

"Bullshit." Rip made no reply. "You see it, too. I know you do."

"What, the linked portals?" Rip shrugged. "I didn't know it was you. Not for a long time."

"That time in the hospital room, when I came back and you got burned."

"What about it?"

"You tried to use your own ace on me somehow, while I was lying there in a coma, didn't you? *That* was why my ace finally finished its turn. That's why the flames went out of control. I remembered seeing those mirror flashes then, too. From when you left—"

"When I returned, actually."

"—it forced my own portal open—"

"—and I got caught in the blast. Yeah."

"So the accident was *your* fault. Not mine."

Rip gave him a sidelong look. There wasn't enough ambient light here for John to read his expression. "I'd love to reminisce with you some more, old buddy, but I could use some of that green flame of yours right about now."

John snorted. "Dream on."

"Really?" Rip demanded. "Really. You're going to let me bleed out. Come on!" John only looked at him. He slumped back to rest his head on the ground. "Well, god *damn*. Didn't think you had it in you."

More time ticked past.

"What's your body count, Titus?"

Rip looked over. "I lost count." He was breathing heavily now.

"I don't believe you. I think you know *exactly* how many. In fact, I'm willing to bet you have a little shrine for each of your victims. A death garden you lovingly tend."

Rip gave him a sharp look. *Uh-huh. Thought so.*

A helicopter passed overhead, shining its searchlight. Rip tried to lift an arm to wave at it, but he'd grown too weak. The searchlight missed them and moved on.

"Come on," John urged him. "Brag a little. You know you want to."

No answer.

"I've been wondering," John said, "exactly when *your* ace must have turned. I remember in eighth grade when you befriended me, back in Boston, and how everyone warned me away from you. Said you were cruel. A bully. I thought *they* were the bullies. I couldn't believe you'd do all the things they said. You were so nice to me, and at a bad time, after my father died.

"Did you really try to kill your little brother?"

Rip's head drooped lower. John saw him smile. "He deserved it."

"Had your card turned by the time we met?" Rip didn't respond. "It had, hadn't it?" Rip looked over at him, and John saw the answer in his gaze. It had.

"So I was . . . what? A lab experiment?"

"My first," Rip said. "My very first."

"Your first what? Your first love? First victim? First time you fucked a guy?"

"All of the above." Rip shook his head, as if he were trying to stay awake. "It's just no good, though. Not unless I can . . ."

"*What's* no good? Unless you can *what*? Kill? Torment? Ruin lives?"

Rip giggled. "And they have no idea. You, Fagan, everybody. No fucking clue." His laugh was a rattle. John leaned closer, to hear better. "Everything that happened. Those little *twists* of fate that kept . . . messing things up for you." He shook his head. "Even your card turning." He leaned close. "Even your dad's." His eyes glittered in the dark.

John's hands spasmed into fists. "You caused my *dad's* card to turn?"

Rip pressed a bloody finger to John's lips.

"Shhh," he whispered. "Wrecked your perfect little world, didn't I, Juanma? Your perfect little family. Made you end up on the streets. Made you a criminal. A slave to Fagan. Ha! I was just a kid—and I did all that. You were my fucking *masterpiece*." Another delirious giggle. "God, I've wanted to tell you this for so long, Juanma. But you were too easy. A perfect target. So needy! So anguished! Afraid to come out. Sure your dad would disown you. I solved that one for you, though, didn't I?" John jerked. He wanted to choke the life out of Titus with his bare hands. "And after he died, you were *so grateful* for my attention . . . 'Somebody *loves* me!' And then so afraid I'd leave you if I found out you also liked banging girls. Such drama! I had you running in circles, worrying about how to protect poor, sensitive Titus . . .

"Really, Juanma, you were so much more fun to play with than Tiffani. That one . . ." He sighed. "She saw right through me, from the start."

After a minute he looked over. "Does it feel cold to you?"

He released a long, slow breath, and didn't inhale.

John snarled. "*Motherfucker*." He gripped Rip by the shoulders—slapped his face. "I'm not done with you." No response. "All right, we'll do it *your* way. For old times' sake." John *twisted* back, drew in green flame, and returned, and gave him a few drips of it. Just enough to give him another few breaths' worth. Rip gasped. His eyes fluttered open, and grew wide with fear. "Don't . . ."

"'*Don't?*' Don't what, Titus? Don't toy with you? The way you've toyed with everyone else? *The way you've done with me?*"

John shook him again, hard. Then he set his head down, gently, and sat there cross-legged, looking at his face. Seeing the boy inside the man. The blond-haired, green-eyed boy he'd given up everything for, and then given up, to save his own life.

I knew. I did know. Some part of me knew what he was. And wanted him anyway.

"Did you ever love me, Titus?" he asked. But Rip's green-eyed gaze had gone glassy. John sighed. "Don't answer that. It was rhetorical."

He buried his face in his hands and stayed that way for a long while.

Finally he stood and dragged Rip's body back out into the water, hefted it up onto the iceberg and shoved it to the middle of the wedge with more gouts of red. He harvested more ice-blue flame to seal it deep inside. Rip's transport would need to last a good long time, to make it out to the Atlantic. John gave the iceberg a good, hard shove and a kick.

He thought about their earlier fight, and Titus's amputated arm, lying at the edge of the water. He had an overpowering urge to go over and torch it all. Erase all evidence of Titus's presence. But crime scene; duty to preserve the evidence. All that.

Consciousness of guilt, much, Juanma?

Rashida materialized next to him. "Well, you look like shit."

He looked her over. "And you don't! It's not fair."

"Patina hath her privileges." She shifted her outfit into something more casual: a pink leather jacket over gray silk, charcoal gray leggings, and flats. They both watched the iceberg recede into the dark.

"I wonder if some boat is going to run into it."

"Most likely, with your luck."

They looked at each other. "You saw?" he asked.

"I saw. I heard." She paused. "You going to be all right?"

John looked at his hands. His remembered them gripping Titus's shoulders, just now, and last night, his ass. Remembered the taste of Glenlivet on Titus's tongue then, and the faces of his own men, slackened and bloodied in death, just now. He had no words. Instead, after a moment, he flexed the fingers of his right hand, curled the fingers up like flower petals, and brought a different-color flame to each. They spun, little ballerinas—cherry flame, and lemon, mint and royal and periwinkle, and in the center, a will-o'-the-wisp of winged, smoky, crackling black.

All the power I can imagine at my fingertips—more yet, if I ever decided to risk it—and in the end, I was nothing more than a lover's broken toy, all these years. He shook his head and blew the flames out. *Jeez, Candle-man—no wonder you gave up on relationships. And on your art.*

"I'm going to quit," he told Rashida.

She stared. "You *what?*"

"I'm going to quit, and recommend you as my replacement."

"Don't get me wrong; I'm flattered," she said. "But . . . why?"

He shrugged. "I . . . hate paperwork?"

She threw her head back and laughed that belly-deep laugh of hers. It summoned a smile that he hadn't thought he had in him. "Don't quit *just* yet. For one thing, I'm not sure I want the job. And second, I don't think we're done with all the 'ripple effects' left over from that evil fuck." She lifted her chin toward the berg, now nearly invisible at the far end of the bay. "You'll want Chubb to have your back when and if the shit hits the fan."

"I doubt they will, anyway."

"Oh, I dunno. We'll see."

John built them a staircase to the top of the retaining wall and they walked together toward the amphitheater. The statue towered overhead, casting a soft, reflected glow that lit their way. He could see the Beef's silhouette, where she stood silent sentry over the bodies of Gil and Horace, with the trumpet strapped to her back. The edges of his mouth pulled down.

Rashida paused. He turned back to her.

"Did you mean it about leaving the company?" she asked.

He thought it over. "Yeah. Maybe. I think so."

"Well, then! Close enough."

"Close enough to what?"

She slapped him on the arm. "Close enough to when you're at the you-think-so-maybe-not-my-boss-anymore point that we won't get dinged by HR. Besides which, fuck it."

"Uh . . . I'm still not following."

"Wow, you *are* out of it. Fine, I'll spell it out. We'll be up all night dealing with the fallout of this night's horror show, of course." She waved her arm to encompass their fallen team members, the shredded mass of the airship, the sirens and lights. "And then you are going to authorize three days of PTO for you, me, and Arry."

"Makes sense. Not to mention six months of company-sponsored, top-notch trauma therapy."

She nodded. "At a minimum! And, once all *that* is all lined out, you're going to grab your fifth of fancy scotch and meet me at my place. Whereupon we shall throw back a couple of drinks, snort some purple sparkly shit, and get frisky."

"Wait. What?" He blinked, confused. "I thought you were mad at me."

"That's right, John. I'm mad as hell. And I'll probably swear at you a lot."

"That's fair . . ."

"And I'll want your life story." She poked him in the chest. "The real version, this time. Which I've more than earned."

"You really truly have."

"But the important thing is that we're going to fuck each other's brains out, John. We're going to climb into bed and fuck each other. We're going to fuck and fuck until we forget what a horrible shitty day this has been." She crooked her pinkie at him. "What do you say?"

He eyed her pinkie. "I dunno, Ras . . . that'd take an awful lot of fucking."

"Exactly." She wiggled the finger. "C'mon, Candle-man. Don't wait till sunrise to light me up, here. You in or you out?"

He laughed. "All right. Good plan." He lifted his own pinkie, but she pulled hers back. "On one condition. You have to shower first."

"Deal," he said, and took her pinkie in his.

♠ ♥ ♦ ♣

Skin Deep

by Alan Brennert

DAVE BRUBECK'S "TAKE FIVE" was playing on the jukebox, filling the Menagerie with its cool syncopation as the clock ticked toward two a.m. Trina, wending her way through tables carrying a tray of drinks, hated working the late shift. Most of the nats were long gone, leaving only the drunkest of jokers, and the drunkest were also the grabbiest—but none grabbier than a cephalopod. She felt a lithe tentacle trying to loop around her waist but managed to wriggle away from it even as she balanced her wobbling tray.

"Bongo, please," Trina said in exasperation, "stop kidding around?"

Bongo K. was a skinny kid with reddish-brown skin, wearing dungarees and a gray sweatshirt with holes for his eight happy-go-lucky tentacles: one was holding a shot of Jim Beam, another was coiled around a bongo drum, and a third drummed in surprisingly good time with Brubeck's horn. Bongo was usually rather shy, but after two drinks he became a bit frisky—and loquacious:

"Baby, I dig you, that's all," he said imploringly. He used a fourth appendage to snap up some abandoned flowers from a nearby table and waved the bouquet in Trina's face, forcing her to stop in her tracks. "Just listen to this poem I've written in testament to your ever-loving beauty—"

Beauty? Trina wanted to puke. She didn't know which she hated more: men who were repulsed by her face, or those who found such deformities arousing. She pushed aside the flowers, her exasperation flaring into anger.

"Doug!" she called. "A little help here?"

Doug was the club bouncer. Sprawled on the floor next to the bar, he resembled the top half of a giant jellyfish; unlike Bongo he had no tentacles but a compensatory telekinesis that he was using to scoop beer nuts off the bar and pop them into the orifice that passed for his mouth.

>*Gotcha!*<

Bongo started to object: "Hey, cool it, man, I—"

Doug wrested Bongo's tentacle from around Trina's waist using invisible tendrils of his own. He forced Bongo to put down his Jim Beam gently on the table but let him keep his hold on the bongo drum. Then, as if it had been yanked aloft by a winch, Bongo's whole body was jerked up into the air with his tentacles pinned against his body, hovering like a helicopter without rotors.

The chromatophores below the surface of Bongo's skin turned him literally white with fear. "Aw, man—"

>I'll take him home, Trina. Almost quitting time anyway.<

"Thanks, Doug."

>Later.<

Doug floated up off the floor and toward the door, with Bongo trailing him like a tethered balloon. Trina went to the door and watched them head up the boardwalk to the building that was once the warehouse and loading dock for Santa Monica Seafood but was now a hotel for most of Los Angeles's amphibious jokers, with easy access to the ocean and to refrigerator units for those tenants sensitive to heat.

In minutes Trina was off duty herself and outside taking a deep breath of the cool, briny air. It was a beautiful summer night, a full moon floating above the Santa Monica Pier. The food and amusement concessions were all closed, deserted except for the carousel, where one or two desperate joker hookers straddled wooden horses, smoking cigarettes as they waited forlornly for johns. A pair of masked jokers—one wearing a royal-purple cloak and hood, the other a cheap plastic likeness of Marilyn Monroe—staggered tipsily past the merry-go-round, giggling and pawing at each other as they headed, presumably, to one or the other's accommodations.

During the day Trina sometimes wore a mask herself to hide her face from tourists, but at this hour of the morning the tourists were long gone. Rather than returning to her apartment above the carousel, Trina climbed down a side ladder, onto the sand. Under the pier, she kicked off the three-inch heels the manager made the girls wear along with her tacky cocktail dress. Beneath it she wore her swimsuit; excitedly she padded out from under the wooden crossbeams and pylons that supported the pier and onto the beach. It was empty this time of night and the rippling moonlight beckoned from across Santa Monica Bay. Here there were no nat eyes to gape at her misshapen face in horror or laughter; no screams from children too young to understand what the wild card virus had done to her.

She dove into the water and immediately felt calmer, at ease. She swam toward the distant moon, then flipped onto her back, floating on the night tide. Here she was a child again at play, or a teenager swimming out to meet her boyfriend Woody—after fourteen years his tanned face, bright blue eyes, and blond crew cut still tender in her memory—as he straddled his surfboard waiting for the next set of waves, smiling at her as she swam toward him. He kissed her as she swam up, running his hand along the side of her swimsuit, giving her gooseflesh.

She could barely remember what a kiss felt like.

She swam for the better part of an hour, until, exhausted but happy, she returned to the beach. She retrieved her shoes and clothes, scrambled up the ladder, and headed for the Hippodrome, the castle-like building that housed the carousel. The old Looff Hippodrome dated back to 1916 and was an architectural goulash of Byzantine arches, Moorish windows, and Spanish Colonial turrets, all painted a bright mustard yellow. Trina hurried inside a side door, up two flights of rickety stairs, through narrow corridors to one of the seven small apartments above the merry-go-round.

She opened the door to find her cat, Ace, waiting. He greeted her with a familiar *miaow* that Trina knew meant both "Where have you *been*?" and "Feed me!" She went to the kitchen, opened a can of Puss'n Boots, and smiled as he attacked the food. Then she went into the bathroom to take a shower. The room was the same as it was when she moved here fourteen years ago, except for the vanity mirror, which she had taken down soon after moving in.

It was an airy, one-bedroom apartment, and the living room—inside one of the building's turrets—enjoyed a view of the surf lapping at the beach. She ate a sandwich as Ace finished his dinner, then sat down on the divan next to the windows. Ace jumped into her lap, purring as she stroked his orange fur. She gazed out at the waves rolling to shore, their white crests iridescent in the moonlight, and at the beautiful but forbidden lights of Santa Monica. She was born and raised in this city but was now virtually an exile from it, like a blemished princess hidden away in a high castle.

Trina picked up her subscription copy of *Time* magazine and grimaced at the lead story about Richard Nixon securing the Republican nomination for president. She didn't know much about his opponent, Kennedy, but she remembered Nixon's venal attacks—as a member of the House Un-American Activities Committee—on the legendary Four Aces, heroes whose lives and reputations were casually destroyed by HUAC. Trina was willing to don a mask and walk over hot coals, if necessary, to the polls, in order to cast a vote against Nixon.

The other news story that caught her interest told of how the Woolworth's in Greensboro, North Carolina—the subject of sit-down protests for the first five months of 1960—had finally capitulated and would allow Negroes to join white patrons at its lunch counter. She was happy for their victory but despaired of any similar civil rights movement for jokers.

Ace rubbed his head against Trina's chest and purred.

Tears filled her eyes—her human eyes, one of the few human features remaining in her face. Why couldn't people be more like cats, who didn't care what you looked like as long as you were kind to them?

When she finally went to bed, Ace curled up against her hip, the two of them sharing each other's warmth as they slept.

♣

Prior to September 15, 1946, Trina Nelson's world was a quietly ordinary, if privileged, one. She was a pretty, popular sixteen-year-old who lived in a ranch-style home on Ashland Avenue in Santa Monica; was an A student at Santa Monica High School (known as "Samohi" to students and faculty alike) and a cheerleader for the school football team, the Mighty B's, on which her boyfriend, Woody, played as a halfback. The war was over and no one Trina knew had been killed in combat. Life was good, and everyone was expecting it to get even better.

But on September 15, Trina's world expanded explosively to include a cosmos of horrors darker than her worst nightmares, delivered to the Nelson home by the big RCA console radio in the living room. Trina and her parents, Harry and Karen Nelson, listened in astonishment to the news bulletins of a battle raging above Manhattan between Jetboy and someone in a weird blimp-like airship that was said to be carrying an atomic bomb. But when the airship blew up, no mushroom cloud blossomed over Manhattan, and briefly there was celebration that Jetboy had saved the city (though tragically died in the effort).

"Oh God, no." Trina had Jetboy's picture, from *Life* magazine, taped up on her wall alongside one of Frank Sinatra.

Then came the other deaths. Massive, widespread deaths radiating like shock waves across the city and the whole Northeast.

And not just ordinary deaths. People were dying in the most horrifying ways, ways never before seen on Earth. They burst into flame and were incinerated instantly. They dissolved into puddles of protoplasm or died screaming as blood poured from every cavity in their bodies. It sounded so outlandish that Trina's father doubted at first that it was really happening—thought it a hoax, like Orson Welles's invasion from Mars. But it was on every channel: CBS, NBC, Mutual, ABC.

And then the news that we *had* been invaded, not from Mars but definitely from outer space, and what had been released over Manhattan was some kind of alien germ that was killing thousands of people—and even worse, transforming others into monsters.

Chaos erupted in New York and all that people on the West Coast could do was listen helplessly, disbelievingly.

"This is impossible," Harry said. "Things like this just don't happen."

"All those people," Karen said softly. "Those poor people . . ."

Soon there were scientists on the news talking about this virus—they called it the "wild card" virus—and how it had likely been swept up into the jet stream and was by now on its way eastward, across the Atlantic. They could not rule out the possibility that some of the viral particles might circle the earth on winds of up to 250 miles an hour, eventually arriving on the West Coast in perhaps three or four days.

That was all it took to spark panic and chaos up and down the coast. In Los Angeles there was a run on grocery stores as people bought up, then stole, food against the coming apocalypse. Military surplus stores were quickly stripped of their supplies of gas masks. Fires and looting broke out across the city. Doomsayers and kooky cultists—of which LA had a ready supply—declared that the end was nigh, and it was the doing of either God or fugitive Nazis planning a comeback.

Some families piled their belongings into station wagons, slapped a MOVED sign on their houses, and headed south for Mexico—with no guarantee the virus wouldn't find its way there too. Others flooded into air raid shelters or began duct-taping shut the doors and windows of their homes so that the virus could not get in. Trina's family was one of the latter: she helped her parents tape the smallest crack in the house even as she wondered whether they would die of suffocation before the virus could even get to them.

And then all that was to be done—was to wait.

One, two, three days of waiting for the end of the world, or something like it, to arrive. Listening to reports of the virus infecting the passengers and crew of the ocean liner *Queen Mary* in the mid-Atlantic, turning it into a literal death ship. Then sporadic reports of outbreaks in Europe—followed by a day's silence that raised Trina's hopes that perhaps the virus had blown out to sea, might *never* arrive here . . .

Until, on the fourth day, the sirens began screaming.

Air raid sirens, police sirens, fire and ambulance sirens . . . a rising chorus of wails both near and far.

Her parents were upstairs; Trina ran to the living room window and pulled back the drape to look outside. Ashland Avenue was deserted and peaceful, at odds with the blare of sirens in the distance. But within moments she could hear people screaming up the block, and as Trina looked up the street, she saw what they were screaming at.

Running down the street was a coal-black wolf—but it was enormous. At least ten feet long by four feet high, with legs longer than Trina's arms. And yet that was not its most salient characteristic.

The wolf had two heads.

Two identical heads, both with wide jaws open to expose long razor-sharp teeth . . . and it was *howling*. Not a snarl of aggression but a howl of confusion, of pain, as if it was trying to communicate with anyone who could hear it—

A police car, siren blaring, came speeding down the street and screeched to a halt only about ten feet away from the wolf, which came to a sudden stop. SMPD officers jumped out of the car, weapons drawn.

The wolf seemed to understand. It did not advance on the car.

Trina's heart pounded in her chest, but she couldn't look away.

Now a second police cruiser careened around the corner of Ashland and Twenty-First Street and stopped on the other side of the creature. Two officers burst out of the car and leveled rifles at the beast.

The wolf's two heads took in both cars at the same time, and Trina was certain she saw an almost human fear and helplessness in its eyes.

It howled, crying out in terrible knowledge of its own fate.

The police fired. Dozens of rounds of bullets ripped into the wolf, blood spouting from its wounds; the animal staggered, fell to the ground.

Tears filled Trina's eyes as she listened to the creature's death howl.

"No! No!"

A woman came screaming up the street, running toward the fallen animal, then collapsed at its side. With no fear she put her arms as far around the wolf's torso as she could, and Trina heard her sob:

"Henry . . . *Henry* . . ."

Trina's heart seemed to stop as she took in the words and what they implied. The woman's tears fell on the soft fur of the wolf's body.

By now Trina's parents had come pounding down the stairs and were standing in the vestibule.

"Trina, get away from the window!" her father shouted.

Trina closed the drape. She couldn't bear to look anymore.

Then, behind her, her mother screamed.

Trina turned—and was horrified to see that her mother's arms were *dissolving* into some kind of blue vapor.

"Karen!" Harry cried in horror. "Jesus Christ!"

"Mom!" Trina ran across the living room toward her.

It only took seconds for Karen's arms to dissipate into plumes of blue mist, and then her feet and legs began to evaporate. With nothing but smoke to support them, her head and torso fell to the floor.

No, no, Trina thought, *this can't be, it isn't real!* She and her father fell to their knees beside what remained of Karen's body.

"Karen! Honey!" Harry grabbed onto his wife's torso as if to halt the spread of whatever was consuming her. Through tears he said, "*Hon—*"

As her torso was dissolving into wisps, Karen had only seconds to look at her family and gasp, "Harry . . . Trina . . . love you both . . . so *mu—*"

The last of her dissolved before she could finish—leaving only a blue mist behind.

Trina was in shock. Harry sobbed helplessly, taking in deep breaths of the blue vapor, all that was left of his wife of twenty-two years.

Harry started coughing . . . then choking.

His hands went to his throat as he struggled to take in air.

"Daddy, no! No!" Trina screamed, slapping him on the back as if he had something caught in his esophagus. But it was no use. The blue toxin that was once his wife was poisoning him, and in seconds he collapsed. He was no longer breathing.

Unlike what it had done to his wife, the wild card virus had not vaporized him, but had killed him just as quickly.

"Mama . . . Daddy . . ." Trina held on to her father's limp hand and sobbed, weeping and calling out for the parents she loved. *This isn't happening, please God, let me wake up, please God please!*

She wept unconsolably for fifteen minutes, torn between grief and disbelief . . . until, unable to bear the sight of her father's body or the absence of her vanished mother, she stripped off the duct-taping around the front door, flung it open, and ran out.

She ran to the home of their next-door neighbors. Emma and Lou Boylan, both in their fifties, were standing on their lawn (as were other neighbors) gaping at the dead two-headed monster in the street being loaded into a police truck.

Trina embraced Emma and wailed, "They're gone! Mom and Dad— Mom is *gone,* there's nothing *left,* and Dad—Daddy—"

Emma enfolded Trina in her arms. "Oh Lord, Trina, what—"

"They're gone. They're *dead!*" And she broke down sobbing again.

Lou Boylan said to his wife, "Bring her inside. I'll get her a shot of Jack Daniel's to calm her down."

"She's only sixteen, Lou!"

"I think she just aged a couple of years, hon," he said, and went ahead to get them all drinks.

"We're so sorry, honey," Emma told Trina as she led her into their home and toward a couch. "My God, this is all so terrible."

Lou came over with three shot glasses. "You've had a shock, Trina, take this. It might seem strong at first if you're not used to it."

Trina didn't bother to tell them that this was not her first glass of whiskey. She drank it down, and though it calmed her nerves a little, it took away none of her grief. Then—remembering suddenly that this madness was happening all over—she asked, "Have you heard from Judy and Gary?"

Yes, Lou assured her, their two married children were fine in their homes in San Diego and Mill Valley—at least for the moment.

"What did you mean," Emma asked with trepidation, "that your mother—that there was nothing left?"

Trina explained what had happened and the Boylans' eyes went wide. If there hadn't been a giant, two-headed wolf in the middle of Ashland Avenue, they might even have doubted her. But as the radio droned on about the alien virus, the world seemed much larger—and much more terrifying—than it had three days ago.

The Boylans did the necessary business of calling for an ambulance for Harry's body, but it would be seven hours before one arrived; there were simply too many bodies, scattered from Santa Monica to El Monte, from Castaic to Long Beach, for the authorities to handle all at once. There was widespread rioting, and looters breaking into closed-up stores and abandoned homes. Radio reports estimated that at least fifteen hundred people had died across Los Angeles County and perhaps a hundred more had been—transformed. Some into monsters, some only slightly deformed, and a few into something . . . more than human. No one would ever know how many "aces," as these super-powered individuals would come to be called, were birthed that day—if people had special powers, they were keeping it a secret for now.

With one exception: in West LA, a young man could be seen rocketing into the air, crying out "I can fly! I can fly!" as he rose straight into the stratosphere and out of sight—until his frozen, lifeless body came plummeting back to earth, crashing into the fountain at the corner of Wilshire and Santa Monica Boulevards. Newspapers were quick to name him Icarus, as there was not enough left of him to identify.

Trina numbly listened to the radio reports, barely ate any of the dinner Emma prepared, and felt drained and exhausted by six p.m. She gratefully accepted the Boylans' offer to stay in what was once their daughter's room.

It took more than an hour for her to fall asleep, and her dreams were tense and frightening, but she slept past dawn. When she got up, she padded into the small attached bathroom. Inside she passed the bathroom mirror, saw something not right, and turned to look into it.

There was a monster in the mirror.

She screamed.

It was a swollen, bestial face with a thick brow, sunken eyes, a pig-like snout of a nose, ridged cheekbones, and a twisting slash of an upper lip . . . all of it grotesquely framed by a stylish crop of bobbed brunette hair.

Her hair, she realized with a jolt.

Instinctively her hands went up to her face, and now she could *feel* the same deformities she saw in the mirror.

She screamed again. She kept on screaming until the Boylans rushed in to see what was wrong. When she turned to face them, their confusion and concern had become shock . . . and revulsion.

She looked back into the mirror, hoping to see something different, but when the monster continued to stare back at her, she fainted, falling into Lou's arms as her body went limp.

She woke a few minutes later in bed and as her eyes fluttered open, she saw Emma and Lou staring down at her, the same mix of pity and revulsion in their eyes. She couldn't blame them, she felt it herself, but it was still unbearable to see.

She jumped out of bed and ran past them, down the stairs.

"Trina! Trina, we only want to help you!" Emma called after her.

But Trina ran out of the house, without even a thought that she was still wearing her pajamas. She ran next door to her own house; its door was unlocked but after entering she locked it behind her. She saw the empty floor where her parents had died so horribly, and she ran from that too, rushing up the stairs and into the one safe place remaining to her: her room. She fell onto her bed, sobbing, anguished, overwhelmed—grieving for her parents, for herself, and for the life she had loved, a life she knew would never, ever be the same again.

♠

Trina kept the window curtains drawn and took down every mirror in the house. There was enough food in the kitchen to last at least a month. Whenever the phone rang that day—relatives or friends, probably, checking in to see if the family was okay—she let it ring. In the middle of the night, as the neighborhood slept, she cracked open the front door, taped a MOVED sign on it, then quickly shut and locked it again. Over the next several days people came by and rang the doorbell, and through a crack in the upstairs curtains she recognized her cousins from Covina and the school truant officer—but they all went away, eventually. The hardest one to watch was her boyfriend, Woody, who showed up one day, rang the bell, called her name: "Trina! Trina!" He went all the way around the house, searching for signs of life, and Trina wanted so much to let him in. She wanted him to hold her, to tell her everything was all right, tell her he still loved her—but she knew that would not happen. And she couldn't bear to see the look of revulsion and horror in his eyes when he saw her face.

The only ones she let in were the Boylans, who, bless them, continued to look in on her despite her grotesque appearance. Emma Boylan brought home-cooked meals to Trina's back porch and talked with her when she needed someone to talk to.

During the next several days she listened to the radio reports about people like her, who were now being called "jokers." That was rich—this *was* a joke, a cosmic joke, and she was the butt of it. Worse, public fear of the transformed was hardening into prejudice. Stories of jokers being driven out of their houses, neighborhoods, and towns terrified Trina. Experts talked about isolating all the jokers in asylums, but the hundred-odd jokers in Los Angeles County either left with no forwarding address or quickly went into hiding. Like Trina.

The Boylans tried to give her hope: "That spaceman in New York, Dr. Tachyon, has been treating people like you," Emma told her. "In a lot of cases he can cure them. Maybe he can cure you, honey."

"And how do I get to New York?" Trina asked. "Take the bus? A plane? You think anybody is going to be willing to sit next to me—even have me on a bus with them at all?"

"We could drive you," Lou offered, and Trina was touched by that.

"Thank you," she said gently, "that's very sweet of you to offer. But people like me are dangerous to be around. I couldn't ask that of you."

By the following week, the authorities had succeeded in quelling most of the panic and rioting and were doing their best to assure the public that there would be no further disruptions from the wild card virus. Trina sat listening to these assurances on the radio one evening—the radio on low, the living room dark, the window curtains drawn—

When she heard a crash of breaking glass from the kitchen.

She jumped to her feet. She stood stock-still, listening to the unmistakable sound of a window being raised, followed by two thumps ... and the sound of voices:

"Fuck. I got cut by the goddamn glass."

"Stop whining, it's just a scratch. There's silverware in that hutch, get moving."

Looters, Trina realized. The MOVED sign had worked too well. She listened to the chiming of silverware being thrown into a bag. Paralyzed with fear, she didn't know what to do. Run outside to the Boylans' house? No, she couldn't endanger them too. Run upstairs and lock the bedroom door behind her? No. What if they broke the door down?

She was looking around for something she could use as a weapon when one of the men suddenly entered the living room. "What the fuck?" he blurted out, swinging his flashlight in her direction.

Trina winced as the beam struck her directly in her face.

The burglar saw clearly her deformed, horrible features and yelled, "Jesus H. Christ!"

The second looter, carrying the bag full of silverware, came in behind his accomplice and said, "She's one of them jokers!"

Instantly the men abandoned all further interest in looting, turned tail, and ran the hell away, out the back door.

Trina was relieved, though it depressed her that she was so repulsive she caused two hardened criminals to flee in terror ... and afraid that this would not be the end of it. They were hardly likely to call the police, but what if they told someone she was there—anyone?

For a week or more it seemed as if they had not. Then she woke up one morning to find that someone had painted the words GET OUT JOKER! on the front of the Nelson house.

She immediately began to make plans if the worst should happen, packing every perishable food item she could find into the trunk of the family Buick in the garage, along with water, blankets, a pillow, and extra clothes. Emma and Lou gave her what canned food they had.

Three nights later, someone threw a rock, wrapped in a burning rag, through the living room window. The drapes instantly caught fire. Rather than try to save the house, Trina ran to the garage and backed the Buick into the driveway as flames crackled and consumed the living room.

"Goodbye, house," she whispered, with tears in her eyes for the only home she had ever known.

She drove through side streets until she reached the California Incline, then down the sloping road to Pacific Coast Highway. There was a stoplight at PCH and another car in the lane next to her, so Trina took her mother's big floppy sunbathing hat and put it on, slanting it so the man in the car next to her couldn't make out her face. The red light seemed to last for years, but finally it turned green and Trina headed up the coast highway toward Malibu.

She and Woody had spent enough time at Malibu's beaches that she knew that despite its reputation as a mecca for Hollywood celebrities, much of Malibu was still quite rural. There were enough sparsely populated canyons and secluded side streets to provide some degree of concealment from prying eyes. For each of the next ten days she would find a deserted spot off Trancas or Latigo Canyons, eat cold canned food, sleep during the day with a blanket hiding her face, then at night drive to a deserted beach and swim alone, relieving some of her stress and grief in the rocking cradle of the waves.

One evening she was parked along a deserted road in Solstice Canyon, eating canned tuna, when she heard:

"Miss?"

Trina heard a man's voice and saw the sweep of a flashlight beam across the front seat. She grabbed her floppy hat, hiding her face.

"Leave me alone," she begged. "I'm not bothering anyone!"

"I know you're not," the man said gently. "And there's no need to hide your face. I know what you look like."

"You—you do?" Hesitantly she lowered the hat. A tall man in a police uniform stood outside the car. He saw her hideous face but didn't flinch or even look surprised. "How?"

The policeman raised the palm of his hand. At first it looked perfectly ordinary, but then a fold appeared in the flesh of the palm and, to Trina's astonishment, opened to reveal a *human eye* staring at her.

Trina sat bolt upright. "What the *hell* is that?" she blurted.

"My third eye. It sees more, and farther, than the other two—it showed me that you were hiding here, and what you looked like."

"You're like Icarus," Trina said softly. "The virus gave you—powers." The randomness of the virus suddenly hit home: if things had gone only a *little* differently, she might be able to fly, or turn invisible, instead of . . .

"I may have powers," the policeman said, "but believe me, if anyone on the force saw this, I'd be just another joker on the run, like you. But I use it to help out where I can."

She felt a pang of hope. "How can you help me?"

"About a week ago, the eye showed me that there's a refuge, of sorts, for our kind. On the amusement pier in Santa Monica. Go there tonight and ask for Dr. Pink."

"Dr. Pink," she repeated. "At the—Santa Monica Pier?"

"That's right. You'll be safe there. Here, take this."

He handed her a cheap plastic Hollywood mask of Betty Grable. "These are all the rage among jokers in New York—so they can hide their faces from 'nats,' naturals. They may catch on here, too." She took the mask and he added urgently, "Now go, before the pier closes for the night. If you stay here, someone will eventually discover you and it won't end well."

"Thank you so much, Officer—what do I call you?"

"You don't," he said with a smile. "But I'll keep an eye on you."

The eye in his palm winked at her.

He closed his hand and moved away into the shadows.

Trina put on the mask but was still terrified at the thought of driving all the way to Santa Monica at nine in the evening, when there would be plenty of other cars on the road—but thirty minutes later she made it, without incident, to the famous arched sign at the pier that read SANTA MONICA in bright red letters, and below that, YACHT HARBOR * SPORT FISHING * BOATING * CAFES.

She parked in the nearby beach lot and, mask on, made her way up to the pier. No one gave a second glance to "Betty Grable" because she wasn't the only one here wearing a mask of some kind. She heard the Wurlitzer organ in the carousel building playing the "Blue Danube" waltz, which brought back comforting childhood memories of the pier—merry-go-round rides and cotton candy—and slowly made her way past the cafés, bait and tackle shops, seafood retailers, concession booths, "palm reader and adviser" Doreena, and a building that announced itself as—

DR. PINK'S SHOW OF FREAKS.

Oh my God, thought Trina.

Posters advertised a frog-faced man, a human torso, a bearded lady, a weightlifter with biceps bigger than his head, and other acts.

This was her "refuge"? To work in a *freak* show?

"Step right up," cried the tall, ruddy-faced man at the barker's stand, "see the most amazing collection of human oddities this side of—New York City!" That brought a laugh from the large crowd. It made Trina sick, but it drove people up to the ticket stand with their dollars.

Trina was embarrassed, afraid, angry. She waited until the crowd was on their way inside, then went up to the barker and said in a tone edged with resentment and sarcasm: "Are you—Dr. Pink?"

She raised up her mask, exposing her face to him, and he took in her features with—not horror, not revulsion, but actual sympathy.

"Oh, you poor girl," he said softly, and the pity in his voice was not what she had expected. "Come with me, dear. Come inside."

"Why? Just to be another 'human oddity' to be gawked at?"

"No no, of course not," he said. "Please, come into my office, we can talk there." He turned to the ticket taker. "Jack, take over the pitch, will you? I'll be back as soon as I can."

He took Trina around the building that housed the freak show to the rear, where he led her into a small office and shut the door behind them. "May I get you something? Water? Food? A shot of tequila?"

She wasn't sure if that was a joke but replied, "I'll take the tequila."

He smiled, took out a bottle from a desk drawer, poured two shots. "I'm Irving Pinkoff. And your name is . . . ?"

"Trina. Trina Nelson." The warmth of the tequila took a little of the edge off her anger. "I was told to come here for—'refuge.'"

"Yes, my dear, that is what we offer. But let me explain.

"My show has been on this pier for five years, and I assure you, I don't really think of my employees as 'oddities.' They're all human beings, all friends. This is the only way most of them can make a living and they know what I have to do to sell them to the public. It's all show business."

He downed his shot. "The owner of this pier, Walter Newcomb, came to me a few days after the virus hit LA. A relative of his had been—changed—and was hounded out of his neighborhood. He asked me if I would take the young man in to protect him and I said yes, of course. He's the frog-faced lad, Robby, on the poster.

"Word somehow got out that there was a real joker in the show—and business actually increased. People may not want jokers living next door, but apparently, they're happy to pay money to see them as entertainment.

"Next thing I knew, more jokers were coming out of the woodwork, begging me to take them in. What could I say? Mr. Newcomb provides living quarters for them—some above the Hippodrome, some downstairs where the lifeguards used to stay until they became 'uncomfortable' with their new neighbors. A lot of the vendors here were uncomfortable, too, and abandoned the pier . . . and jokers with money took over the leases. Why, there's even talk of opening a joker nightclub next to the carousel."

"And the owner is fine with all this?" Trina asked skeptically.

"As long as the pier turns a profit, yes. Walter's met my performers; he knows they're just people who have been dealt a bad hand."

"Why are *you* doing this, Mr. Pinkoff? Someone set my house on fire. This is risky for you, too."

"I had family who died at Dachau," he said, and didn't need to say more. Trina nodded. "Now, let's get you some living quarters, all right?"

He showed her to her new home, an apartment above the carousel building with a turret room overlooking the surf lapping up Santa Monica Beach. The sight of the beach and the city beyond greeted her like an old friend thought forever lost. And for the first time in weeks, she began to feel—*safe*. Protected. Tears welled in her eyes, unbidden.

"Thank you," she told him. "Oh God, *thank* you, Mr. Pinkoff."

As the tears turned into sobs, Mr. Pinkoff wrapped his arms around her and let her cry. "Call me Irv."

Being in the freak show was hard at first, but the other performers—both jokers and non-jokers—made her feel welcome. She put up with the gawks and catcalls ("Oink! Oink!" the kids liked to shout at her) for three months until the Menagerie nightclub opened, and she quickly secured a job as a cocktail waitress. The skimpy costume was straight out of Frederick's of Hollywood, but it was a small price to pay; the clientele was both jokers and nats and the gawking was somewhat more tolerable here.

Her friend with the third eye had been right about something else: within weeks a new store opened on the pier, opened by a once-famous French character actor, now known only as Anonyme (Anonymous) and constantly masked to hide his presumably deformed features. La Jetée de Masques carried everything from plush hooded cloaks, dark veils, Halloween fright masks, Hollywood movie star masks, to even macabre replicas of actual plaster "death masks" of Hollywood celebrities, the latter starting at a hundred bucks a pop. La Jetée de Masques was an instant success with jokers who wanted a respite from the gawkers who came to the pier, or who simply ached to go out to a movie or take a walk without being shunned or taunted.

Trina tried going out wearing her Betty Grable mask a few times, but the mask itself practically announced she was a joker and she could still feel people's apprehension and fear as they passed her with a sideways glance. And when HUAC (and later, Joseph McCarthy) began attacking the aces—genuine American *heroes,* for God's sake—she realized that none of them, aces *or* jokers, was truly safe, and she only donned a mask and left the pier to buy groceries or visit doctors.

Fourteen years after she arrived, she was still at the Menagerie, and the pier had evolved into a full-blown Jokertown, reviled by the bluenoses in LA but self-supporting and profitable. Walter Newcomb died in 1955, but his family remained committed to the pier's independence even in the face of the vitriol of anti-joker columnists like Hedda Hopper.

These days she worked the late shift on weekends and first shift—afternoons—during the week. This made it easier for her to avoid Bongo's ardent tentacles (in the heat of day he was cooling his heels in one of the refrigerated hotel units up the pier). In the afternoon, the customers were less drunk and more intent on watching joker dancers like Iris, whose invisible epidermis allowed her blood, skeleton, and internal organs to be seen twirling around the stripper's pole. Her billing was "Iris, the Human X-Ray."

On Trina's first late shift of the next weekend, Bongo was back—but quick to apologize for his behavior the previous weekend. "I'm, like, on the wagon, I promise," he said. She accepted the apology and was impressed when Bongo ordered club soda instead of Jim Beam—and did so for the rest of the evening. He still gazed at her like a lovelorn calf, but he kept his arms to himself, and that was just fine with her.

Celebrities were nothing new to the pier, whether it was actors with a casual curiosity about what went on here, or those like the late Brant Brewer, star of the *Captain Cathode* TV show, whose sexual proclivities for jokers had been well known here. But the short, dark-haired man who strode up the pier today was someone new.

It was a hot August day and he was comfortably wearing slacks and a polo shirt and not the suit and tie most of America was used to seeing him in—but there was no mistaking his face, his voice, or the lit cigarette he held clenched in one hand. Bob Louden—once the frog-faced boy at Pink's freak show, now the concessionaire who ran the shooting gallery—saw him and quipped, "Hey, man, you're too late. We're already *in* the Twilight Zone."

Rod Serling laughed a warm, hearty laugh, approached the frog-faced man, and extended a hand without hesitation. "Call me Rod."

"I'm Bob."

"Let me try my hand at your game. See if my shooting has improved any since the war."

Word quickly spread that the man behind *The Twilight Zone* was here, shaking hands with everyone he met—jokers or nats—chatting, laughing, signing autographs. Irv Pinkoff gave Serling a guided tour of the freak show, and he greeted everyone in it as the professional performers they were and, most importantly of all, as people. He seemed absolutely genuine and totally unlike the usual Hollywood assholes who visited Jokertown.

By the time he walked into the Menagerie, Trina had heard he was here and thought maybe he was too good to be true. When he sat down at one of her tables and lit a cigarette, she duly approached him with her standard question: "Hi, I'm Trina. Get you something to drink?"

He took in her face and just smiled warmly. Not even a flicker of disgust. "Nice to meet you, Trina, I'm Rod. I'll have a scotch."

She nodded, got his scotch at the bar, and when she returned, he had already smoked his cigarette down to a nub. He stubbed it out in an ashtray, thanked her for the drink, then downed it in one swallow.

She studied him a moment, then couldn't help noting, "You don't . . . sound like you do on your show."

He laughed, a warm, infectious laugh. "You mean my 'television voice'? That's what my daughters call it."

She smiled. "Can I ask you something?"

He lit another cigarette. "Sure."

"Why are you here? At the pier?"

He took a drag on his cigarette and exhaled a plume of smoke. "Ah. Short question, long answer. Set me up again and I'll tell you."

She obliged, but when she brought him another shot, he didn't down it right away. "As you obviously know," he said, "I produce a show called *The Twilight Zone*."

"Yes, I've seen it, when I'm not on shift here." She hesitated, then added, "I think my favorite is the one about the man who . . . walks back in time. To his childhood. I . . . I really liked that one."

Serling seemed to take in the wistfulness in her tone and nodded. "Yes. I think we all yearn to return to our youth, for one reason or another. I know I do." He took a swallow of scotch. "*The Twilight Zone* has been extremely fortunate. It's been a Top Ten show ever since its debut. And I think that has a lot to do with the world we've all been living in since September of 1946. If people hadn't already seen the reality of spacemen and people with strange abilities, *Twilight Zone* might be languishing in the ratings right now, instead of being at the top."

"So?"

"So . . . I'd like to acknowledge that. I'd like to do something for those of you who have been most adversely affected by the wild card virus. I want to break the blacklist against jokers appearing on TV."

Trina was taken aback by that. "Wow. Really? What about Hedda Hopper?"

Serling grinned. "Fuck Hedda Hopper."

Trina laughed. Serling went on, "Our ratings give me a certain amount of capital with the network, and this is how I choose to spend it."

Another customer came in, Trina apologized and went to take the man's order. When she came back, Serling startled the hell out of her by asking, "Trina, have you ever done any acting?"

"Uh . . . I played Patty in *Junior Miss* in high school. But there is no way in hell I'd show *this* face on television!"

Serling said gently, "It's not your features that got my attention. You have kind eyes and a sweet voice. That's what I need in this particular story. It's a parable about the dangers of conformity . . . it's called 'The Eye of the Beholder.' I wrote it specifically with the joker situation in mind. I hope you won't be offended by it—it's meant to shock, but then to play against viewers' expectations.

"I can have the script messengered to you tomorrow, and if you're interested, I'd like to bring you in to audition for the director, Doug Heyes."

Audition? *Her?* For a TV show? Was this real? But this man wasn't like the usual producer who came to the club, promising stardom to joker women (or men), then inviting them back to his place to talk it over. Rod Serling was all business.

"You don't understand. I—we—we're all safe here. I don't want to do anything to jeopardize that."

"I do understand that, Trina. But wouldn't you like more out of life than you can have on this pier? This—pardon my expression—ghetto?"

Trina had never described the Jokertown on the pier with that word, but hearing it come from Serling it sounded . . . sadly appropriate.

She hesitated before replying, "Well . . . it couldn't hurt to read the script."

"That's great. Thank you, Trina. Write down your address and it'll be delivered tomorrow morning."

Trina scribbled down her name and address on his bar chit. He took the chit and paid for his six dollars of scotch with a fifty-dollar bill. "Keep the change. I'll write my office number on the script . . . call me if you have any questions."

He left, leaving Trina shocked, bewildered, and a little terrified.

The next morning a messenger rapped on the door to her apartment. The young man had obviously been warned about her appearance, but she still saw a glint of fear in his eyes as he stared at her. "Uh, delivery from MGM Studios," he said, handing her a manila envelope, then beating it out of there as quickly as he could.

She had three hours before her shift began at the club, so she sat down and opened the envelope. She slid out the twenty-six-page script, and there was a note attached to it:

> Trina, I hope you'll be intrigued by this story. The role you'd be auditioning for is the Room Nurse. Also enclosed are the "sides," the scene that will be used for your audition.
>
> Best Wishes,
> Rod Serling

Trina started reading. The story was set in a hospital in what appeared to be some sort of future society that prizes "glorious conformity" and condemns "diversification." The main character, Janet Tyler, is a woman whose face is wrapped in bandages. We never see her face, nor, according to the script, do we get a clear view of the nurses and doctors around her. Apparently, Janet is horribly deformed, and the other characters talk about her behind her back with a mix of pity and disgust. But her doctor and the room nurse are kind and sensitive when dealing with her. As Janet waits for the day when the bandages are removed to see if her treatment was successful, we learn that in this society only eleven such treatments are allowed—after that the patient must be sent to "a special area where others of your kind have been congregated." The parallels were clear: the "special area" is a ghetto, not unlike the one in which Trina was living.

But then Janet's bandages are removed, and contrary to expectations she is a "startlingly beautiful" woman—and when we finally see the doctors and nurses, *they* are the deformed ones: "Each face is more grotesque than the other."

Trina felt a flash of anger that she had been offered this role because of her own "grotesque" appearance. But who was she kidding? That's what she was. And by the end of the script—after Janet tries to run away, only to be gently captured by the doctor and nurse—Serling's intent became crystal clear. Janet is introduced to a handsome man from the "special" area where her kind are segregated. At first, because she shares the same cultural standards of her society, she is repulsed by his appearance. But he gently reminds her of an old saying: "A very, very old saying . . . beauty is in the eye of the beholder."

Trina put the script down. She was buzzing with nervous apprehension at the idea of showing her face on network television after hiding here on the pier for fourteen years. But maybe, she thought, America needed to see her face. Needed to see themselves as the monsters and to see jokers like her as real people and not freaks. It seemed to her that this script—this show—could be the equivalent of those sit-ins in Greensboro, North Carolina, for Negro civil rights. Not a solution, but a necessary first step.

When she looked at it that way . . . she could hardly say no.

◆

Even so, she asked permission from her fellow residents on the pier: "This could affect you too," she said. The majority of them told her to do it: "What more can they do to us?" Iris the dancer asked. "Screw 'em if they can't take the heat." Trina called Serling and said she'd audition; his secretary told her to come in at one p.m. the next day, and a car would be sent to pick her up at noon.

The following day, Trina put on a Doris Day mask—*Que será, será!*—as she waited at the foot of the pier. At noon, a big black limousine picked her up, the driver studiously betraying no reaction when she took the mask off once inside. He drove her through downtown Santa Monica on their way to the MGM Studios, where *Twilight Zone* was filmed, in Culver City. The car windows were tinted so no one could see in, but Trina could look out without fear of being seen. She felt a thrill, tinged with melancholy, as she gazed out at the familiar streets of her childhood. Even more thrilling was when the limo approached the entrance gate to MGM, a grand mock-Greek colonnade with a sign proclaiming it as METRO-GOLDWYN-MAYER. All at once it was 1939 again and she was nine years old, sitting in Loew's Theatre as the MGM lion roared at the start of *The Wizard of Oz*. But this part was far from Oz, just a collection of drab, nondescript office buildings and soundstages; it was here the limo driver dropped her off, at the production offices for *Twilight Zone*.

Trina took a deep breath and entered. Inside it looked like an ordinary business office with secretaries sitting at desks typing or answering phones. She stopped at the first desk, cleared her throat, and said, "Excuse me. I'm Trina Nelson, I'm here to see Mr. Heyes?"

Clearly the staff had been prepared for her and the secretary just smiled at her. "Of course, they're waiting for you. Follow me." She led Trina to Mr. Heyes's office and opened the door.

"Miss Nelson is here."

Serling got up from a chair and clasped her hand in welcome. "Trina, thanks for coming in. We're all excited to hear you read."

There were a lot more people here than she had expected. "You mean I'm supposed to do this out loud?" she joked. Everyone laughed.

Serling introduced her to the producer, Buck Houghton, a distinguished-looking man with silver-gray hair; the casting director, Ethel Winant, who wore black spectacles and had conservatively cropped brown hair; and the episode's director, Douglas Heyes, a handsome man with a high forehead. "Thank you for coming in, Trina," Heyes said, shaking her hand. "I know this couldn't have been an easy decision for you."

They all sat in chairs opposite one for Trina.

"It's a really good script," Trina said nervously. "I hope my reading won't embarrass you, Mr. Serling."

"Please—Rod. And I'm sure it won't."

Ethel Winant explained, "I'll be reading the part of Janet Tyler in the scene with you, Miss Nelson."

Trina nodded and took out her "sides." This was it—showtime.

Heyes noted, "Rod's description of the room nurse is 'firm first, kindly second.' Firm, not hard—we want to hear that kindness, that sympathy in her voice. And since we don't see her face for much of the story . . ."

Surprisingly, he got up, turned his chair around, and sat facing *away* from Trina. "I'm doing this with all the actors. I want to hear their voices only, as if we were casting a radio play."

Trina, startled, looked to Serling, who saw her unease, smiled, and said, "I started in radio and now I seem to be back in it." He laughed that infectious laugh of his, which eased Trina's nervousness.

She and Ethel Winant ran through the scene together:

Ethel said, "Nurse?"

Trina fought back a flurry of anxiety and read the line: "Brought you your sleeping medicine, honey."

"Is it night already?"

The dialogue was mostly chitchat for the next page, until they came to Janet's line "When . . . when will they take the bandages off? How long?"

Trina put hesitation, awkwardness, and yet a gentleness in her reply: "Until . . . until they decide whether they can fix up your face or not."

"Janet" talked about how bad she knew she looked, remembering how people had always turned away from her and how the first thing she remembered was a little child "screaming when she looked at me."

Tears welled in Trina's eyes as Ethel read Janet's speech about never wanting to be beautiful, or even loved—she just wanted people not to scream when they looked at her. Trina struggled to keep her emotions in check. Then "Janet" asked again when the bandages would come off, and that was Trina's cue.

The sympathy, the kindness, in Trina's voice was more than just acting.

"Maybe tomorrow," she said. "Maybe the next day. You've been waiting so long now . . . it really doesn't make too much difference whether it's two days or weeks now, does it?"

And that was the end of the scene. Trina exhaled in relief. She looked up to see Serling and Miss Winant gazing raptly at her. Did that mean she did well or did terribly?

Doug Heyes got up, turned around, and said quietly, "That was very nice, Trina. Would you excuse us a moment as we compare notes?"

Oh God, Trina thought as she stepped out of the office. *They hated me! Will they give me a second chance?*

She waited by the secretary's desk for thirty long seconds, and then the office door burst open and Doug Heyes, a big smile on his face, extended a hand to her and said, "Welcome to the Twilight Zone, Trina."

Serling smiled and quipped, "He stole my line." Everyone laughed. "Congratulations, Trina."

There was barely time for her to feel her elation before business matters took over. Ethel produced a contract and explained, "You'll be paid six hundred dollars for a three-day shoot. Is that acceptable, Miss Nelson?"

This sounded like a fortune compared to what Trina made at the Menagerie. "Yes. Fine."

"We built an extra day into the schedule," Heyes said, "so I can give you a crash course in acting for television. I'll be blocking out the actors' moves more than usual, to avoid tipping the ending to the audience." He put a reassuring hand on her shoulder. "Now we've got to get you to makeup so we can cast a mold of your face."

"A mold? Why?"

"Because we'll be basing the makeup on your features, and from the mold we'll be making rubber appliances for the other actors . . ."

He took her to the makeup department and introduced her to the makeup artist, William Tuttle, a friendly man with dark hair, a mustache, and glasses. She sat in a chair as plaster was applied to the top half of her face—everything but her mouth and eyes—and then sat there as the plaster hardened. To keep her relaxed, Tuttle told her about some of the movies he'd worked on: *Singin' in the Rain, The Time Machine, North by Northwest, Jailhouse Rock* with Elvis Presley . . .

"You worked with Elvis?" she gasped, and Tuttle regaled her with Elvis stories until the plaster mold had hardened and was removed.

By the end of the day Trina was exhausted but exhilarated. The limo got her home at seven o'clock; she fed Ace and was putting a Banquet chicken dinner in the oven when there was a knock on her door.

She opened it to find Irving Pinkoff standing there, looking at her expectantly. "Well?"

"I got the part!" she nearly shouted. "I'm going to be on television!"

He embraced her proudly. "Good girl, I knew you would!"

"I didn't! I was terrified."

"Trina, this is so important what you're doing," he said, smiling. "For everyone on this pier, and . . . everywhere else."

"I wouldn't be here—literally—if not for you, Irv. All of us."

"I'm the one whose life has been the richer for that," he said, and hugged her again. Then, with a wink: "Break a leg, my dear."

♥

In that extra day of pre-production, Heyes coached Trina in the craft of acting for the camera—how to hit your marks and "not bump into the furniture"; how, in close-ups, to ignore the sound of the camera as film runs through the sprockets—and she quickly grew to trust this smart, talented, nice man. On a coffee break she asked what other shows he had worked on, and she was delighted to discover that he had written and directed some of the best episodes of her favorite show, *Maverick*.

Trina now also had more time to memorize the script. It had been a long time since that class production of *Junior Miss* and even though "Eye of the Beholder" was shorter, it was a long way from a supporting role in a high school play. She sat at her dining table overlooking the beach and read—and re-read, and read again—not only her lines but those of the other actors, so she knew her cues.

There was a standard day of rehearsal, at which Trina met her fellow actors—Maxine Stuart, playing the role of the bandaged Janet Tyler, and Donna Douglas, who would play Janet after the bandages came off; William Gordon, who played Janet's doctor; George Keymas, who portrayed (on TV screens) the Leader of this conformist society; Edson Stroll, the handsome outcast; and Joanna Heyes, Doug's wife, who had a small part as the reception nurse. They all seemed like lovely people and treated Trina like one of them—that is, a nat.

The blocking was complicated, and Trina tried not to show her anxiety as she watched, listened, and followed instructions. Heyes's plan was to not show the faces of any of the doctors and nurses, without making it seem as if that information was being deliberately withheld: "The way I see it is this is Janet Tyler's viewpoint; she can't see anyone around her, so the viewers can't either. Here's hoping they buy into that, however subconsciously." This involved some fancy camerawork and cinematography:

the set was shadowed, reflecting Janet's "inner darkness," and in certain scenes those shadows would obscure characters' faces. Overhead shots would show only the top of their heads; in others, only the back of their heads, which looked perfectly normal, especially in shadowy rooms. Actors would also pass in front of one another, obscuring each other's faces, or walk behind screens that revealed only a silhouette. She was relieved to see that even the seasoned cast found the blocking challenging to memorize.

She had a seven o'clock call the next morning and when she showed up on the soundstage, she found the rest of the cast already there—they had been there for hours, having the makeup prostheses applied. Trina stopped short when she saw seven people—nine, if you counted a couple of background extras—all of whom looked *exactly like her*. It was shocking, disorienting—and somehow highly amusing.

"We look like a family reunion!" she cried out, and everyone, including crew, broke into laughter.

Trina was in the first scene, playing opposite poor Maxine Stuart, her head wrapped in bandages. But it got off to a bumpy start when Trina flubbed her line in the first take, then missed her mark a few camera setups later, during a tracking shot. Feeling (or imagining) the eyes of everyone on the set on her, she quipped, "Who's the joker that screwed up that shot?"—a familiar kind of joker self-deprecation around nats, but it got the laugh she sought, dissipating the tension.

"Back to one!" the assistant director called out, and all the actors went back to their starting positions. And Trina made damn sure not to miss her mark again.

During the next setup, one of the extras—a young woman in her twenties whose makeup made her almost a twin of Trina's—came up to her: "It's no big deal, honey, everybody flubs a line now and then."

"Thanks," Trina said, "but I just feel like such an amateur."

"They knew you were inexperienced when they hired you, but they wouldn't have done that if they didn't think you could deliver the goods." This made Trina smile gratefully. The woman held out a hand. "I'm Suzie. Suzie Ludwick."

"Trina Nelson."

"This your first time on a movie lot?"

"This is my first time *anywhere*, almost."

"Well you picked a good place for your first job. Listen, when we break for lunch, I'll show you around the lot, okay?"

None of the actors in "joker" makeup could eat a normal lunch, only milkshakes or chocolate malts they could sip through straws. (Maxine's "bandages" had a zipper in back and she could remove them as needed.) Trina, of course, could eat anything she wanted—she took a sandwich off the craft services table as Suzie, sipping her milkshake, led her out of the soundstage and onto the MGM backlot. Trina felt self-conscious at first, but she quickly realized that of everyone they passed—actors, crew carrying equipment, people driving golf carts to and from soundstages—none of them was paying Trina and Suzie the slightest attention, though they both looked as if they'd dropped in from Jupiter.

"This is Hollywood," Suzie said with a shrug. "Nothing's real."

Trina basked in her newfound anonymity.

Suzie took her over to Lot 2, one of six backlots that MGM owned, and into a genuine wonderland. First Trina marveled at a partial re-creation of New York City's waterfront docks and a ship's gangway that led up to a convincing replica of the midsection of an ocean liner. Next, they walked down ersatz New England streets—a filling station, a malt shop, a tree-lined village square—that Trina recognized from old Andy Hardy movies. She passed the empty shells of typical American houses that achingly reminded Trina of her old neighborhood on Ashland Avenue, and stood there a moment, wishing this could be real, wishing one of the front doors would open and her parents would come out and wave to her. She quickened her pace as they passed a faux but depressing cemetery, to a delightfully French courtyard used in *The Three Musketeers*.

They continued past a small-town railroad depot to an amazing mock-up of Grand Central Station (where a film crew was shooting in the working interior set). A few steps later Trina was on a Chinese street lined with pagodas, palaces, docks, even sampans floating on the man-made waterfront. Just beyond the Chinese street was a horseshoe-shaped space that at one end was a stunning re-creation of a street in Verona, Italy—fountains, ornate colonnades, mosaics—and at the other, the Moorish architecture of a street in Spain, which made Trina think of the Hippodrome, which itself was kind of a set.

Trina was amazed at the sheer size, the vastness of these lots—and they only had time to see half of what was here on Lot 2!

"Well," Trina joked, "I always did want to travel the world."

Suzie smiled a little sadly at that. "There's lots more on this lot and the others. We can do this tomorrow at lunchtime too if you want."

"Yes, I'd like that."

Suzie glanced at her watch. "We'd better be getting back."

The rest of the day's shoot proceeded smoothy, but before they broke for the day new script pages were distributed—and Trina quailed to see that it was a new scene between herself and Bill Gordon, who played the doctor. "Rod felt we needed someone who, in private at least, challenges the rules of conformity," Doug Heyes explained to her, "and who better to do that than you?"

Trina gulped but managed a thin smile. Oh God, more lines to memorize!

The studio limo picked her up and whisked her home to the pier. A crowd of friends gathered around her, curious as to how the day had gone; she answered their questions as quickly as she could before hurrying into her apartment, feeding Ace, and studying her new lines over a pastrami sandwich. And as she read the lines, she understood what Doug had meant, and why she had to say them. She only hoped she could do justice to Rod's dialogue.

♣

The next day she arrived palpably nervous, even more so when she saw that her new scene with Bill Gordon was first up to shoot. Maxine Stuart tried to calm Trina's jitters by telling her about her own acting debut, at the age of nineteen, in a short-lived ("We closed after a week!") Broadway play called *Western Waters*. "I was so nervous the first night, I thought I was going to throw up on Van Heflin," she admitted. "Today is your second day, you're practically an old veteran."

Trina laughed along with her, grateful for her kindness.

The new scene was set in a hospital "break room" where Trina's nurse spoke sympathetically of her patient:

"I've seen her face, doctor, under those bandages ... I've seen deeper than that pitiful, twisted lump of flesh."

Trina was glad the camera couldn't see the tears in her eyes as she delivered this line.

"I've seen her *real* face," she went on. "It's a *good* face. It's a *human* face. What's the dimensional visual difference between beauty and something we see as repellent? Skin deep? No, it's more than that."

Then, with a righteous anger she didn't need to fake, she implored, "Why, doctor? Why shouldn't people be *allowed* to be different?"

When the doctor warns that such talk is considered treason, the nurse backs off. "Don't be concerned, doctor, I—I'll be all right."

A short scene, but for Trina it was as if Serling had seen inside her mind and put into words all of her pain, rage, and resentment.

She had occasion to tell him this in person when Serling dropped by the set unannounced at the end of the day and said to her, "I hope you don't have plans for lunch tomorrow. I've made reservations for us at the MGM commissary." She looked startled and he explained, "It's your last day. We need to commemorate it in appropriate style."

"But—I'm a joker," she said.

"So? Besides, when you walk in with Rod Serling, the kook who writes that kooky *Twilight Zone,* everyone will assume you're in makeup and not give you a second thought. What do you say, are you up for it?"

Though still nervous at the idea, Trina assured him she was.

♠

Trina was expecting to be taken to a small studio cafeteria and was shocked to be ushered instead into a palatial dining room with high ceilings and arched doorways, the décor a resplendent chrome and green. The maître d' widened his eyes when he saw Trina's face but, as predicted, he then looked at Rod and smiled. "Ah, Mr. Serling. We have your table waiting for you and your guest." He led them to a small table in the center of the packed crowd; on the way Trina was astonished to see sitting at tables such luminaries as Shirley MacLaine, Laurence Harvey, Lana Turner, and—oh my God, she thought, was that Bob Hope?

A few of them stared back with evident revulsion at her face, but then, seeing Serling, they simply turned back to their lunches.

She was so starstruck that Serling had to take her by the elbow and guide her into her chair. The maître d' handed them both menus. Trina smiled at Serling and said, "I can't believe I'm sitting here with all these stars. It's like a fairy tale."

"I felt that way too, at first. I still like walking around the lot, seeing sets from movies I watched when I was a boy growing up in Binghamton, New York." He opened up his menu. "I highly recommend the chicken soup, it's the best this side of the Carnegie Deli."

Trina was even starstruck by the menu, featuring items like the "Elizabeth Taylor Salad" and the "Cyd Charisse Salad." Though she was tempted by the "Barbecued Alaska Black Cod," she knew this would be the only time in her life she would be able to utter the words "I'll have the Elizabeth Taylor Salad," and so she did. Serling ordered the corned beef sandwich on rye and a bottle of champagne.

"We have ample reason to celebrate," Rod said, lighting the latest in a succession of cigarettes. "The dailies are looking terrific and your performance is everything I'd hoped it would be. I think this will be a—"

"Rod Serling!"

A woman's angry voice cut through the din of conversations around them. Trina looked up to see an elegantly dressed woman in her seventies, wearing a flamboyant hat and a mink stole wrapped around her shoulders like a game trophy, with bleached blond hair.

"How dare you disgrace this venerable old studio like this!" she accused.

Serling looked surprised but said dryly, "Lovely to see you too, Hedda. Is that the pelt of one of your victims you're wearing?"

"Hedda"? Jesus, Trina thought, it was Hedda Hopper! A shiver of fear ran through Trina at this woman who destroyed careers and people with words like poison darts.

Hedda ignored the insult and snapped, "So it's true—you *are* employing a 'joker' in one of your trash television shows!"

"Which one of your little spies ferreted out that information for you, Hedda?" Serling asked.

"I have my sources, and they're all good Americans. But *this*—it's bad enough you're breaking the blacklist by employing a joker, but to actually bring this revolting creature in here, while people are eating—"

Trina's hackles went up, her fear forgotten.

"She's an actress working for my company and MGM," Serling shot back, "and she has every right to be here. And 'revolting creature' is an appellation that more aptly suits you, dear Hedda."

Hedda's eyes popped: she was clearly not used to being talked back to with such amiable contempt. "Get this disgusting *freak* out of here now," she demanded, "or I'll call Sol Siegel so fast it will make your head spin!"

Trina, enraged, found herself jumping to her feet and saying: "Oh, I see. No jokers allowed. Just like those Negroes in Greensboro, North Carolina, who were refused service at the lunch counter—is that it?"

Hedda certainly didn't expect the target of her venom to fight back and was momentarily at a loss for words.

Trina was not. "Well I've got news for you, Miss Hopper," Trina said evenly. "Right now, there *are* Negroes sitting at that lunch counter in Greensboro, as is their legal right. Just as *I* have a legal right to be sitting here with Mr. Serling. And I have no intention of leaving until I've had my lunch—and maybe dessert, too!"

Unexpectedly, Trina heard—applause.

She looked around and saw at least a dozen people—among them Shirley MacLaine and Lana Turner—on their feet and applauding in solidarity with *her.*

Trina was stunned—and touched. She nodded at the people applauding her, then slowly sat back down.

Serling was grinning at this turn of events. "Now, Hedda," he said, "if you don't mind, as you yourself noted—people are eating."

Hedda, fuming, stared daggers at him but said nothing, just turned and stalked away, out of the commissary.

Serling, still grinning, said, "Trina, that was brilliant. And it took extraordinary courage."

Trina shook her head. "No, I was just pissed off."

Serling laughed. "That's what courage is sometimes—being pissed off at what's not right."

"Now I'm worrying, though. Rod, the whole country reads what that woman writes. She could do real damage to you and your show."

"I doubt it. Her rants against Dalton Trumbo and *Spartacus* haven't stopped the filming. In any event, it's worth the risk if it breaks the joker blacklist as *Spartacus* has broken the Red Scare blacklist."

Trina smiled. "You're the brave one, I think."

Serling shook his head and took a draw off his cigarette. "I'm not doing this for altogether altruistic reasons, Trina. Yes, I want the blacklist to end, but also—" He thought a moment and went on, "Look, we all like to think that writers write because they have something to say that is truthful and honest and pointed and important. And I suppose I subscribe to that, too. But God knows when I look back over my career thus far, I'm hard-pressed to come up with anything that's important. Some things are literate, some things are interesting, some things are classy, but very damn little is important.

"You—what we're doing together—this may be important. I hope it helps you and others like you. Someday, at the end of my time on this earth, that would be a fine comfort, to have been a part of this."

Trina, moved, picked up her champagne glass and held it aloft. Serling took his shot glass of scotch—and they toasted to that.

At the end of the shoot, the cast and crew surprised Trina with a goodbye cake prepared by craft services and broke open yet another bottle of champagne. Maxine Stuart told her it was an honor to have worked with her, which touched Trina deeply. Everyone wished her well and Suzie promised to drop by the pier between gigs—and she made good on her promise several times, she and Trina eating fish and chips in one of the little cafés. She even came to the viewing party the night in November that "Eye of the Beholder" aired. The Menagerie's manager closed the club for a "private party" and most of the pier's residents, many, like Anonyme, clad in festive masks, jammed inside to watch the episode. It was a powerful story and Trina was relieved that she hadn't embarrassed herself—she'd held her own with more seasoned actors. And she was proud to be the first joker in a network television series.

Hedda Hopper tried to sabotage the episode by writing venomous screeds about it and how it was another attempt by jokers and Communists to undermine American values—but it backfired, and "Eye of the Beholder" got the highest rating of any *Twilight Zone* that season. Rod gave her this news himself when he, his wife, and two daughters visited the pier that weekend. "The mail has been largely positive," he said, "except for the ones that sound as if Hedda had dictated them personally. But contrary to her dire warnings, the world as we know it has not ended."

The episode did what was intended of it: it broke the joker blacklist. The following year Reginald Rose and Herbert Brodkin cast a joker in their law series *The Defenders*, in an episode that openly discussed jokers' rights. Floodgates did not open; there wasn't so much a rush of jokers onto TV as a slow trickle. But it was a start.

The show had two unforeseen impacts on Trina's personal life. One evening after her afternoon shift, Trina looked out at an empty beach—this was November, after all—and decided to chance going for a short (if bracing) swim. When she got out of the water, she was startled to see a woman and an eight-year-old boy standing on the beach, having just come from the pier. The boy stared wide-eyed at Trina's face and she braced herself for a scream—

But instead he burst into a big smile and asked breathlessly, "Are you the *Twilight Zone* lady?"

Trina felt relief wash over her like a wave—relief and an unexpected pleasure. "Yes," she told him, "I am."

"He loves that show," the mother said. "Would you mind having your picture taken with him?"

Where am I, Trina thought, *what world is this?* But she just smiled and said, "Of course."

The little boy came running over, wrapped his left arm around Trina's legs, and smiled into the camera. A flashbulb popped, and Trina's life changed forever.

After that, whenever she was outside on the pier, tourists would stop her—"Are you the girl from *The Twilight Zone*?"—then ask for an autograph or a photo, and Trina was happy to oblige. She became popular enough that Irv Pinkoff—now getting on in years—asked her if she would come back to work for him, not inside the building but outside, helping him sell tickets. He thought her presence might boost sales, and he was right. Trina could live her life in the sun again and not inside the dark confines of the Menagerie.

The other change came at the viewing party for "Eye of the Beholder." When the episode was over, everyone applauded and congratulated Trina on her performance... including Bongo, who came up and said in the sincerest voice, "You were beautiful, Trina. You were the most beautiful one on the show."

Trina smiled at hearing this again. "Bongo, what is it about me you think is so beautiful?"

He didn't hesitate. "You have kind eyes and a sweet voice. They're, like, windows to your soul."

The words were an echo, and they shamed her into looking, really looking, at Bongo for the first time. She'd always found his attraction to her so off-putting that she never really examined his face—but now that she did, she saw that he was really kind of a sweet-looking kid, with a shy, endearing smile.

Had she been the one all along who had something to learn from "Eye of the Beholder"?

"Bongo," she asked, "do you have a real name?"

Hesitantly he admitted, "It's Harold."

"That's a nice name, Harold." She smiled. "Would you like to get some coffee later at that little espresso shack up the pier?"

Harold's eyes lit with surprise—and a happiness that made Trina awfully glad she'd asked. "I would dig that the most, Trina," he said.

What was that line of Rod's dialogue she had spoken?

Skin deep? No, it's more than that.

She was embarrassed that she, of all people, needed to be told this. A lesson to be learned, she thought... in the Twilight Zone.

♠ ♥ ♦ ♣

Hearts of Stone

by Emma Newman

Note from the author: This story contains references to, and characters from, Russia and Ukraine. It was written in 2020, and was inspired by my fear of what was then a potential war, rather than any of the devastating events unfolding in Ukraine as a result of the Russian invasion in 2022.

St. Albans, England, September 2005

"**STORIES FROM THE GREAT WAR?**" Captain Flint picked up one of the books piled on the sofa, opened it to find the library label, and then flipped through the pages. *"What made you choose this?"*

Kerry turned to look at him. He stood in the middle of the living room, a stone giant who made everything else around him seem tiny and flimsy. His eyes glowed red from deep in the sockets, and from the slight tilt of his head she deduced that he was puzzled.

She nudged the fridge shut with her backside and shrugged. "It looked interesting." She didn't tell him that she'd spotted it at the library when she was hunting for another book to feed her schlock-thriller habit and had grabbed it in the hope of finding some morsel in its pages with which to impress him.

Flint dropped the book down on the sofa and opened the French doors out onto the small patio. There was a stone bench by the fish pond that he preferred to sit on when the weather was good, and it was a fine autumn day.

"It made me think about what the men must have felt like, when they went into battle," she said, following him out with her drink.

Flint sat on the bench with a dull thud and rested his elbows on his knees, the closest he ever came to appearing relaxed. She sat on the grass next to him, her head level with his knees, and put her glass next to the pond. He stared down at the koi turning in their slow circles. *"A lot of fear before each push, and a lot of boredom in between, I imagine."*

She wondered how much of that was based on his own experience of combat. She wanted to ask him what it was like, how he'd coped, whether he'd ever been scared. But she had to pick her moments with Flint, and she had the sense that this wasn't the time. He usually visited every couple of weeks, work permitting, and it had only been six days since his last visit.

"*You had a psych evaluation a few days ago,*" he began, and her stomach sank into the grass. "*I received the report.*"

Kerry chewed her lip and pulled a lock of her curly black hair from her ponytail to twist it around her fingers. She too looked down at the koi, nervous about what he was going to say. She hadn't liked that evaluation. It was only because Flint had ordered it that she actually stuck it out.

"*She was very impressed with you.*"

Her head snapped up. "She was?"

"*You've had a lot to adjust to. And as she points out in the report, there aren't many eighteen-year-olds who have lived alone for several years and adapted so well considering the . . . challenges you have.*"

Kerry plucked a strand of grass and tore it down the middle. She had tried, very hard, to play down all the negatives. She'd shut down any discussion of what had happened with her parents. She resented even being made to think about it and for days afterward had been left with a grim emotional hangover that only miles of running and a lot of trashy movies had been able to lift.

She looked up at Flint, whose glowing eyes were now focused on her. "Well, I had a lot of help, didn't I? There are lots of people who've been through a lot worse and didn't have you to look after them."

"*Kerry . . .*"

"No, I'm serious. You gave me a safe place to live." She waved a hand at the cottage. Yes, it was a mile away from the edge of St. Albans, which had to be one of the most boring towns in England, but it was safe and secluded, and when the briefest touch could turn any living thing to granite, that was a definite advantage. "You gave me an education, and personal trainers, and . . . and you never used me."

He looked away from her then, up at the sky, leaning back and breaking the moment of connection. "*I think you credit me too much,*" he finally said. "*I facilitated these things, using resources awarded to me by my position.*"

"Yeah, but you could've done it differently. What I'm trying to say is . . ."

And then all words left her, replaced by a chaotic tumble of images, memories, snippets of days she'd worked so hard to put behind her. The first time she'd met Flint and how terrifying he was. The sight of her parents as the granite statues she'd made them into broke their bed under their weight. Waking in the cupboard beneath the stairs after her father had knocked her out, the surge of despair and physical pain in her chest when she realised that they'd used her to murder people and disguised it as art.

The breath in her lungs burned and she squeezed her eyes shut and grabbed handfuls of grass and forced herself to be where she was now. She listened to the birds and the buzzing bugs and felt the breeze in her hair and the sunlight on her face. She was safe. She was at home, and she was with Flint, and he had made sure nothing bad happened to her since the day they met. He'd only asked to see her ability once, just so he could understand. When the fox with its mangled leg was turned to stone and its suffering ended, she'd sobbed. He'd gathered her into his arms and held her. For the first time since her card had turned, she had felt safe.

"What I'm trying to say is thank you."

Flint looked back down at her and then rested his stone hand on her head and smiled. Even though he was being as gentle as he was able to be, being made out of flint meant he was still heavy and sharp in places. She knew there would probably be a few severed locks when she freed the chaotic mass of curls from the ponytail. She didn't care though.

"So," he said as he stood, in a tone that marked the end of that conversation and the beginning of a new, less emotional one. "Now that you've had your exam results and I've seen the report, I want to know what you want to do next."

"You know that. I want to join the Silver Helix."

"It's dangerous."

"Well, so am I."

"This isn't something to be flippant about."

"I'm not! I've thought about this. A lot."

He slowly paced to the middle of the lawn, leaving crushed grass and imprints in his wake. "You're bright . . . there are all sorts of opportunities in data analysis and—"

She stood too. "Oh no you don't. I want to be at the front, with the other aces. You can't keep me tucked away here forever. I want to go out there and make a difference." When he said nothing, she sat on the stone bench, trying to appear calm. "You've done so much for me. Let me contribute something for a change."

"You're sure you want to work in the field?"

"Yes! I know I won't be doing the really exciting stuff right away, but I want to have the chance to learn! You know I can take care of myself.

I've been working hard on my fear . . . I've been into London a few times. I know how to minimise the risk to other people." She didn't mention how hard it was. How she had nightmares about accidentally turning someone she brushed against into stone. How she'd taken up running so she always knew that she could get away fast.

"Mmmm . . ." Why didn't he sound convinced? *"The report did talk about how keen you are . . ."*

She held her breath, waiting for him to decide. She wanted to be in the Silver Helix and be a hero, not a monster. But more than that, she wanted to see him every day. She wanted him to need her as much as she needed him.

"There is something that would be a good first mission for you," he said slowly, as if still deciding whether it was a good idea.

Her heart fluttered at the sound of "first mission," but she stayed silent. She didn't want to seem too excitable, or he'd decide she wasn't mature enough.

"There's someone we need to put under surveillance. Came in just this morning. He's a nat, so low risk for you."

"Where is he based?"

"Central London."

Fear stabbed at her gut. Central London was crowded and chaotic and she'd only been there a handful of occasions at the quietest times of day. Her surveillance training had been in St. Albans. She didn't want to admit that the thought of a mission in London horrified her as much as it thrilled her, so she took another sip of her drink to cover as she gathered her thoughts. "Would I be working alone?"

"You'd be sharing the assignment. It might turn out to be nothing more than overcaution on our part. You'd be given a hotel room close to the target." He came over and put a hand on her shoulder. *"There's no shame in saying you're not ready yet, Kerry."*

That clinched it. She looked up into his burning coal eyes, standing as straight and tall as she could. "I'm ready."

◆

Kerry wasn't sure what she'd been expecting, but it wasn't a tiny hotel room in a converted Victorian townhouse that had seen better days. The Russian embassy was only a two-minute walk away though, and the target's accommodation less than a minute.

Three days into the assignment, all of the things she'd been worried about hadn't come to pass. It was relatively easy to avoid close contact with people in the hotel as she wasn't going in and out at peak times. The surrounding area had wide pavements and it was easy to keep her distance from other pedestrians. It had turned unseasonably cold and people were wearing scarves and gloves early, making her need to wear gloves to feel safe completely unremarkable. Everyone was so caught up in their own lives that they universally ignored her.

However, all the things she'd hoped for hadn't happened either. There were two other people involved in the surveillance, but she hadn't met them and probably wouldn't. She didn't even get to speak to them over the phone; everything was being run through two pagers, which had surprised her. When she asked Flint why they didn't use a mobile phone instead, he'd bristled at her and said the pagers were far more reliable than phones and less of a security breach if lost. She wondered if he just didn't like mobiles, but either way, there was no further discussion. She was given a pager that connected her to Flint and one that connected her to the other two agents, both of which had a simple acknowledgement button for her to press when she'd seen a message.

Flint hadn't been in touch since he briefed her, and the other pager only beeped to let her know when the target had left either a work setting or his accommodation and where she needed to pick up his trail. She was assigned to monitor his movements outside. Where he went, what he did, and who he spoke to. In the past three days he'd gone out to eat once, alone, and that was it. She was actually bored.

The target was an aide to a Russian diplomat who was in town to assist in negotiations regarding a tricky trade deal. His name was Kazimir Nazarenko, and he seemed to be the dullest man in London. Everything about him was bland, from his suit and coat to his neatly clipped greying brown hair. His face was eminently forgettable, and the only thing she thought when she first saw him was that she was going to have to work hard not to lose him if he went anywhere busy because he seemed just like any other relatively successful businessman in London.

For all his dullness though, he'd been seen coming out of a Twisted Fists hideout five days ago, which had put him on Flint's radar. There were no known connections between the Russians and the joker terrorist group. Flint was concerned that Nazarenko had delivered a message on behalf of his boss, a diplomat who had direct links to the most powerful men in Russian politics. Without any other evidence of conversations happening between the two, he was hoping that they'd caught it early.

She was hoping that her target would be more interesting over the weekend. He worked long hours and didn't seem to be interested in exploring the city. Maybe he'd been there before. She was just glad she'd bought lots of books and her Game Boy.

A knock on the door made her leap from the bed to her feet and ready to fight in moments. There was a DO NOT DISTURB notice on the door and Flint wouldn't come to see her here, he'd summon her through the pager. She breathed in deep and went to the door's spy hole as quietly as possible.

The woman standing in the hallway was definitely not a hotel employee. She was utterly beautiful with long black hair and was wearing sunglasses inside, after sunset. Kerry chewed her lip, instinctively staying quiet in the hope that the woman would go away. Maybe she had the wrong room.

The stranger ducked down out of sight, sending Kerry into a panic. There was no keyhole to look through, thankfully, just the thin gap under the door, but she was definitely still there and—and then she was inside the room.

Kerry squeaked in surprise and threw herself into the corner without thinking. Then her brain kicked into gear and realised the woman had to be an ace . . . one who could teleport, one who had found her out!

Just as Kerry was weighing up how to take her down nonlethally, the intruder smiled. "So you're Flint's latest ace in the hole. So to speak."

"Who are you?"

"Hasn't Kenneth told you about me? I'm his favourite." When Kerry shook her head, she put a hand over her heart and feigned being wounded. "That hurts. But then again, our mutual friend likes to play his cards close to his chest, doesn't he?"

"I didn't invite you in. Get out!"

The woman took off her sunglasses, revealing silver eyes. "That was rude of me. I apologise. Looks like you've realised I'm not here to kill you." She smiled, but Kerry didn't relax. "You must be Stonemaiden. You can call me Lilith."

"What do you want?"

"Two things. I needed to visit so I can extract you in an emergency. Now that I've been here, I can come and get you instantly, as soon as you need me. If something goes wrong, get back here if you can, then I can pull you out even if there are people surrounding the building or waiting for you to come out."

Flint had mentioned another ace would be brought in if there was an emergency. How else would Lilith have been able to find her? A warning would have been nice. Kerry frowned. "Do you need to touch me to do it?"

Lilith nodded. "Oh," she said at the sight of the fear that must have been blasting from her eyes. "That's a problem, is it?"

"Yeah." Why hadn't Flint mentioned that? They couldn't be absolutely certain that clothing would protect anyone from her curse and she'd refused to experiment with it.

"A fatal sort of problem, I gather, from the look on your face. What would happen if I touched you?"

Kerry pressed her lips together, her hands balling into fists tucked under her armpits.

"So you don't trust easily. I respect that. It's a good way to be in our line of work. Though you're not an official recruit yet . . . that first mission . . . ah, nothing like that buzz at being let off the leash for the first time."

The way the woman spoke unnerved her. She was so casual and calm, as if they were just passing the time like two farmers chatting over a gate. Kerry felt on edge and ready to run at any moment, but then she remembered that she could kill Lilith so very easily, if she really needed to. "What was the second thing you wanted?"

"Just a chat. I'm not going to hurt you. We're on the same team!" Somehow, even though the words were reassuring, there was something mocking in her tone.

Kerry folded her arms. "What about?"

Lilith glanced around the room, at the book that had slid onto the floor, a YA romance that made her right eyebrow twitch with amusement. She sat on the bed and undid the buttons of her coat, revealing a slinky black dress underneath. She was so graceful and . . . gorgeous. Her beauty made Kerry feel like a potato. "You. I've been hearing whispers about you for a long time. Then the whispers became arguments and the curiosity became unbearable."

She was obviously trying to suck Kerry in and make her ask more questions. She wanted something, but what?

"Flint and Enigma were arguing about you only this morning," Lilith continued nonchalantly, leaning back so she could rest against the wall. "Flint's quite emotional when it comes to you. His desk took a beating. I think he misses being able to shout."

The thought of Flint not only talking about her with someone else, but also being passionate about her, made Kerry feel . . . wait, why was Lilith bringing this up? Did she want to work out why Flint had been looking after her? Kerry couldn't fathom why she'd be so interested.

"Did Enigma say something to annoy him?"

"Mm." Lilith's eyes were scanning the pile of books on the tiny bedside cabinet, making Kerry feel horribly self-conscious. "Something about a psych report. He seems to think that Flint has been keeping you wrapped in cotton wool."

"What's that supposed to mean?"

"You tell me. I can only compare it to how Flint had me trained. How did Banger and Mash treat you?"

"Who?"

Lilith's eyes were suddenly very much focused on her. "You didn't get any physical training?"

Kerry thought of the hours of running, the punchbag sessions, and the awkward noncontact combat training that they'd tried and then written off, when they decided that progressing to anything more useful was too risky to the trainer. Besides, if anyone who was a problem got that close to her and she needed to defend herself, they would always come off worse. "Of course I did. Lots."

Lilith was all smiles again. "We don't know each other, so it must seem that I'm being horribly nosey. But the truth is . . ." She paused a little, as if hoping Kerry would reveal her real name. She didn't. "The truth is, Stonemaiden, being a newbie is hard. I don't want you to make the same mistakes I did. Flint can be really tough on new recruits, and if he's been gentle with you so far, it'll only hurt all the more when you see the . . . other side of him."

Kerry knew better than to trust anyone pretending to be kind to her. Only Flint had shown any genuine interest in her wellbeing. "Why do you care?"

Lilith shrugged. "Hearing about the new kid on the block brought back some memories. And we're going to be working together, aren't we? I want to make sure the people I work with don't get hurt."

Kerry edged around the room, keeping as far away from Lilith as possible without looking like she was trying to, until she reached the dressing table. She pulled out the stool, a rickety thing with a stained chintz cover, and perched on it. "I want this to be a success. I don't want to disappoint Captain Flint."

Lilith's smile was dazzling. "Of course you do and of course you don't. But let me give you a bit of advice. This is a surveillance mission, right? Just writing down where the target goes and what time and all that. They could get any grunt to do that. Hell, it's a nat, so even a bloody plod could handle it. No. This is actually a test."

She leaned forward. "To see how I handle boredom?"

Lilith laughed. "Only if you're doing it wrong. They're testing your initiative. It's obvious. If this were really serious, there would be three of you tailing him on the street, not just you. Just the fact that they're handing him off to you when he leaves his flat or the office speaks volumes. It's a training-wheels exercise at most, if you take it at face value."

"I don't take mission briefings at 'face value,'" Kerry said, bristling at how condescending she was being. "I listen to what they want and I do the job."

The smile turned into a smirk. "If you trail this guy for a few weeks and send in dull reports that any plod could write, they're going to conclude that that's all you're good for. You're an ace. Flint's latest recruit. He needs to see if you've got what it takes to really find out who this guy is and what he's up to. The only way to do that is to befriend the target."

"But Flint said I wasn't allowed to make direct contact. Observation only!"

"Of course he did. That's the test, don't you see? He doesn't want bloody robots in the Silver Helix. He wants bright, brave, and resourceful aces who are willing to take risks to get the intelligence he needs to keep queen and country safe. This man you're watching might be a nat, but he visited the Twisted Fists. How can you find out why he did that just by watching which restaurant he goes to? Knowing how he likes his steak isn't going to reveal whether he was opening a line of communication to the Russian government or if he's simply a bit of a prat who got tricked into going into the only bar in Guildford that gets you an audience with a joker terrorist."

Kerry didn't want it to, but what Lilith said made a lot of sense. And she had wondered about her part in the surveillance . . . it certainly didn't seem as robust as some of the more hardcore thrillers she'd read, but she'd dared not question it. For all she knew, the stuff in the novels was just totally made up. And besides, Flint might have people tapped into the London CCTV network, checking his movements too. But if that was the case, why assign her at all? Was it really a test?

Lilith had nothing to prove and couldn't possibly see her as a threat. Kerry couldn't see why she'd take the trouble to come here and give her bad advice. What if she did as Lilith suggested? She could find out so much more, and prove that she was overcoming her fear of interacting with people in close proximity. The Russian was only a nat, Flint had said, and she'd make sure he didn't get too physically close. She imagined being able to tell Flint, confidently, that he was either no risk at all . . . or the first sign of Russian collaboration with domestic terrorists. That could be huge. He'd be so impressed that she'd gone the extra mile.

"Okay," she said.

Lilith looked pleased. She pulled a small slip of paper from her pocket and put it on the bed. "That's my mobile number. Get a burner phone, put this number in it, and label it as 'home,' okay? Text me so I have your number. Don't leave this room without it. If you get into trouble, call me, any time, day or night."

Kerry nodded, thinking through the advice she'd given. "How do you find things out from people without them realising that's what you're trying to do?"

Lilith smiled broadly. "Oh, I can give you some excellent tips, don't you worry about that."

♥

It took another week of waiting and watching Kazimir read newspapers in three coffee shops before the opportunity she'd been hoping for arose.

Even though the week had been dull, it had given her a chance to think through the advice Lilith had given her and even practise it a bit. For her it was quite revelatory; most people don't assume the worst when someone strikes up a conversation with them, the woman had said. "Especially men. In fact, men like it the most."

For Kerry, any initiation of social contact sent her heart racing. What did the person want from her? What were they trying to get her to do? She found it hard to imagine that anyone would *not* feel that way, but in most cases, Lilith had argued, people felt open and curious. And if it was a young woman striking up a conversation with a man, he often felt intrigued and excited. "But why?" she'd asked.

"Because they think it could turn into something more."

"Yeah, but not every time, not every conversation, surely?"

Lilith had shrugged. "Maybe not consciously. And maybe they just like the thought of it, but know it won't be anything more. But trust me . . . men like talking to young women, and most spend a huge amount of time and effort working out how to make young women want to talk to them. You see everyone as a threat. They see every woman as a prospect. It's a fundamentally different worldview."

"Not *all* men, though," she said, thinking of Flint. But Lilith had just remained silent.

She tried it out at the coffee shop across the street from the restaurant where Nazarenko had been eating. She asked the man at the next table if he'd finished with his newspaper—an older man in his fifties, a similar age to her target. He'd smiled, passed it over, and made a comment about how there wasn't much news today, just gossip. That had been her opening. She'd agreed with him—another tip from Lilith—and made a comment about how much attention was paid to celebrities when there were real problems to focus on.

And it had worked! They chatted for twenty minutes, until the man finished his coffee and cake, got up, wished her a good day and said how much he'd enjoyed talking with her, and left! It was the boost in confidence that she needed.

On a rainy Thursday evening, Kerry followed Nazarenko to a large bookshop with late opening hours and decided to take the risk of going in to browse near him.

He went to the thrillers section. Heart thrumming, Kerry picked a book off a nearby shelf and pretended to read the blurb on the back as she kept an eye on his movements. She wondered if he was looking for a dead drop, or a specific edition of a book in order to crack a cipher. Then she reined her thoughts in. This was real, not some schlock spy rubbish.

Another man came in and drifted over to the same section. She couldn't help getting excited at the prospect of some sort of exchange or meetup with a Twisted Fists contact. She did her best to memorise everything about what the second man was wearing: a perfectly nondescript suit and wet overcoat, similar to the target. It being a working day in London, neither of them looked out of place at all. Nazarenko plucked a book out that she'd read and flipped to the opening chapter. The other man picked up the latest from one of the big-name authors and browsed some more.

"Excuse me," Nazarenko said to the other man, his Ukrainian accent soft and pleasant. "Have you read this book? Is it good?"

Kerry held her breath. Was this a coded message to identify each other?

"Oh, yeah, it's crap," the man said disparagingly. "Don't bother. Stick with the greats." He waved the book he was holding up. "You know what you're getting, and there's none of that politically correct crap in it, know what I mean?"

Nazarenko nodded politely, but the initial friendliness she'd seen in his face had gone. The other man grabbed a second book and went off to the till while her target continued to browse. "I've read that one," she said with a shy smile. "I liked it. I don't think it's as good as his second series though. I think he got better as a writer."

Nazarenko turned and smiled at her. She found herself warming to him immediately. He was in his late fifties, not particularly handsome but not terrible to look at either, with kind grey-blue eyes. "What is first book of other series?"

She scanned the shelf and tapped the spine before drawing back, not daring to take it out and pass it to him. "That one."

He pulled it out and read the back. "It look interesting."

"Oh, it is. I read it after a whole bunch of Scandi-noir and it was really refreshing."

"I'm sorry . . . Scandi-noir? I'm not familiar with that word."

And then they chatted about books for a while, and it was . . . easy. She felt like a normal person, the sort who goes out and has friends. She was working so hard to be all the things that Lilith had told her to be, while in the back of her mind she was absolutely fizzing with the thrill of conversation with another human being. One who wasn't made of flint.

The conversation reached its natural conclusion and they both bought books and smiled at each other when they left. She took care to go in the opposite direction, rounded a corner, and then pulled out a tragic anorak from her rucksack. She put it on, tugged the hood over her hair, and then doubled back to pick up his trail. As hoped, he was heading straight back to his apartment building, where she handed over to the other agent on duty there with her pager.

That night she barely slept. She replayed the conversation in her head, even though she'd written down as much of it as she could remember as soon as she got back to her room. On Lilith's advice, she kept the movement log exactly as she'd been maintaining it before, using a separate notebook to keep track of her extra efforts. She planned to keep up the pretence of following the mission briefing to the letter, and then delivering the big report at the end of the assignment. Then she could demonstrate she'd done both. Captain Flint would be so impressed.

But it wasn't fantasising about Flint's approval that kept her awake. It was how much she'd enjoyed the conversation. She knew it was sheer luck that her bookish ways had helped to break the ice, and that it wasn't actually that big of a deal, compared to the average person. But she wasn't average. Since her card had turned, she'd had an in-person conversation that lasted longer than one minute with . . . six people . . . seven if she included Nazarenko.

When she followed him on his usual walk to work, she desperately wanted to talk to him again, and knew that she shouldn't be feeling that way. The need eased as the days went by, and it helped that the book she'd bought was really good. She managed to focus on the mission, mindful of Lilith's advice.

♣

Then, five days later, Nazarenko went to a coffee shop and she saw her chance to find out more.

Kerry pretended not to notice him when she went up to the counter to order her drink and continued the pretence as she sat a couple of tables away. It was pouring rain again and the place was less than half full, leaving a clear table between them. She sat side-on to him, took off her gloves, pulled her book from her rucksack, and started reading.

"Ah, hello again!"

The accent was unmistakeable. Her smile was genuine when she looked across at him. "Oh, hi! How was the book?"

"Excellent, thank you for recommendation. I'm two chapters from end."

She held up her book. "Same."

"Apologies. I leave you to read."

"No, it's fine." She closed the book and put it away.

"May I join you?" He gestured to her table. When she nodded, he picked up his coffee and coat and sat opposite her. "Thank you. It's nice to have someone to share coffee with."

"I don't know anyone in London either," she said.

"Oh, I know people here. I just don't want to have coffee with them." They both chuckled at that. "No, my colleagues are good people. They just want to talk about work. Not books."

"What do you do?"

"I'm diplomatic aide. My boss is here for big trade talks, maybe you see them on news?"

She shook her head. "I don't watch the news. It sounds important. Do you help with the negotiations?"

He smiled. "No. I am not diplomat. I am good at legal documents and looking for loopholes. It is quite important but also very boring. My name is Kazimir."

He held his hand out across the table and she almost panicked. She gave a small, awkward wave and picked up her mug, a giant one that merited the use of both hands, thankfully. "I'm Clare."

After the briefest moment he covered the rejected handshake by reaching for the sugar. "Do you work in London?"

"No, I'm looking at colleges. I'm thinking about studying here."

The conversation flowed so easily between them. She actually enjoyed the lies she told, like it was a game, pretending to be someone else. They talked about the differences between coffee shops in Moscow and in London, and the similarities too. They discussed books and life as a diplomatic aide. Kazimir was so friendly that she almost felt guilty that she was spying on him.

They ordered a second drink and talked about films and what to do in London as a tourist. He was unmarried; when he told her, he hastily added that he wasn't looking for a young wife, that he was old enough to be her grandfather. The way he insisted that he had no designs on her was endearing. But how was she supposed to find out what he was doing when he went to that hideout?

"What are you going to study?" he asked.

"I was thinking about English lit, or history. Not sure."

"What do your parents think?"

"They're dead."

It just came out. She'd relaxed so much, even when lying, that the truth sounded harsh and ugly.

"I am sorry you lost so much so young," he said softly and reached toward her arm.

She was so busy worrying about having revealed something too personal that she didn't notice until he was mere millimetres away. She pulled back and, adrenaline surging, she was on her feet, grabbing her rucksack and coat and running out of the coffee shop.

There were tears on her cheeks when she got back to her room and she didn't know if they were of grief or shame. Then she was sprinting and now she was back at the hotel and she'd screwed it all up. She locked the door behind her, dumped her gear on the floor, and flopped onto the bed. Why did she think she could take on this assignment? If Lilith had known how dangerous she was, she'd never have suggested Kerry try to get close to the target. She grabbed the pillow, curled herself around it, and sobbed. It wasn't just the failure. It was the fact that Kazimir seemed like a nice guy. He was only trying to comfort her, like any normal person would. She'd seen people do that on TV and in films, just reaching out and touching someone's arm when they wanted their companion to know someone was there for them. And every time she watched that happen she ached for it.

She'd ruined the mission.

No . . . she hadn't ruined it; she could still watch him and turn in the basic report, but she'd failed the test. Should she write all of this up now? She wanted to show how much she'd learned about the target, how well she'd done to get closer, but how could she do that without revealing how she'd royally cocked it up?

"Miss Johnson?"

The receptionist called Kerry's pseudonym as she was leaving the next day to get some lunch. Kazimir was installed at work and would be there until six, if his normal schedule was upheld.

She went over to the desk as the receptionist held out an envelope. "A man left this for you yesterday evening."

"Thanks." *Clare* was written on the envelope in a spidery scrawl.

She opened it there and then, knowing it could only be from Kazimir; everyone else who knew her cover name had direct access to her through the pagers.

> *Dear Clare,*
> *I am sorry I scare you. I think I know why you are scared. I will be at coffee shop every night this week at 6:30 p.m. Please come. I was scared like that too. I know how bad it is. I want to help.*
> *Kazimir*

It was written on her hotel's notepaper; there was a pad on the table in the corner. He must have followed her there after she ran. She crushed it to her chest. She was so stupid! Her target knew where she was staying! Did that mean she had to abort?

Appetite gone, Kerry went back to her room. She read the note again, then pulled her case from under the bed and started to chuck her clothes into it, shaking and nauseated. She'd have to tell Flint how badly she'd messed up. He'd be angry. He'd say she wasn't good enough to be in the Silver Helix, and then what was she going to do? She had no money and nowhere to live without Flint's support. How was she going to survive?

Legs wobbling, she sat at the dressing table and rested her head on the aged wood. There was the farm. She could go back there . . . No, just the thought of seeing it again made her feel sick.

She read the note again. Why had Kazimir sent this? If she took it at face value, he was telling her he understood why she was so afraid. But he was a nat. How could he know? He probably assumed she'd been attacked in the past or had some sort of phobia.

Maybe she didn't have to abort, if she was really careful. She could ask what he meant by the note, an easy way to find out more about his life and why he'd been scared too. The breath eased in her chest. This wasn't a disaster. It was an opportunity.

♠

He was sitting in the same place as before, a large cup of black coffee in front of him. She watched from across the street until she mustered the courage to go in. There was no pretending she hadn't seen him this time. His face transformed from a worried glower to a happy and relieved smile. That same warmth was there, and she started to wonder if maybe he could help her, even without knowing what she was really afraid of.

Once she had her hot chocolate, she went to sit opposite him again. There were a few more people than before, with just enough ambient noise from their conversations to make it feel more private. "I'm so glad you come," he said. "I feel bad for scaring you. And I know I can help."

She slipped off her coat, tucked her bag under the table within easy grabbing range, and sipped the chocolate. "But you don't know anything about me."

"I know you are scared of touch. And I know it not because someone hurt you. It because you have hurt someone else, and not wanted to, when you touch."

Her stomach clenched. It was like she could feel the blood sink inward from her cheeks and lips. What if he really did understand?

"There is point in diplomatic talks, when deadlocked, when one party has to make decision to be vulnerable," he continued, his voice soft and low. "It is risk, yes? But to find solution, risk must be taken."

"Solution? Don't you need a problem to need a solution?"

He smiled sadly. "Clare, you are scared of people, all the time. Is that not problem?"

She didn't reply; she knew she wouldn't be able to get the words around the lump in her throat. She couldn't even keep looking at him, at his kind eyes, so she stared down at the hot chocolate instead.

"So, I take risk," he continued softly. "I know that fear because I too can kill people with touch. How you say . . . my card turned. But is secret. Yes?"

Her head snapped up. He wasn't a nat?! This changed everything. She searched his face for any sign of a lie, but he looked the same as before. Kind. Concerned.

"But . . ." Slowly her brain came back online. "But you tried to touch my arm! Were you trying to—"

"*Nyet!*" He looked appalled. "No, no, you have to understand . . ." He became aware of the other patrons who'd looked over at his outburst and lowered his voice again. "I control it now. But in start, I had no control. I . . ." He looked up, eyes shining with unshed tears. "I kill my brother," he whispered. "When I was more young than you. When card turned I did not know, I did not look or feel different, but then one morning, I got out of bed, I went to eat breakfast, I . . ." His voice cracked. "I just want to pat him on shoulder, to say good morning . . ."

He was telling the truth. She knew it. And in that moment, more than anything in the world, she wanted to reach across and touch his arm, to express that she understood without the need for clumsy, stupid words. Kerry wrapped her arms around herself, gripping her elbows, squeezing tight, fighting the urge to cry as she felt his pain.

"I turn him to dust." A single tear broke free, rolled down his cheek, and landed on his coffee spoon. He looked down at it, swiped a hand across his face, and sniffled, dragging himself from the memory to look at her again. "So I know what it is to be scared of touch."

The coffee shop chatter faded into the background as she reeled from the feeling that someone finally understood. She'd been comforted by Captain Flint as much as anyone can be comforted by a strong man of sparse words, but now she realised it hadn't been comfort, merely the removal of that constant fear in his presence. She'd mistaken the absence of that tension as something soothing, when it wasn't at all. Here was a person who really did understand, who wanted to help her.

A person who had found a way to control his curse.

His status as a surveillance target, his motives for contacting the Twisted Fists, his part in whatever game was being played between the UK and Russia, all of it faded into the background. She didn't care about what Flint wanted her to do; all she wanted was to stop feeling scared.

"I turn people to stone."

She'd crossed a line. It was one thing to decide to speak to the target, it was another to reveal her true nature. With five words, it felt like she'd betrayed Flint and set herself on a path that could take her away from him.

Kazimir nodded slowly. "Is this why parents are dead?"

She pressed her lips together to stop the lower one trembling, breathed in deep to push the lump in her throat down, then swallowed to keep it there. "Yes."

He murmured something in Russian. Then he seemed to make a decision. "We both take risk in telling this to each other. I promise I will not tell another what we say here."

Kerry nodded. "I promise too." And she meant it. None of this was going into her report. Right now, she wasn't even sure if she was going to write one. It felt weird confessing something so private while she was supposed to be spying on him. But she couldn't tell him about Flint and the mission without jeopardising her chance to learn from him.

She pushed down the discomfort with that and sipped the hot chocolate to cover her hesitation. "You're not scared of touching people anymore . . . Did someone teach you how to control it?"

He shook his head. "I teach me."

"But . . ." She let the rest of the question die off, unable to think of a way to ask it without sounding horrible.

"But how learn, when I kill so easy?" He sighed and leaned back in his chair, his gaze moving from one patron to the next. "I think conversation is dangerous for us if overheard. Shall we go to my apartment?"

Her heart flipped with panic. If she went there with him, the agent posted there would see her! "I . . . would rather stay somewhere public."

He nodded. "I understand. Shall we walk in park?"

It would be dark in less than an hour, but it was better than being seen by one of Flint's people. She agreed, and they finished their drinks and left. As they headed toward Kensington Gardens she wrestled with her guilt, feeling like she was betraying Flint, even though she wasn't quite sure if she actually was. The silence between them was giving her fear too much room to grow, that was all.

"Do you keep it a secret from your colleagues?" she asked.

He took so long to reply that she thought he hadn't heard her. "Some. It is . . . complicated."

"I worry that I won't be able to find a job, being the way I am."

He glanced at her, frowning. "Your government does not know? I thought there was register here."

She shook her head.

"Do not tell them."

"Why?"

They'd arrived at the nearest entrance to the park. He pointed to an empty bench nearby. "Are you happy to talk there?"

She nodded and once they sat down, he leaned back, thoughtful. "Have you heard of Chernobyl?"

"I read about it." It was some of the history she'd devoured over the past few years since escaping the farm. "It happened before I was born. It must have been scary."

"Before you were born . . ." he muttered. "You make me old. I grew up in village ten kilometres away. When accident happened, I live in Moscow. I was sent to . . . 'help.' Not help people there . . . help Communist Party to control information. It was my job to make sure Party's secrets stay secret."

The tone of his voice suggested the job was deeply unpleasant. "Did you have that job because of your curse?"

"Curse?" He frowned a moment and then seemed to understand. "Yes. I can make anything turn to dust. Document. Report. People. Useful for KGB."

She stayed very still, fearful that her racing thoughts would somehow become visible on the surface. He was a member of the KGB?! That wasn't in the briefing! She'd read a few Cold War thrillers, and many more modern ones that had former KGB agents who, for the sake of flimsy plots, refused to recognise that the Cold War was over. Was that why he went to the Twisted Fists? Because he still worked for whatever branch of the Russian government used to be the KGB? Why was he telling her this?

"That was when I see how much harm I do. Not because of gift. Because of how government use it." He twisted to face her. "You can kill too. Fast, yes?"

"Yes." The word was just a croak.

"You can kill fast, with one touch. If they know about you, your government see you as weapon, like me."

"But if they wanted me to kill people, leaving a statue behind as evidence would be rubbish!"

He smirked. "Statue is easy smashed. No evidence of life. No body to bury. No bones to find. If outside, in right place, people would not think it real person before. If I wanted to kill that way, I would wait until they were posed somewhere. Look like art."

The hot chocolate was shooting up her gullet in a sudden rush of nausea. She pressed a fist against her lips, breathing in through her nose and desperately trying to suppress the urge to vomit. Captain Flint wouldn't ask her to kill anyone! He knew she'd never be able to do that again, not after what her parents put her through.

"Apologies. I scare you in different way. I want to stop what happen to me, happen to you, yes? When I young, like you, I want to be hero. To help my country be great. The KGB tell me I do that, but not true. At Chernobyl, I see many people—my people, Ukrainian—not get help."

"So did you leave them? Is that why you're a diplomatic aide now? To do more good?"

He laughed, but it was bitter. "There was no way for me to leave KGB. Then KGB end, but new government find way to keep me useful. I help diplomatic corps, yes, but not in way people think."

So he was still making things—and maybe people—disappear for his government. And he was just . . . chatting about it? "I don't understand why you're telling me this. Surely you're supposed to keep it a secret?"

With a sigh, he nodded. "I have old friends who have no idea what I do, who know me almost all of my life. But I am tired and . . ." He patted his chest as he fumbled for words. "Heartsick. I hope that after end of Soviet Union, things get better for Ukraine. But I learn something here that . . ." Another sigh as his gaze focused on a nearby tree. "I am sick of loyalty to powerful men who not care for people. I try to ignore so many things, all my life. I just do job. But no more. I change. And . . ." His gaze returned to her. "And I see me in you and I wish I have someone to help me when I am young. Then I might not be where I am now. But what I learn in London I cannot forget and I cannot carry on same."

So he was having some sort of crisis of loyalty to the Russian government and thought she was just some scared girl that good fortune had brought into his life so that he could help her. But what had he learned in London? The Fists hideout he'd visited was outside of the city, in Guildford, so it wasn't their existence, or what had happened there—if he was telling the truth. It felt like he was. She was desperate to know more but paralysed with uncertainty: how to pursue it without giving herself away?

"And," he added, "there is relief to talk to someone, yes? It is lonely in my job."

"Yes," she replied, and the agreement was genuine. At the sight of a park attendant approaching the gates, she stood. "They're about to lock the park. We should go." As they walked to the exit, she stuffed her hands in her pockets and clenched them into fists. "Do you think you'd be able to teach me how to control my curse?"

"Yes." He sounded very confident. "It all in mind. You are smart and you want to learn. That all you need."

It sounded too simple. How could he really know? "Have you helped anyone else?"

"Yes. But that person has different gift."

"What could they do?"

"Ah, that is secret I must keep. But same in most important way; touch was problem."

The man smiled at them as they left and the gates were locked behind them. Once he'd moved off, she turned to face Kazimir. "Will you teach me?"

"Yes."

She looked, but there was only kindness in his eyes. Could she trust her instincts though? "What do you want in return?"

"Nothing. It only take time, and I have many evening and British TV is terrible. We can start now, yes?"

Surely it wasn't that simple? Surely he wanted something? Then her attention was pulled away by a vibration in her inside coat pocket. Flint's pager! "Um, I have to go . . . I have to . . . think about it."

"It is hard to trust. I understand. Meet at café again tomorrow? Same time?"

She felt wretched as she nodded and gave a little wave before heading off.

◆

"I've read through your activity logs and it doesn't seem like the target has met with anyone or been anywhere suspicious."

Everything seemed completely normal, the way Captain Flint sat, the way he looked at her. And yet Kerry's heart was racing as if she were sprinting up a hill. Was this a trap?

"He just goes to get food, or books or coffee. That's it. When he's not at work."

Flint nodded. *"I think it's as I suspected and he just delivered a message to the Fists rather than acting of his own volition. We're keeping a close eye on his boss, but there's been no more communication between that cell and the Russians."* He closed the file on his desk. *"I think it's time for us to wrap up the surveillance."*

"But . . ."

He frowned at her. *"You think we should continue? I see no reason to do so from this data."*

"I . . . I just feel it's good training in a low-risk scenario, like you said."

He leaned back, scrutinising her. *"You're enjoying it."* It was a statement, rather than a question.

She feigned embarrassment. "Yeah. It's the first time I've felt like I could be useful. I guess it might be boring for the other agents."

"Those duties have been folded into CCTV monitoring. It's only one person at a time and easy to share with other assignments. I'm not concerned about that."

And the whole time she'd been thinking that there were actual people posted outside his flat and workplace. If Flint knew that Kazimir was really an ace though, that would change. It felt wrong to keep so much from him, but she kept silent. If he knew what Kazimir could do, she'd be pulled off the assignment and lose her chance to learn how to control her curse.

"I'm going to be away for a few days," Flint said, breaking her internal

guilt spiral. "We'll keep it up for another week, to be on the safe side. I want you to keep the activity log going and then write a report at the end on any issues you overcame and any potential problems for future assignments. I want that on my desk seven days from now. I should be back by then."

A week to learn everything she could from Kazimir. "Thanks." She stood and was surprised when he did too.

He moved round from behind his desk to come over to her, putting a hand on her shoulder and squeezing just enough for one of the sharp edges to hurt. "I'm glad this has been going well. I know being in the city is hard. I'm proud of you."

Tears welled, but Kerry didn't know why. "Thank you," she croaked, trying so hard to be the professional young woman she wanted to be. Then she threw her arms around his waist and shut her eyes, desperate for something she couldn't name. She felt his stone hands resting lightly on her back and for a moment, just a moment, it felt like she had a father again.

♥

She watched Kazimir draw an outline of a human body, reminding her of the chalk line drawn around murder victims in TV shows. They were back in the coffee shop, but this time tucked into the corner of the basement area.

"This sound strange, but listen to all and"—he smirked slightly—"and trust me. It work."

"I'm listening."

"This all about mind over matter, yes? But not silly American firewalk thing. This about using our mind to control something virus make us do. Now, when you touch and turn person to stone, it is skin to skin, yes?"

She nodded.

"But look at cup." He pointed at the hot chocolate in front of her. "Not stone. You touch with hand but still ceramic. Yes? And your clothes, and your bed, yes?"

She frowned. "Yeah. My power only works on living things."

"But what about your eyes? Your hair. All living."

"But they're mine."

He smiled broadly. "Yes! They are part of you. Good."

She wondered if something was being lost in translation. "I don't see how—"

"I try to show you that there are . . . limit to power. And what we do now is think about how to change limit. There is no . . . thing in your skin that make this happen. It is all mind."

"It *might* be something in my skin for all we know."

He looked briefly frustrated. "Trust me. I know this."

She chewed on her thumbnail as he put the black pen down and picked up a blue one.

"Now, I want you to imagine thing inside you that turn people to stone is like . . . ghost that fill you up."

"What?!"

"No, listen, it make sense. I think of my power like this. Like . . . soul? Not physical, but fill whole body before I learn control, like this." He began to fill the outline of the body with blue ink. "It not matter which bit of skin touch another person, because this"—he waggled the blue pen at her—"fill me up, yes?"

She nodded but still felt a bit lost.

He picked up the black pen, drew a second body outline and then a third. "Then I think, *What if I can . . . pull it in . . . stop it from filling all of me?*"

He coloured in the second outline, but this time not right to the edge, leaving a narrow band of white between the blue and black ink. He tapped the white strip with the pen. "This . . . gap, this mean power not touch other person, or thing. It is deeper inside, so protect other person. Yes?"

It suddenly made sense. If she pulled the power inward, somehow, shrinking it, it would no longer be able to turn people to stone. If it worked the way he seemed to think it did. "I think I understand."

He looked so happy. "Good! Is so hard in English!"

"But if it works this way, do you have to concentrate on making it . . . smaller inside you all the time?"

"At first, yes. Is tiring. But after practise, no." He pointed at the third outline he'd drawn. "Now, it feel like this, all the time." He coloured in the core of the drawn body and no blue ink in the limbs or head at all. "Is like deep inside. When I want to turn something to dust, I imagine pulling power from inside to hand." He added a blue line from the core to one of the hands, set the pen down and picked up his teaspoon. "Now I am second picture." Nothing happened.

Then he stared at the spoon and she watched its shiny surface turn dull before the spoon crumbled to dust, as if it had never been metal. "That is what happen when I am third picture, yes? Send power to hand." He picked up a packet of sugar. "Pull in, all good. Now . . ." The sachet's paper turned to powder and a couple of sugar granules slipped out before all of them were turned to dust too. "Sent to hand."

She blinked at the smears of dust on the table, and his other hand, which had been resting on the wooden surface the whole time. He had so much control! "And you can turn anything to dust? Living or not?"

He nodded. "But first only living things, like you. Maybe one day you be same, turn coffee cup to stone for party joke."

She attempted a smile.

"You think it won't work. That I talk rubbish. I understand. It take practise."

"It's pretty hard to practise something when people die if you get it wrong."

"That is not practice, that is test. Practice is for thinking of power this way." He tapped the paper. "Spend time to change way you think about what is you and what is power and how they not same. *Test* is get something very small, like bug, and see if work. Test is not think about this and then touch *person* to see if work."

"Yes, of course." She felt stupid again. "Okay, I'll try."

♣

For the next three days she practised thinking about the curse in the way Kazimir had described. It was a frustrating process. It felt too much like doing nothing but a weird sort of focused daydreaming, a slippery, dissatisfying activity with no way to tell if she was doing it right. She imagined the curse like a second soul filling her body—even though it seemed stupid to do so—and imagined shrinking it inward.

They arranged to meet at the coffee shop in three days' time. She hated the fact that there was so little time left on the assignment, but she couldn't think of a good enough reason to hurry Kazimir along. She soon realised why he'd made the arrangement; it seemed he knew someone who'd been taken to hospital and visited them there two days in a row. At first she'd thought he was seeking medical help, especially as she saw him use an asthma inhaler for the first time that day. But the second time he went, he took a small bunch of flowers and left the hospital without them. She couldn't face following him in to see which ward he went to. It was too busy, and too easy for Kazimir to spot her if she screwed up.

After a couple of days of frustration, she decided to test her progress. She went back to Kensington Gardens in the afternoon, while Kazimir was at work, and spread out her anorak on the damp grass next to a flower bed.

It was mercifully quiet, it being a weekday morning during the school term. She sat watching the soil for a while, soon seeing all sorts of bugs bustling about in their own muddy world. She took a moment to focus her thoughts and then put her hand on the soil next to a few ants.

She concentrated on imagining the curse pulled inward so intently that she didn't initially see the ant crawling across her hand; it was the tickling that drew her attention.

It hadn't turned to stone! She watched it patter across the back of her hand and felt such a surge of excitement that she laughed out loud. Then the ant froze, turned a dark grey colour and tumbled off, no more than a tiny chip of granite.

Appalled, she bit her lip, wondering if she'd imagined it being alive while touching her before. She grounded herself, helped by the feeling of the cold, damp earth beneath her palm, and went back to imagining the power shrinking inward. Another ant ventured onto her thumb, crawled onto the back of her hand, and she knew she wasn't imagining it. It was working!

But as soon as she'd thought that, and let the excitement fracture her concentration, the ant turned to stone and tumbled off.

It was all the proof she needed though! Kerry jumped up, grabbed her anorak, and sprinted out of the park, past the coffee shop, back to her hotel. She had to run, she had to release the sheer joy and excitement at seeing an end to this hellish life. Kazimir's technique worked and it would just be a matter of time and practice, and then she could live something like a normal life!

She was panting when she got to the hotel. The same receptionist who had given her the letter from Kazimir was on duty. Kerry stopped, feeling something jar in her brain. Kazimir had followed her from the café to her hotel after he'd almost touched her arm. She had sprinted, probably faster than she just had. He was asthmatic, in his late fifties, possibly early sixties for all she knew. How did he keep her in sight round the three corners between here and the café?

She went to the desk. "Hi . . . I don't suppose you remember me, but you gave me a letter that was left by a man."

The receptionist smiled. "I remember. I was on duty when he came in and wrote it. It doesn't happen every day." She lowered her voice and leaned in a little. "I keep an eye on the men who want to speak to a young woman staying alone at the hotel. You know, just in case."

Kerry nodded. She knew. All women knew. "Was he very out of breath? Like he'd been running?"

The receptionist shook her head. "No. He looked worried, came to the desk and asked if I had a spare envelope because he wanted to leave a message for someone staying here. I think he was Russian. He seemed kind. I gave it to him, and he sat over there to write it and handed it in."

So he hadn't chased after her, as she'd assumed. Which meant only one thing; he'd already known where she was staying before she befriended him.

♠

She was so nervous before their next meeting at the café that she couldn't eat. She didn't know how to handle this, and she couldn't ask for help. She didn't want to ask Lilith because she didn't know the woman well enough; she had the feeling Lilith would look down on her if she confided her fears. If she managed to salvage this mission and earn her place in the Silver Helix, they'd be colleagues and she didn't want Lilith to know how badly she'd screwed up. So she went down into the basement area carrying an unwanted hot chocolate after trailing Kazimir from his apartment, knowing he was down there waiting for her.

He looked pleased to see her, and she couldn't help smiling back at him. "How is practise?"

She'd been so worried about what to say that her success had been pushed to the back of her mind. "It worked! Only for a few seconds when I was really concentrating, but it worked!"

He beamed at her, genuinely pleased. "Tell me all."

She told him about the ant and—after a brief translation issue—about her excitement, how she ran all the way back to the hotel afterward. As he chuckled at the thought of her gleeful sprint, she took a breath and readied herself for what was to come. "It made me think, actually," she said as he sipped his coffee. "About when I last ran to the hotel, after I panicked with you. Remember? When we first chatted here?" At his nod, she looked him in the eye. "It made me realise that you couldn't have followed me back. I run very fast when I want to, and I wanted to that day. There are three corners, two close together . . . easy points for you to lose me if you weren't right behind me. And given your age and"—she almost mentioned the inhaler—"and the fact that you tend to cough a little when we go outside after sitting in the warm, I don't think you could have kept up with me."

He didn't look away, didn't smile, didn't do any of the things she expected him to do. "And what does that make you think?"

"That you knew where I was staying before that day. And that . . . worries me."

"It worries you. That I might do to you what you were doing to me? Following me."

She gave a tense nod.

"I am glad you thought about this. I wait for this, for many days now, and I know you not stupid. But you are young and have no experience. That is why it was easy for me to notice you follow me, days before we talk in bookshop."

She felt her cheeks flush red and hated it.

"Do not feel bad. I have been agent for longer than you live. This is new for you, yes?"

She nodded. "Oh, God, I've really screwed this up."

He smiled. "Drink chocolate. All not lost. I do not want to hurt you. We talk, work it out."

She wrapped her shaking hands around the giant mug and found the chocolate a small comfort. "I feel so stupid. You knew, the whole time?"

"*Da.*"

"But you've been so kind. And it wasn't all . . . I mean . . . you've really helped me. I don't understand."

"When I see how young you are, I not worry. I can kill very quick, remember. So I decide to wait and see what else being done. But I work out only you on street, and cameras to watch me come and go from apartment and office. Not good operation. Training for you. But why me? And then I realise why and I know you are with Silver Helix. Perhaps first mission. Wanting to know why boring Russian man go to Fists' place."

The more he said, the more incompetent she felt. She had really believed that she had been doing a brilliant job and yet he'd been one step ahead of her the entire time. "I don't suppose you'll tell me why," she said with an attempt at a cheeky grin.

Kazimir laughed. "Because of thing I learn in London. But now not time to talk about that."

"So you let me befriend you to learn about what we knew, and then you saw me panic when you nearly touched me."

"*Da.* I tell you truth. I see me in you. Then I know I must help. Because you work for government now, but still young, still new. Still time for you to get out and not be like me."

It had felt true at the time, and it still did. That was a relief. "But why did you tell me about when you were in the KGB, and what you still do now, even when you knew I was spying on you?"

He shrugged. "All game, no matter now. If I care about Russia and how they use me, then I say nothing. But I do not care now. Loyalty to Russia is gone. And helping you more important than both governments. They only care about power and money for them, not people."

She believed him. But should she? She felt like a silly little girl playing grown-up games, and she hated it. What should she do?

"We finish drink," he said, as if sensing her indecision. "We go back to our rooms. You make decision. I tell you truth; your government will use you to kill. If you can get out, do. If you need help to get out, I give it. And do not worry about Fists. I speak once to them, they are fools, nothing more. No risk. No terrorist plan with Russian government. My government does not need *those* British fools to do evil."

The emphasis made her wonder if there were other British fools he had in mind who were helping the Russians. But it was clear this was all he was willing to say now, and that all she could do now was decide what to tell Flint.

♦

Four days later Kerry was perched on the edge of a chair in the waiting room close to Captain Flint's office, her stomach cramping, trying not to cry. She didn't want to, but her eyes were stinging and her cheeks were still burning after the brief exchange with him that morning. She'd known she'd done something wrong the moment she walked in, her report laid out on the desk in front of him. Even though his flinty features couldn't show the nuances of human expression, there was nothing nuanced about his anger, and it burned from his hellish eyes when he'd looked up at her.

She'd been so certain that he'd be thrilled by how much she'd discovered, that he'd be so proud of her. She couldn't have been more wrong.

His anger had ended the moment she mentioned Lilith's name. Now she feared she'd got the other agent into trouble, but she had to tell the truth about the advice Lilith had given; otherwise Flint wouldn't understand her disobedience. Now, waiting to be summoned back in, she could see how stupid she'd been. Lilith's advice had sounded so ridiculous when she said it to Flint. How could she have believed that he'd be happy with anything other than what he had asked for?

Was Flint letting her stew or just trying to manage his temper? She'd worked so hard to impress him and received the worst dressing-down she'd ever experienced. Perhaps he was working out what to do with her. It might be the best time to run, to strike out on her own, but she wasn't prepared. First lesson learned: expect the worst, be ready for it. It had taken her nearly two years to live without a grab bag of stuff by the door, ready to bolt if needed. And now her complacency had denied her a quick escape. She wouldn't make that mistake again.

Her burner phone vibrated in her pocket, making her jump. Only Lilith had that number. She left it for a few moments, fearful that if she answered, she'd just get another telling off. But then Lilith might turn up in person when she least expected it. Better to get it over with. She pulled the phone out and accepted the call.

Before she'd even got it to her ear she could hear Flint's fist pounding on his desk. "—as Lilith, not to mention the risk to the public as well as to her! What possessed you to interfere with a green recruit's first mission?!"

"Would you have preferred me to reveal everything about myself on a first meeting?" A soft male voice spoke. Who the hell had Lilith's phone? "I thought appearing as Lilith would be less scary than a man finding her. Is that sound your teeth grinding? Why, Captain, you're so upset."

"Don't derail this, Noel!"

This "Noel" and Lilith were the same person? A shapeshifter who could teleport? Wow. That explained how he had the phone number that only Lilith knew, and why he was confident about who would pick up and listen in. But why risk a breach of Flint's trust in him? Why did Noel want her to hear their private conversation?

"All right, if you want the truth, I wanted to make sure she understood what she's getting herself into."

"By telling her to befriend an ex-KGB assassin?!"

"No one knew that at the time, not even you. I wonder if you're so upset because it's such a royal cockup on your part, not because I encouraged her to get some real experience. Even if she was just tailing, he would have clocked her."

"Real experience? And you're the better judge of how to train her, are you?"

"You're mistaken, Captain. Not real experience of spycraft. Real experience of you."

In the long pause that followed, Kerry realised she was holding her breath. She moved her thumb over the mic, just in case she gave away the fact that she was listening in.

"She has no idea what you're really like," Noel continued. "What you'll make her do. She's a kid. Like I was."

"So this, unsurprisingly, is all about you."

Another pause. "You wrap her in cotton wool, hide her away, and then give her some bullshit assignment to build her confidence. At what point were you going to drop the kindly father act?"

"Ah, so you're upset that she didn't get the same treatment as you, without considering that she is a completely different person with different skills and—"

"I had hoped, for maybe all of five minutes, that you might have regretted how you had me trained, but no. This is you manipulating a vulnerable kid all over again, just without the beatings. She has no idea what the psych said about her, I take it."

"And how would you know? That report was confidential."

"I overheard Enigma warning you that the psych said she was too keen to please you and it would impede her judgement. That you have too much power over her."

Kerry remembered Flint's words in her garden . . . he'd only said she was keen . . . he'd manipulated her?

"Look, you might not be happy with what I did." Noel's change in subject didn't escape her. "But she uncovered a Russian ace who wasn't even on your radar and handled it all brilliantly."

"She's arguing for him to join us!"

"Poor kid. She's really clueless, isn't she?"

The sound of Flint's fist hammering the desk again made her jump. "This is far more complex than you realise! And now I have to clean up the mess you made!"

"Oh, drop it! We both know why you're so angry, and it's not because I interfered with your new pet. It's because she's found another man who's taken her under his wing and wants to train her. You've got competition, and you can't stand it!"

There was a pause. "You have your assignment," Flint finally said. "Don't go near Stonemaiden again, and don't come back until your assignment is complete."

She feared the assignment had something to do with Kazimir. There was a snort from Noel. "I'm amazed you managed to find something that takes me thousands of miles away from her so quickly. Don't worry, I'm sure she's learned what she needs to."

He ended the call then, and clearly didn't leave via natural means. She made sure that the phone was set to airplane mode, and barely had time to process what Noel had enabled her to listen in on, when the expected summons came.

Shaking, she walked back into Flint's office, not even able to look at him.

"Sit down, Kerry. I'm not angry with you."

She looked up at his face, tried to gauge whether that was true, but it was impossible to deduce from the angles of his stone features. She sat down, willing herself to stay quiet and calm. She knew more than he realised, but not enough to control this conversation at all.

Flint sighed. "While I disagree—strongly—with the methods you employed, I can't deny that you've brought me very valuable intelligence."

Her chest tightened. Was he about to make her a full member?

"And that intelligence has cleared up a few questions from previous cases, and cast a new light on the findings from other, simultaneous operations. The thing about our line of work, Kerry, is that you might only know a small part of a bigger picture. That's why it's important not only to follow orders, but to understand that your conclusions may not be correct when combined with information from other operations."

"You think I'm wrong about him not being a threat."

Flint nodded, and seemed relieved that she was quick on the uptake. "I think he's actually one of the most dangerous men alive. And I'm convinced that he's involved in a plot to kill several key members of the government, and potentially the extended royal family."

She almost laughed. It sounded ridiculous. "No, he hates the Russians and what they made him do. He doesn't want to kill anyone."

"I know you don't believe me. He's manipulated you brilliantly. We're extraordinarily lucky that he decided to recruit you rather than kill you."

"He doesn't want to do that! He wants to help me!"

"Kerry . . . your family kept you hidden away. I did the same. Our motives may have been very different, but it had the same impact. You're better educated now, but you're not worldly. You have to trust me when I tell you that Nazarenko is very skilled at putting you at ease and making you think of him as a kind man. He's not. And regardless, Nazarenko would never be able to work for the Silver Helix, and I would never be able to trust him even if he could. His presence in London constitutes a terrible threat, and it's our responsibility to stop him."

Their eyes met and it felt like the world fell away from under her chair. "You want him to . . . to be killed?"

"That's the only way to ensure he can't do any more harm to our leaders and national interests. Men like him can't be arrested and put in prison. There is no kind way to deal with this, Kerry. It's a struggle to defend our country."

"But . . . but . . ."

"Have I ever lied to you?"

"No." But he had left out that detail from the psych report.

"Have I ever pressured you into wanting to join the Silver Helix?"

"No."

"The only thing I'm guilty of is wanting to ease you into this life slowly. Gently, I suppose. I made mistakes when I recruited . . . Lilith, I know that. I didn't want to make the same mistakes with you. But I fear I've been too protective, and all of that is going to come to naught."

He had something in mind, but she couldn't fathom it. "I don't understand."

"It has to be you, Kerry. You need to eliminate the threat."

Her ears began to ring. She shook her head. She was missing something, surely. He'd never ask her to kill.

"Nazarenko trusts you, and you're the most likely to be able to get close enough to do it. You'd be very fast, and that's critical, given his own power."

The ends of her fingers started to tingle, along with her lips. Tiny dots sparkled at the periphery of her vision. Then Flint's hand was gripping her shoulder and he was looming over her and it felt like she snapped back into her body again. "Kerry. I'm so sorry. I never wanted your first assignment to come to this. But if you really want to be a member of the Silver Helix, you have to be prepared to do your duty."

There was a surge of emotions—anger, betrayal, rage, despair, all so strong and terrifying that the blood roared in her ears—and then, all of a sudden, nothing. She felt so calm. So . . . numb. "Do I have a choice?"

"The choice is whether you join us or not. Not whether he has to die. If you're not prepared to do it, tell me now. There's no shame in this not being the life for you."

But she couldn't imagine any other life. It all revolved around Flint. And the thought of turning her back on the dream of being in the Silver Helix, of getting up and walking out and never seeing him again, never being able to feel his hand on her shoulder or see that look of pride when he spoke to her . . . she couldn't bear it.

"I'll do it," she said. "I was a stupid girl. I thought I knew him, and . . . and I see how he manipulated me." She listened to the words coming out of her, detached, almost like another person was speaking them. "I won't let you down."

Flint's hand moved from her shoulder to brush the top of her head before he stepped back. *"I know you won't."*

♥

All the way to Kazimir's apartment she tried to make a plan, but her thoughts just kept sliding off it. She couldn't keep focused on anything more than which tube to catch and keeping as far from other people as possible. She had to get to Kazimir. Once she arrived, hopefully the next thing to do would become clear.

And then she was ringing the bell to his apartment.

He buzzed her in after only the slightest pause. Perhaps he'd been expecting her. Having been sent there by Flint, she wasn't concerned about being spotted on CCTV, but she wore a baseball cap with her unruly hair tied and pinned under it, just in case there were interior cameras run by

Kazimir's people. She wore the anorak she hated, and it would go in the bin the moment she left.

The communal area was clean, tidy, and impersonal. She knew Kazimir's apartment was on the top floor, one of only three in the small converted townhouse, and so she headed up the staircase at the far end of the small lobby.

He was waiting at his open doorway and smiled at her. "I am glad you come. I worry I not see you again."

She reached the uppermost stair, saw the kindness and warmth in his eyes, and her knees buckled beneath her. She sat heavily, tears welling, unable to go any farther.

"Come in," he said softly.

"I can't."

"He want you to kill me."

Her head whipped round at the sound of the truth, but he was still just standing there, like an old uncle waiting for his niece to come inside so they could cook together. Like it was the most normal thing in the world to be welcoming to your own assassin.

"It is okay," he said softly. "I expect this. Come inside. We talk. We work it out."

Was he trying to lure her inside to kill her instead? She couldn't just sit there and cry and she couldn't leave without doing anything, so she picked herself up and followed him inside.

After closing the door behind her, she followed him through the small hallway to a large living room. It looked like there was a kitchen, a bathroom, and two other closed doors leading off to what were presumably the bedrooms. She went to the living room doorway and lingered, uncertain what to do.

It was a spacious room with a high ceiling, neutral décor, and large windows. The curtains were drawn against the dusk and a single lamp was lit in the corner, giving the large room a cosy atmosphere.

He gestured at a plump sofa as he sat in one of the two armchairs, both covered in beige brocade. She perched on the edge and glanced at the picture on the wall behind him of a street in a beautiful city.

"St. Petersburg," he said. "Interesting place but does not feel Russian. I kill four men there in one night."

When she realised her jaw had dropped open, she shut her mouth.

"I am dangerous. He tell you this, yes? I am threat. Must be eliminated. I understand."

"Why are you so calm about this?" she blurted out.

He shrugged. "It happen before. Someone come to kill me. But this first time I want to talk to person first. Because this is not same."

"Because you're not scared of me?"

"*Nyet*. Because I care about you. I tell you they will make you kill. It come true, yes?" At her nod, he leaned forward. "And how you feel about that?"

The same surge of emotions rose within her as they had in Captain Flint's office, but this time it was harder to push them back down again. She clasped her hands together, pushed the palms against each other until the heels of her hands hurt. She had to get a grip!

"He said you're dangerous, yes," she began. "But he thinks you want to kill important people, and that's why you should be stopped."

Kazimir nodded. "He is right. I do."

She groaned. "Why are you agreeing with the man who wants you killed?!"

"Because I do not lie to you. The only lie is not telling you that I know you have been sent to follow me. I want you to make decision for yourself. This is life junction . . . intersection . . . no, *crossroads*, yes? When I am at same crossroads, many years ago, I have no one to help me. I want you to see you have choice."

She felt sick. Was this all just a ploy to stop her from killing him? "Okay . . . then tell me what you learned in London that made you stop being loyal to your government."

"I come with diplomatic corps in case government want something . . . cleaned up. The trade talks in press are just cover for real talks happening between top negotiator and UK arms dealers. The Russian government want to buy lot of guns, lot of tanks. This not new. But I hear conversation by accident between our diplomat and our negotiator. Guns and tanks are to use against Ukraine, my homeland, if Ukraine decide to join NATO. Russia still see Ukraine as their place, like in days of USSR. But Ukraine want to join West, not East."

His hands balled into fists. "When I hear this, I know that Russian government never care for people. But worse; no government care for people. The UK arms dealers in talks, they have many deals with UK government. Many ministers take money from them, many ministers make decision about overseas policy to keep arms dealers happy, not to help British people. Same in Russia, many decision made for money, not people. That why loyalty die." He looked down at his hands, distant for a moment. "I realise many thing, here in London. There are only two type of people; super rich and rest of world. Countries, borders, rules . . . I start to see how it is all lies to keep control of masses. Super-rich—funded by arms deals and out-of-control capitalism—can go where they want, do what they want, kill who they want. They use press to tell everyone else what to feel, who to hate. They tell people to hate each other, so super-rich can make more money. I am part of that machine, and I want to break it. I hoped Fists would be allies, but no. Silver Helix is British part of same machine. I do not want you to be cog in machine like me."

She believed him. But she believed that Captain Flint felt he was doing the best thing for his country too.

"Is Flint, yes, who send you?" She didn't answer, but he nodded at her silence anyway. "Flint is military man. Questions trained out of him. He salute queen and never question. He more dangerous man than I and definitely more dangerous for you. Does he deserve your loyalty?"

"Yes!" she replied without hesitation. "He's done so much for me! He saved my life. I don't know how I could have survived without him."

"And he give you safety in return for love?"

"Urgh, no, that's gross!" He didn't love her. But she did love him.

"Then why help you? Because he kind?"

He had been kind to her, but she wouldn't say he was a kind man. He was cold and hard to read and to love. To say he'd done everything out of kindness felt wrong.

"Your face say lot of things, Clare," Kazimir said sadly. "This man see young girl, scared, no family, and sees weapon in future."

"No!"

"Yes. Men like Flint only see war. They are made from war. They only see targets and weapons. You are weapon that need kindness and help for long time, then when ready, weapon can be used to kill."

His face was distorted by her tears so she looked away. "He's done so much for me."

"Not for love. If it was love, Clare, he would give it all to you like daughter, and not ask you to kill man in return."

"But it wasn't like that! He didn't say I had to do this because of everything he's done for me!"

Kazimir shook his head. "Many ways power can be used with no words. If you say no to him, do you have somewhere to live? Will you have money? Be safe?"

A heavy tear plopped onto her boot.

"That is power over you. Now you see it, you have choice. I can give you money to survive."

"Oh, pay me not to kill you? That doesn't sound very noble!"

He laughed. "When I say I am noble? I give you money, no strings. You have money, you can leave Flint, so money gives you power to decide. Or do you want to kill me? When he point at next person and tell you they are danger to queen, will you turn them to stone too? Will you do that for rest of your life?"

She saw the woman's back in the studio, her pale pink flesh, the tiny hairs and pores of her skin as she posed for her father in the Grecian-style dress. How it turned grey at her touch. All those times she killed because she was told it was good, that it was right, that it made the world better.

She'd vowed she would never do that again. And yet here she was, talking to a man she had been sent to kill by the man she thought would keep her safe. A second tear dripped onto her boot. "I don't want to," she said. Her voice sounded reedy and small and she felt like she was fourteen again.

"I am sorry. This hard. But good for you to see how things really are. Like surgery. It hurt, but will let you heal. Better you feel this now, so young, with whole life to live, than like me, old and many times murderer."

"But . . ." She sniffled. "If I don't do what he wants, will you kill more people?"

"I see your problem. Hm. How would you solve?"

"Well . . . Captain Flint would argue that I already know the solution to that."

He smiled. "Remember, I kill with touch too. Flint expect you to get close without me expecting, but not possible now."

He was reminding her she was not the only deadly person in the room. She had no idea whether she would be turned to dust before he was turned to stone, but she didn't want to risk it, for either of their sakes.

She wiped the tears from her eyes. "I don't want to kill you. So I'd make a deal with you. I'd say that if I let you live, you have to let your targets live too."

"Better. Tell me flaws in plan."

It was like he was training her, more than Flint himself had, having just managed the provision of other trainers. She pushed that thought away. "I'd have to trust that you'll keep your word. But . . . these people you want to kill aren't Russian targets, they're *your* targets, so it's more likely you would be able to keep your word and find another way to solve your problem. Like turning tanks to dust, instead of people."

His smile was radiant. "Good, good. But what about biggest flaw in plan?"

"Oh." Her stomach twisted painfully. "Flint. He'd know I didn't kill you. He'll be monitoring the building . . . he'll be waiting for a statue to be removed or something . . . or will send someone in to prove it's been done."

"So if stone man was here when he look, problem solved?"

"Yeah . . . but I turn living things into granite. It's heavy and hard to work, and it would be too difficult to have one made and bring it into the building and . . ." She saw an interesting look on his face. "Wait . . . you've got something in mind, haven't you? Don't tell me you've got a bloody statue here already?"

"Even I cannot make that happen. But I do have another man."

"Oh, God! A body? Here?!" She jumped up, hating the thought of there being a corpse somewhere in the apartment the whole time they were talking.

"*Nyet*, calm, calm." He stood too, patting the air between them. "Listen. I expect this, so I make plan too. We help each other. I give you statue for Flint, so he think you are good girl and do what he say. Give you time to make plan to leave if you want, be safe, yes? But also give me freedom too. If statue here, Russians think I killed by Silver Helix. They will not make fuss as I am not supposed to be real, yes? They be angry, but not start war. Everyone think I am dead, but I am not. I am free."

It made a lot of sense. "I don't want you to die, but I'm not willing to kill another man to save you. It kinda defeats the point, y'know?"

"What if man already dying?"

♣

Behind one of the closed doors was indeed a bedroom, and lying within was a man of a similar age to Kazimir who was in the late stages of cancer. His skin had a dreadful yellow pallor and his breath was laboured, but he still smiled when he saw her. "Ah, the angel," he said at the sight of her, his Ukrainian accent far softer than Kazimir's. "My angel of death."

She sat by his bedside and they talked. His name was Nikolai and he'd known Kazimir for over thirty years, through "work"—a comment that was not elaborated upon and one she didn't push. They had saved each other's lives at least twice though, so they were probably both in the spy trade.

Kazimir had explained his situation, and as the man wheezed his way through the tale, pausing occasionally to press the button that delivered more morphine, Kerry was painfully aware of how many steps ahead of her Kazimir had been throughout this entire assignment. The visits he'd made to the hospital were to visit his friend, but rapidly turned into a plan to buy Kazimir's survival and freedom, whilst giving a faster and painless death to Nikolai.

"There is no hope for me now," Nikolai said. "Just palliative care, they call it. I ask them to let me go faster, but no. It is not allowed. And my body is fighting to stay when my mind want to go." His smile brought more tears to her eyes. "It will be kindness to me and gift to my friend. No burden on your soul, angel. No guilt for you. Kindness. Kindness."

Kazimir watched the conversation from the doorway and when it was over, he went back into the living room as Kerry shut the bedroom door quietly. For a few moments she crouched in the hallway, trying to stop herself from crying, but the swell of grief and guilt and the pressure of so many memories that had been trapped behind the dam she'd built inside herself was too strong. She buried her face in her hands and wept as quietly as she could, not wanting this choice, this life, this dreadful crossroads where none of the choices led to peace. If she saved Kazimir and reconciled herself to euthanizing Nikolai, she would still have to lie to Flint, betraying the man who'd saved her. *But then again,* said a tiny voice at the back of her mind, *hasn't he already betrayed you by asking you to kill again?*

And then, like before, it all just . . . stopped. She felt nothing. She stood, wiped her face, blew her nose on a tissue she'd stuffed into the anorak pocket days before, and went into the living room.

"What if the people watching the flats saw you bring him in?"

Kazimir looked up from the armchair. "He come by taxi when I at work and neighbour in flat below let him in. Your people probably think he is relative of hers. Nothing to link us."

"Can you leave without anyone finding out you're still alive?"

He gave her a weary look. "I have multiple identities, disguises, and money in many currencies."

"You've thought of everything, haven't you?"

"I am good at my job," he said sadly. "So, have you made decision?"

"You have to promise to leave the UK. Tonight. And not kill any of the people involved in this arms deal, or in the government or royal family. Otherwise the ruse with Nikolai is useless because Flint will know it's you."

He nodded. "I protect you as you protect me."

"Let's do it then."

Kazimir dressed Nikolai in some of his own clothes, even putting false eyebrows and a toupee on Nikolai's bald head to mimic his own hairstyle, and then carried him into the living room as Kerry stood in the corner and watched silently. The two friends talked to each other in their own language, softly, with occasional chuckles. She imagined they were reminiscing, judging by the open affection between the two of them.

She took the opportunity to examine the differences between the two men. They were a similar height, but Nikolai was frail while Kazimir was still solidly built. Another jumper was added to pad him out, like preparing for a bizarre photo shoot, Nikolai wheezing throughout. Kazimir's nose was bigger, but if they posed him . . .

Was this what her father did before he asked her to murder those people? Did he stand back and look at them with the same critical eye and wonder about how to make sure the statues looked lifelike but not incriminating?

She swallowed down a bubble of bile and stared down at her shoes instead. Flint and his people would not look at the statue with the same critical eye as she was.

"I am ready," Nikolai finally said to her.

She went over to him. "Are you absolutely sure?"

"Yes."

"It will be very quick. I don't think it will hurt."

"I already hurt. Please. It is time."

He shook hands with Kazimir, who murmured something in his ear as he let go. Whatever it was made Nikolai throw his head back and belly laugh and she touched his hand in that moment of pure joy on his face, looking away as soon as she felt contact. The laughter was cut off so abruptly that the last echoes of it rang off the glass cabinet behind him.

Kazimir gasped and said something in Russian and then she was running, out the door to the apartment, down the stairs to burst out of the building and vomit in the gutter outside.

EPILOGUE

THREE WEEKS LATER, KERRY—aka Stonemaiden, the newest member of the Most Puissant Order of the Silver Helix—lay on her stomach on the grass in her garden and watched a worm crawl across her palm. She clenched her teeth, fighting to keep control of her excitement as the creature expanded and contracted itself across her skin to the other side.

The TV was on in the living room behind her, the familiar sound of the lunchtime-news-headlines music barely making an impression as she grinned at her progress.

". . . continue for one of the world's largest arms manufacturers." Her attention focused on the newsreader when she heard those words. "Share values have plummeted following reports of a severe metal fatigue problem in several shipments," the male newsreader said. "The company denies responsibility, saying they have proof that the shipments left their factories in perfect working order. In other news . . ."

She rolled over onto her back and laughed. Mysterious severe metal fatigue? She imagined crates of guns being opened only to reveal well-packaged dust. "Good luck, Kazimir."

♠ ♥ ♦ ♣

Grow

by Carrie Vaughn

Spring 1994
Leeds

"**GIVE ME THAT**," **MARYAM** said, reaching for Elaine's cigarette and plucking it out of her hand. She took a long drag off it, then dropped it on the grass and stamped it out.

"Hey, I wasn't finished with it!"

Maryam ignored her, watching the cricket field on the other side of the chain-link fence. The match was maybe half done. Boys in trousers and jumpers ran about, yelling, though as far as she could see there wasn't a ball in play. There'd be no better time to do this. She unclipped her black hair so it fell past her shoulders, pulled her jumper and bra off, and shoved down her school skirt, stockings, knickers, and shoes. Naked now, she handed all her clothes to Elaine, who was suddenly looking skeptical.

"You really going to do this?" Elaine had dirty-blond hair wrapped up in a purple scrunchy at the top of her head, with maybe a quarter of it falling out to frame her pale, freckled face. Her eyes always seemed to get really round and shocked whenever Maryam cooked up a plan like this. You'd think she'd be used to it by now.

Maryam grabbed the nylon fabric of the ripped-up tent she'd rescued from the bin that was exactly the right size for her purpose and wrapped it around her waist. "Yeah, I am."

She closed her eyes and focused. She had practiced this, but never in public and never with a target in mind. Go big, bigger than she ever had. Huge, or there'd be no point to it. Her skin started to tingle, which grew into a heat that went all the way to her bones. A hiss and a crack sounded from nearby power lines as her body grabbed hold of that electricity.

Grow, grow, *grow*.

Elaine let out a squeak and stumbled back, and Maryam opened her eyes on a world turned distant. Small. Like looking down from a balcony.

Elaine blinked up at her with a stupid owl-like expression, and Maryam grinned madly.

She stepped right over the fence, planting her bare foot on the grass on the other side, her brown skin contrasting with the bright green, and went striding across the back field of the pitch in just a few steps. She could break into a run and cover miles in a few minutes. She could pick up cars and shove them out of her way. Knock over poles. She could do anything. But right now, she merely walked, like she was strolling through the park, letting people get a good look at her.

The screaming from the spectators was *extremely* satisfying.

Her long hair stayed draped past her face and over her chest. Not that she had much in the way of breasts to show off, and she rather expected that all joking aside, the fact that she was *so very tall* would draw more attention than her toplessness.

Be interesting to find out, anyway. Which was only part of why she was doing this.

She didn't linger. This was just an experiment. A bit of dabbling, to see what would happen. Just enough time to let people take photos, maybe a bit of video if someone was taping the match. She had her exit strategy all mapped out, stepping over the fence on the opposite side of the field while the panicked shouting continued behind her. However much she wanted to glance over her shoulder to enjoy the chaos she'd caused, she resisted temptation. The air of mystery was more important.

Across the street was a park surrounding a duck pond, lined with enough tall trees to offer a bit of shelter. Plunging into them, she offloaded energy, and size, with a flash and a crack of static, returning to her normal height in almost an instant. Now that she was hidden among the trees, no one would notice.

Wrapping the tent fabric tightly around herself, she jogged off, and no one was even looking for her. Elaine was waiting right where they'd agreed to meet, in the yard outside a water tower about half a kilometer from the cricket field.

"Well?" Elaine asked, handing her back her clothes and keeping a lookout as she rushed to put them on.

"I did it!" Maryam grinned madly.

"Brilliant!" Elaine grabbed her arms, and together they hopped up and down in a quivering dance of teenage enthusiasm.

That evening, the house was its usual chaos. Her two older siblings—both on break from university, which seemed a bit much—were arguing at the kitchen table about rail passes or the price of beef or some nonsense.

Their mother was simultaneously fixing supper and yelling at their father in Farsi. Maryam only knew that she'd told him "please turn on the news" because he got up to turn the television on immediately. Maryam had only been two when the family left Iran, and her grasp of her native language was flimsy at best. She sometimes thought she ought to repair that, but never seemed to find the time, between studying for A-levels and figuring out her power. Nobody but Elaine knew she'd turned an ace. *Well, nobody until today.*

She went to the sitting room to join her father. From the sofa, he smiled a fond but absent-minded greeting at her, half watching the television while reading a newspaper. She took the chair near the sofa. This was the moment she'd been waiting for, but she couldn't seem too eager. She didn't usually watch the news, hiding away in her upstairs bedroom instead. She couldn't exactly tell everyone to just shut up now without giving herself away.

Her mother wandered in, wiping her hands on a towel, and her brother and sister were still arguing in the kitchen. "Be quiet!" her mother told them when the BBC News logo came up.

The lead story was about some turmoil or other in American politics. The second about an oil spill someplace in Africa. Maryam began tapping her feet. What if she hadn't made the news at all? But finally there it was, halfway through the broadcast.

"And here in Britain, a cricket match outside of Leeds was disrupted when a previously unknown ace made an appearance—"

God, she'd made the news. And yes, there was some grainy home video footage of a towering otherworldly creature taking long deliberate steps across the grass and away. It was marvelous, like something out of a bad movie. Her siblings had come in from the kitchen to watch and stood with their mouths open in disbelief. Maryam had to be very still. Not react at all.

Her father stroked his chin. "Leeds? That's just near the school, isn't it?"

Gaping at the television, her mother asked, "Anyone we know?"

"Of course not, we don't know any of those kinds of people."

Me, Maryam wanted to yell at him. Those kinds of people were *me.*

Maybe she ought to keep this secret. Not be such an exhibitionist. But the newscast was still going on, interviewing spectators who'd been at the match. "A giant! She came out of nowhere!" one of them said.

"How does a fifteen-foot-tall woman come out of nowhere!" her mother exclaimed. "She had to have come from somewhere."

The video showed gigantic Maryam leaving the other side of the field, then cut out. So no one had really seen where she went. She'd ducked behind a building and that was that. At no point had her face been visible.

"Well," her mother said, then wandered back to the kitchen.

Maryam had been sitting right there and neither of them recognized the giant girl on the screen as their own daughter. Well, indeed.

She ran up to her room to phone Elaine, who answered on the first ring as if she'd been waiting. "Did you see it?"

"That was *fantastic*," Elaine said. "I can't believe it."

"You know what this means?"

"What?"

"I'm doing it again."

Fifteen feet. That was as tall as she'd ever gotten. Almost five meters, the commentator said. She could go taller. She knew she could.

♣

Maryam had done some reading when this first started happening to her. Growing to an immense height, or changing shape into something much larger than one's self, was a fairly common wild-card power that had been studied and classified, and she was introduced to the concept of proportional strength. A larger frame required more strength to carry itself around, much less be able to move or run or do anything at all. There had been cases of wild-card victims who'd grown to twelve, fifteen, twenty feet—but still maintained the proportional muscle mass and strength of a normal human. They were incapacitated. They couldn't move. But some got the strength they needed, and it made them powerful. Radha O'Reilly, Elephant Girl, was a case Maryam had particularly studied. A woman who could transform into a full-grown Asian elephant, who couldn't just move normally, but fly. Researchers agreed that telekinesis was involved.

Maryam was lucky. Her strength grew with her height. She hadn't been able to really test this yet, but she planned to.

The second exhibition—experiment, she still thought of it—was even better. A children's football match, so there were sure to be enthusiastic parents with video cameras on hand. She started on the other side of the school and then casually strolled across the end of the field, as if she were just having a ramble and the game happened to get in the way. Didn't even look at the screaming crowd and fleeing children. She heard them well enough. Continuing past the field, she went on to a wooded greenway and ducked into the trees, where she let off a clap of energy, and then ran before anyone could connect that disturbance with the giant woman who'd just marched across the way.

On that evening's newscast, she was the second story. "Another sighting of Britain's newest ace! This time at a student football match, where spectators were shocked—"

"Is that woman even wearing any clothes?" Maryam's mother exclaimed at the television.

"Yeah, she's got a thing around her," Maryam said, then shut up. She wasn't supposed to be interested.

"The police should do something," her father said.

"She isn't breaking any laws," she shot back. Actually there was probably a law against toplessness. But not against just *walking*, even if you were fifteen feet tall.

Her mother snorted a laugh. "How're they going to arrest her, then?"

Maryam smiled to herself. Ultimately, that was the thing that was going to save her. Who could possibly stop her? Who would ever try?

♦

Maryam lay on her bed, papers spread out around her, checking schedules for highly public, high-profile events. Local sports matches were all well and good, but she couldn't just keep popping across obscure fields and expect people to continue paying attention. She was also on the phone with Elaine.

"You should go public," Elaine stated.

Maryam didn't know that she could. *Those people,* her father had said, scorn in his voice. That raised the question: What if she had turned up a joker, and grown horns out of her head or five extra legs? What if she hadn't been able to keep it secret, what then?

She didn't want to think about that.

"And then do what?"

"Charge for autographs. Get a sponsorship. Make a little money off these stunts."

"It's not about making money," Maryam grumbled. Then what was it about? She hadn't really thought that far ahead. Just . . . she could do this *thing,* she was an ace, she ought to *do* something with it, right? Make a splash, get attention.

Was that all she wanted? Attention? She hadn't thought herself so shallow.

Elaine huffed at her in disgust. "But I bet you could make *a lot* of money."

"Doing what, being a freak?"

"Well I don't know, you work it out!"

"Wait, I found something." Maryam sat up and read the story more closely. "This is it. This is perfect."

"What?"

"There's a new hospital opening, a big charity event. Prince Edward will be there. Can you imagine the press? They'll get some *amazing* video."

"Prince Edward? Em, you can't. That's . . . there'll be so many police there. Security will be *really* serious."

"And you think they can stop me?"

"That's not the point! They might not try to stop you, they may just shoot you!"

"They wouldn't. It's not like I'll actually get close or anything. I'll just show up at the end of the street and wave or something."

"So what, you'll just keep doing this until someone figures out who you are?"

"No one'll figure it out. They haven't yet, have they?"

"Maryam Shahidi, you're addicted! You're a thrill-seeking addict!"

"You going to help me or not?"

"Fine. Where do you want me to meet you?"

♥

Maryam was thrilled. The crowd was stupendous, and TV cameras were everywhere. The royal motorcade had already made its way to the front of the hospital. She'd get close enough to wave to the prince, then walk off again before anyone even knew what was happening.

She and Elaine got as close as they could, outside the barricades of the police cordon. Maryam had the routine down by now, stripping off her clothes and shoes, arranging her hair loose down her chest, hitching the nylon fabric around her hips and between her legs like some makeshift loincloth, like she was some biblical Goliath. Ha, maybe that could be her ace name, Goliatha . . .

"When you start making money at this, I need a cut," Elaine said, gathering up her clothes.

"You do, do you?"

"I'm your assistant. I deserve something for handling your stinking knickers."

"My knickers do not stink!"

Elaine rolled her eyes.

"Just meet me down by the river. I'm counting on you, Elaine." She said it like this was some secret mission upon which the fate of the nation depended. Elaine rolled her eyes again and backed away.

Maryam closed her eyes and pulled energy into herself.

Grow. Bigger. *Even more.*

A great thrilling charge passed through her body, down to her bones. Like she had taken in a breath, and the breath just kept going, her lungs expanding. Like stretching a muscle that had never been stretched before.

When she opened her eyes again, the ground seemed far away. Elaine, who now didn't come up any higher than her hips, backed away, wide eyed, before turning and running like a girl in a bad horror movie.

Maryam could look inside second-story windows. She could step on cars. Kick over trees. She laughed, and her voice came out *big*. Time for her moment.

She came around the building, stepped over the police barricade, took another long stride that brought her into the open—and had no place to go. The street was packed with onlookers, news vans, rows of photographers, and the sleek black limousines of the royal motorcade. The glittering party in orbit around Prince Edward himself stood before the front entrance of the new hospital. Impeccably dressed in a medal-festooned Royal Navy uniform, Prince Edward posed for the endless pictures and video being taken, caught in the middle of cutting the ribbon tied in front of the doors.

Someone screamed. Maryam couldn't tell where exactly the scream had come from; noises from the crowd seemed tinny and mashed together. The extra height made a difference in all her perceptions. Then came another scream, and another, and the crowd lurched, as every single person tried to move away from her. Chaos ensued, and the police moved in, trying to manage the sudden stampede. All the cameras were suddenly on Maryam, and she had *no place to go*. At least not without actually *stepping* on people. A deeply unpleasant prospect in bare feet.

All this attention. Pandemonium, all because of her. This was what she wanted, wasn't it?

The moment she spent frozen in place, undecided about what to do, her face turned full to the crowd, and what seemed like a million camera shutters went off. Prince Edward, his navy cap settled over a studiously curious brow, merely blinked back at her.

If she could just get across the street, to the car park past the row of shops, she could catch her breath.

Maryam set down a foot and the concrete of the pavement cracked. More screaming followed. Well, this wasn't good.

Uniformed police and security were replacing the civilian crowd. Only a matter of time before someone arrived with a gun. Maybe that was enough of a show for one day. Maryam turned on a heel and ran back the way she had come, behind the new hospital building, hoping the structure would hide her. Not bloody likely.

She kept running, her footfalls pounding like a jackhammer. Glancing behind her, she saw that a couple of intrepid photographers chased after her. Oh, that really wasn't good. She needed to get away, to hide just long enough to shrink back to normal—and then what, run around the streets with tent fabric wrapped awkwardly around her? This was ludicrous.

Well, at this height her strides carried her away fast, so she kept going, dodging down narrow lanes and around buildings until she reached the riverside park where Elaine should have been waiting for her.

Elaine was not waiting for her.

"Dammit!" she muttered and let off the burst of energy that dissipated her power and brought her back to normal size. Only this time was she aware that a lightning burst like that in the middle of a cloudless day was like sending up a signal flare.

Normal size weirdly made everything seem big. The trees were too big, the buildings on the other side of the street seemed far away. It was disorienting.

She started pacing. Her heart was thudding a million times a minute and all her nerves were electric wires, waiting to blow out. A car drove past, and she ducked down behind a shrub, hoping she couldn't be seen from here.

Still no Elaine.

This was not unsolvable. She could figure this out. Walk home, while avoiding any attention. Wait until everyone was occupied, then sneak inside and up to her room, wash and dress and act like nothing at all was wrong. Pretend to be shocked when the news showed a giant girl attacking a member of the royal family.

She kept pacing. She couldn't seem to get herself to move out of the trees and find a path that would take her home.

"Em!" shouted a voice, followed by a crashing through undergrowth.

Maryam jumped, startled. "Bloody hell, where were you!"

Elaine appeared, gasping for breath, sweat matting her hair to her face. She carried Maryam's clothes in a plastic grocery bag. "Trying not to be followed, there're police and news vans and cars everywhere! What the hell did you do?"

"I didn't do anything! Basically just stood there! There were a lot more people there than I thought there'd be."

"I told you! Didn't I tell you? You can't fuck around with the royals without something like this happening." Elaine's face was turning red, furious.

Their voices were going to carry up to the street if they weren't careful. Maryam closed her eyes a moment to steady her breathing. Then she looked right at Elaine. "You need to calm down. Nothing actually happened, did it?"

Elaine threw the bag of clothes at Maryam, who ducked, but not fast enough, and it hit her shoulder, then plopped to the ground.

"I'm finished!" she shouted. "I'm not doing this anymore!" She turned and marched back through the trees and up the slope leading to the street.

Maryam's first thought was of what she would need to say to Elaine to make her stay, convince her that she shouldn't leave, that what Maryam was doing was good and worthwhile and Elaine would stick with her if she knew what was good for her. What could Maryam say to her? That wasn't an outright apology, of course, because she would never apologize for this.

Maryam's second thought was that she could do this on her own from now on. "Coward!" she shouted after Elaine, who never once turned around.

At least Maryam had her clothes and could dress now. Go home, wait for the news, and see where she stood before planning the next outing.

♣

Sweaty and exhausted, Maryam got home on foot, hopped the low brick wall into the back garden, dumped the wadded-up tent by the door, and snuck inside. She was able to get upstairs and into the bath to clean up before anyone saw her, and strolled back down the stairs with a magazine in hand as if she'd been in her room reading all afternoon.

Turned out she didn't need to wait for the news—a special broadcast was already playing, and the whole family was gathered to watch. When Maryam appeared in the front room, her parents and siblings looked at her, wearing expressions of pure shock that she'd never seen in her life.

"What?" she said, though a chill passed over her.

Her brother pointed weakly at the television, and Maryam watched. A now familiar style of impromptu video was playing, the viewpoint maybe half a street up from the new hospital's front doors. And there Maryam was, striding into the frame, followed by screaming, and something like a stampede. The image shook, jostled by people running past. The person with the camera seemed to be torn between fleeing themselves and staying to record the moment.

Then giant Maryam turned toward the camera, exposing a clear view of her face, framed by a fall of black hair. The newscast froze this image and put it in the background while the very serious newscaster read from her page.

"The Towering Teenager, as she is now being called, has been identified as Maryam Shahidi, of Horsforth, near Leeds . . ."

Beside the image from that afternoon's hospital opening, a second photo appeared, an innocuous black-and-white school picture, in which she was wearing a white shirt and necktie and a stupid, toothy smile. The two were very clearly the same girl, and very clearly Maryam.

"Authorities now believe this was *not* an assassination attempt against Prince Edward as initially believed, but may be nothing more than a schoolgirl prank. In any case, police are looking for Maryam Shahidi, and anyone who has any information should contact—"

That was when the knocking at the door started.

She stared back at her family and wondered if it was too late to simply run as far and fast as she could and never come back.

Her father got up to move toward the door.

"Don't answer that!" Maryam called. Meanwhile, her brother and sister were pulling aside the curtains to look out the front window. Gasps followed.

"Look at that!" her brother announced, laughing a little.

The front street was filled with cars, vans, and a seething crowd, all pointed toward the Shahidi house. Once the name was out, Maryam wasn't at all hard to find, it turned out. Noticing the curtains parted, dozens of people with cameras lunged through the front shrubbery to put lenses up to the glass.

"Close those curtains!" Maryam said. Miraculously, her brother did so, and the room went dark, except for the television, where the video footage from the hospital was playing over again. This time, there was a clip of Prince Edward being escorted to his waiting limousine. His expression was serene, as if he'd merely been interrupted by a bit of rain. As if this sort of thing happened all the time. Maryam had to admire him a bit.

From the front door, someone was shouting, "Are you Mr. Shahidi? Is your daughter Maryam? Is she here? I can pay you for an exclusive interview, just let me inside—"

The door slammed shut. Her father wandered back to the front room in a daze.

Her mother was not in a daze. "Maryam, what have you done!" she shouted, hands out, pleading. She was a middle-aged woman, soft and tired, in a smart blue skirt and a nice blouse, her black hair tied back in a prim bun. Very presentable. Maryam had stopped being able to talk to her about anything years ago.

"It was just for fun!" she pleaded. "I didn't hurt anyone! I just wanted to see what I could do, how big I could get!"

"You could have been hurt, you could have been killed, if someone decided to shoot at you—"

"I had it all planned out, I wasn't going to get hurt!"

Her mother put her hands on her hips. "And how will you ever find a husband, when people see you walking around naked like that!"

"God, Mum, this isn't about finding a husband!"

"Don't 'God, Mum' me! What do you think you're doing? When did this happen? *How* did this happen? We are a good family!"

"That's got nothing to do with anything! It's a virus, that's it! The wild card! It just happened, I don't know how, I woke up one day with my legs hanging off the foot of the bed, how am I supposed to know how that happens!" Her father was a cardiologist, her siblings were medical students, shouldn't everybody in this family know how viruses worked, for God's sake?

The banging at the front door continued. The voices were shouting loud enough to be heard through the window, and her brother and sister kept stealing glances. Next, a police siren rattled from the end of the street. Her father stood before her, his expression hurt and lost. "Maryam, I don't understand."

Her whole family was arrayed around her, and they all looked so confused. She didn't know what to do about that.

"I'm an ace, all right? That's it, that's all it is, I'm an *ace*."

Her mother said, "But why do you have to go running all over the countryside—"

"Because I could! I just . . . I wanted to see if I could." Her eyes were stinging, and if she started crying now she would hate herself forever.

The sirens were getting closer.

This was too much. She didn't want to deal with her family, and her family didn't deserve this mess. Maybe she could at least get the police and media circus away from them.

"Look, I'm sorry. I'm just sorry." She went through the kitchen to the back door, pulling off her shirt as she went. She was already growing, gaining a foot of height with every step. She grabbed the old ripped tent from where she'd abandoned it, then easily stepped over the brick wall, and by then she was visible from the front of the house. She turned and waved, to make sure everyone saw her. That nearly started a riot, and just as she hoped, the crowd surged away from the house, back to their vehicles, trying to race away to follow her and getting tangled up with one another in the meantime.

She didn't know where she was going, so she just ran, from the yards behind the row of houses to the next street over. She was big enough and heavy enough now that she was leaving cracks in the pavement and asphalt.

If she could get to someplace without roads, the cars and vans couldn't follow her, or at least would get even more tangled up and turned around trying to follow her. A mile or so on was a bit of pastureland, fenced in, with rambling trails along the River Aire. She could lead them on a big chase, put on one last show, then hide. Then—she didn't know what. Maybe the Towering Teen would never appear again. She was getting this out of her system, she could vanish, and then be done with it all.

Except that this was *glorious*. Even with the stress and panic and the police sirens screaming after her, she was *thrilled*. The landscape swept by her at speed; she was covering entire blocks in just a couple of strides. Her head was above it all. She could see for miles, and the tiny faces of the tiny people pointing at her and screaming went by too fast for her to really see them, and she didn't care. Nothing could catch her.

The Towering Teenager? Schoolgirl prank? She'd show them.

She stepped into an intersection just as a police car sped up the road, gunning its motor to cut her off, spinning a one-eighty as it slid ahead of her, a move worthy of the cinema. A man in a suit jumped out of the passenger side and held up his hands. At first she thought he was pointing a gun at her—she was quite sure she was still vulnerable to gunfire, even at this height. But no, he just raised his arms, beseeching. He shouted at her, but sounded faraway and tinny; she couldn't make out the words. Not like she wanted to talk to him anyway.

Maryam rocked back on a heel and veered to her right. The greenway was close and getting closer. Nothing could catch her.

That didn't stop them from trying. She only just caught sight of the van out of the corner of her eye as it careened down the lane after barely making the turn. A photographer hung out the open passenger-side window, holding a video camera. The car wasn't slowing down. It raced straight toward her, as if it intended to ram her. And why not? She didn't look as if anything would knock her over, after all. If they wanted to stop her, running into her seemed reasonable.

This was all mad. She planted her feet, legs apart to brace herself, and when the car came within reach, she put her hand on the roof and pushed.

The metal dented. The car stopped, its tires squealing on the asphalt, burning rubber and raising a stink.

Then she shoved it out of the way. Not hard, just to get it to the side of the lane so she could run past it. The passenger was screaming something about property damage and suing her; the driver appeared to just be screaming.

Yeah, she was probably going to get in trouble for that. She kept running, and finally made it to the pasture. Her steps sank into the muddy grass, which felt soft and soothing on her bare feet after scraping against asphalt. She kept going, toward the trees. The noise and sirens and screaming faded behind her. Once she hit the trees she could shrink back down and find a place to lie low. Maybe wait for nightfall, though the reporters would probably be camped out at her house for days. She'd have to find a phone somewhere. Maybe Elaine would let her stay over—

No, that wasn't likely, was it? She'd be lucky if Elaine ever spoke to her again.

And then she tripped. Her foot hit a soft spot that was a little too soft, a slope where her increased weight was just a little too much, and the muddy grass gave way. Too distracted with all her tangled thoughts, she didn't catch herself in time and crashed down.

A wrenching, shocking pain ran up her left leg, settling into a deep throb in her ankle. She cried out, lying flat on the grass, gasping for breath and staring miserably up at the cloudy sky. She was afraid to move, absolutely certain that when she did, pain would wrack her ankle again. She'd broken her ankle. Fifteen feet tall, incredibly strong, and she'd broken her bloody ankle with a bad step. Fantastic.

Finally, she sat up to look at it. The pain throbbed in time with her pulse, and she still couldn't catch her breath. She was sitting in the middle of a pasture filled with sheep shit, and what had she done to deserve any of this? The ankle was already swelling, looking gross and puffy compared to the normal shape of the other. From her point of view, her legs, her own body, looked normal, in proportion, nothing to be alarmed about. She had no idea what her swollen, broken ankle looked like from the outside.

She'd have to go to the hospital, she supposed.

This had been a terrible idea. It had all been a terrible idea. That was obvious *now*.

Supposing it would be easier to get to the hospital as a normal-sized person, she took a deep breath and released that burst of energy to let go of her size, returning to where she started.

And she *screamed*. She'd never felt anything so incredibly painful, like her whole foot was being twisted fiber by fiber. It faded into a merely vicious throbbing ache, but she was still left sitting there, all her muscles clenched, gasping for breath. It was clear what had happened: this was the damage of a fifteen-foot-tall woman compacted into a five-foot-five woman's ankle. Exponential.

For future reference: never, ever get injured while super tall. Or if I do, don't bloody well shrink immediately after.

She was still sitting on the ground, wrapped in nylon tent fabric and whimpering, when the police found her, a whole squad of them charging down the hill that had betrayed her. Not a single one of them slipped, which seemed horribly unfair. They all stopped and stared at her a moment, as if uncertain what to do. They had been expecting a giant ace, not a miserable teenage girl. While Maryam wasn't crying, not really, she was sniffing hard and feeling very sorry for herself.

"Maryam Shahidi?" said a woman in a smart police uniform, short hair under her cap. "You ready to come with us now?"

She could only nod.

♠

It happened that her ankle was merely sprained, not broken, which amazed her. How badly would it have hurt if it had actually broken? The doctor assured her that soft-tissue damage could be extremely painful, but he was probably just trying to make her feel better.

The hospital wrapped her ankle, put it on ice, gave her a raft of painkillers, and kept her overnight "for observation," though Maryam was fairly certain the police had asked them to hold her.

Her parents hadn't yet been to visit her, and she was shocked at how much she wanted to see her mother right now. Even if she yelled at Maryam about finding a husband, she'd also stroke her hair and cry all over her and make her feel that *somebody* liked her. Maryam had told the nurse on duty that she wanted to see her mother.

The policewoman standing next to the nurse had said, "Not just yet." Which seemed like a bad sign.

Maryam wasn't sure how much trouble she was in. While she knew she ought to try to sleep, she couldn't, and lay in the hospital bed staring up at the ceiling. She was completely unable to remember why she had started all this exhibitionist business in the first place. It had seemed like such fun. She was an idiot.

Close to suppertime, the door opened, and Maryam was all ready to demand that the nurse, or policewoman, or whoever it was, let her mother come see her. But the visitor was none of these.

He was a middle-aged man wearing a nondescript suit with an old-fashioned hat tucked low on his head. The skin of his face had a strange quality to it, a kind of flat, matte look that didn't seem natural, and he wore gloves. For a moment, he seemed to be studying her, his brow furrowed skeptically. He stepped forward, carefully shutting the door behind him. She shrank back against the bed, growing increasingly uneasy.

"Miss Shahidi," he said finally. "A very impressive bit of spectacle."

"Who're you?"

"I wonder if I could ask you what you hoped to accomplish? You didn't seem to have any particular goal in mind on any of your outings except causing chaos. Which you succeeded at, I must admit."

"You didn't answer my question."

He ducked his gaze, chuckling lightly. "Be patient, we'll get to that momentarily. May I make an observation first? You wanted to be seen. You wanted to be noticed. But you didn't necessarily want to cause trouble, or even be identified. With a power such as yours, you could have robbed banks, destroyed power lines, any and all matter of destruction and disturbance. But you didn't. Also, I speculate that you've had these abilities for a number of years. Onset came at puberty, yes?"

She thought that was a rhetorical question, but he waited for her answer, and she felt the heat of a blush on her cheeks. "Yes."

"So the timing wasn't random. You waited until after you'd taken your A-level examinations before starting these escapades. Whatever happened would not affect your exams or the results. From this I infer that you care about your future and don't want to damage your prospects."

She'd thought she was just blowing off steam after exams. Working out all that stress. But he was right. It had been safer, doing this after exams were done.

"Oh, I have your results, by the way," he said, offhand.

"We're not supposed to see them until next week. How did you—" He raised an amused eyebrow and smiled thinly, as if to say what a foolish question that was. She snuggled back against the pillow and crossed her arms. The man waited calmly. Finally, she couldn't stand it any longer. "So how did I do?"

"You did very well, Miss Shahidi. You're a smart girl. Surely you've guessed by now that I represent a government agency that seeks out talents like yours. You seem like someone who might appreciate the chance to use your abilities for a higher purpose. To help people and your country, rather than simply make a scene that will be forgotten when the next new spectacular ace comes along."

"The government? The British colonialist government?" she scoffed, trying to poke him, to get a rise out of him.

"Ah, a crusader." He smiled, unperturbed. "I'm simply presenting alternatives. And letting you know that I could put in a word. If you had your eye on, say, Oxford or Cambridge. There are doors that could be made to open." He gave a noncommittal shrug.

"And what would you want from me in exchange?" she asked.

"You are still technically underage, so I can't officially make any offers, and I can't hold you to any promises you might make now. But let's say in exchange for my good word, you will be open to meeting with me or one of my colleagues when you've finished your degree. My card."

He walked to the bed and held out a business card. Of course she took it, how could she not? It was expensive-looking, cream-colored card stock with an embossed royal seal on the left and lettering in a subdued, professional typeface to the right: ALAN TURING, ENIGMA, ORDER OF THE SILVER HELIX. And a phone number.

A higher purpose. Was he joking? No, he wasn't. One of her A-levels was in history. She knew the name Alan Turing and exactly who he was.

"Lovely meeting you, Miss Shahidi," he said.

"Yeah," she said a little breathlessly. "Same."

He opened the door, but paused and turned back around. "Oh, and you'll need to come up with a better name than the Towering Teenager. Do think about that over the next year or so."

"Yeah, okay."

The door shut, and the room fell suddenly, deeply quiet. Maryam could hear the blood rushing in her ears. She considered her future. And what else she might grow into.

♠ ♥ ♦ ♣

About the Editor

GEORGE R. R. MARTIN is the author of the acclaimed, internationally bestselling fantasy series A Song of Ice and Fire, which was the basis of HBO's popular *Game of Thrones* television series. Martin has won multiple science fiction awards, including four Hugos, two Nebulas, the Bram Stoker, the Locus, the World Fantasy, the Daedelus, the Balrog, and the Daikon (Japanese Hugo) Awards.

georgerrmartin.com
Twitter: @GRRMSpeaking